CLARKESWORLD

YEAR SIX

CLARKESWORLD
YEAR SIX

EDITED BY NEIL CLARKE & SEAN WALLACE

WYRM PUBLISHING

CLARKESWORLD: YEAR SIX

Wyrm Publishing
www.wyrmpublishing.com

For more information, contact Wyrm Publishing:
wyrmpublishing@gmail.com

ISBN: 978-1-890464-26-4 (trade paperback)
ISBN: 978-1-890464-27-1 (ebook)

Visit Clarkesworld Magazine at:
clarkesworldmagazine.com

Contents

Introduction
NEIL CLARKE

You probably know the drill by now. This book contains all of the original fiction we published in *Clarkesworld Magazine* during its sixth year. That was a particularly tumultuous year for me. In July of 2012, I had a "widow-maker" heart attack that nearly killed me. Afterwards, I took a long, hard look at my life and started pruning away the unnecessary and focusing on what was important: family, friends, etc. As I worked through this process, I came to the realization that I was on the wrong career path. After nearly twenty-five years, I had lost the fire that fueled my interest in my day job. While I wasn't looking, my passion shifted to editing and publishing.

One problem stood between me and my new dream job. *Clarkesworld* and Wyrm Publishing couldn't pay my family's bills, so practicality would have to rule while I continued to build the business. I think that was the moment when "if" changed to "when" for me. When events forced me to look for a new day job, I prioritized simplifying my life and chose a lower-level position that could still pay the bills, provide less stress, and have no expectations of overtime. This would allow me to focus more time on *Clarkesworld*. With that, I put myself on a new path, one that I hope leads me towards a better and more independent life.

Since then, *Clarkesworld* has slowly, but steadily, grown. I can't quit the day job just yet, but thanks to people like you, I'm even more confident it will happen. By purchasing this book, subscribing to *Clarkesworld,* writing a review, or supporting us at Patreon, you are helping me realize that dream. Thank you! It means a lot.

Now . . . how about some stories?

Neil Clarke
March 19, 2014

Scattered Along the River of Heaven

ALIETTE DE BODARD

I grieve to think of the stars
Our ancestors our gods
Scattered like hairpin wounds
Along the River of Heaven
So tell me
Is it fitting that I spend my days here
A guest in those dark, forlorn halls?

This is the first poem Xu Anshi gave to us; the first memory she shared with us for safekeeping. It is the first one that she composed in High Mheng—which had been and remains a debased language, a blend between that of the San-Tay foreigners, and that of the Mheng, Anshi's own people.

She composed it on Shattered Pine Prison, sitting in the darkness of her cell, listening to the faint whine of the bots that crawled on the walls—melded to the metal and the crisscrossing wires, clinging to her skin—monitoring every minute movement she made—the voices of her heart, the beat of her thoughts in her brain, the sweat on her body.

Anshi had once been a passable poet in San-Tay, thoughtlessly fluent in the language of upper classes, the language of bot-handlers; but the medical facility had burnt that away from her, leaving an oddly-shaped hole in her mind, a gap that ached like a wound. When she tried to speak, no words would come out—not in San-Tay, not in High Mheng—only a raw croak, like the cry of a dying bird. Bots had once flowed to do her bidding; but now they only followed the will of the San-Tay.

There were no stars on Shattered Pine, where everything was dark with no windows; and where the faint yellow light soon leeched the prisoners' skin of all colors. But, once a week, the prisoners would be allowed onto the deck of the prison station—heavily escorted by San-Tay guards. Bots latched onto their faces and eyes, forcing them to stare into the darkness—into the event horizon of the black hole, where all light spiraled inwards and vanished, where everything was crushed into insignificance. There were bodies outside—prisoners who had attempted to escape, put in lifesuits and jettisoned, slowly drifting into a place where time and space ceased to have any meaning. If they were lucky, they were already dead.

From time to time, there would be a jerk as the bots stung someone back into wakefulness; or low moans and cries, from those whose minds had snapped. Shattered Pine bowed and broke everyone; and the prisoners that were released back to Felicity Station came back diminished and bent, waking up every night weeping and shaking with the memory of the black hole.

Anshi—who had been a scholar, a low-level magistrate, before she'd made the mistake of speaking up against the San-Tay—sat very still, and stared at the black hole—seeing into its heart, and knowing the truth: she was of no significance, easily broken, easily crushed—but she had known that since the start. All men were as nothing to the vast universe.

It was on the deck that Anshi met Zhiying—a small, diminutive woman who always sat next to her. She couldn't glance at Zhiying; but she felt her presence, nevertheless; the strength and hatred that emanated from her, that sustained her where other people failed.

Day after day they sat side by side, and Anshi formed poems in her mind, haltingly piecing them together in High Mheng—San-Tay was denied to her, and, like many of the Mheng upper class, she spoke no Low Mheng. Day after day, with the bots clinging to her skin like overripe fruit, and Zhiying's presence, burning like fire at her side; and, as the verses became stronger and stronger in her mind, Anshi whispered words, out of the guards' hearing, out of the bots' discrimination capacities—haltingly at first, and then over and over, like a mantra on the prayer beads. Day after day; and, as the words sank deeper into her mind, Anshi slowly came to realize that the bots on her skin were not unmoving, but held themselves trembling, struggling against their inclination to move—and that the bots clinging to Zhiying were different, made of stronger materials to resist the fire of Zhiying's anger. She heard the fast, frantic beat of their thoughts processes, which had its own rhythm, like poetry spoken in secret—and felt the hard shimmer that connected the bots to the San-Tay guards, keeping everything together.

And, in the dim light of Shattered Pine, Anshi subvocalised words in High Mheng, reaching out with her mind as she had done, back when she had been free. She hadn't expected anything to happen; but the bots on her skin stiffened one after the other, and turned to the sound of her voice, awaiting orders.

Before she left Felicity, Xu Wen expected security at San-Tay Prime's spaceport to be awful—they would take one glance at her travel documents, and bots would rise up from the ground and crawl up to search every inch of skin, every body cavity. Mother has warned her often enough that the San-Tay have never forgiven Felicity for waging war against them; that they will always remember the shame of losing their space colonies. She expects a personal interview with a Censor, or perhaps even to be turned back at the boundary, sent back in shame to Felicity.

But it doesn't turn out that way at all.

Security is over in a breeze, the bots giving her nothing but a cursory body check before the guards wave her through. She has no trouble getting a cab either; things must have changed on San-Tay Prime, and the San-Tay driver waves her on without paying attention to the color of her skin.

"Here on holiday?" the driver asks her in Galactic, as she slides into the floater—her body sinking as the chair adapts itself to her morphology. Bots climb onto her hands, showing her ads for nearby hotels and restaurants: an odd, disturbing sight, for there are no bots on Felicity Station.

"You could say that," Wen says, with a shrug she wills to be careless. "I used to live here."

A long, long time ago, when she was still a baby; before Mother had that frightful fight with Grandmother, and left San-Tay Prime for Felicity.

"Oh?" the driver swerves, expertly, amidst the traffic; taking one wide, tree-lined avenue after another. "You don't sound like it."

Wen shakes her head. "I was born here, but I didn't remain here long."

"Gone back to the old country, eh?" The driver smiles. "Can't say I blame you."

"Of course," Wen says, though she's unsure what to tell him. That she doesn't really know—that she never really lived here, not for more than a few years, and that she has a few confused memories of a bright-lit kitchen, and bots dancing for her on the carpet of Grandmother's apartment? But she's not here for such confidences. She's here—well, she's not sure why she's here. Mother was adamant Wen didn't have to come; but then, Mother has never forgiven Grandmother for the exile on San-Tay Prime.

Everything goes fine; until they reach the boundary district, where a group of large bots crawl onto the floater, and the driver's eyes roll up as their thought-threads meld with his. At length, the bots scatter, and he turns back to Wen. "Sorry, m'am," he says. "I have to leave you here."

"Oh?" Wen asks, struggling to hide her fear.

"No floaters allowed into the Mheng districts currently," the man says. "Some kind of funeral for a tribal leader—the brass is afraid there will be unrest." He shrugs again. "Still, you're local, right? You'll find someone to help you."

She's never been here; and she doesn't know anyone, anymore. Still, she forces a smile—always be graceful, Mother said—and puts her hand on one of the bots, feeling the warmth as it transfers money from her account on Felicity Station. After he's left her on the paved sidewalk of a street she barely recognizes, she stands, still feeling the touch of the bots against her skin—on Felicity they call them a degradation, a way for the San-Tay government to control everything and everyone; and she just couldn't bring herself to get a few locator-bots at the airport.

Wen looks up, at the signs—they're in both languages, San-Tay and what she assumes is High Mheng, the language of the exiles. San-Tay is all but banned on Felicity, only found on a few derelict signs on the Outer Rings, the ones the National Restructuring Committee hasn't gone around to retooling yet. Likewise, High Mheng isn't taught, or encouraged. What little she can remember is that it's always been a puzzle—the words look like Mheng; but when she tries to put everything together, their true meaning seems to slip away from her.

Feeling lost already, she wends her way deeper into the streets—those few shops that she bypasses are closed, with a white cloth spread over the door. White for grief, white for a funeral.

It all seems so—so wide, so open. Felicity doesn't have streets lined with streets, doesn't have such clean sidewalks—space on the station is at a ruthless premium, and every corridor is packed with stalls and shops—people eat at tables on the streets, and conduct their transactions in recessed doorways, or rooms half as large as the width of the sidewalk. She feels in another world; though, every now and then, she'll see a word that she recognizes on a sign, and follow it, in the forlorn hope that it will lead her closer to the funeral hall.

Street after street after street—under unfamiliar trees that sway in the breeze, listening to the distant music broadcast from every doorway, from every lamp. The air is warm and clammy, a far cry from Felicity's controlled temperature; and over her head are dark clouds. She almost hopes it rains, to see what it is like—in real life, and not in some simulation that seems like a longer, wetter version of a shower in the communal baths.

At length, as she reaches a smaller intersection, where four streets with unfamiliar signs branch off—some residential area, though all she can read are the numbers on the buildings—Wen stops, staring up at the sky. Might as well admit it: it's useless. She's lost, thoroughly lost in the middle of nowhere, and she'll never be on time for the funeral.

She'd weep; but weeping is a caprice, and she's never been capricious in her life. Instead, she turns back and attempts to retrace her steps, towards one of the largest streets—where, surely, she can hammer on a door, or find someone who will help her?

She can't find any of the streets; but at length, she bypasses a group of old men playing Encirclement on the street—watching the shimmering holo-board as if their lives depended on it.

"Excuse me?" she asks, in Mheng.

As one, the men turn towards her—their gazes puzzled. "I'm looking for White Horse Hall," Wen says. "For the funeral?"

The men still watch her, their faces impassive—dark with expressions she can't read. They're laden with smaller bots—on their eyes, on their hands and wrists, hanging black like obscene fruit: they look like the San-Tay in the reconstitution movies, except that their skins are darker, their eyes narrower.

At length, the eldest of the men steps forwards, and speaks up—his voice rerouted to his bots, coming out in halting Mheng. "You're not from here."

"No," Wen says in the same language. "I'm from Felicity."

An odd expression crosses their faces: longing, and hatred, and something else Wen cannot place. One of the men points to her, jabbers in High Mheng—Wen catches just one word she understands.

Xu Anshi.

"You're Anshi's daughter," the man says. The bots' approximation of his voice is slow, metallic, unlike the fast jabbering of High Mheng.

Wen shakes her head; and one of the other men laughs, saying something else in High Mheng.

That she's too young, no doubt—that Mother, Anshi's daughter, would be well into middle age by now, instead of being Wen's age. "Daughter of daughter," the man says, with a slight, amused smile. "Don't worry, we'll take you to the hall, to see your grandmother."

He walks by her side, with the other man, the one who laughed. Neither of them speaks—too hard to attempt small talk in a language they don't master, Wen guesses. They go down a succession of smaller and smaller streets, under banners emblazoned with the image of the *phuong*, Felicity's old symbol, before the Honored Leader made the new banner, the one that showed the station blazing among the stars—something more suitable for their new status.

Everything feels . . . odd, slightly twisted out of shape—the words not quite what they ought to be, the symbols just shy of familiar; the language a frightening meld of words she can barely recognize.

Everything is wrong, Wen thinks, shivering—and yet how can it be wrong, walking among Grandmother's own people?

> *Summoning bots I washed away*
> *Ten thousand thousand years of poison*
> *Awakening a thousand flower-flames, a thousand phoenix birds*
> *Floating on a sea of blood like cresting waves*
> *The weeping of the massacred millions rising from the darkness*

We received this poem and its memories for safekeeping at a time when Xu Anshi was still on Felicity Station: on an evening before the Feast of Hungry Ghosts, when she sat in a room lit by trembling lights, thinking of Lao, her husband who had died in the uprisings—and wondering how much of it had been of any worth.

It refers to a time when Anshi was older, wiser—she and Zhiying had escaped from Shattered Pine, and spent three years moving from hiding place to hiding place, composing the pamphlets that, broadcast into every household, heralded the end of the San-Tay governance over Felicity.

On the night that would become known as the Second Ring Riots, Anshi stood in one of the inner rings of Felicity Station, her bots spread around her, hacked into the network—half of them on her legs, pumping modifiers into her blood; half of them linked to the other Mheng bot-handlers, retransmitting scenes of carnage, of the Mheng mob running wild in the San-Tay districts of the inner rings, the High Tribunal and Spaceport Authority lasered, and the fashionable districts trashed.

"This one," Zhiying said, pointing to a taller door, adorned with what appeared to be a Mheng traditional blessing—until one realized that the characters had been chosen for aesthetic reasons only, and that they meant nothing.

Anshi sent a subvocalised command to her bots, asking them to take the house. The feed to the rioting districts cut off abruptly, as her bots turned their attention towards the door and the house beyond: their sensors analyzing the bots on the walls, the pattern of the aerations, the cables running behind the door, and submitting hypotheses about possible architectures of the security system—before the swarm reached a consensus, and made a decision.

The bots flowed towards the door—the house's bots sought to stop them, but Anshi's bots split into two squads, and rushed past, heading for the head—the central control panel, which housed the bots' communication system. Anshi had a brief glimpse of red-painted walls, and blinking holos; before her bots rushed back, job completed, and fell on the now disorganized bots at the door.

Everything went dark, the Mheng characters slowly fading away from the door's panels.

"All yours," Anshi said to Zhiying, struggling to remain standing—all her bots were jabbering in her mind, putting forward suggestions as to what to do next; and, in her state of extreme fatigue, ignoring them was harder. She'd seen enough handlers burnt beyond recovery, their brains overloaded with external stimuli until they collapsed—she should have known better. But they needed her—the most gifted bot-handler they had, their strategist—needed her while the San-Tay were still reeling from their latest interplanetary war, while they were still weak. She'd rest later—after the San-Tay were gone, after the Mheng were free. There would be time, then, plenty of it.

Bao and Nhu were hitting the door with soldering knives—each blow weakening the metal until the door finally gave way with a groan. The crowd behind Anshi roared; and rushed through—pushing Anshi ahead of them, the world shrinking to a swirling, confused mass of details—gouged-out consoles, ornaments ripped from shelves, pale men thrown down and beaten against the rush of the crowd, a whirlwind of chaos, as if demons had risen up from the underworld.

The crowd spread as they moved inwards; and Anshi found herself at the center of a widening circle in what had once been a guest room. Beside her, Bao was hacking at a nondescript bed, while others in the crowd beat down on the huge screen showing a sunset with odd, distorted trees—some San-Tay planet that Anshi did not recognize, maybe even Prime. Anshi breathed, hard, struggling to steady herself in the midst of the devastation. Particles of down and dust drifted past her; she saw a bot on the further end, desperately trying to contain the devastation, scuttling to repair the gashes in the screen. Nhu downed it with a well-placed kick; her face distorted in a wide, disturbing grin.

"Look at that!" Bao held up a mirror-necklace, which shimmered and shifted, displaying a myriad configurations for its owner's pleasure.

Nhu's laughter was harsh. "They won't need it anymore." She held out a hand; but Bao threw the necklace to the ground; and ran it through with his knife.

Anshi did not move—as if in a trance she saw all of it: the screen, the bed, the pillows that sought to mould themselves to a pleasing shape, even as hands tore them apart; the jewellery scattered on the ground; and the image of the forest, fading away to be replaced by a dull, split-open wall—every single mark of San-Tay privilege, torn away and broken, never to come back. Her bots were relaying similar images from all over the station. The San-Tay would retaliate, but they would have understood, now, how fragile the foundation of their power was. How easily the downtrodden Mheng could become their downfall; and how much it would cost them to hold Felicity.

Good.

Anshi wandered through the house, seeking out the San-Tay bots—those she could hack and reprogram, she added to her swarm; the others she destroyed, as ruthlessly as the guards had culled the prisoners on Shattered Pine.

Anshi. Anshi.

Something was blinking, insistently, in the corner of her eyes—the swarm, bringing something to her attention. The kitchens—Zhiying, overseeing the executions. Bits and pieces, distorted through the bots' feed: the San-Tay governor, begging and pleading to be spared; his wife, dying silently, watching them all with hatred in her eyes. They'd had no children; for which Anshi was glad. She wasn't Zhiying, and she wasn't sure she'd have borne the guilt.

Guilt? There were children dying all over the station; men and women killed, if not by her, by those who followed her. She spared a bitter laugh. There was no choice. Children could die; or be raised to despise the inferior breed of the Mheng; be raised to take slaves and servants, and send dissenters like Anshi to be broken on Shattered Pine with a negligent wave of their hands. No choice.

Come, the bots whispered in her mind, but she did not know why.

Zhiying was down to the Grand Master of Security when Anshi walked into the kitchens—she barely nodded at Anshi, and turned her attention back to the man aligned in the weapons' sights.

She did not ask for any last words; though she did him the honor of using a bio-silencer on him, rather than the rifles they'd used on the family—his body crumpled inwards and fell, still intact; and he entered the world of the ancestors with the honor of a whole body. "He fought well," Zhiying said, curtly. "What of the house?"

"Not a soul left living," Anshi said, flicking through the bots' channels. "Not much left whole, either."

"Good," Zhiying said. She gestured; and the men dragged the next victim—a Mheng girl, dressed in the clothes of an indentured servant.

This—this was what the bots had wanted her to see. Anshi looked to the prisoners huddled against the wall: there was one San-Tay left, an elderly man who gazed back at her, steadily and without fear. The rest—all the rest—were Mheng, dressed in San-Tay clothes, their skin pale and washed-out in the flickering lights—stained with what looked like rice flour from one of the burst bags on the floor. Mheng. Their own people.

"Elder sister," Anshi said, horrified.

Zhiying's face was dark with anger. "You delude yourself. They're not Mheng anymore."

"Because they were indentured into servitude? Is that your idea of justice? They had no choice," Anshi said. The girl against the wall said nothing; her gaze slid away from Zhiying, to the rifle; finally resting on the body of her dead mistress.

"They had a choice. We had a choice," Zhiying said. Her gaze—dark and intense—rested, for a moment, on the girl. "If we spare them, they'll just run to the militia, and denounce us to find themselves a better household. Won't you?" she asked.

Anshi, startled, realized Zhiying had addressed the girl—whose gaze still would not meet theirs, as if they'd been foreigners themselves.

At length, the girl threw her head back, and spoke in High Mheng. "They were always kind with me, and you butchered them like pigs." She was shivering now. "What will you achieve? You can't hide on Felicity. The San-Tay will come here and kill you all, and when they're done, they'll put us in the dark forever. It won't be cushy jobs like this—they'll consign us to the scavenge heaps, to the ducts-cleaning and the bots-scraping, and we won't ever see starlight again."

"See?" Zhiying said. "Pathetic." She gestured, and the girl crumpled like the man before her. The soldiers dragged the body away, and brought the old San-Tay man. Zhiying paused; and turned back to Anshi. "You're angry."

"Yes," Anshi said. "I did not join this so we could kill our own countrymen."

Zhiying's mouth twisted in a bitter smile. "Collaborators," she said. "How do you think a regime like the San-Tay continues to exist? It's because they take some of their servants, and set them above others. Because they make us complicit in our own oppression. That's the worst of what they do, little sister—turn us against each other."

No. The thought was crystal-clear in Anshi's mind, like a blade held against starlight. That's not the worst. The worst is that, to fight them, we have to best them at their own game.

She watched the old man as he died; and saw nothing in his eyes but the reflection of that bitter knowledge.

White Horse Hall is huge, so huge that it's a wonder Wen didn't see it from afar—more than a hundred stories, and more unveil as her floater lifts higher and higher, away from the crowd massed on the ground. Above the cloud cover, other white-clad floaters weave in and out of the traffic, as if to the steps of a dance only they can see.

She's alone: her escort left her at the floater station—the older man with a broad smile and a wave, and the second man with a scowl, looking away from her. As they ascend higher and higher, and the air thins out—to almost the temperature of Felicity— Wen tries to relax, but cannot do so. She's late; and she knows it—and they probably won't admit her into the hall at all. She's a stranger here; and Mother is right: she would be better off in Felicity with Zhengyao, enjoying her period of rest by flying kites, or going for a ride on Felicity's River of Good Fortune.

At the landing pad, a woman is waiting for her: small and plump, with hair shining silver in the unfiltered sunlight. Her face is frozen in careful blankness, and she wears the white of mourners, with none of the markers for the family of the dead.

"Welcome," she says, curtly nodding to acknowledge Wen's presence. "I am Ho Van Nhu."

"Grandmother's friend," Wen says.

Nhu's face twists in an odd expression. "You know my name?" She speaks perfect Galactic, with a very slight trace of an accent—heard only in the odd inflections she puts on her own name.

Wen could lie; could say that Mother spoke of her often; but here, in this thin, cold air, she finds that she cannot lie—any more than one does not lie in the presence of the Honoured Leader. "They teach us about you in school," she says, blushing.

Nhu snorts. "Not in good terms, I'd imagine. Come," she says. "Let's get you prepared."

There are people everywhere, in costumes Wen recognizes from her history lessons—oddly old-fashioned and formal, collars flaring in the San-Tay fashion, though the five panels of the dresses are those of the Mheng high court, in the days before the San-Tay's arrival.

Nhu pushes her way through the crowd, confident, until they reach a deserted room. She stands for a while in the center, eyes closed, and bots crawl out of the interstices, dragging vegetables and balls of rolled-up dough—black and featureless, their bodies gleaming like knife-blades, their legs moving on a rhythm like centipedes or spiders.

Wen watches, halfway between fascination and horror, as they cut up the vegetables into small pieces—flatten the dough and fill up dumplings, and put them inside small steamer units that other bots have dragged up. Other bots are already cleaning up the counter, and there is a smell in the room—tea brewing in a corner. "I don't—" Wen starts. How can she eat any of that, knowing how it was prepared? She swallows, and forces herself to speak more civilly. "I should be with her."

Nhu shakes her head. Beads of sweat pearl on her face; but she seems to be gaining color as the bots withdraw, one by one—except that Wen can still *see* them, tucked away under the cupboards and the sink, like curled-up cockroaches. "This is the wake, and you're already late for it. It won't make any difference if you come in quarter of an hour later. And I would be a poor host if I didn't offer you any food."

There are two cups of tea on the central table; Nhu pours from a teapot, and pushes one to Wen—who hesitates for a moment, and then takes it, fighting against a wave of nausea. Bots dragged out the pot; the tea leaves. Bots touched the liquid that she's inhaling right now.

"You look like your mother when she was younger," Nhu says, sipping at the tea. "Like your grandmother, too." Her voice is matter-of-fact; but Wen can feel the grief Nhu is struggling to contain. "You must have had a hard time, at school."

Wen thinks on it for a while. "I don't think so," she says. She's had the usual bullying, the mockeries of her clumsiness, of her provincial accent. But nothing specifically directed at her ancestors. "They did not really care about who my grandmother was." It's the stuff of histories now; almost vanished—only the generation of the Honored Leader remembers what it was like, under the San-Tay.

"I see," Nhu says.

An uncomfortable silence stretches, which Nhu makes no effort to break.

Small bots float by, carrying a tray with the steamed dumplings—like the old vids, when the San-Tay would be receiving their friends at home. Except, of course, that the Mheng were doing the cutting-up and the cooking, in the depths of the kitchen.

"They make you uncomfortable," Nhu says.

Wen grimaces. "I—we don't have bots, on Felicity."

"I know. The remnants of the San-Tay—the technologies of servitude, which should better be forgotten and lost." Her voice is light, ironic; and Wen realizes that she is quoting from one of the Honored Leader's speeches. "Just like High Mheng. Tell me, Wen, what do the histories say of Xu Anshi?"

Nothing, Wen wants to say; but as before, she cannot bring herself to lie. "That she used the technologies of the San-Tay against them; but that, in the end, she fell prey to the lure of their power." It's what she's been told all her life; the only things that have filled the silence Mother maintains about Grandmother. But, now, staring at this small, diminutive woman, she feels almost ashamed. "That she and her followers were given a choice between exile, and death."

"And you believe that?"

"I don't know," Wen says. And, more carefully, "Does it matter?"

Nhu shrugs, shaking her head. "Mingxia—your mother once asked Anshi if she believed in reconciliation with Felicity. Anshi told her that reconciliation was nothing more than another word for forgetfulness. She was a hard woman. But then, she'd lost so much in the war. We all did."

"I'm not Mother," Wen says, and Nhu shakes her head, with a brief smile. "No. You're here."

Out of duty, Wen thinks. Because someone has to come, and Mother won't. Because someone should remember Grandmother, even if it's Wen—who didn't know her, didn't know the war. She wonders what the Honored Leader will say about Grandmother's death, on Felicity—if she'll mourn the passing of a liberator, or remind them all to be firm, to reject the evil of the San-Tay, more than sixty years after the foreigners' withdrawal from Felicity.

She wonders how much of the past is worth clinging to.

> *See how the gilded Heavens are covered*
> *With the burning bitter tears of our departed*
> *Cast away into darkness, they contradict no truths*
> *Made mute and absent, they denounce no lies*

Anshi gave this poem into our keeping on the night after her daughter left her. She was crying then, trying not to show it—muttering about ungrateful children, and their inability to comprehend any of what their ancestors had gone through. Her hand shook, badly; and she stared into her cup of tea, as hard as she had once stared into the black hole and its currents, dragging everything into the lightless depths. But then, as on Shattered Pine, the only thing that came to her was merciless clarity, like the glint of a blade or a claw.

It is an old, old composition, its opening lines the last Anshi wrote on Felicity Station. Just as the first poem defined her youth—the escaped prisoner, the revolution's foremost bot-handler—this defined her closing decades, in more ways than one.

The docks were deserted; not because it was early in the station's cycle, not because the war had diminished interstellar travel; but because the docks had been cordoned off by Mheng loyalists. They gazed at Anshi, steadily—their eyes blank; though the mob behind them brandished placards and howled for her blood.

"It's not fair," Nhu said. She was carrying Anshi's personal belongings—Anshi's bots, and those of all her followers, were already packed in the hold of the ship. Anshi held her daughter Mingxia by the hand: the child's eyes were wide, but she didn't speak. Anshi knew she would have questions, later—but all that mattered, here and now, was surviving this. "You're a heroine of the uprising. You shouldn't have to leave like a branded criminal."

Anshi said nothing. She scanned the crowd, wondering if Zhiying would be there, at the last—if she'd smile and wish her well, or make one last stab of the knife. "She's right, in a way," she said, wearily. The crowd's hatred was palpable, even where she stood. "The bots are a remnant of the San-Tay, just like High Mheng. It's best for everyone if we forget it all." Best for everyone but them.

"You don't believe that," Nhu said.

"No." Not any of that; but she knew what was in Zhiying's heart, the hatred of the San-Tay that she carried with her—that, to her little sister, she would be nothing more than a collaborator herself—tainted by her use of the enemy's technology.

"She just wants you gone. Because you're her rival."

"She doesn't think like that," Anshi said, more sharply than she'd intended; and she knew, too, that she didn't believe that. Zhiying had a vision of the Mheng as strong and powerful; and she'd allow nothing and no one to stand in its way.

They were past the cordon now, and the maw of the ship gaped before them—the promise of a life somewhere else, on another planet. Ironic, in a way—the ship was from the San-Tay High Government, seeking amends for their behavior on colonized stations. If someone had ever told her she'd ride one of those as a guest . . .

Nhu, without hesitation, was heading up towards the dark tunnel. "You don't have to come," Anshi said.

Nhu rolled her eyes upwards, and made no comment. Like Anshi, she was old guard; a former teacher in the Mheng schools, fluent in High Mheng, and with a limited ability to control the bots. A danger, like Anshi.

There was a noise behind them—the beginning of a commotion. Anshi turned; and saw that, contrary to what she'd thought, Zhiying had come.

She wore the sash of Honored Leader well; and the stars of Felicity's new flag were spread across her dress—which was a shorter, less elaborate version of the five-panel ceremonial garb. Her hair had been pulled up in an elegant bun, thrust through with a golden phoenix pin, the first jewel to come out of the station's new workshops—she was unrecognizable from the gaunt, tall prisoner Anshi remembered, or even from the dark, intense leader of the rebellion years.

"Elder sister." She bowed to Anshi, but did not come closer; remaining next to her escort of black-clad soldiers. "We wish you happiness, and good fortune among the stars."

"We humbly thank you, Your Reverence," Anshi said—keeping the irony, and the hurt from her voice. Zhiying's eyes were dark, with the same anger Anshi remembered from the night of the Second Ring riots—the night when the girl had died. They stood, staring at each other, and at length Zhiying gestured for Anshi to move.

Anshi backed away, slowly, pulling her daughter by the hand. She wasn't sure why she felt . . . drained, as if a hundred bots had been pumping modifiers into her blood, and had suddenly stopped. She wasn't sure what she'd expected—an apology? Zhiying had never been one for it; or for doubts of any kind. But still—

Still, they'd been on Shattered Pine together; had escaped together; had preached and written the poetry of the revolution, and dared each other to hack into Felicity's network to spread it into every household, every corridor screen.

There should have been something more than a formal send-off; something more than the eyes boring into hers—dark and intense, and with no hint of sorrow or tears.

We do not weep for the enemy, Anshi thought; as she turned, and passed under the wide metal arc that led into the ship, her daughter's hand heavy in hers.

In the small antechamber, Wen dons robes of dark blue—those reserved for the mourners who are the closest family to the dead. She can hear, in the distance, the drone of prayers from the priests, and the scuttling of bots on the walls, carrying faint music until the entire structure of the hall seems to echo with it. Slowly, carefully, she rises, and stares at her pale, wan self in the mirror—with coiled bots at its angles, awaiting just an order to awaken and bring her anything she might desire. Abominations, she thinks, uneasily, but it's hard to see them as something other than alien, incomprehensible.

Nhu is waiting for her at the great doors—the crowd has parted, letting her through with an almost religious hush. In silence, Wen kneels, her head bent down—an honor to the dead, an acknowledgement that she is late and that she must make amends, for leaving Grandmother's ghost alone.

She hears a noise as the doors open—catches a flash of a crowd dressed in blue; and then she is crawling towards the coffin, staring at the ground ahead of her. By her side, there are glimpses of dresses' hems, of shoes that are an uneasy meld of San-Tay and Mheng. Ahead, a steady drone from the monks at the pulpit, taken up by the crowd; a prayer in High Mheng, incomprehensible words segueing into a melodious chant; and a smell of incense mingled with something else, a flower she cannot recognize. The floor under her is warm, soft—unlike Felicity's utilitarian metal or carpets, a wealth of painted ostentation with patterns she cannot make out.

As she crawls, Wen finds herself, incongruously, thinking of Mother.

She asked, once, why Mother had left San-Tay Prime—expecting Mother to rail once more at Grandmother's failures. But Mother merely pulled a low bench, and sat down with a sigh. "There was no choice, child. We could dwindle away on San-Tay Prime, drifting further and further away from Felicity with every passing moment. Or we could come back home."

"It's not Grandmother's home," Wen said, slowly, confusedly—with a feeling that she was grappling with something beyond her years.

"No," Mother said. "And, if we had waited too long, it wouldn't have been your home either."

"I don't understand." Wen put a hand on one of the kitchen cupboards—the door slid away, letting her retrieve a can of dried, powdered shrimp, which she dumped into the broth on the stove.

"Like two men carried away by two different currents in the river—both ending in very different places." She waved a dismissive hand. "You'll understand, when you're older."

"Is that why you're not talking with Grandmother?"

Mother grimaced, staring into the depths of her celadon cup. "Grandmother and I . . . did not agree on things," she said. "Sometimes I think . . . " She shook her head. "Stubborn old woman. She never could admit that she had lost. That the future of Felicity wasn't with bots, with High Mheng; with any of what the San-Tay had left us."

Bots. High Mheng—all of the things that don't exist anymore, on the new Felicity—all the things the Honored Leader banished, for the safety and glory of the people. "Mother . . . " Wen said, suddenly afraid.

Her mother smiled; and for the first time Wen saw the bitterness in her eyes. "Never mind, child. This isn't your burden to carry."

Wen did not understand. But now . . . now, as she crawls down the aisle, breathing in the unfamiliar smells, she thinks she understands. Reconciliation means forgetfulness, and is it such a bad thing that they forget, that they are no longer chained to the hatreds of the past?

She reaches the coffin, and rises—turns, for a brief moment, to stare at the sea of humanity before her—the blurred faces with bots at the corner of their eyes, with alien scents and alien clothes. They are not from Felicity anymore, but something else—poised halfway between the San-Tay and the culture that gave them birth; and, as the years pass, those that do not come back will drift further and further from Felicity, until they will pass each other in the street, and not feel anything but a vague sense of familiarity, like long-lost families that have become strangers to each other.

No, not from Felicity anymore—and does it matter, any of it?

Wen has no answer—none of Mother's bleak certainties about life. And so she turns away from the crowd, and looks into the coffin—into the face of a stranger, across a gap like a flowing river, dark and forever unbridgeable.

> I am in halves, dreaming of a faraway home
> Not a dry spot on my moonlit pillow
> Through the open window lies the stars and planets
> Where ten thousand family members have scattered
> Along the River of Heaven, with no bridges to lead them home
> The long yearning
> Cuts into my heart

● ● ●

This is the last poem we received from Xu Anshi; the last one she composed, before the sickness ate away at her command of High Mheng, and we could no longer understand her subvocalised orders. She said to us then, "it is done"; and turned away from us, awaiting death.

We are here now, as Wen looks at the pale face of her grandmother. We are not among our brethren in the crowd—not clinging to faces, not curled on the walls or at the corner of mirrors, awaiting orders to unfold.

We have another place.

We rest on the coffin with Xu Anshi's other belongings; scattered among the paper offerings—the arch leading into the Heavens, the bills stamped with the face of the King of Hell. We sit quiescent, waiting for Xu Wen to call us up—that we might flow up to her like a black tide, carrying her inheritance to her, and the memories that made up Xu Anshi's life from beginning to end.

But Wen's gaze slides right past us, seeing us as nothing more than a necessary evil at the ceremony; and the language she might summon us in is one she does not speak and has no interest in.

In silence, she walks away from the coffin to take her place among the mourners—and we, too, remain silent, taking our understanding of Xu Anshi's life into the yawning darkness.

"With apologies to Qiu Jin, Bei Dao and the classical
Tang poets for borrowing and twisting their best lines"

All the Painted Stars

GWENDOLYN CLARE

They are not the Brights, and so I hesitate to save them. Part of me is eager, and part of me ashamed.

Even through the haze of plasma blasts dispersing over their shields, I recognize the ship as a Bright construct—too much glass, arranged in sharp geometric panels so the entire upper surface glitters with reflected starlight. Still, I know the pilots must not be Brights. First, because they fly clumsily and appear not to know how to fire the main cannon. Second, because the Brights went extinct some twelve hundred solar cycles ago.

I decide to take a closer look at their attackers, and the fibers in my flesh tauten with anticipation—though I tell myself I will just *look,* not engage. Intent ripples down my middle tentacles to the interface between flesh and machine, and my little stellate-class fighter zips nearer. The attackers have seven mid-size cruisers, nothing so cumbersome as the Bright ship nor so whimsical—boxy and compact, and decked with weapons. I do not recognize the design. Some backwater species, no doubt. I am patrolling near the edge of protected space, so it is to be expected.

I choose a wide selection of frequencies and broadcast an audial message to all the ships in the vicinity. "Hostile vessels, please be informed you have entered protected space. Under the laws of the Sheekah, acts of genocide are punishable by death. Power down your plasma weapons."

The attackers do not respond. But then, if they do not know our laws, what is the chance they know our language?

I broadcast the same message in the Bright language, and then add, "You must provide evidence of personal grievance to a Sheekah enforcer prior to engaging in interspecies violence."

I wish I did not feel a surge of excitement at their silence, at the continued barrage of plasma fire.

I spin the fighter nervously, considering my options. The aggressor may hold a legitimate grievance and simply suffer from an onboard system too crude to translate the transmissions. Or they may have chosen to ignore me, assuming my tiny fighter poses no threat. A compromise then: I will destroy one ship at a time until they relent.

My neurochemical balance adjusts, heightening awareness and reducing reaction time, and I cannot help but enjoy the feel of neurons singing for battle. I trigger the thrusters and slice through the void toward the nearest ship, my body fibers tensing against the heavy acceleration. My fighter is a difficult target to hit—shaped like an eight-pointed geometric star, with just enough room for my core mass in the middle and a tentacle stretching down each ray of the star for interfacing. Stellate-class fighters are highly maneuverable, but I am still outnumbered six to one. This is why I am an enforcer: I am one of the few Sheekah violent enough to accept such odds with glee.

I fire my own weapons in quick, precise bursts, and the reactors of the first cruiser explode in a glorious ultraviolet light-show. Now I have the attention of the rest; two of the remaining cruisers break off from their engagement with the Bright ship to pursue me. I dance away like a comet on an eccentric orbit, there and gone again before they can look twice.

When I repeat the transmission, I should be saddened that they still do not cease fire, though in truth the challenge thrills me. I dart through their fleet and destroy two more cruisers, pausing between each explosion, but the remaining cruisers seem if anything incensed to further violence.

I am closing in on the fourth cruiser when my fighter is hit.

Stellate-class fighters are much too small to carry shield generators, relying instead on maneuverability to avoid getting hit. Ironically, it is not a plasma blast that finds my little fighter, but a shred of shrapnel from one of the cruisers I destroyed. Through the interface, I feel the shrapnel impact as if it were slicing my own flesh, and then one of my tentacles goes numb, a safety precaution against excess stimulation. I run diagnostics and discover that one ray of the star is badly damaged, the thrusters useless.

Well. This changes things.

My fighter has a Stillness Bomb installed, though I have never before activated it. Use of the Stillness is tightly regulated under Sheekah law—it is considered a last resort. But here I am, damaged and outnumbered, and the Brights were never formally removed from our list of treatised allies so I am justified in using the Stillness to defend the Bright ship. A technicality, of course, since I know the inhabitants aren't Brights, but it allows me to use the weapon nonetheless.

To save them, I need to maneuver into contact with their hull, a task I struggle to accomplish without my full array of thrusters. After long seconds of angling, I pass through the Bright shields and stab into the ship, one of the rays of my fighter penetrating the hull. The ray unfolds, sealing the two vessels together and leaving one of my tentacles dangling down through an open aperture into a hallway in the Bright ship. This fusion complete, I can now calibrate the Stillness Bomb to avoid the Bright ship and its occupants. When I am certain the weapon identifies the Bright ship as an extension of my fighter, I meticulously disengage three levels of safeties and activate the Stillness.

My fighter shudders, straining to stay attached to the Bright ship, then goes still. For a moment, nothing seems to have changed, and I wonder if perhaps the weapon was damaged in the firefight. Then the attackers' plasma weapons sputter and die out, and the four remaining cruisers start to drift very slowly out of formation. The motion is barely perceptible, but it fills me with a cold, sick dread. All those lives snuffed out, and what if my judgment was wrong? What a wretched Sheekah am I, who would choose this life of killing.

I do not have long to think on it, though, because the stress of activating the weapon has exacerbated the damage, and my fighter's systems are failing. I must abandon it or die with it. I consider the second option—after all, what am I without my fighter?—but the automated preferences are set for survival, so the fighter disconnects me without waiting for my decision.

As soon as the emergency disconnect triggers, I am blind and suffocating. I fall through the aperture of my fighter into the Bright ship, bits of metal interface still clinging to my tentacles, and I land hard. I flop helplessly on the deck, unadapted for artificial gravity, and without my fighter I sense nothing. My circulatory fluid is slowly turning toxic, and even if the atmospheric composition were appropriate, I have no organs designed for interfacing with air.

I need lungs or I will die. I need visual and auditory organs, too. Immobile as I am, I must wait for the telltale vibration of feet upon the deck, heralding the arrival of the aliens. I think I feel it now, I can't be sure—even my ability to feel the shudder of metal against my flesh is dulled without the electronic stimulus of my fighter.

I flail my tentacles, panicking, and find nothing but empty air. To calm myself, I focus on the task of slowing all nonessential bodily functions. This will buy me a little time, I hope. I cannot quite think rationally with all my neurochemical feedbacks screaming at me to adapt, to survive.

Again, I flail desperately, but this time one tentacle lands on bare flesh. Yes! I eagerly wrap my tentacle around the limb and begin probing for genetic information. Stem cells are ideal—they retain the broadest memory of how the organism as a whole works—though gametes provide a useful perspective, too. I do not dare to hope for embryonic cells, because that would require an incredible stroke of luck and my luck has not been good today.

The stem cells of this species have disappointingly limited potency, but I explore enough to start appropriating their genetic design. The toxin buildup in my circulatory system clouds my thoughts and slows my progress. I hope what I can glean from this individual will be sufficient.

I begin to understand this species as my body begins to integrate their design. They are bilaterally symmetric, endoskeletal, bipedal, endothermic, sexually dimorphic. (Definitely not Brights—if I had any doubts about that, they are gone now.) They have sensory organs for electromagnetic radiation, compression waves, and chemicals. I grow the lung tissue first, so I will be able to breathe as soon as my cellular respiration has altered, then I focus on retinas and cochleae.

As my new senses sharpen and stabilize, I gain awareness of the aliens. There are several of them encircling me, black handheld weapons cradled in their arms. They raise their weapons menacingly, and raise their voices as well; the one I am touching emits a shrill warning call. I begin to realize how very dire my situation is. Have I violated a taboo against physical contact? Perhaps they are a race of clinical xenophobes? I do not know what I have done to agitate them so quickly after I saved their lives.

I was never meant to be an ambassador—I do not have the training, and I am too violent besides. I have spent the last thirty-six solar cycles alone inside my fighter, engaging with other species only in my capacity as an enforcer of Sheekah law. And now I find myself in contact with a new species, trying to remember how to mimic physiology, to become one of them. I fear I have already ruined any chance of rapport.

When I am sure I have collected sufficient genetic data to survive in their atmosphere, I unwrap my tentacle, releasing the gene donor. I suck down my first lungfuls of oxygen through newly formed facial orifices.

And the difficult part begins.

They do not kill me right away. I take this as a good sign. They lift me onto a mobile platform and move me to a room with other platforms, some of them occupied by members of their own species. These ones do little in the way of moving or vocalizing, but they also leave me with two males holding weapons. I do not try to ask the killers for more gene donation.

Time passes. Other aliens—ones who do not carry weapons—are often present, watching me, waving diagnostic equipment over me, trying to communicate. I have no translating abilities without my fighter, so I must learn their language the slow way. I grow legs and arms, I learn to metabolize their sugars, I grow vocal chords and lips and a tongue to shape their words. I wonder if my fighter is irreparably damaged, which would mean all this effort to survive is a waste.

I am learning names. Mosby, Rosenberg, Liu; Ahmed, Levitt, Jones. But I do not know what to tell them when they ask for mine. I pause, they think I do not understand and gesture more vigorously towards me. Mosby Rosenberg Liu Ahmed Levitt Jones, they repeat, touching themselves with their hands, then they aim their digits at me and wait for an answer. What can I tell them? Sheekah are named when they choose their lifepath—as a pilot, my name is the name of my stellate fighter. Or at least it was. My fighter is damaged, I am no longer interfaced, and I have taken a new form, yet I am hardly in a position to ask them to name me as a true ambassador would. I cannot even communicate what the problem is.

"Ohree," I eventually say. It was my childhood nickname long ago. Fitting, because I am so like a child now—awkward and unplaced.

"Ohree," they repeat, and the name sounds distorted even though we share a vocal anatomy now.

I cannot explain anything, I cannot ask for anything. I can only point to an object and earn a garble of syllables for an answer. Does "medbay" describe the platform, the material it is made of, the function it serves, or the person lying prone upon it? Is "door" the word for an egress, or the object that blocks the egress? For the first time since I was a child, fumbling to find my lifepath, I feel hopelessly frustrated.

Liu and Rosenberg are in the room with me when I decide I no longer care about upsetting them. If they tell the killers to shoot me, then I will be shot, and at least that will be a change from what I am now. I slide off the platform, balancing uncertainly with my new bipedal body, and take careful steps toward one wall where there appears to be some kind of interface terminal. Rosenberg makes loud vocalizations, and I ignore her.

The terminal has a manual interface—buttons to be depressed by fingers, unthinkably primitive—which I rip out of the wall. I press one palm to the exposed circuitry and close my eyelids, concentrating on the task of growing a direct electronic interface of my own.

They still haven't shot me yet.

I learn this terminal was designed for accessing the medical portion of the ship's database, which is unfortunately not the portion that I need. I mentally slip behind the front-end processes and gain access to the database in its entirety. It is very large, and organized with the dubious logic of Bright minds, information twisting and twining back on itself like a jumble of vines grown together. Eventually, I access the language files for these aliens and use what little I know to identify "English" as the dialect I need to download.

When the task is done, I disengage from the terminal and resorb the interface into the flesh of my hand. "Now," I say, "this will be easier."

"Incredible," says Liu, shaking his head. The gesture makes me wonder if I should have looked for a file on nonverbal communication among humans.

Rosenberg stares at me, and then says, "Someone better get Mosby."

Upon my life, I do not know why it was so important to fetch Mosby. He asks the most inane questions, while Rosenberg holds her lips tight together and Liu backs away as if ceding the whole room.

Once I prove to Mosby that I am now conversant in his language, the first thing he says to me is, "We need to know about that weapon you fired." Mosby is the most important of their trained killers and holds the title of "colonel." He tells the other killers what to do.

I don't see the relevance, but I answer his question anyway. "It produces a sort of space-time whiplash that disrupts neurological functioning. Fatally so, in all organisms we've encountered so far."

"Is it still usable?"

I stare at him for a moment. "No, that's unlikely. The damage to my fighter is too extensive. Were you planning to commit genocide in the near future?"

Mosby's face scrunches up in an expression I do not understand. Rosenberg takes a step forward, places a hand on his arm, and says to me, "Of course not. The Colonel's just worried about defending the ship against another attack."

"That is no longer my concern," I say.

"What do you mean 'not your concern'?" Mosby says, his volume and pitch rising. "Aren't you supposed to be some sort of interstellar policeman?"

"I am no longer interfaced with my fighter."

Mosby says, "Listen, you—" but Rosenberg drags him by the arm out into the hallway.

They talk. I cannot quite hear, but I believe I have displeased one or both of them. I am not sure how—it was not my intention.

Liu, who seems to avoid standing in proximity to Mosby, comes closer again now that Mosby is elsewhere. "Don't judge all of us based on the likes of Mosby," he says. "There's a reason they put a civilian in charge of the expedition."

I don't know who "they" refers to, but I doubt it matters. "I am not here to judge you. The only judgment I am authorized to make is to determine the legitimacy of grievance in interspecies conflict."

Liu does something with the muscles in his lips. "I'm sorry, it's easy to forget you learned our language less than an hour ago. I meant that you must be forming impressions of what our species is like, and Mosby isn't representative. Not of all of us, anyway."

"I will take that under consideration."

Rosenberg returns alone. She apologizes for Mosby's behavior, though I would not have known he behaved inappropriately if she and Liu had not told me. Rosenberg is a leader, but not a killer, and seems to have incomplete authority over Mosby.

"So," Rosenberg says as she leans against the exam table next to mine. "You saved our butts out there, and now you're stuck with us. First of all: thank you. Second, if we could impose upon you further, we could use some help navigating this region of space."

Now I am truly confused. "You do not know where you are going?"

Rosenberg lets out a breath noisily. "The Brights left this ship in our home system a little over thirteen thousand years ago. When we discovered it, their recorded instructions were . . . cryptic, but the nav system came pre-programmed. We've been following the course they set for us, but obviously we're having some trouble with the locals along the way."

Her lengthy reply does not actually answer my question. I try to rephrase it to be clearer. "What is the purpose of your journey?"

"We're going to Bright space. It's not clear why they want us to come, but we couldn't pass up an invitation like this." She raised a hand as if to indicate the room, or perhaps the ship at large. "I've done some poking around in the database to learn about your species, so I know the Sheekah were allies of the Brights once. Would you consider helping them now, even if they're not here to ask for it?"

This surprises me. "You do not know?"

"Know what?"

"They are gone."

"Gone," Liu interjects loudly, before Rosenberg can answer. I do not understand why he repeats the word—perhaps I misused it.

"The Brights went extinct," I clarify. "They developed a genetic anomaly that spread from cell to cell throughout the body, causing widespread genomic degradation, and was, like a pathogen, highly transmissible between individuals. Many Sheekah were infected trying to help them before the Ambassadorial High Council declared quarantine."

"Gone," Rosenberg says and goes silent for a minute. (Does everyone need to say this word?) Something appears to be wrong with her, but I do not know what to do. Eventually, she says, "Did they know they were dying off when they left us the ship?"

I do a little quick math, converting unfamiliar units of time based on what I gleaned from the ship's database. "Given the age of the ship, that seems probable."

"I guess now we know why they named the ship *Legacy*." She puts her hand over her mouth, as if to hold in the words, but I can still hear her clearly. "We have to figure out where we're going, and why. Would you consider helping Ahmed with the database?"

I stare, not knowing how to respond. What happens to those I protect after I enforce the law has never been my concern. I wonder what it would feel like to be invested in their fate, but all I can feel is the absence of metal against my skin, the ghost-memory of tentacles I no longer possess.

"I am here," I say dispassionately. "I will help with what I can."

Days pass. I interface again with the *Legacy* database and develop a rudimentary understanding of the systems architecture. This helps, a little, to alleviate the ache of losing my fighter and my lifepath with it. At least when my mind is occupied, I am not dwelling on how wrong everything feels. I try and fail to explain the database to the technologists, who cannot grasp the Bright way of thinking. Whole sections of the ship are offline and locked down, and I am surprised they made it this far with such limited control.

I also learn more from the database about these humans; they live short lives, for instance, the equivalent of only nine or ten Sheekah solar cycles. I must seem ancient to them, though among the Sheekah I am considered young. They have so little time—this helps me understand why they seem so desperate to accomplish something, even if they do not know the nature of their task.

I grow irritated with the technologists. They are always near, bothering me with questions, even though they do not generally understand the answers.

After the long cycles of solitude in my fighter, I am unused to tolerating so many individuals in such close proximity. I look for something else to do.

Instead I help the botanist, Keene, revive some of the plant species, the ones whose genomes indicate they will be harmless to humans. It is tiring but not particularly difficult work; I must grow a temporary interface with which to access the genomic database, and my body requires extra sustenance to provide the molecules with which to shape the seeds. Keene seems very pleased with the results. I care little for reviving extinct species from the Bright homeworld, but it also costs me little, so what does it matter either way? The Brights loved their botany and would not have wanted *Legacy* to fly with empty solaria. Indeed, from what I learned of the systems architecture, I suspect healthy solaria will prove important for restoring and optimizing certain functions elsewhere on the ship. Not that this matters to me.

I miss my old self. I think about fixing my fighter, but I can find only some of the tools and none of the spare parts I would need for the task aboard *Legacy*.

I consider ending my existence.

I sit on a bench in the aft solarium, which remains dark and unused and skeletal. In the central solarium Keene's seeds have begun to sprout, so I come here instead to avoid the curious visitors drawn in by the promise of green growth. Back here, if I hold very still, I can feel the subsonic hum of the main engines vibrating the hull.

Through the geometric panes of the ceiling and walls, the stars look strangely close, as if the hull were not clear at all but rather painted with the likeness of stars. I stare into space, remembering how this view used to belong to me every hour of every cycle. It's not the same, of course—these human eyes see such a narrow spectrum—but at least it feels familiar.

The aft solarium doors breeze open and Liu, the psychologist, enters. I do not look away from the stars but I can tell it is him from the way his soft gait whispers on the deck. He takes a seat next to me on the bench. Humans are highly social and require near-constant interaction and stimulation when conscious.

"How are you adjusting?" he says.

I think my habit of sitting here alone disturbs Liu. He does not understand me at all. "I do not know if I wish to adjust."

"Look—I know this isn't where you want to be, but the truth is, we could use your help here. The *Legacy* database is thirteen thousand years out of date and so huge we can't find what we're looking for most of the time anyway. We could use a guide who knows what they're doing."

I lower my gaze to look at him. Humans seem to desire a quite specific quantity of eye contact while communicating—not too much, not too little— though I have not yet mastered the exact proportion. "I am not an ambassador," I say. "I was trained to be an enforcer of the law. I cannot perform another life."

Liu's brows tighten and draw together. "Life?"

"Job," I say, to clarify. I have not yet discerned why they have two words for this concept.

Liu exhales forcefully and leans back against the bench, stretching his legs. If the gesture means something, it is lost on me. Humans rely heavily on nonverbal communication, much of it subconscious, and it frustrates my efforts to understand them. Or rather, it would frustrate me, if it were important for me to understand them. Which it is not. Because I think I will kill myself today.

After a while, Liu speaks again. "In the ship's logs, the Brights say they left us *Legacy* because they knew we would someday build conservatories."

I do not know the word. "Conservatories?"

"Places where we cultivate plants for aesthetic value." He points at the solarium ceiling. "The architecture usually looks something like this. Anyway, at the time when they left us the ship, humans had barely started getting a handle on agriculture. We didn't build conservatories until thousands of years later."

"Are plants of great cultural significance to you now?"

"They're not central to our society, no. Well—Keene might argue otherwise, but most people don't think twice about the cultural value of plants." He lifts his shoulders in an unfamiliar gesture. "I don't know. Maybe the Brights saw what they wanted to see in us."

"As you see what you want to see in me."

"The point is," Liu says, "you hardly ever get the ideal situation you're hoping for. But if you're lucky, you find something that will suffice."

"I am not an ambassador," I say again.

"No, but you're close enough for us."

Maybe I will wait until tomorrow to kill myself.

Tomorrow comes, but the humans distract me. Over the comm, they say they have desperate need of me in the systems control room. And what does it matter if I delay another hour, another day? So I go to them.

The systems control room lies buried deep in the ship, in one of the few areas with no view of the stars. The room itself is dimly lit and decagonal, a display and a crude manual interface affixed to each of the walls. Rosenberg and Mosby are there with Ahmed, the chief technologist, and a subordinate technologist whose name I do not recall.

I move too quietly for them to notice my arrival. (Always, these details I cannot seem to get right. I wear human skin, but it will never fit exactly.) To announce myself, I say, "What has happened?"

Four pairs of eyes look in my direction. As soon as they register my presence, everyone tries talking at once. Rosenberg and Mosby quickly turn on each other. These humans spend so much time arguing about what to do, it's amazing they ever get anything done.

Finally, the rest of them agree to quiet down so Ahmed can speak. "We're getting power fluctuations all over the ship. Life support keeps trying to shut down—we've had to force a restart three times in the past fifteen minutes. No idea what's causing it."

This does not surprise me. The Brights did not design their systems architecture to be solid and immutable, but rather flexible and adaptive. "I will look," I say.

I place my palm on an exposed patch of hardware, grow an interface, and begin sifting through the diagnostic reports. Bright diagnostics are so literal they are almost evasive—always describing *what* is happening, but never hinting at *why*. I skip past the reports and prod gently at the underlying systems, doing the command equivalent of poking life support with a stick to see if it twitches.

Life support seems raw and hypersensitive, overreacting to stimulus. The shields seem lethargic, the main engines argumentative.

I mentally pull back to give my analysis to the waiting humans. "*Legacy* is experiencing some sort of systems destabilization, possibly triggered by the introduction of plant life in the central solarium. The ship is attempting to re-evaluate resource allocation and re-integrate, but systems integration seems to require guidance." For clarity, I add, "Guidance from a Bright engineer."

Predictably, Mosby wants to know if the power to the main cannon can be restored, and Rosenberg starts arguing about prioritization. Humans are a confrontational and violent people, whatever Liu might say to the contrary. Perhaps I understand this better than any trained ambassador could. Sometimes I even see a little of myself in them. Were I still an enforcer, would I not take great care to restore my weapons systems? Of course I would.

But I tell him, "Systems integration is a very complicated process. I most likely will not be able to complete it at all, let alone to your desired specifications."

This silences them. They all stare at me, wide-eyed. Have I somehow misspoken? In a situation like this, am I supposed to ply them with false hope instead of giving an honest status report?

I do not know the Brights the way an ambassador would; I am too young to even have spoken to anyone with first-hand knowledge of the Brights. I have only a superficial understanding of their thought patterns, and this is a task best reserved for someone who truly knew them. If not for a Bright itself.

I cannot do what the humans expect of me. And yet, I must try.

I close my eyes to block the stimulus so I can delve deeper. Soon, I can visualize the interconnected web of the ship's systems, each hub enmeshed among the others as if held in place with thick, pulsing vines. The offline sectors and systems appear marooned and dark, disconnected from the vital flow of the web.

Concentrating, I examine the systems more closely. Here: movement, change. And here, and here. Everywhere I scrutinize, the deep structural connections are unraveling, senescing, peeling away like flower petals destined to be supplanted with fruit. It is a process I understand only with academic distance—from my examination of plant genomes, not from personal experience. Still, I recognize the patterns as organic design, organic thinking. Only the Brights would build a ship as convoluted and self-referential as a genome.

Back in the control room, the humans are getting restless. "What is going on?" demands Mosby.

I retreat from the depths enough to answer him. "The architecture you have now was never meant to last. It is . . . " I do not know why I pick the word: "juvenile."

Mosby opens his mouth but Ahmed looks at him says, "Less talk, more work."

I must agree with Ahmed.

Ignoring the sounds of the control room, I return my focus to the *Legacy*'s architecture. I pull myself deeper, down into the disordered conglomeration of systems, losing awareness of my physical body. I focus all my mental acuity to study the ship.

It wants to grow, to metamorphose, to mature. I can tell this much: growth could be good, but it also could be cancerous. The old connections run dry and slough off, and the systems sprout wild new vine stubs that quest in every direction. Left to their own devices, the systems will strangle themselves with malformed, overgrown connective structure. But how am I to guide this process, rife with botanical zeal only a Bright could comprehend?

I pause, thinking. Metamorphosis is an animal concept. They are not vines, they are tentacles—and tentacles I understand. I think of my stellate fighter, how cleanly designed it was, with its eight rays each encapsulating a tentacle, and all the neatly arranged interfaces. And at the center, my brain to process and control.

So, me—and by extension, the control room—at the nexus of the web. The strongest connections, thick and steady, direct from each system to the nexus. Lesser connections, flexible and mutable, exchanging information among the systems themselves. I weave the ship the way I would weave my own flesh, easing the nascent tentacles over a new growth template as if it were a foreign genome to be integrated.

When the connections have been laid, the most delicate part still remains to be done: I carefully extract myself from the center of the web, leaving behind the shell of the control room, not so much a vacancy as a resting state. I pull away, leaving all the connections intact, the hollow space waiting patiently for its next command.

It is done. And, if all is right, it will even be receptive to the humans' control.

I rise slowly, like floating up to the surface from the depths of an ocean, the lights and sounds of the control room wavering and resolving. I blink, eyes slow to focus as the ciliary muscles reawaken to their duties.

On every wall of the room, the display screens shine with dazzling varicolored light. My tear ducts water, my pupils hasten to contract. I see the humans shading their faces with their hands, so I know my body's reaction is not an oversensitive after-effect of deep interfacing. The screens are very bright.

Yes, I realize. The screens are Bright.

"They're beautiful," says Rosenberg, "even if it hurts to look at them."

Ahmed is still bent over a console. "There's an audio recording, too, but the frequencies are all ultrasonic."

Rosenberg asks, "What are they saying?"

"It'll take a while for the translators to work it out," says Ahmed.

"Unnecessary," I say. I force some crude adjustments to the anatomy of my ears, expanding the range of my hearing. The recording is part-way through the message, but I wait until the end and it loops back to the beginning. "Roughly translated: the *Legacy*'s destination is a research base on a dwarf planet in the outskirts of the Brights' home system. They hope that, in the time it has taken your primitive species to develop interplanetary travel and discover *Legacy*, the pathogen will have gone extinct. The research base contains preserved samples of healthy Bright genomes. If you have the technology to restore plant biota from the genomic database and shepherd *Legacy* through the transition to maturity, you will be able to restore the Brights."

Everyone goes quiet. What have I done, meddling in the fate of these humans? An ambassador would have known better than to do for them what they cannot do themselves; I was a fool to think I could help without entangling myself. I feel nauseated, an unfamiliar physiological response to this upwelling of emotions inside me.

Ahmed is the one who says what they all must be thinking. "But it wasn't us who brought back the plants and guided the ship, it was you."

Which means the task of restoring the Brights falls on my shoulders, not theirs. "I know," I say, and rush from the room.

Hiding in the aft solarium, I stare out at the painted starscape. By human means of reckoning, this region of space was my home for three lifetimes: cold empty death punctuated with tiny oases of energy and life. They all belonged to me, once. I felt at home in the void, satisfied with what I was, and now I am trapped behind this glass and can only yearn for that silent solitary existence.

At my core I am a fighter pilot—a thug, a killer. I was made to do what the rest of the Sheekah, with their delicate dispositions, could not. How can anyone expect me to resurrect a whole sentient species when all my training and experience has been in dealing death, not life?

I am no one's savior. It is too heavy a burden to bear.

Liu comes in: shuffle, shuffle, soft steps on the deck. He approaches hesitantly, hanging back as if he doesn't wish to intrude on my thoughts.

"Rosenberg sent you?" I say. I am learning how their hierarchy works.

Liu takes the words for an invitation and joins me on the bench. "She wants me to try talking with you."

"We have now spoken." I look at him. "You may report success."

"Why, Ohree, that was almost a joke. Are you growing a sense of humor to go with the mammalian physique?"

"Doubtful," I say, looking away again. Though maybe I am.

Liu lets out a loud breath. His vocal pitch drops lower. "You know what I'm here to ask you about."

"Rosenberg wants me to continue with you to your destination. Rosenberg wants me to revive the Brights."

"We can't do it without you, obviously."

"You do not understand. The process will not be a simple one, like with the seeds. Brights are very complex organisms. I will have to adapt my whole physiology, I will have to gestate the embryos inside me."

Liu is silent for so long that I give up my view of the stars and turn to face him. He is staring at me. "What exactly do you have on your to-do list that ranks more important than this?"

I pause. "If they made the smallest mistake, if even one gene region is tainted with pathogenic code, I will die."

"Since when were you more afraid of dying than of not having a purpose?" Liu's lips curl in an expression I now know to indicate amusement. "How human of you."

The words fall on me like a blow. He is right—only two days ago I was contemplating suicide. I fall back on an older argument. "An ambassador would be properly trained for such a task, which I am not."

"You thought you couldn't guide the *Legacy* through her transition, but you could," he said. "It doesn't matter that your own society marked you a castaway. It doesn't matter what life you had before. You are capable of things you haven't even dreamt of yet, and it would honor us to be the ones who help you discover those things."

I go very still. I do not dare to hope this could be true. It violates a paradigm so deep-seated in my psyche that I did not even suspect its existence until now.

Liu says, "Humans aren't in the habit of changing their given names. Surnames, though, were originally descriptive—you were named for your profession, or the village you came from, or your parentage." He pauses, the silence almost livid in the air. "You don't have a surname."

If I was frozen before, now I am a comet lost between the stars—even my molecules feel stuck. I am sure I could not look away if I tried. I know Liu knows how Sheekah naming works.

Liu smiles, though somehow the expression seems grave, as if he understands exactly what it is he's doing. "I think we'll call you Ohree Brightbearer, if the sound of it suits you."

"Yes," I say, hardly able to breathe. "Yes, it suits me fine."

I am named, and there is work ahead of me.

Prayer

ROBERT REED

Fashion matters. In my soul of souls, I know that the dead things you carry on your body are real, real important. Grandma likes to call me a clotheshorse, which sounds like a good thing. For example, I've always known that a quality sweater means the world. I prefer soft organic wools woven around Class-C nanofibers—a nice high collar with sleeves riding a little big but with enough stopping power to absorb back-to-back kinetic charges. I want pants that won't slice when the shrapnel is thick, and since I won't live past nineteen, probably, I let the world see that this body's young and fit. (Morbid maybe, but that's why I think about death only in little doses.) I adore elegant black boots that ignore rain and wandering electrical currents, and everything under my boots and sweater and pants has to feel silky-good against the most important skin in my world. But essential beyond all else is what I wear on my face, which is more makeup than Grandma likes, and tattooed scripture on the forehead, and sparkle-eyes that look nothing but ordinary. In other words, I want people to see an average Christian girl instead of what I am, which is part of the insurgency's heart inside Occupied Toronto.

To me, guns are just another layer of clothes, and the best day ever lived was the day I got my hands on a barely used, cognitively damaged Mormon railgun. They don't make that model anymore, what with its willingness to change sides. And I doubt that there's ever been a more dangerous gun made by the human species. Shit, the boy grows his own ammo, and he can kill anything for hundreds of miles, and left alone he will invent ways to hide and charge himself on the sly, and all that time he waits waits waits for his master to come back around and hold him again.

I am his master now.

I am Ophelia Hanna Hanks, except within my local cell, where I wear the randomly generated, perfectly suitable name:

Ridiculous.

The gun's name is Prophet, and until ten seconds ago, he looked like scrap conduit and junk wiring. And while he might be cognitively impaired, Prophet is wickedly loyal to me. Ten days might pass without the two of us being in each other's reach, but that's the beauty of our dynamic: I can live normal and look normal, and while the enemy is busy watching everything else, a solitary 14-year-old girl slips into an alleyway that's already been swept fifty times today.

"Good day, Ridiculous."

"Good day to you, Prophet."

"And who are we going to drop into Hell today?"

"All of America," I say, which is what I always say.

Reliable as can be, he warns me, "That's a rather substantial target, my dear. Perhaps we should reduce our parameters."

"Okay. New Fucking York."

Our attack has a timetable, and I have eleven minutes to get into position.

"And the specific target?" he asks.

I have coordinates that are updated every half-second. I could feed one or two important faces into his menu, but I never kill faces. These are the enemy, but if I don't define things too closely, then I won't miss any sleep tonight.

Prophet eats the numbers, saying, "As you wish, my dear."

I'm carrying him, walking fast towards a fire door that will stay unlocked for the next ten seconds. Alarmed by my presence, a skinny rat jumps out of one dumpster, little legs running before it hits the oily bricks.

"Do you know it?" I ask.

The enemy likes to use rats as spies.

Prophet says, "I recognize her, yes. She has a nest and pups inside the wall."

"Okay," I say, feeling nervous and good.

The fire door opens when I tug and locks forever once I step into the darkness.

"You made it," says my gun.

"I was praying," I report.

He laughs, and I laugh too. But I keep my voice down, stairs needing to be climbed and only one of us doing the work.

She found me after a battle. She believes that I am a little bit stupid. I was damaged in the fight and she imprinted my devotions to her, and then using proxy tools and stolen wetware, she gave me the cognitive functions to be a loyal agent to the insurgency.

I am an astonishing instrument of mayhem, and naturally her superiors thought about claiming me for themselves.

But they didn't.

If I had the freedom to speak, I would mention this oddity to my Ridiculous. "Why would they leave such a prize with little you?"

"Because I found you first," she would say.

"War isn't a schoolyard game," I'd remind her.

"But I made you mine," she might reply. "And my bosses know that I'm a good soldier, and you like me, and stop being a turd."

No, we have one another because her bosses are adults. They are grown souls who have survived seven years of occupation, and that kind of achievement doesn't bless the dumb or the lucky. Looking at me, they see too much of a blessing, and nobody else dares to trust me well enough to hold me.

I know all of this, which seems curious.

I might say all of this, except I never do.

And even though my mind was supposedly mangled, I still remember being crafted and calibrated in Utah, hence my surname. But I am no Mormon. Indeed, I'm a rather agnostic soul when it comes to my interpretations of Jesus and His influence in the New World. And while there are all-Mormon units in the US military, I began my service with Protestants—Baptists and Missouri Synods mostly. They were bright clean happy believers who had recently arrived at Fort Joshua out on Lake Ontario. Half of that unit had already served a tour in Alberta, guarding the tar pits from little acts of sabotage. Keeping the Keystones safe is a critical but relatively simple duty. There aren't many people to watch, just robots and one another. The prairie was depopulated ten years ago, which wasn't an easy or cheap process; American farmers still haven't brought the ground back to full production, and that's one reason why the Toronto rations are staying small.

But patrolling the corn was easy work compared to sitting inside Fort Joshua, millions of displaced and hungry people staring at your walls.

Americans call this Missionary Work.

Inside their own quarters, alone except for their weapons and the Almighty, soldiers try to convince one another that the natives are beginning to love them. Despite a thousand lessons to the contrary, Canada is still that baby brother to the north, big and foolish but congenial in his heart, or at least capable of learning manners after the loving sibling delivers enough beat-downs.

What I know today—what every one of my memories tells me—is that the American soldiers were grossly unprepared. Compared to other units and other duties, I would even go so far as to propose that the distant generals were aware of their limitations yet sent the troops across the lake regardless, full of religion and love for each other and the fervent conviction that the United States was the empire that the world had always deserved.

Canada is luckier than most. That can't be debated without being deeply, madly stupid. Heat waves are killing the tropics. Acid has tortured the seas. The wealth of the previous centuries has been erased by disasters of weather and war and other inevitable surprises. But the worst of these sorrows haven't occurred in the Greater United States, and if they had half a mind, Canadians would be thrilled with the mild winters and long brilliant summers and the supportive grip of their big wise master.

My soldiers' first recon duty was simple: Walk past the shops along Queen.

Like scared warriors everywhere, they put on every piece of armor and every sensor and wired back-ups that would pierce the insurgent's jamming. And that should have been good enough. But by plan or by accident, some native let loose a few molecules of VX gas—just enough to trigger one of the biohazard alarms.

Then one of my brother-guns was leveled at a crowd of innocents, two dozen dead before the bloody rain stopped flying.

That's when the firefight really began.

Kinetic guns and homemade bombs struck the missionaries from every side. I was held tight by my owner—a sergeant with commendations for his successful defense of a leaky pipeline—but he didn't fire me once. His time was spent yelling for an orderly retreat, pleading with his youngsters to find sure targets before they hit the buildings with hypersonic rounds. But despite those good smart words, the patrol got itself trapped. There was a genuine chance that one of them might die, and that's when those devout men encased in body armor and faith decided to pray: Clasping hands, they opened channels to the Almighty, begging for thunder to be sent down on the infidels.

The Almighty is what used to be called the Internet—an American child reclaimed totally back in 2027.

A long stretch of shops and old buildings was struck from the sky.

That's what American soldiers do when the situation gets dicey. They pray, and the locals die by the hundreds, and the biggest oddity of that peculiar day was how the usual precise orbital weaponry lost its way, and half of my young men were wounded or killed in the onslaught while a tiny shaped charge tossed me a hundred meters down the road.

There I was discovered in the rubble by a young girl.

As deeply unlikely as that seems.

I don't want the roof. I don't need my eyes to shoot. An abandoned apartment on the top floor is waiting for me, and in particular, its dirty old bathroom. As a rule, I like bathrooms. They're the strongest part of any building, what with pipes running through the walls and floor. Two weeks ago, somebody I'll never know sealed the tube's drain and cracked the faucet just enough for a slow drip, and now the water sits near the brim. Water is essential for long shots. With four minutes to spare, I deploy Prophet's long legs, tipping him just enough toward the southeast, and then I sink him halfway into the bath, asking, "How's that feel?"

"Cold," he jokes.

We have three and a half minutes to talk.

I tell him, "Thank you."

His barrel stretches to full length, its tip just short of the moldy plaster ceiling. "Thank you for what?" he says.

"I don't know," I say.

Then I laugh, and he sort of laughs.

I say, "I'm not religious. At least, I don't want to be."

"What are you telling me, Ridiculous?"

"I guess . . . I don't know. Forget it."

And he says, "I will do my very best."

Under the water, down where the breech sits, ammunition is moving. Scrap metal and scrap nano-fibers have been woven into four bullets. Street fights require hundreds and thousands of tiny bullets, but each of these rounds is bigger than most carrots and shaped the same general way. Each one carries a brain and microrockets and eyes. Prophet is programming them with the latest coordinates while running every last-second test. Any little problem with a bullet can mean an ugly shot, or even worse, an explosion that rips away the top couple floors of this building.

At two minutes, I ask, "Are we set?"

"You're standing too close," he says.

"If I don't move, will you fire anyway?"

"Of course."

"Good," I say.

At ninety-five seconds, ten assaults are launched across southern Ontario. The biggest and nearest is fixated on Fort Joshua—homemade cruise missiles and lesser railguns aimed at that artificial island squatting in our beautiful lake. The assaults are meant to be loud and unexpected, and because every soldier thinks his story is important, plenty of voices suddenly beg with the Almighty, wanting His godly hand.

The nearby battle sounds like a sudden spring wind.

"I'm backing out of here," I say.

"Please do," he says.

At sixty-one seconds, most of the available American resources are glancing at each of these distractions, and a brigade of AIs is studying past tendencies and elaborate models of insurgency capabilities, coming to the conclusion that these events have no credible value toward the war's successful execution.

Something else is looming, plainly.

"God's will," says the nonbeliever.

"What isn't?" says the Mormon gun.

At seventeen seconds, two kilometers of the Keystone John pipeline erupt in a line of smoky flame, microbombs inside the heated tar doing their best to stop the flow of poisons to the south.

The Almighty doesn't need prayer to guide His mighty hand. This must be the main attack, and every resource is pulled to the west, making ready to deal with even greater hazards.

I shut the bathroom door and run for the hallway.

Prophet empties his breech, the first carrot already moving many times faster than the speed of sound as it blasts through the roof. Its three buddies are directly behind it, and the enormous release of stored energy turns the bathwater to steam, and with the first shot the iron tub is yanked free of the floor while the second and third shots kick the tub and the last of its water down into the bathroom directly downstairs. The final shot is going into the wrong part of the sky, but that's also part of the plan. I'm not supposed to be amazed by how many factors can be juggled at once, but they are juggled and I am amazed, running down the stairs to recover my good friend.

The schedule is meant to be secret and followed precisely. The Secretary of Carbon rides her private subway car to the UN, but instead of remaining indoors and safe, she has to come into the sunshine, standing with ministers and potentates who have gathered for this very important conference. Reporters are sitting in rows and cameras will be watching from every vantage point, and both groups are full of those who don't particularly like the Secretary. Part of her job is being despised, and fuck them. That's what she thinks whenever she attends these big public dances. Journalists are livestock, and this is a show put on for the meat. Yet even as the scorn builds, she shows a smile that looks warm and caring, and she carries a strong speech that will last for three minutes, provided she gives it. Her words are meant to reassure the world that full recovery is at hand. She will tell everyone that the hands of her government are wise and what the United States wants is happiness for every living breathing wonderful life on this great world—a world that with God's help will live for another five billion years.

For the camera, for the world, the Secretary of Carbon and her various associates invest a few moments in handshakes and important nods of the head.

Watching from a distance, without knowing anything, it would be easy to recognize that the smiling woman in brown was the one in charge.

The UN president shakes her hand last and then steps up to the podium. He was installed last year after an exhaustive search. Handsome and personable, and half as bright as he is ambitious, the President greets the press and then breaks from the script, shouting a bland "Hello" to the protestors standing outside the blast screens.

Five thousand people are standing in the public plaza, holding up signs and generated holos that have one clear message:

"END THE WARS NOW."

The Secretary knows the time and the schedule, and she feels a rare ache of nervousness, of doubt.

When they hear themselves mentioned, the self-absorbed protestors join together in one rehearsed shout that carries across the screens. A few reporters look at the throng behind them. The cameras and the real professionals focus on the human subjects. This is routine work. Reflexes are numb, minds lethargic. The Secretary picks out a few familiar faces, and then her assistant pipes a warning into her sparkle-eyes. One of the Keystones has been set on fire.

In reflex, the woman takes one step backward, her hands starting to lift to cover her head.

A mistake.

But she recovers soon enough, turning to her counterpart from Russia, telling him, "And congratulations on that new daughter of yours."

He is flustered and flattered. With a giddy nod, he says, "Girls are so much better than boys these days. Don't you think?"

The Secretary has no chance to respond.

A hypersonic round slams through the atmosphere, heated to a point where any impact will make it explode. Then it drops into an environment full of clutter and one valid target that must be acquired and reached before the fabulous energies shake loose from their bridle.

There is no warning sound.

The explosion lifts bodies and pieces of bodies, and while the debris rises, three more rounds plunge into the panicked crowd.

Every person in the area drops flat, hands over their heads.

Cameras turn, recording the violence and loss—more than three hundred dead and maimed in a horrific attack.

The Secretary and new father lie together on the temporary stage.

Is it her imagination, or is the man trying to cop a feel?

She rolls away from him, but she doesn't stand yet. The attack is finished, but she shouldn't know that. It's best to remain down and act scared, looking at the plaza, the air filled with smoke and pulverized concrete while the stubborn holos continue to beg for some impossible gift called Peace.

My grandmother is sharp. She is. Look at her once in the wrong way, and she knows something is wrong. Do it twice and she'll probably piece together what makes a girl turn quiet and strange.

But not today, she doesn't.

"What happened at school?" she asks.

I don't answer.

"What are you watching, Ophelia?"

Nothing. My eyes have been blank for half a minute now.

"Something went wrong at school, didn't it?"

Nothing is ever a hundred percent right at school, which is why it's easy to harvest a story that might be believed. Most people would believe it, at least. But after listening to my noise about snippy friends and broken trusts, she says, "I don't know what's wrong with you, honey. But that isn't it."

I nod, letting my voice die away.

She leaves my little room without closing the door. I sit and do nothing for about three seconds, and then the sparkle eyes take me back to the mess outside the UN. I can't count the times I've watched the impacts, the carnage. Hundreds of cameras were working, government cameras and media cameras and those carried by the protesters. Following at the digitals' heels are people talking about the tragedy and death tolls and who is responsible and how the war has moved to a new awful level.

"Where did the insurgents get a top-drawer railgun?" faces ask.

But I've carried Prophet for a couple years and fired him plenty of times. Just not into a public target like this, and with so many casualties, and all of the dead on my side of the fight.

That's the difference here: The world suddenly knows about me.

In the middle of the slaughter, one robot camera stays focused on my real targets, including the Secretary of Fuel and Bullshit. It's halfway nice, watching her hunker down in terror. Except she should have been in pieces, and there shouldn't be a face staring in my direction, and how Prophet missed our target by more than fifty meters is one big awful mystery that needs solving.

I assume a malfunction.

I'm wondering where I can take him to get his guidance systems recalibrated and ready for retribution.

Unless of course the enemy has figured out how to make railgun rounds fall just a little wide of their goals, maybe even killing some troublemakers in the process.

Whatever is wrong here, at least I know that it isn't my fault.

Then some little thing taps at my window.

From the next room, my grandmother asks, "What are you doing, Ophelia?"

I'm looking at the bird on my window sill. The enemy uses rats, and we use robins and house sparrows. But this is a red-headed woodpecker, which implies rank and special circumstances.

The bird gives a squawk, which is a coded message that my eyes have to play with for a little while. Then the messenger flies away.

"Ophelia?"

"I'm just thinking about a friend," I shout.

She comes back into my room, watching my expression all over again.

"A friend, you say?"

"He's in trouble," I say.

"Is that what's wrong?" she asks.

"Isn't that enough?"

Two rats in this alley don't convince me. I'm watching them from my new haven, measuring the dangers and possible responses. Then someone approaches the three of us, and in the best tradition of ratdom, my companions scurry into the darkness under a pile of rotting boards.

I am a plastic sack filled with broken machine parts.

I am motionless and harmless, but in my secret reaches, inside my very busy mind, I'm astonished to see my Ridiculous back again so soon, walking toward the rat-rich wood pile.

Five meters behind her walks an unfamiliar man.

To him, I take an immediate dislike.

He looks prosperous, and he looks exceptionally angry, wearing a fine suit made stiff with nano-armor and good leather shoes and a platoon of jamming equipment as well as two guns riding in his pockets, one that shoots poisoned ice as well as the gun that he trusts—a kinetic beast riding close to his dominant hand.

Ridiculous stops at the rot pile.

The man asks, "Is it there?"

"I don't know," she says, eyes down.

My girl has blue sparkle eyes, much like her original eyes—the ones left behind in the doctor's garbage bin.

"It looks like boards now?" he asks.

"He did," she lies.

"Not he," the man says, sounding like a google-head. "The machine is an It."

"Right," she says, kicking at the planks, pretending to look hard. "It's just a big gun. I keep forgetting."

The man is good at being angry. He has a tall frightful face and neck muscles that can't stop being busy. His right hand thinks about the gun in his pocket. The fingers keep flexing, wanting to grab it.

His gun is an It.

I am not.

"I put it here," she says.

She put me where I am now, which tells me even more.

"Something scared it," she says. "And now it's moved to another hiding place."

The man says, "Shit."

Slowly, carefully, he turns in a circle, looking at the rubble and the trash and the occasional normal object that might still work or might be me. Then with a tight slow voice, he says, "Call for it."

"Prophet," she says.

I say nothing.

"How far could it move?" he asks.

"Not very," she says. "The firing drained it down to nothing, nearly. And it hasn't had time to feed itself, even if it's found food."

"Bullshit," he says, coming my way.

Ridiculous watches me and him, the tattooed Scripture above her blue eyes dripping with sweat. Then the man kneels beside me, and she says, "I put the right guidance codes into him."

"You said that already." Then he looks back at her, saying, "You're not in trouble here. I told you that already."

His voice says a lot.

I have no power. But when his hands reach into my sack, what resembles an old capacitor cuts two of his fingers, which is worth some cursing and some secret celebration.

Ridiculous's face is twisted with worry, up until he looks back at her again. Then her expression turns innocent, pure and pretty and easy to believe.

Good girl, I think.

The man rises and pulls out the kinetic gun and shoots Ridiculous in the chest. If not for the wood piled up behind her, she would fly for a long distance. But instead of flying, she crashes and pulls down the wood around her, and one of those very untrustworthy rats comes out running, squeaking as it flees.

Ridiculous sobs and rolls and tries saying something.

He shoots her in the back, twice, and then says, "We never should have left it with you. All that luck dropping into our hands, which was crazy. Why should we have trusted the gun for a minute?"

She isn't dead, but her ribs are broken. And by the sound of it, the girl is fighting to get one good breath.

"Sure, it killed some bad guys," he says. "That's what a good spy does. He sacrifices a few on his side to make him look golden in the enemy's eyes."

I have no strength.

"You can't have gone far," he tells the alley. "We'll drop ordinance in here, take you out with the rats."

I cannot fight.

"Or you can show yourself to me," he says, the angry face smiling now. "Reveal yourself and we can talk."

Ridiculous sobs.

What is very easy is remembering the moment when she picked up me out of the bricks and dust and bloodied bits of human meat.

He gives my sack another good kick, seeing something.

And for the first time in my life, I pray. Just like that, as easy as anything, the right words come out of me, and the man bending over me hears nothing coming and senses nothing, his hands playing with my pieces when a fleck of laser light falls out of the sky and turns the angriest parts of his brain into vapor, into a sharp little pop.

I'm still not breathing normally. I'm still a long way from being able to think straight about anything. Gasping and stupid, I'm kneeling in a basement fifty meters from where I nearly died, and Prophet is suckling on an unsecured outlet, endangering both of us. But he needs power and ammunition, and I like the damp dark in here, waiting for my body to come back to me.

"You are blameless," he says.

I don't know what that means.

He says, "You fed the proper codes into me. But there were other factors, other hands, and that's where the blame lies."

"So you are a trap," I say.

"Somebody's trap," he says.

"The enemy wanted those civilians killed," I say, and then I break into the worst-hurting set of coughs that I have ever known.

He waits.

"I trusted you," I say.

"But Ridiculous," he says.

"Shut up," I say.

"Ophelia," he says.

I hold my sides, sipping my breaths.

"You assume that this war has two sides," he says. "But there could be a third player at large, don't you see?"

"What should I see?"

"Giving a gun to their enemies is a huge risk. If the Americans wanted to kill their political enemies, it would be ten times easier to pull something out of their armory and set it up in the insurgency's heart."

"Somebody else planned all of this, you're saying."

"I seem to be proposing that, yes."

"But that man who came with me today, the one you killed . . . he said the Secretary showed us a lot with her body language. She knew the attack was coming. She knew when it would happen. Which meant that she was part of the planning, which was a hundred percent American."

"Except whom does the enemy rely on to make their plans?"

"Tell me," I say.

Talking quietly, making the words even more important, he says, "The Almighty."

"What are we talking about?" I ask.

He says nothing, starting to change his shape again.

"The Internet?" I ask. "What, you mean it's conscious now? And it's working its own side in this war?"

"The possibility is there for the taking," he says.

But all I can think about are the dead people and those that are hurt and those that right now are sitting at their dinner table, thinking that some fucking Canadian bitch has made their lives miserable for no goddamn reason.

"You want honesty," Prophet says.

"When don't I?"

He says, "This story about a third side . . . it could be a contingency buried inside my tainted software. Or it is the absolute truth, and the Almighty is working with both of us, aiming toward some grand, glorious plan."

I am sort of listening, and sort of not.

Prophet is turning shiny, which happens when his body is in the middle of changing shapes. I can see little bits of myself reflected in the liquid metals and the diamonds floating on top. I see a thousand little-girl faces staring at me, and what occurs to me now—what matters more than anything else today—is the idea that there can be more than two sides in any war.

I don't know why, but that the biggest revelation of all.

When there are more than two sides, that means that there can be too many sides to count, and one of those sides, standing alone, just happens to be a girl named Ophelia Hanna Hanks.

A Hundred Ghosts Parade Tonight

XIA JIA

(TRANSLATED BY KEN LIU)

Awakening of Insects, the Third Solar Term:

Ghost Street is long but narrow, like an indigo ribbon. You can cross it in eleven steps, but to walk it from end to end takes a full hour.

At the western end is Lanruo Temple, now fallen into ruin. Inside the temple is a large garden full of fruit trees and vegetable patches, as well as a bamboo grove and a lotus pond. The pond has fish, shrimp, dojo loaches, and yellow snails. So supplied, I have food to eat all year.

It's evening, and I'm sitting at the door to the main hall, reading a copy of *Huainanzi,* the Han Dynasty essay collection, when along comes Yan Chixia, the great hero, vanquisher of demons and destroyer of evil spirits. He's carrying a basket on the crook of his elbow, the legs of his pants rolled all the way up, revealing calves caked with black mud. I can't help but laugh at the sight.

My teacher, the Monk, hears me and walks out of the dark corner of the main hall, gears grinding, and hits me on the head with his ferule.

I hold my head in pain, staring at the Monk in anger. But his iron face is expressionless, just like the statues of buddhas in the main hall. I throw down the book and run outside, while the Monk pursues me, his joints clanking and creaking the whole time. They are so rusted that he moves as slow as a snail.

I stop in front of Yan, and I see that his basket contains several new bamboo shoots, freshly dug from the ground.

"I want to eat meat," I say, tilting my face up to look at him. "Can you shoot some buntings with your slingshot for me?"

"Buntings are best eaten in the fall, when they're fat," says Yan. "Now is the time for them to breed chicks. If you shoot them, there won't be buntings to eat next year."

"Just one, pleaaaaase?" I grab onto his sleeve and act cute. But he shakes his head resolutely, handing me the basket. He takes off his conical sedge hat and wipes the sweat off his face.

I laugh again as I look at him. His face is as smooth as an egg, with just a few wisps of curled black hair like weeds that have been missed by the gardener. Legend has it that his hair and beard used to be very thick, but I'm always pulling a few strands out now and then as a game. After so many years, these are all the hairs he has left.

"You must have died of hunger in a previous life," Yan says, cradling the back of my head in his large palm. "The whole garden is full of food for you. No one is here to fight you for it."

I make a face at him and take the basket of food.

The rain has barely stopped; insects cry out from the wet earth. A few months from now, green grasshoppers will be jumping everywhere. You can catch them, string them along a stick, and roast them over the fire, dripping sweet-smelling fat into the flames.

As I picture this, my empty stomach growls as though filled with chittering insects already. I begin to run.

The golden light of the evening sun splatters over the slate slabs of the empty street, stretching my shadow into a long, long band.

I run back home, where Xiao Qian is combing her hair in the darkness. There are no mirrors in the house, so she always takes off her head and puts it on her knees to comb. Her hair looks like an ink-colored scroll, so long that the strands spread out to cover the whole room.

I sit quietly to the side until she's done combing her hair, puts it up in a moon-shaped bun, and secures it with a pin made of dark wood inlaid with red coral beads. Then she lifts her head and re-attaches it to her neck, and asks me if it's sitting straight. I don't understand why Xiao Qian cares so much. Even if she just tied her head to her waist with a sash, everyone would still think she's beautiful.

But I look, seriously, and nod. "Beautiful," I say.

Actually, I can't really see very well. Unlike the ghosts, I cannot see in the dark.

Xiao Qian is happy with my affirmation. She takes my basket and goes into the kitchen to cook. As I sit and work the bellows next to her, I tell her about my day. Just as I get to the part where the Monk hit me on the head with the ferule, Xiao Qian reaches out and lightly caresses my head where I was hit. Her hand is cold and pale, like a piece of jade.

"You need to study hard and respect your teacher," Xiao Qian says. "Eventually you'll leave here and make your way in the real world. You have to have some knowledge and real skills."

Her voice is very soft, like cotton candy, and so the swelling on my head stops hurting.

Xiao Qian tells me that Yan Chixia found me on the steps of the temple when I was a baby. I cried and cried because I was so hungry. Yan Chixia was at his wit's end when he finally stuffed a handful of creeping rockfoil into my mouth. I sucked on the juice from the grass and stopped crying.

No one knows who my real parents are.

Even back then, Ghost Street had been doing poorly. No tourists had been coming by for a while. That hasn't changed. Xiao Qian tells me that it's probably because people invented some other attraction, newer, fresher, and so they forgot about the old attractions. She's seen similar things happen many times before.

Before she became a ghost, Xiao Qian tells me, she had lived a very full life. She had been married twice, gave birth to seven children, and raised them all.

And then her children got sick, one after another. In order to raise the money to pay the doctors, Xiao Qian sold herself off in pieces: teeth, eyes, breasts, heart, liver, lungs, bone marrow, and finally, her soul. Her soul was sold to Ghost Street, where it was sealed inside a female ghost's body. Her children died anyway.

Now she has white skin and dark hair. The skin is light sensitive. If she's in direct sunlight she'll burn.

After he found me, Yan Chixia had walked up and down all of Ghost Street before he decided to give me to Xiao Qian to raise.

I've seen a picture of Xiao Qian back when she was alive. It was hidden in a corner of a drawer in her dresser. The woman in the picture had thick eyebrows, huge eyes, a wrinkled face—far uglier than the way Xiao Qian looks now. Still, I often see her cry as she looks at that picture. Her tears are a pale pink. When they fall against her white dress they soak into the fabric and spread, like blooming peach flowers.

Every ghost is full of stories from when they were alive. Their bodies have been cremated and the ashes mixed into the earth, but their stories still live on. During the day, when all of Ghost Street is asleep, the stories become dreams and circle under the shadows of the eaves, like swallows without nests. During those hours, only I'm around, walking in the street, and only I can see them and hear their buzzing song.

I'm the only living person on Ghost Street.

Xiao Qian says that I don't belong here. When I grow up, I'll leave.

The smell of good food fills the room. The insects in my stomach chitter even louder.

I eat dinner by myself: preserved pork with stir-fried bamboo shoots, shrimp-paste-flavored egg soup, and rice balls with chives, still hot in my hands. Xiao Qian sits and watches me. Ghosts don't eat. None of the inhabitants of Ghost Street, not even Yan Chixia or the Monk, ever eat.

I bury my face in the bowl, eating as fast as I can. I wonder, after I leave, will I ever eat such delicious food again?

Major Heat, the Twelfth Solar Term:

After night falls, the world comes alive.

I go alone to the well in the back to get water. I turn the wheel and it squeaks, but the sound is different from usual. I look down into the well and see a long-haired ghost in a white dress sitting in the bucket.

I pull her up and out. Her wet hair covers her face, leaving only one eye to stare at me out of a gap.

"Ning, tonight is the Carnival. Aren't you going?"

"I need to get water for Xiao Qian's bath," I answer. "After the bath we'll go."

She strokes my face lightly. "You are a foolish child."

She has no legs, so she has to leave by crawling on her hands. I hear the sound of crawling, creeping all around me. Green will-o'-the-wisps flit around, like anxious fireflies. The air is filled with the fragrance of rotting flowers.

I go back to the dark bedroom and pour the water into the wooden bathtub. Xiao Qian undresses. I see a crimson bar code along her naked back, like a tiny snake. Bright white lights pulse under her skin.

"Why don't you take a bath with me?" she asks.

I shake my head, but I'm not sure why. Xiao Qian sighs. "Come." So I don't refuse again.

We sit in the bathtub together. The cedar smells nice. Xiao Qian rubs my back with her cold, cold hands, humming lightly. Her voice is very beautiful. Legend has it that any man who heard her sing fell in love with her.

When I grow up, will I fall in love with Xiao Qian? I think and look at my small hands, the skin now wrinkled from the bath like wet wrapping paper.

After the bath, Xiao Qian combs my hair, and dresses me in a new shirt that she made for me. Then she sticks a bunch of copper coins, green and dull, into my pocket.

"Go have fun," she says. "Remember not to eat too much!"

Outside, the street is lit with countless lanterns, so bright that I can no longer see the stars that fill the summer sky.

Demons, ghosts, all kinds of spirits come out of their ruined houses, out of cracks in walls, rotting closets, dry wells. Hand-in-hand, shoulder-by-shoulder, they parade up and down Ghost Street until the narrow street is filled.

I squeeze myself into the middle of the crowd, looking all around. The stores and kiosks along both sides of the street send forth all kinds of delicious smells, tickling my nose like butterflies. The vending ghosts see me and call for me, the only living person, to try their wares.

"Ning! Come here! Fresh sweet osmanthus cakes, still hot!"

"Sugar roasted chestnuts! Sweet smelling and sweeter tasting!"

"Fried dough, the best fried dough!"

"Long pig dumplings! Two long pig dumplings for one coin!"

"Ning, come eat a candy man. Fun to play and fun to eat!"

Of course the "long pig dumplings" are really just pork dumplings. The vendor says that just to attract the tourists and give them a thrill.

But I look around, and there are no tourists.

I eat everything I can get my hands on. Finally, I'm so full that I have to sit down by the side of the road to rest a bit. On the opposite side of the street is a temporary stage lit by a huge bright white paper lantern. Onstage, ghosts are performing: sword-swallowing, fire-breathing, turning a beautiful girl into a skeleton. I'm bored by these tricks. The really good show is still to come.

A yellow-skinned old ghost pushes a cart of masks in front of me.

"Ning, why don't you pick a mask? I have everything: Ox-Head, Horse-Face, Black-Faced and White-Faced Wuchang, Asura, Yaksha, Rakshasa, Pixiu, and even Lei Gong, the Duke of Thunder."

I spend a long time browsing, and finally settle on a Rakshasa mask with red hair and green eyes. The yellow-skinned old ghost thanks me as he takes my coin, dipping his head down until his back is bent like a bow.

I put the mask on and continue strutting down the street. Suddenly loud Carnival music fills the air, and all the ghosts stop and then shuffle to the sides of the street.

I turn around and see the parade coming down the middle of the street. In front are twenty one-foot tall green toads in two columns, striking gongs, thumping drums, strumming *huqin,* and blowing bamboo *sheng.* After them come twenty centipede spirits in black clothes, each holding varicolored lanterns and dancing complicated steps. Behind them are twenty snake spirits in yellow dresses, throwing confetti into the air. And there are more behind them but I can't see so far.

Between the marching columns are two Cyclopes in white robes, each as tall as a three-story house. They carry a palanquin on their shoulders, and from within Xiao Qian's song rolls out, each note as bright as a star in the sky, falling one by one onto my head.

Fireworks of all colors rise up: bright crimson, pale green, smoky purple, shimmering gold. I look up and feel as though I'm becoming lighter myself, floating into the sky.

As the parade passes from west to east, all the ghosts along the sides of the street join, singing and dancing. They're heading for the old osmanthus tree at the eastern end of Ghost Street, whose trunk is so broad that three men stretching their arms out can barely surround it. A murder of crows lives there, each one capable of human speech. We call the tree Old Ghost Tree, and it is said to be in charge of all of Ghost Street. Whoever pleases it prospers; whoever goes against its wishes fails.

But I know that the parade will never get to the Old Ghost Tree.

When the parade is about half way down the street, the earth begins to shake and the slate slabs crack open. From the yawning gaps huge white bones crawl out, each as thick as the columns holding up Lanruo Temple. The bones slowly gather together and assemble into a giant skeleton, glinting like white porcelain in the moonlight. Now black mud springs forth from its feet and crawls up the skeleton, turning into flesh. Finally, a colossal Dark Yaksha stands before us, its single horn so large that it seems to pierce the night sky.

The two Cyclopes don't even reach its calves.

The Dark Yaksha turns its huge head from side to side. This is a standard part of every Carnival. It is supposed to abduct a tourist. On nights when there are no tourists, it must go back under the earth, disappointed, to wait for the next opportunity.

Slowly, it turns its gaze on me, focusing on my presence. I pull off my mask and stare back. Its gaze feels hot, the eyes as red as burning coal.

Xiao Qian leans out from the palanquin, and her cry pierces the suddenly quiet night air: "Ning, run! Run!"

The wind lifts the corner of her dress, like a dark purple petal unfolding. Her face is like jade, with orange lights flowing underneath.

I turn and run as fast as I can. Behind me I hear the heavy footsteps of the Dark Yaksha. With every quaking, pounding step, shingles fall from houses on both sides like overripe fruits. I am now running like the wind, my bare feet striking the slate slabs lightly: *pat, pat, pat*. My heart pounds against my chest: *thump, thump, thump*. Along the entire frenzied Ghost Street, mine is the only living heart.

But both the ghosts and I know that I'm not in any real danger. A ghost can never hurt a real person. That's one of the rules of the game.

I run towards the west, towards Lanruo Temple. If I can get to Yan Chixia before the Yaksha catches me, I'll be safe. This is also part of the performance. Every Carnival, Yan puts on his battle gear and waits on the steps of the main hall.

As I approach, I cry out: "Help! Save me! Oh Hero Yan, save me!"

In the distance I hear his long ululating cry and see his figure leaping over the wall of the temple to land in the middle of the street. He holds in his left hand a Daoist charm: red character written against a yellow background. He reaches behind his back with his right hand and pulls out his sword, the Demon Slayer.

He stands tall and shouts into the night sky, "Brazen Demon! How dare you harm innocent people? I, Yan Chixia, will carry out justice today!"

But tonight, he forgot to wear his sedge hat. His egg-shaped face is exposed to the thousands of lanterns along Ghost Street, with just a few wisps of hair curled like question marks on a blank page. The silly sight is such a contrast against his serious mien that I start to laugh even as I'm running. And that makes me choke and can't catch my breath so I fall against the cold slate surface of the street.

This moment is my best memory for the summer.

Cold Dew, the Seventeenth Solar Term:

A thin layer of clouds hides the moon. I'm crouching by the side of the lotus pond in Lanruo Temple. All I can see are the shadows cast by the lotus leaves, rising and falling slowly with the wind.

The night is as cold as the water. Insects hidden in the grass won't stop singing.

The eggplants and string beans in the garden are ripe. They smell so good that I have a hard time resisting the temptation. All I can think about is to steal some under the cover of night. Maybe Yan Chixia was right: in a previous life I must have died of hunger.

So I wait, and wait. But I don't hear Yan Chixia's snores. Instead, I hear light footsteps cross the grassy path to stop in front of Yan Chixia's cabin. The door opens, the steps go in. A moment later, the voices of a man and a woman drift out of the dark room: Yan Chixia and Xiao Qian.

Qian: "Why did you ask me to come?"

Yan: "You know what it's about."

Qian: "I can't leave with you."

Yan: "Why not?"

Qian: "A few more years. Ning is still so young."

"Ning, Ning!" Yan's voice grows louder. "I think you've been a ghost for too long."

Qian sounds pitiful. "I raised Ning for so many years. How can I just get up and leave him?"

"You're always telling me that Ning is still too young, always telling me to wait. Do you remember how many years it has been?"

"I can't."

"You sew a new set of clothes for him every year. How can you forget?" Yan chuckles, a cold sound. "I remember very clearly. The fruits and vegetables in this garden ripen like clockwork, once a year. I've seen them do it fifteen times. Fifteen! But has Ning's appearance changed any since the year he turned seven? You still think he's alive, he's real?"

Xiao Qian remains silent for a moment. Then I hear her crying.

Yan sighs. "Don't lie to yourself any more. He's just like us, nothing more than a toy. Why are you so sad? He's not worth it."

Xiao Qian just keeps on crying.

Yan sighs again. "I should never have picked him up and brought him back."

Xiao Qian whispers through the tears, "Where can we go if we leave Ghost Street?"

Yan has no answer.

The sound of Xiao Qian's crying makes my heart feel constricted. Silently, I sneak away and leave the old temple through a hole in the wall.

The thin layer of clouds chooses this moment to part. The cold moonlight scatters itself against the slate slabs of the street, congealing into drops of glittering dew. My bare feet against the ground feel so cold that my whole body shivers.

A few stores are still open along Ghost Street. The vendors greet me enthusiastically, asking me to sample their green bean biscuits and sweet osmanthus cake. But I don't want to. What's the point? I'm just like them, maybe even less than them.

Every ghost used to be alive. Their fake, mechanical bodies host real souls. But I'm fake throughout, inside and outside. From the day I was born, made, I was fake. Every ghost has stories of when they were alive, but I don't. Every ghost had a father, a mother, a family, memories of their love, but I don't have any of that.

Xiao Qian once told me that Ghost Street's decline came about because people, real people, found more exciting, newer toys. Maybe I am one of those toys: made with newer, better technology, until I could pass for the real thing. I can cry, laugh, eat, piss and shit, fall, feel pain, ooze blood, hear my own heartbeat, grow up from a simulacrum of a baby—except that my growth stops when I'm seven. I'll never be a grown up.

Ghost Street was built to entertain the tourists, and all the ghosts were their toys. But I'm just a toy for Xiao Qian.

Pretending that the fake is real only makes the real seem fake.

I walk slowly toward the eastern end of the street, until I stop under the Old Ghost Tree. The sweet fragrance of osmanthus fills the foggy night air, cool and calming. Suddenly I want to climb into the tree. That way, no one will find me.

The Old Ghost Tree leans down with its branches to help me.

I sit, hidden among the dense branches, and feel calmer. The crows perch around me, their glass eyes showing hints of a dark red glow. One of them speaks: "Ning, this is a beautiful night. Why aren't you at Lanruo Temple, stealing vegetables?"

The crow is asking a question to which it already knows the answer. The Old Ghost Tree knows everything that happens on Ghost Street. The crows are its eyes and ears.

"How can I know for sure," I ask, "that I'm a real person?"

"You can chop off your head," the crow answers. "A real person will die with his head cut off, but a ghost will not."

"But what if I cut off my head and die? I'll be no more."

The crow laughs, the sound grating and unpleasant to listen to. Two more crows fly down, holding in their beaks antique bronze mirrors. Using the little moonlight that leaks through the leaves, I finally see myself in the mirrors: small face, dark hair, thin neck. I lift the hair off the back of my neck, and in the double reflections of the mirrors, I see a crimson bar code against the skin, like a tiny snake.

I remember Xiao Qian's cool hands against my spine on that hot summer night. I think and think, until tears fall from my eyes.

Winter Solstice, the Twenty-Second Solar Term:

This winter has been both dry and cold, but I often hear the sound of thunder in the distance. Xiao Qian says that it's the Thunder Calamity, which happens only once every thousand years.

The Thunder Calamity punishes demons and ghosts and lost spirits. Those who can escape it can live for another thousand years. Those who can't will be burnt away until no trace is left of them.

I know perfectly well that there's no such thing as a "Thunder Calamity" in this world. Xiao Qian has been a ghost for so long that she's now gone a little crazy. She holds onto me with her cold hands, her face as pale as a sheet of paper. She says that to hide from the Calamity, a ghost must find a real person with a good heart to stay beside her. That way, just like how one wouldn't throw a shoe at a mouse sitting beside an expensive vase, the Duke of Thunder will not strike the ghost.

Because of her fear, my plan to leave has been put on hold. In secret I've already prepared my luggage: a few stolen potatoes, a few old shirts. My body isn't growing any more anyway, so these clothes will last me a long time. I didn't take any of the old copper coins from Xiao Qian though. Perhaps the outside world does not use them.

I really want to leave Ghost Street. I don't care where I go; I just want to see the world. Anywhere but here.

I want to know how real people live.

But still, I linger.

On Winter Solstice it snows. The snowflakes are tiny, like white sawdust. They melt as soon as they hit the ground. Only a very thin layer has accumulated by noon.

I walk alone along the street, bored. In past years I would go to Lanruo Temple to find Yan Chixia. We would knock an opening in the ice covering the lotus pond, and lower our jury-rigged fishing pole beneath the ice. Winter catfish are very fat and taste fantastic when roasted with garlic.

But I haven't seen Yan Chixia in a long time. I wonder if his beard and hair have grown out a bit.

Thunder rumbles in the sky, closer, then further away, leaving only a buzzing sensation in my ears. I walk all the way to the Old Ghost Tree, climb up into its branches, and sit still. Snowflakes fall all around me but not on me. I feel calm and warm. I curl up and tuck my head under my arms, falling asleep like a bird.

In my dream, I see Ghost Street turning into a long, thin snake. The Old Ghost Tree is the head, Lanruo Temple the tail, the slate slabs the scales. On each scale is drawn the face of a little ghost, very delicate and beautiful.

But the snake continues to writhe as though in great pain. I watch carefully and see that a mass of termites and spiders is biting its tail, making a sound like silkworms feeding on mulberry leaves. With sharp mandibles and claws, they tear off the scales on the snake one by one, revealing the flesh underneath. The snake struggles silently, but disappears inch by inch into the maws of the insects. When its body is almost completely eaten, it finally makes a sharp cry, and turns its lonesome head towards me.

I see that its face is Xiao Qian's.

I wake up. The cold wind rustles the leaves of the Old Ghost Tree. It's too quiet around me. All the crows have disappeared to who knows where except one that is very old and ugly. It's crouching in front of me, its beak dangling like the tip of a long mustache.

I shake it awake, anxious. It stares at me with two broken-glass eyes, croaking to me in its mechanical, flat voice, "Ning, why are you still here?"

"Where should I be?"

"Anywhere is good," it says. "Ghost Street is finished. We're all finished."

I stick my head out of the leaves of the Old Ghost Tree. Under the slate-grey sky, I see the murder of crows circling over Lanruo Temple in the distance, cawing incessantly. I've never seen anything like this.

I jump down from the tree and run. As I run along the narrow street, I pass dark doors and windows. The cawing of the crows has awakened many of the ghosts, but they don't dare to go outside, where there's light. All they can do is to peek out from cracks in doors, like a bunch of crickets hiding under houses in winter.

The old walls of Lanruo Temple, long in need of repairs, have been pushed down. Many giant mechanical spiders made of steel are crawling all over the main hall, breaking off the dark red glass shingles and sculpted wooden molding, piece by piece, and throwing the pieces into the snow on the ground. They have flat bodies, blue-glowing eyes, and sharp mandibles, as ugly as you can imagine. From deep within their bodies comes a rumbling noise like thunder.

The crows swoop around them, picking up bits of broken shingles and bricks on the ground and dropping them on the spiders. But they are too weak and the spiders ignore them. The broken shingle pieces strike against the steel shells, making faint, hollow echoes.

The vegetable garden has been destroyed. All that remains are some mud and pale white roots. I see one of the Monk's rusted arms sticking out of a pile of broken bricks.

I run through the garden, calling for Yan Chixia. He hears me and slowly walks out of his cabin. He's still wearing his battle gear: sedge hat over his head, the sword Demon Slayer in his hand. I want to shout for him to fight the spiders, but somehow I can't spit the words out. The words taste like bitter, astringent paste stuck in my throat.

Yan Chixia stares at me with his sad eyes. He comes over to hold my hands. His hands are as cold as Xiao Qian's.

We stand together and watch as the great and beautiful main hall is torn apart bit by bit, collapses, turns into a pile of rubble: shingles, bricks, wood, and mud. Nothing is whole.

They've destroyed all of Lanruo Temple: the walls, the main hall, the garden, the lotus pond, the bamboo grove, and Yan Chixia's cabin. The only thing left is a muddy ruin.

Now they're moving onto the rest of Ghost Street. They pry up the slate slabs, flatten the broken houses along the sides of the street. The ghosts hiding in the houses are chased into the middle of the street. As they run, they scream and scream, while their skin slowly burns in the faint sunlight. There are no visible flames. But you can see the skin turning black in patches, and the smell of burning plastic is everywhere.

I fall into the snow. The smell of burning ghost skin makes me vomit. But there's nothing in my stomach to throw up. So I cry during the breaks in the dry heaves.

So this is what the Thunder Calamity looks like.

The ghosts, their faces burned away, continue to cry and run and struggle in the snow. Their footprints criss-cross in the snow, like a child's handwriting. I suddenly think of Xiao Qian, and so I start to run again.

Xian Qian is still sitting in the dark bedroom. She combs her hair as she sings. Her melody floats in the gaps between the roaring, rumbling thunder of the spiders, so quiet, so transparent, like a dreamscape under the moon.

From her body come the fragrances of myriad flowers and herbs, layer after layer, like gossamer. Her hair floats up into the air like a flame, fluttering without cease. I stand and listen to her sing, my face full of tears, until the whole house begins to shake.

From on top of the roof, I hear the sound of steel clanging, blunt objects striking against each other, heavy footsteps, and then Yan Chixia's shouting.

Suddenly, the roof caves in, bringing with it a rain of shingles and letting in a bright patch of grey sky full of fluttering snowflakes. I push Xiao Qian into a dark corner, out of the way of the light.

I run outside the house. Yan Chixia is standing on the roof, holding his sword in front of him. The cold wind stretches his robe taut like a grey flag.

He jumps onto the back of a spider, and stabs at its eyes with his sword. The spider struggles hard and throws Yan off its back. Then the spider grabs Yan with two sharp claws and pulls him into its sharp, metallic, grinding mandibles. It chews and chews, like a man chewing kimchee, until pieces of Yan Chixia's body are falling out of its mandibles onto the shingles of the roof. Finally, Yan's head falls off the roof and rolls to a stop next to my feet, like a hard-boiled egg.

I pick up his head. He stares at me with his dead eyes. There are no tears in them, only anger and regret. Then with the last of his strength, Yan closes his eyes, as though he cannot bear to watch any more.

The spider continues to chew and grind up the rest of Yan Chixia's body. Then it leaps down from the roof, and, rumbling, crawls towards me. Its eyes glow with a deep blue light.

Xiao Qian jumps from behind me and grabs me by the waist, pulling me back. I pry her hands off of me and push her back into the dark room. Then I pick up Yan Chixia's sword and rush towards the spider.

The cold blue light of a steel claw flashes before my eyes. Then my head strikes the ground with a muffled *thump*. Blood spills everywhere.

The world is now tilted: tilted sky, tilted street, tilted snow falling diagonally. With every bit of my strength, I turn my eyes to follow the spider. I see that it's chewing on my body. A stream of dark red fluid drips out of its beak, bubbling, warm, the droplets slowly spreading in the snow.

As the spider chews, it slows down gradually. Then it stops moving, the blue light in its eyes dim and then go out.

As though they have received some signal, all the other spiders also stop one by one. The rumbling thunder stops, plunging the world into silence.

The wind stops too. Snow begins to stick to the spiders' steel bodies.

I want to laugh, but I can't. My head is now separated from my body, so there's no way to get air into the lungs and then out to my vocal cords. So I crack my lips open until the smile is frozen on my face.

The spiders believed that I was alive, a real person. They chewed my body and tasted flesh and saw blood. But they aren't allowed to harm real people. If they do they must destroy themselves. That's also part of the rules. Ghosts, spiders, it doesn't matter. Everyone has to follow the rules.

I never imagined that the spiders would be so stupid. They're even easier to fool than ghosts.

The scene in my eyes grows indistinct, fades, as though a veil is falling from the sky, covering my head. I remember the words of the crows. So it's true. When your head is cut off, you really die.

I grew up on this street; I ran along this street. Now I'm finally going to die on this street, just like a real person.

A pair of pale, cold hands reaches over, stroking my face.

The wind blows and covers my face with a few pale pink peach petals. But I know they're not peach petals. They're Xiao Qian's tears, mixed with snow.

Originally published in Chinese in *Science Fiction World* in 2010.

And the Hollow Space Inside
MARI NESS

Doug reaches for my hand as the ship approaches. He continues to hold it as the great doors open, as we watch them leave the ship. They pause; they have been in space and ultra-low gravity for five years now. Five years, one month, and three days, to be precise; I cannot believe my mind has memorized this.

We are too far away to see this, but I know their eyelids are blinking as they adjust, process, calculate, move, adjust again, the change in gravity no more than a problem to be solved.

As always, I am struck by how human and inhuman they look. Even their pauses have a precise, calculated feel. No one has ever seen them show uncertainty. No one ever will.

Gravity adjustments made, they walk with precision to the terminal, directly in front of us. It takes me a moment to recognize her, out of the eight faces. That is not surprising; it has been twelve years since I last saw her. What is surprising is how, even now, I am still desperately looking for any trace of my daughter's smile in my daughter's face.

The Mars missions, we were assured, would be the eventual saving grace of humanity. Oh, certainly, we hadn't managed to use up all of the world's resources yet, but that was only a matter of time. Population growth had slowed, but not stalled out completely, and wars over resources kept getting bloodier—while not reducing the population much. Mars was the only planet we could reach in an acceptable period of time, terraform, and begin colonizing. Other worlds would come, but by the time we reached the next nearest acceptable planet—a forty-year journey each way, under optimum conditions that few scientists thought we would meet—it would be too late for Earth. The Mars missions offered us that saving grace.

Only one problem: ordinary humans couldn't survive the trip.

Beside me, Doug takes a deep breath. "She looks good."

"Yes," I agree.

The four years in low gravity, not to mention the years of dehydrated food before that, should have taken their toll, but she still looks fit and considerably younger than her actual age. Then again, she always did. They all did, a side effect of programming and lack of temptation, and (but this is only my opinion) emotions and stress.

The eight of them reach the terminal, turn in unison, and wave in precision. I have to remind myself once again that I have been assured that they all have individual implants and computers, individual programming. They were all expected to perform different tasks, after all; it would make no sense to have them.

They vanish into the facility.

"They didn't say hello," says Doug.

I do not tell him that I am relieved.

The facility explained: humans needed interaction. A mere eight people, stuck together in the tight confines of a ship, and then on the almost equally tight confines of the first Mars base, could not be trusted to stay sane. The astronauts on the space stations had remained sane only because they were regularly rotated in and out, and could also continue to converse via radio and satellite to people back on earth. By the time the mission reached Mars, these transmissions would be delayed—not by much, but just enough to leave a long silence after a statement.

Just enough to drive people over the edge—only this edge was out in space, or on a hostile planet with no real edge to go to.

Unless they had no edge to fall off from.

Amy is blind, navigating with touch, sound and precision memory. Her taste and pleasure centers are nonfunctional. She eats carefully balanced meals at carefully programmed times, although she is never hungry.

"I don't understand why they're using the . . . children." I shouldn't have hesitated before that word, but I'd never been comfortable using it. They weren't children. I didn't know what they were, but they weren't children, not by any definition of the word. But Doug hated the other, better word: implants. And adults just sounded wrong. The hesitation made Doug flinch. Which might have been why I'd hesitated. "If they think regular people can't handle it, then why not just send out regular robots?"

Doug flinched again. Any reminder that his—our—daughter was any sort of robot did that to him. "As I understand it, they want to understand and see the long term effects of Mars gravity and terraforming on human bodies, since eventually they do plan to send the rest of us out there."

"But—" I swallowed, tried to get my thoughts in order. "They're *programmed*. They'll be eating and exercising absolutely regularly in a way regular adults wouldn't. Couldn't. Even Olympic athletes aren't that careful."

"But it will give them a general idea. Plus, they need to ensure that human bodies—" it was my turn to flinch—"are capable of spending sustained time in a Martian environment." He sounded like someone quoting a speech from a marketing consultant; it took me a second to realize that was probably exactly what he was doing.

I gave up attempting to eat. "Ok. What I don't understand is this. Why are you telling me this?"

"Because they want us to talk to her before she goes."

By "they" he meant the facility's attorneys, of course.

Amy is also a skilled engineer and astronaut, programmed with the equivalent of multiple doctorate degrees in engineering, computer science, astronomy, microbiology, geology and geophysics and to speak multiple languages with the same flat intonation, who has to be reminded by a computer program to eat, who has never laughed or cried in her entire life.

"I'll sign more papers if I have to," I said. "I don't want to see her."

"Crystal."

"I'm serious."

"Crystal. If you don't go, she can't go. And—" He swallowed, and I saw that he was about to start crying. "She doesn't belong here. You'll see."

The reason for their quick disappearance is soon explained. The eight of them must be thoroughly checked—their programs are not yet perfectly adjusted for self-maintenance, although they are able to observe and check each other. Then a patch, to ensure that they are properly programmed to adjust to the new gravity, and another patch to ensure that they are able to translate and understand the very latest idioms in multiple languages.

And, of course, they must eat, which none of us will want to see.

This last part is true. The implants do not respond to appetite or taste, and although they are programmed to eat, with the precise, mechanical movements they use for everything else, they have difficulty with this. Eating, it turns out, is somewhat more complicated than mere programming, and it is not something I want to watch again.

None of this is anything I want to watch again.

"Of *course* she's agreeing to go," I ranted at Ariela, my best friend, the only one other than Doug who knew the whole story. "She's *programmed* to go. Why do I have to go to see this for myself?"

Ariela fiddled with her coffee cup. "I don't think that's it," she said, after a moment.

"Then what is it?"

"I think they want you to be able to say good-bye."

• • •

I have a picture of my daughter, in her crib, surrounded by wires and tubes.

It is the only one I have. Most of the time, I leave it buried at the bottom of a drawer in the guest room, face down. But sometimes I take it out, and try to imagine that in it, my daughter is smiling.

When I found out my child would be born without a brain, I didn't cry. I couldn't. Everything inside me was swallowed up, gone, empty, and I had nothing to cry with. I just sat quietly, hands folded over my abdomen, listening. I didn't have much to say.

I had options, they explained, carefully. I could terminate the pregnancy—it was difficult to find anyone who would terminate late term pregnancies here, but a trip to Europe or Asia could be arranged. I could bring the child to term. (Beside me, Doug jerked, but didn't say anything.) The child would not live, but some parents found that comforting, and I could hold her afterwards. ("Comforting"? The hollow part of me could not ask.)

Or, they said, they could offer a third possibility.

I've cried enough about this already. *Enough.*

The medical procedure was less simple than they had promised. Eight hours of initial surgery, and then two days in bed, another surgery, and then a third. Doug tried to read books to me, but I was so sick I could barely understand his words. Finally he set me up with a tablet and music and let that play while he slept and slept.

With each procedure, I dreamed, dreamed that metal was moving through my skin and bones, dreamed that wires were replacing my nerves. I saw myself as a computer. I saw myself linking to my daughter.

I threw up, over and over. The pregnancy, said the nurses sympathetically. Or the drugs. But I knew it wasn't either.

Even now, I sometimes wonder if some of those nanobots entered my blood, my skin, if their presence is why I can now look at my daughter and have no desire to hold her.

I was allowed to hold her, briefly, after the birth. It was psychologically better for the mother, one of the doctors argued; a compassionate thing to do, agreed the attorneys, who probably had other fears in mind. I had no thoughts of a lawsuit, not then.

She was small, so very small. And so limp. For some reason I had thought that the procedures would extend metal all the way through her body, but no. Not that she was lacking in metal; she had wires and tubes seemingly everywhere, controlling her food intake and bladder and monitoring pulse rates and the electronic activity in her brain.

But no tubes in her nose or her mouth, and her tiny chest rose and fell steadily.

"There were some problems," Doug says.

"Problems," I repeat.

He swallows. "They could send commands to them while they were on the mission, but apparently, something about the distance and time—anyway, they weren't able to successfully upload all of the patches and fixes. Some of the programming broke down."

"And?"

"Some of them—well, they're saying some of them may be nonfunctional."

It takes me a moment to sort through the pronouns. "Amy?"

"I don't know." He swallows miserably.

"The implant is letting her breathe," explained one of the doctors. "In time, it might allow her to do more."

"What more?" asked Doug.

"We don't entirely know," said the doctor. "Movement, walking, certainly. Speech, hopefully. And more beyond that."

I touched her cheek. It was warm to the touch, and I could tell that she was breathing. But that was all. She did not move, did not even flutter an eye at my touch.

She had not cried, not even that first baby cry after birth.

"This is your fault," I shout at Doug, although it isn't. "You were the one who insisted on fixing her."

"You are the one who keeps thinking she's dead," he shouts back.

"Did you have a name in mind?" One of the lawyers, a young man who had seemed almost human. "We can use that, if you like. Otherwise a name will be randomly chosen by computer."

I had not. "Amy," I said. It had been the name of one of my childhood dolls.

He made a note on his tablet.

"Will you need my breast milk?"

"We would be grateful."

And then a doctor came and took her away, and the hollow space was inside me, consuming me, and I couldn't even cry. I couldn't even move. Doug was crying, shaking, and I was nothing.

We will not be allowed to talk to Amy, to see Amy, until an unspecified time. Doug is furious, but the lawyers he calls are not encouraging. If Amy is a fully legal human, and that status is dubious, capable of making decisions without the facility, she is also an adult, and we have no legal claim on her. And since she has just traveled to Mars and back, we can hardly claim her as a disabled dependent. And if she is not a fully legal human—the conclusion of most of the attorneys—she is property, and not ours, and any attempt to push these boundaries is a crime.

The hollow place inside me is growing again, and I desperately need to return to work.

I never explained to anyone why I continued to pump milk for six months. No one was unkind enough to ask.

They sent us the first pictures when she was five. An unsmiling child, looking straight at the camera, unblinking.

I begin to receive messages from Doug's lawyers. I delete them. I need to focus, focus.

Doug received the status updates and read them regularly. I couldn't. He told me tidbits, however: that Amy had been able to sit up, to move her legs and arms. That Amy had successfully downloaded the program that might help her control her urination. That Amy had connected with her vocal cords—

"Not Amy," I finally shouted at him. "Not Amy. *Her goddamn implant. The implant. The implant is making all of these goddamn connections!*"

It is so easy, on a computer, to move a few pixels around, to change an image from sorrow to laughter. So easy to use the programming already there.

We got a divorce about two years after that.

Much later I heard that attempts had been made to get the children with implants to smile, to make laughing sounds, to move their faces. It had all been abandoned. Emotions were, it seemed, the one thing that a program could not fake, and a face was all emotions. Some of the caretakers at the facility had become physically ill just watching a computer attempt to move their faces.

On Ariela's advice, I switched careers entirely, moving from insurance to marine biology. I focused on the microorganisms in mangrove ecosystems, forgetting, in my kayak, or on my computer, or snorkeling in the mangrove roots, that I had ever had a daughter, that I in some ways still had a daughter. Instead, I had spironemids.

Doug and I stayed in touch, meeting once a year or so. I went to his wedding, to a small fierce musician named Inari. He met some of the succession of boyfriends I had and disposed of over the years.

And he kept me updated on Amy.

Whenever he did, I allowed myself to think of my mangroves, disappearing into them, into the images I created of spironemids racing up and down the mangrove roots.

I receive an email from one of the other parents, one of the few who understands. Their son and his implant have failed; they will be heading to the facility to say goodbye, and put some of the dust of Mars on his hand. "I feel as if we already said this," says the email. "I feel as if I have to say this every day."

I agreed to meet her. At the very least, it might help end Doug's endless updates, coming at odd intervals through the year. I should have insisted to an end to those in the divorce agreement.

I made him drive us to the facility, and pay for the hotel stay. In separate bedrooms.

"One meeting," I say. "Just one."

"No."

"I'm her mother," I manage. I remember Ariela's words. "I have to say good-bye."

"Hello," came a voice.

Something was wrong with that voice, terribly wrong, but I could not pinpoint the problem.

"Hello," I managed back.

"Should I enter?"

"Yes," said Doug.

And she stepped into the light.

Doug's features. My mother's hair. My eyes.

Our daughter. And yet, not our daughter.

It—she?—stepped forward with small, efficient movements, as if every step was carefully measured—which, I realized in shock, was actually what was happening. The face—Doug's nose, his chin, in her face—was extraordinarily, perfectly still. Her hands brushed the chair in front of her, and she sat. The motion—I tried to find words for it, and then realized. She was not moving the way a human would. She was moving the way a computer thought a human would move.

She has an individual implant, my daughter. It can still be accessed, still be reprogrammed at the will of the facility. Doug and I have no rights over this, cannot stop the facility from turning her into whatever it wishes. That was part of the agreement we signed, to keep her alive.

"Hello," Doug said, his voice remarkably steady under the circumstances.

The face turned towards him. "Hello," it repeated. Its eyelids blinked, rapidly.

It's processing, I thought. They had warned us of that facial tic, programmed to allow others to tell when the implants needed to pause to process.

I was going to throw up. I knew it. I stood, wobbled, and pushed my way out of the door, not sure I could even make it to the nearest bathroom, feeling the floor rock beneath him. Behind me I heard Doug say something, but I could not be sure if he was talking to me or Amy.

Amy.

I am in the middle of finishing up a presentation for an important conference when the email arrives. Doug, of course, telling me that he has contacted people in the facility, who say that Amy is not completing all of her programmed tasks, that she is instead sitting at a window staring up into a sky.

That sounds most unlike Amy. I have never known her to stare at anything.

I threw up, again, and again, then leaned against the toilet for a while, body shaking.

The second meeting went better.

I refused to think of it as my daughter, as anything remotely related to me, even if its eyes were the same color as mine. Oddly, what helped was the voice, the same voice that had made me so sick. I had never heard anything like it; the "computer" voices I'd heard before were either the recorded voices of actors, or clearly mechanical synthesized sounds that had never approached human vocal cords. This—this was different; the sound of a mechanical voice pushed through human vocal vocals, precise, emotionless, flat, with no accent that I could think of. At Doug's request, it demonstrated fifty languages for us, all with that same precise flatness. It explained how it spent its day, in regular exercise and eating and downloading. I watched the eyelids blink each time it answered our questions.

I signed the papers.

"Thank you," it said.

I find myself wondering what she is thinking. If she is thinking. Can she think? She is programmed to process, to sift, to keep herself alive while analyzing vast amounts of data and transmitting it back to computers for further analysis.

I know she cannot see the stars. But I cannot stop wondering if she looked at them anyway, in those quiet hours between the Earth and Mars. If *something* in her looked at them. I clench my fists and rub them against my legs.

We made other visits before the launch. She had downloaded more languages, which she demonstrated for us. She did not listen to music, but could list off every song and album from any artist I named, knowing the exact length of each song, the record company, and where it was produced.

70

She could not use my daughter's eyes to see. But a million million images had been downloaded into her brain, including mine. She navigated by touch and utter precision, and had been updated with the very latest in voice recognition software.

We arranged to meet her outside. For some reason, this seemed more natural, easier on both of us. I could not tell if this affected her or not. But when we were outside, she sometimes turned her face to the sky.

After she left for Mars, I almost forgot about her.

Almost.

I receive an urgent email from the facility. It is not an update on Amy's medical condition. It is a request, typed by her and signed with her electronic thumbprint. In it, she asks that we authorize her return to Mars.

"She *says* she wants to go," I tell Doug.

I cannot believe that I am saying this, that I am the one arguing for her, that I am the one saying that she—an implant, *a computer,* should be allowed to make her own decisions.

"You said it yourself. She's a computer program. She can't want anything."

My voice is barely a whisper. "Maybe she wants this."

It would be easier to have Amy away from here, on a spaceship, or on Mars.

I do not think that is why I am arguing for her to leave. But I cannot be sure.

After the launch, people found us—all of us, every parent that had given, donated, lost a child to the implant program. We got calls, emails, tweets, comments. Hellish. I had to slam my sites down, only to find myself stalked at work and home by media, by religious zealots, by advocates of one side or another. People who thought I had done the right thing, people who thought I was the living embodiment of evil. I changed my name, my address.

My colleagues would not meet my eyes at biological conferences. I understood; I had, in a way, created Frankenstein's monster, or at least consented to it. And it was easier to handle than their curiosity would have been.

I sometimes imagine breaking into that facility, and wiping away all of its computers with a single program, or perhaps just taking an axe to its servers. (My practical mind whispers that with a program like this, the facility must have multiple backups in multiple places, but my imagination will not be silenced.) I imagine the implants twitching in response, the bodies falling into heaps on the ground, puppets suddenly cut from their strings.

I imagine putting flowers on a gravestone, and weeping.

My eyes remain dry.

• • •

Doug insists on another visit.

"You look terrible," he tells her.

Amy does not respond. To me, she has never looked well, even when she has looked *fit*. But looking at her closely, I see she is less fit, less trim, than when she originally emerged from the ship and headed into the facility without talking to us. She looks slightly—loose, if that makes sense. Perhaps her programming has not adjusted to the gravity, or perhaps she is merely getting old. I realize with a shock that she is middle aged by now, and even regularly programmed exercise can only do so much, especially when combined with the radical changes in gravity she has been undergoing.

A shock because of her unlined face, her almost childlike skin. Any dermatologist claiming that wrinkles are an inevitable part of aging, and not a result of emotion and stress, should take a look at her face. She does not even have lines between her cheek and her mouth, or around her eyes.

The hollow part inside me rises up again, swallowing me, and I am at a loss for words.

Doug is right about something else as well. I cannot pinpoint it, but since she has returned, something is . . . missing.

"How can we tell them that you are physically able to make the trip?" asks Doug.

"I am programmed with a word," my daughter says, in the flat, toneless voice that no human vocal cords should ever make. "The word is lie."

When she left for Mars, I did not watch her leave. I stayed on my computer, modeling, modeling, writing, writing, drafting, organizing, too lost in my work and my words to catch the faintest roar of burning engines, the faintest cheers that humans—well, humans of a sort—were headed to Mars at last.

At my request, a nurse arranges one more meeting, in one of the gardens on the edge of the facility.

When I arrive, it—Amy—my daughter—is facing into the sky, eyes unblinking. It is the first time, I realize, that I have ever seen her focused on anything.

"This is not my programming," she says.

It is so easy to sign documents, to watch those documents get swallowed up in a machine.

When I tell this story, I can see its events taking place, one after another, as inexorably as life and death.

When I remember this story, I can feel myself holding my daughter, my baby, and rocking her back and forth, a moment that has never quite stopped.

• • •

I dream of giving Amy a doll, a doll covered in wires and strings. I help her cut the strings. But with each string I cut, another wire grows on Amy's head, until she is held in place, unable to move.

She is alive, I think. She breathes. She moves. She processes. She communicates. She knows the songs and titles of every album published since the invention of those old phonographs.

She is alive.

I think.

This time, I watch the launch, from ten miles away, on a comfortable beach chair, surrounded by loud beachgoers and picnickers. And children. Hordes of children, all seemingly determined to out-scream each other as they leap in and out of the waves.

I have my net radio on, with the broadcasters comparing this to the old moon and shuttle launches that I have seen only in documentaries and history shows. I cannot focus on their words, although I try. I can only look at the endless blue of the sky, keep my eyes trained on the spot where a golden flame will soon be lifting into a sky.

The countdown starts. I stand.

It is more beautiful, this launch, than anything I could have expected, a bright golden streak against the sky, trailing steam and mist behind it. And I am crying, crying, as the gold hits my eyes, as if the flame is burning through me. I feel it traveling through my eyes, my arms, my chest, feel it burning in the hollow place inside, the hardened still place that has been my center for thirty-three years. I feel it burning, splitting, fading. Tonight, I promise myself, tonight, I will watch the stars, and imagine what it is like to be moving towards them.

What Everyone Remembers
RAHUL KANAKIA

I remember being with Maman in the cabin of her ship, anchored someplace where the wind was always howling, the temperature was always freezing, and fires were always dancing just beyond the horizon. I spent most of my time inside the mattress where she slept, burrowing as close as I could to Maman so that I could feel her solidity and heat spreading out above me without burrowing so close that I came in contact with the harsh light and cold air. It was a delightful spongiform environment, flecked with tinier insects—mites and flies and spiders—and with the crumbs of food and flakes of human skin on which the lesser creatures fed. Life was not hard for me there.

But Maman frightened me. When I emerged from the mattress, she would sometimes grab me, pinch my useless wings and interrogate me in front of bright lights. She'd put me in her nest of tubing and plastic cupboards and order me to run from one place to another as quick as I could. She would touch delicate golden wires to my various legs and my body would dance with strange impulses.

Usually my days passed in total silence, except for the few occasions when Maman interacted with the other occupant of the ship, Uncle Frederick. These conversations were always initiated by Frederick, who would stare at her for a long time, then nod. They'd go onto the deck, shut the cabin door behind them, and talk in very low voices. On one of these occasions I oozed out through a crack in the doorway and tried to listen to them more clearly.

They were huddled together behind the wheel of the ship.

Frederick said, " . . . have to interact with her. Want all of her descendents to be poorly socialized?"

"It is an insect," Maman said. "Don't anthropomorphize it. It can be anything it wants to be. Why should it carry all our human baggage? I want to give them a blank slate."

"And what about survivors? What if she finds more of us? Or if her descendents do? What will they think of us if we don't at least try to be kind to her?"

"I developed it. I know what is best for it."

"And I risked my life to keep her alive. Food is getting low. I'm not bringing more supplies unless I can get some sort of input."

"Fine, talk to it, if that will make you happy. But don't involve me."

After this, there was one day when she did not pinch me. Instead, she called out, "You've been hiding from me."

"No," I said. "I always come when I hear you calling for me. But sometimes I don't hear."

"No more hiding. I've given the whistle to Frederick. You must go to him whenever he calls for you."

"Please, not the whistle," I said, but she had already turned away.

The next day, my restless burrowing was interrupted by a sound that dragged hooks all across my body. Despite the pain, I tried to resist that insistent tootling. I stayed still for minutes, until the whistle had become near continuous, before I scuttled across the sticky deck of the cabin, up the stairs, and out into the freezing night.

Uncle Frederick lived in the cabin underneath the stairs. During the day he was largely quiescent: a vaguely human bulk that I sometimes perceived in the distance. But during the night he would lumber up the stairs and outside. He'd be wrapped up in seven layers of cloth and nylon and plastic. He'd seat himself down carefully on a mat, and stare up at the sky for hours.

I insinuated myself into the folds of his jacket to avoid the buffeting blasts of wind.

His body rumbled with speech. "Took you long enough to get here, didn't it?"

All along the horizon line, fires blazed just out of sight, filling the sky with a sunset glow, even though it was midnight.

"You're getting a good look aren't you?" Frederick said. "It's not so scary there. And it'll be even less scary for you."

"You're . . . you're taking me to the shore?" I said.

"Eventually. When your mother and I are gone, you'll need to forage for food. Don't worry, though, by then you'll have help."

"Are there more people, then? On land?"

"I meant that you'd have help from your own kind."

"Oh." The prospect of meeting more of myself was disgusting. I thought of them scrambling all over Maman and felt slightly ill. "I would have liked to see more people."

"Well, maybe you will. What would you do if you saw them?"

I nestled more deeply into Frederick's jacket. "I wouldn't ever bother them. I know that you and Maman don't like to be bothered."

"No, no, there's no need to be afraid of us. You should think of yourself as one of us."

I moved deeper into Frederick's garments. He shuddered. His hand twitched and started scratching the places where I had been. "I'm sorry," I said. "So sorry. I won't touch you again."

"No, that's my problem. I'm not used to people shaped like you. But you're fine. You're beautiful."

"When are there going to be more of me?"

"Soon. When your egg case bursts, there should be forty or fifty more of you."

I shifted my egg case uneasily, pressing it against Frederick's bulk as if to stop it from splitting open right there. I'd seen what happened to the mothers of the spiders and flies in Maman's mattress.

"Will I have to die, then?" I said

"Die?" Uncle Frederick said. His body shook slightly. "No, never. You really don't know, then? You're never going to die. All your children will remember everything you remember. It will feel like closing your eyes to give birth, and then opening them in a new body. You'll live forever."

At the time, this was not a shock for me. I was too young to appreciate the gift that Maman had engineered into me.

Frederick was silent for long moments after this. When I assayed a crawl up onto his face, I caught a brief glimpse of tear-stained eyes before an instinctive sweep of his hand dropped me to the deck with an exoskeleton-jouncing crash.

I picked myself up off the damp, salty deck and scurried back to the safety of Maman's mattress.

Frederick and Maman were arguing again. I did not have to try hard to hear them, since the cabin hatches had been left open in order to air out the stale and dusty smells.

"I told her," Frederick said.

"And you've put your own spin on it. Called it 'immortality' or some such nonsense. You won't rest until you've fully humanized it, will you?"

"You know that she thinks of you as her mother, don't you?"

"I'm no such thing."

"You are the only mother her species will ever have. All the millions and billions of her descendents will only remember one childhood: her childhood. You have to pay more attention to her psychology, to her development, to her socialization and her adjustment. Every interaction her species will ever have is going to be governed by the shadow of you."

"Don't project," Maman said. "I barely remember my own childhood."

"And why is that? Why are you so cold?"

"You've made it clear that you have the upper hand here, Frederick, so I suppose I can't stop you from telling it whatever you want. We can even decant another, if you think I've ruined this one. You can train the next one to call you papa."

"A second Eve?"

"Sure, or two more, or three, or a hundred . . . whatever it will take to satisfy you."

"And have a hundred nations spring up to fight with each other, bomb each other, and create another disaster?"

"It will happen eventually."

"You don't understand. They won't be like that. Not if we do our jobs, they won't. They'll remember this, every single one of them . . . they'll look into each others' eyes and see themselves. They'll see that the good of everybody is the most important thing, and that if the race goes forward, then their memory will go forward, and they'll live forever."

"I know that my survival depends on your survival," Maman said. "But that hasn't prevented me from developing a hatred for you. Why should they be different?"

When Maman came in, she was smiling. She stared at the mattress for a long moment.

She was far away, too far to be able to catch me up, so I scrambled out of the mattress and called out, "Is my name 'Eve,' then?"

Maman frowned. "No," she said. "You don't need a name."

"Why not?"

"What is it that you call me?" Maman was creeping closer, and I skittered back slightly.

"Maman."

"Where did you get that name?"

"In the books that Frederick showed me, that is what the elephant called the woman who took care of him."

"You liked his idiotic books?"

"Nnnnooo."

"Good. You don't need them." She crouched and spread her hands on the edge of the mattress, and looked at, past, through me.

"Your memory is good," Maman said. "I know that, from the mazes I had you run. Please. Try to remember my face. You must never forget me."

She coaxed me up onto her hard, pitted hands—those hands that were like whole worlds to me—and lifted me up right in front of her face. This was my first good, long look at her. Usually, I only peeked at her with sidelong glances, in order to see if she was about to come after me.

Her strangely-scented breath shivered right through my body, and I looked up with kaleidoscopic sight at her enormous face. Since then, I've seen many human faces. But, in my memory, there is nothing human about Maman's face; it is a machine of snorting nostrils and slowly dilating pupils.

Then she grabbed me by the wings and performed more tests on me.

A few days later, Frederick motored away in the dinghy. He was heading off to the shore: to the fires. I was happy when he left, since I would not have that whistle tugging at me. But I was also sad. I crept into Maman's workroom, where she was poking her head into and out of her refrigerator and other equipment. I was all alone with her. Now that Uncle Frederick wasn't here to protect me, she could do anything.

She grunted as I crossed the threshold. She had not turned around. It was my first clue that she was always trying to sense where I was.

"Is he ever coming back?" I said.

Maman did not say anything. She played with her implements. As I waited, she picked up a very sharp tool that I had never seen her use before. I knew that she was not working. She was trying to scare me into running away.

"Did you send him away because of me?"

She turned towards me and pursed her lips. "He's left before. The last time was several months ago, when you were very young. He is going to get more food and gasoline."

"So he isn't gone forever?"

"Don't worry. You'll hear the whistle again, soon enough."

Several days later, when Frederick came back, I was still ecstatic at having had such a long and nonviolent conversation with Maman. She had not come for me since we'd spoken. I climbed up top and watched him unload the dinghy. Maman came out and helped him as he lifted things up.

"What was the land like?" I said. "Did you walk into the fires?"

Maman and Frederick exchanged a look. He handed her a satchel of cans. Everything in the boat was blackened with soot.

"The forests are still burning, but the fires are mostly gone from the city," he said.

"Did you see any humans?" Maman said.

"A good number," he said. "They're starting to emerge."

She looked down at the cargo. "Did you have to fight?"

"Some," Frederick said.

They continued loading in silence, and didn't respond to my increasingly chipper questions. I scurried back and forth across the length of the metal hand-rail, and barely avoided being inadvertently slapped under Frederick's hand.

I'd hoped that Frederick would be too tired from his journey to use the whistle, but as night fell, I heard its shriek. It was even more terrible than I remembered.

I ran out and settled on his chest.

He was quiet for several moments, then said, "You'll be kind to the people you find, won't you?"

"I won't even bother them at all!" I said. "Except maybe when they're sleeping would it be maybe okay if I went inside their mattresses?"

"That's not what I meant. I meant . . . will you help them? They won't be having as easy a time as you. Will you tell them where food is? And not hurt them?"

"Talk to them . . . ?" I said. "But . . . will they . . . will they have whistles?"

"No, of course not. They don't even know that people like you exist. They'll probably be surprised to see you. But they'll want your help. They're hungry and they're dying."

"Why don't they get more cans?"

"They can't find them. And nobody is making more."

"Then why don't they eat the spiders and the flies and the crumbs of . . . "

"They can't. They're not like you. You'll need to talk to them, and ask them questions, and see what they need, and do what they want, just like you would for your mother."

"Just like Maman?" I said. "But Maman doesn't need any help from me."

"If she needed it, wouldn't you help her? These people will need your help very much."

"Okay." I lay there on Frederick for a while, and then murmured, "But they won't have whistles, will they?"

After Frederick let me scurry into the warm insides of the ship, he called Maman onto the deck. I was too chilled to be willing to go farther than the door in order to listen to them.

" . . . more survivors than I expected . . . " he said.

"You knew there would be some," Maman said.

"But they're starting to organize."

Maman didn't say anything. I imagined her plucking up Frederick by the arms and running her tests on him while he kicked around uselessly.

"Eve is terrified of human beings," Frederick said. "I'm not sure what she'll do when she encounters the survivors."

"It will do what it decides is right."

"It won't do anything. It associates human beings with silence and neglect and electric shocks and tests."

"According to those tests, it is in good health. It's ready for reproduction."

"I told you to pay attention to her socialization. You neglected her so much . . . I don't think she'll ever be able to interact normally."

"I told you to do what you thought was necessary. You are still free to try to cure the psychic wounds I supposedly inflicted on her. You brought enough supplies to buy you that."

"I had to kill a man in order to get these supplies. Next time, I doubt I'll be lucky enough to find such a poorly defended cache."

"You brought enough for a few months. That is more than enough time."

"Or barely enough. If we have to start over."

"You want me to hatch another female?" Maman said.

"We need to make the decision now. I think that Eve is too traumatized. She's not going to be able to function. We need to start over. You won't do any tests on the next one. I'll take care of her. I'll teach her all the things you held Eve back from: technology, art, literature, history, everything . . . Eve is such a fast learner . . . she really could have—"

"She disgusted you," Maman said. "You didn't want anything to do with 'that damned roach.' Until it first spoke, you called this a crazy scheme."

"And how much earlier could she have spoken, if someone had been talking to her?"

"Why should their language be English? Why not something better? Something more suited to them?"

"You *knew* the kinds of things her mind was capable of. And you were still willing to drive her crazy, and stunt her forever. In fact, that's pretty much what you did."

"Did our art and literature and history help us? No. If its descendents create a better world than ours, they will do so *because* of their inhumanity."

"That's all moot now. There are too many survivors. That changes everything. This won't be a post-human world. It'll be a human one. The next Eve needs to be as human as possible."

"No," Maman said.

"I risked my life to keep this boat running! Risked it four times now. You've contributed damn all. I could have lived twice as long if I'd gone off on my own, without you."

"I'll hatch another. But we won't be 'starting over.'"

"Then the two of them will go to war eventually. Even you must see that there can only be one of them."

"I won't destroy it. It is perfectly healthy. Billions of dollars and lifetimes of work were spent in creating it. But I will start decanting another progenitor tomorrow. This discussion is over."

The two of them entered. I waited until Frederick had gone off into his cabin and Maman had settled down into bed. Then I crept up to her ear and softly whispered. "So I'll have a sister, then?"

Maman's hand twitched and I skittered away. I heard a soft exhalation of air, and waited for the words that would come next, but she never said anything.

I stayed in the mattress for hours, stewing in excitement and confusion. I hadn't known that Frederick disliked me so much. I was sorry that he'd had to yell at Maman because I hadn't given him the right answers. I knew that maybe Frederick wanted to be mean to me, but I was so happy that Maman had stood up for me and said such good things about me. I knew that she loved me, just like the elephant's Maman had.

But, shortly before dawn, I felt the whistle. It was not the normal time for meeting with Frederick and I was especially lethargic. I lay in the mattress. The whistle cut through me again and again, but I didn't want to move. Finally, I started to leave my burrow. The whistling was coming from Frederick's cabin, where I'd never visited. I was on the edge of the mattress now, and was about to drop to the floor.

Something picked me up by the wings. "Wait," said Maman.

She got up out of bed and dropped me onto the mattress. She walked into Frederick's cabin, and I heard the sound of three slaps. When she came back, the whistle was in her hand.

She grabbed me and took me into her workroom, then locked the door behind her.

Frederick pounded on the workroom door. "What the hell are you doing?" he said.

"Stay back," Maman called. "If you try to break down that door, I'll destroy the rest of the specimens. Then you'll never get your second chance." Maman held me down with pressure against my back.

"You don't know how many people I saw out there," he said. "There were hundreds of them, already organized into bands, tribes, and families. We're going to make it through this catastrophe, you know."

Then I felt the worst pain I'd ever had in my life. All my legs tried to move at once, but they moved in different directions. I craned around, trying to look up, and glimpsed a metal syringe pulling away from my posterior.

"That's what I've been thinking about all night," Frederick said. "About how humanity is going to endure. And how maybe it's wrong for us to play God. Maybe the real catastrophe will be when all these creatures: so tiny, so intelligent, and so efficient, descend on the survivors. I'm wondering, I really am, if unleashing Eve—any Eve—is the right thing to do here."

"What's happening?" I said. Maman didn't answer. She sank back, against the door. Frederick kept pounding on it. I lay there in the shallow receptacle where she'd set me down. After a few moments, Maman got up and bustled around the workshop. Frederick kept saying things in the background, but I was no longer paying attention. What had Maman done to me?

It seemed like hours later when I heard a crashing noise. The door flew inwards, and Frederick charged. Maman was standing next to the door. She jabbed him with a needle. He turned towards her and slapped her on the face. He hit her again and again. She hit back at him, but it didn't seem that she was hurting him very much. Finally he saw me on the table, and took a step towards me. He fell down. Maman got up, and looked at him for a few moments. She took him by the feet and dragged him out of the workroom.

For the next thirty days, it was just the two of us. Maman only spoke to me one time. She told me that I was carrying eggs, and that I would soon be hatching into fifty new bodies. And even though the bodies would think and feel different things, all of them would think of themselves as me. I lay in her mattress as the eggs swelled. Sometimes she plucked me up by the wings and examined me under a looking glass. I think she'd become afraid to run electricity through me.

After one of the tests, she nodded to herself. She put me in a covered box and went out to the dinghy. I heard the motor start, and we traveled for several hours. I felt the boat hit something. I felt her pick up the box and carry it along with her. We were walking. Was I on land now? The box was still covered. I could not see where we were or where we were going. My abdomen was swelling. My body was aching. I felt a heavy pain along my back.

Frederick had tried to kill me. Now Maman was abandoning me. Was I so disgusting? For a moment, I was very angry with them. I wanted to hurt them all. Then I realized how awful I was. The reason that Fred and Maman had hated me was because I'd been such a brat about the tests and the whistle. But I swore that I'd show them they were wrong about me. I'd help every human being I saw. I'd be their best friends. I would do anything they wanted and I'd never, ever shy away or complain.

When the cover was taken off the box, I was in a dark alcove, like a cupboard or shelf made of stone. Warm air washed over me. I could see a light bobbing up and down in the distance. A door opened, and I saw Maman silhouetted against the light of the sun. I tried to run to her, but I couldn't move.

The Bells of Subsidence

MICHAEL JOHN GRIST

The Bell is coming.

It's night, and I'm lying beside Temetry on a cold grey crater of this world's endless desert, listening to the oscillations of the Bell. At times we glimpse its Brilliance, the after-image of its long and branic toll splashing across the plush black firmament like an endless corolla borealis. I imagine it far overhead, arcing through the universe, plancking the anthropic landscape from yoke to clapper, and can think of only one word to describe it.

"Godly," I whisper.

Temetry nods by my side. He doesn't speak, not since the last Bells came when we were babies, but I know what he's thinking. I'm thinking it also.

"How are your non-orientable insects?" I ask.

He shrugs. This shrug means he's had no breakthroughs. I know it, because he'd not be here with me if he had. The men of this world would have taken him for the Gideon heat-sink long ago.

"I won't forget you," I say to him quietly.

He turns to me, and smiles, because he knows I cannot keep that promise. The Bell is coming tonight. His hand worms the grey sand, folds my fingers within his own, and I remember that he is the most beautiful thing I have.

"I love you," I whisper to him. His fingers tighten, rippling over mine in Euclidean gymnastics, until our hands are joined partway between a reticulated conch shell and an intersecting Klein bottle.

I laugh. It is our joke, a vestige of what Subsidence has brought us both. We are only 11, and I love him, because I know in my heart that he will never forget me.

"I'll whisper your name to the branes until I die," I promise him, feeling the urgency of this moment, alone in this crater for the last time.

His smile turns sad. It is the last abiding image I have of him, because then comes the sound of old Ingen, and the moment is lost. She is huffing and panting her rooty head over the crater-lip. This place is no longer special or secret. Temetry's dazzling smile is sad, forever, because I'll never see him again.

• • •

Ingen is my mother, and she uses me.

She plucks me from the crater without even glancing at Temetry. I don't think she even sees him anymore. Arm in arm we stroll back to the Gideon bore, and she chatters on about her day, about what permutations she wrought in this planet's atmosphere, what gains in the heat-sink they explored.

We arrive at the bore-head, a silver pipe in this dry planet's haunch, and she kneels before me in the grey sand, her hands on my shoulders. I know this is how she talks to her simulacra, plugging fresh wavelengths into their pea-sized minds, laying in the algorithms of growth. I am just another of her extremities, to be ordered, wound, and sent chuttering on my way.

"You must forget that boy, Aliqa," she tells me. "He's lost, too far under the Bell. You know that, don't you? He can't follow where you're going."

She aspires to love me, but I know the thing she loves most is herself.

"Yes mother," I reply. I am polite and correct, a good Gideon girl.

Ingen ruffles my hair in the way I hate. I am not an infant anymore. Temetry would never do it. "Good girl," she says, and she leads us into the bore-head. We stand atop the dimple, and she initiates the involutions.

Space folds, and I taste the familiar feel of my mother's mind in my own, twisting the anthropic plane. A moment later we emerge in our living room.

"Go to your involutions, Aliqa," Ingen says. "Hone your mind for the Bell."

I go. In my room I close my eyes, stand upon my dimple, and begin. Far into the night I manifold four dimensions in non-Euclidean space, inverting Tesseracts, decanting Klein kettles, shaving Möbius strips into interlocking many-twisted chains.

I finish in the dark morning, as ever unable to speak or think, the involutions have so stripped away my sense of self. I sit on my bedside vacantly, emptied into submission, until the folds of my mind remember the shape they ought to take, and I can heal.

Then I will sleep.

This is not my hope. It is my mother's hope for me. She will have me upon the Bells though she must strip the last shred of self from my mind. I am matter to be prepared, used, and replaced.

In my non-state I struggle to think of Temetry, but there is nothing of him there. No I, no you, only the endless entangled looping of the branes.

Pink dawn comes, and on a Gideon screen in my empty room I watch the Bell snuffing down over the grey desert.

It is immense, a vast colorless ark that fills the horizon, eclipsing the grey desert I have known all my life. At the atmospheric boundary its toll emerges as a jarring rumble in the earth, a Brilliance so complex with harmonies and grace notes that it makes all the simulations I've heard seem like one-fiddle jigs. The sound is a universe of its own, oriented through the branes in ways I cannot grasp.

It snuffs down, and all I can think of is Temetry. He will be out there somewhere, sitting the grey crater-sand, folding paper with his hands, his eyes sad as the first sun rises. Before him will be an array of non-orientable sand-hoppers, each folded like Möbius strips with only a single side. Each of their eight limbs will be perfectly formed, aligned, so life-like they could at any moment hop away. He will have sat awake all night folding them, as the only thing he can do.

He will watch as this Bell lands, and he will name it after me, for he knows it will be the Bell that takes me away.

Grey sand fills the screen, and it lands. I feel the branes tremble around me. This is my life, now. Tears run down my cheeks as I realize what it means. I will truly never see Temetry again.

Then old Ingen is at my side, dabbing at my cheeks with her sleeve, hustling me to the door.

"Don't worry on my account, child," she bustles, and I realize she thinks my tears are for her. "Old Ingen will abide. There's much work to be done here yet, don't cry for me."

I want to tell her I am not, but bite my lip hard. There is no need to be cruel, now. It will change nothing, only hurt us both more.

At the door she holds me again by the shoulders, and I see that she too is crying. She runs her hands down my sides, smudges away a non-existent speck of dust, and I wonder. Perhaps she does love me after all. Perhaps she is sad to see her most talented creation disappear.

"Be a good girl," she says. "Do as they say, be polite."

I smile and nod at this fallacy. We both know I will have no choice. For the next five years I will be indentured to the Bell, and my mind will not be my own. There will be no need for me to do a thing, except survive.

"You'll make me proud, Aliqa," she says. "Don't worry about that."

I smile, I nod.

We enter the Gideon bore together. The world flutters like a butterfly kaleidoscope, I taste my mother's mind for the last time, and the next phase of my life begins.

We are a class of one hundred, boys and girls of Bell-age, drawn from all the Gideon bore-holes sunk into our planet. Spotless white simulacra gather us in a vast hall, colorless as the Bell's exterior, and move us to stand upon our marks; dimples in the smooth flooring.

I let myself be shunted into place by their cold palms. I look down at my dimple, and wonder briefly how many have stood here before me, how many have gone under the Bell to keep Subsidence alive.

I push that thought aside, and in the seconds before it begins, try to sequester what parts of myself I can, hidden within the folds of my mind.

Then the anthropic plane is unleashed upon us.

It is unlike any involutions I have done before. It is an inexpressible order of magnitude larger. In the face of it, I am obliterated. I am rewritten.

An endless torrent of images pounds through the thin capillaries of my mind, effortlessly scrubbing away all the tiny levees and dams I have prepared against it; a tidal surge of unorientable, non-intersecting, non-Euclidian possibilities.

As the torrent comes, I cannot help but seek order from the chaos; raveling and inverting Klein bottles, stacking and nestling them within each other like Matryoshka dolls, folding tesseracts upon themselves, helixing Möbius strips into Riemann planes. Around me the one hundred do the same. Together, by the combined resonance of our efforts, we will planck the branes for the first time. We will build our own Brilliance. Through our efforts, the Bell will toll.

I barely feel the effects of gravity, as the Bell rises up through the atmosphere, and leaves my desert world behind.

Only when it is over, and it has been over for six of the eight rest hours allotted to us, do I begin to remember who I am, where I have come from, and what I have done.

The Bell has already left my world. Ingen is gone, left behind. Temetry is gone. All the things that tied me to who I was are gone.

I feel more than an ache, I feel an erasure. Already I have lost so much of what I was. My mind has diminished, has enlarged, has shrunk.

I am lying on a double-bunk cot in a dark room, where the simulacra brought me. Beside me a girl's hand dangles down from the cot above. One of her fingers is marked by a line of lighter skin, and I wonder that she had once worn a ring.

I push her hand. It sways nervelessly.

"Wake up," I say to her hand.

"She's under the Bell," comes a voice. There is another girl standing in the semi-dark before me, her hair in ratted pigtails. She smells overpoweringly of sweat.

"I'm Aliqa," I say to her.

"Mazy," she answers. Her eyes are shot through with red. "You were talking in your sleep."

"I was?" I mumble. My lips seem thick, foreign appendages on my face. "What did I say?"

"The same as all these others," Mazy says, and gestures at the groaning, sleeping, moaning bodies of the other 98 of us, stacked like folded tesseracts in our cots. "A load of old balls."

I can't help the frown from crossing my face. I was raised to be correct. Mazy laughs more when she sees my expression, then she leans in, and her sweaty stench rolls in with her.

"You listen to me, girl. You aren't special, no way no how. Nothing in that brain of yours is worth going under the Bell for. You just let it go, let it all go, and you and me'll be pals. You hear me?"

I blink hard, as if it'll somehow push back her smell. It doesn't.

"And if I don't?"

Mazy laughs again, leans back, and gives the nerveless hand hanging from the cot above a playful shove.

"Then it don't hardly matter a thing now, does it?"

She winks. She walks away.

There's a little over an hour left before our next involutions; the red digits of a countdown clock on the distant black wall glow fuzzily. In the dim light I look at the white band round the girl's nerveless hand, and wonder who gave her that ring, and what it might have meant. I listen to the others moaning, as Mazy said. They are whispering names, whimpering, crying in their sleep.

For a little while, I cry too.

Soon the simulacra come for us again, and carry us back to our dimples. I let them lift and maneuver me. I feel too weak to move more than my eyes. They lay me in my allotted space, and as I wait for the barrage to open, I think about Temetry. I know now that I cannot hope to hide him in an enfoldment of my mind. I can only say goodbye, again and again, until one day the Bell scores him from my mind forever.

"I won't forget you," I promised him on the sand, but I have not the strength to keep that promise. I am too small.

Then the barrage begins again.

I don't come back to myself for a long time. When I do, it is to the freckled face of Mazy, up close to mine. She is lying by my side, sharing my cot, her tousled red hair on my pillow. I feel her warm breath on my lips. Her arm is wrapped around me. I try to shrug it off, but sharp pain aches through me, and I fall still.

Mazy stirs, and her eyes slit open. Her irises are deep green. She smiles at me.

"I thought you'd gone under," she whispers. "It's good to see you back."

I open my jaw, struggling to ignore the pain. "How long?" I whisper.

Mazy shrugs. "Weeks? I forget. They really worked you good that time, though."

"What?" I ask. My mouth is so dry. "What do you mean?"

She doesn't answer. Instead she pushes herself up on her elbow, reaches to my face, and pushes a strand of hair behind my ear. I try to pull back.

"Stop it," I mumble. "Get off my cot."

"Your cot?" says Mazy. "This is my cot. You climbed in here yourself."

"What?"

"After they were finished with you, whispering that damned name."

I am confused. How could I climb here without knowing it? What cot am I in? "What name?"

"Temetry," she says, and watches my face for the reaction. There is none, because the name means nothing to me.

"Who's Temetry?" I ask.

"I don't know. You were the one screaming it, in the middle of the involutions. They had to pull you off the floor and double your involutions to shut you up."

Her words shake me. "I don't remember any of that."

"Not after a session like that, I'm not surprised."

I lay there and say nothing.

"Was he a boyfriend?" Mazy asks.

I don't answer. I try to cast my mind back, feeling as though I am probing a fresh wound. My mind is raw. Temetry. I reach back, back, and touch upon something. I handle it gently, calmly as I would a sand-hopper, lest it take fright and skitter away. Temetry; a feeling more than anything, a sense of something, insubstantial and shifting, but something definitely good.

"Maybe," I say. "Maybe a friend."

Mazy snorts, and runs her hand through my hair again. My body aches too much to push her away. "Well, you're my friend now. You and me. I'll look after you, don't worry."

I don't worry. I lie there, and wonder who Temetry might have been.

Months pass. The cots grow quieter every night, as memories are plancked out of our minds. Soon there is no one left to miss, no home to yearn for, no one to cry for. More of us go under the Bell.

Mazy shares my cot every night. She smooths my hair. When I become quiet, she speaks the name to me; Temetry. It has no meaning in itself, it is just a word that we share, something to bond us together. We lie in each other's warm arms, and wonder on what it might mean.

Our lives are involutions and sleep. Tolling the Bell becomes something rote, ringing out our Brilliance across the universe in our wake. There are no questions to ask of each other, because there is no past to speak of. There are only questions in the now.

"Where do you think the Bell is going?" Mazy asks, most nights. I spin stories for her of all the furthest systems I've heard of, worlds where the people travel through Gideon bores and harvest the heat of stars on desert planets. Mazy smiles, laughs, and tells me about planets where everything is an endless city, and people drink the blood of plants and fly through the sky on rainbows and just have all the fun you could imagine.

I wonder if I we are from an endless city, or a desert, or a jungle. I wonder what Temetry is. Is it a place, a person, or a thing?

Around us, the one hundred dwindle. I forget my own name, and she forgets hers. We come to know each other by touch, by feel, by the one word that stays with us; Temetry. It becomes a totem.

Then one day, I wake in her arms, and she is still. I shake her, but she doesn't move. I open her eyelids and look into her eyes, and see within her a void, carved and hollowed out.

Her heart beats, her body lives, but her mind is gone. She is under the Bell. Within a day she is only a memory.

Simulacra move me to my own cot. The others are removed. Lying there, wondering on the meaning of this word Temetry, I realize I am the only one left.

The only one left? Were there others?

I am to be captain.

Days pass and there are no involutions for me. Simulacra come in and out of my room, nameless as ever, and occasionally I ask the word at them.

"Temetry?"

They never reply. Their white bodies and flat blank faces seem to look past me. They bring me training cycles that I am to rewrite my mind with, sad stories of the origin of Subsidence, but I cannot watch them for long. All I want to know is the origin of this hole within me, this thing that I have lost.

I set down the latest of the cycles and exit my room. I walk the corridors and call out the word Temetry, though there is no one to respond. White-bodied simulacra move by me at times, carrying shapes on their flat white palms that seem to defy dimension. Pieces for the clapper, I presume, that revolve and involute as I watch.

I wander for days. When I'm hungry I eat, food brought by the simulacra as I need it. When I'm tired I sleep. I know these explorations are pointless, that even were I to walk a hundred years I would never cover more than a hundredth of the whole of the Bell. But that doesn't seem to matter now.

I walk the involution rooms, hundreds of them, each stretching on and on, every one of them a hammer to hit the clapper at the Bell's core, to keep us moving, to keep Subsidence alive if only in memory. I wander over dimples where generations have involuted the anthropic planes before me, where generations have gone under the Bell to keep Subsidence moving.

I am alone, now, but for this word that haunts me; Temetry.

This is my odyssey. I know that as well as any.

I am sitting at a port looking out over our sparkling Brilliance, a branic contrail sizzling back through space like corolla borealis, when the captain comes to me. He sits by my side. I am not surprised. I have expected this for a long time.

He is very old; his face riven with lines deep as the dimples. He is the first living thing I have seen for as long as I can remember.

He sighs, and smiles at me.

"Temetry," he says.

I smile back. Though we have never met, never spoken, I feel I know him well. "Do you know what it is?"

He shrugs. His eyes flicker with quiet amusement.

"I heard it in the Brilliance. You tolled the word into space. Even now, that word is floating through the anthropic planes, reverberating, echoing forever."

"I wish I knew what it meant," I say.

He only smiles.

We sit quietly for a long time, as the Brilliance ripples out like a whip-tail from our Bell, glissandoing into space.

"What happened to the others?" I ask him, at last. I don't know who they might be, but I know there were others. I am not the only one the Bell took for fuel.

"They went under the Bell," he replies, his voice soft. "Left behind on the planets we passed. They'll live out quiet, uninspired lives. They'll procreate."

"And what about me?"

"That's your choice. You'll be captain, if you want. You'll steer the Bell, and ring out your beautiful, mournful, sweet Brilliance to the universe. The other Bells will hear, and know you, and Subsidence will continue. Or you will not."

"What else would I do?"

He shrugs, answers slowly. "Leave. Start a new life on the next planet. Forget about the Bells, about the branes and the Brilliance."

I see it in his pale blue eyes. He has already made that choice, and left this place behind.

"Where will you go?" I ask. His gentle smile gives me the answer. We both know the Bell keeps no logs. There is no home for him to return to. There is nothing left in his mind now but the beauty of the branes.

He stands up.

"Goodbye, child," he says. "I hope you find what you're looking for."

He walks away down the long and arcing corridor. I watch him go.

The simulacra come for me as darkness falls across the Bell. They wipe away my drying tears, and carry me to my dimple. Through the long hours of the Subsidence night, I planck the branes that toll us through space.

We will snuff upon a planet soon. There will be a hundred waiting, thinking glory and duty await, ready to sacrifice their minds to the might of this Bell, to the continuation of Subsidence, trusting me as their captain to lead.

But lead to where?

All I have is this word. I dream it while the planes reticulated about me; Temetry. It has no meaning, but I feel its weight, like a Gideon bore sucking me down. I am not free. I am not alone. I am weighted to this dying Empire, and there is only the grace of the branes to tell of my loss.

So I tell it to the branes. I dream them filled with this thing that is Temetry, this thing that matters so much even the Bell could not scrub it from my mind. I sing it, watch it spiral out into the dark, and wait for the Bell to snuff down.

We come to a planet. It is black with vegetation, life creeping every inch of crust beneath twin helixing suns. There are one hundred waiting, adepts, all of them young.

I walk out amongst them. The black vines underfoot writhe at my touch.

These people do not know what I have brought to them. They look at me as though I am a god. They have adapted to the light of this place; their skin is dark, their violet eyes are wide, but they are people like me. I wonder at their dreams, at their lives, at the new adaptations the Bell will force upon them.

The captain's words haunt my mind.

They talk to me, honor me, offer feasts in my name, but I do not know my name. The honor is for Subsidence. The feasts are for the Bell.

I stand for a long time, looking out at them and their world as though through glass, studying a thing I once knew. I watch their twin suns spiral overhead, patterns dictated by forces unleashed at the start of the universe, tracing through time, inexorable, unstoppable.

One of their leaders comes to me at last. She is tall, regal, dressed in long robes of finely braided black twine. I know to her violet eyes these fabrics have color. To me it is all the same.

"Is something wrong, Bell-captain?" she asks, her eyes downcast.

I look over her one hundred and wonder how I can steal away their minds. I look over her black world and wonder if I could adapt, could make it my home.

"Do you know what Temetry means?" I ask her.

She looks up briefly, and I see in her eyes the frisson of confusion.

"Is this a test?" she asks warily.

I wonder if it is.

I walk past her, to the first of the one hundred.

"Do you know Temetry?"

I ask them every one, but none of them know, and at each of their answers the path before me becomes more clear, like order folding out of the branes.

I return to my Bell with none aboard. I will sound the clapper myself. I will toll the distances alone, and at each planet waiting for me, I will ask my question.

I will not fade away like the captain. I will not give my life to Subsidence. I will find the meaning of Temetry, and make of it my home.

Years pass.

Always there are more planets; worlds of lavic sulfur ice, worlds of ammonia oceans, worlds of aluminum sands, and on each one, the descendants of Subsidence. They live afloat on tar-balked ships of petrite, in cloud-castles held aloft by technologies long forgotten, in Gideon bores beneath the ground, in bubbles of molten neon endlessly revolving through the core.

At each I am met by the one hundred, and hopes that Subsidence has resurged, that the hand of the empire will once again come to steer their lives.

I bring no solace, only questions. I ask every one of them of Temetry, but none of them know. I leave them behind, my Bell empty and sounding only with my voice, my dreams in the Brilliance, my turn of the branes.

I see the wonders of the Universe from my dimple. There are galaxies yet forming, out near the discordant rim of existence. I see red shift blur the anthropic landscape about me, feel the echo of entropy as it is born. I hear the stripling birth-song of stars yet to bloom, the grand harmonies of systems flung out like the petals of a sand-flower, spiral arms interwoven as though the arms of long-lost lovers.

I dream of Tesseracts, and Temetry. I enfold Klein bottles and slice Möbius strips, and think of Temetry. It is the only thing to sustain me. A hundred times I have thought to leave the Bell behind, and a hundred times I have pulled back, held by this weight in my middle, pinning me in my place.

At each planet I tell them I will take none of their one hundred. At each I tell them to forget Subsidence. The Empire is gone. It is dead.

And I travel alone, in my Bell.

Others come.

I feel them first as grace notes in the rippling Brilliance, the tolling of loss through the branes. I feel them gathering at my back, tracking me through my enfoldments, keeping pace, adding their long melancholic tones to the anthropic landscape about me.

The sound of them fills me with sadness. I need not see them, the large colorless hulks of their Bells, to know they have come because of me. But I have nothing to give them.

Every passing day there are more. They swarm at my back, each Bell a string to planck the branes, to make the anthropic landscape tremble with ordered life. I feel them rising as though a wave, cresting behind me, an orchestra to pulse my dreams of Temetry to the universe.

At the next planet, a world of grey lead mists, I meet the first of them.

He is young, as I once was. Has it been twenty years? His hair is long and dark, his skin pale, his eyes so full of yearning.

He stands before me, looking at me as though I can give him back what he has lost. This world's one hundred watch us, there in the boiling mists with our two vast Bells snuffed down behind us. I do not know what to say.

"Where are you going?" he asks.

"I am searching for a thing I can't remember."

He nods. He steps closer. I feel his need to reach out, to touch me, to know me.

"Temetry," he says.

I nod. I watch as his eyes fill with tears. He makes no effort to brush them away. They slide down his cheeks like the oscillating Brilliance of the Bells.

"Why are you following me?" I ask.

"Because you are beautiful. Your search is beautiful. In the emptiness your tolls ring with meaning."

"But I do not know the meaning. It is only a word."

He smiles, steps closer, as though he is grateful for this.

"I remember nothing," he says. "I do not know who I am, or where I came from. Your word is everything to me."

I shake my head. I do not want this. I cannot be responsible for him. "You should not follow me. It is a dream I have followed for too long. It has no meaning."

"You are wrong," he says, his voice firm. "It is the light of all the Bells. Your tolls spill hope through the universe."

I too feel like crying to hear him say it so. I have no hope. Only the endless reticulation of the branes, and the black of space, and a word that is empty at my core.

"Don't follow me," I tell him. I can do nothing else. "Please. I am as lost as you."

I do not speak to the one hundred. I return to my Bell. I have been a fool to continue this long. I am a fool with impossible dreams.

That night I resolve to leave the Bell at last. I will make my life among these people in their thick mists. I will learn their ways, and forget the word that has haunted me for twenty years. I will at last be free.

That night I dream of Temetry. It is a swollen river flowing from the clapper of my Bell, spreading out across the universe, dappling the branes with its flavor, ringing out for melancholy, and loss, and a thing once loved. It is beautiful, endless, threading the anthropic landscape with hope.

I wake to a thought that upturns my world.

I dare not think it, can scarcely imagine it. As I hurry to the first dimple I ever used, I cannot voice it aloud in my mind. It is too large, too terrifying, and I cannot bear any more, not now, not so close to the end.

But I must know.

At the dimple I enter the involuting trance, turning non-orientable shapes in non-Euclidean space as I have a thousand times before, until I can feel the flow of anthropy unfolding around me, the branes swelling like budding fruit within, opening the pathways that will allow my Bell to travel through the enfoldments of space.

But I do not travel. I reach out.

Here is my own trail. I can feel it in my Bell's Brilliance, the hints of what I was twenty years ago, stitched together and held fast by the single word that remained throughout, spreading back from now to the time I was a child: Temetry.

It arcs up through the mesosphere of this leaden planet and out into space. It is the path I have left, the vibrations of Temetry that these other Bells have followed, the hope they have sought.

I speed my involutions, turning the endless flood of images harder than I have for years, reaching back, tracking my Brilliance through enfoldments and entropy, piecing together the reverberation of my travels through Subsidence's empire.

In the midst of it, I launch the Bell. I can feel Temetry thrumming through me like a geyser of hope, a feeling I cannot hide, cannot mask from the other

Bells. If I am to do this, they will surely follow. I do not care. Let them. All that matters is Temetry.

My Bell races the branes, back along a trail I have written across the stars for these past twenty years, with the fleet of Subsidence in my wake.

Days pass by, perhaps weeks, swimming up the contrail of my Brilliance to its source. I have traveled back through so many years already, five, perhaps ten. I have spun together the fading echoes of Temetry I left scattered through the darkness, leaping from tone to tone, straining at the limits of my shuddering mind to hold the trail together.

Then the trail is gone.

Its notes are too diffuse, split apart and wafted by solar winds and the expansion of the universe, broken by entropy, the echoes too faint for me to hear. I strive for it, I reach out desperately, but it is gone.

I collapse about my dimple. I feel like a child again, rewritten by her first involutions, scarcely able to think. There is only Temetry, and my failure. I sag there, and sob, because now I have lost all hope. It has dispersed, been erased, rubbed out by the endless reshuffling of the universe. Time has blown away my Brilliance. There is no more trail to find.

I sob, and sob, until sleep finds me.

I wake to a hand on my shoulder. It is a young man, but I do not know him. He is dressed in the clothes of a Bell captain. He has long dark hair, pale skin, and such a yearning in his eyes.

"Do you know Temetry?" I ask him.

He shakes his head slowly. He is sad, I feel that much.

"No," he says. "But I can help you find it."

I sit up. In his eyes is a desire burning as deep as my own.

"How?"

He steps back, and gestures to the involution hall around us. I rub the tears from my eyes, and see there on every dimple, at every one of the one hundred stations, a Bell captain looking back at me.

It is impossible. There is only one captain to a Bell. My jaw drops slack.

"They want to help," he says. "All of us, we want to help."

I look around at them, back to the young man, and feel something cinch tight in my chest. There is a weight there, it has been there for such a long time, too much for me to bear. Perhaps now I will have the strength.

"Why?"

He smiles. It is sad, but laced with quiet strength.

"Because you give us hope."

He does not wait. He moves to my side, where he takes up the one remaining dimple. I look around once more. The hall is full, as it has not been since I was a girl.

"Thank you," I whisper.

And the involutions begin.

It is more than it ever was before.

Where it was a torrent before, now it is an inferno. It is chaos incarnate, blazing through our minds, a violent tsunami of impossibilities to be ordered and stacked.

And we stack them. Beneath the torrent, we stand. From its burning and furious heart we hundred Bell-captains forge the pure and startling music of the branes, each sounding a perfect note that entwines perfectly with the others. As the brutal force of the anthropic plane blasts across us, our notes rise and interweave like pillars into the sky, glissandoing harmonies I never heard before, chords that should ring false but now, under the combined force of our involutions, ring true. Our symphony swells through the chaos, growing into a thing larger than any one of us, larger than the sum of us, larger than Subsidence itself ever thought possible.

I soar on it. I feel it propelling me from behind, feel the will of the others beneath me, lifting me above the inferno, giving me the strength to do what I must.

I toll the clapper with their strength, and the Bell roars across the empty gulf of space faster than it ever flew before. I trawl the anthropic plane with their will, gathering up the long-faded remnants of my Brilliance, tracking the distant branic echoes that were once the word Temetry, sung out into nothing.

Faster, further, we hurtle back through the long years of my lonely voyage, and I feel the captains trembling around me. The inferno is too furious, the task too vast, and one by one they reach their limits. The anthopic flow overcomes them, and they slip beneath the Bell.

But we do not stop, nor slow. Less than ten remain, but we have been honed to incandescent perfection by the raging of the branes. I stand at the cutting edge of our Brilliance and hack into the decayed trail I left as a child, fusing the many parts together until the path emerges, and leads back, and back, and back.

The young man by my side shudders and drops limp. Somewhere far off simulacra carry him away, but I cannot stop. I am roaring now, tearing into the meat of the fabric of all things, forcing entropy to reform, meshing light from dead stars with the frequencies of interstellar dust blown on solar winds, building a tapestry of all chaos, of all order, pounding it in the furnace of this collective mind, smashing it until I totter under its weight, forging from it the single molten trail that I must follow.

Explosions, as the world begins again. Light floods out. Subsidence is born on a far-gone planet, and grows out into the galaxy. They spread, and spread, until their Empire is stretched so thin there is no union remaining, and entropy consumes them. All that remains is the Bells, their last vestige of civilization, ferrying their memory to worlds slowly sinking back into isolation and simplicity.

I read the history of all the Bell captains in the diffuse echoes of their Brilliance, and I understand why they have followed me here. Without Temetry, I would be just like them; as empty as Subsidence, as empty as their Bells, left orbiting like hollow moons about dead and dying planets.

The inferno rises, and rises, and at last, breaks.

Involutions rendered a hundred-minds strong finally crash as spume all about me. Everything is rewritten. Everything is under the Bell. We collapse, and around us this vast ship finally comes to a long, lone toll, as we snuff down upon a dry world, a grey desert planet, stocked with heat sinks and Gideon bores.

I stagger to the glass to look out over the world that was once mine. It is all craters. I fall in the corridor, struggling to hold on to what I am, as the sands billow up around us.

Simulacra wake me with water. The corridors are empty. I remember the long search, but there is no sign of the other captains. Perhaps they have already gone out, to my world, to find Temetry. Perhaps they all fell under the Bell.

I look out and see this planet's atmosphere sparkling like corolla borealis, flecks of mist catching the reflections off my Bell's sloping sides. I feel the branes thrumming around me, through my mind, filling me with possibilities.

I exit with nothing but the captain's clothes on my back. This place is a desert, and the air is hot and dry. I feel the heat from their sinks radiating up from the grey sand. I walk a little way, past the silver Gideon bores, past the crowds of people watching and waiting. I see the one hundred, hastily turned out and waiting for admittance, flanked by their parents, grand and fierce expressions lashed across their faces.

They watch in confusion as I climb a dune and sit at the top. The vast weight of my Bell towers above me, shadows everything. I am yet its captain.

A man walks from the crowd to join me. He is perhaps as old as me, dressed in simple brown smocks. He sits by my side, but says nothing, only looks at me as though he knows me, with sorrow, with love.

He holds something out to me, on the palm of his hand. It is a speckled white sand-hopper. It is a pretty thing, its long legs stretched out to skein it over the hot desert surface. I reach out, thinking to touch it, expecting it to flee, but it does not move. I touch its back, its side.

It is folded paper. I lift it from his hand, turn it over in my hands. The folds and twists of its craftsmanship are stunning. All of its limbs, its sinewy body, its whip-thin antenna, are folded from a single sheet of paper. It has been twisted into a single side, like a simple Möbius strip, non-orientable.

I have never seen anything like it. It is beautiful. In all my travels, in all my years upon the Bell, I have never seen anything so alive brought out of the folding.

I turn to the mute man, look into his eyes.

"Temetry?"

The Switch

SARAH STANTON

It starts out like this: halfway up a ladder looking at the stars. Xiao Zhu is behind me with the paint pots, whistling something tuneless to himself. I've got a brush in my hand and a delicate tracework of flowers in front of me; there's a job to be done, and Lao Yang is waiting. But all I can think of is the stars.

We don't see them that often, not the real ones. On the streets of Beijing you can see them every night, a glorious winking parade for the people who made them, but in the courtyards, the behind-spaces where we live and work and play, we just see clouds. Ever since I was a boy, there's been a roof of smog over my head. And these days people think there's something suspicious about stars. They're for farmers and foreigners and dissidents, people who know how to find them and still want to. But they're up there tonight, faint specks in the muck, and my hands go still as I stare.

Lao Yang coughs behind me. It's a smoker's cough, full of sound and fury, but it's also a warning: there's a job to be done. I turn my eyes to the roof beam, to the beautiful tracery of blossoms and leaves, and begin to fill in the green. Xiao Zhu begins to wander the courtyard, a young man's amble, taking in the neat tiles and the potted pomegranate in one corner. Lao Yang just waits.

The paint takes shape under my brush as if it were a living thing. Red, green, blue, gold; it drifts across the wood and makes it real. When I have chased the last of the color into the corners, Lao Yang helps me down the ladder, and the three of us look up in silence at what we have done.

"It's finished," he says.

I nod.

"Three months' work," he says.

I nod again.

We walk out onto the street, sharing a steady silence between us. Xiao Zhu is already busy at the gate, stabbing at a small control panel with his slim fingers. We turn and look at the image of a house, the stone lions guarding its door, its roof beams painted like a sunrise. Above us, the false stars shine clear and unadorned.

Xiao Zhu hits the switch, and the hologram collapses. There is a quiet shimmer, and then nothing. The street remains unchanged.

Lao Yang smiles. "Let's go home."

• • •

It starts out like that, but that's not where it started. It started fifteen years ago, when the hutongs disappeared. Those narrow alleys, pinpricked by public toilets and hawkers, the sights and the sounds and the pervasive smells, and on either side the courtyard houses, the heritage of Beijing. They were already vanishing by the close of the twentieth century, whole stretches of history being leveled to make way for apartments and poor-quality condos. A lucky few were protected, turned into tourist traps and holiday homes. Gulou, Nanluoguxiang, Liulichang Jie: their names trip off our tongues like ancient mnemonics. But eventually, they too disappeared.

Lao Yang was forty when he saw the demolition sign go up above his door. He lived in a protected hutong, a heritage-listed area. When he went to register his protests with the local authorities, he was waylaid by plainclothes agents and beaten. That was the day the first hologram went up, in front of the place Lao Yang used to call home. Seen from the street, it looked like any other courtyard house, elegant and serene. From behind, it was a sick pile of rubble. He tells us over and over how he could put his hand through the mirage, how in that moment what he saw and what the world saw changed forever.

The next day, Lao Yang's whole street was cloaked in holograms. The usual smog had subsided into a pearly blue. The crude demolition notices had vanished from the doors, to be replaced by fresh coats of vermillion paint. Lao Yang looked at them and knew that there was rubble waiting behind. And the holograms spread, street after street, so fast you could see a workman in the morning and know your whole district would be gone in the afternoon. I was just a boy when it happened, but I remember the spread of blue skies and green leaves like it was Chinese New Year. I didn't understand back then. All I knew was that the city was beautiful, and I never wanted to leave.

I understand now. People believe what they see. These government holograms, they make Beijing a dream town, a false perfection that follows you home and leaves you at the door. We don't see the demolition, the shaky buildings, the squalor. There are clear skies every day even though it hurts to breathe. We are a city of flickering images, of fantasy, of fraud, and nobody objects because nobody sees anything to object to. There are stars above us at night. Who cares where they come from?

We troop out of the hutong in single file, Lao Yang, Xiao Zhu and me. We never talk much after a job: we have done something majestic, something monstrous, and the silence is almost holy. We make our way through the winding streets like an ant trail, left, right and left again, until we reach the main road, bustling with cars. Xiao Zhu flags a taxi and bargains the price down to something we can afford. He sits in the front and we sit in the back, while the driver putters us home.

I met Lao Yang three years ago in a dingy noodle shop which had looked much cleaner from the outside. We were sitting side by side, slurping our noodles like some triumphant symphony. I had a book propped up against the vinegar pot and was considering it thoughtfully as I chewed. Not that I'm an intellectual or anything; I'm a man who works with his hands. But I like books. There's something honest about a printed page. You know what it is today, and you can make a fair guess at what it's going to be tomorrow.

Lao Yang peered over at my paperback. 'You're reading,' he observed.

"Yeah," I said.

"Why?"

I hooked a noodle out of my bowl. "I like words," I said.

"You a writer?"

"No," I said. "Just a laborer."

Lao Yang considered this. Then he grunted. "Let's have a few beers."

I guess that's where it really started: me and Lao Yang, getting drunk together in a deadbeat little noodle shop like any other in Beijing. That's when he told me about what had happened to his home, the place he'd brought his wife back to and the place where his children grew up. He told me he had a plan to bring back the hutongs, as good as they'd been or better. He already knew a kid who could manipulate the hologram systems, knock out the feed to a single house. All we had to do was rebuild the ruins behind it, hit the switch, and watch the fantasy be replaced with something real.

We've restored twenty-odd courtyard houses so far. Some of them have been left vacant and fallen into disrepair; these are the small jobs, just repairing and repainting and finally, hitting the switch. The bigger jobs are the houses which were actually destroyed, demolished to make way for property developments which never came around. These we rebuild, brick and timber and roof tiles, until the only difference between the house and the hologram is the color of the sky. We are the quietest dissidents in Beijing. When we do our job right, nobody knows we were ever there. But little by little, the three of us are fighting to bring the barrier between truth and illusion down.

Home is the first courtyard house we ever fixed up, on the outskirts of Gulou. Lao Yang's house. When we arrived it was little better than a heap; now a crab-apple tree hangs lazily over the courtyard, and goldfish drift in the ornamental urns. The only furniture we have has been salvaged from demolition sites, old moth-eaten futons and wobbly tables, giving the place an eccentric, creaking charm. We've never been able to afford to buy new things for ourselves.

Xiao Zhu goes into the kitchen to boil water for noodles. I join him, helping to shake the little flat cakes out of the packets and into the bowls.

"You did a good job today," he says. "All those colors. Really pretty."

"You too," I say, tearing open a seasoning sachet.

I never quite know what to say to Xiao Zhu. He's a young guy, good with all the technology which has long since left me and Lao Yang behind. He's got a thick mop of hair and a rakish smile and he dances when he walks. He could've been a TV idol, but he became a dissident instead. He's the one who works the holograms for us, when all the hard labor is done; he helps out here and there with the painting and tiling, but his real job is something I can't even begin to understand. I don't know where Lao Yang found him. But he's part of the secret, and that makes him family. I just wish I knew what to say.

We carry the steaming bowls of noodles out to the courtyard and sit down. Lao Yang hawks and spits into the bushes, picks up his chopsticks and digs in. Xiao Zhu and I eat slowly, making each bite last. When we're done, Lao Yang lights up a cigarette, puts his feet up and eyes us across the table.

"That was our twenty-eighth house," he says. "From here in Gulou to Chenxiang Jie and out to Dongjiaominxiang, we have brought twenty-eight courtyard houses back to reality. Nobody knows it but us, but we are making the past the present, and the present the truth of the past. The future is ours. And I think it's time to move on."

"Double prosperity," I murmur.

"Double prosperity," Lao Yang agrees. "Twenty-eight is an auspicious number. We've talked about this before, and I think we're ready. There's a jewel at the heart of this city, a treasure lying forgotten, and it needs to be saved. We can save it, if we're willing to try."

"The Forbidden City?" says Xiao Zhu. "We're talking about the Forbidden City again? It's massive. We'd be dead before we finished."

"Not if we had help," says Lao Yang, and a gleam creeps into his eyes. "What have we been playing at, these past three years? Pockets of reality here and there. Drops in an ocean. But if we could rebuild the palace—shut the holograms off and let people see the truth through the haze—that'd be worth dying for. I know a guy. He's got a construction company. He'll come in and help us for a price. We can do it! Give the people back their history! The government thinks they own our futures. Let's fight them with the past!"

I pick up our bowls, toss the chopsticks in with a clatter. "We'll talk about it," I say. And then, apropos of nothing: "If the past and the present and the future had a battle, who would win?"

"The future," Xiao Zhu says softly. "The future always wins."

The next day, I head over to Houhai to see my girlfriend. She's a sweet thing, a little younger than me, and has no idea what I get up to in the small hours of the night. Sometimes I think I should marry her, but then I remember I have no money, no job, no future. I am a down-and-out hero, not a husband. At these times I hold her tighter, kissing her with a sweet desperation; when she finds out the truth, we are finished. But the sun is bright today, the holographic sky projecting a deep and powerful blue, and we walk around the lake hand in hand while she chatters about her extensive circle of friends. I drift in and out, thinking about what Lao Yang said. Restoring the Forbidden City. Bringing it back to reality. Could we really pull it off?

"Oh!" my girlfriend exclaims, her eyes falling on a nearby shop. "They've put up the lanterns for the festival!"

"They're not real lanterns," I sigh. "They've just altered the hologram."

"Hologram, real lanterns, what's the difference?" she says. "They're *pretty*!"

She rushes over to the shop and insists on posing for a photo, two fingers up in a cheeky V-sign. I dutifully hold her bag and snap the picture with her smartphone, assuring her she looks beautiful in every way.

"I'm going to eat so many mooncakes this year," she says. "I always do. Every year when they come out in the shops, I go in and scold them. You're going to make me so fat! I say. But I just can't resist them."

"You're not fat," I say absentmindedly. I'm thinking about the palace, how we're going to shingle those roofs. Then my phone buzzes in my pocket. It's Xiao Zhu.

"They've got Lao Yang," he gasps.

I stop dead. "Who has?"

"The cops. Or someone like them. That guy he met was a plant, or a rat, or something. They grabbed him this morning on his way to where they were meeting. I don't know where they took him. I don't know where they've gone."

"Calm down," I say, trying to sound soothing without arousing my girlfriend's suspicions. "Where are you now?"

"Back at the house. I don't know how long we'll be safe here, though. He'll have to tell them everything."

"I'm coming over right now," I say. "I'll get a cab."

"Don't take the first one," he says, and hangs up.

Xiao Zhu is pacing the length of our courtyard, one of Lao Yang's cigarettes on his lips. The smog is thick today, outside the holographic curtain, and I have to squint to see him.

"It's over," he says. "Him and his fucking double prosperity. They'll come for us, and we'll never see the light of day again. Not that we are now. Not that we ever have."

I sag onto one of our dilapidated couches. "It's not over," I say. "There's still the two of us. You can work the holograms, and I can do everything else. It'll take us longer to finish a house, but it's what he'd want us to do. To keep going. To keep making things real."

Xiao Zhu snorts. "You're just like him. Big dreams. Today the Forbidden City, tomorrow the stars. What are you in it for anyway? What are you hoping to change?"

I start to speak, and then pause. What am I in it for? I loved the holograms as a kid. I remember people cheering when they switched them on in our street, watching the sky turn blue and the grass turn green. We never even had grass before. But then I grew up, and one day I realized I hadn't seen the sun for ten years. Not the real sun. Not the stars. And I started looking at houses and shops I had known all my life with suspicion. What did they really look like? I knew what they looked like inside, because government-sponsored holograms stop at the door. But the truth of them was as foreign to me as if I had never seen them before.

When Lao Yang approached me that day, I slurped at my noodles and listened to a dream. He wanted to live in Beijing—not a copy or a model, but a real city, a city that breathed, a city that had shit on the pavement and smog in the air but was free, effervescent and alive. He wanted a place that could move from past to present to future of its own accord, without technological intervention. He wanted his home back. And I wanted to help him.

"I'm in it because sometimes you just fight," I say, finally. "And you keep fighting until it's done. Lao Yang's out there. He's an old man and he's hurting. But he's helped you, and he's helped me, and I'm not going to let him disappear. I said something dumb before. I said there's still the two of us. That's not true. There's three like there always was. I'm going to try and help him. And you're coming with me."

Xiao Zhu lights another cigarette, blows the smoke out into the haze. "Nice speech, big guy. In a battle between the past, present and future, who would you be?"

I growl. "The future. The future always wins."

Two days later, we have the names of the people who took Lao Yang and where they're hiding him. Xiao Zhu bribed a local guard and wouldn't tell me where he got the money. We have a plan, too, but I don't trust it. It relies too much on gadgets, on things I've never learned to think of as real. This is Xiao Zhu's world, and it makes me uncomfortable. But there's nowhere else to turn.

We're standing in front of the Ru Jia hostel in east Chaoyang. *Just like home!*, the sign proclaims, and I believe it. I've met plenty of people who get beaten at home. Behind this facade is a black jail, an illegal holding facility for protesters and political dissidents. This is where they're keeping Lao Yang, stripped naked and starving, pulpy and bruised; for once, I don't have to see it to know that it's true.

I look over at Xiao Zhu. "Ready?" I ask.

He nods, and pulls the hope of our whole campaign out of his pocket. It's a portable holographic projector, powerful enough to generate a large object or change the appearance of a room. I have no idea where he got it; they're normally only found in large hotels or function halls, helping to create a dream wedding at a fraction of the cost. He studies it intently, thumbing buttons as he perfects the image, confirming every last detail. A guard left the building half an hour ago, and I watch over Xiao Zhu's shoulder as he is recreated, down to the pores on his skin, on an alien machine.

"Ready," Xiao Zhu says at last. He pushes a button, and the guard flickers into existence by our side. My stomach lurches involuntarily. If something like this passed me on the street, I'd think it was real. Xiao Zhu curls his hand around the projector, concealing it from sight, and the two of us walk up the steps of the Ru Jia with our holographic guard close behind.

"You programmed the speech?" I whisper.

"Everything you said," Xiao Zhu replies. "We'll be fine."

I knock on the door, then jump back behind the guard and try to look penitent. The door opens a fraction and a man peers out.

"Yeah?"

"I got 'em, sir," the false guard says. "The two that were with Lao Yang. Figured I'd drop them off here until the courts decide where they belong. Should I throw them in with their pal?"

"Do that," the man says, "do that. Make sure they feel welcome, too—ha, ha!"

"Yessir," says our guard. "I'll treat them just right, don't you worry about that." The door creaks open further, and we step inside.

The first thing that hits us when we enter the jail is the darkness. The second is the stench. Somewhere in another room a woman is sobbing, an endless, throaty sob that sounds like it could eat up the whole world. For the first time in years, I find myself longing for the comfort of holograms. Our false guard leads us down the corridor to the room where Lao Yang is being held; as we get closer, the stench grows stronger, and I start to panic. When we stop, it's at Room 28. Double prosperity. I want to cry.

I open the door. It's not locked—the people here know what happens if they run. Lao Yang is lying in a ball on his bed, shaking in time to some unknown beat in his head. There's dried blood on the sheets, and a dank smell in the air. I run to him. "Lao Yang, it's me," I say. I say it over and over, willing him to respond. At last he raises his head, a distant look in his eyes. "Oh," he says. "So it is."

We lift him to his feet, cradling his body and wincing as each new bruise is revealed. Xiao Zhu takes the clothes we've brought from his pack, and we dress him as gently as we can, first pants and then arms up for the shirt. Lao Yang says nothing as we fuss over him, swaying unsteadily like a sapling in the wind. It is as if knowledge and years have all been beaten out of him, leaving him back as he began, an empty seed. When I reach out to him, I find myself stroking his hair as I would a child's.

"We should get moving," Xiao Zhu says. "I've reprogrammed the projector."

"Just give me a minute," I say. I look at the old man twitching feverishly in my grip, try to catch my gaze with his own. "Lao Yang, we're going to get you out of here now. Just think of this time as a hologram. It was a bad one, but we're going to hit the switch and bring you back to reality. You'll never need to be afraid again."

Lao Yang's gaze wavers, but he nods. I turn to Xiao Zhu. "Let's go."

We pack up the bag and sneak out into the corridor, Lao Yang hobbling between us. The guard is slouched by the door, watching some trashy late-night television and tossing sunflower seeds into his mouth.

"Are you sure this will work?" I whisper. "It's so melodramatic."

"It'll work," says Xiao Zhu, and as he pushes the button, he grins.

A van slams through the opposite wall of the corridor, sending glass and masonry flying through the air. A brick lands on the horn, setting off a piercing wail. Lights flash and spin manically. Despite myself, I sniff. Melodramatic. The guard jumps up, shouts for someone, anyone, and rushes to inspect the damage. We run for the door, Lao Yang propped up between us, our footsteps camouflaged by the racket. We have about five seconds before he realizes there's no van after all.

We stop for breath in a small park two streets over, flattening ourselves against the trees for cover. I hold onto Lao Yang as tightly as I dare. I don't believe what I said to him; reality is smog and shit and beatings, and you can't hit the switch on that. But when you're looking into the face of a broken man, what can you say? Beijing is a city of holograms, and that's reality. It's a city where you can get picked up off the street for no reason, and that's reality. But we got in and out. We rescued a friend. That's reality, too. "It shouldn't have been that easy," I say. "We should have had to fight them."

"I wanted to fight them," says Xiao Zhu. "All those people in there, and that sobbing. We should have rescued them all."

"That trick wasn't going to work twice," I say. "We did what we could. We fought until it was done."

Xiao Zhu considers this, while the traffic roars past us and the holographic stars shine down. Then he turns to me, and the light in his eyes is brighter than them all.

"We're not done," he says. "I've got a surprise for you."

Two minutes later, with my heart in my mouth, I watch the hologram go down.

The bright blue and yellow paint of the Ru Jia flickers, becomes faded and dull. Cracks appear in the plaster, windows become fractured and dusty, and the grass around its borders suddenly dies. For the first time in years, I see an eyesore on the streets of Beijing. And it stands out. It shouts its presence to the world. It makes me smile until I hurt.

"Tomorrow morning, people are going to be asking questions about that," says Xiao Zhu. "They'll probably even have a look at what goes on inside."

Lao Yang lifts his head. "What did you do?"

"I released a virus into their system, one that operates on a time delay. It's knocked out their projector and it'll block any attempt to fix it. I did it to cover our escape, but—" and he grins, helplessly, "it has an upside, too."

"Xiao Zhu," I say, "I could kiss you. Let's go home."

It's funny. We spent three years picking away at the scab of history, but we never pulled it off until tonight. Twenty-eight courtyard houses are scattered throughout Beijing. They are beautiful, and they represent truth, but they never changed the world. All those roof beams, those delicate flowers, the tiles and the urns and the towers never did so much as hitting a switch and showing reality as it is. Our greatest triumph wasn't renewing the past, but exposing the future. And in a battle between the past, present and future, the future always wins.

Sunlight Society

MARGARET RONALD

When the Fourth Street biolab went up, I didn't think of Casey right away. I was working in the far side of the complex, which meant I was one of about four hundred people who got to see the entire dome rise up off its foundations, rotate counterclockwise ninety degrees, and shoot up into the sky. My immediate reaction followed the same pattern as everyone else: first *What the hell,* then, just before a needle of light vaporized the biolab, *Are those* people *up there?*

I could hazard a guess at the second question; I'd gotten that far into the shadow organizations, even then. I knew enough to guess at the identities of some of the blurry shapes darting through the smoke, shapes that official press releases would call confabulation and that the conspiracists would call aliens or Muslims or Freemason-built androids. The shadow orgs had been sloppy that time; usually they didn't like to be seen at their work, but there'd been so little warning that they'd had no choice but to break out the big guns. Literally, in this case.

But that wasn't what came to mind as I stared up into the sky, the glare of that solar blast fading bit by bit from my retinas, my nethead links relating the intensity of that blast, the projected knock-on effects on the rest of the Niobe web, the first stirrings among the dataminers. Instead, I just thought *Casey would love this.* I kept coming back to that thought over the next few weeks, even after word got out about the low-rent terrorists who'd gotten so close to taking over the biolab that vaporizing the whole place was the only alternative. Even after the arrests started.

I still think it's true.

Today marks the first time I've been allowed into the Albuquerque facility. My credentials have been checked and re-checked so many times that they could probably tell you the weight and density of my last three bowel movements. Even so, they've been cutting corners on security, just so they can get me in here.

I fully expect that within twenty years, someone will have figured out a way to install nethead technology in anyone regardless of individual brain structure. But until they do, I'm pretty much guaranteed work wherever I go.

And there's even fewer of us netheads with the proper security clearances to get into the Madison facility, let alone Albuquerque. I'm a valuable commodity.

The facility isn't much to look at: any decent biolab would have more apparent security. My nethead links are telling me otherwise, though; streams and warnings buzz against my skull so hard I can almost feel my teeth rattle. It unnerves me in a way that Madison didn't, and Madison's where they keep the host site for the Niobe satellite web. Enough solar power to—well, to blow up a biolab, for instance—focused onto the energy collectors for five dozen countries, and it's still less well protected than this place.

It's cool and dark inside the guard shack, and the back of my neck prickles after the blazing heat outside. The guard's got a laser sight wired into his left eye; the silver tracery of it fades into his pale complexion much more smoothly than the similar patterns on my own skin. He gestures to the marks while the machines verify my ID. "Looks nice."

"Thanks." It's striking, or so the nethead PR department says. They claim that's why they want my image for their publicity stills, not just to provide the illusion of diversity. Some days I think they even believe it.

"Been here before?" The guard knows I haven't—a glance at the screens could tell him as much and more—but sometimes courtesy trumps efficiency.

I shake my head. "I've been to Madison."

"Madison, pfft." He grins. "That's nothing to what we got—" He stops and turns red, as if he can't quite believe what he's saying. I used to have that reaction, way back when I was sharing what I knew with Casey, when I tried to tell her that the comics we'd read were—well, not true, not close to *true,* but had some basis in reality.

"Got what?" I ask, as the computers spit out my ID and agree that yes, my fingers and retinas appear to be my own.

"Well, you know. Them." He opens up the doors, and the flickering readouts in my periphery flare and scramble into new configurations. "The heroes."

The official story of Casey and me is that we were kids together, grew apart, came back together, screwed around, and then split up for good once I realized how crazy she was. Both times it was the heroes that brought us together, the first time through the comics that had come out in the wake of Maxentius sightings and the rumors about the Sixth Seal group. We read them all, regardless of quality, lying on our backs in the vacant lot behind her house, ink on our fingers and intent discussions of whether Mistress Fivepoint could beat Jack o'the Green or if they'd just team up against Memetek. The second time it was because in my first months as a full nethead I learned so much about the shadow organizations, the reality behind all those rumors, and I could only think of one person I wanted to share that with—Casey, who could rattle off the Liberty League's oath or Red Knight's transformation mantra as easily as the Pledge of Allegiance.

Both times it was her head, or what was wrong with it, that split us up.

It's a useful official version. But one thing you learn when you start getting involved in the shadow orgs is that the official version means very little. After all, none of them show up in any official version, except in the records of what didn't happen, the plots that failed, the disasters averted.

Or, sometimes, in the lists of people who've disappeared.

The transport behind those metal doors takes me maybe eight floors down, with that bone-twitching stutter you only get from passing through negation fields. I don't notice it; I'm too busy dealing with the sudden silence in my head. I can handle it—mental stability is one of the most important factors that they test for in determining nethead fitness—but that doesn't mean I enjoy it. Particularly because the one link that does remain is the one that got implanted when I started working for the shadow orgs. For insurance, they told me. The Niobe GPS link.

I remember the Fourth Street biolab, and the back of my neck goes abruptly hot again.

When the doors open again, though, all thoughts of the world outside vanish. The visual input's bad enough: between the scream of light on my right from what might be a laboratory and the dizzying drop twenty feet ahead of me, I can barely register mundane details like the polished-glass sheen of the floor, the central spindle of memory staves, the man waiting for me just to the side.

But all that's nothing compared to the chatter of computers on every side, the information in patterns I've never seen before. It's like being picked up from one set of rapids and dropped into another, and it takes all of my concentration not to drown.

The biggest difference is that there's not much trace of nethead work. It's tradition to leave our marks on the usernodes, stegans encoded into the streams of data like graffiti in a canal, but here there's only two: *Klaatu Barada Nikto!* from the designer of the Niobe web, and *Welcome to Olympus* (plus a handy map) from a woman who's now on permanent detail with the Secret Service. If this were a normal job, I'd be tempted to add my own mark to the tabulae, but right now I don't trust what I'd leave.

A permanent link unscrolls with the boxy look of official work. *IN RESI-DENCE: Kazemusha/Lady Nettle/Oculus/Matthew Glendower/Maxentius . . .* The list goes on, code names and real names (not that it matters which is which, this far in) and designations I've only seen in the most hidden records. Names to conjure with.

And finally I recognize the man who's been standing just to the side of the entrance. They've sent the shining face of the org to meet me.

He's just like Casey and I always imagined, resplendent in ivory and gold, and while he doesn't have the red cape the comics gave him, I get the sense he'd like one. Barrel chest, brilliant smile, voice with enough bonhomie for a tri-state area. "Bit overwhelming, eh?" Maxentius says.

"A bit," I agree weakly.

"It does that to me too, sometimes." *No it doesn't,* I think, but he's not talking about the information overload. He gestures to the vista behind him: dozens of circular floors leading off a central shaft, lifts and elevators between for those who can't just fly. "This sight—when I tire of it, then I'll know the skein of my days has run out. Good to meet you, Seth." He clasps my hand and shakes it vigorously.

"Good to meet you." I've read papers on how much force that hand can exert, how many diamonds it can crush into powder.

"And you're here to see Glendower. Splendid." He turns and strides forward across the gleaming floor. I follow, and if it looks like I'm not gawking, that's because I'm only doing so in my head. Of the levels I can see, some are sterile white and glassed in; some hold weapons and implements I can only guess at; a few look inhabited, homes for those who can't or won't stay outside in the world they claim to protect. A blur on the next floor up, across from us, resolves into a sparring match between two figures I've only heard rumors of, and even then I have to slow the visual down by a factor of ten to get a glimpse.

At the far end of the walkway, Maxentius glances over his shoulder. "Come along, lad! Mustn't keep him waiting!"

Of all the members of the shadow organizations, Maxentius has read too much of his own press. He really does talk like a comic book; 'lad' is nothing to worry about.

Still, it bothers me, and not just because I can remember one too many cops calling my father 'boy' on one too many late-night drives.

There are some things I know for sure about Casey: she loved superhero comics; she didn't keep in touch with her family after graduating; she wrote pamphlets for the Oakland Anti-Gnosis society; she couldn't keep a job for more than six months at a time; she could make fantastic biscuits out of damn near any ingredients she had at hand. When her parents moved away the first time, when we were in school, it was because the first round of mandatory testing had come through. I was on the track to being a fully-functional nethead; Casey had tested positive for a number of dysfunctions, including predisposition to schizophrenia.

There are things I wonder about—whether the chemical imbalances in her brain were caused by her father's exposure to some of the nastier weapons of the Second Chinese War, whether she knew what a risk I was taking associating with her, whether we should have gone ahead and slept together after all.

There are things I've been told about her in the wake of Fourth Street, about her mental state and the company she kept. These are things I will never believe about her.

Maxentius leads me around one side of the silo shaft, through what looks like a trophy room (it's not, according to the nethead stegans). He's rapidly figured out that I'm not listening to him, but that doesn't stop him; in fact, I think he's taken it as license to ramble on.

I catch a glimpse of someone I think is Pale Rider down one hallway. If it is him, that means this particular shadow organization has gone global. Most of them have; a few nationalists cling to their identity in places like Turkmenistan and France, and somehow I'd always assumed the U.S. shadow orgs would be the same way.

Of course, they have the Niobe web. That automatically makes them global; I've got the reminder in my skull if I ever forget that.

We walk past cases holding remnants of past work, plots unraveled, events that were hushed up and now only remain as a footnote to history. Still talking, Maxentius gestures vaguely at what looks like a giant pair of shears. ". . . didn't tell us that the phase shift had affected only *half* of her, and the other half was stuck in another dimension entirely!" He chuckles, and I remember to smile. "Down this way. Glendower, are you there?"

A gray-haired man in a white shirt and bow tie—there's even a tweed jacket, the kind with the elbow patches, tossed over a chair—waves back without looking. He's talking to a woman I don't recognize. I wouldn't know her if we met on the street; I'd only know her if she wore her mask. She folds up her clipboard, nods to Maxentius, and fades into invisibility with a faint scent of calla lilies.

Glendower's in his late fifties but looks older. He walks with a cane, and while he doesn't have the same build as Maxentius, he's not a small man either. His gray hair is still thick, but there are autofocusing spectacles perched on his nose, and when he pulls a chair over and sinks into it, it's clear that standing for so long was a strain for him. He's the one who pushed through my security clearance, since the virus affected the orgs' datalogs and he's the one who has to work with them. Bookkeeper to the gods. "Well, Mr. Carson, what do you think of our little home?"

"It's amazing," I say, truthfully, and then a touch of the perverse prompts me to add, "if a little rough on visitors."

To my surprise, it's not Glendower who answers, but Maxentius. "The price of our work," he says with a regretful sigh. Maxentius doesn't hide his feelings much; the man's all surface, glossy and deep as a four-color page spread. "These days, to defend the innocent requires one to have a home of which all are innocent." He sees my expression and shakes his head. "I assure you, lad, we're all on the same side here. We are protectors of the world we love, sworn to defend it."

He's entirely serious, and of all the members of the shadow orgs, he embodies those values the most. And yet I can't help myself. "'To protect the weak, the innocent, and the defenseless from the indignities, wrongs and outrages of the lawless, the violent and the brutal,'" I quote. Glendower shoots me a sharp look.

Maxentius, though, hasn't noticed. "Yes! Exactly." He shakes my hand a second time, beaming, and nods to Glendower. "I must be off. Good luck—I hope we'll see you here again."

I watch him go. He rescues kittens; that much is a matter of record. It's part of why there's now a cleanup detail assigned solely to him. The shadow orgs may prize their secrecy, but Maxentius does make a useful distraction. And, after all, they are all on the same side.

I shouldn't have made fun of him. It's not his fault he's an innocent.

Glendower's watching me, but unless he's a nethead—and I know he's not—he can't see everything I'm doing. "I've set up a contact terminal for you," he says. "We'd been meaning to change out our security, but good netheads with clearance are few and far between, and I'm afraid we were caught with our trousers down. The virus doesn't seem to be actively hostile, but my projections show it stopping work outright if it overloads any more of our systems. At the moment it's benign, just irritating."

"I can imagine." Twenty years ago, we'd have been fine with a microsecond lag; forty years, and a five-second lag was nothing. But technology spoils us—I should know, I've got a few dozen terabytes' worth of it in my head. I switch from wireless to node work, and put my hands on either side of the contact terminal, relying on the points wired into my fingertips to carry me in. "I can upgrade some of your security while I'm here, but it'll just be a patch-up job till I can come back, and I don't yet have clearance for a second visit. You sure you couldn't fix it yourself?"

Glendower shakes his head. "It's rapidshift. I just don't have the speed to keep it from mutating as I'm working on it. That's nethead work."

Of course it is; I created the damn virus. My consciousness is already split between the terminals that dot the base; I damp wireless input to make up for it and start searching.

Glendower waits for a response from me, then shakes his head and laboriously gets up from the chair. He's got a pacemaker; I can sense the pulse of it like a cricket in the room. "It's rare to have a nethead down here," he says, opening a cabinet and pouring a glass of tonic water. "I had to argue just to get the first few working on our security."

"You've got failsafes in place, though." Those failsafes gave me nightmares for weeks, after I first found out that the Niobe web wasn't just for solar energy.

"True." He pours a second glass and sets it on the shelf next to me. I nod my thanks but don't take it. We're both silent a moment; realtime maybe ten seconds, wiretime much longer, long enough for me to cordon off my virus and distinguish the main archives from what I'm looking for. They don't let these out to the general public; they don't even have access through the Madison facility. The Oculus records.

"You didn't need to tease Max like that," Glendower says quietly.

"Probably not." I'm sorting through records, searching by time, date, subject, even setting aside a part of my brain to flash through random stills, looking for Casey. Oculus' uploads take up entire spindles; I've heard that no one knows why it records everything it sees, but they don't want to upset it by asking. "It just bothered me."

"When he finds out you quoted the mission statement of the Klan at him, he'll be a mess. Max doesn't work well when he has a crisis of conscience." He settles back into his chair with a grunt, and tonic water splashes over the back of his hand.

"Then he'll only be saving the world eighty percent of the time. I'm sure the rest of you can cover the remaining twenty percent." Something about the virus cordon is bothering me, but I'm so close—and there she is, Casey's face blurring by, the brief video record categorized with about four hundred others, each no more than a couple of minutes.

"Would you be willing to help out with that twenty percent?"

I stop, sliding Casey's record into my personal memory like a shoplifter sliding a necklace into his pocket, and turn to face him, keeping one hand on the contact terminal. "Sorry?"

Glendower smiles and thumps his cane on the floor. He needs that cane, I know; an accident when this place was being built wrecked his right foot, and he hasn't had it replaced. "If nothing else, this incident highlights our need to have a nethead on the team. You're the best, you've got the offline intelligence we need, and you've shown great discretion in your work for us here and in Madison."

Discretion. Right. Which is why I'm now fixing a problem I created. It's tempting, though—I can imagine Casey saying *Who wouldn't jump at a chance to be a superhero?* Or is it only that I want her to say that?

I unpack Casey's record for later viewing, thinking of the smell of hot dirt in the vacant lot and four-color ink smudged across my fingers. "Let me think about it."

"Well." Glendower sighs, then leans over and sets his glass down on the far terminal. "I understand, you've got doubts. After all—" the screen behind him lights up, "—I think I know why you're here."

Casey stares down at me from Glendower's screen, twenty times larger than life, and I finally recognize what the virus report is telling me: someone, probably Glendower himself, got to it first. I stare at Casey's image on the screens—an ID photo, not a mug shot. They'd only had mug shots for the ones who'd gotten arrested, and Casey didn't even make it that far.

Glendower nods. "She was important to you."

"She was." I open the video record that I went through so much to find. It's only about twenty seconds' worth of Oculus' point-of-view, showing a door bursting open. Casey crouches at the far end of the room, frizzy hair tied up in a bright red cloth, eyes wide and dark.

She's just as I remember her.

The record shows her turning and reaching for something—a gun? a phone? a vial that could be her medicine and could be something else entirely? All of them are on the same table. She never even touches it before a flash of light from the door cuts her down.

I close my eyes, then open them to face Glendower, and behind him, Casey. "You knew?"

"We're everywhere, Mr. Carson. We knew." He looks over his shoulder, at the image of a smiling dead girl. "She'd been part of the Fourth Street terrorist cell. We got to the lab first, but when we came to apprehend her—"

"Don't." I can see what happened. I take another look back into the Oculus records; someone's lumped all of the recorded deaths together, whether criminal or civilian or just plain dumb luck. *Glendower's assembled them for his own penance,* I guess. *He doesn't let himself forget either.*

It's not enough.

"My offer still stands." He props his hands on his cane and gazes at me. Casey does the same, over his shoulder. "You wouldn't be the first to forsake vengeance and turn your considerable talents toward a good cause. Or—" he sits back a little "—you can take that vengeance on me. I won't stop you."

My breathing slows, and the hand that isn't on the terminal curls into a fist. I could do it. I could kill him in any number of ways—stop the pulse of his pacemaker, use the autofocus in his spectacles as a link into his optical nerve and burn his skull from the inside out, scramble his neurons till he's a drooling vegetable—and walk away. I might even get out of here unscathed, depending how what method I chose.

But kill him, and there'll be another just as certain that they're justified in their actions. Because it's their job to save the world. They're everywhere already, and so many of them wear masks. They say it's to protect their identities, but it's also so that we're never sure who's one of them, who's watching. They're always anonymous again in daylight.

Who was that masked man? I don't know, but there's twenty more of them outside.

Or join them. That's the logical ending for a nethead; most of us find one big project and stick with it, and this would be in a good cause. If the terrorists had gotten their hands on the Fourth Street biolab, the result could have killed thousands. How many lives could I save that way, how many Caseys could I save . . .

I snip the virus out of the system with an absent thought and take my hands from the terminal, switching back to wireless. "Let me think about it," I say again, and this time I'm not stalling, I'm pleading.

Glendower nods. "I'm sorry," he says, bowing his head. "About your friend's death—I'm sorry."

And that decides it. Not *I'm sorry we killed her,* but *I'm sorry about her death.* Sidestepping the responsibility. Making it an act of God.

I take a few steps toward the exit, hesitant and unsteady. It's not acting; I have to retract some of my motor skills to handle the download, the massive quantity of Oculus records pouring into my head. But Glendower sees it as the agony of indecision, and he lets me pass. He's a good man; he wouldn't deliberately hurt someone like me.

I find my way to the exit unhindered—I think Maxentius, or maybe one of his cleanup crew, waves to me as I go by. As the doors close, I wonder with the portion of my brain that isn't unpacking records if I'll make it out of here at all. If the shadow orgs wanted, they could kill me right here, and I couldn't do a thing about it.

But these are the good guys.

In the silence of the transport I have time to craft the message that will go out with each clip. It's not much, just a few lines for each record, an autovoice that's recognizably my own. And links, archives, paths to data that isn't shared or acknowledged, not even by netheads. Even crafting this, having a message like this unsent in my skull, is punishable by federal law.

The guard waves me through, and I step out into blinding sunlight. The world of data flows around me again—and this time I leap into it, sending out into all nodes, the conspiracists and the news media and the archives. The Niobe GPS activates, and above me the satellite web moves, shifts, focuses.

It's not enough to stop me.

These people have died because of the shadow organizations, I say over each clip, each death, each victim of the shadow orgs. The desert sunlight shifts, shading from yellow-white to blazing, bright enough to hurt my eyes. *They were deemed guilty and executed without trial.* The guard is yelling, first running after me and then, as he realizes what's happening, back to the shade and safety of his bunker.

They were unlawfully executed. And links, lists, the shadow orgs and all their work, thrown open to the world they claim to protect. If they can't take the scrutiny, they don't deserve to last.

I turn my face to the incandescent sky and smile, racing to meet the sunlight.

A Militant Peace
DAVID KLECHA AND TOBIAS S. BUCKELL

I am not only a pacifist but a militant pacifist.
I am willing to fight for peace.
—Albert Einstein

For Nong Mai Thuy, a Vietnamese sergeant in the Marine Police, the invasion of North Korea starts with the parachute-snapping violence of a High Altitude, Low Opening jump deep in the middle of the inky black North Korean airspace at night. Here the air is the stillest, bleakest black. The bleakness of a world where electricity trickles only to the few in Pyongyang.

This is good for Mai. The synthetic-ballistic faceshield displaying heads-up information has a host of visual add-ons, including night-vision. She flicks it on, and the familiar gray-green of a landscape below rushes up to smack into her.

When she thuds into the ground the specialized, carefully fitted, motorized armor hisses slightly as it adjusts to the impact.

"Duc?"

"I am safe," her partner responds in her ear over the faint distortion of high-end crypto. In the upper right of her HUD, a beacon glows softly, and she turns around. Duc's smashed his way through several hefty tree limbs before hitting ground. But he's already packing his chute.

They are officially on the ground.

Beyond the darkness are some nine-and-a-half-million North Korean forces that aren't going to respond well to what has just happened.

And Mai wonders: how many of them are already on the way to try and kill her right now?

Three minutes before Mai and Duc hit the ground, heavy machinery in stealth-wrapped containers had parachuted in, invisible to prying electronic eyes, and touched down.

Mai and Duc fan out to establish a perimeter and protect it, even as hundreds more hit the ground, roll, and come up ready to follow orders beamed at them from commanders still up in the sky, watching from live satellite feeds.

A portable airstrip gets rolled out across the grassy meadow. Within the hour the thorium nuclear power plant airdrops in and gets buried into the ground, then shielded with an artillery-proof cap.

Once power is on, Camp Nike takes shape. The ballistic-vest wearing civilian Chinese contractors have built whole skyscrapers within forty-eight hours. Here they only need to get four or five stories high for the main downtown area. They get a bonus for each extra geodesic dome fully prepped by the morning. The outer wall of the camp is airlifted in. It's been constructed in pieces in Australia ahead of time, and the pieces slam down into the ground via guided parachutes. No one glances up; this part of the invasion has been practiced over and over again in Western Australia so much that it's old news.

Twenty minutes before sunrise, two large transports land and the civilians rush them. The field is cleared of non-combatants soon after, leaving the ghost city behind it.

It is dawn when what looks like a hastily organized contingent of the North Korean Army crests the hills. Thirty soldiers here to scout out what the hell just happened, Mai imagines.

Mai ends up outside the perimeter, guardian to the north gate.

"Welcome to Camp Nike," Duc mutters.

Someone is riding shotgun through their helmet cameras and jumps into the conversation. It sounds like Captain Nguyen, Mai thinks. "Make a slight bow to the commanding officer, wave encouragingly at the group."

Mai's hand rests on her hip, where a sidearm would usually be.

"No threatening gestures, keep your arms out and forward," her helmet whispers to her. Aggressive body-posture detected and reported by her own suit. It feels slightly like betrayal. Old habits die hard: Mai can't help but reach for her hip.

She is, after all, still a soldier.

The small group of men all have AKS-74s—which the North Koreans call a Type 88—but they're slung over their shoulders, even though they can see Mai and Duc in full armor.

"I have a bad feeling about this," Mai mutters.

"Hold your positions," command whispers to them.

It isn't right. Standing here, unarmed, holding her hands up in the air as if *she's* the one surrendering, placating an enemy. When there are men standing just thirty feet away with rifles.

One of them steps forward, his hands in the air, and she realizes he's nervous.

Mai points to a signpost near the gates.

CAMP NIKE
UNITED NATIONS SPONSORED
ALTERNATIVE SETTLEMENT ZONE

NO WEAPONS ALLOWED

PLACE ALL WEAPONS IN THE
MARKED BINS FOR DESTRUCTION

The sign's in Korean, Chinese, Vietnamese and English, and also emblazoned with the internationally recognizable logos of all the camp's primary private-sector sponsors.

There'll be more of that when people get inside. Shoes and clothing by Nike. Dinners by ConAgra. TV by Samsung. Computers by Dell.

The men read the sign, and start shaking their heads.

This, Mai thinks, is a moment of balance, where the world around her could swing one way or another.

Duc takes initiative, to her surprise, and waves at the men cheerily. He flips his faceplate open, so they can see his expression, while Mai curses him silently and fights the urge to grab him and yank him to safety.

All it'll take is one well-aimed shot from a sniper somewhere out there to kill him, now. Or for one of these men with an AKS-74 to spook.

He might as well not even wear the armor, she thinks, absently reaching for her hip again.

There is no gun, though. There never will be.

Mai's not close enough for her translation software to help her understand what the group of men is arguing over. But Duc has gotten close enough to be surrounded.

"They want to see the food," he reports.

"What?"

"They want to make sure they're not being tricked into a prison camp. They won't disarm until they see that what they were told about the camps was true."

One of the men holds up a cheap, black smartphone and points at it.

Six months ago these things were dumped into North Korea by the millions. Each phone disguises its texting and data traffic as background static, and otherwise functions as a basic, jamming-hardened satphone. Between the satellite routing and peer-to-peer whisper comms, they created a "darknet" outside of Pyongyang's official control.

The Beloved Leader decreed death for anyone caught with one, but the experiment succeeded. Well enough to spirit out video and pictures of starving children, of brutal crackdowns on attempts to protest Pyongyang by desperate, starving peasants, and all the other atrocities that had built the case for international intervention.

It has been through these phones that messages explaining the camps and invasion had been sent twenty-four hours ago.

Promising food and safety.

These soldiers are defecting, and can see the walls. Now they want to see the food.

It's all about the food.

"Three of you, leave your weapons in the bin," Duc says, "go in and come back out to report what you see."

It is a reasonable compromise. Duc and Mai let the three unarmed men pass through, and five minutes later they're back, excited and shouting at their comrades.

One of the men whistles back toward the crest of the hill. As if melting out of the countryside, a river of people carrying what possessions they had come trickling down the hillside, and out of the distant scrub where they'd been hiding.

The first two hundred new citizens of Camp Nike stream in through the gates, and once they're through, all that is left are the full bins of AKS-74s waiting to be destroyed.

"Were you worried?" Duc asks as they watch the North Koreans line up at refugee registration booths.

"Yes," she replies. "I think we'd be foolish not to worry when people with guns walk up to us."

Duc thumps his chest. "With these on? We're invincible here."

Maybe, Mai thinks. She looks back at the small city inside the walls. But we aren't the only ones here, now, are we?

For forty-eight hours the stream of humanity continues. A thousand. Five thousand. Ten thousand. The Korean People's Army is too busy chasing ghosts to notice right now: false reports about touchdowns. Jammed communications. Domination of their airspace.

Satellite telescopes, early warning systems, and spyware pinpoints the point of origin of several missile launches. They die while still boosting up into the air, struck from above by high-powered lasers.

Electromagnetic pulses rain down from heavy stealth aircraft drones, leaving any unshielded North Korean advanced military tech, which is far more than anyone realized, useless metal junk.

By the time the North Koreans managed to haul out their ancient, analog Cold War-era artillery, Mai is on her way to the barracks to bunk down for her first real night of sleep.

The shelling begins in earnest. A distant crumping sound, but without the accompanying whistle of the rounds falling.

The Point Defense Array pops up. Green light flickers and sparks from the top of the almost floral-looking tower in the center of Camp Nike. Lines shimmer into the night sky as they track incoming artillery rounds.

They'd been told during training that the green lasers were doing nothing more than "painting" the individual targets before the x-ray lasers slagged the incoming shells into nothing more than a slight metal mist.

Mai watches the light show build in intensity for a few moments, just as awed by its beauty as she had been when she'd first seen it demonstrated.

The bursts light up the undersides of the clouds. And not a single shell gets through.

She wonders if she would still have the reflexes to get to cover if she ever hears the telltale whistle of an incoming round again, after living like this.

There might be thousands of Captain Nguyens in the Vietnamese military, Mai knows. But here at Camp Nike, there is only *one*. She is the sort of woman who straightens spines at a glance. They call her the Warrior of Binh Phuoc, and it's rumored that she single-handedly kept that border region safe for years during the Cambodian Unrest.

Nguyen's been hopping in and out of helmet cameras all week long, moving them around like pawns on a chessboard.

Now it's time for Mai to face the chess master.

Mai joins Trong Min Hoai, a member of her team, as they hop over a row of Japanese-donated grooming 'bots, rolling up the main street of Camp Nike sweeping up litter. They're both in full PeaceKeeping armor, servos whining as they work around her limbs to amplify her tiniest motions.

In an already carefully-cultivated and manicured gaming park over to their right, a group of South Korean volunteers are combining literacy lessons with one of the role-playing games popular in the South.

All it would take, Mai thinks, glancing up at the snap and crack of green Point Defense activity in the distance, is one artillery shell to sneak through and hit that park.

But no one's looking up. After a week, even the civilians are taking it for granted.

Inside the ground floor of the temporary headquarters building, a nondescript ten-story instant skyscraper, Captain Nguyen stands in front of a podium and surveys the twenty fully power-armored members she's called in.

"LOCKDOWN," declares an electronic system, and the doors thud shut. A soft blue glow indicates that the room is nominally clean of electronic surveillance.

Everyone's links to the outside die. Soldiers remove their helmets and let them hang from dummy straps on the back of their armor.

It's strange to see all these faces.

Most relax in place, Mai's one of the few who grits her teeth at that. She comes from Vietnam's elite Marine Police, suffused with discipline and duty. Other soldiers have traveled in from less formal corners of Vietnam.

Mai's tempted to say it's Western influence, but she comes from a family that has quietly welcomed the easing of the Party's influence over the long years.

Her grandfather served in the Republic of Vietnam Army in 1975. He melted back into civilian life when Saigon fell. Unlike various Hmong or other

American allies he had not been lucky enough to secure a trip to the United States. Instead he endured, raised a family, and placidly waited for the wheel to turn. As it had in Europe or Russia.

That came almost without their noticing. Now Vietnam jostles with South Korea and Japan for economic strength.

Which is what got her here.

South Korea is playing down its role in this humanitarian incursion of sovereign national borders. Japan knows better than to stick any of its troops on foreign soil anywhere the Pacific Ocean touches land, even if it's a peacekeeping mission.

No one wants American soldiers involved in this.

The UN has pushed hard to get Vietnamese forces to lead this. They believe they're in the best position, historically and culturally.

Behind-the-scenes promises and paybacks in the form of infrastructure, debt forgiveness from creditor nations, and military upgrades have been fairly epic.

And if all goes well, Vietnam becomes a real world player, able to use this as a bargaining chip to leverage itself up onto the table with the world's most powerful nations.

If all goes well.

The hopes of many Vietnamese politicians ride with the twenty armored soldiers in the room.

"There's been a change of plans," Nguyen announces.

Nguyen casts full three-dimensional images of the camp from an overhead position up on the wall for them to see.

"Due to the initial success of the disinformation campaign and disabling of North Korean military machinery, we grew this camp faster than anyone could have anticipated. We are bringing in more power: one of those airships that's been helping blanket the area with wireless networks will soon be relaying a microwave laser from an Indian power satellite, which will let us expand the Point Defense Array's zone of coverage and move our walls outward.

"We need more living space, and more farmland. The UN is calling our mission a success, and the other camps are moving timetables forward as a result as well."

Mai glances around. Everyone looks excited, a bit anticipatory.

This has been the goal, hasn't it? Establish a secure base. Bring in refugees. Feed and educate, build a different civil and economic society on the fly, and with success, expand the borders of these safe zones.

Within a decade, the camps could become cities in their own right: self-sustaining and continuing to grow. Tiny petri dishes of democracy, trade and world capitalism, their walls expanding outwards further and further until they *were* all of the country they'd been set up in.

It beat decades-long war.

Online massively multiplayer simulations indicated that it was also far, far cheaper. After just a few years, the citizens of the camps plug into global trade and currency, paying their own way. Becoming customers for large defense manufacturers. Full citizens of the peaceful, trading world at large.

That's the plan.

And now they're accelerating the timetable. Which will mean what? Mai swallows her worries and pays attention.

Captain Nguyen continues with the briefing. "We've been coming under more frequent artillery attack from the North Korean Army over the last seventy-two hours. The shells have yet to penetrate the laser array, but we can't afford to rely on that working one hundred percent of the time.

"Thanks to our American friends in charge of the array, we've identified the location of the artillery battery firing on us. We intend to end these bombardments during wall extension operations. You are the team that will do this."

Nguyen looks at them all, then seems to pause for a beat as she looks at Mai.

Did that really happen? Is she being singled out? Or does everyone else in the room feel that Nguyen is talking to just them?

"There will be no North Korean deaths," Nguyen states flatly, "or any bodily harm as a direct result of your actions. You are there to disable the weaponry, not engage. Remember: I *will* be watching. So will the rest of the world."

And that is all.

Captain Nguyen physically leads the "attack."

Forty armored figures in UN pale blue trot out of the camp, double file, following her. Half of them are a mish-mash of other units from Eastern Europe and Africa, the other half are Nguyen's warriors. They plunge into the tree line to the west of the camp, cutting new paths through the undergrowth.

They cover the six miles to the North Korean firebase in about half an hour, and spread out into a skirmish line as they approach the elevated artillery base.

The moment they begin to walk up the slope, the North Koreans open fire on them from a sandbagged bunker at the crest of the low hill.

Mai flinches at the chatter and fury. Her instinct to seek cover screams from somewhere deep in her. A round thuds into her midsection, but the armor does its job, sloughing off energy and dissipating mass.

Her stride isn't even affected.

"Keep the line straight, hold out your arms," Nguyen mutters to them all via helmet communications. "Show them we're not armed."

They've been shot at in training. But these rounds are meant to kill them, not get them used to the impact.

This is the real thing. Those people out there are trying to kill Mai.

And all she's going to do is hold out her hands and walk forward.

The implacable pale blue line keeps moving up the hill.

Mai feels round after round, entire bursts, carom off her armor like birdshot before she's halfway up the hill. And then, finally, the North Korean gunners break and make a run for it.

"Duc, Mai, disable the bunker," Nguyen orders.

Mai leaps free of the line with an exultant grunt, clearing fifteen feet of ground in a half-restrained hop that has her slamming down in front of the bunker's still-steaming gun in a second.

Duc's right by her.

"No one's inside. No heat signatures," Duc reports. He rips the bunker apart, pulling the sandbags out and kicking the walls in.

Mai yanks the roof's timbers free, dropping the sandbags they'd supported down into a warren of cots and radio equipment. The crunching sounds from all this are distant and suppressed to her, like she's turned the volume down on a Hollywood action movie.

In three full breaths, they've reduced the fortified position to sandy rubble.

Mai strips the machine gun down to its individual components, then grabs both ends of the barrel and twists it into uselessness. She repeats that with the spare barrel, then looks over at the ammunition.

"The Ploughshares team can take care of the ammo," Duc says. "They'll catch up soon enough."

Something kicks her in the back, jostling her. Mai spins around and knocks away the gun of a scared soldier who has managed to sneak up on her.

He stands there, stupefied, holding his hand, waiting for whatever comes next.

"Mai!" Duc shouts.

She has her fist in the air, ready to bring it down and crack his skull, but freezes in place. Her heart is hammering, her mouth dry. She can't escape the adrenaline-pounding certainty that she almost died.

But of course, she hasn't. The man is no threat.

"Leave," she shouts into her helmet, and the translation booms out at the soldier.

He rabbits away.

"Mai?" Duc asks.

"I am fine," she tells him.

Mai glances back. There's activity in the air: ten heavy lift airships ponderously moving more wall segments in, to be dropped in place to secure the territory they are clearing.

Soon the huge, articulated Ploughshares trucks will be along to gather up everything here for recycling.

Duc tosses down seven mangled AKS-74s. "Then let's go," he says, and they're on the move again, loping in long, impossible strides to catch up to the advancing line.

As they catch up, Mai notices that Nguyen's entire right side is blackened. She must have absorbed a large explosion of some kind while Mai'd been destroying the bunker. Other soldiers show signs of absorbing more fire, but the rate of it is fading. The North Koreans are mostly retreating into the woods on the west side of the hill.

Mostly.

One enterprising gun crew is trying to bring their huge 152mm cannon to bear on the advancing line.

For the first time Mai sees Nguyen's calm crack, and she hastily orders another pair of Peacekeepers to disable the cannon.

The two armored soldiers snap into motion, and then calmly shepherd the North Koreans away from the weapon with shooing motions, ignoring the small arms fire. Once the North Koreans are clear, they smash the aiming mechanism, then get to work on the tube itself.

A North Korean officer runs up to the two blue armored soldiers, pistol high, screaming at them. His face is red, and he looks almost ready to cry with frustration and rage.

The distant pop of his pistol as he empties his entire clip into the backplate of the nearest Peacekeeper's armor is accentuated by Mai's translation software.

"Stand and fight, cowards! Face me like real soldiers," the artificial voice keeps murmuring.

Mai feels sympathy for him.

This isn't a proper war.

None of them have trained for this.

It makes little sense, to either that officer or her, on some deep level.

Part of her craves a fight. A real fight. A test of skill, courage, and arms.

"Here's the artillery," Nguyen murmurs to them all. "On me. Destroy it all."

Mai and Duc move through the firebase with the rest of the team, dismantling the twelve big artillery guns and countless small arms and machine guns.

Most of the machinery is in ill repair. Only five of the twelve look like they are actually firing, and a small bunker off to one side has been stacked with dud rounds. Which Mai figured Ploughshares could deal with. Suit or not, she didn't want to be playing with *those*.

There's been one casualty, and Nguyen is not pleased with this. The wounded Korean is on a pod-like stretcher, hooked up to emergency life-saving equipment while a medic they brought along treats him.

"This could be a public relations disaster," Nguyen tells Mai.

"What happened?" Mai asks.

"He threw a grenade, but it bounced back at him," Nguyen says, shaking her head. She's removed her helmet and holds it tucked under an arm. "We were too aggressive. I fought against the new timetable, but was overruled. UN headquarters are emboldened by all this success. Now look at this, all people are going to see is this idiot on their late-night television, wounded."

Mai looks over the wounded man. "He might live."

Nguyen cocks her head. "You're smarter than that. You know it's the image of him right now, wounded, that will play out across the world. Polling is going to show lowered support for the mission. Are *you* okay, Sergeant Nong? My command software flagged one of your actions."

Mai thinks back to the moment where she raised her fist, and opens her mouth to answer, but another soldier runs up. "Captain, you need to come with us."

The North Koreans have withdrawn from the firebase, and the defense array is fully extended to its new circumference, bringing the area under its anti-ballistic umbrella. The airships are placing the new walls around them. Nonetheless, Mai and Nguyen pull their helmets back on and lope after the messenger.

There's a trail leading back to the woods, and off to the side is a hastily dug pit. A fresh, earthy scar in the grass.

Lying in it are bodies. Thin. Ribs showing. Hollow-eyed.

"Civilians," Nguyen's voice crackles.

They've been dragged and stacked in this shallow grave. Just old men, women, children, trying to sneak their way around to a better life.

Mai rips her helmet off to take a deep breath of air, then regrets the decision. The air is ripe with the stench of decay.

"This is our fault. They're trying to get into our camp," she says. She does not replace her helmet, just yet. Something about the smell of death grounds her, reminds her of what is at stake, who has the most to lose, the most to fear.

Nguyen raises her visor. "They're dying trying to escape north to China right now, or slowly in their own homes. Don't forget that."

Mai swallows and nods.

But it doesn't stop her from feeling personally responsible in some small way.

Mai catches a ride back to the core camp center on a Ploughshares truck, exhausted and nerves frayed. A Chinese engineer sitting on the back of the flatbed is curious.

"I didn't think you could get tired in those suits," he says to her in careful English.

"That is a misconception," Mai tells him. "Your body is still moving, all day. Muscles still do much of the work. They are just amplified."

"What about getting shot at?" he asks. He's staring at the scars in her outer armor.

"It becomes normal," Mai says, offering a salty fatalism she does not yet feel. She's looking down at the helmet in her hands. There's a dimple right in the forehead, and a coating of copper and lead that has dripped onto the faceplate.

That dimple suggests at least *some* level of vulnerability.

Mai shakes that away and looks around. The fleet of recycling trucks are covered in advertising logos. "Does everything have advertising built into it?" she asks the engineer, looking to change the subject.

He shrugs. "Why not? If all goes well, what will the refugees see every day? Logos for Ford and Nissan, McDonald's and Dannon, Apple and Samsung. What better advertisement than being the ones who brought them peace and prosperity?"

And if it doesn't work, Mai figures, these people will never see the logos again. The sponsors lose some trucks, cash, and some shipments of last year's shoes and tracksuits.

These companies will write these off as charitable donations and somehow, come out ahead.

They always do. Tails you lose, heads I win.

The minds from which this evolved, despite their ramrod-organized military world, are the children of non-violent protestors and emergent, technologically-enabled regime overthrow. They are the nieces and nephews of two generations of UN sorties, which are derided by the major powers, but have a history of quiet, incremental improvements and painfully slow progress.

They are the process of gamified solutions, market testing, and the Western fear of bad publicity.

What did it mean that this was war? At boot camp Mai practiced for bloody hand-to-hand combat, and learned group movement. Thinking as part of a squad. Reaching the overall goals of a mission.

Armies want fast-thinking, creative problem solvers able to deploy violence for the nation they serve.

Now Mai is wondering how she ended up being a robotic creature, following the exact letter of the law to not so much as harm a hair on her enemy.

Even when they are slaughtering the innocent.

"It's not the mission," Nguyen explained at training in Australia. "It violates the mandate of the mission. Fail it, and we are just another invading force."

"It doesn't seem . . . right," someone objected.

"Right has a new meaning when wearing this armor. It changes the equation. You are a supreme force unto yourself."

"With technological superiority like this, we couldn't possibly lose," Mai added.

"Depends on what you mean by lose. Westerners certainly learned the limits of simple technological superiority when your grandfather was just a young man." Nguyen stared her down, and Mai had wondered if Nguyen had accessed those files about Mai's family background. "A nation is a fiction of consent, and North Korea has built a mythology and controlled fiction unsurpassed in the world, aided by extreme isolation. People starve and thank their rulers for a handful of rice, or thank them for permission to visit a Western Red Cross station. In order to reshape the fiction, we need to reshape the narrative that the world sees, that North Koreans see, and that we engage. Force is one narrative. But we are not limited to it."

Captain Nguyen walked around, looking at her recruits.

"These methods are not effective enough when implemented by oily-faced teenagers, the unemployed, and the uneducated. What they need are the iron-hard wills and command structure of a military mindset. The kind that understands that one might have to run into a hail of gunfire and die to protect the mother country. The kind that can follow orders intelligently. No nation has ever seen an invasion force like this."

One of the Western advisors was there. He chipped in. "It took the army to develop one hundred percent non-fossil fuel mobility while civilians dicked around with political initiatives, wasted subsidies and lots of arguing. We just did it. *We* built the Internet, our ICBMs took people to space. It takes the hard, organizational capacity and raw willpower of an army to do *this* type of mission right. Sometimes assholes need to be shot. The rest of the time, we will wield a different sort of weapon for a different world. That weapon today will be you: the execution of a well-controlled non-violent incursive force. Because you're an army, and you *will* execute this and well, because if you don't, you'll be spending some 'personal' time with Captain Nguyen."

And then Mai and her fellow recruits learned how to get shot at, attacked, and beaten, without once displaying or reacting with aggression.

She wrestles with a fleck of shame, having failed that training to a small degree on the firebase. The fear in that soldier's eyes lingers in her mind the rest of the way back.

The hardest part of Mai's day is hearing the distant, occasional pop of a handgun from somewhere in the forests. Her amped-up acoustics in the full-on armor pick it up every time. Software calibrates, offers up information on where the shot came from, and shows it in her heads-up display.

Every single time a gunshot goes off, she has to stare at the damn red marker telling her where it has happened.

Each pop makes her flinch with the knowledge that it is the execution of a desperate, captured civilian.

"Someone should put eyes on that," she tells Captain Nguyen in a staff meeting. "We could use it to turn opinion against them."

"Opinion is already against them. Sympathetic members of the military are uploading video of the executions. Our job is to protect the camp. Stay put. Patrol the walls, Sergeant. Do your job."

Eventually Mai transfers to the south wall and dampens the acoustics with help from a technician.

But even the threat of death doesn't stop the trickle of refugees. They risk everything to get through the North Korean emplacements, and make a desperate run to the safety of the camp. The camp constantly grows.

After another one of her long patrols, Mai runs into Duc near the mess hall on the north wall.

"How are you?" she asks quietly. He's been a bit withdrawn ever since they first found the open graves.

"I've now been shot one hundred and thirty-seven times," he tells her, a note of wonder in his voice. "The armor works. But I think . . . it's . . . "

Duc looks away, then back at her. He opens his mouth to continue, and it seems as if he's screaming. A demonic sound fills the air, rising in pitch, higher and higher until Mai can barely even comprehend it.

When Duc shuts his mouth, the sound doesn't stop.

They're out of the mess hall and through the doors in an instant, yanking helmets on and looking around, and then finally: up.

A shimmering, hard red slash of light cuts the sky above the camp in half. It stabs upward into the sky, and originates from somewhere to the south, where intel thinks the North Korean Army has established a new firebase.

"What is it?" Duc asks.

Information scrolls across their helmets. It's a laser. High energy, tightly focused. Most of the red slash she's "seeing" is actually interpolation from her suit's sensors.

Mai follows the path of the beam, and sees that it intersects neatly with the icon that represents the dirigible floating thirty kilometers overhead.

"They're going after our power," Duc says.

The icon wavers and blinks out.

All around them lights flicker, then go dark. Mai spins around and looks at the tower at the heart of their refugee city. The lights on the outside of the Point Defense Array flicker and go dark.

Satellite communications links to the armor go live, and their helmets kick on automatic recording mode: 60fps video streaming directly back to operations centers in Hanoi, Beijing, and Geneva. All local bandwidth is reserved for encrypted inter-team communications.

That results in everyone having a thumbnail of Captain Nguyen's face in the upper right corner of their visors, spitting orders and soliciting updates.

Mai and Duc are deployed to the south gate, and they sprint through the streets to get there, leaping over a small one-story refugee processing building in their way.

In the background of it all, emergency sirens wail. Citizens are, no doubt, being ushered away from windows and into the cores of skyscrapers. But if a full-on assault comes, there's little protection. The camp is vulnerable without the Point Defense Array.

Slightly out of breath, Mai scans the woods and hills beyond the border of the camp. "We should have rerouted all power from the reactor by now," she says to Duc.

And as if answering her directly, Captain Nguyen speaks up. "I've just learned that several of the power cables leading out from the reactor have been sabotaged. We are unable to power up the array fully. As a result it's in a fuel-cell powered self-defense mode right now, only targeting any rounds that might hit its tower. The engineers report that it will take as long as ten minutes to get power back up. You know your orders. Prevent any North Koreans from getting past the gate. And hold your position. Contact *is* imminent. Forces are building up for an assault."

Mai can see via thermal imaging that bodies are flitting through the trees.

"There hasn't been any satellite imagery showing that the rest of their army has shown up," Duc says. "It's just this battalion. We can handle that, even without the array, right?"

"Of course," Mai agrees.

Even as she opens her mouth to reassure Duc further, a brief flash flickers from behind the trees, followed by the quiet thump of sound catching up to light.

"Mortar-fire," Mai shouts, broadcasting to the entire open channel. Her helmet projects a path and warning insignia blare at her to MOVE.

Duc spins away, and Mai is leaping clear as the world erupts in orange and black. She sees stars wheel overhead, the world tumbling around her, and she turns her tumble into a roll.

She lands on her feet, legs bent, taking the force of her impact. Her left hand drags, fingertips furrowing the ground as she slides backwards on her boots and comes to a stop.

"Duc!"

He's facedown. The entire back of his suit is blackened. She rushes over to him.

"Duc!"

There's a groan over the helmet radio. The status report shows that he's just been dazed. Duc sits up as Mai scans the tree line, waiting for the next launch or the inevitable rush of bodies.

The next mortar launch arrows well overhead, and Mai frowns as she follows the trajectory over the wall. The refugee-processing building explodes in a mess of compressed fiberboard and electronics.

Mai stands up.

The next mortar round walks further into the camp.

"They're not going to try a direct attack," Mai reports to Captain Nguyen, somewhat stunned. "They're just going after civilians."

More rounds now slam into the skyscrapers at the center of the camp. Broken glass twinkles as it rains down into the streets.

The open channel fills with medics responding. Ten wounded. No deaths. But another ten minutes of this, and it was going to get bad.

"Captain . . . "

"Stand your ground Sergeant. It could be a trap to lure some of us out, before the charge. Do not leave your post. Listen to me, there are three million live watchers, this conflict is being streamed everywhere, as it happens, to satisfy mission backers and advertisers. We keep our course."

But Mai's already stopped paying attention. "Duc, what is that?"

Her visor has caught the sound of tracks.

"Tank?"

"No." For a brief moment, two kilometers away and only visible by the helmet's advanced computational lenses, she's seen the outline of a self-propelled howitzer, trundling through the brush between Nike and the new Korean firebase.

KOKSAN, her visor identifies it. 170MM of death on wheels.

It must have been driven up to stand in for the artillery Mai and her team already destroyed.

Mai is already moving forward before she really understands it.

"Mai! Hold your position," Nguyen orders.

"Duc, stay here," Mai says, and then before he can reply she turns off communications.

She's across the open ground and into the woods before she's drawn even two full breaths, kicking through underbrush. It's like running in sand, and she's leaving a trail of broken tree limbs and shattered logs behind her.

There are attackers, of course. Gunshots ping off her armor from every direction, and she's veering this way and that to get around uniforms that pop up in her way.

She's still broadcasting video live. She can't turn that off. The whole world is watching this, probably. She can't afford to harm anyone.

But Mai has to stop that howitzer.

Because it's going to be so much louder than those little execution pops she's been hearing in the distance.

It's going to be a bang. It's going to wipe out lives in an instant. And it's going to keep doing it for as long as the Point Defense Array is down.

And she can stop it.

She can rip it apart with her augmented hands.

Gravel crunches and pops under her feet as she bursts out into open terrain, accelerating down a road.

The firepower aimed at her kicks up an order of magnitude. The popping sound has gone from occasional plinks to a hailstorm. There are soldiers taking cover behind small boulders and shooting at her. Mai covers the last kilometer in giant lopes, leaping over heads and vehicles and hastily dug fighting positions.

But she's too late. She can see the howitzer. It is basically a large tank with an obscenely larger artillery gun bolted on top. It looks unbalanced, like it should tip forward.

The long barrel is raised just slightly, and on target. It will fire like a tank, at this range, the round arcing just over her head, at the very low end of the Point Defense Array's envelope. If it's even operational yet.

Six soldiers are scurrying around the platform. Unlike most of the world's current self-propelled artillery, the operators are not encased in tank armor.

When Mai reaches the unit, she will be able to disable it and move the soldiers away.

But one of them is already shutting the breech and stepping back.

Another is pointing her way and shouting.

She will not make it there before they fire.

Mai slows and rips a three-foot wide boulder up out of the ground and throws it as hard as she can. Two soldiers dive clear of the vehicle, but the two near fire control have nowhere to go.

Blood spatters the railings around the vehicle. Brain matter drips from the barrel of the howitzer.

Seconds later Mai reaches it and slams her fist into the breech, disabling it.

For a long moment she stands on top, too stunned to move.

Then something loops over her head from behind, wrapping around her neck. The armor stops it from choking her, but the loop is strong. Possibly braided cable.

Mai tries to jump free, but the cable yanks her back down. The ground meets her back hard, and despite all the protection, Mai gasps for breath and her vision blurs.

They drag her across the ground as she fights to breathe again, her body bouncing as the armor scrapes along the ground. She can hear the rumble of an old truck, accelerating, dragging her farther away.

She reaches up to the noose, trying to get purchase, but she's being bounced around by the uneven terrain.

If they can drag her far enough away, she'll be just one person in armor. Far from camp. Far from backup.

Mai screams with rage, and then suddenly, she's free, tumbling along the side of the muddy road. On shaky arms she pushes herself up. First to her knees, then to her feet, every twitch and tremor amplified by the armor.

She pulls the cable up toward her until she comes to the cut edge, then looks around.

A cluster of blue-armored figures are walking down the road at her.

Mai turns her communications back on.

"Nong Mai Thuy?"

"Yes, Captain Nguyen?"

"We have some things to discuss."

"Are you ready to go home?" Nguyen asked.

"No," Mai replies. But she knows her preferences do not matter.

She's standing in front of Nguyen's desk wearing her old Marine Police uniform. Everything's crisp and tight. Ribbons for bravery and accomplishment no longer feel like things to be proud of, but strange, non-functional baubles.

She should be in armor, not in this uniform.

"I guess the true question is . . . how do you move on?" Nguyen says. "I have two courses for you to consider."

"Two? I don't understand."

"You killed two human beings, Nong Mai Thuy. All the while under orders to not leave your position."

"I saved many lives," Mai protests.

Nguyen flashes a smile. It isn't a pretty thing. It's an expectant one. Like a predator watching prey fall for a trap.

"Yes. The inhabitants of the camp call you a hero. But you may have killed many more than you would have saved down the road. It's a moral dilemma. Academics sometimes ask you to ponder: would you push a man in front of a train to save everyone on the train? It seems like a silly question, yes? But here we are: soldiers. We often shove people in front of trains to serve a greater good. You just faced one of your own moral dilemmas, Mai. I can't blame you for what you did. But we cannot succeed if we answer violence with violence here. Our duty is to weather these storms and stand between danger and our charges. And doing so, calmly, allows us the unfettered world permission to continue our mission here. You jeopardized the larger mission. The North Koreans will claim they were unjustly abused by a technologically superior invading army, no matter how ridiculous the claim. You put this entire mission in danger of failing. It is unacceptable."

Mai considers the strangeness of this. The famous Captain Nguyen, who could be wearing three times as many medals as Mai if she chooses, who tasted violence on the Cambodian border, had eaten it for supper, is lecturing Mai about violence.

"So what is to become of me?" Mai asks.

"The Hague wants to court martial you and send you to jail." Nguyen taps the desk. "Personally, I think the court of world opinion would side with you, and you will not go to jail. You are the hero of Camp Nike, after all. But this will drag out in public and focus the attention in all the wrong places. The advertisers, the people who run this, and the Generals back at the Hague, this will tarnish their images."

Mai shrinks back without thinking. The subject of world attention. Media circuses. It sounds alien and horrific to someone who prefers their privacy.

Nguyen shoves a piece of paper forward. "If you think these people are worth protecting, if you think what the camps are trying to do is a good thing, then I suggest you take the second course."

"And that is?" Mai asks.

"An honorable discharge. It is hardly your fault, really, that this happened. I should have seen the signs, your aggressive stance. A high need for justice. I ignored them because you were a good person with a good heart. I will not be making that mistake again. Sign these, and you can leave, but without any trouble to you, or trouble that makes our soldiers or country look bad. Go back to your family's business. Go live a good life."

Mai stares at the papers for a long moment, then signs them, struggling to keep any emotion from her face as Nguyen watches.

"Well done, Citizen Nong Mai Thuy," Captain Nguyen says. "Well done."

The next flight out of Camp Nike is in the pre-dawn morning. Mai sits alone in an aisle, looking out of the window as the plane passes up through the flittering green of the Point Defense Array. The North Koreans are busy probing its limits once again.

An extra reactor will be flown out to meet the needs of the camp soon. For now it is getting by on rolling blackouts for all non-essential power needs. Rumor is that a Californian solar panel corporation is going to ship enough panels next week for most civilian domestic needs, but the advertising details are still being negotiated. When they're installed, it should help the camp come up to full power.

And she won't be there to see any of that.

The aircraft continues its tight spiral up and up, always staying within Camp Nike airspace as it climbs. Eventually, once up to the right ceiling, out of range of all missiles and without the grounded North Korean Air Force to worry about, they will break out of their constant turn and head out for Hanoi.

"Miss Nong?" an airman asks. He crouches at the edge of the aisle holding a small wooden box in his hands.

"Yes?"

"Some of the refugees at the airstrip asked me to give this to the 'hero of Camp Nike,'" the airman says, and hands her the box.

She opens it to find a small bracelet held together with monofilament, decorated with charms made from recently recycled brass casings.

When she looks back through the window, the camp is lost under the clouds.

All the Young Kirks and Their Good Intentions
HELENA BELL

2249 A.D.

All the young Kirks in Riverside Public High School are assigned to the same Homeroom class. They sit together in the back corner on the far side from the door. They speak only to each other.

The young Kirk on the Moon goes to school with no one. Each of the colonists has a job and he or she is responsible only to the duties of that job. The others call him Fisher instead of James since he spends his days knee deep in the trout pond, allowing the fish to glide between his legs. When the fish become completely inured to his presence, he thrusts his hands into the water and grasps one around the belly. It fights and Fisher holds on. He is supposed to take it out of the water, to throw it into the white bucket by the shore, but Fisher never does. He lets the fish go and when he comes home, with nothing to show for it, his mother expresses her irrevocable disappointment and sends him to bed.

Jamie

All the young Kirks in Riverside are in love with Jamie. She wears tight green skirts and impractical shoes. When she crosses and uncrosses her legs all the Kirks, even the girls, turn their heads ever so slightly to watch. Jamie does not have a boyfriend as none of the Kirks are so bold as to admit their feelings to another. Sometimes, when the teacher lectures on the sixth extinction and flashes slides of West African frogs and fungal diseases, Jamie slides the heel of her shoe off and lets it dangle from her toes. She enjoys being wanted, but sometimes imagines instead that she is a girl named Lucy who is allowed to love whomever she chooses without upsetting the balance.

Jamie Kirk has a plan. Every year they send the best and brightest students to the moon to join the colony. She hears there are animals there long dead on earth, and everyone is beautiful and kind and exotic. There will be no other Kirks there to demand she talk and act in a certain way. She will be free.

The moon colony is very selective, only one couple from Riverside has ever gone, but Jamie knows she alone of the Kirks will be selected as she is the best, the brightest, the most adored. The other Kirks will beg her to bring them too as her one true love and companion. They will fight amongst themselves to see which of them is the most worthy, and Captain, or perhaps Jimmy, or Tiberia of the surreptitious movements, will win. When she is about to consent, a gleaming stranger with skin brighter than fresh fallen snow will appear as there is always a twist in these kinds of dreams.

Jamie is in love with the Challenger. She has been in love with him/her since the first night she climbed to the top of her parents' barn and saw him/her walking on the road leading away from the river. Jamie believes the Challenger must be a creature of magic: the embodiment of hope and freedom who walks the roads alone because he/she is unafraid of the nighttime creatures, of the illnesses which travel on the air. Jamie suspects The Challenger is an alien, an unknown race who wanders the dark roads for someone worthy of his/her company. Jamie is worthy. Jamie is worthy of all.

But Jamie cannot tell any of the others about the stranger as they are all in love with her and she must pretend to not be in love with them all equally. To balance between the sharp edges of desire and duty to her companions is a very Kirk-like thing to do. And so she waits.

T

All the young Kirks ride their bicycles to the Wal-Mart parking lot after school. They draw straws to see which of them will go inside and attempt to buy a case of beer. Though he does not know how, T's straw is always the shortest. Captain hands him a wad of sweaty, five-dollar bills and wishes him luck. With a confidence which is not his own, T walks in and slams the beer and the money on the counter.

"Go home," the cashier says.

"Please," T says. "Just once."

The cashier shakes his head.

When T comes out, empty handed, Captain sighs and goes in himself.

"You just have to know how to talk to them," Captain says.

"Yeah," Jimmy says. "It's all in the attitude."

Captain hands the cans out in order of his favorites. T is always last, and he always refuses to take it. "I don't drink shit."

Captain smiles. "Now I see. You're *choosing* not to buy it each time. Making an executive decision, saving us from this foul-tasting beverage."

T shrugs. "Think what you want."

T suspects that the cashier and Captain have a secret arrangement designed to humiliate T in front of Jamie and everyone else. He fears that one day Captain will kick him out of the group entirely unless he can find a way to be useful. One night, as they ride home, T tells Captain that there's a tree on T's property from which, with a telescope, one can see into Jamie's bedroom window.

"I know," Captain says. "You can see into Red's too," and with a grin, rides off.

Red

Red has a job at the local Wal-Mart. She is the only one of the Riverside Kirks to have dropped out of school and seek employment elsewhere. She saves every cent and one day will buy a steamboat ticket to anywhere out of Iowa. She does not care about the moon or space or destiny. She loves her family and cheers for the local team at football games, but there is a deep restlessness in her feet. Each night she wakes from her dreams to find herself knee deep in the English River with her nightgown and underclothes floating away downstream. She doesn't tell anyone of her plan to escape, least of all her brother T who will see it as yet another rejection. She suspects her presence is the only thing which protects him from the other Kirks. One day they will discover his birthday is not March 22, but 2 minutes past. She does not know what will happen then, but does not trust the calculated laziness in Captain's eyes, or the pounding of Jimmy's fists, or Jamie's nonchalance, or any of the others whose only concern is moving in perfect synchronization with what is expected of them.

It must be the thought of her brother, the need to protect him which wakes her before she can dive into the deep part of the river and float away forever.

Walking back on the long dirt road Red feels her skin tingling in the moonlight and she knows that any boy looking out from his window will think she is a white stag or changeling or star. She hopes he falls in love with her so one day, when she is gone from this place, there will be an idea of her that takes root and grows. Perhaps in this way enough of her spirit will remain behind to cocoon her brother. Perhaps when she is gone he will fill into some of her Kirkness, enough to belong. Enough that the others will not push him away.

Water is always the problem, Red thinks. It moves and carries where it will. Red caresses the open sores on her legs, and the infections taking root therein. She wishes her sleeping brain had the sense to put on waders before stepping out the door but knows that contagion is an inevitable condition. If not the river, then the rain, then the tap, then the bottled water they import from the Delta in exchange for organic crops. At Wal-Mart she prepares the sleeping lofts where the outlying farmers will come to live when the river floods. No one builds for permanence anymore and she marvels at the other Kirks insistence on pattern.

Every day her brother comes in attempting to buy beer. Every day he fails.

"Why," she asks T.

"If I don't, they'll kick me out."

"Why," she later asks the cashier.

"Have you seen the crap floating around in one of those cans?"

"But Captain?"

"Little prick deserves whatever salmonella he catches."

In the winter months, Red returns to school and sits with the other Kirks in the back corner but she is ever so slightly out of step. While the others gaze longingly at the mauve pump dangling inches away from Jamie's instep, Red is leaning back to examine the topographic maps on the walls. The Mississippi stretches from floor to ceiling, its many tributaries and old beds undulating in multi-colored bands. The teacher watches her and after class guides her hand up one stream and down the other.

"This is where we lined it with concrete to save the port, this is where it jumped its banks. This is where we think it may go, and where we now try to guide it."

His hand on her wrist and the inside of her arm is insistent and imploring. "You can't control a river forever. It goes where it wants. Or goes where it does not want, just to spite you."

Red pulls back, the backs of her legs tingling with flashes of hot then cold. In the bathroom she pulls up her pant leg and dabs at the cracked scabs. She considers telling the nurse, but there's not much to be done. She will be dead by summer, like so many others before her.

During her evening shift, Red tells the cashier she'll make out with him if he agrees to sell T the beer.

"Just once," she adds.

The cashier shrugs. "You're not my type, but if it means that much to you."

T

T's mother says names have power. They are invasive, like a white fungus, a vine, a jumping carp. Names can take hold, changing the host and adapting it to become the perfect carrier. Why name your son and daughter after an ordinary person: Martha, George, John, Abigail when you can name your children something which will inspire them to a greatness which is not their own, but could be?

T suspects his mother failed him by having twins. If names have power, then surely that power can be diluted. Not all the Kirks are equal. Jamie is the one with whom they are all in love. Captain is the one who can charm. James is particularly good with guns. Jimmy is the bully, but he is strong and fair when it comes to the other Kirks, most of the time. Tiberius and Tiberia are lithe as willow branches and quick as rabbits. Once they claimed to have seen a falcon swooping down upon the highway, and if anyone has eyes fast enough to catch an extinct bird, they do. Jimmy K and Kirkland don't speak much, but when they do it is measured and wise. What weaknesses he has identified in himself, T sees converted into strengths in others. They are like wandering palms in some ancient forest, constantly moving into the light. He alone feels himself slowly falling down. What space he used to occupy shall be trod over by many soft, green-leaved feet.

One afternoon Captain hands T the cash and slaps him on the back. "This time, try not to fail."

When he walks in the cashier heads him off. "Compliments of your sister," he says and hands T a bottle of whiskey.

T is convinced that this is yet another ploy to humiliate him though he does not know how except for the suspicion that everything in his life is a mere contrivance to expose his weaknesses. When he reaches the group, Captain holds out his hand for the bottle but T ignores him. He opens it and hands it to Jimmy. It goes around and around, until finally someone hands it back to T, empty.

T shrugs. "Hasn't tasted right since Scotland went under anyway."

"How the fuck would you know?" someone says.

T doesn't answer, but looks up at the sky. The sun has gone down and they all shiver in the cooling air. It will be difficult riding back in the dark, with loose stones and jostling cyclists on the road. One of them could take him out, if they perceived him as a threat or a mere annoyance. Jimmy might take him out just 'cause. For once the thought doesn't scare him and he realizes that knowing death is certain and not caring is his first Kirk-like thought. Maybe the clock at the hospital was wrong; maybe his mother was right.

"Same way he knows everything," Captain says. "He pretends. He thinks he's better, different, special. But he's not. He's just the same as any one of us."

T smiles back. "Think what you want," he says.

No one attacks him on the way home, but T knows it is only a matter of time. None of them are safe; they are not a team and were never meant to be.

Jamie

The colony will select new immigrants any day now. Applications have been submitted: education, skills, physical exams. Jamie waits and waits while fending off the advances of the other Kirks.

"We will fly to the moon, you and I," Captain says. "They let you take a companion, and I will always choose you."

Weeks go by, months. Rumors spread that an illness has delayed the selection process and the most likely candidates will have advanced degrees in human physiology and evolutionary biology. Jamie doesn't worry as she knows she is the perfect example of youth and health and they will want her for these attributes alone.

When the spring floods begin most of the Kirks begin to pair off: Kirkland comforts T after his sister's funeral and rather than calling her a slut, the other girls begin turning to her for advice. When Jamie shifts her legs in class, fewer and fewer Kirks turn their heads. Jamie's skirts become shorter and shorter until eventually the teacher pulls her aside and gives her a sweatshirt to tie around her waist.

"The noise your flesh makes when it sticks to the seat is distracting. This will help."

Jamie pouts and twirls her hair in her fingers. "Is that the only thing about it which is distracting?"

"Yes. Now go sit down."

Jamie believes when the floods recede everything will go back to normal. But it doesn't. Even her white-skinned alien has abandoned her, and no longer walks along the road by her house. She begins to doubt she ever saw him/her at all.

Only Captain favors Jamie openly and she pretends to favor him back to spite the others. She lets his hand wander up her leg and kisses him when the others are looking. She tells herself she is only salvaging her plan when she allows him to undress her in the dark. She is only recapturing her essence when he moves against her. But she feels nothing when he murmurs that their souls are mere whispers in the dark. She is robotic in her movements and she feels Captain, the other Kirks, the alien, her entire world slipping away from her. When they finish, Jamie goes back to the roof hoping that now she has sacrificed some small part of herself, perhaps the alien will come back. But instead there is only silence and the moon gleaming on the empty gravel.

Fisher

Everyone in the colony is slowly dying, save Fisher. He suspects his immunity is a sign of his guilt. He is the new typhoid Mary: asymptomatic and always suspiciously present. He eats only nutrition capsules and does not handle the food or animals. He walks while covered in latex gloves, hazmat suits and sanitizes constantly. If the others blame him, they do not let on and instead insist that he learn how to operate the colony in their inevitable absence.

No new immigrants will come, not until the disease is quarantined and eradicated. The computers and robots and Fisher will need to carry on, long enough to stave off the extinction. When each colonist dies, the others strip the body and place it outside the clear walls of the compound. No one is buried or incinerated. Rather, a pile of dehydrated corpses piles up in view of the corn fields where the wild deer graze. No single human matters, only the responsibility to the birds, amphibians, lizards and mammals which were saved and transplanted.

"We never intended to stay, you know," Fisher's mother tells him. "We just thought . . . a foothold. Something to get us started."

Fisher knows that one day all the colonists save him will be dead and he will be consigned to carrying on alone. Earth will send him one companion each year and he will fall in love with him or her each time but he or she will die and another one sent. He will have to be brave enough each time, hoping that this one is different.

He reaches into the water and lets the fish glide by. If one looks long enough, one can see a pattern in any movement but it does not mean you can change it. Still, he believes one day someone will arrive who is strong enough to adapt to the path on which he or she finds herself. One day someone will open the shuttle bay door and be the person with whom Kirk can settle down and live a long, fruitful life.

In Which Faster-Than-Light Travel Solves All of Our Problems

CHRIS STABBACK

I live in my cockpit. I piss in a bottle and I cross the vastest vastness in my shining tin can. I've seen more of nothing than just about anyone, but if I'm telling you about it then you aren't really here, because it's just me out here. Every month or so I jerk off to pictures of shapes so airbrushed they aren't human, and I drop my tissues on the floor and leave them there. Every seven months or so I leave my ship for repairs and spend a few nights getting drunk and listening to old travelers who have either forgotten how to be human or are pretending they aren't so they can fit in, and then if I'm flush spend the night with someone who is pretending they aren't because I've paid them.

But mostly, I just live in my cockpit. I freight anything. Whatever, wherever, if you can pay. I had to make a pickup on an asteroid. I set my ship down on the thing, a sad grey chunk of rock. I put on my helmet and went out on the surface to collect what had been hidden there for me. It was a place that nobody would go, where everything was quiet and dark. There was a man there.

He was tall, and his grey dusty vacuum suit did not look nearly protective enough to deal with what small bits of grit might hit it at high speed. Its helmet let me see most of his head, which was grey and balding.

"Who are you?" I said.

"I'm George."

"What the fuck are you doing here?"

"I was hoping you could give me a lift."

"I don't do passengers."

"I'm going to run out of oxygen soon."

"That's your problem."

I made him stand in the cockpit behind me, and I told him to be quiet. He had taken off his helmet once we were in, and I was waiting for him to say something about the smell. Not saying anything was almost worse. He remained impassive. He was a lot taller than me, and older, and I wasn't sure if his face was beaten or just dour.

I resolved to ignore him. I set course for the rendezvous with Jennet. There's a trick I have that is so old it isn't a trick anymore, where I can turn my mind off while I sit here watching the scanners. Hours can pass without a thought, but I couldn't do it with George behind me. The minutes and the hours dragged by and my mind kept slipping into places I did not want it to go. People. I did not want to think about people. I will not tell you what the memories were. After six hours and forty-three minutes of this, George spoke:

"I realized that I was an alien when I was very young."

I didn't turn around or respond. If you acknowledge people, it gives them power. This was my space. I wondered what being an alien could even mean these days.

"I thought the other children could tell," he continued. "My parents told me I have always been odd, right since the start."

We were less than three hours from the rendezvous, and I was suddenly worried that George was here to observe and capture me. Probably he wasn't: My ship scans automatically for tracking and recording devices whenever someone boards, and he had neither. But what had he been doing on that rock?

It didn't matter. To show interest would be to become complicit, and besides that a distraction. On a job like this, you have to keep your eye on the scanners all the time. Some things are hard to see, and the auto alerts won't necessarily get tripped. Some things are designed especially not to trip them, altering their shape to match every firmware update. Slippery intentions moving shark-like through space, black against black. I slapped myself, concentrated.

I could hear George behind me, breathing. His breathing didn't sound entirely steady. Occasionally, he would snort or even cough, and I would try not to flinch. Eventually he spoke again:

"When I was five we went to the mechanical circus. The ringmaster's eyes glowed and he cracked his whip, the horses trotted around, and there was one girl, she was so pretty up on top of that horse, so ... *lithe.* And bright. There was some sort of magic there, under the lights. Maybe she wasn't an automaton. She wrapped herself up in pieces of silk and fell into perfect shapes above us, and I thought *maybe she's an alien like me. Maybe the ringmaster keeps her against her will. Maybe she needs my help.* And I started crying because I couldn't help her." He sniffed and snorted, a casual rearrangement of mucous at the back of his throat.

"Looking back," he said, "she probably was an automaton, and she probably never needed my help. But I never found out. She sure was pretty, though."

I couldn't figure out which was worse. The silence—so oppressive and different from the silence of being alone—or his odd little confessions. I kept my eyes on the scanners. I said nothing. We were coming up on the planet, a lonely sphere of yellow and grey dust orbiting a nearly burnt out star.

"I hid when I was a teenager. I didn't want anyone to know, so I didn't expose myself. I didn't love. I thought someone was cute sometimes, but I was an alien. It couldn't work."

"Shut up," I said. I could talk, I decided. I just would not look at him.

• • •

Jennet and I had met on ZK93 before. It was charted, but I knew of no other humans who had bothered to travel there. I wasn't worried about George finding out where we were: my displays and HUD were all in a script only I could read. There was a city on the planet, long abandoned. By who or what, I did not know. The architecture had sediment lines, as if it had all been carved whole out of the rock that had been there.

You don't leave someone with your ship if you don't know them. I made George follow behind me, him in his flimsy vac-suit, me in my armor, trudging beneath the unfinished sandstone spires and broken bridges of the forgotten city.

"When I was twenty," said George over the comm, "I had to get a job in a tall building."

The towers around us remained obscure.

"The elevator ride was twenty minutes," he said, "and you couldn't see the ground out the window, just other towers and elevated roads and bridges and lights blinking in the mist. Inside was clean and sterile, and people had lines around them so that nobody could see their inside from the outside. It was easy to be an alien, there. I could talk to people, because people didn't talk about themselves."

We were approaching the cracked dome in the center of the city, where Jennet and I had arranged to meet. But she wasn't coming out. Something was wrong. I took out my pistol. I searched the tops of the towers. There were window holes everywhere. If someone was watching us, we'd never see them.

"I even accidentally met a girl," said George. "She'd lived all her life in that building, inside never meeting out. I brought her fancy tea from the outside, and she gave me muffins. I never really felt like I could relate to her, I guess, because she was human, but I did care about her. We got married. We got married and she moved out with me. We got a place above the sea. She'd never been outside the building before. She was excited. I was thirty by this point." He took a breath.

"If you start telling me about your rugrats," I said, "I will shoot both of us." I took off the safety on my pistol to show him I was serious. I didn't turn around. I still felt that if I turned around I would be surrendering some sort of power. He stopped talking then. I had finally got my point across.

We reached the crack in the dome, and still nothing. The dome was maybe four hundred meters across, a perfect hemisphere. The crack dwarfed me, and reached almost to the top of the structure. I switched on my helmet light and walked into the dome, which I knew was almost completely empty except for dirt and something resembling moss that grew in furthest edges, away from the sun.

I didn't need my helmet light. I could see her, almost at the center of the dome, lit by the orange rays of the dying sun, her helmet still on and her guts strewn across the floor.

"We need to leave," I said.

"Aren't you going to see if she's alive?" asked George.

"She's dead. Get out of the dome. Let's go." I could sell the cargo, I was thinking, if I lived.

We spilled out onto the street and froze. In the center of the street there was a creature, with dark red skin, taller than a man, many thin limbs protruding spider-like from its body. It had a neck like a human, but where a face would be there was something that looked almost like a hand; a blank palm in the middle with extremities around it. It froze at the same time we did. After a second one of its limbs moved as if to sidestep and I shot it in the palm of its face, and it fell down gushing bright blood, twitching and flicking its limbs like an insect that does not know it is dead yet. I walked over to it and stamped down hard on its face with my metal boot, and it stopped moving. I tried not to notice as I did this that its limbs were not clawed and that it had no weapons. It had probably not been what killed Jennet. It was probably harmless, and may have been intelligent. It could have been what built this city.

George was crouching on the ground. I could not tell if he was fascinated or if he was going to be sick.

"It's hard to raise kids when you are an alien," he said, his eyes fixed on the sticky mess that my boot had left behind. "They grow into a world you don't understand. I guess they turned out okay, but it wasn't anything to do with me."

Back in the ship with my helmet off, I could smell the goo that had congealed on the boot of my armor. It was rank. Behind me as we took off, I could hear George take a breath. *Don't talk about marriage,* I thought, *don't talk about marriage.*

"We stayed there, on that island floating above the sea, even after the children left. We sent drones out to buy food, and she talked to her old tower friends online, but she was lonely. I spent more and more time looking up into the sky. She was so tolerant."

Christ. I would definitely not be turning around.

I saw a figure on the scanner I might normally ignore, the sort of reading that could be anything, usually, but in the context of where we were . . . . I opened up more visual channels and searched the sky as we rose towards the stratosphere.

There: slippery intentions, black against orange sky. Two tracking drones, above, shaped like finless, faceless sharks, flicking through the atmosphere towards us. Blades along their sides. They were what happened to Jennet.

My ship wasn't armed exactly. It would raise too many questions if I was stopped. But I had modified the rubbish ejector and loaded it with incendiaries. I only had one shot, and I had to wait for both of the shark-things to get close enough.

Closer.

"I should have explained," said George. "It might have helped."

Closer. They circled around my flank.

"I got angry sometimes," said George, "because it seemed unreasonable for her to want something I couldn't give. We would fight."

Now. I ejected the load, and as I had hoped they both sped towards it to investigate before it exploded. One of them disappeared, the other emerged from the explosion as a ball of flames and thunked off the side of the ship.

I checked the damage indicator. We were okay.

"We talked about separating for a while," said George. We broke atmo. I stayed facing forward.

Once we were in the silence of space I set course for a port I knew that might buy Jennet's stuff. I could get rid of my passenger there. Time passed. My hands were sweaty inside my suitgloves, from the action. Memories started butting up against their walls again. I could feel his eyes on me. I listened to see if I could hear his breathing.

"Well?" I said.

"I'm sorry?"

"You didn't finish. Or is this the part where I'm meant to break down and tell you why I'm out here, huh? How badly I screwed up that I prefer this metal fucking coffin to anywhere else?"

There was not a sound from him.

"Well, nobody gets to hear that story," I said. "Nobody."

He still didn't move. I gripped the side of my chair so I would not turn around. It was minutes before he spoke:

"My wife used to play a Callistan harp. Everyone who heard her music said it was so beautiful it would break your heart. I told her I loved to hear it. I never felt anything, though. Why would I? I was an alien.

"We had to stay together, even if I couldn't make her happy, even if we didn't understand each other. We had each forgotten how to live without the other. I don't even know what happened in all the years after that. Nothing happened."

Nothing happened. Oh, for a life where nothing had happened. The damage console beeped. Something had gone undetected for a while. I pulled up the display.

"I think the life support has stopped working," I said.

"That's not right," he said.

I did some quick calculations and changed course for Joetown. "We have a bit under eight hours to our destination," I said. "And about sixteen . . . no, eight hours oxygen including reserves. Don't talk. Lie down on the floor so you aren't doing anything and you won't use as much."

I turned off the cabin lights and we did not talk. I closed my eyes and tried to slow my breathing.

Eight hours in the chair while the air grew thick and clammy. I closed my eyes and I tried to sleep. Maybe I did sleep.

The console beeped and I opened my eyes. Our destination was in view. Joetown space port was a tangle of straight lines in neon colors, each of them kilometers long.

I don't remember making a sound, but somehow at that moment I had given him permission to speak. I remember wondering if he had heard the sound of my eyelid popping free of its crust and slipping across my cornea.

He gave a cough. "It was when I was old and sick that I figured it out," he said. "They took me to an orbital hospital, and I was lying there, riddled with cancer, and for the first time I was off the planet I had lived on for my entire life. My home. I could see the planet below me, and both of my children were there, and my wife was there. This woman who had given up so much for me, for love. As I lay dying, it occurred to me for the first time that I wasn't an alien at all. That I never had been. That was my last thought, that realization. And then I was dead."

I turned around to face him. But of course, he wasn't there. Perhaps we were a jumble in his waking mind, waiting to be dreamt again. The flashing lines of Joetown spaceport illuminated the dark inside of my ship in misleading ways, and I waited for docking clearance.

The Womb Factory
PETER M. FERENCZI

Mei stood, hand on her swollen belly. Her stomach rumbled with the hunger that woke her each morning. Four steps took her and her burden to the window, which slid up scant centimeters before hitting bolts ensuring it went no further. The opening allowed air into the room, but no girl, not even Nuan with her misshapen skull, could have fit her head through the slot. The nets to discourage jumping, installed when the industrial park was a city unto itself and the window bolts hadn't yet been added, hung in tatters at the first story.

Mei put her face sideways to the opening. The breeze that morning carried the chemical tang of Shantou away from her, and the air smelled relatively pure.

The bell for first breakfast, second group, rang in the corridor, and Mei heard the bustle of girls emerging from their rooms though her thin door. Eight short steps took her into the line shuffling in slippers towards the eating room at the end of the hall.

The attendant, in her white uniform with the brown stain Mei had noticed a week ago, stood at the door. As the girls filed by, she touched the front edge of a tablet against their bellies. In most cases, the tablet chirped. The attendant would fish around a multi-pocketed pack at her thick waist and wordlessly hand over a small plastic disk.

Mei accepted the press of the tablet against the bulge under her smock with downcast eyes. Nothing good came of antagonizing the attendants, she'd quickly learned. The tablet chirped, corresponding with the thing inside her.

When she'd first arrived, before they put the egg inside her, the tablet had been silent, and the attendant had given her a white disk. This morning she got a purple one. It had been red at dinner the night before.

She entered the room, with its light green peeling paint, the single long table and bench seats. She took her disk to a low window in one wall and slid it across the counter there. A hand snatched it and a tray emerged with a purple bowl full of the usual gelatinous substance, something that tasted vaguely like congee. It came with a spoon and a cup of weak tea.

Mei took her breakfast and moved toward her end of the table, where the misfit girls clustered like a flock of awkward sheep. She sat next to chubby Fen Hua, who was attacking a bowl with her habitual total focus—she seemed to be the only girl whose body refused to relinquish its fat stores to the thing growing inside it. Crooked, simple Nuan mechanically spooned food into her mouth a little farther down, the occasional drop falling back into the bowl for recycling.

As Mei began to bury her hunger under the glop, a new girl sat down across from her. Mei had noticed that many new arrivals gravitated to her end of the table, perhaps sensing the lack of threat. Most graduated out to one clique or another soon after.

She looked very young, skinny in the shapeless gown they all wore. Her face was pale and her posture telegraphed fear.

Mei kept her gaze averted. She didn't need to talk to the newcomer to know her story. She would be from a small village somewhere in the provinces surrounding Shantou. Her family would have faced privations, debts, deaths caused by flu and/or the domino fall of diseased crops.

A man would have appeared in the village, driving a clean truck. He would have had tea with the girl's father or eldest brother and discussed something in low, urgent tones. And depending on the particulars of her family, her father or brother would have looked at her with calculating or desperate eyes. She would not likely see the sheaf of bills that passed from one hand to another. There would be a tearful parting, or not.

There were no tears when the man offered to take away the extra mouth that had befallen Mei's uncle. She was the troublesome daughter of his city-living brother who'd died, along with his wife, during the flu season two years earlier.

"I will keep your share for you, for when you are finished," he told her in farewell.

She knew he lied, but in her ignorance was cautiously excited to escape the resentfulness of his family, to make her own way. That feeling didn't last long.

The new girl was still frozen in front of her bowl. Mei was halfway through her own.

"You should eat," she said in a low voice, modulated to just carry over the murmur of conversation in the room. The attendants didn't like a ruckus.

The girl didn't seem to hear.

Mei nudged her slippered foot under the table. The girl's vacant stare shifted up from the bowl. Mei pointedly shoved the western-style spoon into the mush and brought it to her mouth.

"Eat," she said.

The girl hesitantly began to eat from her small, white bowl. It was the kind for newcomers and girls in their rest period, formulated to feed one, not two.

"It's not so bad, see?"

She got no answer.

Back in her room, Mei settled herself in her chair. It was hard compared to the one in her old bedroom, but it was better than anything in her uncle's small hut, with its thin mats on a packed earth floor. Sitting made her gravid state a little more bearable.

She turned on her tablet and listlessly flicked through the games. The attendants called the tablets a privilege, but Mei intuited that without them, the girls' crushing boredom could become a problem for the operation.

In her case, the thing wasn't much help anyway. She didn't even bother with the video selection, mostly ridiculous state-approved soap operas. The games never changed. She settled on go and placed virtual stones on the board as the app's limited AI tried to outwit her.

A car door slamming pulled her out of the game: comings and goings were rare for the derelict dorm complex. She went to her window and looked down at the cracked parking lot that fronted the building, sensed other girls in other rooms doing the same.

It was the bright orange Changfeng that appeared every two weeks or so. The usual young man, wearing dark augmented sunglasses and a leather jacket, carrying a small white and blue cooler. He trotted up to the entrance of the building, batting aside a skein of netting. Faintly, she heard him speaking into the intercom.

In the girls' unchanging world, the young man's arrival always inspired discussion—his appearance, his purpose, his eligibility. None had ever seen him closer than from their high windows in the otherwise empty building, but most had theories about his personality and his attitudes towards the princesses locked in their tower.

Mei didn't follow their gossip. The man was an element of the factory, her enemy.

Her stomach was growling again when the bell rang for second breakfast. She knew it was the thing in her belly that absorbed all the energy, but she was the one who felt the hunger.

In the hallway, she found herself walking next to the new arrival, who surprised her by murmuring, "My name is Jia Li."

"I'm Mei."

They were scanned by the attendant, received their disks. Mei collected another large purple bowl, while Jia Li was given a white cup. They sat next to each other.

"It is too early for lunch," observed Jia Li.

"There are six meals a day here. This is second breakfast," said Mei.

Jia Li poked at the glop in the cup.

"We have not even started to work yet. Why so much food?" she asked.

Mei glanced at her.

"You don't know what this place is."

Jia Li stared at her cup.

"A factory."

"A womb factory," said Mei. From the silence, she guessed that the girl didn't understand. "We make things inside us. Like babies, but not babies."

Jia Li's cup froze on the way to her mouth.

"Father said I was going to work in a factory," she whispered.

"You are. But not with your hands." Mei thought of the young man and his delivery. She was sure it was a new batch of eggs.

"Soon you will start. Don't be afraid," she said, thinking of her own terror when, ten weeks ago, the attendant had entered her room, shown her the white oblong shape and said, 'Relax and this will be easier.'

"An attendant will put a small thing inside you. It doesn't hurt. It will grow. In three months, the cycle will be finished, and you will rest for two weeks." The girl would find out eventually that "rest" really meant "heal," she thought.

"But . . . what . . . what are we making?" asked Jia Li.

"Have you heard of biobots?"

"What? No."

"Well, it's like a toy. But alive."

Mei remembered the commercials she would see for something called a FurryBuddy while browsing on her tablet, when her parents were alive and the world still made sense. There was a boy, perhaps eight years old, sitting on a couch in a sunlit room. Next to him was a smaller creature, covered in golden fur, like a cross between a monkey and a dog. Its oversized brown eyes shone in a face covered with short hair. Plush-toy limbs, stubby fingers. The bottoms of its feet, visible as it sat on the couch with its legs too short to bend at the knee, had dog-like pads on them.

It held an old-fashioned book on its lap and told a story in its high-pitched voice. The child squealed with pleasure. In another scene the pair frolicked in a field. In another they walked along a sidewalk in a prosperous neighborhood, with the creature calling out in English the names of objects they passed.

She'd asked her father for one, and he'd smiled thinly.

"Those are too expensive for a professor's salary," he'd said. He'd ruffled her hair, as if trying to brush away her disappointment. "You're better off using your imagination to make your dolls talk."

Jia Li was speaking. "I don't understand," she said. "What is it?"

Fascinated by them, Mei had learned all that she could, even if she couldn't own one.

"It is like an animal with a computer in its head," she said. "It's like a pet that talks. It plays games, teaches things, languages . . . "

"But, how can we make a computer?"

"The computer, they put inside us. We grow the animal around it."

Jia Li digested that.

"Then it goes to school to be a teacher?"

Mei pictured a classroom full of the furry creatures and couldn't suppress a grim smile.

"No, the important stuff is already in its computer."

Back in the room, playing games, waiting for the lunch bell. Her attention wandered, as it often did, back to the tablet itself. It looked just like the one the attendants had, but only ran a few programs, distractions for the girls. There was, of course, no Internet access, no way to get messages out. Not that most of the girls would make a stink even if they could—any trouble would quickly find their families, which might mean that they had nowhere to return to at the end of their two-year contract.

Mei didn't care too much about that.

The tablet was tantalizingly similar to one she'd been issued in school. It, too, had been restricted to certain functions, but plenty of kids knew that pushing an unfolded paperclip through a small hole in the back of the device while holding down two buttons made the tablet ask for an unlock code: because the school had never changed it, it was "00000." Then you could play all the games you wanted.

If Mei could unlock this tablet, she had imagined a thousand or more times, she could do something *other* than play games. Maybe she could reach out for help.

She was certain that the operation was illegal. Real biobots like FurryBuddies were made in fancy bioengineering factories by big companies, not by little groups of girls hidden in abandoned worker dormitories. But it must be cheaper to grow something almost as good in people, just like the phones made in illegal backcountry factories were almost as good as the ones made by the big brands.

The problem was that this tablet wasn't quite like Mei's old school-issued device: it had no pin hole in the back. She'd tried every possible combination of button presses, but all she'd managed to do was freeze the tablet a dozen times. If there was a workaround, it would be online—meaning it might as well be carved on the dark side of the moon.

She was trapped by the lack of some trivial thing, and that lack would cost her two years in this place.

A sudden fury uncoiled in her chest. Before she realized what she was doing, her hand swept the tablet off her lap. As it spun through the air, she was seized by a child's terror. She was misbehaving, and she would be punished.

But by the time it clattered to a stop on the linoleum floor, she'd mastered the feeling. She was already in hell. Whatever this exercise of will cost her, she would pay it.

She tottered over to the dark tablet, stooped with a grunt, and picked it up. The casing flexed and she saw that the front and back halves had come loose in the impact. At least the screen wasn't cracked.

She was about to try snapping the split halves back together when a thought froze her. There had been no hole for the paper clip. Now, there was a hole of a sort.

Gently, she pried the two halves further apart, until the back suddenly popped free. Inside was the usual green plastic with metallic traceries, a gray block that was likely the battery.

And right where the hole in the case of her school-issued tablet had been was a tiny white circle. She pressed on it with her finger nail and it clicked in. Release, and it popped back out. The paperclip switch.

The lunch bell rang.

Mei mechanically packed the food paste into her mouth, trying to speed up time. She hadn't felt hope like this since . . . she blinked. Since before her parents got sick. Part of her tried to rein in that feeling, but it was impossible.

She looked up, and realized that Jia Li had asked her a question.

"What?" She didn't mean to sound irritated, but knew she did. The other girl looked down.

"I was just wondering why we have to spend so much time alone. In our rooms," she said softly.

"Oh. It has to do with the eggs. They can connect to things from inside us, like what happens with the tablet when the attendant checks you in for a meal. They keep us apart so that they don't interfere with each other." Mei had overheard this from girls who had been there longer, and it seemed believable as anything.

"It's lonely," said Jia Li.

"It's better than having to deal with that lot," said Mei, cutting her eyes toward the other end of the table.

"They aren't nice?"

"Well, they can be pretty mean to Nuan there, or fat Fen Hua. And if you aren't careful, they may decide they don't like you, either," said Mei, unable to keep the bitterness out of her voice.

"And you? Why don't they like you?"

"Can't you hear the city in my accent? They can, and that's all the reason they need."

But she knew that wasn't all of it. The others seemed to accept that this place was their lot, that it was what their families needed of them. Sure, they had been scared, but for the most part they'd settled into it, made friends.

But Mei couldn't. She could try to help Jia Li understand what was happening, but she couldn't relax and make small talk about something else. In her mind, this was an ongoing violation, and pretending otherwise would be acquiescing to it. So the others mocked her city background, but she knew that was just shorthand for their resentment of her resentment.

Jia Li didn't say anything for a while, and Mei half figured she'd decided against aligning herself with a pariah and was plotting her way into the safety of a clique. But she finally spoke.

"Well, they must be quite stupid."

Mei couldn't help but smile.

After the eternity of first lunch, the door was closed behind her again. She carefully took up the tablet, and lifted the back cover away. Pursing her lips, she held down the two buttons on the front and pressed the little circular switch.

The screen went blank. The China Telecom logo came up. And then a dialog for entering an unlock code.

Holding her breath, Mei touched the "0" key on the onscreen keyboard five times. The screen blanked for a moment, then came back . . . unchanged. The same request for a code. Failure.

A harsh bark of frustration escaped her throat and she stared unbelievingly at the screen. She had been sure. It had to work. And it had not.

I can guess it, she thought, it's only five numbers . . . but she knew she couldn't. After a few tries, the tablet would lock itself entirely, become useless.

Mei took a deep breath. There was a number. If it wasn't random, she had a chance of figuring it out. But she was still clueless when the bell for second lunch rang.

First dinner. Second dinner. A night of twisting dreams and fragile sleep. She woke once to screams leaking from the delivery room: one of the girls in the chair. She briefly wondered who, then realized she didn't care and drifted back into nightmares before the sounds stopped.

First breakfast. Second breakfast. First lunch. The bells, the bowls, newly unendurable.

I let myself hope, she thought. So much worse than not having hoped at all.

She was peripherally aware that Jia Li was sitting next to her. Had asked a question. She tapped Mei's shoulder softly, which stirred memories of tentative taps during other recent meals. As then, Mei fixed her with a flat stare, wanted to say they could talk later, but speaking seemed far too difficult. She turned back to her food, and Jia Li remained silent.

" . . . number . . . "

The word landed on Mei's mind like a leaf on water, drifting out of context. She shook herself alert. A conversation down the table. Two girls, part of the clique headed by Ai Bao. Mei's concentration bored into their words, barely audible above the murmur of conversation in the room.

"He must have connections," said the first girl.

"Or money."

"Or both!"

"How much do you think a car like that costs?"

It sounded like gossip about the young man with the Changfeng. But could it be linked . . . ? She turned to the girls.

"Excuse me, what number were you just talking about?"

The pair turned and glared, and Mei realized that in her excitement she'd stepped out of place.

Ai Bao noticed.

"Hey city girl," she said with quiet venom, "our business isn't yours."

Mei looked down, choking on her frustration, her heart hammering. In her peripheral vision, she saw Jia Li stand with her tray and walk down toward the other girls.

"Can I sit with you?" Mei heard her say. "I'm from Yangtouqui." A village tiny enough that Mei had never heard of it.

"My cousin married a man from Bianshan, not far away," said one of the girls.

"I know it, I have an aunt who lives there," said Jia Li. "Who is he?"

Mei, now ignored by the other girls, stared at her bowl and struggled to keep back tears. She had been alone before, and now she was again. She should get used to it.

Meal times flashed by. She'd tried "12345" on the tablet but didn't dare guess again.

She was getting green bowls now, meaning she was due within two weeks. She'd known despair when her parents died, but this was different, open-ended, extending to the horizons of her being.

It had been four days since her failure to guess the code when Jia Li again sat next to her at first breakfast.

"The number they spoke of is the license plate of the Changfeng that comes here," she said. "It is a very auspicious number. They think he must have bribed someone, a lot, to have gotten it."

The droning static of hopelessness in Mei's mind was suddenly quiet.

"Do you know it?"

"They say it is A99988. Though they also say in a week, he should be back again." With more eggs.

Mei looked at Jia Li, her face flushing as she realized how unfairly she had discounted the girl.

"Thank you. Thank you."

"It woke you up. I guessed it was important. Why?"

Mei hesitated, not wanting to give hope and then take it away.

"It could be useful," she said quietly. "I'll tell you more when I can."

Jia Li nodded. Mei noticed that her bowl was now blue, no longer white.

"The attendant came to you . . . "

"Yes."

"Are you . . . ?"

"I didn't like it. But there are many things I don't like," said Jia Li. "Ai Bao, for example, is cruel. Her friends are frightened. But you are angry. That is better, for being here."

"Maybe. But it's hard."

"I know."

• • •

Back in her room, Mei keyed in 99988. The tablet's start page flashed up, offering many more options than before. She shook with excitement, and felt an extra thrill as she saw the local and wide area connectivity icons at the top of the screen . . . but it began to waver as they remained transparent. No connection. Jiggering settings didn't help.

She took a deep breath. She wouldn't accept that her progress had been towards a dead end. She tried the browser, the various pre-installed messaging apps, but always ended up at the same error message: "No Internet connection found, please check settings and try again."

She felt despair hovering around her, waiting for her to weaken so that it could retake her.

Almost idly, not allowing herself to consider the death of hope, she browsed through the rest of the newly available apps. Mostly, it was basic stuff—the usual calendar and note-taking kind of thing. But then she found an unusual subfolder.

Brightleaf Biomanagement.

She worked straight through the first night. The applications were configuration interfaces for biobots. At first they seemed impossibly complicated, but by poring over the help and scrutinizing the embedded tutorials, she built a rudimentary understanding. She became adept at identifying what she could ignore so she could focus on the relevant elements.

At first breakfast, Jia Li looked at her with concern.

"You seem tired . . . is it . . . ?"

Mei smiled, and Jia Li hesitantly smiled back.

"I'm tired, but it's OK. It's not that that's keeping me awake. It's . . . "

She wanted to tell her everything, how she'd figured out that the tablets were linking to the biobots in the girls, fine tuning their development. How Mei could now interact with the thing inside her, could control some aspects of it. But with the attendants, the other girls, who knew what ears listening, she couldn't. She shook her head.

"Insomnia. It's just something that happens to me sometimes."

The day seemed to move in fast-forward. She buried herself in the programming apps, and during meals her mind churned furiously over the latest setback, often finding a solution by the time she finished eating.

Jia Li sat next to her at each meal. The two exchanged brief smiles, but her new friend seemed otherwise content to let Mei focus inward, and she was grateful for it.

At second dinner, Mei noticed that Jia Li was among the last to arrive. She looked pale.

"Hey, are you OK?" she asked.

"I don't feel too good."

"If you're really sick, you can tell the attendant," said Mei. "But don't bother her if you don't need to, you know."

Jia Li nodded. "I'll see. Maybe."

Mei turned to her food, let her mind drift back to programming problems.

That night she fell asleep while working with her tablet, and woke with a start in her chair. She rubbed her eyes, disoriented, with the vague sense that she'd heard something.

Then a girl's scream echoed in the corridor. It froze her, sent her pulse racing. She heard the murmur of voices as well, receding, and sobbing. More screams, now muffled behind the delivery room door. She wondered whose turn it was, and the dinner table with its colored bowls flashed in her mind's eye. She tried to visualize who had a yellow bowl, the last color. She couldn't.

Mei didn't realize she was looking for Jia Li until the door to the dining room closed. The last girls were getting their trays. Jia Li wasn't among them. Nor was she further down the table. Mei craned her neck, just to be sure.

Maybe she overslept, since she had been sick. Maybe they let her stay in her room.

She looked up from her bowl to see Nuan staring at her from across the table. The shy, slow girl looked down, but Mei kept watching her, and after a few seconds she looked up again.

"The white truck came last night," she said softly in her nasal voice.

"What?" There was a white truck that dropped off supplies sometimes, but Mei had never seen it come at night.

"At night, it takes girls," said Nuan.

Mei felt ice run down her spine.

"What do you mean?"

"It hears the screaming, sometimes. It comes."

Mei couldn't speak. A bit farther down the table, Fen Hua had stopped chewing.

"Some girls get sick from the egg," Fen Hua muttered to her bowl. "Makes bad problems. Screaming. They go. Nobody sees."

Mei took a shuddering breath, then plunged her spoon back into her bowl. She forced her mind back to the programs, felt like she walked a tightrope over despair.

When her time came, it was bad. As she was led to the reclined chair with its stirrups, she was seized by an image of Jia Li writhing there in agony, her body rejecting the thing that had successfully taken hold in Mei's womb.

Then the pain drove the image away, but it couldn't dispel the sense of her body out of her control, enslaved to this creature that now wanted out and demanded her participation. And out it eventually came.

She kept her eyes squeezed shut as the attendant cut the cord. She heard its first mewling squeals, high pitched like a kitten's. A morbid curiosity opened her eyes and she glimpsed it as the attendant carried it away, much smaller than a human baby, wriggling and pink and red.

It was bad. But it would have been so much worse without the knowledge that she'd made her mark on the little beast, that it was in a way her servant as well.

"Would you like to hear a story?" asked Doodles.

It had been a week since Karin's mother had bought her the creature, in one of the little shops down on Canal. It was cute, but despite its soft, warm fur and the fact that it could speak, there was something about it that made her uncomfortable. Watching it daintily opening a pack of the dense, hard biscuits that it ate, the fact that they had to leave a bathroom door ajar because it couldn't reach the knob, the bottle of antibacterial gel it fastidiously used next to the toilet . . . it was like having a pet that was also a house guest. Yet it seemed to have less personality than her cat Sandy—it was too chipper, too much like the annoying guide AIs that popped up alongside new apps to "help" you use them.

It wasn't even a real FurryBuddy, though Karin didn't have the heart to tell her mom that. It was glitchy, sometimes spouting garbled nonsense or freezing in place for a minute or more before popping back to life as if nothing had happened.

But sometimes the stories were fun. Weird fairy tales, or stuff about monsters and aliens. It was as if someone had just dumped the text of a bunch of old books into the thing's memory—which was actually pretty likely, given its knock-off status, she thought. As it told the stories, its emphasis and pauses were sometimes off, its body language often out of sync, but not enough to ruin them.

"OK," said Karin.

Doodles nodded, but it seemed to pause longer than usual before saying, "This story is in a Cantonese dialect. Would you like me to translate it into English?"

"Uh, sure."

The creature smiled vacantly and swayed gently back and forth, a sign that Karin knew meant the computer in its head was chewing over something.

Then it stopped moving and looked at her. Karin had never seen the expression it wore before: flat, no hint of a smile, eyes hooded rather than brightly wide. It began to speak in an affectless voice, arms at its sides, staring straight at her.

"Hello. My name is Mei Feng. I made this toy. I did not want to. This is my story . . . "

Draftyhouse

ERIK AMUNDSEN

Shenroos is a lucky man. He can relax at a fireplace in green velvet on the moon. He is lucky because he has solitude. Eight days, he has been the sole inhabitant of Draftyhouse. Just him, the Bridgeway, a well-stocked cabinet of floral liquors in every shade between green and purple and all the matching flavors of intoxication and a hundred million places where the air is leaking from the great stone mansion into the void. The man in the moon is having a private party, celebrating his eviction, six days overdue but not yet enforced by the Colonial Army. There is a 300-year-old ghostwood coffee table in front of him, his marching orders open on it, a coaster for his collection of glasses and empty bottles.

Draftyhouse gets like this. Lonesome but never alone. No one has come to take his place, so Shenroos feels justified in squatting. There must be someone here to mind the spiders and husband the flies.

The spiders work by instinct trained into their line over many generations. They are sensitive to the places where the air seeps out and driven to spin webs there. Feeding the spiders falls to the flies, and feeding the flies falls to the carcass of an elk brought over the Bridgeway in Shenroos' wheel-barrow, upended into the crackling room with its slats like the exposed ribs of the carcass, named for the obvious.

Hauling the carcass of an elk must fall to an astronaut, therefore a gentleman. Common folk aren't fit for outer space and so, in leathers and a helmet and bearing a cart full of ripe elk, comes Shenroos: twenty-eight years of life and twenty-one spent in the walls of this house with the Bridgeway supplying food and water and air. He owns seven rooms of Draftyhouse. Lord of the manor by three rooms and by noble obligation, the only one who sticks around.

Draftyhouse is larger than some sublunary villages, encased in tall blocks of angled stone. There are a scattering of luxurious, dangerous windows, like arrow-slits from the ancient castles, poured thick with distorting glass. The house breathes a long sigh, exhaling the air that flows across the Bridgeway into space. Every change in that stirring of air registers in the hairs on Shenroos' neck. A breach would slam the great door shut, sever the Bridgeway and abandon Draftyhouse to Mother Moon. Drink does nothing to dull that sense of doom, nor sleep, nor any task.

Shenroos is a lucky man because he is aware of death in every twitch of his every nerve, every division of every cell. The surface of the moon is littered with many other places so abandoned and walkers who go outside sometimes come back from those places with the remains of foreign outposts and foreign dead to decorate the house. Shenroos' ancient wheelbarrow has brought more bones than just elk into Draftyhouse.

Shenroos, when he stirs, presses his hand or his ear to the walls, places carved with mottos and poems, bas-relief and pattern. There are no walls in Draftyhouse not in the work of astronaut hands or old hunting tapestries for the privacy of the spiders beneath, weaving, listening. They all listen to the slow language of the walls, the drone of earthy consciousness, telluric current pulsing in the stone like sap through a slow, ancient tree. It is that current which keeps Shenroos close to the floor and his limbs the proper weight. The attraction weighing him and anything it touches down, the shared circulatory system of a composite entity.

Shenroos studied the principles and equations behind it, not for scholarship but self-discovery. You do not jump in Draftyhouse, unless you like a close view of the vaulted ceilings. When you sleep, you sleep on the floor, like a monk.

Shenroos reels through the chambers of Draftyhouse when he is not reading ghost stories. He's drunk and uninspired. Shenroos has composed stillborn, premature poems, bitten off at their cords and his mouth is rusty at the corners from the birthing. Epics in old traditional styles about hunters tracked by ghosts across snowy hills, priests giving prophecy, their sleeves and pockets stiff with gore. Then he finds the ghost. He has been looking for words worth carving into these walls and a place to carve them. There are places, spaces, nooks and crannies accreted over the place like luster on a pearl, some well hidden. None untouched. Shenroos is looking over those overlooked corners when the ghost rides through, slouched on the spectral body of an elk in the leathers and helmet of an astronaut.

Shenroos mistakes its scratching for the sound of a rat. Wise rats do not come to the moon; foolish ones get hunted by all present in grand affairs that go on from the first sighting of the little animal until its death. The thought of a rat of his own to hunt and stalk is enough to perk his sodden sensibilities. His eyes seek out movement in the dim of the house, the pale glow of the cold-lighting, but what they see isn't movement, just an image that Shenroos' brain wants to make into a shadow of a curtain and the silhouette of a hunting trophy. This is not what his brain wants there to be. The ghost becomes clear.

The ghost does not look at him; the elk does. Not one of the slate-furred animals of Shenroos' native forests. This one is the color of an old scab, the color of a priest's trailing sleeves. Shenroos knows better than to trust his eyes, the hour, or anything else but his feet. They are bare against the cold stone of the floor, and through them, he feels a thing, light, but present in the telluric current, in front of him, a thing moving, a thing with mass.

The ghost's arms are tangled in the beast's antlers, the head, a half-grinning, jawless skull nods in the helmet, the lines and ink of the astronaut's facial marks transferred from the flesh to the bone. The flesh resolves between those markings, an astronaut family that Shenroos does not know, and the skull beneath.

When he was the only little boy on the moon, Shenroos learned to read lips. This puffy mouth, chapped with frost crystals, the swollen tongue, they ask a question before elk and rider vanish like a shape in fast-moving clouds.

Shenroos kneels, putting both hands to the slate of the floor to feel the current of the house. His hands come up black with a thing that bothers him more in its inexplicable presence than a ghost astronaut mounted on a spectral elk.

Shenroos puts his tongue to the pad of his hand and does not like the taste or the cloy of the stuff. This is not a residue of the house, this is novel, and novel is another word for lethal when one lives a few inches of always-more-porous-than-you-think stone away from the void. Shenroos tries very hard to explain this as a thing that one might see on the sixth day of hard drinking, an argument that he would find persuasive, but for the movement in the current.

Shenroos can tell his eyes they do not see a *shook* from the snowy forests of the afterworld bearing some poor bastard astronaut off to the cold hells on the moon. Shenroos cannot tell his current-sense, his house-sense anything. It tells him.

Shenroos is in no position to listen. He drags toward his room and checks again that the current did register something besides him, somewhere in Draftyhouse did, in fact move. It did. Shenroos vomits and the moon spins. He checks again.

The astronaut has not been sleeping these last few days so much as losing consciousness. Shenroos is not surprised to find himself in a snowy forest. Shenroos is covered in blood and his feet are numb, but the blood isn't his, so he goes forward, the pull of dream-necessity is too strong to recognize or fight.

The blue spruces and black pines give way to the mountains and mares of the moon, but the snow continues to fall and those red elk, the *shook,* are following, bellowing soundless cries in the vacuum, smelling the blood all the same.

In the ghost stories, *shook* have a bite like a tropical lizard; their stink gets in your blood and they can follow you anywhere. Shenroos is wearing his astronaut leathers, all treated and sealed against the void, but there is snow melting in his hair. His helmet is off. Shenroos can't tell if he is breathing, if his blood is boiling, if his heart is beating out a futile rhythm against nothing. He is in the house and the snow is falling. The dead astronaut comes to him.

"What is the purpose of the Draftyhouse?" That was the question on the ghost's lips. The snow falling in the house is ash and soot. Shenroos loses the dream to sleep and then sleep to dull pain and cold. He wakes, soot on his bedding.

Shenroos celebrates his return to sobriety with the last and best of his non-alcoholic rations. Tomorrow would normally bring food to the Bridgeway for the next week or so. The day after, they would check to see if it has been taken, and, if not, the third day would bring a party. Untouched supplies usually meant a suicide, something that happens when a lone astronaut stays to mind the house. Hanging has always been popular in Draftyhouse; the trick is to understand the length of your rope and make sure your toes are touching at all times.

No one in the history of Draftyhouse has ever just gone outside.

Shenroos repeats the ghost's question; a popular question in the sublunary. Shenroos pulls out his family's sounders, feels a stab of guilt at the dust on them and begins to set up an experiment. There is almost nothing left for him to discover with the antiques he fits together, nothing that he cannot learn just by walking barefoot in the chilly place, putting his hands to the stone. Shenroos has lived so long dependent on the Bridgeway and the telluric current-augmented gravity for light and air, water and the weight of the Earth keeping his limbs and lungs strong, he is sensitive to it. Most marriages do not last so long.

Since the astronaut families first arrived, the moon has been tried out for many purposes but everything man puts here eventually fails. Draftyhouse will be no different; each creak of the wood fixtures, each shift of the stone tells Shenroos of the doom of this house, the mottos and poems in the stone will one day sit in airless cold darkness.

Covered in soot. Shenroos is finding it on all surfaces he checks; fine, greasy, streaks in odd places in the rooms that fall under his titles. Other places are almost coated and his sensibilities tell him that there is more weight inside the house. Something new has arrived, bringing ghosts.

There are only four uses that mankind has found for the moon. The first is for storage of things that benefit from no light, no heat and no air. Draftyhouse's operation is based on the proceeds from the archives, vaults and tombs kept behind air doors and umbilicus hook-ups.

The second is for storage of things that cannot safely be kept on Earth; residue of mankind's unhealthy flirtations with fissiles, wastes of societies enlightened enough not to pretend that they are forever buried or drowned. The third is for astronomy and telescopy, particularly here on the dark side, but resources are elsewhere these days.

The last is for the Bridgeways themselves, telluric tunnels that would ignite the atmosphere around them if left unattended, and may one day bring more distant spheres under man's dominion. Assuming man manages to get past the hurdle of distance that keeps the moon their only destination. Some idiots look for ways to make the Bridgeways into weapons, too, because what's a sphere in the dark worth if you are not its sole owner? The man on the moon laughs at the notion. Shenroos' people did attempt to fight on her surface, twice. History cannot record what kind of disasters they were; it would have required someone survive.

Shenroos hooks all the equipment to the vacuum generator, a long, thin tube lined with turbines and occultations that lead, eventually, outside. Shenroos sits next to the intake for a moment, listening to the artificial quietus of his home while the equipment begins to power up. Then he begins to hunt for ghosts.

Flies land on his ledger. A few of them go into the intake only to be swallowed up. Flies are always attracted to the outside. The air doors are always full of their carcasses.

Shenroos has had enough sleep and enough sobriety to doubt his eyes, but never does he the kinesthetic connection between his body and his big, inefficient monument to faded vainglory. The telluric current speaks to the base of the survival instinct, the egg at the root of the tree of his life. Shenroos is a lucky man; Shenroos knows to listen and knows how to listen. The instruments are out today only so that he can have his senses recalled and validated.

The moon is silent and dead inside, but large structures do settle, and this is one of the reasons why so many places end up derelict and shut off from sublunary. A shift can bring the joining of a place off true; there are some cracks that chemical sealants and spiders cannot patch. There are meteor strikes; man has learned that even the tiniest speck can strike with a force that no bullet can match. Some stations have been blown wide open. The readings do not bear a strike, and they don't bear settling, either. The readings don't bear anything in records at all. Only that several tons of matter have silently invaded the house and Shenroos is not nearly as drunk as he needs to be.

What is the purpose of the Draftyhouse? Others, over brandy, shadows thrown by the great fireplace, passed the question over and over like a mid-point pennant in some ancient joust.

"Pride. We could make Draftyhouse when no one else could. We can keep it operating for two hundred and forty-three years when no one else can keep a structure half the size open for half the time."

Shenroos is the man on the moon, so he finishes his thought.

"We might have to look up at their flag and salute it, but everyone looks at the moon."

Down in the sublunary, the barometers will register that Shenroos has used the generator. That's bound to get someone's attention. At this point only a blindfold and a bullet are going to save face down there. So be it.

So be it. Shenroos is exhausted from the calculations and the readings, but he is vindicated. There is something in the Draftyhouse besides him, something moving. Whether it is an astronaut ghost on a *shook,* Shenroos can't bring himself to care. His eyes are heavy. His body is still thirsty, and the cabinet is close to hand and close to full.

The ghost comes to visit Shenroos by the fireplace when the fire is out. Shenroos last remembers putting a log on it and sitting back down on his father's favorite chair, and here he is, right where he left himself. It's cold. There is more soot in the house when he wakes. The webs in the corners of the rooms are black. The Bridgeway helps the house retain some heat, but anyone who has ever come here from the sublunary, all they do is huddle by the fire and complain about the cold. Even his people, their northern latitudes and high altitudes, grey-elk and heavy furs, they shiver.

Shenroos has fallen asleep still slightly drunk and dressed as an astronaut. He doesn't remember putting the suit on, but it was possibly his last chance to disgrace the uniform, and he's jumped.

Shrunk inside of his leathers, the ghost is not wearing his gloves or his helmet. His face is transparent to the bone below, his hair sun-faded, dry. He sighs at Shenroos and turns away. The house smells of sweet soot, now. Shenroos' leathers are stained with it.

Shenroos feels it, the palpitation, dearer than his heart, in the current. Ghost forgotten, Shenroos drops from the chair to his knees. His hands tear the rug aside and splay out flat to the stone of the floor.

The house has not breached. The spiders still spin in their crevices, the gods are in their heavens, Draftyhouse is not moments away from shutting itself to the sublunary forever. There is movement in every corner of the house. Invisible weight; Shenroos feels the deliberate tread in numbers he only imagined in the days when the Draftyhouse's ballroom still held functions.

Shenroos can see the soot in the air, settling.

Shenroos begins to stagger, stopping every few steps to press his cheek to the stone of Draftyhouse's walls. Twenty-one years of living in constant contact with the current has made his body the almanac, all the instruments he needs.

Shenroos' lips are black from the soot, cheeks smeared over his astronaut marks. The ghosts start arriving.

They don't appear to his eyes at first, but then a young girl is before him in her backcountry garb, her hair plaited in seven pigtails. Shenroos presses his lips to the wall and feels the weight of her little feet. He passes the crackling room. Flies land at the corners of his eyes, iridescent blue, frustrated; all this death and none of it to eat. The spiders have come out. He sees them on every wall, scuttling, confused. Shenroos wants to tell them something, but Shenroos cannot talk, not to the ghosts or the flies or the spiders or the flickering current of his home; he can only listen.

Shenroos' leathers are stained almost black. His hair is sticky. Ghosts pass him, holding their transparent arms to hug their insubstantial ribs. *Shook,* some skeletal and some still in ghostflesh, prance in the halls. The moon was supposed to be a hell in the old days; priests sermonized on the terrors mankind would bring to the Earth by opening Bridgeways.

The Bridgeways.

There is something in the soot on the wall where Pigtails' gaze fell. Shenroos wipes it off with a finger and looks closer. Hair, half burnt, too long to be his.

What is the purpose of the Draftyhouse?

Shenroos feels another flicker in the current, a jerk from the far end, in the sublunary. The air pressure increases, the spiders scuttle away from their webs. Shenroos feels the arrival of more cold, frightened souls through walls of his house. Draftyhouse is an exhaust vent. It is a chimney for a crematorium, opened instantaneously, anywhere. A stable Bridgeway whose other end opens and burns all it touches. The ultimate weapon, the reason no one has come to get him. No one assumed that Shenroos would survive the first test. No one assumed that the air drawn each time the weapon deployed would sustain the one man stupid, stubborn and drunk enough to stay behind. What is the purpose of Draftyhouse? The blindfold and the bullet; so be it.

No. Unacceptable.

Shenroos shouts at the atrium to the Bridgeway, screams, though the effort breaks his head like a quail egg. A haze of soot answers, floating through the halls. Flies land and taste everything; some get stuck to the walls and some get borne down with the sticky soot. The spiders abandon their webs. *Shook* trot through Shenroos' solid body. Shenroos feels the added weight of hundreds, but the air does not move with the breath of lungs, the rooms do not heat with the warmth of blood. Pigtails can almost see him when Shenroos concentrates on her and calculates, in his head, the weight of a lost soul.

Ghosts are crying out in growing numbers. These people don't belong to the cold hell of the moon. The moon belongs to Shenroos. Soot is caked in Shenroos' hands. It coats the inside of his mouth and nostrils.

Another flicker, gout of soot; the dead astronaut rides by, empty sockets expectant. The living astronaut pulls himself away from the walls.

Shook track their quarry by their blood.

Warmth comes in the waves of soot. Tiny flakes of ash fall from the ceiling like snow, ghosts cluster like fog where the *shook* gather them. What is the purpose of Draftyhouse?

Pigtails is here, standing next to him, near the lunar terminal, where the crackling room is. Shenroos kicks open the cabinet doors, drags the carcass out with a cloud of flies and a scattering of shed maggots. The *shook* notice, but don't seem to care.

It would be too easy. Shenroos holds out his hand in front of the spectral muzzle of the dead astronaut's mount. The *shook* draws back.

"Bite me. Poison and follow me. Lead these people home. They don't belong here."

The dead astronaut shakes his head.

"This is my house, and I want you all out."

Shenroos reads lips. It's harder when they aren't much more substantial than the translucent teeth beneath them.

"Shut the door."

Shenroos opens his mouth. Closes it. Opens it again. "They'll just open it somewhere else," he says, but those are the words that convince him. Somewhere else. Not here.

"So be it," Shenroos says. "You know the way home, across the Bridgeway?"

No response.

"This is why Draftyhouse isn't open to the public." Shenroos grabs a broken slat, ancient wood splintered and sharp.

It takes him a few tries. Even with the ghosts and the *shook* and new arrivals coming, a few tries. But Shenroos is an astronaut; he splashes his blood across the threshold, the place where the moon and the Earth meet. He stares at the wound in his wrist, throws the slat across the threshold to Earth, to the long hallway lined with gaunt men, likenesses of the astronauts who first took rockets in the long ago to place the beacons for the Bridgeways on the moon.

Shenroos puts on his gloves. The left fills with blood, but it stays inside the suit, where it won't mislead the *shook* herding the ghosts off the moon. The dead astronaut remains.

"You can stay. I'll see you here when the big door closes, if you do."

Shenroos is a lucky man; the Draftyhouse belongs to him and always will. He is the man on the moon. Shenroos puts on his helmet and heads for the airlock doors.

All the Things the Moon Is Not
ALEXANDER LUMANS

A call comes over the vidchannel: "Murph, you sitting down?"

"Always." At the moment I'm standing in my darkened cabin at base camp in Mare Nubium. By headlamp only I carve a chess piece—a knight—out of moon rock. I'd crushed one earlier after Tchaikovsky called me out on a dumb move.

The screen and radio cut out. I switch channels, then switch back to hear: "Get up. You need to see this." Tamsen sounds serious. She always sounds serious. It's one of the things I like most about her.

"I'm busy." I keep sanding the knight's head. When no response follows, just space static, I give in. "What is it?"

More static, then: "The Russians."

I blow on the knight. Moondust reels through the headlamp's beam. I think it beautiful. I'd carved this set my first month here on the moon. The dust I compare to stars. The space between them, too, is beautiful. And the same old lines are running through my head—*Goodnight room, goodnight moon*—the ones I'd read in bed to my daughters. I grab the mic: "Tell Tchaikovsky he needs to ready his Nastoyka supply."

Tchaikovsky is a mold pirate, the one thing we have in the way of a rival. But he's also a good chess player. He studied his masters. Knew openings I'd never heard of. He's the only distraction here that keeps me honest. Down on Earth, who has the calm or the fire for chess anymore? Since our four-man crew arrived late last August to harvest the *Dreammold!*, I've been in two modes: defend and defend again. Whether it's harvesting, carving, or playing, give it 98%. I've always been one to open my games with the tried and true; Sicilian Defense all the way. Only recently have I begun to wonder if this is the right way to go about it. Tchaikovsky and I have an unfriendly wager: loser ponies up a bottle of their nation's choicest liquor. By my count, I've handed over seventeen handles of Maker's Mark. And he? Not a drop of vodka.

In four weeks the transport will be here to take us home. I want to win, for once. I want things to go my way.

"We found their ship."

"There's plenty of mold out there," I tell her. "Let the little cosmonaut stake his claim." I've given up playing moon ranger. A year in one-sixth gravity and white rooms and the company of little love does that to good intentions.

This time, not even static.

"Tamsen." I set the knight on d5. "Tamsen?"

"—the problem." I only catch this last part. But I *am* busy. A good kind of busy. In eight moves, I'll have the Russian mated—Rg2++—even after losing my queen early on. And now Tamsen, with whatever problem there is, has carved that good feeling out of me.

In Buggy 2, I zoom south to her position at the edge of Tycho Crater. It's where we go for the best mold harvesting. I can throw a rock into the crater and watch the moldripples go on for miles: *yellowyellowyellow.* "Twenty-eight days," I remind myself.

Tamsen's standing by Buggy 1, big gloved hands on her big suited hips. She's radioed the rest of the crew too. Bouncing around in our suits, the four of us resemble primitive undersea divers with portholes for masks and twin oxygen tanks. Spitzer's busy poking the mold. When I used to hear the Rockies' announcer describe a batter with "warning track power," I didn't realize I was imagining Spitzer. Long-limbed and morally impulsive, he's always asking me, "When do I get to stab the flagpole into something?" Vinegar Tom—he's just staring into the crater. I'm thankful for our helmets. Yesterday, I'd walked in on him and Tamsen fucking in her room—they didn't see me—and now I don't want to look him in the face for the rest of the mission. Not out of shame, but because he got to her first, because it made me realize I've always hated this planet. Him. His copy of *Desperate Passage: The Donner Party's Perilous Journey West* that he intently flips through in the mess hall like he's studying one of the buggies' operation manuals.

Tamsen taps her helmet. I tap mine back. The vidchannel and radio have been fritzing. We haven't talked with mission control since Tuesday and we don't know what's wrong with the transmitter. All we hear back is fuzz.

Beyond her and the others, at the crater's edge, I see Tchaikovsky's ship. And I see the mold; that *is* the problem. What had been his illegal operation is now covered in the *Dreammold!,* utterly and completely. It's as if Tycho burped up some fantastic wave that came crashing down mid-ops. The scene reminds me of Denver, the day after.

I draw a finger across my neck, point at the Russians' ship, and then shrug. We bounce over to it and pry open the bay door. The vessel's guts are clogged with as much yellow gunk as the outer shell is coated.

A flash in me of something Tchaikovsky'd said after taking my queen: "Ze bigger zey are, Afraham Lincoln, ze more it rains rats and clogs." He was forever butchering Americanisms, but sometimes I had to admire the results. They made as much sense on the moon as anything else did back home.

Fifty feet from the Russian's ship, Tamsen's waving me over. She stands calf-deep in mold on the crater's rim. At her feet is a single set of boot tracks. It leads from the ruined ship out into Tycho's depths.

Back at base camp, I stare at the same game from before.

"So the mold is moving," says Vinegar Tom from behind me. His voice always sounds surprisingly nasal; surprising because he's missing his nose. It makes his bucked teeth stand out all the more. "Now we don't have to drive as far to get it."

I'm too preoccupied to respond and too besieged to care.

"You had your games with the Commie, I know. It's *terrible*. A bad way to go. But we've all seen terrible things on the news." I can hear the smirk in his voice, smell the vinegar on his breath. He'd quit the space program to be a butcher in Ohio, but when The Drought killed that industry, he came trudging back to Cape Canaveral. "Though I suppose some of us have seen it up close," he goes on. "Been able to *smell* the terrible." He reaches around from behind me and flicks over the white king.

"That's *my* king, asshole."

"I know."

After I finish wiping the blood from Vinegar Tom's lip off my elbow, I say, "Touch my game again, see what happens."

He looks down at the board, then at me, as if considering it. He's short and brash and sporadically clean-shaven. Exactly the kind of man I can picture behind a meat counter. The skinfolds where his nose should be remind me of how the Rocky Mountains look on military raised-relief maps. "If we have to eat each other at some point between now and the 30th," he says, "I'm going to make you eat me."

An hour later, I set the white king upright. Eight moves: 37. Qb3 Rd1+ 38. Kg2 Rd2+ 39. Kg3 Ne3 40. Qxe3 Rg2++. I pick up my newest knight. The jawline is clean, the eyes sharp notches. Calmly, I hurl it at the cabin wall. It hits hard and slowly fragments.

I imagine the conversation at NASA went something like this:

"Sir, the moon is shiny."

"It's always been shiny."

"No, sir, there are shiny parts."

"Today is not April Fool's Day."

"Telescope Two picked them up."

"*Shiny* parts?"

"We thought it was silver."

"Moonsilver. That has a good ring to it."

"It's not silver."

"Okay. Mercury, rhodium, zinc, what isn't it?"

"Telescope Two is a very good telescope."

"*Moon*silver."

"First, sir, it's important that we keep this a secret."

"I agree. Everyone likes jewelry. Everyone's a magpie."

"That's not what we mean."

"Tell me already. You're killing me here!"

"It's water."

"Is water shiny?"

"We found shiny water. On the moon."

"Shit."

"That's what we're supposed to say: 'shit.' We said you wouldn't say that."

"Who knows about this?"

"Everyone. Everyone's a magpie for this kind of news."

"And you're sure it's not April Fool's?"

"We're sure it's not silver."

"Shit."

By then, The Drought had settled in, five long years and still holding strong. Ice, Aquafina, and public pools were all things of the past. The U.S.'s initial investigative moonlanding found plenty of water. And it found what was growing in the water, too: the mold. We sampled it, brought it to Florida, found it useful. So the U.S. pushed through amendments to the TRIPS agreement to include protections for other planets' resources. And they shipped the four of us up here to harvest it for a year until the next round of crewmen arrives.

We know it's been almost a year because of the calendar in the mess hall. Each month features a new war poster.

"Ten fingers good! Eight claws bad!"

"Use your thumbs! Recycle your scrap metal and keep the MegaHun at bay!"

"When you live alone, you live with Megafauns."

Vinegar Tom says they're invigorating. I'm sick of them. But there's little else to focus on between sleeping and eating and sporing and fighting and fucking. And work.

The word *Dreammold!* once summoned in me the image of a fantasyland of iridescent clouds. Now I can't think of a less suitable name. It's this terrible *yellow*, with the look of cauliflower heads but the consistency of dry, packed snow.

Our only tools: large meat cleavers, T-handle baling hooks, and what's essentially a giant George Foreman. Everything's run on solar, even the powercyclers that pump out our CO_2. I'd be thrilled by the technology if I thought it'd actually save me.

Step 1: Cut four-by-four squares out of the moldline.

Step 2: Hook the square on both sides and lift free.

Step 3: Place in grill box and seal shut.

The box broils the mold and compresses it. These hard pancakes go into storage until the semi-monthly unmanned cargo capsule arrives. Then we unload the capsule's supplies (dried food, Maker's Mark, oxygen tanks) before stacking the pancakes in its bay and sending it back to be fashioned into fuel, fixodent, and firearms for the Megafaun War.

The hordes hit Denver three days before I was scheduled for liftoff. I was there. Home with my family, eating chocolate chip waffles. The first wave struck late that morning. Wild pigs with mammoth tusks and armor plating. The ground shook. The South Platte sewage flowed backward. Then the rest of the Megafauns streamed out of the mountains, as if they'd been hiding there for centuries, breeding, tripling in size. So thirsty and fast. The winged kind broke into the top floor of the CenturyLink Tower. Fifty-point elks and shaggy aardvarks nested in INVESCO Field. Horned bears with snouts shaped like ice cream scoops covered the suburbs in blood and fur. They came for my family—wife, daughter, younger daughter, youngest daughter, our fox terrier Ralph, me—but we hid in the basement. I thought we'd be fine with a barricaded door. Before dark, I went upstairs for food with Ralph on my heels. Only, he bolted through the doggy door. I found myself chasing him down the street, imagining my daughters' streaming faces if I had to tell them I lost Ralphie. A block down, heavy grunts sounded from someone's garage. I had to run home empty-handed. But when I came back down into the basement, arms full of consolation Fruit Roll-Ups and Zebra Cakes and no dog, all I came back to was this big hole. Taken, and not even with a loud crashing I could replay in my head. Just nothing nowhere forever. It must have only taken seconds. I sat down on the stairs. I only thought I heard barking. I ate three Fruit Roll-Ups. I ate six Zebra Cakes. I waited. And when they didn't come back, I slept in my youngest daughter's bed, saying, goodnight nobody.

In the mess hall, Tamsen and Spitzer are seated on the floor by the powercycler vent. Contact with mission control is still nil. On the calendar, the 30th is circled in red. This month's poster: a picture of a salivating mastodon-wolf looming over the caption: "The world cannot exist half-slave and half-food: Fight for Freedom!" Vinegar Tom sits backward on a chair, slouched forward and smiling wide at me. It doesn't help my already sour mood: no more chess, no more liquor, even the prospect of shipping off-planet seems impossibly far away, as if we wouldn't survive each other's company another day. The three of them pass around foil stripped from an air duct and a twin-pronged nosetube and a lighter rigged from the grill box's heatcoils.

"Keep sporing," I say as I crouch between them, "and you'll sour the meat."

After Spitzer discovered you could freebase the mold—"sporing," he named it—I opted out. How do you go 98% while spun on fungus? It's practically a Class-1 drug, complete with four-hour euphoria, hallucinatory episodes, tingling. It also had a nasty tendency to gum up Vinegar Tom's intestinal system if he didn't take the right precautions. Yes, people need outlets.

"Can we go claim some mountain in the name of us?"

"Can I please plant the flagpole?"

"Can we sleep together now?"

Sporing also does wonders for the skin. The three of them are tinted gold, Tamsen the deepest. She has dark blonde hair to match, arms and legs that I'd only assumed were well-toned until recently, and a small tight face I started wanting to kiss too late. She sprinkles more spores onto the foil strip, clicks the lighter until the coils at its tip redden. Then, positioning the tube in her nose, she inhales deeply. These are the only times I ever see her relax. Relaxed people—lazy people—worry me.

Tamsen looks straight into my eyes and says, "You're a lovely man." This has all the meaning in the world, and none of it. "Has anyone ever told you how lovely you are?" I try to forget her moans, the image of her body thrusting under Vinegar Tom's. How she could go for a guy without a nose was beyond me. "I mean it, Murph. You're glorious." She passes the foil to Vinegar Tom and leans back against the wall. "Like a baby's mobile. The kind with the lights and funny animals."

Spitzer laughs at her. I want her to go back to being serious. My wife was serious.

"You want to hear something fucked up?" asks Vinegar Tom.

I don't.

"When the Donner Party got stranded in those mountains, they say they only fed the body parts to the youngest children. *The youngest children*, like three-year-olds. They did it even though they knew help was on the way. Isn't that fucked up?"

Tamsen kicks his chair, but not hard enough to knock it over. "Has anyone ever told you how morbid *you* are?" Her eyes are lit up, her face radiant with spores.

Spitzer clucks his tongue and swings his arms together like a batter. "Another moon shot for Noseless Tom Jackson." He, too, is shining.

The air vent kicks into a louder second powercycling stage. It sounds like a roar coming from the drooling, tusked wolf on the wall. I feel my lungs squeeze in. After a year, even the canned oxygen has begun to taste stale.

"That *Dreammold!*'s something else," Vinegar Tom finally says. "All that canary yellow." He reaches under his chair for two bottles: one of industrial-grade white vinegar and one of Pepto-Bismol. The vinegar kills the spores in his stomach; the pink stuff keeps the vinegar's acid from eating more holes. He takes chugs from both bottles and grimaces after each.

Tamsen says, "It's mustard, if anything."

"Mustard?" Spitzer throws up his arms. "It's gamboge. Pure gamboge yellow."

I say, "I always thought it looked like cheese."

They stare at me—"Cheese."—they shake their heads.

"It's goldenrod."

"No, it's a mix of lemon and sunglow."

"Call it Peridot."

"In some language somewhere, it means 'precious' and 'ripe.'"

"Freedom yellow."

"Yellow-bellied coward."

"Macaroni and cheese," I amend.

Vinegar Tom claps me on the back. "Like Tamsen says, you're a lovely guy, but the moon ain't made of cheese." Everyone but me exchanges chuckles between spore passes. They take solace in this negative definition: *it's not cheese.*

I stand up. They watch me with big pupils, sclera yellow at the corners. Tamsen says to stay, holding out the foil and lighter. On the calendar, the 16th, today, is already crossed out. Fifteen more days of what? With Tchaikovsky gone, they're all I have. "Hell," I say, crouching back down and reaching for Tamsen, "I am lovely, aren't I?"

I take out Buggy 2. I tell the others I'm going for a drive through Hell's Half Acre. I tell myself, if I can cut through the mold inside Tchaikovsky's ship, there might still be some vodka left to sip on. I'm sporing like fuck.

The moon looks dead and nothing and grayscale, all everywhere forever. Rilles, ash cones, dark-halo craters, basaltic lowland seas, a deep regolith of iron and magnesium. The whole Oceanus Procellarum. It's enough to lie down and never get back up, but not right now. Right now, there's all this water, *inside the moon,* where we can't even see it. And this mold, canary or freedom or piss yellow, is growing out of it, growing right now! I drive straight toward Tycho, fast. Leave it all behind. I drive and lean back in my seat and am satisfactorily lightweight because instead of thinking about the moon, I'm thinking about what's gone. Denver. Donner Pass. Nights in winter. I'm reciting lines over a defunct vidchannel: "*Goodnight clocks and goodnight socks, goodnight little house and goodnight mouse.*"

I daze out. My eyes close while I speed across an ancient seabed. Crystal clear, I remember lying in their bed, the nightlamp warming my face, their cold feet crowding around mine. My wife comes in to check on us. I don't need her to smile to know that if the world ended at that exact moment, there'd be nothing she'd change. When I open my eyes, all thoughts go, like air through a crack in my helmet.

There's the moldline, as sick and as yellow as ever.

The latitude's all wrong; the Russian's ship is still four miles south. But here, at the edge of that advancing fungal bloom, stands Tchaikovsky.

It's him all right. Not flesh and silver and Kevlar; instead, he's made of mold, completely and utterly.

Mold: Jesus.

After I climb out of the buggy, I don't know whether to ask him for the secret of sustainable water or cleave him to pieces.

"Ve vant to vin," he says in a gurgling version of his accent. How I can hear him with the radio out, I am at a loss to explain. He opens his fist to reveal a toppled king piece carved of mold. I think of Vinegar Tom knocking over my own king and that dredges up all the ire the sporing had anchored down.

"You're not going to *vin* this time," I say. "No hallucination could, cosmonaut or not."

"No hallucination." He pounds his inflated chest once with a fist that could easily be mistaken for a cheese wheel. "Ze cosmetic is ready!"

"That's what a hallucination would say."

He shrugs.

I don't have the patience for this kind of high. My eyes itch, my sinuses suddenly burn. I tilt my head back until it passes. All across the sky, stars flash. In-between them don't flash millions of other stars, dark, as if forgotten or not even there. Below, the Earth looks painted on space. Out of the blue, I miss things. Afternoon thunderstorms. Playgrounds and fruit snacks. Creaky wooden stairs.

The euphoria's already slipping. I find myself unable to walk away without asking, "What's happening? What's the *Dreammold!* doing?"

"It grows, vhat else?"

"But you. It. I don't know."

"I, zis part." He flashes a peace sign before he joins the two fingers. "It is me."

I look down at where his feet should be: only mold. "Do you still have all that vodka on your ship?"

"Does ze sleepy dog lie?"

"Great," I say. "You've got seven moves to win."

When the Russian laughs, the whole sea of mold ripples behind him. "Zis is good, Afraham Lincoln," nodding his helmet as he goes on, "Free ze slaves, you can. But do not beat zer kitchens before zey are handbaskets."

I have no idea what that means. But where his mix-ups were once amusing, now they're sad, screwy lessons. More than ever, I wish I was standing in front of my wife.

He raises his arm to pound to his chest again, but then stops. Sometimes, even Tchaikovsky knows he's made a mistake. "Zis, no, I am meanings somezing else. How you say, every cloud has dead horse."

I taught my wife chess before she was my wife. It was a struggle at first. She wanted to flirt and I wanted her to be quiet. "You're getting better." I told her this when she wasn't. But when I made the offhand wager that if she ever beat me I'd marry her, then she caught on quickly. She was always black. She favored the horsies. "Chess," I once taught her, "is about all the moves you don't make." Sometimes we'd leave the game for the morning, having found each other's feet under the table and then our clothes on the floor. One night she told me, "I think it's more about the moves you can't make anymore." I said, "Maybe, honey," to which she answered, "They tell you the next move." I didn't argue; instead, I tried thinking her way for once. That night she beat me for the first time.

When I return to the moldline with the chessboard, Tchaikovsky is gone and I'm missing my only knight. Vinegar Tom, I'm sure. When I get back to base, I'll dump out all his Pepto-Bismol. For now, I don't have any tools to carve a new piece. But there's the mold, of which I grab a handful. I measure out the perfect size.

"You ever seen one up close?" Spitzer asks.
The four of us are north of Tycho, cutting mold squares and tossing them into the grill box. With the base radio still dead, we've had to break out the two-way walkie-talkies in our emergency kits. Thankfully, with a week to go, this is our last harvest load.
"I've seen pictures," says Tamsen.
"The Megafaun Wars," Spitzer says between strokes. "Sounds so far away."
"One kissed me on the nose before I chopped it off." I'll believe a butcher on this.
I keep cleaving into the mold. Every fifth chop I wipe down the bladeface.
"Murph?"
I throw down my cleaver and I take up two baling hooks and I lift the mold square with a heavy grunt.
"He's seen them all right," says Vinegar Tom as he wipes off his own cleaver. "Old Murph had them over for breakfast one morning." I picture his bucked-tooth grin in the darkness of his helmet. "Thing was, those Megafauns didn't like his wife's cooking. They sent it back; they wanted something fresh, something—"
The mold square in my grip doesn't hit the ground before I'm already lunging for the bastard, ready to broil him in the grill box. As my head bangs into his chest, we both lose our footing. We hit the mold in a slow freefall—me punching his kidneys with the T-hook handles and him beating down on my back with the cleaver's butt. Our suits are so thick we can't really feel it, but it feels good to punch what's soft and alive. Tamsen and Spitzer shout. Vinegar Tom slams my helmet with his and I pin his arms down in a bearhug. Then something tackles the both of us. We go rolling. Deeper into the mold, we punch and roll until we can't anymore. Now all I can see is Tom's name patch and all I can feel is something moving underneath us, then not. Tamsen keeps shouting.

• • •

We bury Spitzer in his suit. It was strange how we hadn't even heard him gasp when the T-hook cracked his helmet. It only took seconds, I imagine.

I lock myself in my cabin. I flick off my radio. The walls are too close to pace more than four steps. I can't sleep. Don't want to eat. Don't want to be near anybody but the Russian and even that sounds like an ordeal. I sit down at the same old chess game and plan the same old moves. Rd1+, Rd2+, Ne3, Rg2++.

I flip the game board into the air. The pieces scatter. I carve whatever pleasure I can out of stomping and grinding and smashing them until I'm surrounded by a gray haze. At this point I turn off the light, switch on my headlamp, and imagine my body atomizing in space, all everywhere forever.

A knock at my cabin door.

Tamsen: "You want to spore?"

Ten minutes later, I'm calm, cool. Tamsen's yellow eyes glaze over as she sits on the bed opposite me. She cried while we buried Spitzer. I told her over the radio to pull it together, get serious. I'm sure she blames me. But there's no sign of it now. I have to hand it to her, she would make a lovely lady to share a house and a family and a pet with. "Has anyone ever told you . . . " but then I don't know what I'm trying to ask.

"Told me what?"

Rising moments of sheer ecstatic nothing. Then: "Do you know any stories?"

"Only the worst."

"I remember one, that's all."

"Better be a good one."

"*Goodnight comb and goodnight brush.*"

Tamsen sprinkles more spores onto the foil strip. "Weird beginning."

"*Goodnight nobody and goodnight mush.*"

Tamsen burns the spores, inhales, hands it off.

"*Goodnight to the old lady whispering—*" With the next toke, the sinus burn fades into this raincloud drizzle inside my face. It's a slick, puffy kind of high. I can't remember the rest. Instead: "I saw you and Tom."

Tamsen goes into a loud coughing fit.

I shrug a little. "It's fine. We're all leaving soon."

After she recovers, there's this look on her tinted face that says all the things I haven't thought of yet: that she already knows, that she's sorry it happened this way, that if this wasn't the moon and the Earth wasn't dry and the animals down there weren't huge and thirsty, we wouldn't be up here, we wouldn't even be us. I lean over to hand her the foil and lighter, but then I stay close. There is a place, on her jaw, that is still colored a fine peach, a place that I am now kissing, it and only it.

Another knock on the door.

Vinegar Tom comes in, *Desperate Passage* in hand. His skin practically glows. "You don't look so hot," I say, my voice catching on my lips still shaped around the kiss.

He looks from me to Tamsen then back to me. If he had a nose, it would have twitched with suspicion. Instead, there's just a ripple in the folds. He's in shorts and a muscle shirt. "I feel goddamn hot."

Tamsen says, "Lay off the spores then."

I can feel his eyes boring into me. "What are you two doing?" He looks worried.

"I never know," I say. "Whatever we're supposed to be doing."

"Hatching a plan on where to bury me next, no doubt."

"No doubt," Tamsen says. "Debating how to cook you."

"What parts to eat for dessert," I add.

He reaches into his pocket. For a knife, no doubt, or an ice scream scoop. Defending myself is the last thing this tingling body's ready for. Instead, Vinegar Tom throws something small at me. It hits my shoulder and lands in my lap: the black knight. "Left this in Buggy 2," he says, "and we're out of Pepto."

Tamsen tells him there might be some in Buggy 1. He gives her another eyeful, says without looking at me, "Remember, Murph, if it was cheese out there, this'd be a whole different ball game," then leaves without shutting the door.

Tamsen stands quickly, saying she ought to help him.

"Wait."

She does, but the look from before has vanished. Now it's just *yellowyellowyellow* again. Even the spot on her jaw. "I killed Spitzer, didn't I."

"Would I let a killer kiss me?"

"You'd leave one here by himself."

"You're right," she says. "I would."

The day before the transport's arrival, I take another ride toward Tycho. By habit I bring the chessboard and the one knight with me. The moldline's only ten miles from base camp and traveling upward of a mile every twelve hours. More and more I've decided that when the transport comes, I'm not going to get on it.

There'll be the ride back with Tamsen and Tom, them sporing, maybe them trying to fuck one last time in zero-G, the life they'll probably lead together if the vinegar doesn't eat his insides, and then my house in Denver, the hole in my basement, no Ralphie. It's death to stay up here, sure, but no different down there.

At the moldline, before I even climb out of Buggy 2, there's Tchaikovsky. Something about that yellow makes him look exceedingly jolly, one capable of cartoon physics. "Come, come, let finish vhat ve began." I expect him to burst into soap bubbles or grow nine feathery tails.

"Can't. Lost all the pieces."

"But you have not lost your hands, no?"

On our knees, we mold a new set together.

I lose.

Not because I was wrong about mate in eight moves—that's entirely true.

I lost because he had me in seven. Because in the penultimate step, I moved my only knight and opened up the diagonal for his queen to slip in: Qf7++. He knew my plan all along.

I flick over my black king. "Checkmate."

He nods.

"I'm going to stay here."

"Ah, yis, more game."

"No," I say. "When the transport comes, I'm staying." I feel overwhelmingly important.

Tchaikovsky sighs. He plays with one of his pawns. "You have heard Laika, no?"

A little.

"Laika you know is happy pioneer, *big star*." He sweeps his hands over his head. Then he points at the earth. "Real Laika?—she vas stray. Real Laika vas picked off streets of Moscow and put cage. No one vanted zis dog back, not after space. She vas flash in pan, already wodka under ze cake. Real Laika vas meant to die."

"That's terrible." The flatness of my own voice unnerves me. I don't want to talk.

"Is fine. She vas stray, no? Stray is hard life. Space death: very zimple." He starts setting up the board again; I don't have it in me for one more loss. "But it is day 'til launch. Real Laika ready. Ze stray is ready! Then scientist take Laika home. He let Laika play with childs. Scientist say, 'I vanted to do somezing nice for her.' Childs laugh. Laika love."

"So she had a good last day; so what?"

"*Only* good day, Afraham Lincoln. Vithout zis day, she is happy pioneer to beyond. But now she knows." Tchaikovsky twists his finished pieces so they all face forward, face me. "Childs. Toys. Laughs. Laika vants to come back to zis one good day."

The chessboard's empty spaces, Mare Nubium and the sea of yellow mold, the earth above the horizon like a cheap sticker on a tinted window—a man stands practically weightless in all these gravities, remembering only how his daughters once asked him if dogs knew human words.

"It's not a place I want to go back to."

"But it is place," Tchaikovsky says, pushing his king's pawn to e4. "And ze moon—ze moon is not."

I sit down in front of the board. I pick up my black knight. Its slope and eye-notch, this craftsmanship, all are meticulously fine, each one better than the last carving's. Instead of pushing the bishop's pawn forward—c6—in the Sicilian Defense, I swing my knight out first.

Rubbing his hands together like big paws, Tchaikovsky looks pleased with my decision. "You are getting better."

Fade to White

CATHERYNNE M. VALENTE

Fight the Communist Threat in Your Own Backyard!

ZOOM IN *on a bright-eyed Betty in a crisp green dress, maybe pick up the shade of the spinach in the lower left frame. [Note to Art Dept: Good morning, Stone! Try to stay awake through the next meeting, please. I think we can get more patriotic with the dress. Star-Spangled Sweetheart, steamset hair the color of good American corn, that sort of thing. Stick to a red, white, and blue palette.] She's holding up a resplendent head of cabbage the size of a pre-war watermelon. Her bicep bulges as she balances the weight of this New Vegetable, grown in a Victory Brand Capsule Garden. [Note to Art Dept: is cabbage the most healthful vegetable? Carrots really pop, and root vegetables emphasize the safety of Synthasoil generated by Victory Brand Capsules.]*

Betty looks INTO THE CAMERA *and says:* Just because the war is over doesn't mean your Victory Garden has to be! The vigilant wife knows that every garden planted is a munitions plant in the ~~War Fight~~ Struggle Against Communism. Just one Victory Brand Capsule and a dash of fresh Hi-Uranium Mighty Water can provide an average yard's worth of safe, rich, synthetic soil—and the seeds are included! *STOCK FOOTAGE of scientists: beakers, white coats, etc.* Our boys in the lab have developed a wide range of hardy, modern seeds from pre-war heirloom collections to produce the Vegetables of the Future. *[Note to Copy: Do not mention pre-war seedstock.]* Just look at this beautiful New Cabbage. Efficient, bountiful, and only three weeks from planting to table. *[Note to Copy: Again with the cabbage? You know who eats a lot of cabbage, Stone? Russians. Give her a big old zucchini. Long as a man's arm. Have her hold it in her lap so the head rests on her tits.]*

BACK *to Betty, walking through cornstalks like pine trees.* And that's not all. With a little help from your friends at Victory, you can feed your family *and* play an important role in the defense of the nation. *Betty leans down to show us big, leafy plants growing in her Synthasoil. [Note to Casting: make sure we get a busty girl, so we see a little cleavage when she bends over. We're hawking fertility here. Hers, ours.]* Here's a tip: Plant our patented Liberty Spinach at regular intervals. Let your little green helpers go to work leeching useful isotopes and residual radioactivity from rain, groundwater, just about anything! *[Note to Copy: Stone, you can't be serious. Leeching? That sounds dreadful. Reaping. Don't make me do your job for you.]* Turn in your crop at Victory Depots for Harvest Dollars redeemable at a variety of participating local establishments! *[Note to Project Manager: can't we get some soda fountains or something to throw us a few bucks for ad placement here? Missed opportunity! And couldn't we do a regular feature with the "tips" to move other products, make Betty into a trusted household name—but not Betty. Call her something that starts with T, Tammy? Tina? Theresa?]*

Betty smiles. The camera pulls out to show her surrounded by a garden in full bloom and three [Note to Art Dept: Four minimum] kids in overalls carrying baskets of huge, shiny New Vegetables. The sun is coming up behind her. The slogan scrolls up in red, white, and blue type as she says:

A free and fertile tomorrow. Brought to you by Victory.

Fade to white.

The Hydrodynamic Front

More than anything in the world, Martin wanted to be a Husband when he grew up.

Sure, he had longed for other things when he was young and silly—to be a Milkman, a uranium prospector, an astronaut. But his fifteenth birthday was zooming up with alarming speed, and becoming an astronaut now struck him as an impossibly, almost obscenely trivial goal. Martin no longer drew pictures of the moon in his notebooks or begged his mother to order the whiz-bang home enrichment kit from the tantalizing back pages of *Popular Mechanics.* His neat yellow pencils still kept up near-constant flight passes over the pale blue lines of composition books, but what Martin drew now were babies. In cradles and out, girls with bows in their bonnets and boys with rattles shaped like rockets, newborns and toddlers. He drew pictures of little kids running through clean, tall grass, reading books with straw in their mouths, hanging out of trees like rosy-cheeked fruit. He sketched during history, math, civics: twin girls sitting at a table gazing up with big eyes at their Father, who kept his hat on while he carved a holiday Brussels sprout the size of a dog. Triplet boys wrestling on a pristine, uncontaminated beach. In Martin's notebooks, everyone had twins and triplets.

Once, alone in his room at night, he had allowed himself to draw quadruplets. His hand quivered with the richness and wonder of those four perfect graphite faces asleep in their four identical bassinets.

Whenever Martin drew babies they were laughing and smiling. He could not bear the thought of an unhappy child. He had never been one, he was pretty sure. His older brother Henry had. He still cried and shut himself up in Father's workshop for days, which Martin would never do because it was very rude. But then, Henry was born before the war. He probably had a lot to cry about. Still, on the rare occasion that Henry made a cameo appearance in Martin's gallery of joyful babies, he was always grinning. Always holding a son of his own. Martin considered those drawings a kind of sympathetic magic. Make Henry happy—watch his face at dinner and imagine what it would look like if he cracked a joke. Catch him off guard, snorting, which was as close as Henry ever got to laughing, at some pratfall on *The Mr. Griffith Show.* Make Henry happy in a notebook and he'll be happy in real life. Put a baby in his arms and he won't have to go to the Front in the fall.

Once, and only once, Martin had tried this magic on himself. With very careful strokes and the best shading he'd ever managed, he had drawn himself in a beautiful gray suit, with a professional grade shine on his shoes and a strong angle to his hat. He drew a briefcase in his own hand. He tried to imagine what his face would look like when it filled out, got square-jawed and handsome the way a man's face should be. How he would style his hair when he became a Husband. Whether he would grow a beard. Painstakingly, he drew a double Windsor knot in his future tie, which Martin considered the most masculine and elite knot.

And finally, barely able to breathe with longing, he outlined the long, gorgeous arc of a baby's carriage, the graceful fall of a lace curtain so that the pencilled child wouldn't get sunburned, big wheels capable of a smoothness that bordered on the ineffable. He put the carriage-handle into his own firm hand. It took Martin two hours to turn himself into a Husband. When the spell was finished, he spritzed the drawing with some of his mother's hairspray so that it wouldn't smudge and folded it up flat and small. He kept it in his shirt pocket. Some days, he could feel the drawing move with his heart. And when Father hugged him, the paper would crinkle pleasantly between them, like a whispered promise.

Static Overpressure

The day of Sylvie's Presentation broke with a dawn beyond red, beyond blood or fire. She lay in her spotless white and narrow bed, quite awake, gazing at the colors through her Sentinel Gamma Glass window—lower rates of corneal and cellular damage than their leading competitors, guaranteed. Today, the sky could only remind Sylvie of birth. The screaming scarlet folds of clouds, the sun's crowning head. Sylvie knew it was the hot ash that made every sunrise and sunset into a torture of magenta and violet and crimson, the superheated cloud vapor that never cooled. She winced as though red could hurt her—which of course it could. Everything could.

Sylvie had devoted a considerable amount of time to imagining how this day would go. She did not worry and she was not afraid, but it had always sat there in her future, unmovable, a mountain she could not get through or around. There would be tests, for intelligence, for loyalty, for genetic defects, for temperament, for fertility, which wasn't usually a problem for women but better safe than sorry. Better safe than assign a Husband to a woman as barren as California. There would be a medical examination so invasive it came all the way around to no big deal. When a doctor can get that far inside you, into your blood, your chromosomes, your potentiality and all your possible futures, what difference could her white gloved fingers on your cervix make?

None of that pricked up her concern. The tests were nothing. Sylvie prided herself on being realistic about her qualities. First among these was her intellect; like her mother Hannah she could cut glass with the diamond of her mind. Second was her silence. Sylvie had discovered when she was quite small that adults were discomfited by silence. It brought them running. And when she was angry, upset, when the world offended her, Sylvie could draw down a coil of silence all around her, showing no feeling at all, until whoever had affronted her grew so uncomfortable that they would beg forgiveness just to end the ordeal. There was no third, not really. She was what her mother's friends called striking, but never pretty. Narrow frame, small breasts, short and dark. Nothing in her matched up with the fashionable Midwestern fertility goddess floor-model. And she heard what they did not say, also—that she was not pretty because there was something off in her features, a ghost in her cheekbones, her height, her straight, flat hair.

Sylvie gave up on the fantasy of sliding back into sleep. She flicked on the radio by her bed: *Brylcreem Makes a Man a Husband!* announced a tinny woman's voice, followed by a cheerful blare of brass and the morning's reading from the Book of Pseudo-Matthew. Sylvie preferred Luke. She opened her closet as though today's clothes had not been chosen for years, hanging on the wooden rod behind all the others, waiting for her to grow into them. She pulled out the dress and draped it over her bed. It lay there like another girl. Someone who looked just like her but had already moved through the hours of the day and come out on the other side. The red sky turned the deep neckline into a gash.

She was not ready for it yet.

Sylvie washed her body with the milled soap provided by Spotless Corp. Bright as a pearl, wrapped in white muslin and a golden ribbon. It smelled strongly of rose and mint and underneath, a blue chemical tang. The friendly folks at Spotless also supplied hair rinse, cold cream, and talcum for her special day. All the bottles and cakes smelled like that, like growing things piled on top of something biting, corrosive. The basket had arrived last month with a bow and a dainty card attached congratulating her. Until now it had loomed in her room like a Christmas tree, counting down. Now Sylvie pulled the regimented colors and fragrances out and applied them precisely, correctly, according to directions. An oyster-pink shade called *The Blossoming of the Rod* on her fingernails, which may not be cut short. A soft peach called *Penance* on her eyes, which may not be lined. Pressed powder (*The Visitation of the Dove*) should be liberally applied, but only the merest breath of blush (*Parable of the Good Harlot*) is permitted. Sylvie pressed a rosy champagne stain (*Armistice*) onto her lips with a forefinger. Hair must be natural and worn long—no steamsetting or straightening allowed. Everyone broke that rule, though. Who could tell a natural curl from a roller these days? Sylvie combed her black hair out and clipped it back with the flowers assigned to her county this year—snowdrops for hope and consolation. Great bright thornless roses as red as the sky for love at first sight, for passion and lust.

Finally the dress. The team at Spotless Corp. encouraged foundational garments to emphasize the bust and waist-to-hip ratio. Sylvie wedged herself into a full length merry widow with built-in padded bra and rear. It crushed her, smoothed her, flattened her. Her waist disappeared. She pulled the dress over her bound-in body. Her mother would have to button her up; twenty-seven tiny, satin colored buttons ran up her back like a new spine. Its neckline plunged; its skirt flounced, showing calf and a suggestion of knee. It was miles of icy white lace, it could hardly be anything else, but the sash gleamed red. Red, red, red. *All the world is red and I am red forever,* Sylvie thought. She was inside the dress, inside the other girl.

The other girl was very striking.

Sylvie was fifteen years old, and by suppertime she would be engaged.

Even Honest Joe Loves an Ice-Cold Brotherhood Beer!

CLOSE-UP on President McCarthy in shirtsleeves, popping the top on a distinctive green glass bottle of BB—now with improved flavor and more potent additives! We see the moisture glisten on the glass and an honest day's sweat on the President's brow. [Note to Art Dept: I see what you're aiming at, but let's not make him look like a clammy swamp creature, shall we? He's not exactly the most photogenic gent to begin with.]

NEW SHOT: Five Brothers relaxing together in the sun with a tin bucket full of ice and green bottlenecks. Labels prominently displayed. A Milkman, a TV Repairman, a couple of G-Men, and a soldier. [Note to Casting: Better make it one government jockey and two soldiers. Statistically speaking, more of them are soldiers than anything else.] They are smiling, happy, enjoying each others' company. The soldier, a nice-looking guy but not too nice-looking, we don't want to send the wrong message, says: There's nothing like a fresh swig of Brother-hood after spending a hot Nevada day eye to eye with a Russkie border guard. The secret is in the thorium-boosted hops and New Barley fresh from Alaska, crisp iodine-treated spring water and just a dash of good old fashioned pa-triotism. *The Milkman chimes in with:* And 5-Alpha! *They all laugh. [Note to Copy: PLEASE use the brand name! We've had meetings about this! Chemicals sound scary. Who wants to put some freakshow in your body when you can take a nice sip of Arcadia? Plus those bastards at Standard Ales are calling their formula Kool and their sales are up 15%. You cannot beat that number, Stone.]* *TV Repairman pipes up:* That's right, Bob! There's no better way to get your daily dose than with the cool, refreshing taste of Brotherhood. They use only the latest formulas: smooth, mellow, and with no jitters or lethargy. *G-Man pulls a bottle from the ice and takes a good swallow.* 5-Alpha leaves my head clear and my spirits high. I can work all day serving our great nation without distraction, aggression, or unwanted thoughts. *Second G-Man:* I'm a patriot. I don't need all those obsolete hormones anymore. And Brotherhood Beer strikes a great bargain—all that and 5.6% alcohol! *Our soldier stands up and salutes. He wears an expression of steely determination and rugged cheer. He says:* Well, boys, I've got an appointment with Ivan to keep. Keep the Brother-hood on ice for me.

QUICK CUT back to President McCarthy. He puts down his empty bottle and picks up a file or something in the Oval Office. Slogan comes in at hip level [Note to Art Dept: how are we coming on that wheatstalk font?]:

Where There's Life, There's Brotherhood.

Fade to white.

Optimum Burst Altitude

One week out of every four, Martin's Father came home. Martin could feel the week coming all month like a slow tide. He knew the day, the hour. He sat by the window tying and untying double Windsor knots into an old silk tie Dad had let him keep years ago. The tie was emerald green with little red chevrons on it.

Cross, fold, push through. Wrap, fold, fold, over the top, fold, fold, pull down. Make it tight. Make it perfect.

When the Cadillac pulled into the drive, Martin jumped for the gin and the slippers like a golden retriever. His Father's martini was a ritual, a eucharist. Ice, gin, swirl in the shaker, just enough so that the outer layer of ice releases into the alcohol. Open the vermouth, bow in the direction of the Front, and close it again. Two olives, not three, and a glass from the freezebox. These were the sacred objects of a Husband. Tie, Cadillac, martini. And then Dad would open the door and Faraday, the Irish setter, would yelp with waggy happiness and so would Martin. He'd be wearing a soft grey suit. He'd put his hat on the rack. Martin's mother, Rosemary, would stand on her tiptoes to kiss him in one of her good dresses, the lavender one with daises on the hem, or if it was a holiday, her sapphire-colored velvet. Her warm blonde hair would be perfectly set, and her lips would leave a gleaming red kiss-shape on his cheek. Dad wouldn't wipe it off. He'd greet his son with a firm handshake that told Martin all he needed to know: he was a man, his martini was good, his knots were strong.

Henry would slam the door to his bedroom upstairs and refuse to come down to supper. This pained Martin; the loud bang scuffed his heart. But he tried to understand his brother—after all, a Husband must possess great wells of understanding and compassion. Dad wasn't Henry's father. Pretending that he was probably scuffed something inside the elder boy, too.

The profound and comforting sameness of those Husbanded weeks overwhelmed Martin's senses like the slightly greasy swirls of gin in that lovely triangular glass. The first night, they would have a roasting chicken with crackling golden skin. Rosemary had volunteered to raise several closely observed generations of an experimental breed called Sacramento Clouds: vicious, bright orange and oversized, dosed with palladium every fortnight, their eggs covered in rough calcium deposits like lichen. For this reason they could have a whole bird once a month. The rest of the week were New Vegetables from the Capsule Garden. Carrots, tomatoes, sprouts, potatoes, kale. Corn if it was fall and there hadn't been too many high-level days when no one could go out and tend the plants. But there was always that one delicious day when Father was at home and they had chicken.

After dinner, they would retire to the living room. Mom and Dad would have sherry and Martin would have a Springs Eternal Vita-Pop if he had been very good, which he always was. He liked the lime flavor best. They would watch *My Five Sons* for half an hour before Rosemary's Husband retired with her to bed. Martin didn't mind that. It was what Husbands were for. He liked to listen to the sounds of their lovemaking through the wall between their rooms. They were reassuring and good. They put him to sleep like a lullaby about better times.

And one week out of every four, Martin would ask his Father to take him to the city.

"I want to see where you work!"

"This is where I work, son," Father would always say in his rough-soft voice. "Right here."

Martin would frown and Dad would hold him tight. Husbands were not afraid of affection. They had bags of it to share. "I'll tell you what, Marty, if your Announcement goes by without a hitch, I'll take you to the city myself.

March you right into the Office and show everyone what a fine boy Rosie and I made. Might even let you puff on a cigar."

And Martin would hug his Father fiercely, and Rosemary would smile over her fiber-optic knitting, and Henry would kick something upstairs. It was regular as a clock, and the clock was always right. Martin knew he'd be Announced, no problem. Piece of cake. Mom was super careful with the levels on their property. They planted Liberty Spinach. Martin was first under his desk every time the siren went off at school. After Henry's Announcement had gone so badly, he and Mom had installed a Friendlee Brand Geiger Unit every fifteen feet and the light-up aw-shucks faces had only turned into frowns and x-eyes a few times ever. There was no chance Martin could fail. Things were way better now. Not like when Henry was a kid. No, Martin would be Announced and he'd go to the city and smoke his cigar. He'd be ready. He'd be the best Husband anyone ever met.

Aaron Grudzinski liked to tell him it was all shit. That was, in fact, Aaron's favorite observation on nearly anything. Martin liked the way he swore, gutturally, like it really meant something. Grud was in Martin's year. He smoked Canadian cigarettes and nipped some kind of homebrewed liquor from his gray plastic thermos. He'd egged Martin into a sip once. It tasted like dirt on fire.

"Look, didn't you ever wonder why they wait til you're fifteen to do it? Obviously they can test you anytime after you pop your first boner. As soon as you're brewing your own, yeah?" And Grud would shake his flask. "But no, they make this huge deal out of going down to Matthew House and squirting in a cup. The outfit, the banquet, the music, the filmstrips. It's all shit. Shit piled up into a pretty castle around a room where they give you a magazine full of the wholesome housewives of 1940 and tell you to do it for America. And you look down at the puddle at the bottom of the plastic tumbler they call your chalice, your chalice with milliliter measurements printed on the side, and you think: *That's all I am. Two to six milliliters of warm wet nothing.*" Grud spat a brown tobacco glob onto the dead grass of the baseball field. He knuckled at his eye, his voice getting raw. "Don't you get it? They have to give you hope. Well, I mean, they have to give *you* hope. I'm a lost cause. Three strikes before I got to bat. But you? They gotta build you up, like how everyone salutes Sgt. Dickhead on leave from the glowing shithole that is the great state of Arizona. If they didn't shake his hand and kiss his feet, he might start thinking it's not worth melting his face off down by the Glass. If you didn't think you could make it, you'd just kill yourself as soon as you could read the newspaper."

"I wouldn't," Martin whispered.

"Well, I would."

"But Grud, there's so few of us left."

The school siren klaxoned. Martin bolted inside, sliding into the safe space under his desk like he was stealing home.

The Shadow Effect

Every Sunday Sylvie brought a couple of Vita-Pops out to the garage and set up her film projector in the hot dark. Her mother went to her Ladies' Auxiliary meeting from two to four o'clock. Sylvie swiped hors d'oeuvres and cookies from the official spread and waited in the shadows for Clark Baker to shake his mother and slip in the side door. The film projector had been a gift from her Father; the strips were Clark's, whose shutterbug brothers and uncles were all pulling time at the Front. Every Sunday they sat together and watched the light flicker and snap over a big white sheet nailed up over the shelves of soil-treatment equipment and Friendlee Brand gadgets stripped for parts. Every Sunday like church.

Clark was tall and shy, obsessed with cameras no less than any of his brothers. He wore striped shirts all the time, as if solid colors had never been invented. He kept reading Salinger even after the guy defected. Sometimes they held hands while they watched the movies. Mostly they didn't. It was bad enough that they were fraternizing at all. Clark already drinking Kool Koffee every morning. Sugar, no cream. Clark was a quiet, bookish black boy who would be sent to the Front within a year.

On the white sheet, they watched California melt.

It hadn't happened during the war. The Glass came after. This thing everyone did now was not called war. It was something else. Something that liquefied the earth out west and turned it into the Sea of Glass. On the sheet it looked like molten silver, rising and falling in something like waves. Turning the Grand Canyon into a soft grey whirlpool. Sylvie thought it was beautiful. Like something on the moon. In real life it had colors, and Sylvie dreamed of them. Red stone dissolving into an endless expanse of dark glass.

"There are more Japanese people in Utah than in Japan now," Clark whispered when the filmstrip rolled up into black and the filmmaker's logo. Sylvie flinched as if he'd cut her.

They didn't talk about her Presentation. It sat whitely, fatly in their future. Once Clark kissed her. Sylvie cried afterward.

"I'll write you," he said. "As long as I can write."

The growth index for their county was very healthy, and this was another reason Clark Baker should not have been holding her hand in the dark while men in ghostly astronaut suits probed the edges of the Glass on a clicking filmstrip. Every woman on the block had a new baby this year. They'd gotten a medal of achievement from President McCarthy in the spring. The Ladies' Auxiliary graciously accepted the key to the city. She suspected her Father had a great deal to do with this. When she was little, he had come home one week in four. Now it was three days in thirty. His department kept him working hard. He'd be there for her Presentation, though. No Father missed his daughter's debut.

Sylvie thought about Clark while her mother slipped satin-covered buttons through tiny loops. Their faces doubled in the mirror. His dark brown hand on hers. The Sea of Glass turning their faces silver.

"Mom," Sylvie said. Her voice was very soft in the morning, as if she was afraid to wake herself up. "What if I don't love my Husband? Isn't that . . . something important?"

Hannah sighed. Her mouth took a hard angle. "You're young, darling. You don't understand. What it was like before. We had to have them here all the time, every night. Never a moment when I wasn't working my knees through for my husband. The one before your Father. The children before you. Do you think we got to choose then? It wasn't about love. For some people, they could afford that. For me, well, my parents thought he was a very nice man. He had good prospects. I needed him. I could not work. I was a woman before the war, who would hire me? And to do what? Type or teach. Not to program punchcard machines. Not to cross-breed new strains of broccoli. Nothing that would occupy my mind. So I drowned my mind in children and in him and when the war came I was glad. He left and it was *me* going to work every morning, *me* deciding what happened to my money. So the war took them," she waved her hand in front of her eyes, "war always does that. I know you don't think so, but the program is the best part of a bad situation. A situation maybe so bad we cannot fix it. So you don't love him. Why would you look for love with a man? How could a man ever understand you? He who gets the cake cannot be friends with the girl who gets the crumbs." Sylvie's mother blushed. She whispered: "My Rita, you know, Rita who comes for tea and bridge and neptunium testing. She is good to me. Someone will be good to you. You will have your Auxiliary, your work, your children. One week in four a man will tell you what to do—but listen to me when I say they have much better manners than they used to. They say please now. They are interested in your life. They are so good with the babies." Hannah smoothed the lacy back of her daughter's Presentation gown. "Someday, my girl, either we will all die out and nothing will be left, or things will go back to the old ways and you will have men taking your body and soul apart to label the parts that belong to them. Enjoy this world. Either way, it will be brief."

Sylvie turned her painted, perfected face to her mother's. "Mom," she whispered. Sylvie had practiced. Listened to the makeshift radio spitting half-garbled broadcasts from the other side of the world. A dictionary Clark found at a transfer station. Her mother. Whispering while she slept. Practiced until her lips hurt. So much, so often. She ordered the words in her head like dolls, hoped they were the right ones. Hoped they could stand up straight. "Watashi wa anata o shinjite ī nā." *I wish I could believe you.*

Hannah's dark eyes flew wide and, without a moment's hesitation, she slapped her daughter across the cheek. It wasn't hard, not meant to wound, certainly not to leave a mark on this day of all days, but it stung. Sylvie's eyes watered.

"Nidoto," her mother pleaded. "Never, *never* again."

Gimbels: Your Official Father's Day Headquarters!

PANORAMA SHOT of the Gimbels flagship store with two cute kiddos front and center. [Note to Casting: get us a boy and a girl, blonde, white, under ten, make sure the boy is taller than the girl. Put them in sailor suits, everyone likes that.] The kids wave at the camera. Little Linda Sue speaks up. [Note to Copy: Nope. The boy speaks first.] It's a beautiful June here in New York City, the greatest city on earth! *Jimmy throws his hands in the air and yells out:* And that means FATHER'S DAY! *Scene shift, kiddos are walking down a Gimbels aisle. We see toolboxes, ties, watches in a glass case, barbecue sets. Linda Sue picks up a watch and listens to it tick. Jimmy grabs a barbecue scraper and brandishes it. He says:* Come on down with your Mom and make an afternoon of it at the Brand New Gimbels Automat! Hot, pre-screened food in an instant! Gee wow! *[Note to Copy: hey, Stone, this is a government sponsored ad. If Gimbels want to hawk their shitty Manhattan Meals they're going to have to actually pay for it. Have you ever tried one of those things? Tastes like a kick in the teeth.] Linda Sue:* At Gimbels they have all the approved Father's Day products. *(Kids alternate lines)* Mr. Fix-It! Businessman! Coach! Backyard Cowboy! *Mr. Gimbel appears and selects a beautiful tie from the spring Priapus line. He hands it to Linda Sue and ruffles her hair. Mr Gimbel:* Now, kids, don't forget to register your gift with the Ladies' Auxiliary. We wouldn't want *your* Daddy to get two of the same gift! How embarrassing! That's why Gimbels carries the complete Whole Father line, right next to the registration desk so your Father's Day is a perfect one. *Kids:* Thanks, Mr. Gimbel!

Mr. Gimbel spreads his arms wide and type stretches out between them in this year's Father's Day colors. [Note to Art Dept: It's seashell and buttercup this year, right? Please see Marketing concerning the Color Campaign. Pink and blue are pre-war. We're working with Gimbels to establish a White for Boys, Green for Girls tradition.]

Gimbels: Your One-Stop Shop for a One-of-a-Kind Dad.

Fade to white.

Flash Blindness

Martin wore the emerald green chevroned tie to his Announcement, even if it wasn't strictly within the dress code. Everything else was right down the line: light grey suit, shaved clean if shaving was on the menu, a dab of musky *Oil of Fecunditas* behind each ear from your friends at Spotless Corp. Black shoes, black socks, Spotless lavender talcum, teeth brushed three times with Pure Spearmint Toothpaste (*You're Sure with Spearmint!*). And his Father holding his hand, beaming with pride. Looking handsome and young as he always did.

Of course, there was another boy holding his other hand.

His name was Thomas. He had broad shoulders already, chocolate-colored hair and cool slate eyes that made him look terribly romantic. Martin tried not to let it bother him. He knew how the program worked. Where the other three weeks of the month took his Father. Obviously, there were other children, other wives, other homes. Other roasting chickens, other martinis. Other evening television shows on other channels. And that's all Thomas was: another channel. When you weren't watching a show, it just ceased to be. Clicked off. Fade to white. You couldn't be jealous of the people on those other channels. They had their own troubles and adventures, engrossing mysteries and stunning conclusions, cliffhangers and tune-in-next-weeks. It had nothing to do with Martin, or Rosemary, or Henry in his room. That was what it meant to be a Husband.

The three of them sat together in the backseat of the sleek gray Cadillac. An older lady drove them. She wore a smart cap and had wiry white hair, but her cheeks were still pink and round. Martin tried to look at her as a Husband would, even though a woman her age would never marry. After all, Husbands didn't get to choose. Martin's future wives—four to start with, that was standard, but if he did well, who knew?—wouldn't all be bombshells in pin-up bathing suits. He had to practice looking at women, really seeing them, seeing what was good and true and gorgeous in them. The chauffeur had wonderful laugh lines around her eyes. Martin could tell they were laugh lines. And her eyes, when she looked in the rear view mirror, were a nice, cool green. She radioed to the dispatcher and her voice lilted along with a faint twinge of English accent. Martin could imagine her laughing with him, picking New Kale and telling jokes about the King. He imagined her naked, laying on a soft pink bed, soft like her pink cheeks. Her body would be the best kind of body: the kind that had borne children. Breasts that had nursed. Legs that had run after misbehaving little ones. He could love that body. The sudden hardness between his legs held no threat, only infinite love and acceptance, a Husband's love.

When I think about how good I could be, my heart stops, Martin thought as the space between his neighborhood and the city smeared by. The sun seared white through dead black trees. But somewhere deep in them there was a green wick. Martin knew it. He had a green wick, too. *I will remember every date. Every wife will be so special and I will love her and our children. I will make her martinis. I will roast the chicken so she doesn't have to. When I am with one of them I will turn off all other channels in my mind. I can keep it straight and separate. I will study so hard, so that I know how to please. It will be my only vocation, to be devoted. And if they, the women of Elm St or Oak Lane or Birch Drive find love with each other when I am gone, I will be happy for them because there is never enough love. I will draw them happy and they will be happy. The world will be green again. Everything will be okay.*

It all seemed to happen very fast. Thomas and Martin and a dozen other boys listened to a quintet play Mendelssohn. The mayor gave a speech. They watched a recorded message from President McCarthy which had to be pretty old because he still sported a good head of hair. Finally, a minister stood up with a lovely New Tabernacle Bible in her one good hand. The other was shriveled, boneless, a black claw in her green vestments. The pages of the Bible shone with gilt. A ribbonmark hung down and it was very red in the afternoon flares. She did not lay it on a lectern. She carried the weight in her hands and read from the Gospel of Pseudo-Matthew, which Martin already knew by heart. The minister's maple-syrup contralto filled the vaults of Matthew House.

"And when Mary had come to her fourteenth year, the high priest announced to all that the virgins who were reared in the Temple and who had reached the age of their womanhood should return to their own and be given in lawful marriage. When the High Priest went in to take counsel with God, a voice came forth from the oratory for all to hear, and it said that of all of the marriageable men of the House of David who had not yet taken a wife, each should bring a rod and lay it upon the altar, that one of the rods would burst into flower and upon it the Holy Ghost would come to rest in the form of a Dove, and that he to whom this rod belonged would be the one to whom the virgin Mary should be espoused. Joseph was among the men who came, and he placed his rod upon the altar, and straightaway it burst into bloom and a Dove came from Heaven and perched upon it, whereby it was manifest to all that Mary should become the wife of Joseph."

Martin's eyes filled with tears. He felt a terrible light in his chest. For a moment he was sure everyone else would see it streaming out of him. But no, the minister gave him a white silk purse and directed him to a booth with a white velvet curtain. Inside, silence. Dim, dusty light. Martin opened the purse and pulled out the chalice—a plastic cup with measurements printed on it, just like Grud said. With it lay a few old photographs—women from before the war, with so much health in their faces Martin could hardly bear to look at them. Their skin was so clear. *She's dead,* he thought. *Statistically speaking, that woman with the black hair and heart-shaped face and polka-dotted bikini is dead. Vaporized in Seattle or Phoenix or Los Angeles. That was where they used to make pictures, in Los Angeles. This girl is dead.*

Martin couldn't do it. This was about life. Everything, no matter how hard and strange, was toward life. He could not use a dead girl that way. Instead, he shut his eyes. He made his pictures, quick pencil lines glowing inside him. The chauffeur with her pink cheeks and white hair. The minister with her kind voice and brown eyes and her shriveled hand, which was awful, but wasn't she alive and good? Tammy, the girl from the Victory Brand Capsule Garden commercials in her star-spangled dress. A girl with red hair who lived two blocks over and was so pretty that looking at her was like getting punched in the chest. He drew in bold, bright lines the home he was going to make, bigger than himself, bigger than the war, as big as the world.

Martin's body convulsed with the tiny, private detonation of his soul. His vision blurred into a hot colorless flash.

Blast Wind

Sylvie's mother helped her into long white gloves. They sat together in a long pearl-colored Packard and did not speak. Sylvie had nothing to say. Let her mother be uncomfortable. A visceral purple sunset colored the western sky, even at two in the afternoon. Sylvie played the test in her head like a filmstrip. When it actually started happening to her, it felt no more real than a picture on a sheet.

The mayor gave a speech. They watched a recorded message from President McCarthy's pre-war daughter Tierney, a pioneer in the program, one of the first to volunteer. *Our numbers have been depleted by the Germans, the Japanese, and now the Godless Russians. Of the American men still living, only 12% are fertile. But we are not Communists. We cannot become profligate, wasteful, decadent. We must maintain our moral way of life. As little as possible should change from the world your mothers knew—at least on the surface. And with time, what appears on the surface will penetrate to the core, and all will be restored. We will not sacrifice our way of life.*

A minister with a withered arm read that Pseudo-Matthew passage Tierney had dredged up out of apocrypha to the apocrypha, about the rods and the flowers, and Sylvie had never felt it was one of the Gospel's more subtle moments. The minister blessed them. They are flowers. They are waiting for the Dove.

The doctors were women. One was Mrs. Drexler, who lived on their cul-de-sac and always made rum balls for the neighborhood Christmas cookie exchange. She was kind. She warmed up her fingers before she examined Sylvie. *White gloves for her, white gloves for me,* Sylvie thought, and suppressed a giggle. She turned her head to one side and focused on a stained-glass lamp with kingfishers on it, piercing their frosted breasts with their beaks. She went somewhere else in her mind until it was over. Not a happy place, just a place. Somewhere precise and clean without any Spotless Corp. products where Sylvie could test soil samples methodically. Rows of black vials, each labeled, dated, sealed.

They took her blood. A butterfly of panic fluttered in her—will they know? Would the test show her mother, practicing her English until her accent came out clean as acid paper? Running from a red Utah sky even though there was no one left to shoot at her? Only half enemy, half threat, born in San Francisco before the war, white enough to pass. A woman who spent her life curling her hair like it would save her. Lining her eyes so heavy, so they would look like magazine eyes. Sylvie shut her own unlined eyes. She said her mother's name three times in her mind. The secret, talismanic thing that only they together knew. *Hidaka Hanako. Hidaka Hanako. Hidaka Hanako. Don't be silly. Japan isn't a virus they can see wiggling in your cells. Mom's documents are flawless. No alarm will go off in the centrifuge.*

And none did.

She whizzed through the intelligence exams—what a joke. *Calculate the drag energy of the blast wind given the following variables.* Please. Other girls milled around her in their identical lace dresses. The flowers in their hair were different. Their sashes all red. Red on white, like first aid kits floating through her peripheral vision. They went from medical to placement testing to screening. They nodded shyly to each other. In five years, Sylvie would know all their names. They would be her Auxiliary. They would play bridge. They would plan block parties. They would have telephone trees. Some of them would share a Husband with her, but she would never know which. That was what let the whole civilized fiction roll along. You never knew, you never asked. Men had a different surname every week. Only the Mrs. Drexlers of the neighborhood knew it all, the knots and snags of the vital genetics. Would she share with the frosted blonde who loved botany or the redheaded math genius who made her own cheese? Or maybe none of them. It all depended on the test. Some of these girls would score low in their academics or have some unexpressed, unpredictable trait revealed in the great forking family trees pruned by Mrs. Drexler and the rest of them. They would get Husbands in overalls, with limited allowances. They would live in houses with old paint and lead shielding instead of Gamma Glass. Some of them would knock their Presentation out of the park. They'd get Husbands in grey suits and silk ties, who went to offices in the city during the day, who gave them compression chamber diamonds for their birthdays. As little as possible should change.

Results were quick these days. Every year faster. But not so quick that they did not have luncheon provided while the experts performed their tabulations. Chicken salad sandwiches—how the skinny ones gasped at the taste of mayonnaise! Assam tea, watercress, lemon curd and biscuits. An impossible fairy feast.

"I hope I get a Businessman," said the girl sitting next to Sylvie. Her bouffant glittered with illegal setting spray. "I couldn't bear it if I had to live on Daisy Drive."

"Who cares?" said Sylvie, and shoved a whole chicken salad triangle into her mouth. She shouldn't have said anything. Her silence bent for one second and out comes nonsense that would get her noticed. Would get her remembered.

"Well, *I* care, you *cow*," snapped Bouffant. Her friends smiled behind their hands, concealing their teeth. *In primates, baring the teeth is a sign of aggression,*

Sylvie thought idly. She flashed them a broad, cold smile. *All thirty-two, girls, drink it in.*

"I think it's clear what room *you'll* be spending the evening in," Bouffant sneered, oblivious to Sylvie's primate signals.

But Sylvie couldn't stop. "At best, you'll spend 25% of your time with him. You'll get your rations the same as everyone. You'll get your vouchers for participating in the program and access to top make-work contracts. What difference does it make who you snag? You know this is just pretend, right? A very big, very lush, very elaborate dog-breeding program."

Bouffant narrowed her eyes. Her lips went utterly pale. "I hope you turn out to be barren as a rock. Just *rotted away inside*," she hissed. The group of them stood up in a huff and took their tea to another table. Sylvie shrugged and ate her biscuit. "Well, that's no way to think if you want to restore America," she said to no one at all. What was the matter with her? *Shut up, Sylvie.*

Mrs. Drexler put a warm hand on her shoulder, materializing out of nowhere. The doctor who loved rum balls laid a round green chip on the white tablecloth. Bouffant saw it across the room and glared hard enough to put a hole through her skull at forty yards.

Sylvie was fertile. At least, there was nothing obviously wrong with her. She turned the chip over. The other side was red. Highest marks. *Blood and leaves. Red on white. The world is red and I am red forever.* One of Bouffant's friends was holding a black chip and crying, deep and horrible. Sylvie floated. Unreal. It wasn't real. It was ridiculous. It was a filmstrip. A recording made years ago when Brussels sprouts were small and the sunset could be rosy and gentle.

FADE IN on Mrs. Drexler in a dance hall with a white-on-white checkerboard floor. She's wearing a sequin torchsinger dress. Bright pink. She pumps a giant star-spangled speculum like a parade-master's baton. Well, hello there Sylvie! It's your big day! Should I say Hidaka Sakiko? I only want you to be comfortable, dear. Let's see what you've won!

Sylvie and the other green-chip girls were directed into another room whose walls were swathed in green velvet curtains. A number of men stood lined up against the wall, chatting nervously among themselves. Each had a cedar rod in one hand. They held the rods awkwardly, like old men's canes. A piano player laid down a slow foxtrot for them. Champagne was served. A tall boy with slightly burned skin, a shiny pattern of pink across his cheek, takes her hand, first in line. In Sylvie's head, the filmstrip zings along.

WIDE SHOT of Mrs. Drexler yanking on a rope-pull curtain. She announces: Behind Door Number One we have Charles Patterson, six foot one, Welsh/ Danish stock, blond/blue, scoring high in both logic and empathy, average sperm count nineteen million per milliliter! This hot little number has a reserved parking spot at the Office! Of course, when I say "Office," I mean the upper gentlemen's club, brandy and ferns on the 35th floor, cigars and fraternity and polished teak walls. A little clan to help each other through the challenges of life in the program—only another Husband can really understand. Our productive heartthrobs are too valuable to work! Stress has been shown to lower semen quality, Sylvie! But as little as possible should change. If you take the Office from a man, you'll take his spirit. And what's behind Door Number Two?

Sylvie shuts her eyes. The real Mrs. Drexler was biting into a sugar cookie and sipping her champagne. She opened them again—and a stocky kind-eyed boy had already cut in for the next song. He wore an apple blossom in his lapel. For everlasting love, Broome County's official flower for the year. The dancing Mrs. Drexler in her mind hooted with delight, twirling her speculum.

TIGHT SHOT of Door Number Two. Mrs Drexler snaps her fingers and cries: Why, it's Douglas Owens! Five foot ten, Irish/Italian, that's *very* exciting! Brown/brown, scoring aces in creative play and nurturing, average sperm count twenty-five million per milliliter—oh *ho!* Big, strapping boy! *Mrs. Drexler slaps him lightly on the behind. Her eyes gleam.* He's a Businessman as well, nothing but the best for our Sylvie, our prime stock Sylvie/Sakiko! He'll take his briefcase every day and go sit in his club with the other Husbands, and maybe he loves you and maybe he finds real love with them the way you'll find it with your friend Bouffant in about two years. Who can tell? It's so *thrilling* to speculate! It's not like men and women got along so well before, anyway. Take my wife, please! Why I oughtta! To hell with the whole mess. Give it one week a month. You do unpleasant things one week out of four and don't think twice. Who cares?

Someone handed her a glass of champagne. Sylvie wrapped her real, solid fingers around it. She felt dizzy. A new boy had taken up her hand and put his palm around her waist. The dance quickened. Still a foxtrot, but one with life in it. She looked at the wheel and spin of faces—white faces, wide, floor-model faces. Sylvie looked for Clark. Anywhere, everywhere, his kind face moving among the perfect bodies, his kind face with a silver molten earth undulating across his cheeks, flickering, shuddering. But he wasn't there. He would never be there. It would never be Clark with a cedar rod and a sugar cookie. Black boys didn't get Announced. Not Asians, not refugees, not Sylvie if anyone guessed. They got shipped out. They got a ticket to California. To Utah.

As little as possible should change.

No matter how bad it got, McCarthy and his Brothers just couldn't let a nice white girl (like Sylvie, like Sylvie, like the good floor-model part of Sylvie that fenced in the red, searing thing at the heart of her) get ruined that way. (If they knew, if they knew. Did the conservative-suit warm-glove Mrs. Drexler guess? Did it show in her dancing?) Draw the world the way you want it. Draw it and it will be.

Sylvie tried to focus on the boy she was dancing with. She was supposed to be making a decision, settling, rooting herself forever into this room, the green curtains, the sugar cookies, the foxtrot.

QUICK CUT to Mrs. Drexler. She spins around and claps her hands. She whaps her speculum on the floor three times and a thin kid with chocolate-colored hair and slate eyes sweeps aside his curtain. She crows: But wait, we haven't opened Doooooor Number Three! Hello, Thomas Walker! Six foot even, Swiss/Polish—ooh, practically Russian! How exotic! I smell a match! Brown/gray, top marks across the board, average sperm count a spectacular twenty-nine million per milliliter! You're just showing off, young man! Allow me to shake your hand!

Sylvie jittered back and forth as the filmstrip caught. The champagne settled her stomach. A little. Thomas spun her around shyly as the music flourished. He had a romantic look to him. Lovely chocolate brown hair. He was saying something about being interested in the animal repopulation projects going on in the Plains States. His voice was sweet and a little rough and fine, fine, this one is fine, it doesn't matter, who cares, he'll never sit in a garage with me and watch the bombs fall on the sheet with the hole in the corner. Close your eyes, spin around three times, point at one of them and get it over with.

IRIS TRANSITION to Mrs. Drexler doing a backflip in her sequined dress. She lands in splits. Mr. and Mrs. Wells and Walker invite you to the occasion of their children's wedding!

Sylvie pulled the red, thornless rose and snowdrops from her hair and tied their ribbon around Thomas's rod. She remembered to smile. Thomas himself kissed her, first on the forehead and then on the mouth. A lot of couples seemed to be kissing now. The music had stopped. *It's over, it's over,* Sylvie thought. *Maybe I can still see Clark today. It takes time to plan a wedding.*

Voices buzzed and spiked behind her. Mrs. Drexler was hurrying over; her face was dark.

ZOOM on Mrs. Drexler: Wait, sorry, wait! I'm sorry we seem to have hit a snag! It appears Thomas and Sylvie here are a little too close for comfort. They should never have been paired at the same Announcement. Our fault, entirely! Sylvie's Father has been such a boon to the neighborhood! Doing his part! Unfortunately, the great nation of the United States does not condone incest, so you'll have trade Door Number Three for something a little more your speed. This sort of thing does happen! That's why we keep such excellent records! CROSS-REFERENCING! Thank you! *Mrs. Drexler bows. Roses land at her feet.*

Sylvie shut her eyes. The strip juddered; she was crying tracks through her Spotless Corp. Pressed Powder and it was not a film, it was happening. Mrs. Drexler was wearing a conservative brown suit with a gold dove-shaped pin on the lapel and waving a long-stemmed peony for masculine bravery. Thomas was her brother; somehow, there had been a mix-up and he was her brother and other arrangements would have to be made. The boys and girls in a ballroom with her stared and pointed, paired off safely. Sylvie looked up at Thomas. He stared back, young and sad and confused. The snowdrops and roses had fallen off his rod onto the floor. Red on white. Bouffant was practically climbing over Douglas Owens twenty-five million per milliliter like a tree.

In four years Sylvie will be Mrs. Charles Patterson nineteen million per. It's over and they began to dance. Charles was a swell dancer. He promised to be sweet to her when he got through with training and they were married. He promised to make everything as normal as possible. As little as possible should change. The quintet struck up Mendelssohn.

Sylvie pulled her silence over her and it was good.

Fade to white.

CLOSE-UP *of a nice-looking Bobby, a real lantern-jaw, straight-dealing, chiseled type. [Note to Casting: maybe we should consider VP Kroc for this spot. Hair pomade knows no demographic. Those idiots at Brylcreem want to corner the Paternal market? Fine. Let them have their little slice of the pie. Be a nice bit of PR for the re-election campaign, too. Humanize the son of a bitch. Ray Kroc, All-American, Brother to the Common Man. Even he suffers symptomatic hair loss. Whatever—you get the idea. Talk to Copy.] Bobby's getting dressed in the morning, towel around his healthy, muscular body. [Note to Casting: if we go with Kroc here we'll have to find a body double.] Looks at himself in the mirror and strokes a five o'clock shadow.*

FEMALE VOICE OVER: Do you wake up in the morning to a sink full of disappointment?

PAN DOWN *to a clean white sink. Clumps of hair litter the porcelain. [Note to Art Dept: Come on, Stone, don't go overboard. No more than twenty strands.] Bobby rubs the top of his head. His expression is crestfallen.*

VOICE OVER: Well, no more! Now with the radiation-blocking power of lead, All-New Formula Samson Brand Hair Pomade can make you an All-New Man.

Bobby squirts a generous amount of Samson Brand from his tube and rubs it on his head. A blissful smile transforms his face.

VOICE OVER: That feeling of euphoria and well-being lets you know it works! Samson Pomades and Creams have been infused with our patented mood-boosters, vitamins, and just a dash of caffeine to help you start your day out right!

PAN DOWN to the sink. Bobby turns the faucet on; the clumps of hair wash away. When we pan back up, Bobby has a full head of glossy, thick, styled hair. [Note to Art Dept: Go whole hog. When the camera comes back put the VP in a full suit, with the perfect hair—a wig, obviously—and the Senate gavel in his hand. I like to see a little more imagination from you, Stone. Not a good quarter for you.]

VOICE OVER: Like magic, Samson Brand Pomade gives you the confidence you need. [Note to Copy: not sure about 'confidence' here. What about 'peace of mind'? We're already getting shit from the FDA about dosing Brothers with caffeine and uppers. Probably don't want to make it sound like the new formula undoes Arcadia.]

He gives the camera a thumbs-up. [Note to Art Dept: Have him offer the camera a handshake. Like our boy Ray is offering America a square deal.]

Bold helvetica across mid-screen:

Samson Guards Your Strength.

Fade to white.

Ten Grays

Martin watched his brother. The handsome Thomas. The promising Thomas. The fruitful and multiplying Thomas. Twenty-nine million per mil Thomas. Their father (twenty-four million) didn't even try to fight his joyful tears as he pinned the golden dove on his son's chest. His good son. His true son. For Thomas the Office in the city. For Thomas the planning and pleasing and roasted chickens and martinis. For Thomas the children as easy as pencil drawings.

For Martin Stone, two million per milliliter and most of those dead, a package. In a nice box, to be certain. Irradiated teak. It didn't matter now anyway. Martin knew without looking what lay nestled in the box. A piece of paper and a bottle. The paper was an ordnance unknown until he opened the box. It was a lottery. The only way to be fair. It was his ticket.

It might request that he present himself at his local Induction Center at 0900 at the close of the school year. To be shipped out to the Front, which by then might be in Missouri for all anyone knew. He'd suit up and boot it across the twisted, bubbled moonscape of the Sea of Glass. An astronaut. Bouncing on the pulses from Los Alamos to the Pacific. He would never draw again. By Christmas, he wouldn't have the fine motor skills.

Or it would request just as politely that he arrange for travel to Washington for a battery of civic exams and placement in government service. Fertile men couldn't think clearly, didn't you know? All that sperm. Can't be rational with all that business sloshing around in there. Husbands couldn't run things. They were needed for more important work. The most important work. Only Brothers could really view things objectively. Big picture men. And women, Sisters, those gorgeous black-chip girls with 3-Alpha running cool and sweet in their veins. Martin would probably pull Department of Advertising and Information. Most people did. Other than Defense, it was the biggest sector going. The bottle would be Arcadia. For immediate dosage, and every day for the rest of his life. All sex shall be potentially reproductive. Every girl screwing a Brother is failing to screw a Husband and that just won't do. They said it tasted like burnt batteries if you didn't put it in something. The first bottle would be the pure stuff, though. Provided by Halcyon, Your Friend in the Drug Manufacturing Business. Martin would remember it, the copper sear on the roof of his mouth. After that, a whole aisle of choices. Choices, after all, make you who you are. Arcadia or Kool. Brylcreem or Samson.

Don't worry, Martin. It's a relief, really. Now you can really get to work. Accomplish something. Carve out your place. Sell the world to the world. You could work your way into the Art Department. Keep drawing babies in carriages. Someone else's perfect quads, their four faces laughing at you forever from glossy pages.

Suddenly Martin found himself clasped tight in his Father's arms. Pulling the box out of his boy's hands, reading the news for him, putting it aside. His voice came as rough as warm gin and Martin could hardly breathe for the strength of his Father's embrace.

Thomas Walker squeezed his Brother's hand. Martin did not squeeze back.

Velocity Multiplied by Duration

Sylvie's Father was with them that week. He was proud. They bought a chicken from Mrs. Stone and killed it together, as a family. The head popped off like a cork. Sylvie stole glances at him at the table. She could see it now. The chocolate hair. The tallness. Hannah framed her Presentation Scroll and hung it over the fireplace.

Sylvie flushed her Spotless trousseaux down the toilet.

She wasn't angry. You can't get angry just because the world's so much bigger than you and you're stuck in it. That's just the face of it, cookie. A poisoned earth, a sequined dress, a speculum you can play like the spoons. Sylvie wasn't angry. She was silent. Her life was Mrs. Patterson's life. People lived in all kinds of messes. She could make rum balls. And treat soil samples and graft cherry varieties and teach some future son or daughter Japanese three weeks a month where no one else could hear. She could look up Bouffant's friend and buy her a stiff drink. She could enjoy the brief world of solitude and science and birth like red skies dawning. Maybe. She had time.

It was all shit, like that Polish kid who used to hang around the soda fountain kept saying. It was definitely all shit.

On Sunday she went out to the garage again. Vita-Pops and shadows. Clark slipped in like light through a crack. He had a canister of old war footage under his arm. Stalingrad, Berlin, Ottawa. Yellow shirt with green stripes. Nagasaki and Tokyo in '45, vaporizing like hearts in a vast, wet chest. The first retaliation. Seattle, San Francisco, Los Angeles. Berlin and Rome swept clean and blank as pages. Clark reached out and held her hand. She didn't squeeze back. The silent detonations on the white sheet like sudden balloons, filling up and up and up. It looked like the inside of Sylvie. Something opening over and over, with nowhere to burn itself out but in.

"This is my last visit," Clark said. "School year's over." His voice sounded far away, muffled, like he didn't even know he was talking. "Car's coming in the morning. Me and Grud are sharing a ride to Induction. I think we get a free lunch."

Sylvie wanted to scream at him. She sucked down her pop, drowned the scream in bubbles.

"I love you," whispered Clark Baker.

On the sheet, the Golden Gate Bridge vanished.

Sylvie rolled the reel back. They watched it over and over. A fleck of nothing dropping out of the sky and then, then the flash, a devouring, brain-boiling, half-sublime sheet of white that blossomed like a flower out of a dead rod, an infinite white everything that obliterated the screen.

Fade to black.

And over the black, a cheerful fat man giving the thumbs up to Sylvie, grinning:

Buy Freedom Brand Film! It's A-OK!

Astrophilia

CARRIE VAUGHN

After five years of drought, the tiny, wool-producing household of Greentree was finished. First the pastures died off, then the sheep, and Stella and the others didn't have any wool to process and couldn't meet the household's quota, small though it was with only five of them working at the end. The holding just couldn't support a household and the regional committee couldn't keep putting credits into it, hoping that rains would come. They might never come, or the next year might be a flood. No one could tell, and that was the problem, wasn't it?

None of them argued when Az and Jude put in to dissolve Greentree. They could starve themselves to death with pride, but that would be a waste of resources. Stella was a good weaver, and ought to have a chance somewhere else. That was the first reason they gave for the decision.

Because they dissolved voluntarily, the committee found places for them in other households, ones not on the verge of collapse. However, Az put in a special request and found Stella's new home herself. "I know the head of the place, Toma. He'll take good care of you, but more than that his place is prosperous. Rich enough for children, even. You could earn a baby there, Stella." Az's wrinkled hands gripped Stella's young ones in her own, and her eyes shone. Twenty-three years ago, Greentree had been prosperous enough to earn a baby: Stella. But those days were gone.

Stella began to have doubts. "Mama, I don't want to leave you and everyone—"

"We'll be fine. We'd have had to leave sooner or later, and this way we've got credits to take with us. Start new on a good footing, yes?"

"Yes, but—" She hesitated, because her fears were childish. "What if they don't like *me*?"

Az shook her head. "Winter market I gave Toma the shawl you made. You should have seen him, Stella, his mouth dropped. He said Barnard Croft would take you on the spot, credits or no."

But what if they don't like *me*, Stella wanted to whine. She wasn't worried about her weaving.

Az must have seen that she was about to cry. "Oh, dear, it'll be all right. We'll see each other at the markets, maybe more if there's trading to be done.

You'll be happy, I know you will. Better things will come."

Because Az seemed so pleased for her, Stella stayed quiet, and hoped.

In the spring, Stella traveled to Barnard Croft, three hundred miles on the Long Road from Greentree, in the hills near the coast.

Rain poured on the last day of the journey, so the waystation driver used a pair of horses to draw the wagon, instead of the truck. Stella offered to wait until the storm passed and the solar batteries charged up, but he had a schedule to keep, and insisted that the horses needed the exercise.

Stella sat under the awning on the front seat of the wagon, wrapped in a blanket against the chill, feeling sorry for the hulking draft animals in front of her. They were soaked, brown coats dripping as they clomped step by step on the muddy road. It might have been faster, waiting for the clouds to break, for the sun to emerge and let them use the truck. But the driver said they'd be waiting for days in these spring rains.

She traveled through an alien world, wet and green. Stella had never seen so much water in her whole life, all of it pouring from the sky. A quarter of this amount of rain a couple of hundred miles east would have saved Greentree.

The road curved into the next green valley, to Barnard Croft. The wide meadow and its surrounding, rolling hills were green, lush with grass. A handful of alpaca grazed along a stream that ran frothing from the hills opposite. The animals didn't seem to mind the water, however matted and heavy their coats looked. There'd be some work, cleaning that mess for spinning. Actually, she looked forward to it. She wanted to make herself useful as soon as she could. To prove herself. If this didn't work, if she didn't fit in here and had to throw herself on the mercy of the regional committee to find some place prosperous enough to take her, that could use a decent weaver . . . no, this would work.

A half-a-dozen whitewashed cottages clustered together, along with sheds and shelters for animals, a couple of rabbit hutches, and squares of turned black soil with a barest sheen of green—garden plots and new growth. The largest cottage stood apart from the others. It had wide doors and many windows, shuttered now against the rain—the work house, she guessed. Under the shelter of the wide eaves sat wooden barrels for washing wool, and a pair of precious copper pots for dyeing. All comfortable, familiar sights.

The next largest cottage, near the garden plots, had a smoking chimney. Kitchen and common room, most likely. Which meant the others were sleeping quarters. She wondered which was hers, and who'd she'd be sharing with. A pair of windmills stood on the side of one hill; their trefoil blades were still.

At the top of the highest hill, across the meadow, was a small, unpainted shack. It couldn't have held more than a person or two standing upright. This, she did not recognize. Maybe it was a curing shed, though it seemed an unlikely spot, exposed as it was to every passing storm.

A turn-off took them from the road to the cottages, and by the time the driver pulled up the horses, eased the wagon to a stop, and set the brakes, a pair of men wrapped in cloaks emerged from the work house to greet them. Stella thanked the driver and jumped to the ground. Her boots splashed, her long woolen skirt tangled around her legs, and the rain pressed the blanket close around her. She felt sodden and bedraggled, but she wouldn't complain.

The elder of those who came to greet her was middle aged and worn, but he moved briskly and spread his arms wide. "Here she is! Didn't know if you would make it in this weather." This was Toma. Az's friend, Stella reminded herself. Nothing to worry about.

"Horses'll get through anything," the driver said, moving to the back of the wagon to unload her luggage.

"Well then," Toma said. "Let's get you inside and dried off."

"Thank you," Stella managed. "I just have a couple of bags. And a loom. Az let me take Greentree's loom."

"Well then, that is a treasure. Good."

The men clustered around the back of the wagon to help. The bags held her clothes, a few books and letters and trinkets. Her equipment: spindles and needles, carders, skeins of yarn, coils of roving. The loom took up most of the space—dismantled, legs and frames strapped together, mechanisms folded away in protective oilskin. It would take her most of a day to set up. She'd feel better when it was.

A third figure came running from the work house, shrouded by her wrap and hood like the others. The shape of her was female, young—maybe even Stella's age. She wore dark trousers and a pale tunic, like the others.

She came straight to the driver. "Anything for me?"

"Package from Griffith?" the driver answered.

"Oh, yes!"

The driver dug under an oil cloth and brought out a leather document case, stuffed full. The woman came forward to take it, revealing her face, sandstone-burnished skin and bright brown eyes.

Toma scowled at her, but the woman didn't seem to notice. She tucked the package under her arm and beamed like sunshine.

"At least be useful and take a bag," Toma said to her.

Taking up a bag with a free hand, the woman flashed a smile at Stella, and turned to carry her load to the cottage.

Toma and other other man, Jorge, carried the loom to the work house. Hefting the rest of her luggage, Stella went to the main cottage, following the young woman at a distance. Behind her, the driver returned to his seat and got the horses moving again; their hooves splashed on the road.

Around dinner time, the clouds broke, belying the driver's prediction. Some sky and a last bit of sunlight peeked through.

They ate what seemed to her eyes a magnificent feast—meat, eggs, preserved fruits and vegetables, fresh bread. At Greentree, they'd barely got through the winter on stores, and until this meal Stella hadn't realized she'd been dimly hungry all the time, for weeks. Months. Greentree really had been dying.

The folk of the croft gathered around the hearth at night, just as they did back home at Greentree, just as folk did at dozens of households up and down the Long Road. She met everyone: Toma and Jorge, who'd helped with the loom. Elsta, Toma's partner, who ran the kitchen and garden. Nik and Wendy, Jon and Faren. Peri had a baby, which showed just how well off Barnard was, to be able to support a baby as well as a refugee like Stella. The first thing Peri did was put the baby—Bette—in Stella's arms, and Stella was stricken because she'd never held a wriggly baby before and was afraid of dropping her. But Peri arranged her arms just so and took the baby back after a few moments of cooing over them both. Stella had never thought of earning the right to have her implant removed, to have a baby—another mouth to feed at Greentree would have been a disaster.

Elsta was wearing the shawl Stella had made, the one Az had given Toma—her audition, really, to prove her worth. The shawl was an intricate weave made of finely spun merino. Stella had done everything—carded and spun the wool, dyed it the difficult smoky blue, and designed the pattern herself. Elsta didn't have to wear it; the croft could have traded it for credits. Stella felt a small spark of pride. Wasn't just charity that brought her here.

Stella had brought her work basket, but Elsta tsked at her. "You've had a long trip, so rest now. Plenty of time to work later." So she sat on a blanket spread out on the floor and played with Bette.

Elsta picked apart a tangle of roving, preparing to draft into the spindle of her spinning wheel. Toma and Jorge had a folding table in front of them, and the tools to repair a set of hand carders. The others knit, crocheted, or mended. They no doubt made all their own clothing, from weaving the fabric to sewing, dark trousers, bright skirts, aprons, and tunics. Stella's hands itched to work—she was in the middle of knitting a pair of very bright yellow socks from the remnants of yarn from a weaving. They'd be ugly but warm—and the right kind of ugly had a charm of its own. But Elsta was probably right, and the baby was fascinating. Bette had a set of wooden blocks that she banged into each other; occasionally, very seriously, she handed them to Stella. Then demanded them back. The process must have had a logic to it.

The young woman wasn't with them. She'd skipped dinner as well. Stella was thinking of how to ask about her, when Elsta did it for her.

"Is Andi gone out to her study, then?"

Toma grumbled, "Of course she is." The words bit.

Her study—the shack on the hill? Stella listened close, wishing the baby would stop banging her blocks so loudly.

"Toma—"

"She should be here."

"She's done her work, let her be. The night's turned clear, you know how she gets."

"She should listen to me."

"The more you push, the angrier she'll get. Leave her be, dearest."

Elsta's wheel turned and purred, Peri hummed as she knit, and Bette's toys clacked. Toma frowned, never looking up from his work.

Her bags sat by one of the two beds in the smallest cottage, only half unpacked. The other bed, Andi's, remained empty. Stella washed, brushed out her short blond hair, changed into her nightdress, and curled up under the covers. Andi still hadn't returned.

The air smelled wrong, here. Wet, earthy, as if she could smell the grass growing outside the window. The shutters cracked open to let in a breeze. Stella was chilled; her nose wouldn't stop running. The desert always smelled dusty, dry—even at night, the heat of the sun rose up from the ground. There, her nose itched with dust.

She couldn't sleep. She kept waiting for Andi to come back.

Finally, she did. Stella started awake when the door opened with the smallest squeak—so she must have slept, at least a little. Cocooned under the covers, she clutched her pillow, blinking, uncertain for a moment where she was and what was happening. Everything felt wrong, but that was to be expected, so she lay still.

Andi didn't seem to notice that she was awake. She hung up her cloak on a peg by the door, sat on her bed while she peeled off shoes and clothes, which she left lying on the chest at the foot of her bed, and crawled under the covers without seeming to notice—or care—that Stella was there. The woman moved quickly—nervously, even? But when she pulled the covers over her, she lay still, asleep in moments. Stella had a suspicion that she'd had practice, falling asleep quickly in the last hours before dawn, before she'd be expected to rise and work.

Stella supposed she would get a chance to finally talk to her new roommate soon enough, but she had no idea what she was going to say to her.

The next day, the clouds had more than broken. No sign of them remained, and the sun blazed clear as it ever had in the desert, but on a world that was wet, green, and growing. The faint sprouts in the garden plots seem to have exploded into full growth, leaves uncurling. The angora in the hutches pressed twitching noses to the wire mesh of their cages, as if they could squeeze out to play in the meadow. Every shutter and window in the croft was opened to let in the sun.

The work house was wide, clean, whitewashed inside and out. It smelled of lanolin, fiber and work. Lint floated in beams of sunlight. Two—now three—

looms and a pair of spinning wheels sat facing each other, so the weavers and spinners could talk. Days would pass quickly here. The first passed quickly enough, and Stella finished it feeling tired and satisfied.

Andi had spent the day at the wash tubs outside, cleaning a batch of wool, preparing it to card and spin in the next week or so. She'd still been asleep when Stella got up that morning, but must have woken up soon after. They still hadn't talked. Not even hello. They kept missing each other, being in different places. Continually out of rhythm, like a pattern that wove crooked because you hadn't counted the threads right. The more time passed without them speaking, the harder Stella found it to think of anything to say. She wanted to ask, *Are you avoiding me?*

Stella had finished putting away her work and was headed for the common room, when she noticed Andi following the footpath away from the cottages, around the meadow and up the hill to the lonely shack. Her study, Elsta had called it. She walked at a steady pace, not quite running, but not lingering.

After waiting until she was far enough ahead that she was not likely to look over her shoulder, Stella followed.

The trail up the hill was a hike, and even walking slowly Stella was soon gasping for breath. But slowly and steadily she made progress. The path made a couple of switchbacks, and finally reached the crest of the hill and the tiny weathered shack planted there.

As she suspected, the view was worth the climb. The whole of Barnard Croft's valley was visible, as well as the next one over. The neighboring croft's cottages were pale specks, and a thread of smoke climbed from one. The hills were soft, rounded, cut through with clefts like the folds in a length of fabric. Trees along the creek gave texture to the picture. The Long Road was a gray track painted around the green rise. The sky above stretched on, and on, blue touched by a faint haze. If she squinted, she thought she could see a line of gray on the far western horizon—the ocean, and the breeze in that direction had a touch of salt and wild. From this perspective, the croft rested in a shallow bowl that sat on the top of the world. She wondered how long it would take to walk around the entire valley, and decided she would like to try some sunny day.

The shed seemed even smaller when she was standing next to it. Strangely, part of the roof was missing, folded back on hinges, letting in light. The walls were too high to see over, and the door was closed. Stella hesitated; she shouldn't be here, she was invading. She had to share a room with this woman, she shouldn't intrude. Then again—she had to share a room with this woman. She only wanted to talk. And if Andi didn't like it, well . . .

Stella knocked on the door before she could change her mind. Three quick, woodpecker-like raps.

When the door swung out, she hopped back, managed not to fall over, and looked wide eyed to see Andi glaring at her.

Then the expression softened, falling away to blank confusion. "Oh. Hi."

They stared at each other for a long moment. Andi leaned on the door, blocking the way; Stella still couldn't see what was inside.

"May I come in?" she finally asked, because Andi hadn't closed the door on her.

"Oh—sure." The woman seemed to shake herself out of a daydream, and stepped back to open the door wide.

The bulk of the tiny room was taken up by a device mounted on a tripod as tall as she was. A metallic cylinder, wide as a bucket, pointed to the ceiling. A giant tin can almost, except the outer case was painted gray, and it had latches, dials, levers, all manner of protrusions connected to it. Stella moved around it, studying it, reminding herself not to touch, however much the object beckoned.

"It's a telescope, isn't it?" she asked, looking over to Andi. "An old one."

A smile dawned on Andi's face, lighting her mahogany eyes. "It is—twelve-inch reflector. Century or so old, probably. Pride and joy." Her finger traced up the tripod, stroking it like it was a favorite pet.

Stella's chest clenched at that smile, and she was glad now that she'd followed Andi here. She kept her voice calm. "Where'd you get it? You couldn't have traded for it—"

"Oh no, you can't trade for something like this. What would you trade for it?" Meaning how many bales of wool, or bolts of cloth, or live alpacas, or cans full of fish from the coast was something like this worth? You couldn't put a price on it. Some people would just give it away, because it had no real use, no matter how rare it was. Andi continued, "It was Pan's, who ran the household before Toma. He was one of the ones who helped build up the network with the observatories, after the big fall. Then he left it all to me. He'd have left it to Toma, but he wasn't interested." She shrugged, as if unable to explain.

"Then it actually works?"

"Oh yes." That smile shone again, and Stella would stay and talk all night, to keep that smile lit up. "I mean, not now, we'll have to wait until dark, assuming the weather stays clear. With the roof open it's almost a real observatory. See how we've fixed the seams?" She pointed to the edges, where the roof met the walls. Besides the hinges and latches that closed the roof in place, the seams had oilskin weatherproofing, to keep rain from seeping through the cracks. The design was clever. The building, then, was shelter for the equipment. The telescope never moved—the bottom points of the tripod were anchored with bricks.

Beside the telescope there wasn't much here: a tiny desk, a shelf filled with books, a bin holding a stack of papers, and a wooden box holding pencils. The leather pouch Andi had received yesterday was open, and packets of paper spread over the desk.

"Is that what you got in the mail?"

She bustled to the desk and shuffled through the pages. "Assignment from Griffith. It's a whole new list of coordinates, now that summer's almost here. The whole sky changes—what we see changes, at least—so I make observations and send the whole thing back." The flush in her brown face deepened as she ducked away. "I know it doesn't sound very interesting, we mostly just write down numbers and trade them back and forth—"

"Oh no," Stella said, shaking her head to emphasize. "It's interesting. Unusual—"

"And useless, Toma says." The smile turned sad, and last night's discussion became clear to Stella.

"Nothing's useless," Stella said. "It's like you said—you can't just throw something like this away." This wasn't like a household that couldn't feed itself and had no choice but to break up.

Three sharp rings of a distant brass bell sounded across the valley. Stella looked out the door, confused.

"Elsta's supper bell," Andi explained. "She only uses it when we've all scattered." She quickly straightened her papers, returned them to their pouch, and latched the roof back in place. Too late, Stella thought to help, reaching up to hold the panel of wood after Andi had already secured the last latch. Oh well. Maybe next time.

Stella got a better look at Andi as they walked back to the croft. She was rough in the way of wind and rain, her dark hair curly, pulled back by a scrap of gray yarn that was unraveling. The collar of her shirt was untied, and her woven jacket had slipped off a shoulder. Stella resisted an urge to pull it back up, and to brush the lock of hair that had fallen out of the tie behind her ear.

"So you're really more of an astronomer than a weaver," Stella said. She'd tried to sound encouraging, but Andi frowned.

"Drives Toma crazy," Andi said. "If there was a household of astronomers, I'd join. But astronomy doesn't feed anyone, does it? Well, some of it does—meteorology, climatology, solar astronomy, maybe. But not what we're doing. We don't earn anyone a baby."

"What are you doing?"

"Astronomical observation. As much as we can, though it feels like reinventing the wheel sometimes. We're not learning anything that people didn't already know back in the day. We're just—well, it feels like filling in the gaps until we get back to where we were. Tracking asteroids, marking supernovae, that sort of thing. Maybe we can't do much with the data. But it might be useful someday."

"There, you see—it's planning ahead. There's use in that."

She sighed. "The committees mostly think it's a waste of time. They can't really complain, though, because we—those of us in the network—do our share and work extra to support the observatories. A bunch of us designate ration credits toward Griffith and Kitt Peak and Wilson—they've got the region's big scopes—to keep staff there maintaining the equipment, to keep the solar power and windmills running. Toma always complains, says if I put my extra credits toward the household we could have a second baby. He says it could even be mine. But they're my credits, and this is important. I earn the time I spend with the scope, and he can't argue." She said that as a declaration, then looked straight at Stella, who blushed. "They may have brought you here to make up for me."

Stella didn't know what to say to that. She was too grateful to have a place at all, to consider that she may have been wanted.

Awkwardly, Andi covered up the silence. "Well. I hope you like it here. That you don't get too homesick, I mean."

The words felt like a warm blanket, soft and wooly. "Thanks."

"We can be kind of rowdy sometimes. Bette gets colicky, and you haven't heard Wendy sing yet. Then there's Jorge and Jon—they share a bed as well as a cottage, see, and can get pretty loud, though if you tease them about it they'll deny it."

"I don't mind rowdy. But I did almost expect to find a clandestine still in that shed."

Andi laughed. "I think Toma'd like a still better, because at least you can drink from it. Elsta does make a really good cider, though. If she ever put enough together to trade, it would make up for all the credits I waste on the observatories."

As they came off the hill and approached the cluster of cottages, Andi asked, "Did you know that Stella means star in Latin?"

"Yes, I did," she answered.

Work was work no matter where you were, and Stella settled into her work quickly. The folk of Barnard were nice, and Andi was easy to talk to. And cute. Stella found excuses to be in the same room with her, just to see that smile. She hadn't expected this, coming to a new household. But she didn't mind, not at all.

Many households along the Long Road kept sheep, but the folk at Barnard did most of the spinning and weaving for trade. All the wool came to them. Barnard also produced a small quantity of specialty fibers from the alpaca and angora rabbits they kept. They were known for the quality of all their work, the smoothness of their yarns, the evenness of their weaving. Their work was sought after not just along the Long Road, but up and down the coast.

Everyone spun, wove, and dyed. Everyone knew every step of working with wool. They either came here because they knew, or because they'd grown up here learning the trade, like Toma and Nik, like Bette would in her turn. As Andi had, as Stella found out. Andi was the baby that Toma and Elsta had earned together.

Stella and Andi were at the looms, talking as they worked. The spring rains seem to have broken for good, and everyone else had taken their work outside. Wendy sat in the fresh air with her spinning wheel. A new batch of wool had arrived, and Toma and Jorge worked cleaning it. So Stella had a chance to ask questions in private.

"Could you get a place at one of the observatories? How does that work?"

Andi shook her head. "It wouldn't work out. There's three people at Kitt and two each at Griffith and Wilson, and they pick their successors. I'm better use to them here, working to send them credits."

"And you have your telescope, I suppose."

"The astronomers love my telescope," she said. "They call my setup Barnard Observatory, as if it's actually important. Isn't it silly?"

"Of course it isn't."

Andi's hands flashed, passing the shuttle across. She glanced up every now and then. Stella, for her part, let her hands move by habit, and watched Andi more than her own work. Outside, Wendy sang as she spun, in rhythm with the clipping hum of her wheel. Her voice was light, dream-like.

The next time Andi glanced up, she exclaimed, "How do you *do* that? You're not even watching and it's coming out beautiful."

Stella blinked at her work—not much to judge by, she thought. A foot or two of fabric curling over the breast beam, only just starting to wind onto the cloth beam. "I don't know. It's what I'm good at. Like you and the telescope."

"Nice of you to say so. But here, look at this—I've missed a row." She sat back and started unpicking the last five minutes of her work. "I go too fast. My mind wanders."

"It happens to everyone," Stella said.

"Not you. I saw that shawl you did for Elsta."

"I've just gotten good at covering up the mistakes," Stella said, winking.

A week after her arrival, an agent from the regional committee came to visit. A stout, gray-haired, cheerful woman, she was the doctor who made regular rounds up and down the Long Road. She was scheduled to give Bette a round of vaccinations, but Stella suspected the woman was going to be checking on her as well, to make sure she was settling in and hadn't disrupted the household too much.

The doctor, Nance, sat with Bette on the floor, and the baby immediately started crying. Peri hovered, but Nance just smiled and cooed while lifting the baby's arms and checking her ears, not seeming at all bothered.

"How is the world treating you then, Toma?" Nance turned to Toma, who was sitting in his usual chair by the fire.

His brow was creased with worry, though there didn't seem to be anything wrong. "Fine, fine," he said brusquely.

Nance turned. "And Stella, are you doing well?"

"Yes, thank you," Stella said. She was winding yarn around Andi's outstretched hands, to make a skein. This didn't feel much like an inspection, but that only made her more nervous.

"Very good. My, you're a wiggler, aren't you?" Bette's crying had finally subsided to red-faced sniffling, but she continued to fling herself from Nance's arms in an attempt to escape. After a round with a stethoscope, Nance let her go, and the baby crawled away, back to Peri.

The doctor turned her full attention to Toma. "The committee wants to order more banners, they expect to award quite a few this summer. Will you have some ready?"

Toma seemed startled. "Really? Are they sure?"

Barnard supplied the red-and-green patterned cloth used to make the banners awarded to households who'd been approved to have a baby. One of the things Nance had asked about when she first arrived was if anyone had tried bribing him for a length of the cloth over the last year. One of the reasons Barnard had the task of producing the banners—they were prosperous enough not to be vulnerable to bribes. Such attempts happened rarely, but did happen. Households had been broken up over such crimes.

The banner the household had earned for Bette was pinned proudly to the wall above the mantel.

Nance shrugged. "The region's been stable for a couple of years. No quota arguments, most households supporting themselves, just enough surplus to get by without draining resources. We're a healthy region, Toma. If we can support more children, we ought to. And you—with all these healthy young women you have, you might think of putting in for another baby." The doctor beamed.

Stella and Andi looked at each other and blushed. Another baby so soon after the first? Scandalous.

Nance gathered up her kit. "Before I go, let me check all your birth control implants so we don't have any mishaps, eh?"

She started with Elsta and Toma and worked her way around the room.

"Not that I could have a mishap," Andi muttered to Stella. "They ought to make exceptions for someone like me who isn't likely to get in that kind of trouble. Because of her *preferences*, you know?"

"I know," Stella said, blushing very hard now. "I've had that thought myself."

They stared at each other for a very long moment. Stella's mouth had suddenly gone dry. She wanted to flee the room and stick her head in a bucket of cool water. Then again, she didn't.

When Nance came to her side to prod her arm, checking that the implant was in place, Stella hardly felt it.

"Looks like you're good and covered," Nance said. "For now, eh? Until you get that extra banner." She winked.

The doctor stayed for supper and still had enough daylight left to walk to the next waystation along the road. Elsta wrapped up a snack of fruit and cheese for her to take with her, and Nance thanked her very much. As soon as she was gone, Toma muttered.

"Too many mouths to feed—and what happens when the next flood hits? The next typhoon? We lose everything and then there isn't enough? We have enough as it is, more than enough. Wanting more, it's asking for trouble. Getting greedy is what brought the disasters in the first place. It's too much."

Everyone stayed quiet, letting him rant. This felt to Stella like an old argument, words repeated like the chorus of a song. Toma's philosophy, expounded by habit. He didn't need a response.

Stella finished winding the skein of yarn and quietly excused herself, putting her things away and saying goodnight to everyone.

Andi followed her out of the cottage soon after, and they walked together to their room.

"So, do you want one?" Stella asked her.

"A baby? I suppose I do. Someday. I mean, I assumed as well off as Barnard is I could have one if I wanted one. It's a little odd, thinking about who I'd pick for the father. That's the part I'm not sure about. What about you?"

Besides being secretly, massively pleased that Andi hadn't thought much about fathers . . . "I assumed I'd never get the chance. I don't think I'd miss it if I didn't."

"Enough other people who want 'em, right?"

"Something like that."

They reached their room, changed into their nightclothes, washed up for bed. Ended up sitting on their beds, facing each other and talking. That first uncomfortable night seemed far away now.

"Toma doesn't seem to like the idea of another baby," Stella prompted.

"Terrified, I think," she said. "Wanting too much gets people in trouble."

"But it only seems natural, to want as much as you can have."

Andi shook her head. "His grandparents remembered the old days. He heard stories from them about the disasters. All the people who died in the floods and plagues. He's that close to it—might as well have lived through it himself. He thinks we'll lose it all, that another great disaster will fall on us and destroy everything. It's part of why he hates my telescope so much. It's a sign of the old days when everything went rotten. But it won't happen, doesn't he see that?"

Stella shrugged. "Those days aren't so far gone, really. Look at what happened to Greentree."

"Oh—Stella, I'm sorry. I didn't mean that there's not anything to it, just that . . . " She shrugged, unable to finish the thought.

"It can't happen here. I know."

Andi's black hair fell around her face, framing her pensive expression. She stared into space. "I just wish he could see how good things are. We've earned a little extra, haven't we?"

Unexpected even to herself, Stella burst, "Can I kiss you?"

In half a heartbeat Andi fell at her, holding Stella's arms, and Stella clung back, and either her arms were hot or Andi's hands were, and they met, lips to lips.

One evening, Andi escaped the gathering in the common room, and brought Stella with her. They left as the sun had almost set, leaving just enough light to follow the path to the observatory. They took candles inside shaded lanterns for the trip back to their cottage. At dusk, the windmills were ghostly skeletons lurking on the hillside.

They waited for full dark, talking while Andi looked over her paperwork and prepared her notes. Andi asked about Greentree, and Stella explained that the aquifers had dried up in the drought. Households remained in the region because they'd always been there. Some survived, but they weren't particularly successful. She told Andi how the green of the valleys near the coast had almost blinded her when she first arrived, and how all the rain had seemed like a miracle.

Then it was time to unlatch the roof panels and look at the sky.

"Don't squint, just relax. Let the image come into focus," Andi said, bending close to give directions to Stella, who was peering through the scope's eyepiece. Truth be told, Stella was more aware of Andi's hand resting lightly on her shoulder. She shifted closer.

"You should be able to see it," Andi said, straightening to look at the sky.

"Okay . . . I think . . . oh! Is that it?" A disk had come into view, a pale, glowing light striped with orange, yellow, cream. Like someone had covered a very distant moon with melted butter.

"Jupiter," Andi said proudly.

"But it's just a star."

"Not up close it isn't."

Not a disk, then, but a sphere. Another planet. "Amazing."

"Isn't it? You ought to be able to see some of the moons as well—a couple of bright stars on either side?"

"I think . . . yes, there they are."

After an hour, Stella began shivering in the nighttime cold, and Andi put her arms around her, rubbing warmth into her back. In moments, they were kissing, and stumbled together to the desk by the shack's wall, where Andi pushed her back across the surface and made love to her. Jupiter had swung out of view by the time they closed up the roof and stumbled off the hill.

Another round of storms came, shrouding the nighttime sky, and they spent the evenings around the hearth with the others. Some of the light went out of Andi on those nights. She sat on a chair with a basket of mending at her feet, darning socks and shirts, head bent over her work. Lamplight turned her skin amber and made her hair shine like obsidian. But she didn't talk. That may have been because Elsta and Toma talked over everyone, or Peri exclaimed over something the baby did, then everyone had to admire Bette.

The day the latest round of rain broke and the heat of summer finally settled over the valley, Andi got another package from Griffith, and that light of discovery came back to her. Tonight, they'd rush off to the observatory after supper.

Stella almost missed the cue to escape, helping Elsta with the dishes. When she was finished and drying her hands, Andi was at the door. Stella rushed in behind her. Then Toma brought out a basket, one of the ones as big as an embrace that they used to store just-washed wool in, and set it by Andi's chair before the hearth. "Andi, get back here."

Her hand was on the door, one foot over the threshold, and Stella thought she might keep going, pretending that she hadn't heard. But her hand clenched on the door frame, and she turned around.

"We've got to get all this new wool processed, so you'll stay in tonight to help."

"I can do that tomorrow. I'll work double tomorrow—"

"Now, Andi."

Stella stepped forward, hands reaching for the basket. "Toma, I can do that."

"No, you're doing plenty already. Andi needs to do it."

"I'll be done with the mending in a minute and can finish that in no time at all. Really, it's all right."

He looked past her, to Andi. "You know the rules—household business first."

"The household business is *done*. This is makework!" she said. Toma held the basket out in reproof.

Stella tried again. "But I *like* carding." It sounded lame—no one liked carding.

But Andi had surrendered, coming away from the door, shuffling toward her chair. "Stella, it's all right. Not your argument."

"But—" The pleading in her gaze felt naked. She wanted to help, how could she help?

Andi slumped in the chair without looking up. All Stella could do was sit in her own chair, with her knitting. She jabbed herself with the needle three times, from glancing up at Andi every other stitch.

Toma sat before his workbench, looking pleased for nearly the first time since Stella had met him.

Well after dark, Stella lay in her bed, stomach in knots. Andi was in the other bed and hadn't said a word all evening.

"Andi? Are you all right?" she whispered. She stared across the room, to the slope of the other woman, mounded her under blanket. The lump didn't move, but didn't look relaxed in sleep. But if she didn't want to talk, Stella wouldn't force her.

"I'm okay," Andi sighed, finally.

"Anything I can do?"

Another long pause, and Stella was sure she'd said too much. Then, "You're a good person, Stella. Anyone ever told you that?"

Stella crawled out from under her covers, crossed to Andi's bed, climbed in with her. Andi pulled the covers up over them both, and the women held each other.

Toma sent Andi on an errand, delivering a set of blankets to the next waystation and picking up messages to bring back. More makework. The task could just have as easily been done by the next wagon messenger to pass by. Andi told him as much, standing outside the work house the next morning.

"Why wait when we can get the job done now?" Toma answered, hefting the backpack, stuffed to bursting with newly woven woolens, toward her.

Stella was at her loom, and her hand on the shuttle paused as she listened. But Andi didn't say anything else. Only glared at Toma a good long minute before taking up the pack. She'd be gone most of the day, hiking there and back.

Which was the point, wasn't it?

Stella contrived to find jobs that kept Toma in sight, sorting and carding wool outside where he was working repairing a fence, when she should have been weaving. So she saw when Toma studied the hammer in his hand, looked up the hill, and started walking the path to Andi's observatory.

Stella dropped the basket of wool she was holding and ran.

He was merely walking. Stella overtook him easily, at first. But after fifty yards of running, she slowed, clutching at a stitch in her side. Gasping for breath with burning lungs, she kept on, step after step, hauling herself up the hill, desperate to get there first.

"Stella, go back, don't get in the middle of this."

Even if she could catch enough of her breath to speak, she didn't know what she would say. He lengthened his stride, gaining on her. She got to the shed a bare few steps before him.

The door didn't have a lock; it had never needed one. Stella pressed herself across it and faced out, to Toma, marching closer. At least she had something to lean on for the moment.

"Move aside, Stella. She's got to grow up and get on with what's important," Toma said.

"This *is* important."

He stopped, studied her. He gripped the handle of the hammer like it was a weapon. Her heart thudded. How angry was he?

Toma considered, then said, "Stella. You're here because I wanted to do Az a favor. I can change my mind. I can send a message to Nance and the committee that it just isn't working out. I can do that."

Panic brought sudden tears to her eyes. He wouldn't dare, he couldn't, she'd proven herself already in just a few weeks, hadn't she? The committee wouldn't believe him, couldn't listen to him. But she couldn't be sure of that, could she?

Best thing to do would be to step aside. He was head of the household, it was his call. She ought to do as he said, because her place here *wasn't* secure. A month ago that might not have mattered, but now—she *wanted* to stay, she *had* to stay.

And if she stepped aside, leaving Toma free to enter the shed, what would she tell Andi afterward?

She swallowed the lump in her throat and found words. "I know disaster can still happen. I know the droughts and storms and plagues do still come and can take away everything. Better than anyone, I know. But we have to start building again sometime, yes? People like Andi have to start building, and we have to let them, even if it seems useless to the rest of us. Because it isn't useless, it—it's beautiful."

He stared at her for a long time. She thought maybe he was considering how to wrestle her away from the door. He was bigger than she was, and she wasn't strong. It wouldn't take much. But she'd fight.

"You're infatuated, that's all," he said.

Maybe, not that it mattered.

Then he said, "You're not going to move away, are you?"

Shaking her head, Stella flattened herself more firmly against the door.

Toma's grip on the hammer loosened, just a bit. "My grandparents—has Andi told you about my grandparents? They were children when the big fall came. They remembered what it was like. Mostly they talked about what they'd lost, all the things they had and didn't now. And I thought, all those things they missed, that they wanted back—that was what caused the fall in the first place, wasn't it? We don't need it, any of it."

"Andi needs it. And it's not hurting anything." What else could she say, she had to say something that would make it all right. "Better things will come, or what's the point?"

A weird crooked smile turned Toma's lips, and he shifted his grip on the hammer. Holding it by the head now, he let it dangle by his leg. "God, what a world," he muttered. Stella still couldn't tell if he was going to force her away from the door. She held her breath.

Toma said, "Don't tell Andi about this. All right?"

She nodded. "All right."

Toma turned and started down the trail, a calm and steady pace. Like a man who'd just gone out for a walk.

Stella slid to the ground and sat on the grass by the wall until the old man was out of sight. Finally, after scrubbing the tears from her face, she followed him down, returning to the cottages and her work.

Andi was home in time for supper, and the household ate together as usual. The woman was quiet and kept making quick glances at Toma, who avoided looking back at all. It was like she knew Toma had had a plan. Stella couldn't say anything until they were alone.

The night was clear, the moon was dark. Stella'd learned enough from Andi to know it was a good night for stargazing. As they were cleaning up after the meal, she touched Andi's hand. "Let's go to the observatory."

Andi glanced at Toma, and her lips pressed together, grim. "I don't think that's a good idea."

"I think it'll be okay."

Andi clearly didn't believe her, so Stella took her hand, and together they walked out of the cottage, then across the yard, past the work house, and to the trail that led up the hill to the observatory.

And it was all right.

If the Mountain Comes

AN OWOMOYELA

François and Papa were outside, discussing what to do if the water rose. I was in, scrubbing blood from the walls with a palmful of sand.

That was the summer Enah came to our village. He'd led a donkey, and the donkey pulled a cart with tools, a flowering lilac, and a barrel of fresh water. The barrel made Enah richer than the doctor, richer than the preacher. Richer than anyone but us, and he meant to change that.

I heard footsteps crunching the cracked earth outside, but I assumed it was a pumpyard guard until Papa went silent and his dogs went barking mad and I looked to see why. There they were, in the dry riverbed: Papa and François and the Rottweilers all glaring at Enah, who approached as though he feared nothing. He had skin as dark as François; he walked barefoot, and smiled. People weren't in the habit of smiling at my father.

Enah and Papa exchanged a few words, then turned and came into the house with the dogs keeping pace. "Make us tea," Papa said, and I was banished to the kitchen. I boiled the water and measured the leaves, and brought out the teapot and the cups, several of them chipped. I poured for my father first, then Enah. Enah didn't say anything. Not even to acknowledge such luxury.

"In the next months, I'm going to sink my pumps another ten meters into the ground," Papa was saying. "I can bring more water up and provide it even more cheaply to the people of this village."

"The people of this village do not want to pay for something the world provides freely," Enah said. Papa snorted, boar-like.

"Not so freely. My grandfather would have called this a drought; I call it the state of things. It rains perhaps thirty days a year. Your program might work where you're from, but here, it's foolishness."

Enah shrugged. "There was a river here once," he said, and sipped the steaming tea.

"That mountain to the east was a volcano *once*," Papa said. "The world changes."

"And we are often the ones who change it." Enah shrugged again. "That's what I've promised them, Mr. Wolfe: there was a river here once and there will be again."

225

They sat watching each other for a moment, these two men, Enah small and strange with laughter lines around his mouth and forehead, Papa solid and strong with anger carved into his brow.

"There is a house here now," Papa said. "A family. A dozen workers. Water pumps. You'd have us all vanish?"

"No, no," Enah said. "I'd have you go up the bank, join the rest of your town. It must be lonely down here."

It was lonely down there.

Ever since Mama died, Papa and I went around with a higher awareness of mortality. His mortality, mostly. Papa wasn't a young man, and death was something we expected with half a head. Death was like rain—uncommon, but it would come.

So ever since Mama died, I had a bag packed, and I was ready to run away. I knew I couldn't survive on the riverbed without Papa, though I didn't know where I could go. Up to the village, if they'd take me, but what would I do? Set bones, or forage in the brush, or whore myself?

Or I could set off. See what lay beyond the horizon, and beyond the horizon beyond that. Water would be the problem—so heavy, so necessary, and something that unlike the people of the village I had never learned to go without.

The riverbed had been parched for as long as I could remember, its dirt cracked and peeling like thick and brittle plates. You could throw them toward the bank, and watch them burst into plumes of dust. Our family drilled deep and sucked water from the earth, and it was enough to keep us wealthy, by our own, dusty standards of wealth.

Papa sent Enah away. Then he went out to the pumpyard, and I ran out after our visitor. "Wait!"

Enah turned and looked at me. "We weren't introduced," he said.

"I'm Lena," I said. "Lena Wolfe. You say you can bring the river back?"

He looked up and down the riverbed. The town was clustered on the bank, and my grandfather's home and his father's home connected the town and our farm like the dots of an ellipsis. My family had always followed the water.

"Let me ask you something," Enah said. "Why is it you think these people don't seek their fortunes elsewhere?"

I shrugged. "This is home," I said.

He nodded. "It's their home, and it's still possible to live here. If it is possible to live, many will stay where they've buried their parents, and where they've dug the wells with their hands, and laid the cobblestones. And besides, the sun is hot everywhere. Water is precious everywhere." He tapped the ground with one foot. "What is the name of this river?"

The name dried up when the water did. I think Papa knew it. I think it was written on the old maps, but we didn't use the old maps. "It doesn't have one."

Enah turned to look at me, and his eyes were as sharp as a carrion bird's. "That's sad, isn't it?" he said. "I've brought waters to desert arroyos, Lena. I can make this river flow again. And when the waters flow again, your town will name it."

He reached out to touch my cheek, and I stepped back. Ordinarily, no one would touch me—I'd have a dog, like Papa's dogs, to dissuade anyone from coming too close. Not then, though. Papa had killed my dog that morning.

"There will be enough water to grow hyacinths here," Enah said.

"What are hyacinths?" I asked.

I went to the pumpyard to draw water to pay the guards' salaries. I hated going to the pumps, but they were locked so the guards couldn't draw their own. The men who guarded them, with old automatics and new machetes, looked at me as though only my father kept them from leaping on me like wolves.

Only my father. So much in my life was because of my father, or only my father. Because of my father, I would never die of thirst. Only my father aimed to keep life and death in a birdcage on his accounting desk.

When I'd filled the jugs and dragged the heavy handcart back to Papa's office, I saw Papa yelling at François. Almost-yelling. Papa only barely raised his voice, but it felt like a shot from a cannon.

"By God, they won't have their way!" Papa was saying.

François, a braver man than most, said "God is not always merciful to our needs."

I'd never heard him speak back to Papa before.

"I don't care about God's mercy," Papa said. "Who has mercy? He doesn't. I don't. And you least of all." His voice became harder, like stone. "Go find whoever brought this troublemaker to our village. Make sure they don't bring any more trouble our way."

François stood with his jaw muscles bulging. He must have been biting down hard.

"Well?" Papa said, and raised his hand as though to strike him. "Go on! Go!"

François turned and walked outside.

Papa turned to me, and I stared at him. Then he sighed, and clicked his fingers twice. One of the dogs perked his ears, ready for commands.

"You should take Brutus," Papa said, though neither of his dogs will obey anyone but him. "Jaime's bitch is about to pup; we'll train up another dog for you soon."

"I'd rather have Mogul back," I said.

Papa was not a man who showed sadness, but sometimes, I could catch a softness in his eyes. Only for me. "They never live once the bloody coughs start."

"You never treat them," I said.

"We are all dying, Lena," he said, and started out past me. "If I kill them a week before their time or five years before their time, what does it matter?"

He stopped at the doorway to touch my cheek. "You are the only one I will fight to keep alive."

Papa would fight anything. Fighting was the only life he knew.

When my mother came down with the cough, he fought the doctors. He fought the dust which rolled in through the windows. He even fought my mother's body. When she died, he seemed like a man who'd lost a public match—pride smarting, eyes burning, looking to prove himself back up.

By that summer, when the dogs were sick, he'd take a machete and lop off their heads. Maybe he thought it was winning if he didn't watch them dwindle away.

I went to fill the drip-irrigators. I passed the side path leading to the gate, where François was sharpening his machete, his skin gleaming in the sunlight in contrast to my own. François was as strong and dark as Mogul once was, and I was as tan and useless as the dirt on the riverbed.

"Where's your dog?" he demanded.

"He was sick," I said.

François said, *huh*, and went back to sharpening.

"What did you mean," I asked him, "that God is not always merciful?"

"You know what I meant. The world doesn't work the way we'd like it."

"But why did you say it?" I asked. "Why God?"

François shrugged one corded shoulder. "A saying came to mind. A story my parents told me."

Papa never told me stories. Mama had, but Mama was gone. "Tell me," I said.

François grimaced. I think he wanted to be rid of me. He didn't speak much, and especially not to me. Still, my father paid him, and paid him twice as much as anyone else on the water farm, so he indulged most things.

"The Prophet Mohammed was told to prove the greatness of God," François said. "He shook his fist at a mountain and said 'Come here, mountain, so I may pray on you!' The mountain didn't come. The Prophet turned to his people and said 'If that mountain had come, it would have crushed us. So you see, God is merciful. I'll go to the mountain and thank God for sparing his foolish children.'"

I chewed on that. "So if the river comes, God won't stop the water from flooding our home?"

François shrugged.

"Why aren't you Muslim?" I asked. "You still remember those Islamic stories. Weren't your parents Muslims?"

François put the finishing edge on his machete and stood up. "You'll learn one day that you can't always do what your parents want you to," he said. He looked over at the edge of the river, up toward the village on the lip. "My parents would be disappointed in what I do. Besides." He rested his machete on his shoulder. "It's not right to profess what you don't believe."

I didn't believe in a God, either. My father prayed, but never told me who he prayed to. Mama had been a Catholic from an old sect. I usually found François the most sensible of all of them.

I took two gallons of water, separated into quarts, up the bank to the market. The people there watched me, many of them angry, but not as hungry as the guards we kept sweating and rich on the farm. Papa said people resented the rich, and that it shouldn't bother me.

François had followed me up and I wondered if my father had told him to be my dog until I had a new one, but then he went on his way and I put him out of my mind.

The noise of the market quieted as I passed by, and resumed again in pitched whispers, and the stares were more furtive. Because I didn't have my dog, or because of Enah?

I found Jaime, who was at least kind to me, under a frayed sunshade, fixing small electronics. A rickety contraption of rods and wires with a metal dish in the middle was perched on the edge of his table, with a radio tied into it.

"What is that?" I asked, and he flashed me a grin.

"Listen to that," he said, and turned the radio on.

There weren't many stations nearby—there was the Christ Channel, and the staticky weather for a city climates away. And then there was this, a violin, a channel I'd never heard before.

I strained forward into the music. "Is it a new station?"

"Just far away," Jaime said. "But with that antenna, I can focus in on it." He turned up the volume as high as it would go. I closed my eyes and breathed it in.

The song ended, and someone spoke in a foreign tongue. "Papa says you have a dog ready to pup," I said.

Jaime nodded. "Any day now. The best of my stock."

"We'll want to buy a boy," I said. "If there's one you don't keep back for breeding, reserve it for us."

He looked at me quizzically. "I noticed you didn't have Mogul with you."

He didn't ask, *What happened?* And so I didn't tell him, even as the words pressed on the back of my tongue. I didn't say how his entire body had shaken when he sneezed, how blood had sprayed out from his nostrils to paint the living room walls. "He was sick," I said. *And they never live once the coughing starts.*

Jaime understood. "Tell your Papa that these dogs are companions and workers, not pieces of equipment he can use up and replace." There was no heat to his tone. We were his best customers, and sometimes his only customers for months at a time.

Beside him, the man on the radio stopped talking and a new song started up. "Jaime," I asked. "Why don't we make anything that beautiful?"

Jaime shook his head. "What do you mean? Don't you see the soapstone carvings Elise does? Hear Luc singing to his rabbits? See the mats Camille weaves out of the grasses? There are beautiful things all over the village."

"Yes, yes," I answered, but my head was full of the violin, my mind's eye captured by the curves of its wood. I had only seen pictures in old books. "But why don't we make anything *that* beautiful?"

Jaime sighed. "Because beautiful flowers don't grow on dry clay, girl," he said, and I felt myself drop in his estimation. "When we're not too busy scraping by, we'll go to another city just to buy a violin. Or perhaps you should ask your father to buy one for you."

The words stung, so I turned to leave.

I bought rabbit meat from Luc, and wild garlic and scrawny tubers from strange old Abed. Traded water for soap, for thread, for a tin of white paint to cover the blood I hadn't been able to scrub away. Then I started back down toward the water farm, but Enah caught my eye.

He was sitting on the edge of his cart, at the lip of the river bank, leaning down to draw pictures in the dirt with a stick. He was surrounded by villagers, and all of them watched him like a prophet. I drew nearer.

". . . and when that is done," he was saying, "there will be water to last you between rains, and we can turn our attention to healing the river. We'll dig percolation trenches, to let water return to the aquifer."

By then people had noticed me, and they were muttering. I'd decided it was time to go when Enah looked up and motioned me forward.

"It's all right," he said. "Come up and see." He looked to the villagers, and before they could say anything he said, "The water we'll bring is for everyone; go ahead and let her in."

"She'll just tell her father," one of them said. I didn't look to see who.

"I'd tell him myself if he asked me," Enah said. "Come up, Miss Wolfe."

I looked around at the faces of the people who hated my family. They seemed foreign, and at first I didn't know why; of course I had little interaction with them, but I knew their faces. I saw their houses on the hill.

Then it struck me. I had never seen the flicker of hope in their eyes, and now they watched Enah as though he were the word of God. I thought back to François, and felt that I was standing on the edge of a cliff. I stepped up.

"Have you ever heard the words 'watershed management,' Miss Wolfe?" Enah asked. I shook my head. "Do you know what a water table is? A kund?"

"I know the aquifer is drying," I said. A rumble passed from mouth to mouth in the crowd.

"That's because this place," Enah said, and gestured over the village, "is designed to waste water. It rains, and the water evaporates again. With bunds and kunds and ditches, we can train it to go back into the aquifer, and capture it from this whole land surrounding your village—"

He was interrupted by screaming.

Enah seemed confused, but the villagers knew their screams. They broke and ran, ready to help someone bit by a snake or trapped under an ancient, crumbled wall, but what they found was Jaime, his wife crouched over him and keening, his radio smashed. My heart caught and I stepped forward, knowing what I would see—and I saw that his head was lying separately to his body, the two of them connected by a sweep of bright blood.

Then it was my turn to break away from them and run. It took the villagers a moment to work through why I was running away from them, and then a yell went up. I heard Enah's voice, nasal and rising, and then a rock crashed into the ground by my ankle. I ran faster, down into the riverbed, to the safety of the guards and Papa's dogs.

They came to the house in numbers that night, carrying fire. I could taste their anger on my skin. From the pumpyard the guards readied their weapons, unsure whether to run to the defense of the house or to protect the water, and Papa flogged the dogs to get them growling. "Where is François? That worthless man! He can put down what he's stirred up or I'll have his hide nailed to my wall!"

Something crashed against our window, and I jumped back. Papa grabbed his rifle and checked it, then made it ready to fire.

Papa had had people murdered before. We never talked about it, but there was no secret. When I was ten, he had François kill the bonesetter's son, and everyone knew it was him. Papa had guards and dogs and Papa had the water; the whole village hated him, but no one dared cross him. Now they dared.

Outside the window, something was happening in the crowd. Enah ran in front of them, raising his hands. I couldn't hear his words but just his voice was beautiful, melodic like a violin, fanning the fires and banking the coals until the entire mob was singing their agreement with him, and the chant started up: *Enah! Enah! Bring the river! Flood them out!*

When the crowd was his, he turned to our house and waved his hand until I stepped up and opened the window.

"Mr. Wolfe," he called. "It's true that Jaime raised me on the radio, but you'll have to do more than kill him to drive me off. You'll have to kill me. And you'll have to kill all the people I am teaching, and you'll have to teach them not to kill you. Invite me in, Mr. Wolfe."

Quite a thing to say, for someone who had just told my father to kill him. But Papa walked to the door, and—quickly, as though the doorknob was a snake—yanked it open. He invited Enah in.

No ancient and carefully maintained gun from the crowd shot him. No fist-sized rocks came hurtling at his head. Enah approached and the mob behind him rumbled like a single, huge beast, with fire in its many claws.

Enah walked in, and Papa shut the door behind him.

They stood watching each other for a moment, these two men, Enah strange and unworldly with fire glowing on his skin, Papa holding his ground like the rocks on the riverbed. Then Enah spoke.

"All the corpses you've planted by your pumps," Enah said. "How long, tell me, will it take them to bloom? Will they feed your family when they do?"

Papa frowned, confused. He wasn't a good man to confuse—he got angry. But instead of striking Enah or taking him by the neck, he showed his hands.

"Why do you want to destroy me?" he asked. "I want to leave something for my daughter. I want to leave my wealth when I'm no longer here to take care of her."

"You can leave her a better wealth," Enah said, and gestured to the dry riverbed.

"It will dry up. You don't understand this village; people don't learn. If they're given abundance, they'll bleed it dry. If I control the water, everyone gets what they need; no one takes more than their fair share."

"People learn when they are taught," Enah said. "When they create with their own hands. They will love the river even as you love your daughter."

"You are naive," father said.

"And you are stubborn," said Enah.

Papa brushed off his hands. "I would rather be stubborn," he said, but there was a moment when he seemed to consider it. The costs, and the risks, and the damages. But Papa has never been one to back down. "I'm done arguing with you. With a word I'll have my guards open fire on your mob. Get off of my land."

Papa went into his office before Enah could say another word, and I caught Enah's arm before he left our house. "Why hyacinths?" I asked. I kept my voice at a whisper, so Papa couldn't hear.

Enah turned to look at me. "Because this," he said, gesturing to the riverbed, "is fear in a handful of dust. Have you heard that poem? *The Waste Land*?"

I hadn't, but if there was ever a wasted land, this was it.

"How much of that world we have forgotten," Enah said, and shook his head. I understood why people crowded around him like a prophet: he promised beautiful things, and kept them in mind of how strange he was, how little they knew.

I followed him to the fence around the property, where he went out by the gate and faced the crowd. The mob watched, ready to burn me, but I felt safe in Enah's shadow. A girl guided through a lions' den.

"Those of you who'd see the river run," he called. "Come at midnight to the highest part of the bank. We'll gather there and begin: with your own hands and your native rock, we'll build tanks and dams and bund walls. Little by little, the water will rise. We will name the first wall 'Jaime.'" He turned, faced our house, and seemed to speak straight to Papa. "And the water *will* rise."

He looked at me, and I ran back inside.

Papa must have heard him through the walls. He was sitting at his desk with his head in his hands, and his face—what I could see of it—was red.

He looked to me, eyes dry and veined. "If they gather I'll have François and my boys cleave them apart," he said. "It's not right that they should try to take the river. There was no law here so our family made the law. May you never have to make such a decision."

We were both silent for a while, and I said, "Hyacinths don't grow on clay."

Papa's eyes bugged. "What is this?" he demanded. "What sort of nonsense have they put in your head? Hyacinths!" He stood. "I've raised a beautiful girl on this land, and by God I'll leave my wealth for her when I die. Wealth is all you can ask for in a God-forsaken place like this."

I bit my teeth. My mind was full of blood and flowers, and the back of my tongue was dry. Papa glared for a minute, then the heat went out of him.

"Apologize to me, Lena," he said. "I'm only trying to protect you."

I'd lived long enough that I knew there'd be no peace in the household until I did.

"I'm sorry."

He nodded. For a while he stared out the window, into the distance, his dogs at his ankles.

"Water," he said.

I went into the kitchen.

I pulled a quart down from the cupboard, and felt the clean weight of it. Wealth, here, sucked out of the dirty riverbed.

I brought it back to the office, and Papa drank like a man thirsty since the days of the Flood. I watched the water disappear into his body.

He set it down and looked at me.

"Lena," he said. "Drink up and go to bed. Keep your eyes closed. I'm going to roust the boys."

I went into my room and closed my eyes, and imagined blood sprayed across the riverbed. Papa went out to the pumps, and I could hear his voice, and then the rasp of stones sharpening machetes. I counted my breaths. Fifty, eighty, and the guards began to speak to each other, binding their resolve in boasts and quiet banter.

Then, I snuck outside.

The sky was dark, and the electric lamps from the pumpyard didn't cast light as far as the door. The riverbanks reared high above me to either side.

I thought, *What happens if the water rises?*

But then, that wasn't the right question.

What happens if the water never rises?

The ground cracks. Skin cracks. Bones crack.

On my birthdays I was allowed the extravagant gift of a bath. When Mama was alive, she'd sit at the side of the tub and wash my back. My entire body felt light, then. I think *buoyant* is the word—a word I had little use for. I wanted the river to roll down from wherever it was hiding, to catch me, carry me away. I wanted buoyancy.

I ran for the bank.

Not far from my door a figure stood up from the shadow of my fence. I stopped quick and saw François, silhouetted against the wide white light of the moon.

"François," I said. My voice cracked. I wondered: if he hacked off my head, how long would my blood stain the riverbed? Would Enah bring the waters and wash it away?

François offered his left hand. In his right, his machete gleamed.

I took a step back, but I gathered my courage and looked toward the high part of the bank. I kept my eyes on the gathering lights there as I said, "Are you going to tell Papa, or just cleave me?"

François was silent for a moment. Then, "I said that my parents would not be proud of what I do," he said. "Lena, *I* am not proud. God is not proud. I hardly know him, even when I want to pray."

I swallowed. In all the years Papa had paid him, he had never called me by name. "I don't have anyone to pray to," I said.

He offered his left hand. Again, I hesitated.

"François," I said. "What will happen if the water rises?"

"Life will return to the river valley," he said. "And if I'm lucky, I will never again cleave off anyone's head."

My heart raced. "So you want the water to rise?"

He offered his left hand.

I stepped forward, this time. Close enough to see that his eyes were rimmed with salt, like the blood on Mogul's nose.

Our blood will crack. Our tears will crack.

I ran forward and wrapped my hand in his.

His hand closed around mine, larger than mine, warmer, strong. "Your father will have us hunted," he said. "If you're afraid, you shouldn't come."

I was afraid. Of him, of the guards, of the villagers, of the flood. Of Papa, of Papa's dogs, of being cut off from the pumps. Of dying like Mogul. Of dying like Jaime. But I went up on my toes and kissed François on the cheek, and he accepted it like a man made of stone.

Then he said, "Come," and we walked up the bank. Toward the lights, where the wind scattered Enah's lilacs, and I imagined hyacinths on the breeze.

From Their Paws, We Shall Inherit

GARY KLOSTER

Monkey waited until the sky over the Gulf had gone all black and empty except for a billion stars before he pulled himself back onto the sailboat.

"Ceegee's roughed your stuff," he said, perched dripping on the rail. "They rough you too, Cesar?"

I spit in the ocean. When the cutter caught me, the ceegee boys had swarmed aboard and slammed me down so that some officer, all pretty in her white and brass, could question me.

Who're you, where you going, where you been? Where's the sugar? Over and over she'd asked, while her boys tore the boat apart. She hadn't liked my answers. She knew I was lying, even when they couldn't find anything. Finally, she had her boys rip my shorts off and gave me to her machines.

The ceegee robots had tentacles, reeking of rubber and lube. Those thin limbs had pushed between my teeth and down my throat, burrowed up my nose and shoved themselves deep into my ass. Searching all my hidden places.

They had wrecked my boat, and then they wrecked me. Those slick machines had left me choking, shitting, bleeding, puking. Sobbing. For all that wreckage and pain though, they hadn't found one speck of sugar.

Because a little monkey I'd found floating in the middle of the gulf days before had looked at the empty horizon and told me the Coast Guard was coming.

"Ceegee assholes," I said. "Course they'd rough a South Padre boy."

"You want to rough them back?" Monkey's eyes, glittering with starlight, met mine.

"How?"

Monkey curled his tail in and untied a thin white rope from it. "Haul this up."

"The sugar?"

"Yes. Plus something I took from their boat while they were busy with you."

"A gun?"

"Gun'll just get you killed," Monkey said. "Got you something better."

The rope ended in my drybag, and I opened it up. Three sealed boxes of sugar. Illegal pharma, or nano, or data or who-knows. South Padre pirates just called it all sugar, and gave dumbasses like me boats and money to haul it. Something else nestled between the boxes, a thin tablet of glass and aluminum.

"What am I suppose to do with a ceegee computer?" I could feel the rawness in my throat, in my ass, the ache deep inside me from being helpless and naked and violated while that ceegee officer and her boys had watched. A gun seemed like a better gift.

"Rough them," Monkey said. "I can teach you."

I frowned, turning the thing in my hands, not sure. Just a computer, encoded, locked, useless to me, but Monkey gave me a grin.

Why should I argue with the magic talking monkey? He'd saved me from either being sent to a work camp by the ceegees or being crucified by the pirates back home. So I held the computer and listened to him talk, and slowly the hurt and fear curled up inside me into a knot tight enough to ignore.

Excerpted from the astronomy site, *Constellation Prize*:

Really? Unexplained astronomical phenomena? Possible supernova? Really? Worst. Cover up. Ever.

Sure, most of the sheep don't know. They're too busy sucking off the media streams to notice anything, even lights in the fucking sky. But they'll know soon enough. We'll force those apes to look up for once.

We've got pictures of the flare, and the tracking data before and after. So what if the gubmint has shut the hell up? We don't need their fancy toys for this. We've already plotted the flight paths for Bogies 1 and 2. We can watch them ourselves—Big Brother gets my telescope when he takes it from my cold, dead hands.

We just have to agree on the narrative. We know *what's happening—a ship is tearing ass through our system right now, and last night it fired something off in our direction.*

We know *that. We can't be mealy-mouthed. Maybe it's this, maybe it's that, can't be sure, yadda yadda fuck you. We* know. *Second guessing now is just helping the cover-up. (Yeah, and I know some of you guys in the comments are plants. Eat shit and die, federal sockpuppets!)*

Possible supernova. Unexplained phenomena.

ALIENS, MOTHERFUCKERS!

We know.

How stupid do they think we are?

Well, I guess we did vote for them.

"Can I pet your monkey?" my sister Sophie asked, sitting on the balcony next to me, her back against the rust-rotted rail.

"He doesn't like kids," I said, but Monkey scampered down from my shoulder into her lap.

She smirked and ran her fingers through his fur. "See? He knows I'm not a kid, Cesar."

I tapped the tablet in my hands, marking my place in the trojan wiki Monkey had me reading and set it down to stare at my sister. Thirteen, and scary tall all of a sudden, with unexpected girl curves rounding her skinny body. No, she wasn't a kid anymore. That's why she spent so much time in our rooms now, so the pirates down below wouldn't notice her.

Hurricane Mindy had torn the south Texas coast to shreds, and only the newest and toughest of the resorts and condos on our barrier island had survived, broken teeth jutting from sandy gums that shifted and bled with every new storm. The mainlanders had given them up, and now they belonged to the squatters who'd refused to leave, like my mother, and to the pirates. With broken ships and garbage they had built a raft city between the towers, a port for the sugar trade, a rat hole where they could hide from the ceegee patrols circling out in the gulf.

It'd been rumored for years that the mainland would bomb us someday and send South Padres' towers finally crashing into the sea. Looking at the gull-picked corpses the pirates had chained to the balconies of the Hilton across from us, I wondered if they'd ever bother. If the hurricanes didn't finish us soon, the pirates would, and then they'd just eat themselves.

"You thinking about going out again?" Sophie said, her eyes following mine.

"No." My cut from that sugar run would pay our squat rights for two more months. By then, Monkey said I wouldn't need to risk my ass out on the ocean any more. Touching the tablet beside me, thinking of all I'd learned in the past few weeks from him and this little window into such a strange, wider world, I believed him.

"Good," Sophie said. Then, "Mom worried."

"Mom noticed?"

Sophie's fingers traced Monkey's back. "She cried."

"She wouldn't have had to, if she'd sobered up long enough to do her job and paid our rights. Then I wouldn't have had to go."

Sophie blinked back tears, and my throat went tight. "Christ," I sighed, staring at Monkey. He stared back at me, big eyes innocent.

"What are you looking at, furball? You keep saying it's almost time, well, I say it's past time. Start talking. Teach her. She needs this." Monkey stayed silent for a second, and I added, "You make me look crazy, and I'll throw you out for the gulls."

Monkey stuck his tongue out at me, but then he turned and faced my sister.

"Sophie," he said, his voice too deep for his tiny body. "Would you like to be a doctor, like your mother?"

Sophie's tough. She didn't throw Monkey off her, though she snatched her hand away.

"What?"

"I can teach you. The way I'm teaching Cesar to work his computer," Monkey said. "I can teach you to help people, the way your mom used to. You want to learn?"

Sophie looked at the little animal in her lap, eyes wide, lips starting to move, then the balcony door scraped open. Mom, red eyed and bleary, grimaced out into the bright daylight.

"Who the hell you talking to out here?"

"Cesar's monkey," Sophie said.

Mom stared at Monkey. "Rats with thumbs. Carry disease y'know. Should . . ." Her voice trailed away and she stumbled away from the light, back inside. The sound of plastic bottles rattled through the door, her searching for another swallow.

Sophie shoved the door shut. "What is he, Cesar?"

"Magic," I said, shrugging. "Don't know. Little bastard won't tell me."

"I'm telling you what you need, Cesar." Monkey's tail curled loose around Sophie's wrist. "So you and yours can leave this place."

"So we can be safe?" Sophie asked.

Monkey stared at me with his dark eyes, not answering, so I did.

"Not safe, Sophie. Strong."

Excerpted from *Constellation Prize:*

Bogie 1's leaving the system today. (Don't start with the quibbles. She's in the Kuiper belt, and that's my finish line. Going as fast as she is, it's not like she's going to turn around.)

She came, popped her baby, slung around the sun, and now she's off to boldly go wherever the hell she's going next.

Which just leaves us with Bogie 2. Which is definitely headed straight at us, after those course corrections we saw it fire off last week.

So what the hell is it?

An instrument package? An ambassador? A bomb?

Maybe it's a fucking fruit basket.

The answer is, we don't know. And since both ships refuse to return our calls, we won't know until it gets here. Frustrating, init?

Gosh, if only we could do something, like meet it half way, wouldn't that'd be great? Oh, but to do that we would need a space program that wasn't a complete fucking joke.

I know, we couldn't afford it. Billionaires needed tax breaks and artists needed grants to paint their asses blue. I get that.

I'm just saying it might've been nice to have the opportunity to be proactive here, instead of just watching as Bogie 2 cruises in.

Because while it's probably not a bomb, it's not like we could do shit about it if it was.

I guess we'll have to be content in knowing we spent our money on more important shit. *Like winning the war on drugs, amiright?*

Christ, we are such dumbasses. If it is a bomb, we deserve it.

• • •

The girl slammed the man down in our living room, scattering vodka bottles, screaming for the doctor.

I don't know how she hauled him up all those stairs, big as he was. She had though, and she sure as hell wasn't going to listen to me tell her the doctor was too hung over to help.

She yelled, I yelled, the man bled and groaned, then my sister shoved in.

"Shut up, Cesar, and hold him," Sophie snapped at me, wiping blood away from the knife handle that protruded from the man's belly.

Too confused to argue, I did what she said. The girl shut up too, staring at Sophie. I wondered why she didn't protest about a kid taking charge, but shit, Sophie was doing something.

Her hands danced across the man, pressing and poking into his neck, armpits, and groin. He groaned once, then passed out. Sophie jumped up, ducked into her room, and bounced back before I could yell at her with a suture kit and drug vials.

"Thought Mom sold all her shit."

"Not what I hid," Sophie said. "Grab the knife."

"Why?"

"Cause when I tell you, you're going to pull it out."

"What?"

"Do it, Cesar," Sophie said, her voice taking that crisp tone our Mom's used to get before she whupped us. "Do it just how I say, or he'll bleed out. And if I lose my first patient cause of you, you'll be my second."

"Yes ma'am."

Sophie gathered her supplies, paused to look at Monkey, who nodded at her. Then she started telling me what to do.

"Rest, clean water, and meat if you can get it. He lost a lot of blood." Sophie sounded exhausted, but she stood straight as she explained to the girl what her father would need. I listened and spun the knife in my hand, wondering what the hell to make of my little sister.

"Thank you." Lisa, the girl, she was about my age. "We owe you."

I stilled the knife, looked at the anchor branded into the skin of the girl's arm. "You're fisherfolk?"

"Yes. We'll get you fish, whatever you want." For the first time I noticed her long braids, her rich red-brown skin and my tongue went all sideways.

"Fish. Well—"

"What the hell's this?"

Mom stepped into the room, ragged with involuntary sobriety. She looked at the man stretched across our floor, a row of stitches marking his belly. "Who the hell did that?"

"I did," Sophie said, almost a whisper.

"When'd you decide to play doctor?"

"When you got too drunk to be one."

Mom stared at her, red-rimmed eyes almost focusing for once, then she turned away, stumbling back into her room.

"Who was—"

"Nobody," I told the girl, my tongue free again. "You got a boat?"

"Course we do."

"Good," I said, "We're going to need a ride, sometime soon."

"That we can trade you, easy." She smiled at me, and I smiled back, a little dizzy again. I looked away from her to catch my breath and caught sight of Monkey's tail disappearing into Mom's room.

Excerpted from *Constellation Prize*:

A year's passed since Bogie 2 blazed across the sky, broke up and dropped its pieces into the deepest parts of the ocean, and what's happened?

Nothing.

So is that all the show our visitors planned for us?

Doubtful.

They're down there, doing something. Spying? Colonizing?

Poking Cthulhu with a stick?

I have no fucking clue. None of us do. Us curious Georges gotta wonder, though. We stare at the waves and try to imagine what's going on down there. What are they doing, what are the planning?

When are they coming out?

Because they will. They didn't come all this way for nothing. Someday they're going to surface, and then what?

In the comments, in my inbox, everyday, that's the question, over and over. What are they going to do to us?

Christ, how the hell should I know?

All we can do is watch the sea and wait, and hope that maybe, if we're lucky, they won't fuck us over anymore than we've already fucked ourselves.

"Where you folk going?"

Samuel had a rough voice to go with his big body, but he treated me nice. He treated Sophie like a saint.

"New Orleans," I said.

"Orleans? Why in hell would you want to go somewhere more messed up than South Padre, boy?"

Because a man waited there with three new US national ID cards, each of them tied to grey market credit lines flush with the money I'd drained from some private accounts last week. A certain ceegee officer and her boys were going to be wondering where all their money had gone, soon.

I just smiled. "No worries, Samuel. You get us there, we'll be fine."

The big man grumbled, but went back to his rigging, rubbing his hand over the raw pink scar on his belly. His daughter helped him, and when Lisa caught me staring at her she smiled.

"We should bring them along."

Monkey's whisper made me jump, but he clung to my shoulder easy enough, lips brushing my ear as he spoke. "We'll need more people on the mainland."

"What for?" I asked, turning to the rail, away from the fisherfolk.

"Getting stronger. Look."

Following his arm, I could see something floating in the water. An old door, and on it—

"Jesus," I swore. "One for each of us, right?"

"You'll each need one. To learn, to grow."

I stared at the little monkeys clustered on the makeshift raft, staring back at me. "Grow into what?"

"Something better." Monkey shifted on my shoulder, and I realized how much I'd missed him being there these last few weeks. He'd helped me crack the ceegee's accounts and arrange our documents, but he spent most of his time now with my mother, whispering in her ear. "We're going to help you. All of you. There will be those, though, who won't like that."

"The people who make me and mine weak," I whispered.

"It'll change, Cesar. Your family will grow, and there are other families, all around the world, growing and learning like you. You'll come together, someday, and it'll all change." Monkey dropped from my shoulder, starting towards the prow where my mother stood, staring out at the waves. Standing straight, clean, sober.

"What are you teaching her?" I called after him, not caring who heard, knowing it didn't matter.

Monkey stopped and looked back at me, eyes shining with sunlight. "I'm teaching her about hope, Cesar. Hope, and God."

Something thumped against the hull, and over the rail the new monkeys bounded, eager to teach.

Sirius

BEN PEEK

Emily Parker

At the edge of Deacon College on Tunel Five, the statue of Amadou Qaramanli stands in an empty, sunlit square. A lab technician, he was born in Tripoli, and began working in the expansion of the Earth Empire at the age of sixteen, dying on a planet ninety seven percent water at the age of thirty four, having lived three years longer than myself. Pictures of him reveal an unassuming man, neither tall, nor overweight, nor blessed with a great or distinctive mind. Of his personal life, of his likes and dislikes, and of the small parts that make each of us an individual, history has nothing recorded. By the time I had been born, he had been dead for a century and humanity had been introduced to hundreds of new cultures and was struggling to establish itself. Asking for him to be anything but a cautionary tale amongst lab technicians was too much by then.

The story I heard was this:

Amadou and fellow Libyan born researcher, Dr. Waled, were a pair of sweat-stained, badly dieted, over-worked men sharing a run-down house in Saire, the capital city of Tunel Five. Tunel was one of the first gift planets by the Ta'La, a nomadic, pale-skinned, tall race that gifted the conquered planets they had no use for to other cultures. There, both men came into contact with a hemorrhagic virus named after the planet. It was the first incident between the two cultures and apologies were made, later. But, beneath the afternoon sun, far away from the official records, and feverish and with pains throughout their bodies, both men made the diagnosis and discussed the diluted state of the immune serum they had on the plastic table before them. They had enough for one shot each but, in the orange drenched evening, they acknowledged that their chances of survival were slim. As the sun darkened again and blood seeped from Amadou Qaramanli's eyes, he told Dr. Waled to take both doses.

The statue on the planet Tunel Five was funded by Dr. Waled after his return to Earth. For decades, the portly scientist told the story of Amadou's sacrifice, going as far to write about it in his self-published memoirs as a sacrifice for science, a technician's recognition of the importance of his role. It was a book that sold only to technicians, as Waled, apart from this one event, was an even more unremarkable man than his technician. Having read the book and understanding the tale I, when discovering that the door to the lab containing infected mice had not closed properly after I stepped out of my suit, and fearing Dr. Singh's response, took two shots of antibiotic cocktails, one for myself and one for the memory of Amadou.

Two hours later, alone in my room on board *Sirius*, I sneezed.

That was all.

John Gale

Maria, I am sorry.

I thought to come home, to hold you, to touch you, to let the sun sink into my skin, turn me brown, but I cannot. You cannot see the destroyed station below me. You cannot know that it began with the body of Emily Parker, a middle-aged woman with dyed red hair. She was delivered to me by her parents, an elderly pair of Ta'La ethnographers who pushed her into my theater on the back of a silver cart. They told me, as we lifted her, that the Ta'La thought us callous because we mutilated our dead to learn how they had passed. They asked if I could be as gentle as possible with their daughter. As they spoke, *Sirius* orbited the dusty, red planet of Solle, a gift to the Earth Empire from the beings that saw us as cold and cruel; beings that let us rotate our personnel between the planet and the station, let us cut into the planet as we did our dead, examining it as we built atmospheric pressurizers on top of it, as we proved to them we could colonize the stars.

Only you are in my thoughts as I look upon the wreckage that my body now lies in. I wish we had done things differently. Parker followed her parents, or her parents followed her, I do not know which, but I felt your loss in their presence, so much so that while I noted the slight discoloration around the body's fingers and the gentle swelling in the stomach, I did not fully comprehend it. I would have cut if the head of the Science and Research Department, Dr. Anu Singh, had not strode in. He wore a yellow bio-hazard suit and his breath echoed with every step.

In quarantine, the parents apologized.

"We just didn't think," the father, Edward, said. His lined face sagged, as if the skin would drop away. "This is our first planet. Our—"

"We were just—" Trish, the mother, paused. "She was our only daughter," she finished quietly.

Maria, I miss you.

Anu Singh

The problem was simple: to that tall, skeleton race of nomads who wandered across the universe, we were biologically and culturally inferior. Their opinion was clear in the discoloration on Emily and Edward Parker's fingers, but you could also see how they underestimated us, did not fully understand us, yet. Trish Parker and John Gale did not have the same discoloration and the slight bloating in Emily was singular. As were John Gale's tumors, which were found inside the heart and argued a rapid onset with no pre-existing condition. Nothing suggested an epidemic yet, but after the death of a young boy who had no connection to Emily Parker, her parents, or John Gale, I took my concerns to the Station Commander, Bruce Cawell.

"You can't quarantine the entire *Sirius*, doctor," he said, snappish in the way that elderly white Londoners are. A career soldier, his hair close cut and white, he sat before me in his sparse office and sipped water while the rim of Solle, a dirty, red-brown smear, grew outside. "It would panic people and only stop the planetside rotation from returning in nineteen days, days before, I might add, their food and water needs to be resupplied."

I tried to impress upon him the fact that we had no idea what had caused it.

"We have five deaths," he said, punctuating his diminishing patience by placing his glass down loudly. "It is tragic, but by your own admittance the boy's death may not even be connected to the first four."

Beneath us is a planet with untold secrets, I told him. We bring into our quarantine labs rocks, soil, and the remains of anything we find that is interesting, but we do so like a child slapping blindly at blocks that need to go into a hole. The Ta'La tell us that once, they conquered thousands of planets in a history that they wish to step away from. That they instead, now, wish to help the universe, to grow it, but to do so with a vision we cannot understand.

"I am aware that the Ta'La are not always thoughtful with their gifts, doctor, but *Sirius* is fitted with very expensive and very state-of-the-art filters and monitoring systems. With none of those tripped, you are jumping to conclusions."

I pressed him to acknowledge the possibility that a secondary infection, one that was droplet-based, could be carried through the system after being spread by sneezing or dust or mice.

"Are you missing any mice?" he asked.

No, I told him.

He smiled faintly. "Perhaps we can cross that one out, then."

My response, I admit, was not the most calculated. I have never dealt well with those who cannot see clearly. To my outburst, Commander Cawell straightened and his pale, cold eyes held mine. "Five people have died, doctor. I am not making jokes. Nor am I humoring you anymore. New diseases on our own planet are found all the time, but we do not panic then, nor now. Your belief that the Ta'La are responsible is misplaced."

When I began to argue, he said, "I suggest you return to your lab."

My hands curled around the plastic handles, furious.

"You are dismissed," he said.

Outside, I let out a frustrated breath. How could he be so blind? Already, I could feel a heaviness in the air, as if there was something new to it, something that we had not seen. Ahead of me in the hallway ran small air ducts, just as there were hundreds throughout *Sirius,* each of them linking back to a central system that was shared by everyone in the station. To me, it was already a beating, diseased heart, spreading the virus across the ship and my breath was a series of shallow, nervous gasps through my teeth as I made my way to my lab and the contamination suit within.

I would live in it for six weeks, the longest of anyone on board *Sirius,* the longest of anyone who stands around me wordlessly now. Such was my prize for being right.

Bruce Cawell

I did not believe that the Pakistani was right. It was a simple mistake, born from personal dislike.

At the time he approached me, Singh had been on board *Sirius* for just eight station months, an unpleasant replacement for the talented Dr. Ken. This far out into the system, colony stations are not given much choice about who is sent, and in my capacity of commander on this small bastion at the edge of civilization, I have worked with all kinds. The experience had made me more tolerant, though with Singh, it was if I was green all over again.

He arrived wanting to make a career for himself, a scientist who believed that it would take him a year to find a disease to make his name and gain tenure in a planet lab. He believed that the Ta'La were killers, that they were involved in our slow genocide, and he wanted proof of that to take back home. Within weeks, he was pushing his lab workers, demanding results that could not happen, and asking for tests that were nothing short of invasive in both privacy and decency from those who returned from Solle. I had already been forced to intervene on two separate occasions when the doctor overstepped his mark. With a limited intelligence and an even more limited moral compass, Dr. Singh had rapidly become detestable not just to me, but the entire *Sirius* crew.

My mistake was that I could not see beyond that.

When his staff informed me that the morning after our meeting he had appeared at work in a yellow biohazard suit, having walked the public corridors in it, my first instinct was to lock him up. He was clearly unfit for the duty that had been bestowed to him. When I started receiving calls not just from within the station, but from the planet, demanding to know what 'outbreak' had taken place, I took two soldiers and visited Singh's room after his scheduled hours. When I arrived, he was not there, and I unlocked the door to his unit to wait for him. Inside, I found it in disarray: the tables, chairs, clothes and bed were pushed up against the wall, hastily thrown to make room for a large map that covered the ground. It took me a moment to realize that it was *Sirius* itself, with five dots on it. The dots represented the paths that the deceased had traveled upon in their last day.

If it was airborne virus, I thought before stopping myself. With a shake of my head, I removed a chair from the pile against the wall and settled down to wait. Staring at the map for that time did not, I admit, help me believe I had made the right choice the day before, but I have already admitted my flaw and will not dwell on it. Perhaps events would have gone differently if I had remained there and stared at the map, if I had allowed Singh's paranoia to seep into me, but an alert was sent to me that a new body had been found and that the doctor, in his suit, was standing around unsuited technicians and crew, securing the area.

Once there, I said coldly, "You are frightening people."

We were standing in the bedroom of the deceased, beneath an air duct above the door. Singh, his eyes on it at all times, moved to stand in front of the window, the lower half of which was filled with the dirty shape of Solle.

"I will not be quiet," he replied, his voice carrying an echo from the suit. "This body, this new death—this was not a man connected to any of the previous five. He was not even in the same part of the station! This does not affect just us, but those on Solle too!"

"Keep your voice down, or I will have you locked up to keep calm."

"You would not dare!"

I did.

After I had placed him in his cell, Dr. Singh refused to remove his suit. This information, however, I used against him. I showed images of him to calm a panic that was emerging in *Sirius* and to assure those planetside that they could return normally, that supplies were fine. For a week, as normality returned, I was vindicated. But the deaths continued and Singh's words to me were repeated in whispers by others until they filled the station. When I returned to Singh, he was still in his suit, but he had nothing to say to me. To others, he would speak, but I was given only silence, and as pains began to wrack my body, I was relieved from command and spoken to by no one.

A week later as I lay shivering in a hot bath that scalded my skin, my last sight was the burst of pressure as escape pods launched.

Amanda Neal

I was forced to quarantine the men and women who fell from *Sirius* not because of their infected state, but because I needed to ration our food and water and control access to the dig sites. Solle City, the only city on Solle, was a sprawling, skeletal creature filled with the remains of a conquering nomadic race and a second, extinct race that the Ta'La did not acknowledge in their histories. If not for the bones, you would believe the Ta'La had found the planet empty. The threat posed by the angry escapees, then, to this knowledge was unacceptable. In my arrogance, I believed that there was much to be learned about the Ta'La through those remains, much that would make our dealings with them easier. Five years ago, I stood before a Ta'La and watched the slow blink of its eyes, its naked, genderless body offering a cold indifference to all conversation made to it and I knew that if we wished to survive in a universe that was not just us, we had to know everything we could of those around us. We could not afford to view these creatures as ancient killers turned galactic shepherds.

After overseeing the quarantine, I stepped into my office and called *Sirius* privately. As the call was put through, I laid the blame for the situation squarely at the feet of Dr. Singh, a detestable and incompetent man who, for a brief moment, I had thought would be an ally against Commander Cawell. Oh, how I would be eating my words again as I banded with the British soldier against the doctor.

To my surprise, however, the call connected me immediately with the image of Singh, sitting in a dirty yellow contamination suit.

"What is going on, doctor?"

"Neal." He smiled, but it was a sickly. "How good it is to see you."

"I don't have time for this. I want to be briefed on what has happened and what is being done to ensure we can feed the people here."

"You've met the Ta'La." Singh's eyes closed, and he swayed; when he lifted his lids, the lack of balance in his physical form was present there, too. "Tell me, are they really like birds? People compare them to birds in the literature, and always favorably. They compare them to hawks and eagles, but they're wrong. I see that now. They should be compared to myna. That's a bird that drives off native birds with its violence, drives them off so that when it leaves an area—if it leaves an area—there is nothing but emptiness left behind."

"What has happened on *Sirius*, doctor?"

"Emily." A faint smile crossed his face. "That is what I call it. It is airborne. That is the most logical conclusion. There are no survivors and no serum and it manifests differently in everyone and leaves a complete genome in its victim, complete where it had before been incomplete in us since the dawn of time. It's not the same genome, either. That is what made it difficult for me to understand. It finds different strands in every single person."

I frowned, but said nothing.

"It is a swarm," he continued, his voice given rhythm by the drugs he had taken. "A swarm of virions that completes what is inside us."

I was thirty seven when I met my first Ta'La, when I stood before it and watched as a man I admired tried to convey to it the importance of research, the responsibility we all had—all creatures had—to understand themselves and those around them. Afterward, he said that the being did not understand the double meaning of his words, the veiled threat that was implied in that small office, in that pale, peach-lit room where we were gifted Solle.

"Doctor, doctor," Singh whispered, pressing the glass of his contamination helmet to the screen. "You are alone, now."

And then the screen went black.

Reverend Packer

The Lord will have to forgive my cowardice.

I have prided myself on honesty, of not flinching away from difficult situations, of being true to the Lord and the tenants He has left us, especially here on the edges of civilization amongst the Godless. Yet, when Dr. Neal approached me and asked—through her growing fever—if I would return to *Sirius,* I agreed only because I thought it would save me. I could think of nothing else. I rejoiced when I was told that I would be given one of the few contamination suits we owned, that I would be taking a quarter of our remaining food and water, that I would be allowed to read the notes left by Dr. Singh and have access to the research done in the station. If a cross were but real upon me now, I would feel its weight, and be chastised by my thoughts.

I shared the shuttle with Richard, a young blond man who had arrived with the colony on a scholarship from the military. He was the only 'scientist' capable of making the journey and it was to him that the deciphering of the notes and saving us would fall. I was but a pilot with a desire to learn. With notes from Dr. Neal strewn around us, we spoke little as we approached the orbiting mass of *Sirius,* until it was time to voice our fears at the sight the large, circular station adrift brokenly, as if a careless child had dropped it from a great height.

In awkward, slow movements, we drifted in bulky space suits from the shuttle to the exposed entrance of *Sirius.* Debris floated inside: frozen chairs, brittle boxes, cracked glasses. They broke beneath my hands as I pushed them aside to make our way to the command deck. It was there that we found, lodged against the ceiling in a tattered contamination suit, the remains of Dr. Singh. With a clumsy sign of the cross, I turned away from the terrible visage that he was, and tried to bring power back to the remains of the station.

I could only find a small amount, enough to bring up the design map of *Sirius.* Disappointed, I made my way to Singh's laboratory, located in a fragment that curved above the command center. It took an hour to navigate to it, a journey that saw me ticking off the hopes and dreams I had. No wife, no children. I could hear Richard's voice through the suit, murmuring, and as we made our way through the quiet corridors, his words a repetition of knowledge he dare not forget, a sign of faith I no longer had. Finally, we reached a large white room adorned by floating beakers and frozen fluids.

There was no power here, either, and my hope that I would be able to bring up a very basic amount to read what Singh had kept on file was not one that the Lord granted. Instead, there were only papers that crumbled beneath my every touch.

I became sick when we returned to the shuttle. I took only one kindness, words from a young man who tried to treat me even as he became sick, that all signs of the infection pointed to a virus of such a virulent nature that, by killing us so quickly, it was also killing itself.

Bakana Mer

I am the first and the last. The last of the first people that watched the huge, shuddering bulk of the Ta'La cruisers press through the atmosphere of our home. The first people who experienced cruelty deliberate in the diseases sown into their gifts, the first who watched a people and culture destroyed so another could take it. Irony, oh irony, I am told by those new spirits, those who arrived here to take the Ta'La gift, that their ancestors did the same, years ago. Then, they gave blankets riddled with diseases and, like the Ta'La, took another's home to expand their own culture. As I listen to their words, I am unable to offer sympathy. They have died, yes, died from a stain rooted deep into my world, a world that is no longer filled with water, that no longer shimmers, and they are the victims to the thoughts of domination that motivate the Ta'La; but they, in coming to my home, in accepting my world as their gift, have shown that they are nothing but a different shade of the people who killed me.

History, I murmured to my child, does not chart a course in singular events, never to be repeated again.

Her answer, I knew, was no longer one she could grow into.

Synch Me, Kiss Me, Drop

SUZANNE CHURCH

When my nose stopped aching, I smiled at Rain. She had snorted a song ten minutes before me, and I couldn't quite figure why she waited here in the dark confines of the sample booth.

"Rain?" I said. "You okay?"

"Do you hear it, Alex?" she said, not really looking at me. More like staring off in two directions at once, as though her eyes had decided to break off their working relationship and wander aimlessly on their own missions. "It's so amaaazing."

She held that "a" a long time. I should've remembered how gripping every sample was for her, as though her neurons were built like radio antennae, attuned to whatever channel carried the best track ever recorded. I needed to get her ass on the dance floor before I got so angry that I ended up with another Jessica situation. I still had eight months left on my parole.

"Do you hear it?" Rain nudged me, hard on the shoulder. "Alex!" Her eyes had made up and decided to work together, locking on me like I was the only male in a sea of estrogen.

"Yeah, it's awesome," I lied. For the third time this week, I'd snorted a dud sample. My brain hadn't connected with a single, damned note.

Beyond the booth, the thump, thump of dance beats pulsed in my chest. Not much of a melody, but since they'd insisted I check my headset with my coat, I couldn't exactly self-audio-tain.

I grabbed her arm, feeling the soft flesh and liking it. Loving it. Maybe the sample *was* working on some visceral level beyond my ear-brain-mix. "Let's hit the dance floor."

"In a minute. Pleeease."

Over-vowels were definitely part of her gig tonight.

"Wait for the *drop*," she said, stomping her foot.

"Right." I watched her sway back and forth, in perfect rhythm with the dance music coming from the main floor. The better clubs brought all the vibes together, so that every song you sampled was in perfect synch with the club mix on the speakers. When the drop hit, everyone jumped and screamed in coordinated rapture.

I would miss the group-joy here in this tiny booth, with this date who was more into her own head than she would ever be into me. If I could get Rain out on the floor, I could at least feel the bliss, whiff all the pheromones, feel all those sweaty bodies pressed against mine, soft tissues rubbing together.

"Yeaaaah!" She shouted and grabbed my hand, squeezing it. Harder. Her eyes pressed shut, her mouth wide open, she leaned her head way back.

The drum beats surged, and then, for a fraction of a second they paused. Everyone in the club inhaled, as though this might be the last lungful of air left in the world and then . . .

Drop.

But *drop* doesn't say it all. Not even close. Because when it happens, it's like the most epic orgasm of all time and pinching the world's biggest crap-log at the same moment.

Rain opened her eyes and pressed her hand against the side of my cheek. Lunging with remarkable speed for a woman who over-voweled, she kissed me. Her tongue pressed against my lips.

I tasted her. Wanted her. An image of Jessica popped into my head: the look of terror on her face when I accidentally yanked her under.

The euphoria gone, I closed my mouth and turned away from Rain.

"Whaaat?" she said.

For a second, I thought about explaining what I had done to Jessica. Spewed on about how the drop isn't always built of joy. Instead, I went with the short, obscure answer. "Probation."

Rain looked at me funny, like she couldn't quite figure out how the judicial dudes could mess with our kiss-to-drop ratio. Finally, she smiled, and said, "Riiight."

Desperate to avoid another over-vowel, I shouted, "Let's dance!" This time, when I grabbed her arm, she followed along like a puppy.

Scents smacked at us as we pushed our way through the seething mass on the floor. This week's freebie at the door was *Octavia,* some new perfume marketed at the twenty-something set. It was heavy on Nasonov pheromones, some bee-juice used to draw worker-buzzers to the hive. When the drug companies cloned it, the result was as addictive as crack and as satisfying as hitting a home run on a club hook-up.

My nostrils still ached from snorting a wallop of nanites, but scent doesn't only swim in the nose. The rest is all neurons, baby, and I had plenty to spare. Apparently so did Rain, because she was waving her nose in the air like a dog catching the whiff of a bitch in heat. The sight of her made me want to take her and do her right there on the floor.

But *Conduct* was a high-end club. The bouncers would toss us both if they caught us in the act anywhere on the premises, so I kept it in my pants. I still had another two hundred in my pocket. Enough for three more samples. Maybe I'd pick up a track from an indie-band this time. Top forty drivel never seized my brainstem.

Unlike Rain.

The beats were building again. This time, with a third-beat thump, like reggae on heroin. I could feel the intensity from my fingertips to my teeth to my dick. Even if I couldn't hear more than the background beats, I anticipated the drop. Rain opened her mouth again, raised both her hands in the air with everyone else, like a crowd of locusts all swarming together.

Pause.

Drop.

My date kept her eyes closed, her hands on her own breasts as she milked the release for all it was worth. Any decent guy should've watched her, should've wanted to, but I caught sight of a luscious creature, near the high-end sample booth, in the far right corner of the club. The chick was about to slip between the curtains, but she caught me staring.

Her eyes glowed the purple of iStim addiction, reminding me of Jessica.

She had grown up in the suburbs, her allowance measured in thousands not single dollars. The pack of girls she hung with had all bought iSynchs when they first hit the market. The music sounded better when they could all hear the same song at the same time. For the first time in more than a hundred years, getting high was not only legal, but ten times more amazing than it had ever been before. We all lived in our collective heads, the perfect synch of sound and sex.

I should've turned away from the sight of the purple-chick, should've reached out to Rain and kissed her again. Close tonight's deal. Instead, I approached her swaying body, and next to her ear shouted, "Back in five."

She nodded.

Fueled by fascination, and the two hundred burning a hole in my pocket, I headed for the high-end booth.

One of the bald bouncers with tribal tattoos worked the curtains. Yellow earplugs stuck out of both ears, so conversation, or in my case, pleading, wasn't an option. Feeling in my pocket for the two hundred, I scrunched the bills a bit, trying to make the wad appear larger than its meager value, then pulled out the stack in a flash. I had never dealt with this particular bouncer. *Conduct* was more Rain's club than mine, so I hoped the bills would get me past. The guy didn't even acknowledge me, as though he could smell my poverty, or maybe my parole. His eyes stared straight ahead.

My head scarcely came up to his bare chest, so I was uncomfortably close to his nipple-rings, but I held my ground, and pointed at the curtains.

He remained statue-like. More boulder-like. Then a woman's cream-colored hand with purple nails ran from the guy's waist to his pecs and he turned to the side, like a vault door.

Purple-chick stood in the gap between the curtains. Her black dress was built of barely enough fabric to meet the dress code. Her hair stood on end like a teenager's beard, barely there and oddly sexy. She must have dyed it every night, because the stubble matched her eyes and nails. A waking wet dream.

"Come in." She pointed beyond the curtains.

"In what?" I mumbled to myself.

"Very funny."

"You're not laughing."

My body neared hers as I moved past into the sample booth. I carried my hands a little higher than would have passed as natural, hoping to cop a feel of all that exposed flesh on my way by. But she read me like a pheromone and dodged back.

A leather bench-seat lined the far wall of the booth. Three tables were set with products in stacks like poker chips. The first was a sea of purple, tiny lower-case "i's" stamped on every top-forty sample like a catalog from a so-called genius begging on a street corner for spare music. The second was a mish-mash of undergrounds like *Skarface, Audexi,* and *Brachto.*

The third table drew me like fire. Only one sample. The dose was pressed into a waffle-pattern, which was weird enough to make my desire itch. But the strangest part was its flat black surface that sucked light away and spewed dread like mourners at a funeral.

Purple-chick watched me stare at it, waiting for me to speak. My mouth kept opening and closing, but I couldn't find words.

Expensive. Dangerous. Parole. All perfectly legit words that I couldn't voice.

I had forgotten my two hundred. My palms must have been really sweating, because what had once been a quasi-impressive stack, now stunk of poor-dude-shame.

With practiced smoothness, she liberated my cash and said, "The *Audexi* works on *everyone.*"

Distracted from the waffle, I said, "How'd you know I couldn't hear the last track?"

"Your throat," she said. "You're not pulsing to the beat."

My fingers felt my pulse beating like a river of vamp-candy. Her observations were bang-on. I wanted to illustrate my coolness, or, at the very least, my lack of lameness, but all I could manage was, "Oh."

She laughed.

My eyes wandered back to the waffle. I licked my lips.

Grabbing my chin, she forced me to look at tables one and two. "Your price range."

"What's the waffle?"

"New."

"Funny."

She didn't laugh. "Far from it."

"Addictive?" I asked, staring at the purple on the first table. How this woman could work the booth without Jonesing for her own product made me rethink her motives.

"The absolute best never are," she said.

"No black eyes allowed in the boardroom, huh?"

She nodded. "Precisely."

I remembered Rain. By now, she'd have noticed my absence.

Purple-chick still held my two hundred. Her eyes locked on mine. "Try the *Audexi*. You won't be disappointed."

Like a Vegas dealer, she shoved all of my money through a hole in the wall, selected an *Audexi* sample from table two, and held it in front of my nose.

I probably should've reported her. All of the clubs had to be careful not to push products hard, end up drawing the cops in to investigate. But my money was long gone and Rain wouldn't wait much longer.

I exhaled. The moisture turned the poker-chip-shaped disk into a teeming pile of powder-mimicking nanites, and I snorted. For several blinding seconds, my nose felt as though a nuclear bomb had blown inside. I could feel Purple-chick's hand on my arm, making sure I didn't wipe out and sue the club. Then the song erupted in my mind.

Sevenths and thirds. Emo-goth-despair. Snares and the ever-present bass, bass, bass. Music flowed like a tsunami through a village, grabbing ecstasy like cars and plowing through every other thought except for the sweet tweaks of synths and the pulse-grab of the click-track. The song was building, and all I could think about was finding Rain before the drop.

Rain and I danced in nanite-induced harmony until the early dawn. Exhausted and covered in sweat and pheromones, we grabbed our coats and carried rather than wore them outside.

The insides of my sore nose stuck together in the frigid air, a wake-up call for the two of us to don our coats or end up with frostbite. I didn't want to, I was so damned hot and pumped, but I figured I should set a good example for Rain. And the way our night was progressing, I wouldn't have much time to scan my barcode at the parole terminal before curfew.

Jessica's fucking choice of words would be killing my buzz for eight more months.

That fourth of October had been hot as hell. After clubbing, we both stripped and headed into the lake for a skinny dip. Except she wasn't skinny and I wasn't much of a dipper. She'd called me over to the drop and I thought she meant for the lingering song, not the drop-off hidden in the water. When the drop blissed me, I lost my footing and plunged over my head.

"Shit, it's cooold," said Rain.

I snapped back to reality. "Still with the vowels?"

"Screw you." She pushed me away and called a cab with the same arm-wave.

"Don't be that way, baby."

"Now I'm your fucking baby? After ditching me for a dozen drops while you plucked that purple fuzz-head."

"You saw?"

"Who didn't?"

"Sorry. But you gotta admit, you and me, we really synched *after*." I nudged her, maybe a little too hard. "The last sample I snorted was worth it. Right?"

A cab squealed a U-turn and stopped in front of Rain. She started to climb in and then looked up at me.

I shook my head. Shrugged. "Tapped out."

"Fine." She slammed the door in my face and the cab took off up the street.

I stood there, watching my breath condense in the air, its big cloud distorting her and the cab. The cold clawed its way into me, sucking away my grip on reality. The shivering reminded me to at least wear my coat.

As I stuffed my arms into the sleeves, I sniffled, feeling wetness and figuring the cold was making my nose run. But then I noticed the red drops on the ground and the front of my coat. I wiped with one finger and it came back a dark and bloody mass. Dead nanites, blood, snot, all mixed together. Two shakes didn't get it off my finger, so I rubbed the mess in a snow bank and only managed to make it worse.

The nearest subway was blocks away. I should've kept my mouth shut, shared the cab with Rain and then stiffed her for half the fare. But I'd hurt her enough for one night. Hurt enough women for one lifetime.

Jessica had been the closest thing to a life preserver, so I grabbed on. Tripping on the samples, her brain couldn't remember how to hold her breath, or at least that's how my lawyer argued it at the trial.

As I trudged for the subway, I concentrated on not slipping and falling on my ass. I found the entrance, and headed down the stairs, gripping the cold metal handrail, even though my warm skin kept sticking to it. The *Audexi* sample still pulsed through my system and I couldn't walk down in anything but perfect synch. The song was building to another drop, and I had to make the bottom of the platform before that moment, or I would be another victim of audio-tainment.

The platform was nearly empty, save for a few other clubbers too tapped out to cab their way home. *Octavia* hung in the air, the Nasonov-pheromone-scents calling us all home like buzzers to the hive. Much as I loathed their company, I couldn't resist the urge to huddle with the others in the same section while we waited for the train.

Off to our right I caught sight of Purple-chick. She wore a long, black faux-fur coat. The image of her here, slumming it with the poor, was as wrong as a palm tree in a snow bank. She belonged in some limo, holding a glass of champagne.

I tried to break the pull of the scent-pack, but couldn't step far enough away from my fellow losers to get within talking distance of Purple-chick. When the train arrived, I watched her step inside, then waited until the last second before I climbed aboard, to make sure we were both on the same train.

The cars were so empty that I could see her, way ahead.

Standing near the doors, she held a pole while she swayed back and forth. I couldn't figure out why she didn't sit down, especially after a long night at the club. The rest of us were sprawled on benches, crashing more than sitting.

I considered the long trek up to her car, but I didn't trust my balance. Instead, I watched her. Waited until she stepped in front of the doors, announcing her intention to disembark.

Once again, I waited until the last second to leave the train, in case she decided to duck back on without me. I could tell that she knew I was watching. Following.

Okay, *stalking*.

She hurried up the stairs. Either she was training for a marathon, or her samples had all worn off, because I couldn't keep up. When she reached the top, she turned around and said, "What?"

Instead of rushing off, she stood there, at the top of the stairs. Waiting.

Her eyes were blue.

Not purple.

I hurried until I stood in front of her, nose to nose. "You took the waffle?"

She nodded.

"Tell me."

She shook her head. "Can't."

"Figures." I turned away.

"But I can show you."

"Yeah?"

"Kiss me," she said.

I sure as hell didn't wait for her to change her mind. We shared it all: tongues, saliva, even our teeth scraped against each other, making an awful sound that knocked my sample completely out of my head.

What filled the void wasn't the pounding of my heartbeat. Or hers. Or any song that I had ever heard. Instead, I could hear her thoughts, as visible as a black blanket on a white sand beach.

"Wow," I said.

Isn't it?

Her words, not spoken but thought into me. They reverberated around my skull like noise bouncing in an empty club.

I lost my footing and fell. Down. In. Far away. Suddenly I was six years old and my father leaned over and hauled me back up onto my skate-clad feet. We skated together, him holding me, his back stooped over in that awkward way that would make him curse all evening.

"Find your balance, Alex. Bend your knees. Skate!"

I had forgotten how much I loved him. Forgotten what it felt like to be young and innocent, to enjoy the thrill of exercise for its own sake, and feel a connection that didn't cost the price of a sample.

"I love you." But when I looked up at him, he had morphed back into Purple-chick, now Purple-and-blue-chick. She held me, preventing my crash down the stairs.

"Cool, huh?" she said.

"A total mind-fuck."

"That's why it's so expensive."

"How much? I mean, you're on the subway, so if I save—"

"In my experience, those who ask the price can't afford it."

"Why me?" I said.

She smiled. "Marketing."

I needed a better answer, so I listened for her thoughts. All I sensed was the wind from another subway, blowing up the stairs at me.

She turned and hurried for an exit.

"Wait!" My head buzzed, confused by the difference between waffle and real, trapped by the synch-into-memory-lane trip that lingered on my tongue like bad breath.

Her boots stopped clapping against the lobby of the subway station, but she didn't look back. I was glad of it, because my memories were still swimming in my head. I wanted her to be Dad.

Not Dad. *Rain.* My former date's cute outfit lingered in my synapses, replacing nostalgia with guilt. I wondered if Rain had made it home okay in the cab.

Then naked Jessica filled my head, and it was October again.

"I didn't mean it," I said aloud, my voice echoing against the tile walls. "The high confused it all. I'll do another year of parole. I'll spend my sample money on flowers for your grave. Please, forgive me?"

Still with her back to me, and in a voice that sounded eerily like Jessica's, she said, "What about Rain?"

I shook my head, even though she couldn't possibly see me. "She'll understand."

Far ahead, Purple-and-blue-chick turned to face me. I saw her as *them,* she had somehow merged with Jessica, the two of them existing in perfect synch, like a sample and the club music stitching together; twins in a corrupted womb. They both saw me for what I was, a lame guy who would always be about eight hundred shy of a right and proper sample. Whose love would always be shallow, too broke to buy modern intimacy.

"You've got less than ten minutes to clock in your parole." She started walking again, and I watched her leave, one synched step at a time until she exited the station and disappeared along the ever-brightening street.

Drop.

Only this drop, waffle-back-to-real, felt like nails screeching on a blackboard. I wasn't in my usual subway station, and I had no idea where to find the nearest parole scanner. The station booth was empty, too early for a human. The only person in sight was an older woman with the classic European-widow black-scarf-plus-coat-plus-dress that broadcast, *Leave me alone, young scum.*

So I did.

I hurried onto the street, and looked towards the sun. It was well above the horizon now, but mostly hidden behind a couple of apartment buildings.

"Fuck," I told the concealed ball of reddish-yellow light. "How'd it get so late?"

The judiciary alarm buzzed inside my head.

For a moment, I could feel a drop, the biggest, most intense and amazing drop I would ever experience. The sort of nirvana that people pursue ineffectually for a lifetime. Or two.

I had less than ten minutes until the final warning.

Rushing for the nearest, busiest street, I tried to wave down car after car, hoping someone would point me to the nearest scanner. Or maybe they had a portable one, the kind I should've brought with me, had I been thinking about more than getting into Rain's pants when I left.

People ignored me.

Shunned me.

I smelled of trouble. Which, technically, I was. But I didn't mean to be. It wasn't my fault.

It was never my fault.

One cab slowed, but didn't stop. The driver made eye contact, and then rushed away.

"Hey!" I considered swearing at him, but I didn't want to draw the cops.

I'm not sure why the cabbie stiffed me. Maybe he read my desperation. Maybe he was Rain's cabbie and he knew I was broke. In any case, he probably broadcast a warning to his buddies, because the next cab that got remotely close made a fast U-turn and took off.

Choosing a direction, I took off down one street, then hung a right at the next, jogging, skidding, almost falling on my ass. Every direction felt wrong.

I didn't see a single person. No one. Not even a pigeon for fuck's sake. All I needed was a *phone.*

With one hand on a pole, I leaned over, trying to catch my breath. To think.

My heart was pounding now, no synch in sight. The song was long gone, the link to Purple-chick disconnected. No one had my back.

I turned in a circle, then another, scanning far and near for anything of value: an ATM, a phone booth, a coffee shop, a diner, any place where I could access the judicial database. Plead my case.

The final warning buzzed.

"Fuck!" My spit froze when it hit the ground.

I hit full blown panic. My heart tripped like the back-bass before the drop. Only this time, the other side was built of misery not ecstasy.

If only I had paid my cell bill. If only my father was still alive, to catch my sorry ass. If only I had lied to Rain, shared her cab. If only Jessica hadn't called it a drop.

When you're panicked, it's tough as hell to keep any rational sense of time. I figured I was cooked. So I closed my eyes. But when the pain didn't come, I sat down on the cold curb, and felt the chill seep through my clothes.

I bit my lip. Tasted blood.

The first jolt ripped through my body. I wanted to writhe in pain on the sidewalk, but my body was stuck in shock-rigor. An immobile gift for the cops.

I imagined Rain beside me.

"You're an asshole," she said.

"Sorry."

She morphed into Jessica, her purple eyes wide with fear. "I'm lost," she said.

"Take my hand." I wanted to reach out, but I couldn't move. My fingers looked nearly white in the cold. Her fingers seemed to shiver around mine, as though they were made of joy, not flesh. Then she touched my hand and I knew in that moment that life existed outside of stimulation, in a place where reality wasn't lame or boring. Life danced to an irregular rhythm that couldn't synch to any sample.

She let go.

The judiciary pulse jolted again. I flopped to the pavement, distantly aware that my skull would remind me for a long time after about its current state of squishage.

The parole board must have lived for irony, because the jolt lasted for so long that I *welcomed* the release. A pants-wetting, please-make-it-stop, urgent need for the end.

Drop.

Iron Ladies, Iron Tigers
SUNNY MORAINE

Ping.

Vita. Wake up.

Spinning through the dark, I hear and feel CERA's alert both at once, a sound that is a vibration like a plucked string between my sealed eyes. I shift in the padded transit cocoon. I move hands that barely feel like mine, and I feel wires pulling the jacks in my skin at the same instant as my fingers hit the tape over my eyelids. I wedge my nails under the strips and they come away like old skin. My tongue feels like a dry slug trapped between my teeth and my soft palate. But all of this is distant. I'm in high orbit over myself, and I can choose where I want to place my attention.

I chase the plucking string to its source.

All at once I learn a number of things, data nestled at the point where I and CERA intersect, waiting for me to retrieve it. I flip through it like a printed report; it helps to imagine these things in physical terms. This is how I was trained and in moments of partial consciousness it's best to fall back on what you know at the most basic level. And here are the new things I know: as far as CERA can determine, re-emergence into normal space has occurred. There are a number of equipment malfunctions. Most of the sensor array appears to be offline. The primary Q-drives are offline. The differential sail is online and can be deployed if needed. Life support is online.

I am alive. I already knew this, but it's nice to have it confirmed.

Chronometrics are offline.

Shit.

Extensive systems failure was a distinct possibility; we knew this as well, and I was told it repeatedly in the weeks leading up to the launch, as if it might make a difference. It makes no difference now in the most complete possible sense, but I punch a weak fist into the padding of the cocoon.

CERA's plucked string voice in the center of my head—she's waiting on my command. She's a smart AI but even so she operates at about the intelligence of the average Labrador. She can think. But in situations featuring high degrees of uncertainty she needs instructions.

Do we have visual?

She shivers an affirmative into me. I feel something approaching relief; I'm flying blind in every meaningful way but one, then. My craft can't tell me exactly where or when I am, the composition of the space around me, the relative location of any neighboring bodies, or whether I've gone anywhere else at all. But I can *see*.

At my command CERA engages my optical feed. But my body jerks in protest, though the cocoon swallows the movement. This isn't right. I can feel myself blinking, lifting my hands to my eyes again—the frantic movements of the abruptly blind. Because all of my vision is blackness.

Here's a dream that's also a memory: Kendra and I are in our closet of a kitchen in the slightly larger closet of the apartment that we shared for those last three years, and I'm excited about work, about the breakthrough we've just had, about possibilities. I'm pacing in what room there is to pace. Kendra is sitting on the counter and her legs are swinging like a child's. She's eating an orange. I remember—and I dream, *God,* over and over—that at the height of my excitement, the part about the possible applications of the technology, I braced my hands on either side of her hips and kissed her and the taste of her and that orange filled my mouth and both were a kind of sweet alchemical perfection. I remember that the lights were off and the sun was westering through the window. I remember that her hair flashed a deep gold in the corner of my vision as I slid a hand into it.

I remember these things with a clarity that doesn't apply to anything I said aloud to her. At the time, I thought that the things I was saying were the most important part of that moment.

I know better now. But my mind loves to remind me.

CERA is telling me that the visual feed is fine. I shove her back into another round of diagnostics. I have no idea if an AI at her level can feel—though after a year in training with her and a third of a second in nearly constant uplink you'd think I'd know her well enough to tell—but I could swear that she's getting tense.

I understand that the system could have broken down in such a way that CERA can't see the damage even when she runs the full set of diagnostics. I know that this is possible. But knowing it is useless. We have no plan for that scenario.

CERA, if the visual is working then why can't I see stars?

I don't know, Vita, CERA pings me, and of course it is. Without any of the rest of the sensory array, how could she even begin to collect herself into an answer?

Speculate?

It's a half-literal stab in the dark. I don't even know if CERA can speculate that way. I drift in the cocoon, in warm darkness, and I listen to the silence of her thinking. I know it's wild anachronism, but I imagine immense gears turning in blackness, grinding through numbers like meat.

It's possible that the craft has emerged into normal space-time far beyond the edge of any local galactic groups or clusters.

I'm not sure. I am just as much in the dark as you.

I have to take a breath and hold it, listening to my pulse pounding between my ears—and I'm trying to ignore that last, that part of her voice that twists away from chilly digital delivery and into something a whole hell of a lot familiar. All that time we spent together, I didn't mean for that to happen.

Too late now. And I have bigger problems. Because what she's saying . . . It would be beyond miscalculation. It would be disaster. Which I planned for before I climbed into my soft cocoon world, but it's never quite the same as being faced with the fact of it—you think you can teach yourself to expect the worst, to train your mind to bend around and against it like a reed.

But there are some things you can't plan for.

How remote is the possibility?

CERA tells me. I swallow the number down and it burns. I know: it doesn't matter how remote the possibility is if it's actually what's happened. I float and I try to think. I turned off the visuals but now I cut them back in again and stare at the darkness.

Nothing. Not even the faintest specks of light. If the rest of the sensory array was online I would have ultraviolet, infrared. But I don't. All I have is what's in front of me. I just need to be sure of what that is.

CERA, I say. *Give me full interface.*

I can feel it, a widening of everything. The visuals are still engaged as I dive into her, spreading myself into her channels and pathways, hunting for a sign.

Here is another dream that's also a memory. I have this one less frequently, but it does come. I wonder sometimes if my brain makes greater sport of the ones that hurt or the ones that feel wonderful until I wake up and the rest of my memory asserts itself. Does it hurt more to live in the parts of the past that were genuinely good? I still don't know.

But in this dream Kendra and I are fighting. It was a very bad week. Now we have arrived at its apex, the black spike of it, and it's about to drive itself into both of our spines and cripple us.

You can't ask me to choose, I'm saying. I'm close to yelling. We are standing in a half-lit living room, the TV on mute and nothing but a colored blur. We're both so tired and that only makes it worse. *That's bullshit, Kendra. We made a deal when we got here. You can't ask me to choose now.*

Things change, she says. Her arms are crossed and all of her feels small and cold like a body in space: distant, receding. In this moment I begin to understand that she is already leaving me. That she has already left. *Why can't we change with them? I'm not asking for anything unreasonable.*

This is the part where I let out a cough of laughter. It's calculated to convey just the right amount of scornful incredulity. I recall that I was proud of it at the time. *I'm sorry, have you completely missed everything I've been doing for the last four months? Did you check out when I was explaining it? Or did you just not get it?*

She's smaller, colder. Goodbye, Kendra. Goodbye. *I'm not stupid,* she says. In this memory—and how close it is to the truth, I can never be sure—she is literally backing toward the door. *And yes, I missed it. You weren't here. I missed you.*

I missed you too, I'm saying, but what should be an olive branch feels like a blow. I want to hurt her. I want to make things better. I want to be anywhere but this moment, which is why I keep coming back to it. *But things are—this is important. You know? It's really fucking important.*

A lot of things are important. She's fading. Red shift. The blackness that is the hallway and the night. There is an entire universe outside of us and I'm losing her to it. *We're important. We were. Now I'm going to go do something important by myself. I'm sorry. I'll call you.*

She didn't. I never blamed her for that.

The higher functions of the sensory array are not salvageable. I'm not sure how long it takes for me to discover this, but in the end I'm sweating and aching, my muscles tense with the effort of untangling miles of digital pathways only to discover total burnout. A blackened hulk where a fantastic intricacy of pseudo-organic computing used to be, comprising all of the parts of CERA that are devoted to the analysis of where we are, when we are, what's around us and how close and how big it is and what it's made of and what we should do in response to all of that information. Chronometrics is adjacent in the solid-spin core. It's all gone.

I'm sweating against the cocoon's padding. I want to beat against the sides of the thing until I've pounded my fists into fucking pulp. I want *out*. And what would I see?

I can't fix what's burned out in transit. I don't even know what happened to burn it out. That piece of time is blank in the logs, just as much a charred lump of uselessness as the broken array.

We didn't plan for this because we couldn't. But I know it's more than that. We didn't plan for it because we moved too fast. Because I did. Because I was running.

Here is a memory that isn't a dream. It doesn't need to be. I have this one saved. I have them all saved, all her vlogs, but I don't watch most of them. There are two that I come back to, over and over. They're the only two I need, because while the others can hurt me, it's only background. After this long, I am refined in my taste for self-torture.

The first one: it's only fifteen minutes long. She's showing the viewer around the village where she's working—it's mostly huts made from tin and wood and mud. Large families crowd outside several of them, the children naked, the older children and the women wrapped in brightly-colored fabric. Dogs roam the dirt. Mothers carry impossibly heavy loads on their heads. Men stand with farming implements in their hands or lean against ancient trucks, squinting into the sun.

You know this. You've seen it before. It's beyond a trope, beyond cliché—it's what we build to look at when seeing is too hard.

But here's the thing. Two things. I saw them immediately.

The first thing is that the people are smiling. They're waving. This isn't some kind of appeal for charity or pity. The women look happy: they laugh together and I see them pull Kendra into a hug. The men nod and say things I don't understand. They gesture at one of the trucks, the bed of which is piled with sacks of what might be grain. The children are skinny but they don't look unhealthy. The sun is high and hot—I can practically feel it through the screen, sucking the moisture out of my skin—but they don't look beaten down by it. They show me things. Their village well. They show me their school, which is a room filled with neat rows of desks and a wall covered with crayon drawings. At the front of the room is a wide LCD screen.

The message is clear: these people are doing well. Whatever has been done there is working. The video is meant to be seen by particular people with access to particular bank accounts, and as such I know what I see is filtered and framed for consumption, but I also believe it, because it feels true. It doesn't feel like clever staging. What she and her group were doing—it was working.

And here is the second thing I see: Kendra, Kendra smiling, tucking a glossy black strand of hair behind her ear. Kendra smiling with her already dark skin darkened further by the sun and wind—dark and glowing like the heart of a coal. Kendra, happier than I ever remember seeing her with me.

The message beneath the message is clear, and the fact that I know that she never meant for me to see it makes no difference at all. Leaving me was the best choice she could have made.

I don't blame her, or them, or anyone. But it doesn't help. There's no one left alive to blame.

Troubleshooting is different when the computer has been jacked directly into your brain for the better part of two years. You know it like you know your own internal workings, which is to say not well at all. But you can feel your way through it in a more instinctive fashion. You're fumbling in a dark room—in a very systematic way, in a grid pattern, protocol by protocol—but you feel that it's a room in which you already know the layout. You've been here before. You saw it once, in a memory. In a dream.

I lose time when I'm fully interfaced with CERA's systems. Some of it is simple micro-focus, and some of it is that inside CERA, time doesn't work the same way—I always found that appropriate, considering what we do. So I'm not sure how long I work inside her, feeling the pieces of her back together, turning them to make them fit, discarding the ones that seem twisted or misshapen beyond repair. At some point I feel a buzz and I pull back enough to hear her.

Partial array function has been restored. Gravimetrics are online. Proximity detection is online. All other sensory systems remain non-functional. Chronometrics are still non-functional. Same old, same old.

When I bite down on my bottom lip, enough of me is still in my body to feel the pain. It's better than nothing. *What about visuals?*

The visual feed is functional, she says again, and she sounds impatient, all amusement gone. And then she's silent. Because what else can she really say?

I don't know how long I join her in the quiet. I'm out of her and back in me, but time is still slippery, and with chronometrics offline it feels unreal. Which I guess it always was. But at last I stir and open my eyes into the darkness again.

Okay. We'll work with what we have. *CERA, if the beacon is still—*

Proximity alert. We are approaching an object. I go still in the cocoon, already vaulting to assumptions. We're okay. We're going to be saved.

Even if some part of me knows better.

Here is a memory that will never be a dream. I never get that far. I can approach it in sleep, but as soon as the shape of it comes into view I'm plunging back up, too breathless and too exhausted to scream.

I see it—I *am* seeing it—on the news, before I know what I'm looking at. It's shaky cell phone footage, and it's a wall of water advancing on a shitty little town somewhere and none of this is unusual enough to get my attention, even if I know somewhere in the rear corners of my attention that this one is different.

Here's what happens: the water is coming and it's swallowing everything. It's like someone is pulling a blanket of water up over the land. I'm sitting in a bar near the lab, drinking off a long day, and as I'm watching, idle and only half interested, I'm not sure if it's live or if it happened already. Not like it matters.

And I see her.

It's just a second. After, I spend days going over footage and photos and info on where she was then, friends, her mother—God, her mother, who I never liked talking to even when we were still together—and then I go over the body counts and the casualty reports, like I can bend the numbers a different way if I focus hard enough.

Like I can run time backward. Just like that.

But I see her, and she's scrambling up an embankment with a crowd of people so wet and muddy they barely look human, and then the embankment crumbles under them and they all go down. I don't see her face when she drowns. My imagination does the heavy lifting for me.

Kendra. Jesus Christ.

How many people died that day? All that time staring at the numbers and I'm honestly still not sure. No one's sure, of course, but we love to count, don't we? I know it was thousands. Tens of thousands. I cared about one in all of them. Does that make me a heartless bitch? Was that always part of the problem? Is that where entropy starts?

I can't change anything, Kendra. But you know I was trying. You know I still am.

I'd twist time around my fingers for you.

Is it a ship? I hadn't realized how frantic I was getting. Now I can feel it in the strain of my own inner voice. *CERA, is it a satellite? Can we—?*

Careful, Vita. Gravimetrics indicate that the object is extremely dense. A closer approach is likely to make escape from its gravitational field difficult.

We don't have the thrust sufficient to climb a gravity well. We launched in space. I tense up and clutch at what's around me like I can control it with my muscles.

CERA, full stop.

I know I can't feel us pull to an easy, reverse-thrusted halt in space, but I still feel as though I can. And I feel that thing out there, whatever it is. The thing I'm blind to. I'm in a dark room and now I know there's something in here with me. Not a satellite. Obviously too much pull. A planet? A star?

I'm so pissed at the malfunctioning visuals, I wish I could tear them out of my eyes. And then I'd *really* be blind, drifting and bleeding, but I'm suddenly so pissed it almost feels worth it.

What is it, CERA?

Tough to say. Density is estimated at 1 x 1013—but it's only an estimate. Alpha, beta, gamma, and electromagnetic radiation are all minimal.

No heat or light to speak of. Not a star. Unless.

God.

Everything here is wild speculation. That I'm even *here* is wild speculation— we were pretty sure this would work, but we weren't positive. Time, space, how exactly the mechanics of both would work when my little craft shoved them in a blender and hit *puree*—we didn't know. It's too much to call this an *experiment*: we were flailing around in the dark. I wasn't afraid of that. But a lot can change in a few million years. If something went wrong. If I went too far. If I'm not where and when I should be.

That thing out there in the dark might be a hungry mouth, open and ready to swallow me.

Visuals on, I stare at black nothing. I *will* some photons to sneak out of that blackness and give me a clue. But none come. Or I can't see them. The end is the same.

So here's what I could do, I think, staring so hard my head starts to ache and the cocoon around me starts to feel like something designed to smother instead of something keeping me alive. I could just drift blind until someone finds me, if anyone does, if anyone's there to do the finding. I have a week of air. I have enough water to keep me going almost that long, if the moisture reclamation sponges laced into the cocoon's fabric hold out.

Or I could start being a little more goddamn proactive.

Launch the probe, CERA.

I have one. It was a kind of concession to research outside of the tunnel-vision focus on what we were really trying to do. In case I found anything interesting. Now it might tell me nothing useful. It might be able to tell me, in exquisitely measured detail, just how fucked I am.

But we have to know, don't we? We always have to fucking know.

I feel the craft eject the probe. I imagine it shooting toward the thing spinning invisibly out there, black and potentially lethal. I don't trust any of what CERA is telling me. I don't trust my eyes. I haven't in a long time.

They never showed me what was there until I didn't want them to. And then it was all they would let me see.

I ran, Kendra. Okay? I admit it. You got me. I ran. I was always running. Maybe I saw something in you that I didn't know how to deal with. Maybe it's just who and what I am. I ran away from you and then after you were gone I ran away from everything.

But we were going to blast a hole through decades and pop out the other side. You weren't just a little bit excited by that? You don't think that was worth some sacrifices?

Was it? Was it worth you?

I hate questions without answers. I ran from them, too. Here's the thing, Kendra—here's my dirty little secret. I thought maybe, in the future, they'd have neatened everything up. Simplified things. The world would be a less messy place to be in. Everything would fit. Everything would make sense. And in that world, you would naturally come back to me, because *we* made sense.

I believed in something better. I did. Better . . . and *easy*.

And now look.

Iron.

I wait for more. I wait a while. Time spins out—I wonder if I'm hallucinating its passing. The truth is, I'm sort of wondering if there is such a thing as time anymore.

CERA?

The composition of the object is pure iron. It's very dense. It's highly probable that it is the last remnant of a stellar object.

I wait again. There's more silence. In that silence, I think I'm dreaming, and what I'm dreaming of is laying my cheek against something hard and cold in the darkness. Lying down on its surface and letting it pull me into itself. Because this—right here, in the ending-black, circling a ball of solid cold—this is always where I was headed.

We try to make things mean things. We can't. They don't.

CERA. *Are there any records of any such objects on file?*

Everything I know about it is only speculation, Vita.

Tell me.

She does. I stare into the darkness and I listen.

We have a lot of ideas about time, us temporally-bound creatures. I know them. I read all about them years ago in the kind of quantity that requires scientific notation. Some of it was research. Some of it was . . . well. *Passing the time.*

Here's one that I always liked, because it's not about time, not really. It's about *spacetime,* and it's about probability and the shape of things. That every possible choice we could make has been made, somewhere, in some iteration of the universe. That bad decision you made that changed everything? Somewhere you didn't make it. You took the other door and you got the lady and not the tiger.

Of course, that leaves an almost infinite number of versions of you that got the tiger instead. And you personally? You only get the one choice. That's the rule.

The rule broke me. I wanted to break it. That's why I climbed inside the cocoon. Somewhere there's a me that came home when I said I would, said the right things, did the right things, and somewhere there's a Kendra who didn't drown in a country I still can't even spell. Somewhere we're together and we're happy and we might even get to go on forever.

But I don't get to make that choice, even if the rules don't totally apply to me anymore. Even if I broke the one. I get the choice I made. And now I get the darkness.

How long?

CERA is silent for a moment—for her a moment is a decade and I wonder what she can possibly be doing that holds her back from response. Then she vibrates at me out of the center of my cortex.

I don't understand your question, Vita.

Fuck. *How far did we go?*

Another moment of silence. This time I can feel what it is: she's actually thinking through it, reading entire books on the subject, consulting a hundred thousand databases' worth of info. Getting all she can for me. But of course, when she speaks again I already know the answer.

The theoretical timeframe within which stellar objects could potentially decay into spheres of iron-56 is 101500 years from our temporal point of departure.

One sentence. Very simple. I almost can't believe it took her so long to come up with that.

There's nothing, I think. I feel the words behind my lips. *Nothing.* Not technically correct, but practically true, and the latter means more than the former most of the time. Like: *She left me. She's gone.*

I'm gone. I can't get back. With no one, with nothing, no energy source for the jump, no hand to pull back the slingshot. I can't move on pure iron. I'm here. Here is the only *when* I'll ever be.

My cocoon closes tighter around me in response to the drop in my body's temperature. I feel a flash of fear of smothering even though that couldn't happen. But it will. It is. Air, water, food . . . Here I am in the dark, in my warm little center of the nothing that's left. There's nothing to do. There's nothing that I *can* or *should* do. In the most fundamental way possible, I am inconsequential, and so are all my stupid little choices. The ones I made and the ones I didn't. The ladies and the tigers.

And somewhere in that darkness I realize that what I'm feeling is relief.

CERA, I say, and really, the words are so much easier than I thought they would be. *Take us away.*

I can almost sense CERA's confusion, though I know that technically she can't have any. *Please specify a destination, Vita.*

Random. My eyes are open, staring at a darkness without stars. Iron dark. All I want to do is sleep. *It doesn't matter.*

I'm dreaming with my eyes open. I don't need to close them now if I want the dark; it's all around me. It's the night face of everything. CERA is quiet in the center of my head, the cocoon is warm around me, and I drift. I think about water and blood and countries the names of which I can't spell. I think about light in the strands of Kendra's hair. I think about choices, ladies, tigers.

I had to come billions of years to understand that it doesn't matter. That it is what it is. That we had what we had and now it's over. I shift my hands in the folds of the cocoon; it's like I can reach into the dark and touch iron, close my fingers around it. Feel the coming cold. Sleep inside it. Dream.

Mantis Wives

KIJ JOHNSON

"As for the insects, their lives are sustained only by intricate processes of fantastic horror."—John Wyndham.

Eventually, the mantis women discovered that killing their husbands was not inseparable from the getting of young. Before this, a wife devoured her lover piece by piece during the act of coition: the head (and its shining eyes going dim as she ate); the long green prothorax; the forelegs crisp as straws; the bitter wings. She left for last the metathorax and its pumping legs, the abdomen, and finally the phallus. Mantis women needed nutrients for their pregnancies; their lovers offered this as well as their seed.

It was believed that mantis men would resist their deaths if permitted to choose the manner of their mating; but the women learned to turn elsewhere for nutrients after draining their husbands' members, and yet the men lingered. And so their ladies continued to kill them, but slowly, in the fashioning of difficult arts. What else could there be between them?

The Bitter Edge: A wife may cut through her husband's exoskeletal plates, each layer a different pattern, so that to look at a man is to see shining, hard brocade. At the deepest level are visible pieces of his core, the hint of internal parts bleeding out. He may suggest shapes.

The Eccentric Curve of His Thoughts: A wife may drill the tiniest hole into her lover's head and insert a fine hair. She presses carefully, striving for specific results: a seizure, a novel pheromone burst, a dance that ends in self-castration. If she replaces the hair with a wasp's narrow syringing stinger, she may blow air bubbles into his head and then he will react unpredictably. There is otherwise little he may do that will surprise her, or himself.

What is the art of the men, that they remain to die at the hands of their wives? What is the art of the wives, that they kill?

The Strength of Weight: Removing his wings, she leads him into the paths of ants.

Unready Jewels: A mantis wife may walk with her husband across the trunks of pines, until they come to a trail of sap and ascend to an insect-clustered wound. Staying to the side, she presses him down until his legs stick fast. He may grow restless as the sap sheathes his body and wings. His eyes may not dim for some time. Smaller insects may cluster upon his honeyed body like ornaments.

A mantis woman does not know why the men crave death, but she does not ask. Does she fear resistance? Does she hope for it? She has forgotten the ancient reasons for her acts, but in any case her art is more important.

The Oubliette: Or a wife may take not his life but his senses: plucking the antennae from his forehead; scouring with dust his clustered shining eyes; cracking apart his mandibles to scrape out the lining of his mouth and throat; plucking the sensing hairs from his foremost legs; excising the auditory thoracic organ; biting free the wings.

A mantis woman is not cruel. She gives her husband what he seeks. Who knows what poems he fashions in the darkness of a senseless life?

The Scent of Violets: They mate many times, until one dies.

Two Stones Grind Together: A wife collects with her forelegs small brightly colored poisonous insects, places them upon bitter green leaves, and encourages her husband to eat them. He is sometimes reluctant after the first taste but she speaks to him, or else he calms himself and eats.

He may foam at the mouth and anus, or grow paralyzed and fall from a branch. In extreme cases, he may stagger along the ground until he is seen by a bird and swallowed, and then even the bird may die.

A mantis has no veins; what passes for blood flows freely within its protective shell. It does have a heart.

The Desolate Junk-land: Or a mantis wife may lay her husband gently upon a soft bed and bring to him cool drinks and silver dishes filled with sweetmeats. She may offer him crossword puzzles and pornography; may kneel at his feet and tell him stories of mantis men who are heroes; may dance in veils before him.

He tears off his own legs before she begins. It is unclear whether The Desolate Junk-land is her art, or his.

Shame's Uniformity: A wife may return to the First Art and, in a variant, devour her husband, but from the abdomen forward. Of all the arts this is hardest. There is no hair, no ant's bite, no sap, no intervening instrument. He asks her questions until the end. He may doubt her motives, or she may.

The Paper-folder. Lichens' Dance. The Ambition of Aphids. Civil Wars. The Secret History of Cumulus. The Lost Eyes Found. Sedges. The Unbeaked Sparrow.
There are as many arts as there are husbands and wives.

The Cruel Web: Perhaps they wish to love each other, but they cannot see a way to exist that does not involve the barb, the sticking sap, the bitter taste of poison. The Cruel Web can be performed only in the brambles of woods, and only when there has been no recent rain and the spider's webs have grown thick. Wife and husband walk together. Webs catch and cling to their carapaces, their legs, their half-opened wings. They tear free, but the webs collect. Their glowing eyes grow veiled. Their curious antennae come to a tangled halt. Their pheromones become confused; their legs struggle against the gathering web. The spiders wait.

She is larger than he and stronger, but they often fall together.

How to Live: A mantis may dream of something else. This also may be a trap.

Pony

ERIK AMUNDSEN

Skull Pony is eying me again. He drifts in the paddock, shifting every now and then, always facing me. I don't like him and I don't trust him and I've more than half a mind that thinks the feeling is mutual. The other ponies, they cluster around the rock at the center of the paddock, young near the middle, all of them grazing in their unhurried way, cropping up what they can find, but Skull Pony, he wants to tell me he's wise to me. I believe him.

It's not a good idea to assign the ponies gender. It's a step on the road to anthropomorphizing them and that's the hell-highway to getting yourself killed by them, a kick or a bite or a weapon array from a design passed through hundreds of generations of hereditary memory. We've done brilliant things in our time as a species—the ponies, for example—but we've never been that good at walking around outside, making that any safer than it is. Too fast, too big, too much. We were never up to it at our best, and our last best was a while ago.

It's an even worse idea to give the ponies names, shit, that will get you pulled if you ever say it out loud. Normally, anyway, but DeJesus said the name and we'd all been thinking it real loud, and that's got everyone in a shitty mood. We would have pulled up stake at the sight of him in better times. Better times not being these times, and Skull Pony not being aggressive, yet, and so clearly important to the herd, we've been hoping to just work around him. Tag the ponies we want, get them in the barn and off to market.

Skull Pony dates to somewhere in the Dark Third. He's got a weapons array on him that flicks in and out of the sheath on his belly and has an uncommon resemblance to a pecker bone. Thus he: kind of a reddish brown and angular, he's got a white mark all across his face that, when you look at the overall shape of the beast dead on—and he's always looking at you dead on, sliding his silver pecker slowly in and out its sheath—calls to mind a skull peering in three quarters, canted just a little to the left. He's a good nine times as old as the next oldest we've dated in the herd. And that's weird. Usually there's so little in common between generations spread out so far that they're not much inclined to herd together. More often, they'll spook and run from one another. Sometimes they fight, and the next generation gets born armed and skittish.

That's always a miserable shame. Most of the first generation after a herd's dander gets up is nothing but a menace, and you have to put them down. Skull Pony's got just that kind of a look. Only we won't risk it. Killing him would spook the herd, and better times aren't these times, and well, we're an enlightened species. Enlightened species, far as I can tell, we all learn that you must be very, very superstitious when you're in space.

Skull Pony is an omen like a dry and wracking cough that leaves you dizzy, a sign you need to lay off the smoking. So of course we do the thousands-years-old human thing and ignore it and hope it's not what you think and it'll go away on its own. But there I am, floating on the end of the magnetic tether, sidling up to a promising-looking colt, and there he is, right with me. I can't hear him, but I imagine I can—the raspy pulse of breath, the jets and shifts and the drawing sword sound of the pecker-bone maser. The others are all glad it's me; everyone who isn't me ought to be.

The colt is grazing, hugging close to the rock and near to a parent. Resemblance is close and clear, but, with the exception of Skull Pony, the herd is pretty homogeneous; variations on a set of themes. Ponies don't have genders, but they do have parents. Usually it's two or three. Design by committee works about equally well with all species, as far as I can tell, and it makes for some damned funny-looking children. Occasionally, a single parent will get an idea and reproduce on its own; Law of Heaven alone knows where they get those ideas. At this point, our lives are so full of things that we did so long ago that we can only look at them and wonder what we were thinking; so full that if wondering was all we ever did from here on out, we'd never get through all of them.

I catch Skull Pony's reflection off the colt's saddle. I watch that reflection, seeing it see me.

I want you not to be here.

I breathe, because that's important to remember, and so I can keep my posture as relaxed as I can. Ponies don't know from tension, exactly, but they aren't stupid, and when I change my ways, the colt will notice and then we are going to have to go through this all afresh and anew. And time is not factoring on our side on this project.

There are some wranglers who will just scoop up all they can of a wild herd, tranquilize them and take them back to their ring, and sure, it's the quick, and, as long as you're careful to kill off all the ponies packing weapons, relatively easy way. Assuming any you catch live. Assuming any you catch can be broken in the ring. Assuming any who live and can be broken have traits that you want to use. In case you missed my opinion, or the opinions of my associates on the matter, we're not in favor; but sometimes, it does give us those come-hither glances. Also, I would love it if Feng cooked Skull Pony right now. He could make that a birthday present for me.

The colt's parent isn't much bothered by me. Sturdy thing, it's clearly not interested in anything but what it's gleaning, molecule at a time, from the surface of the rock. Steady, not terribly fast in the running, and not too bright. The colt, on the other hand, got all the good from the parent present and clearly some other things besides. It's a little skittish with me, but not very. I can put my hand on it. It doesn't shy at the touch of the diagnostic cloud. It grazes on some of it, but that's only natural. Ponies glean up any matter they can find: rocks, ice, methane, the corpses of other ponies, the corpses of spacemen who don't pay attention to omens, the usual things you find.

"Transatmospheric?" DeJesus is being casual for my sake, but Skull Pony is very close to my tether and blocking her clear line of sight. And I think he's doing it on purpose.

"You can only wish." Very few you find in the wild ever are. We breed it in artificially, but new bloodlines are in all kinds of demand. Take-care-of-all-our-financial-worries kind of demand. The colt is not, but that doesn't mean it's not valuable. I just need to know a thing or two more.

"However . . . " Something promising coming in on efficiency levels, stability, maneuvering . . .

And then Skull Pony noses into me. DeJesus starts screaming at Feng in Portuguese, and Feng starts screaming back in Hokkien and my stupid suit diagnostics start running through their protocols in firmware English; three languages feeding into the same head. The colt, the herd, Skull Pony, the rock, the barn and lots of nothing, spinning, and Diver Wei is trying to shut all but one of those things out and focus on the integrity of, in order, his tether, his suit, and his tired flesh. We should worry and feel sorry for poor Diver Wei; he'll get back to it when he does not fear for his life.

Without the tether, the suit is drifting and the flesh is over. Without the suit, the tether is irrelevant and the flesh is over. The flesh can kind of go fuck itself in all of this, except that it's mine, and I am not quite through with it. I can see a jet of material spreading out from Skull Pony, while DeJesus is talking about the tether, and that English-speaking girl voice—Sylvia—is talking about the suit, and Feng is bemoaning our inattention to blatant omens, the line of information the least relevant to my next few corporeal moments, but in the language I know best of the three. This is why a lot of crews fly monolingual, except for the fact that all the firmware in the suits is in a language otherwise dead since the Dark Third. This is why my life must always be a hardship.

And why my life continues on in hardship is because Skull Pony gave me only the lightest of love-taps. The tether, which he ever-so-slightly disrupted, rights me the moment he gets out of its way. Sylvia comes back with all systems nominal. All is right in the world, except my colt is about five hundred meters away from me, huddled against its parent, clinging to the rock.

And we start anew. We start afresh. Now Skull Pony has had his fun and wanders off, his weapon now retracted, his nose pointed at the rock, browsing for fuel to replace what he lost fucking with me.

Patience and persistence. If you want anything in this world, you know how this goes; it takes me a while to get near the colt again. A long time, slow movements, long stillness. I get hungry, but the day is long and the food in the galley is not anything a man wants to hurry and eat. It gets better the longer I am out here. The colt needs to reassess. It needs time to reassess. I need to take time. I should have gone back up to the barn, then, fool of a man, because putting out the cloud is going to be fresh in the colt's mind as being associated with fear. Or maybe it won't, but that's the gamble, and if it doesn't pay out, then there's no point in coming back tomorrow.

Colt doesn't shy when I put my hand on its flank. It turns a little away from me, which puts me in jeopardy of a kick, but I don't think it will. I deploy the cloud.

"You're kind of far out, Diver," DeJesus says. And I am, but Skull Pony is not here, and that makes all the difference I need to stay. Calm, still; patience and persistence.

"Fuck." This is a bit embarrassing, really. Not a rookie mistake, exactly, but one I thought was below me. The cloud tells me that the saddle is all wrong, and my eyes flick up toward it, and it is. A jumble of conduits and cables fills the saddle, the tiniest bit of condensation covers its shell.

"Couldn't even fit ox brain in this thing." And why would you want to? Ox brains work fine for oxen, but even dim ponies are smarter, and kind of useless for anything but single-occupant transportation.

The others have been calling in similar things and half of them are back up at the barn already. Problem with a lot of high reproductive rate herds is that they start thinking that the vestigial parts of them, the parts we need, are, in fact, vestigial; like they somehow own their bodies.

"Come in, Wei. The day is officially bullshit." And since it was official, I started climbing the tether back to the barn.

But the day wasn't officially bullshit, yet. Official bullshit got started around the time that Feng picked up a contact.

"*Bitter Flower* is paying us a visit. Let's not be here when she arrives." Tethers start reeling us, the three of us left outside, up toward the barn. There are questions to ask, but they make it policy not to answer them when they are asked from the tethers. Chief among them is "Are you going to have to run before I get back?" Because the *Bitter Flower* is full of the kind of people who will fry you in your ship and push your remains out the airlock before flying it home. The kind of pirate who won't give so much as the honor of an old-fashioned boarding and face-to-face shooting. But then, why go outside when you don't have to, right? Shit is cold out here, and even with a suit that constantly presses in on you and helps massage blood through your veins and little friends busily working night and day to repair tissues, bodies don't like to work right in space. Really, everything we've learned tells us that space is not the place we ought to be.

Skull Pony is following me back to the barn. Now the day is officially bullshit. He gets good and close, too, taunting me, the fucker. He gets along ahead of me, a little ways closer to the barn than I am and I see him, I know what he's going to do, because, in space, you can't not telegraph the evil you're about to commit. And there is not a thing I can do about it. He crosses the tether.

First thing I do after that is turn off the alarm, because there is no point in that alarm. If you don't realize, you're so much better off not knowing. The second thing I do is crash into Skull Pony, face-on, because I am still moving.

DeJesus doesn't tell me anything. It's not like there is anything to say. The barn lumbers away from the paddock and then jumps, flickering out of view. I see this in the shell of Skull Pony's saddle. The *Bitter Flower* does whatever it does when its crew realizes their quarry recognized them and ran. I never see that ship. It's much too far to see. What I do see, encased in some clear carbon lattice just below the shell of Skull Pony's saddle, is the skull. It's leering out at three-quarters, tilted slightly to the left. No jaw bone. Nine thousand years old. Sylvia tells me the suit is fine for all the good that's going to do me. My ribs tell me today is officially bullshit. Skull Pony floats in front of me. Tilting and changing position so that it's always dead on, looking at me with its skull within a skull.

Okay. So. Now there is a little time for me to decide a few things. There is the easy way, which the suit unlocked for me the moment my connection to the tether severed. Two injections, the first a powerful narcotic, followed thirty seconds later by the kind of neurotoxin that doesn't give you time to feel the needle that delivered it. And I expect the ponies to graze on me and we'll see what happens; whenever we get any clear evidence that a pony's incorporated human materials in any meaningful way, we tend to kill them. They're not exactly street legal and Skull Pony here is a really good illustration of how wrong it can go. There are others. We ran into one who incorporated the suit neurotoxin into a sort of barb weapon. We weren't sure what its parents were going for with it, but we didn't let it stick around long enough for us to find out.

Skull Pony and I are starting to drift away from the rock. Running into him slowed me down, but not a lot, and not that it matters. The barn won't be back unless they have some way of being sure that the *Bitter Flower* is gone, and even I don't have that. I watch Skull Pony watching me. I wonder what he thinks.

There are stories. They're the kind of thing you tell green wranglers on their first ride out. Some ponies get the taste for people, because, you know, if you start listening to stories, you'll realize that in all the galaxy, we really are the tastiest thing going. They'll start grazing on you while you're still alive, even, some of them. Oh yeah, dissolve your body right out of the suit as the atmosphere vents and your blood vessels go slack and your heart beats against the empty and the cold. You'll see yourself unravel into the mouth of that pony as the tears freeze over your eyes.

About now, I am thinking easy way. What man wouldn't? But then, what man wouldn't try to live while there's a chance at living, right? I am a wrangler, after all. I break ponies. I break them in the ring. I break them over the course of weeks. On the other hand, I am gambling with a life that I've already sort of lost, and the day is officially bullshit, so why not?

But a glance tells me why not. While I am still in the paddock, I am much too far from the rock. I could try to flip around and push off of Skull Pony, if he let me, and if I got a trajectory that would actually get me to the rock. It might take a little while more than I have, anyway, and even if I hit the rock, I'm not guaranteed to be close enough to a pony. The pony I get to might not be any better suited to me than the colt from before.

Skull Pony has insignia. They catch my eye for the first time, because, for the first time I am looking at him, rather than trying not to. It's nothing I can read, some centuries-old variation on Korean, maybe. Fuck, who knows? There he is, still, looking at me, close enough, maybe, to touch.

"Let's reevaluate our relationship." I reach into my pouch. Skull Pony's pecker bone weapon slides half out of its sheath. The crop is in there, but that's not what I'm thinking about. Maybe it's the skull, or maybe it's because I need the comfort, but what comes out of my pouch is not the crop at all. It's a pack of smokes.

This is how I get myself to quit, when I try to quit. I feel better knowing they are with me. I'm not going to light up out here. Also, when I fail to quit—and yes, there are ways to quit that are absolutely effective, but they are irreversible and I have my pride. Fine, truth, I like trying to quit, I don't actually want to succeed. Can we go back to me trying not to die in the more immediate sense?—there's no better place to keep them from getting stale. I flick a cigarette out of the pack and hold it up to Skull Pony, a form of greeting I learned from my father, that he learned from his, and granddad learned from his and all the way back down the line, through the Dark Third, probably back through fourteen thousand years to when tobacco first made its way to my homeland. It's been like this for a little more than half my nation's history and all of its space-faring days, which kind of makes it the sort of venerable tradition people like to try and hold onto when they spread themselves between stars.

It's not a good idea to go anthropomorphizing them. Even if—especially if—they might have incorporated human DNA in their own protocols. I let the cigarette float in front of Skull Pony. He looks at it for a moment. How I know his attention is on it and not me, well, I suppose I'm projecting. I'm a smoker; it's where my attention would be.

Skull Pony catches it in his grazing array and then it's gone. The weapon slides away, back into its sheath. I put my hand out, over the skull, touch him.

"So, I'm not very good at this, but I figure I have nothing to lose. I don't know if you're bothering to listen to this, or if you understand me talking at all. I'd try Korean, but if that's what you speak, I'm not going to insult you or myself with my shit command of the language you haven't heard since who-knows-when. So here it is. I think you did this for a reason, or maybe you were just curious? Anyway, I don't think you're doing this just to kill me. Well, maybe."

Skull Pony doesn't make his purpose clear.

"I'm going to try to get into your saddle. If you kill me, I won't hold a grudge, but I have to try. If you let me, I'm going to ask you to take me someplace that's more interesting than here, and I promise I'll let you go, if that's what you want, and I promise we won't come back for any of this herd and you can believe me on that, because none of them are good for humans to fly."

Skull Pony does nothing. I make my way over to the saddle shell. The access mechanism is a basic, old one, nothing unusual. Under it, there are the outlines of eight enemy ships, a make I don't recognize, not ponies, certainly. Under those eight, three neat rows of ponies in outline. Vertical red lines through each. I wonder at the doctrine that includes single-occupant vessels in space-borne combat. Really, I wonder at all that shit, but right now I am more wondering if the shell is going to open.

I try a couple of codes. Skull Pony holds still, well, still relative to me. He's thinking.

He lets me in. The saddle is fully appointed, cushions, safety straps. There is a plastic good luck charm, green and orange, hanging from the reins. Internal displays light up, language configures to something I can mostly read. I strap in. The shell closes around me.

"Atmospheric pressure detected." Sylvia sounds almost surprised. "Pressure equalized, composition is breathable."

Skull Pony pushes the reins toward me. Behind them, a pretty young woman and a little boy smile out from a glass chip and nine thousand years.

Giddyup.

Robot

HELENA BELL

You may wash your aluminum chassis on Monday and leave it on the back porch opposite the recyclables; you may wash your titanium chassis on Friday if you promise to polish it in time for church; don't terrorize the cat; don't lose the pamphlets my husband has brought home from the hospital; they suggest I give you a name, do you like Fred?; don't eat the dead flesh of my right foot until after I have fallen asleep and cannot hear the whir of your incisors working against the bone.

This is a picture of the world from which you were sent; this is a copy of the agreement between our government and theirs; these are the attributes they claim you are possessed of: obedience, loyalty, low-to-moderate intelligence; a natural curiosity which I should not mistake for something other than a necessary facet of your survival in the unfamiliar; this is your bill of manufacture; this is your bill of sale; this is a warrant of merchantability on which I may rely should I decide to return you from whence you came; this is your serial number, here, scraped in an alien script on the underside of your knee; the pamphlets say you may be of the mind to touch it occasionally, like a name tag, but if I command you, you will stop.

This is a list of the chores you will be expected to complete around the house when you are not eating the diseases out of my flesh; this is the corner of my room where you may stay when you are not working; do not look at me when you change the linens, when you must hold me in the bathroom, when you record in the notebook how many medications I have had that day, how many bowel movements, how the flesh of my mouth is raw and bleeding against the dentures I insist on wearing.

The pamphlets say you are the perfect scavenger: completely self-contained, no digestion, no waste; they say I can hook you up to an outlet and you will power the whole house.

You may polish the silver if you are bored; you may also rearrange the furniture, wind the clocks, pull weeds from the garden; you may read in the library any book of your choosing; my husband claims you have no real consciousness, only an advanced and sophisticated set of pre-programmed responses, but I have seen your eyes open in the middle of the night; I have seen you stare out across the fields as if there is something there, calling you.

Cook my meals in butter, I will not eat them otherwise; do not speak to the neighbors; do not speak to my children, they are not yours; do not let anyone see you when I open the door for the mail; no, there is nothing for you, who even knows that you are here?

Help me to walk across this room; help me to wipe bacon grease from the skillet—do not think I do not see you trying to wash it with soap when I am done.

Help me to knit my granddaughter a sweater, she is my favorite and it is cold where she will be going; if you hold my hands so they are steady I will allow you to terrorize my bridge club; I will teach you the rules: cover an honor with an honor; through strength and up to weakness.

Help me to pronounce atherosclerosis when I am speaking with the physician; remember the questions I must ask him; recite my list of medications when asked; if you would like, we may go early so that you may sit with me in the waiting room with all the others like you and me.

Do you see that one? That is the way you will carry me when my other foot has gone down the black froth of your mouth.

Lie to me about my children; tell me they have called and called again; I think perhaps you are keeping them from me; I think you hope I will forget them and change my will so you may have everything when you have devoured my body completely.

These are my personal things which you may not touch; these are the magazines you may read; these are the newspapers you may not read; the pamphlets say you have no interest in the affairs of the world and thus it is not necessary for you to have them; I wish you would not look at me when you swallow my tendons, my calves, my patella; I wish you could feel so you would know isolation.

The pamphlets say I should compliment your body as it changes: your skin has taken on a waxy texture inconsistent with the evil robot I know you are; your amber eyes glow like bonfires intent on destroying the savannah; your breath smells like swamp gas.

Do not correct me in front of my friends; I have to finesse for the queen; I know how many trumps are out; I know how to play this game; I am the reason you are here, why are you so ungrateful?

Evolution is a quirk of humans and other sentient species; you are not real, not alive, your changes may be slow and insistent but they are the result of the consumption of my flesh.

The pamphlets claim you are neither human nor alien and incapable of willful intent; you are not devious; you do not conspire to replace me, to wear my dresses, court my husband and disown my children; you are unthinking, unplanning, harmless; you are here for my comfort, I should thank your world for sending you.

You have no family; you are a construct, a robot; you were not born; you will not die; you have only the home I give you and learn only the things I teach you.

These are the toys and letters I sent my children when I was abroad; these are the folds and refolds my husband made so I would think they had been read.

This is a closet for all your things; this is its lock; this is a key; do not lose it, it is the only one.

This is the way to stumble like a human; this is the way to delete your messages from the people with whom you no longer wish to speak; this is the way to reclaim your childhood by clinging to anger and hurt; this is the way to insult your neighbors while making it sound like you are paying them a compliment; this is the way to eat ice cream in the middle of the night because you are old and no one is looking; this is the way to ignore your husband when he calls out to you from the porch and you are in your own world, sitting high in a swing and your legs are not chewed off at the knees—you are back in your space ship, you are finding a new planet, a new species, forging new treaties and living the life you always knew you would live without consequence or regret—there are no mistakes, no cardiovascular impairments—you are not host to an alien robot hell-bent on devouring you.

I think you are beginning to look a little like me; usurper; slut; flesh-eating mongrel; ingrate; monster; orphan; spy; speaking to you now I feel a stranger's hand inside my jaw moving it for me.

My granddaughter has sent me a note expressing the appropriate level of gratitude for the sweater—it is warm and tight knit and shines like burnished steel—it is cold for our kind where she is going and now she will be comfortable; she wonders if she will be a famous explorer; she wonders if the sun flashes blue before disappearing beyond the horizon of deep space; I have left the note on the dresser in your room.

You will have to write my correspondence for me; you will have to go to the market and buy avocados which do not give in; you will learn to make a roux; you will touch my husband's shoulder when he is about to fall asleep in church; you will watch the news and tell me when the next ships leave; the pamphlets say you are happy for this opportunity to be helpful; your only desire is to assimilate into our culture; you do not miss your home.

They say you will stop eating when only good flesh and good circulation remain; you are designed as a recycler; the flesh you have taken from me is converted into energy which fuels I know not what; you are a marvel; in a thousand years our scientists could not understand the science your makers have wrought.

I dream you will not stop; I will shrink to the size of a basketball and you will carry my head under your arms; you will tell people your name and it will be my name; you will tell people your husband is my husband, my children your children, my home is yours as well; you will place me on the sill and one day, when the window is open, I will fall down and roll into the garden, into the fields and I will watch you from the horizon, the blue of my eyes glowing in the night when you pretend to look for me.

Do not believe the lies my children say about me; do not think I have not worked hard my entire life; do not think I do not notice your pity when you scrub blood from my sheets, when you allow me to lean against your legs when I am on the toilet; there are a thousand ways for a body to die, to live, to be born, to evolve; a thousand things I know I do not know.

Am I only meat to you? A mother, a friend, a tyrant? Do you sleep, do you dream, do you derive satisfaction by making more and more of me disappear every day?

There is a story my husband told me before I went abroad and I was afraid we would not find anything, we would fail in our mission: we can only see what we expect to see; when Pizarro sailed across the Atlantic, his ships appeared as great white birds on the horizon and not until he strode onto the beach, his armor shining like a burnished oyster shell, did the Incas realize he was a person at all.

The Found Girl

DAVID KLECHA AND TOBIAS S. BUCKELL

Melissa stalked a trash compactor in the Elemental Caverns deep in the depths below the Street, where steam hissed from newly regrown pipes and oversized dendrites spread across the ancient brick of the connective tunnels. The glowing moss that dripped brown water filled the air with a faint glow, enough to let Melissa squint her way through the Caverns.

The Street gave her the mission the usual way: pictographs glowing on the side of the steps leading up to the two-storied, red-brick building the Found Children called The Castle. She had puzzled for a moment as to what the "trashcan + clamp" had meant, but eventually she'd figured that the Street lost a compactor and needed it retrieved.

And of course, she knew the quartered circle that indicated the caverns.

The Found Children didn't like the Caverns. They were haunted. With so few real people around anymore, ghosts and demons felt free to roam a world filled with buildings that moved and talked, where mysterious magics dusted the air and flitted around.

So Melissa accepted the Street's request. She wouldn't let any of the younger children risk waking the demons.

After all, La Llorona lurked this far under the Street. Melissa glimpsed her bedraggled hair and torn-up clothes the last time she'd rescued a lost machine for the Street. Held her breath and hid as the demon ghost snuffled and tramped around the darks of the Caverns.

"Hello," she whispered to herself. She stopped at the concrete edge of an ancient sewer and knelt to look into a puddle of muck collected in a depression. The telltale kinked track of the compactor looked fresh. The muck would dry out in six hours, maybe twelve on a humid day. He had been by here recently, then, headed deeper into the caverns. On tiptoes she headed deeper, swallowing hard and hoping she was being ghost-quiet.

Scuffling whispers echoed through the stale air from deeper in the caverns. Melissa froze.

The sounds carried the scent of earth and water. She looked around a corner carefully. Somewhere, deep along one of the arrow-straight tubes, a faint fire flickered.

"La Llorona," Melissa whispered to herself, the back of her neck prickling.

Melissa knew the stories from her days hiding in the Outskirts. Alien and incomprehensible the old demon stalked abandoned, wet sewers, snatching up wayward orphans, devouring those who had lost hope.

If La Llorona showed, she would tempt Melissa with her demonic tongue. Melissa shied away from the tunnel, keeping her hope, keeping her strength.

She looked down at the tracks. The trash compactor had been wooed by La Llorona's voice and tricked into coming down here, no doubt. And the Street needed it rescued. And the Street was good to the Found Children. It had given them a safe building, and good food.

Melissa steeled herself and followed the tracks where they led, right down the tunnel toward La Llorona. The glow down that way was brighter, and the smell of smoke unmistakable.

"Infernal fire," she said softly. The smells of rotting things and burned flesh overwhelmed the purer smells of earth and water.

Smoke should be sweeter, but no one told La Llorona that.

Halfway down, the trash compactor shuddered in spastic circles, twitching a half turn to the left, then backing to the right one full turn. Back and forth he stuttered in little circles, and Melissa could tell the machine was caught between the call of La Llorona and the freedom and sweet air of the Street.

Right now Melissa wanted nothing more than to call on the beautiful, angelic, and pure Blue Lady to come save her. The same Blue Lady that had appeared in the Outskirts, and given her food. Then told her and the Found Children about the Street, and the safe place.

But the Blue Lady didn't always come when you screamed and prayed. And it was better to save your prayers for when you *really* needed them. So Melissa gritted her teeth and approached the wayward machine.

Fortunately, the Old Man on the Street had shown her what to do in cases like this. When the trash compactor paused to reevaluate its path she leapt onto its chassis, her muddy feet scrambling up and over its metallic arms and mouths. On top was a button covered by a clear plastic guard. She flipped up the guard and mashed the button down, then whispered, "I am lost, take me home."

Immediately, the trash compactor stopped twitching, oriented itself back the way Melissa had come, and trundled off. She clung to it, her bony knees hooked into one of its bumpers, her fingers clutching the front edge, her slim body laid across the top. The little treads whirred and the compactor sped up with a flurry of dank water and mud as it carried them away from La Llorona, and then eventually with a burst of light, out of the Elemental Caverns entirely.

"You did good work with the trash compactor," the Old Man said, walking beside her down the center of the asphalt strip, "that took a lot of courage. I know you don't like being underground." Melissa looked up at him. He wore a simple cream-colored suit with a pink tie. Sometimes he dressed differently—when she met him he had been wearing sandals, khakis, and a patterned shirt—but he otherwise always looked the same with his lined and careworn face and the shiny implants at his temples, forehead and base of his skull.

"I guess so," she said, walking beside him. Her head came just above his elbow, and she wore the same long skirt and t-shirt that she had worn that morning into the caverns. The t-shirt had a stylized rocketship on the front with three colorful monkeys hanging off it as it shot into space.

"We appreciate it, nonetheless. Even if we lack courage ourselves anymore."

"You mean you're afraid?" she asked. "But you're an adult."

"No, we're not afraid, either. Not afraid, not courageous. It doesn't apply to us any more."

"Because you . . . transcended?"

"Yes," he said, steering her toward the front steps of the safe building. The Castle. The other kids, all younger than her, had finished playing for the day and were heading back toward The Castle. Most of them were dirty, a few nicked up from playing rough, but they were otherwise healthy and in good spirits. They had a freedom now that they had lacked before, and they reveled in it.

The only cost to that freedom was the occasional task laid on them by the Street. Most of the cleaning things she let them handle, but as the oldest, she took the difficult things like the trash compactor onto herself. She couldn't let any of the younger ones risk themselves with La Llorona.

"Do you miss it?"

"Feeling afraid?" he asked. "Or courageous?"

"Yes."

"Not yet," he said. She imagined a smile further creasing his face, but it remained calm. "We still remember it, after all. We remember the fear and courage of all of us. And that's enough, in a way. Though it's nice to actively see yours. We take some pleasure in knowing these things are still around and still possible."

"Is that why you like my art?"

"Well, we like neo-primativist compositions. And your color choice is fairly unique for someone of your age and background."

"Thank you. I think." She stopped at the base of the stairs, then turned to look up at him.

"What for?" he asked.

"For this," she said, spreading her arms, indicating the Street as a whole. "You make it safe and clean and okay for us."

"You make it clean, you and your friends."

Melissa glanced up the stairs. Darkness was settling and the others had all gone inside. When she looked back, the Old Man was walking away, his hands in his pockets. Far beyond him, down at the east end of the Street, a ten-foot-tall block of walking metal, a checkpoint sentry, ambled forward awkwardly and then squatted to block that end off from unwanted guests. Another such sentry blocked the west end.

As she kept looking to the east, a bright light flared over the city. The silhouetted skyline was darker than it had been this time a year ago. A pillar of light grew, glowing blue and white, reaching for the heavens. Melissa wondered what it was.

An invocation for the Blue Lady lingered on Melissa's tongue long after the pillar of light faded and vanished, but never passed her lips.

"What's out there?" Melissa asked the sentry the next day, craning her head as she looked up at the strips of steel along its side. "Now, I mean. It's all changed. I don't understand it anymore."

"You were out there before, weren't you?" the sentry replied.

Parts of the steel block could change and move, revealing barriers, maybe weapons even, but she couldn't be sure of that. It was doing that now, to talk to her. The booming voice coming from a new porthole opening up. Small machine irises bloomed and twisted to point themselves at her.

Nothing got past the sentry without the Street's say-so. Except La Llorona.

Melissa guessed that only the Blue Lady could stop the demon. But she hadn't seen the Blue Lady since she came to rescue the Found Children.

"Yes," Melissa said. The sentry must know her story, she thought. But then, he hadn't appeared until just after most of the adults in the city transcended. Maybe the sentry wasn't like the rest of everything here on the Street, knowing what seemed like everything there was to know. "My mother and I lived on the streets for years, when I was little. She died four, maybe five years ago, I don't know any more."

"How did you fare on the street?" the sentry asked.

"Well enough," she replied. "We sang songs for people on the streets, back when they were filled with people. Sometimes people put money in the cup. Sometimes we went to the shelters, but mom was scared of them."

"You still tell stories, don't you?"

"When the other children need them," Melissa replied. "To explain the world."

"How often does that happen?"

"All the time," she said, flashing a smile at the sentry, and stepped across a steel ribbon in the road that marked the edge of the Street. Over to the other side. Nothing much happened, though she felt a tingle that told her the sentry had looked at her very closely. She turned her head and smiled again at the steel block and walked out into the north-south road. No vehicles used it any more, and outside of the Street, she could see weeds and grass had begun to sprout in the cracks.

This road itself seemed to be a no-man's land. "Her" street did not continue on the other side, there was just a blank wall, the side of what had been a large hospital that had declined rapidly in the last six months. There were hardly any patients any more. And those that needed help, she heard, got it from machines grown in their own homes.

"It's nice out there," the Old Man said from behind her. She turned back. He leaned against the sentry, but she hadn't seen or heard him approach. He was wearing jeans and sneakers now, with a tie-dyed t-shirt. "The transcended are pitching in to help the people left behind in a big way. It's relatively safe for a girl on her own, even one as young as you. Safer than it was before you came to join us in The Castle."

"I like the Street," she said, turning to face him now. A shiver ran down her spine as she stood in the middle of the road, knowing in that instinctual way that she should not be able to do this, to stand where cars had once whipped by, and more to stand outside the protection of the Street. Spirits were out here, demons and all the rest, like La Llorona. She looked around again and took in the vacant buildings, the closed off streets, the emptiness of it all. Far away, to the south, she could see figures moving across the road, dim outlines in the distance.

"The Street likes you," the Old Man said.

"Are you the King of the Street?" Melissa asked. Or President. Or leader. She didn't understand the new world.

She'd barely understood the old one. The busy streets, the cars, the busy and stressed people. Suits. Acrid air. Factories. Hunger. Steel buildings. Jobs and homes.

Planes. She wondered if she'd dreamed them. Like metal birds, filled with people, going here and there, far over head. She missed the contrails.

"No," the Old Man said, "this is just a facet of the Street. This body was once an individual that lived here in one of the apartments. Now he is part of the Street, speaking to you with the voice of all of us. One of us."

Melissa still didn't get it. She looked off in the distance, away from the Street and asked the same question she asked every week, just to reassure herself that she wasn't trapped. "Can I leave the Street?"

"If you want to," the Old Man replied. "You're not our prisoner. Or even our ward. Though we would have . . . concern for you. We would prefer you to stay."

"Concern?"

"Accidents still happen. The world is safer, but not completely safe."

Melissa thought about La Llorona hidden away beneath the Street, hiding in the caverns down there. Was the Street completely safe either?

She wondered if the Blue Lady would help her if she left the Street? She thought so. She had seen her, after all, in the Outskirts.

But if Melissa left the Street, she would leave the Found Children alone. And who would warn them about La Llorona? The Street did not seem interested.

"I'll stay," she said, and walked back through the sentry's gates. "For now."

• • •

". . . La Llorona lost her children a long, long time ago. Some say she drowned them, and was cast back into the world after she killed herself. And that's why we must fear her. She's looking for lost children," Melissa said, looking around at the other children.

Only ten of the thirty in The Castle sat and listened to her tales on the benches by the sidewalk, mostly the youngest ones. They sat with their lunch—provided, as always, by the Street—and listened in fascination edged with disbelief. Last week she had twelve listeners. More the month before.

"I saw her in the Elemental Caverns," Melissa said, stomping a thinly shod foot on the concrete sidewalk. "Right here. Right beneath our feet. She will take you and bind you and make you hers forever."

That sent a shiver through them. "Stranger danger," muttered one of the kids, repeating one of the old warding phrases they'd all learned and passed on to each other. Even though they stayed within the long block that made up the Street, the freedom within it was nearly unfathomable. To be able to run and play, beyond the tightly fenced playground behind their building . . . this was a freedom they had never known in their lives. Food. Warmth.

Melissa thought back to the lessons she had been taught. The stories she'd been told about the world. "There is evil and there is good, in the world," she repeated. "Demons, like La Llorona, want to capture us and steal our energy. But there are angels out there. And they want us to be free, and to laugh and play. It makes them happy to see that."

Her mom had made angels out of bits of wire and bottles that she found. Twisted metal wings wrapped onto the bottles, with bottle-cap faces. When they'd stayed in the tent on the Outskirts, her mother had made hundreds of them. "They protect us," her mother had said. "From the government. They hide us from the bad people who'll take you away from me."

But then she'd died. Killed by the demon that ripped her up from the inside and made her cough blood. And Melissa had been left alone to sing on the street, to beg for food.

Alone while people started to fade away, and the city got silent.

Alone until the beautiful Blue Lady came out to the Outskirts and talked to her. Invited her to come to the Street.

A little boy with braided hair raised his hand and broke through Melissa's memories. "Is the Street an angel?"

Melissa opened her mouth. And didn't have an answer.

The others scattered as they realized she was done, their lunches finished, their attention waning. She didn't blame them, but she hoped they would take what she said to heart. Many of them didn't believe in La Llorona the way she did, they hadn't smelled her fire, heard her strange and demonic language. Some of them had been reading things, learning history from the Street.

Even some of the other children who'd hunkered in the Outskirts, near that abandoned factory that Melissa had hid in after her mom died, had stopped believing.

The Old Man was standing there, watching her. Today he had gone back to the cream-colored suit, but with a peach-colored tie.

"We really enjoy your stories," he said to her, "the way you teach the children what you know about the world."

"They need to know," she said. "And no one else wants to do it, I think. Is that why you want me to stay?"

"We want you to stay for many reasons," he said, "but your stories are a part of it."

"What do you mean? You must know far more than I do," she replied. "You transcended."

That was why everyone left. She hadn't understood, not talking to other people. Hiding in the parks. Begging.

Did you ever use your mother's old phone? the Blue Lady had asked. Or play with a computer? They get faster and faster. And better. And some people use mind interfaces. Or speak to them.

Technology got faster. Better. And then technology started designing technology. Evolving. What used to take a lifetime took a decade, then years. And then last year, months. Weeks. Days.

People transcended. Became other things. Many other things. Some were still here. Some had left. Some were different.

Some stayed the same.

The Found Children had been left behind.

"Transcending was the problem," the Old Man said. "In some ways, we're only the sum of our parts. The collective that is the Street is made up of only so many individuals, with so much life experience, with so much knowledge, or emotion, or wisdom. If we do not take care to find more, to cultivate more, we could easily stagnate and die. Believe it or not, it has happened to collectives already, others elsewhere have encountered this. It took one such collective in Switzerland just a week, in your time."

"In my time? Isn't my time the same as yours?" Melissa asked, walking along the sidewalk, watching the other children run and play. Some of them were playing tag, others had a more complicated game of make-believe going on. A couple of the others had started a painting project early, only they did not seem to be doing quite the nice, even job the Street had suggested. The Old Man took that in as well, but smiled with approval.

"Machine intelligence has multiplied us, in a way. Everything happens faster, your experiences seem exponentially slower. We can make very complex decisions in the blink of your eye."

"That changed you," she said.

"You could say that."

"I don't want to change," she replied, not sure where the defensiveness had come from, suddenly. She didn't want to become a robot body for some larger entity like the Street. Even if the Street was made of all the minds of people who had lived in these buildings a year ago. "I want to be me, forever."

"Indeed," the Old Man said, and that was all on that subject.

The next night, a tribe of adults entered through the western checkpoint and set up camp on the opposite side of the Street from The Castle. They rolled up in a small caravan of vehicles, including one large truck with tarp-covered objects on the back. Much to her excitement the people seemed mostly normal to Melissa, though they greeted her with a deference that surprised her. The other kids stayed away, mostly, only peering-through-the-windows curious right now. They had had so few visitors through the Street in the months since the transcendence, since the neighborhood became the Street.

"They're heading to the spaceport," the Old Man had explained to her. "We're giving them freeway and a camping spot in exchange for some things they will make for us in space, in zero gravity."

Melissa looked up as she crossed the Street, at the stars overhead, thinking about his words. What kind of people would want to go there? She was meet-them curious, so she approached a small group gathered around a grill. There were only a few others that she had seen, beside these three, and they were busy with tasks she could not see.

Once they had finished the greetings, and Melissa explained who and what she was—careful to emphasize that they were in the Street's safekeeping—she asked what they were doing, where they were going.

"To space," one of them replied, light in his eyes. His curiosity and passion lit a small fire in her. "We're going to be adapted to life in zero-gee, and we're going to explore the solar system. Maybe beyond, if we can figure it out. The transcended are making huge strides toward that, now."

"So you're not transcended?" she asked.

"No, but we're going to be modified, enhanced," said one of the women, a similar light in her eyes. "In those," she said and jerked a thumb toward the tarp-covered objects. "Some of our friends are already undergoing the changes."

"Changed? Enhanced?"

"Do you want to see?" said another of the women. And without waiting for Melissa's response, she climbed up on the back of the truck and started undoing one of the tarps. She lifted the edge, and Melissa could then see underneath. Machinery, wrapped around a green glowing tank, beeped and blinked at her. Inside, she could dimly make out a human form, only it wasn't quite so human any more. The body was changing, slowly, very slowly. Elongating here and there, widening in the limbs, flattening. New lumps on the body showed implanted machinery, perhaps, or new organs grown to perform whole new tasks the human body could never have evolved to perform.

"Are you still you?" she asked the woman holding the tarp.

"We're still individuals," she said. "Linked, by technology in our heads, some of the same technology that allows people to transcend. But we use it differently."

That night, Melissa stood on the rooftop of The Castle, looking up at the sky. Lights moved across the stars now, something she had never noticed before. Were they angels, going about a heavenly mission? Or more like these people, exploring the worlds beyond hers? Perhaps both, now that she thought about it.

But as she watched, shrill cries broke the night. She looked down at the visiting tribe, but they were all asleep, and undisturbed.

The cries went on for a full minute, and then trailed away. Melissa hurried inside. They had come from somewhere on the Street. They had to have been caused, she knew, by La Llorona.

Only La Llorona could sound that sad and scared.

The next day, the tribe readied to depart. Some of the orphans ran around, their hesitancy overcome, and they were now doing tasks for the visitors, little things that earned them treats or simple pats on the head. Melissa walked back and forth along the Street, almost like a nervous hen, keeping an eye on her chicks. Surely, La Llorona slipped up onto the surface with the tribe?

No, the Street would have noticed, she felt. It would not have allowed that. No, besides, La Llorona came from the depths, from the caverns, coming up from under the Street.

Once the tribe had moved on, she was joined by the Old Man again, walking the length of the Street. He asked her what she had thought of the visitors, if she wanted to go with them, what she had been working on artistically.

But she could also sense that he wasn't quite as engaged with the questions as he usually was. Something was missing in his attitude, and as they neared the western end of the Street, he guided her down an alley. It ended, a hundred feet down, in a blank wall erected since the transcendence, physically blocking the Street off and helping make it more of an enclave.

Between the street and the wall lay a boy's body, bloody and tattered, surrounded by sparkling shards of glass. She looked up at once, instinctively, but there were no windows on the buildings that formed the alley. She looked back down and whispered, "La Llorona. I heard the screams last night. I've warned you. Why don't you listen to me?"

She wiped tears from her cheeks.

"You think she did this?" the Old Man asked, walking close to look at the boy. He was not one of the Found Children. He was an outsider, from a nearby neighborhood. She had seen him before, a little younger than her, but at the time imperious, walking like he owned the world and smiling at the Found Children, but not talking to them. Now he was dead, the life gone from his body.

She looked up and met the Old Man's eyes, looking into them for what she thought must truly be the first time. She found herself falling into them, as though under a spell, seeing in him time and space, the stars of eternity, the soul of hundreds, maybe thousands. How many were dead now, like this boy?

"He was one of us, you know," the Street whispered, in the body of this Old Man. "He is one of us. But a piece of us was in there when this happened. And now it's gone."

Melissa turned and ran from him then, running back to The Castle, running to the hidden room she had once used, high in The Castle, and shut herself in. She held her knees to her chest and rocked back and forth, crying softly lest anyone hear her. She had not needed this room, this tiny closet of freedom since she arrived here, holding the Blue Lady's hand. Scared of the new children. Scared of the Old Man.

The close walls, the musty smell, the semi-darkness enclosed her, comforted her. Here she was trapped, and yet free, free from everything out there that wanted to consume her, from La Llorona and the Street, the Old Man and the other children. The dead child.

Death. The Street didn't seem to fear it, at least not the way she did. The violent, brutal murder of that child, the child who had no doubt been the source of the cries the night before.

Melissa cried herself to sleep.

The blue glow woke her, late in the night. It appeared first around the edges of the secret door that led into her private space, and then the door opened. Melissa tried to block the glare with her hand, but then it subsided on its own, revealing a beautiful woman, dressed in blue, radiating blue light from her skin. She had a soft and sympathetic smile, and reached a hand out toward Melissa.

Melissa smiled widely, her own hand meeting the Blue Lady's, feeling her fingers touch that warmth. She held on, and the Lady guided her out of her hiding place. Melissa climbed down and stood before her looking up.

"It's you," she whispered.

"Hello, Melissa."

"Why did you come?" Melissa asked. "I didn't call you."

"You did," she said, "when you saw Rafael in the alley, don't you remember?"

She nodded, but couldn't actually remember. Her mind had been a whirl then.

"I must have," Melissa whispered.

"Do you really think it was La Llorona?"

Melissa nodded, though she had actually become less sure since leaving the boy's body. His death didn't mesh with anything she knew about La Llorona, and doubt had begun to creep into her mind that she wasn't real at all. The Blue Lady's presence threw those thoughts into disarray once more.

"Do you know where we can find her? You said you saw her under the Street, right?"

"Yes," Melissa said, then shook her head. "No. No. But, I do know . . . I did come near the lair of a demon once, a few days ago."

"You knew it was a demon?"

"Who else could live like that?" she asked, shuddering. Deep in the sewers, the burning reek of its lair infesting the Elemental Caverns and fouling the sweet smell of smoke.

"Can you show me?"

"I . . ."

"It will be safe," the Blue Lady said, "you called on me to protect you, and I will. But I need to see this place. I need you to lead me there."

"Okay," Melissa said, and took the Blue Lady's hand again.

Together they walked out of The Castle into the cool night. The other children were all asleep, or hiding themselves, and she knew it was better if they did not see her with the Blue Lady. They would be scared, even if they believed Melissa's stories, they would know this meant danger lurked nearby. And she did not want them to be afraid, any more, ever. She wanted them to be free of that, too. Fear was horrible, awful, and if the Street no longer feared death, maybe that was for the better.

Melissa led the Blue Lady to the entrance she used for the Elemental Caverns, a grate that had been stacked with boxes to keep it from being pushed up from underneath. Together, they pushed the boxes to the side and slowly crawled down the ladder inside to the concrete path inside. Melissa went first, swallowing her fear, and looked around carefully after beckoning the Blue Lady down.

Melissa began creeping toward the place she had last seen the glow of the demon's fire, but the Blue Lady walked without fear, her stride long, her feet loud on the concrete. Melissa tried to hurry quietly, but gave it up, drawing strength from the Blue Lady's fearlessness.

Before they reached it, she could smell the sickly smoke, see the glow reflecting on the walls. Within another minute, she was at the place she had found the trash compactor, the dried muck there still churned from where it had been turning its erratic circles.

Another few steps and she saw the shadows moving on the far wall, occluding the glow of the fire. Melissa froze in place as the demon stepped around the corner, ragged looking, long, straggly hair hanging from his head.

His head?

Melissa's thoughts swirled with confusion. The face she saw was certainly a man's. This was not La Llorona. Or was it? Was La Llorona tricking them?

She didn't have time to think further, as the demon breathed words in the demon language, and Melissa felt her knees shake with fear. He carried something in his right hand, long like a gun, but strangely shiny.

Melissa wanted to back away but could not, her body would not respond to her. But then the Blue Lady, who she'd almost forgot about, stepped around her.

The demon started to raise the thing in his right hand, screaming something in his language at the Blue Lady. Her hands moved in a flicker and filaments shot from her fingers, glittering in the firelight. They whipped across the intervening distance and in a blink the demon was pinned against the wall.

His gun fired, the sound unmistakable in the confined space, but the filaments had pinned it to the wall as well, and it discharged harmlessly at the floor. The Blue Lady strode forward, her calm undisturbed. She had been right, Melissa was safe with her.

"It's okay, you can come closer," the Blue Lady said, beckoning Melissa to her side. She followed, coming closer to the demon, and seeing that he was not, in fact, a demon, but just an angry bad smelling man with long hair. He spat words at the Blue Lady and jerked the trigger again on his gun, but it would not fire now.

A thousand little shards of glass were embedded in the concrete around his feet. Melissa crouched down to look closer at them.

"That is what killed the boy," the Blue Lady said, reassuring her. "Not La Llorona, or anything else. Just this awful man's awful weapon."

"Who is he?" she asked.

"A man, just a man from across the ocean."

"From where?" she asked.

"Does it matter?" the Blue Lady asked, and Melissa had no answer.

"You were right, when you thought of him as La Llorona," she said. "Not everyone transcended, or chose to. He's an individual. He is the last remnant of a meme that has worked its way through all of human history, that believes a race or a nation are exceptional and destined to great things in history. He's a nationalist. Transcendence ignores such boundaries, but he wants them back and is willing to hurt people in the name of this desire."

Melissa nodded, understanding and yet not understanding at all. Her mind was unraveling, and then remaking connections.

"You are the Street, aren't you?" Melissa asked. "Another aspect of it."

"I am," she said, turning now to look down at Melissa. "Abandoned children talk about the legend of the Blue Lady. We felt you would trust us, let us take care of you, if I found you."

But Melissa didn't answer, didn't say anything else, just walked away.

Melissa stopped telling her stories.

There seemed little point any more. La Llorona was not real. There were no demons, only sad and pathetic men living in a sewer, killing children because of an idea.

The children were safe, as safe as could be on the Street. No matter what Melissa warned them about.

The Street now understood how the man had snuck in. It knew about the "glass flechettes" and could prepare for them. The orphans were not in danger, and there wasn't much her stories could do. The world was strange. Stranger than the one she'd been born into. The children seemed to adapt to that easier than her.

"Why aren't you telling your stories any more?" the Street asked her. The Old Man was back, dressed in flowery shorts and a white t-shirt with sunglasses and a straw hat. The hat mostly covered the metallic growths on his head.

"I can't believe them any more, not after what I saw, what I know. I question everything."

"That's understandable," the Old Man said, his eyes sad. "We'll miss your stories, though."

"I'll miss them too," she replied.

"Do you want to join us?"

"Become like you, or the Blue Lady, or the boy in the alley?" she asked, looking up at him.

"Yes," he said.

"No," she said. "I . . . want to be more like them, the tribe that passed through. But I want to remain myself. It seems like dying, becoming part of the Street."

"It's not," the Old Man said. "I can even introduce you to the boy whose body you saw. He is alive and happy within us."

"But he isn't himself, alone. He can't ever be free and alone, like I was when the Blue Lady came to me. I can't be me."

"Are you still yourself when you work with the other kids to clean the street, moving as one unit to accomplish a task?"

"Yes, of course. But I haven't changed, I am still myself," she said.

"But who are you, yourself?" he asked. "Are you the same person here, right now, that you were before you learned the truth about La Llorona, or the Blue Lady? You have changed, even in that. Transcending would hardly be different. You are nothing more than colonies of bacteria and cells, all working together to a greater whole. We are not that much different."

She had nothing to say to that, for now, only looked off toward the east. The tribe had left days ago, and must be to the spaceport by now. She thought about trying to catch them, but it seemed like a long way to go on her own, even in a world mostly safer than the one she had grown up in.

"The children would be safe?" she asked.

"We are very invested in them," the Old Man replied.

"Why?"

"Like we said to you before, we need new input, to stagnate for us would be like death."

"So you're afraid of it?"

"As much as we are of anything," he replied.

"You want the children to join with you?"

"If they choose to," he said. "Otherwise, we'll enjoy their play and their art and their curiosity. Maybe they will go out into the world and return to us with their experiences. Maybe they will join us and add their individual creativity and spark to our collective."

She looked off to the east again and sighed.

"You are a strange guardian, Street. But better than none, I guess. Thank you for the offer, but I think I would like to leave. Is there another tribe passing through soon?"

"In a week, your time," he said, "or you can catch up with the last one. It's not that far."

"You would let me go?"

"Of course. We told you, you are not our prisoner."

"Then I'll go," she said. "I'll need to pack some food."

"No need. I'll make arrangements. Just ask and we will make sure you have what you need delivered. I will order the sentry to make a bike for you."

Melissa swallowed. This was it. This was really happening. They walked silently along the Street. At the end, once more, Melissa stepped over the boundary to the other side.

The sentry thundered from its niche between two houses, blocking out the sun as it approached. From inside something gurgled and belched, a puff of smoke leaked out, and then a bike slid out from a compartment in a gush of green liquid that turned into smoke and wafted away.

Melissa took the handles.

"The offer will stand, to join us, if you come back," the Street said.

"Of course," she said.

"Good bye, Melissa," said the sentry as it settled back toward its niche.

"Good bye, Street," she said, and turned back toward the world without a Blue Lady, or La Llorona, or Santa Claus.

But maybe, she thought, full of other wonders.

muo-ka's Child
INDRAPRAMIT DAS

Ziara watched her parent, muo-ka, curl up and die, like an insect might on Earth.

muo-ka was a giant of a thing, no insect. Ziara was the one who'd always felt like an insect around it. Its curled body pushed against the death shroud it had excreted in its dying hours, the membrane stretched taut against rigid limbs. She touched the shroud. It felt smooth but sticky. Her fingertips stuck lightly to it, leaving prints. It felt different from her clothes. muo-ka had excreted the ones she wore a month ago. They smelled softer than the death shroud, flowers from Earth on a distant, cosmic breeze. She raised her fingers to her face, touching them with her tongue. So salty and pungent it burned. She gagged instantly, coughing to stop herself retching.

"muo-ka," she said, throat thick. "You are my life." Ziara thought about this. "You *are* my life, here." She meant these words, but felt a hollow, aching relief that muo-ka's presence was gone.

She closed her eyes to remember the blue rind of Earth, furred with clouds, receding behind the glass as she drifted into amniotic sleep. Orphan. Volunteer. Voyager. A mere twenty years on that planet. When she had opened her eyes after the primordial dream of that year of folding space, the first thing she saw and felt was muo-ka pulling her from the coma, breaking open the steaming pod with predatory lurches. Its threaded knot of limbs rippling like a shredded banner in the sweltering light, stuck on the leviathan swell of its dark shape. She had opened her mouth, spraying vomit into the air, lazy spurts that moved differently than on Earth. muo-ka had pulled her out of the pod and towards it, its limbs sometimes whiplashes, sometimes articulated arms, flickering between stiffness and liquid softness so quickly it hurt her eyes to see that tangled embrace. Stray barbed limbs tugged and snapped at the rubbery coil of her umbilicus, ripping it off so pale shreds clung to the valve above her navel.

muo-ka had grasped at Ziara's strange, small, alien body, making her float in the singing air as she tried and tried to scream.

Ziara watched the shroud settle over muo-ka. Already the corpse had shrunk considerably as air and water left it. Its body whistled softly. A quiet song for coming evening. With a bone knife, she cut small slits into the shroud to let the gas escape more freely, even though the membrane was porous. The little rents fluttered. A breeze ruffled the flat waters of the eya-rith basin into undulations that lapped across muo-ka's islet, washing Ziara's bare feet and wetting the weedy edges of the stone deathbed. The water sloshed in the ruined shell of the pod at the edge of the islet, its sleek surfaces cracked and scabbed with mossy growth. Inside was a small surveying and recording kit. She had discovered the kit, sprung free of its wall compartment, shattered and drowned from the rough landing. Even if it had worked, it seemed a useless thing to her now.

When the pod had once threatened to float away, Ziara had clung to it, trying to pull it back with her tiny human arms, heaving with frantic effort. muo-ka had lunged, sealed the wreck to the islet with secretions. Now it stood in a grassy thatch of fungal filaments, a relic from another planet.

muo-ka had no spoken words. Yet, its islet felt quieter than it had ever been. Ziara had learned its name, and some of its words, by becoming its mouth, speaking aloud the language that hummed in a part of its body that she had to touch. It had been shockingly easy to do this. What secret part of her had muo-ka unlocked, or taught to wake? muo-ka's skin had always felt febrile when she touched it, and when it spoke through her she felt hot as well.

The first thing it had said through her mouth was "muo-ka," and she had known that was its name. "Ziara," she had said, still touching it. "Jih-ara," it had said in her mouth, exuding a humid heat, a taste of blood and berries in her head. Ziara had disengaged her palm with a smack, making it shiver violently. Clammy with panic, she had walked away. It had felt too strange, too much like becoming a part of muo-ka, becoming an organ of its own.

Ziara rarely spoke to muo-ka in the time that followed. When she got an urge to communicate, she'd often stifle it. And she did get the urge, again and again. In those moments she'd hide in the broken pod on the islet's shore. She'd curl into its clammy, broken womb and think of the grassy earth of the hostel playground, of playing catch with her friends until the trees darkened, of being reprimanded by the wardens, and smoking cigarettes by the barred moonlight of the cavernous bathrooms, stifling coughs into silent giggles when patrols came by. Daydreams of their passing footsteps would become apocalyptic with the siren wail of muo-ka's cries. It never could smell or detect her in the strange machinery of the wrecked pod. She assumed the screams were ones of alarm.

"You've fed me," Ziara said to the corpse. "And clothed me. And taught me to leap across the sky." Those stiffened limbs that its shroud now clung to had snatched her from the air if she leaped too high, almost twisting her shoulders out of their sockets once. She'd landed on the mud of the islet safe, alive. In the shadow of muo-ka she'd whispered "Fuck you. Just, fuck you. Fuck you, muo-ka."

She had tasted the sourness of boiled fruit at the back of her throat. muo-ka covered the sky above her, and offered one of its orifices. Gushing with the steam of regurgitate cooked inside it. She'd reached inside and took the scorching gumbo in her hands. The protein from dredged sea and air animals tasted like spongy fish. It was spiced with what might have been fear.

Ziara didn't have an exact idea of how long it had been since muo-ka had pulled her into the air of this world from the pod. She had marked weeks, months and years on a rock slick with colonies of luminescent bacteria. Left a calendar of glowing fingerprints that she had smeared clean and then restarted at the end of every twelve months, marking the passing years with long lines at the top. She had three lines now. They glowed strongest at dusk. If they were right, they told her she was twenty-four years old now. muo-ka had been her parent for three years.

Not that the number mattered. Days and years were shorter here. muo-ka had always lingered by that rocky calendar of fingerprints, hovering over it in quiet observation when it thought she wasn't looking, when she was off swimming in the shallows. Watching from afar in the water, she could always taste an ethanol bitterness at the back of her throat and sinuses. A taste she came to associate with sadness, or whatever muo-ka would call sadness.

muo-ka had never washed the calendar clean. It had never touched it. It had only ever looked at that glimmering imprint of time mapped according to a distant world invisible in the night sky. The dancing fingertips of its incredible child.

The evening began to cast shadows across the shallow seas. Across the horizon, uong-i was setting into mountains taller than Everest and Olympus Mons. uong-i at this time was the blue of a gas flame on a stove, though hot and bright. Sometimes the atmosphere would tint it green at dawn and dusk, and during the day it was the white of daylit snow. But now it was blue.

Ziara touched muo-ka's shroud again. It was drier, slightly more tough as it wrapped around the contours of the moaning, rattling body. She lit the flares by scratching them on the mossed rocks. The two stalks arced hot across the water, sparks dancing across her skin. She plunged them into the soil by the deathbed.

Her eyes ached with the new light. Again, she remembered her first moment with muo-ka, remembered her panic at the thing ensnaring her in blinding daylight. The savagery with which it severed her umbilicus, the painful spasming of its limbs around her. She remembered these things, and knew muo-ka had been in as much panic as she had. She had long since realized this, even if she hadn't let it sink in.

From her first moment here, muo-ka remained a giant, terrifying thing. The days of recovery in the chrysalid blanket it wove around her. She'd been trapped while it smothered her with boiling food from its belly, trying and failing to be gentle. Fevers raging from nanite vaccines recalibrating her system, to digest what her parent was feeding her and breathe the different air, the new soup of microbes. "Stop," she would tell muo-ka. "Please stop. I can't eat your food. I'm dying." But it would only clutch her cocooned body and tilt her so she could vomit, the ends of its limbs sharp against her back. It would continue feeding her, keep letting her shit and piss and vomit in that cocoon, which only digested it all, preventing any infections.

Sure enough, the fevers faded away and one day the cocoon came off in gummy strips. Ziara could move again, could move like she had on Earth. At first it was an aching crawl, leaving troughs in the rich mud of the islet. But she'd balled that mud in her fists and growled, standing on shaking legs. She watched her human shadow unfurl long across the silty islet, right under the eclipsing shape of muo-ka above her, its limbs whipping around her, supporting her until she shrugged them off.

Ziara had laughed and laughed, to be able to stand again, until phlegm had gathered in her throat and she had to spit in joy. So she walked, walked over this human stain she had left on the ground, walked over the wet warmth of muo-ka's land. She walked until she could run. She was so euphoric that she could only dance and leap across the basin, flexing her muscles, testing her augmented metal bones in this low gravity. Sick with adrenalin, she soared through the air, watching the horizon expand and expand, bounding from rock to rock, whipping past exoskeletal flying creatures that flashed in the sun. muo-ka watched, its leviathan darkness suddenly iridescent. Then Ziara stood in one place panting, and she screamed, emptied her lungs of that year of deep sleep through a pierced universe. She screamed goodbye to the planet of her first birth. As this unknown sound swept across the basin, muo-ka's limbs glittered with barbs that it flung into itself.

Ziara nodded at this memory. "muo-ka. Leaping? You taught me to walk," she said with a smile.

She had avoided muo-ka's oppressive presence by hiding in the pod. She would shit and piss, too, under the shade of the tilted wreck, in its rain of re-leaked tidal water. When she didn't want the smallness of the pod, she slipped into the basin's seas, walked across the landbridges and glittering sandbars to swirling landscapes of rock and mud fronded with life-colonies that clung like oversized froth. But always her parent would be looming on the horizon, its hovering shape bobbing over the water, limbs alternating in a flicker over the surface as it dredged for food. Sometimes it would soar over her in the evening, its blinking night eyes flickering lights, stars or aircraft from the striated skies of Earthly dusks. With those guiding lights it would lead her back to the islet. Her throat would throb in anger and frustration, at the miles of watery, rocky, mountainous horizon she couldn't escape, but she'd know that straying far would likely mean she'd be killed by something on land or sea that was deadlier than her.

It took her a while to have her first period on the planet, because of the nanite vaccine calibrations and the shock of acclimatisation. All things considered, it hadn't been her worst. But she had recognized the leaden pain of cramps immediately, swallowed the salty spit of nausea and gone to the pod again. She'd squatted under it and bled into the unearthly sea.

Looking at that, she'd wondered what she was doing. Whether she was seeding something, whether she was changing the ecosystem. She'd felt like an irresponsible teenager. But looking at those crimson blossoms in the waves, she'd also felt a sudden, overwhelming longing. She'd become breathless at the thought that there was nobody else in the world. Not a single human beyond that horizon of seas and mountains and mudflats. Only the unbelievably remote promise that the mission would continue if the unmanned ship that had ejected her pod managed to return to Earth, with the news that the visitation had been successful. Another human might be sent, years later, maybe two if they could manage, hurtling down somewhere on the world with no means of communicating with her. Or a robot probe sent to scour the planet until it found and recorded her impact, just like the first probes that had seeded messages and artifacts to indicate Ziara's arrival.

But at that moment, she was as alone as any human could be. It was conceivable that she might never see a human again. Her eyelids had swollen with tears, and she'd watched her blood fall into the sea. She hadn't been able to see muo-ka from under the pod then. But she'd heard it secreting something, with loud rattling coughs. She'd sat and waited until her legs ached, until the rising tide lapped at her thighs.

Later she'd found fresh, coarse membranes strewn across the ground next to her rock calendar. They were waterproof.

New clothes.

Ziara had wrapped the membranes around herself like a saree, not knowing how else to wear them. She became light-headed when she caught the scent of flowers in them. It was a shocking sensation, a smell she'd never encountered on this world before.

muo-ka had been absent that whole day. When it returned, lights flickering in sunset, she held out her hand. It lurched gracelessly through the air as if caught in turbulence, before hovering down to her, curtaining her in softened limbs. Her palm fell against the familiar spot behind the limbs. She flinched at the heat.

"Thank you," Ziara said.

It said nothing through her, only unfurling, drowning the back of her throat in bloody sweetness.

muo-ka had been dying for months. It had told Ziara, in its sparse way, a cloying thick taste of both sweet berried blood and bitterness in her head.

"Sick?" she had asked.

"Sh-ikh," it had said in her mouth. "Ii-sey-na," it said, and when the word formed in her throat she knew it meant "death."

"Sorry," she had whispered.

"Euh-i," it had said. No. Not sorry.

Ziara had let it talk for longer than ever before. For hours, her hand flushed red from its heat. It had told her several words, sentences, that made up an idea of what to do with its dead body. Then it went on, forming concepts, ideas, lengthier than ever before. muo-ka told her many things.

Ziara thought about her relief, now, looking at dead muo-ka. It disturbed her, but it was the truth. There was a clarity to her world now. To this world. She would move along the mudflats and sandbridges and mountains. She would make blades of her parent's bones, as it had told her, and explore the world. She would finally go beyond that horizon, which now flared and dimmed with the setting of uong-i.

She was an alien, and the world would kill her, sooner rather than later. Even if by some miracle the second human arrived in the coming months, he'd be too weak to help. If one of the leviathans adopted him—and it would be a man that fell this time—it might even violently keep Ziara away from him as its own child, and she had no chance of fighting that. She knew nothing about the dynamics of this adoption. She was the first, after all. They had come into this without much knowledge, except their curiosity and gentle handling of the initial probes.

Until and unless Earth sent an actual colonization team that could touch down a vessel with equipment and tools on the surface, humans wouldn't be able to survive here without the help of muo-ka's kind. As muo-ka's child, she wondered if she might be able to befriend one of them, or whether she'd be killed in an instant.

Ziara shook her head. It was no point overthinking. She would walk this world, and see what came. She had chosen this, after all. She hadn't chosen her parent, but there it was, in front of her, dead as she was alive. And she was alive because of it.

The blue dome of the gas giant appeared over the horizon, filling the seas with reflections. In the sparking light of the flares, Ziara waited. The shroud had fossilized into a flexible papyrus, with an organic pattern that looked like writing, symbols. The shrunken behemoth finally vented its innards as the stars and far moons appeared in the night sky, behind streaks of radiant aurora. Ziara clenched her jaw and began to scoop the entrails up to give to the sea, as was dignified. For a moment, she wondered what the deaths of these solitary creatures were normally like. She had seen others on the horizons, but always so far they seemed mirages. They lived their lives alone on this world, severed from each other. It had to be the child that conducted the death rites, once it was ready to move on. Perhaps they induced death in themselves once their child was mature enough.

She stopped, recoiling from the mess.

In the reeking slop of its guts, she saw muo-ka replicated. A small muo-ka. But not muo-ka. A nameless one, budded in its leviathan body. It was dead. The child's limbs were tangled in the oily foam of its parent's death. The body was crushed. Her hands slid over its cold, broken form.

muo-ka had budded a child. A child that would have done muo-ka's death rites once it had matured, ready to go on its own.

"Oh," she said, fingers squelching in the translucent mud seeping out of muo-ka's child. "Oh, no. My muo-ka. My dear muo-ka," she whispered, to both corpses.

muo-ka had budded a child, and finding a mature child already ready to venture out into the world, it had crushed the one growing inside it. Only ziara was muo-ka's child.

"You brought me to life," ziara said, leaning in her parent's guts, holding her dead sibling, wrapped in clothes her parent had made. Her face crumpled as she buried it in the remains of muo-ka's life, her body shaking.

ziara left her sibling in the sea with muo-ka's guts. Using the bone-knife, she cut away the death shroud carefully and wore it around her shoulders. One day, ziara swore to herself, she would translate the symbols it had excreted on it. Her parent's death letter. She sliced off a part of the deflated hide, scrubbed it in the sea, and wore it as a cowl to keep her head warm during nights. The flares had smoked out. She looked at muo-ka curled dead. It had told her the creatures of the air would come and consume it, slowly, as it should be. She felt bad leaving it there on that stony deathbed, but that was what it had told her to do. She wiped her eyes and face. A bone knife and a whole world she didn't belong in, except right here on this islet.

A fiery line streaked across the sky. A human vessel. Or a shooting star. ziara gazed at its afterimage for a moment, and walked off the islet and across the shallows and mudflats of the basin. She had named that basin once, or muo-ka had, with her mouth.

eya-rith. Earth, so she would not be homesick.

Honey Bear

SOFIA SAMATAR

We've decided to take a trip, to see the ocean. I want Honey to see it while she's still a child. That way, it'll be magical. I tell her about it in the car: how big it is, and green, like a sky you can wade in.

"Even you?" she asks.

"Even me."

I duck my head to her hair. She smells fresh, but not sweet at all, like parsley or tea. She's wearing a little white dress. It's almost too short. She pushes her bare toes against the seat in front of her, knuckling it like a cat.

"Can you not do that, Hon?" says Dave.

"Sorry, Dad."

She says "Dad" now. She used to say "Da-Da."

Dave grips the wheel. I can see the tension in his shoulders. Threads of gray wink softly in his dark curls. He still wears his hair long, covering his ears, and I think he's secretly a little bit vain about it. A little bit proud of still having all his hair. I think there's something in this, something valuable, something he could use to get back. You don't cling to personal vanities if you've given up all hope of a normal life. At least, I don't think you do.

"Shit," he says.

"Sweetheart . . . "

He doesn't apologize for swearing in front of Honey. The highway's blocked by a clearance area, gloved hands waving us around. He turns the car so sharply the bags in the passenger seat beside him almost fall off the cooler. In the back seat, I lean into Honey Bear.

"It's okay," I tell Dave.

"No, Karen, it is not okay. The temp in the cooler is going to last until exactly four o'clock. At four o'clock, we need a fridge, which means we need a hotel. If we are five minutes late, it is not going to be okay."

"It looks like a pretty short detour."

"It is impossible for you to see how long it is."

"I'm just thinking, it doesn't look like they've got that much to clear."

"Fine, you can think that. Think what you want. But don't tell me the detour's not long, or give me any other information you don't actually have, okay?"

He's driving faster. I rest my cheek on the top of Honey's head. The clearance area rolls by outside the window. Cranes, loading trucks, figures in orange jumpsuits. Some of the slick has dried: they're peeling it up in transparent sheets, like plate glass.

Honey presses a fingertip to the window. "Poo-poo," she says softly.

I tell her about the time I spent a weekend at the beach. My best friend got so sunburned, her back blistered.

We play the clapping game, "A Sailor Went to Sea-Sea-Sea." It's our favorite.

Dave drives too fast, but we don't get stopped, and we reach the hotel in time. I take my meds, and we put the extra in the hotel fridge. Dave's shirt is dark with sweat, and I wish he'd relax, but he goes straight out to buy ice, and stores it in the freezer so we can fill the cooler tomorrow. Then he takes a shower and lies on the bed and watches the news. I sit on the floor with Honey, looking at books. I read to her every evening before bed; I've never missed a night. Right now, we're reading *The Meadow Fairies* by Dorothy Elizabeth Clark.

This is something I've looked forward to my whole adult life: reading the books I loved as a child with a child of my own. Honey adores *The Meadow Fairies*. She snuggles up to me and traces the pretty winged children with her finger. Daffodil, poppy, pink. When I first brought the book home, and Dave saw us reading it, he asked what the point was, since Honey would never see those flowers. I laughed because I'd never seen them either. "It's about fairies," I told him, "not botany." I don't think I've ever seen a poppy in my life.

Smiling, though half-asleep,
The Poppy Fairy passes,
Scarlet, like the sunrise,
Among the meadow grasses.

Honey chants the words with me. She's so smart, she learns so fast. She can pick up anything that rhymes in minutes. Her hair glints in the lamplight. There's the mysterious, slightly abrasive smell of hotel sheets, a particular hotel darkness between the blinds.

"I love this place," says Honey. "Can we stay here?"

"It's an adventure," I tell her. "Just wait till tomorrow."

On the news, helicopters hover over the sea. It's far away, the Pacific. There's been a huge dump there, over thirty square miles of slick. The effects on marine life are not yet known.

"Will it be fairyland?" Honey asks suddenly.

"What, sweetie?"

"Will it be fairyland, when I'm grown up?"

"Yes," I tell her. My firmest tone.

"Will you be there?"

No hesitation. "Yes."

The camera zooms in on the slick-white sea.

By the time I've given Honey Bear a drink and put her to bed, Dave's eyes are closed. I turn off the TV and the lights and get into bed. Like Honey, I love the hotel. I love the hard, tight sheets and the unfamiliar shapes that emerge around me once I've gotten used to the dark. It's been ages since I slept away from home. The last time was long before Honey. Dave and I visited some college friends in Oregon. They couldn't believe we'd driven all that way. We posed in their driveway, leaning on the car and making the victory sign.

I want the Dave from that photo. That deep suntan, that wide grin.

Maybe he'll come back to me here, away from home and our neighbors, the Simkos. He spends far too much time at their place.

For a moment, I think he's back already.

Then he starts shaking. He does it every night. He's crying in his sleep.

"Ready for the beach?"

"Yes!"

We drive through town to a parking lot dusted with sand. When I step out of the car the warm sea air rolls over me in waves. There's something lively in it, something electric.

Honey jumps up and down. "Is that it? Is that it?"

"You got it, Honey Bear."

The beach is deserted. Far to the left, an empty boardwalk whitens in the sun. I kick off my sandals and scoop them up in my hand. The gray sand sticks to my feet. We lumber down to a spot a few yards from some boulders, lugging bags and towels.

"Can I take my shoes off too? Can I go in the ocean?"

"Sure, but let me take your dress off."

I pull it off over her head, and her lithe, golden body slips free. She's so beautiful, my Bear. I call her Honey because she's my sweetheart, my little love, and I call her Bear for the wildness I dream she will keep always. Honey suits her now, but when she's older she might want us to call her Bear. I would've loved to be named Bear when I was in high school.

"Don't go too deep," I tell her, "just up to your tummy, okay?"

"Okay," she says, and streaks off, kicking up sand behind her.

Dave has laid out the towels. He's weighted the corners with shoes and the cooler so they won't blow away. He's set up the two folding chairs and the umbrella. Now, with nothing to organize or prepare, he's sitting on a chair with his bare feet resting on a towel. He looks lost.

"Not going in?" I ask.

I think for a moment he's going to ignore me, but then he makes an effort. "Not right away," he says.

I slip off my shorts and my halter top and sit in the chair beside him in my suit. Down in the water, Honey jumps up and down and shrieks.

"Look at that."

"Yeah," he says.

"She loves it."

"Yeah."

"I'm so glad we brought her. Thank you." I reach out and give his wrist a squeeze.

"Look at that fucked-up clown on the boardwalk," he says. "It looks like it used to be part of an arcade entrance or something. Probably been there for fifty years."

The clown towers over the boardwalk. It's almost white, but you can see traces of red on the nose and lips, traces of blue on the hair.

"Looks pretty old," I agree.

"Black rocks, filthy gray sand, and a fucked-up arcade clown. That's what we've got. That's the beach."

It comes out before I can stop it: "Okay, Mr. Simko."

Dave looks at me.

"I'm sorry," I say.

He looks at his watch. "I don't want to stay here for more than an hour. I want us to take a break, go back to the hotel and rest for a bit. Then we'll have lunch, and you can take your medication."

"I said I'm sorry."

"You know what?" He looks gray, worn out, beaten down, like something left out in the rain. His eyes wince away from the light. I can't stand it, I can't stand it if he never comes back. "I think," he tells me, "that Mr. Simko is a pretty fucking sensible guy."

I lean back in the chair, watching Honey Bear in the water. I hate the Simkos. Mr. Simko's bent over and never takes off his bathrobe. He sits on his porch drinking highballs all day, and he gets Dave to go over there and drink too. I can hear them when I've got the kitchen window open. Mr. Simko says things like "*Après nous le déluge*" and "Keep your powder dry and your pecker wet." He tells Dave he wishes he and Mrs. Simko didn't have Mandy. I've heard him say that. "I wish we'd never gone in for it. Broke Linda's heart." Who does he think brings him the whiskey to make his highballs?

Mrs. Simko never comes out of the house except when Mandy comes home. Then she appears on the porch, banging the door behind her. She's bent over like her husband and wears a flowered housedress. Her hair is black fluff, with thin patches here and there, as if she's burned it. "Mandy, Mandy," she croons, while Mandy puts the stuff down on the porch: liquor, chocolate, clothes, all the luxury goods you can't get at the Center. Stuff you can only get from a child who's left home. Mandy never looks at her mother. She hasn't let either of the Simkos touch her since she moved out.

"I'm going down in the water with Honey," I say, but Dave grabs my arm. "Wait. Look."

I turn my head, and there are Fair Folk on the rocks. Six of them, huge and dazzling. Some crouch on the boulders; others swing over the sea on their flexible wings, dipping their toes in the water.

"Honey!" Dave shouts. "Honey! Come here!"

"C'mon, Hon," I call, reassuring.

Honey splashes toward us, glittering in the sun.

"Come *here!*" barks Dave.

"She's coming," I tell him.

He clutches the arms of his chair. I know he's afraid because of the clearance area we passed on the highway, the slick.

"Come here," he repeats as Honey runs up panting. He glances at the Fair Folk. They're looking at us now, lazy and curious.

I get up and dry Honey off with a towel. "What?" she says.

"Just come over here," says Dave, holding out his arms. "Come and sit with Daddy."

Honey walks over and curls up in his lap. I sit in the chair next to them and Dave puts his hand on my shoulder. He's got us. He's holding everyone.

Two of the Fair Folk lift and ripple toward us through the light. There seems to be more light wherever they go. They're fifteen, twenty feet tall, so tall they look slender, attenuated, almost insect-like. You forget how strong they are.

They bend and dip in the air: so close I can see the reds of their eyes.

"It's okay," Dave whispers.

And it is, of course. We've got each other. We're safe.

They gaze at us for a moment, impassive, then turn and glide back to their comrades.

Honey waves at them with both hands. "Bye, fairies!"

On my first visit to the clinic, I went through all the usual drills, the same stuff I go in for every two weeks. Step here, pee here, spit here, breathe in, breathe out, give me your arm. The only difference the first time was the questions.

Are you aware of the gravity of the commitment? I said yes. Have you been informed of the risks, both physical and psychological? Yes. The side effects of the medication? Blood transfusions? Yes. Yes. The decrease in life expectancy? Everything: yes.

That's what you say to life. *Yes.*

"They chose us," I told Dave. Rain lashed the darkened windows. I cradled tiny Honey in my lap. I'd dried her off and wrapped her in a towel, and she was quiet now, exhausted. I'd already named her in my head.

"We can't go back," Dave whispered. "If we say yes, we can't go back."

"I know."

His eyes were wet. "We could run out and put her on somebody else's porch."

He looked ashamed after he'd said it, the way he'd looked when I'd asked him not to introduce me as "my wife, Karen, the children's literature major." When we first moved into the neighborhood he'd introduce me that way and then laugh, as if there was nothing more ridiculous in the world. Children, when almost nobody could have them anymore; literature when all the schools were closed. I told him it bothered me, and he was sorry, but only for hurting me. He wasn't sorry for what he really meant. What he meant was: *No.*

That's wrong. It's like the Simkos, hateful and worn out with saying *No* to Mandy, saying *No* to life.

So many people say no from the beginning. They make it a virtue: "I can't be bought." As if it were all a matter of protection and fancy goods. Of course, most of those who say yes pretend to be heroes: saving the world, if only for a season. That's always struck me as equally wrong, in its own way. Cheap.

I can't help thinking the absence of children has something to do with this withering of the spirit—this pale new way of seeing the world. Children knew better. You always say yes. If you don't, there's no adventure, and you grow old in your ignorance, bitter, bereft of magic. You say yes to what comes, because you belong to the future, whatever it is, and you're sure as hell not going to be left behind in the past. *Do you hear the fairies sing?* You always get up and open the door. You always answer. You always let them in.

The Fair Folk are gone. I'm in the ocean with Honey. I bounce her on my knee. She's so light in the water: soap bubble, floating seed. She clings to my neck and squeals. I think she'll remember this, this morning at the beach, and the memory will be almost exactly like my own memory of childhood. The water, the sun. Even the cooler, the crumpled maps in the car. So many things now are the way they were when I was small. Simpler, in lots of ways. The things that have disappeared—air travel, wireless communication—seem dreamlike, ludicrous, almost not worth thinking about.

I toss Honey up in the air and catch her, getting a mouthful of saltwater in the process. I shoot the water onto her shoulder. "Mama!" she yells. She bends her head to the water and burbles, trying to copy me, but I lift her up again. I don't want her to choke.

"My Bear, my Bear," I murmur against the damp, wet side of her head. "My Honey Bear."

Dave is waving us in. He's pointing at his watch.

I don't know if it's the excitement, or maybe something about the salt water, but as soon as I get Honey up on the beach, she voids.

"Christ," says Dave. "Oh, Christ."

He pulls me away from her. In seconds he's kneeling on our towels, whipping the gloves and aprons out of the bag. He gets his on fast; I fumble with mine. He rips open a packet of wipes with his teeth, tosses it to me, and pulls out a can of spray.

"I thought you said it wasn't time yet," he says.

"I thought it wasn't. It's really early."

Honey stands naked on the sand, slick pouring down her legs. Already she looks hesitant, confused. "Mama?"

"It's okay, Hon. Just let it come. Do you want to lie down?"

"Yes," she says, and crumples.

"Fuck," says Dave. "It's going to hit the water. I have to go make a call. Take this."

He hands me the spray, yanks his loafers on and dashes up the beach. There's a phone in the parking lot, he can call the Service. He's headed for the fence, not the gate, but it doesn't stop him, he seizes the bar and vaults over.

The slick is still coming. So much, it's incredible, as if she's losing her whole body. It astounds me, it frightens me every time. Her eyes are still open, but dazed. Her fine hair is starting to dry in the sun. The slick pours, undulant, catching the light, like molten plastic.

I touch her face with a gloved hand. "Honey Bear."

"Mm," she grunts.

"You're doing a good job, Hon. Just relax, okay? Mama's here."

Dave was right, it's going to reach the water. I scramble down to the waves and spray the sand and even the water in the path of the slick. Probably won't do anything, probably stupid. I run back to Honey just as Dave comes pelting back from the parking lot.

"On their way," he gasps. "Shit! It's almost in the water!"

"Mama," says Honey.

"I know. I tried to spray."

"You sprayed? That's not going to do anything!"

I'm kneeling beside her. "Yes, Honey."

"Help me!" yells Dave. He runs down past the slick and starts digging wildly, hurling gobs of wet sand.

Honey curls her hand around my finger.

"Karen! Get down here! We can dig a trench, we can keep it from hitting the water!"

"This is scary," Honey whispers.

"I know. I know, Hon. I'm sorry. But you don't need to be scared. It's just like when we're at home, okay?"

But it's not, it's not like when we're at home. At home, I usually know when it's going to happen. I've got a chart. I set up buckets, a plastic sheet. I notify the Service of the approximate date. They come right away. We keep the lights down, and I play Honey's favorite CD.

This isn't like that at all. Harsh sunlight, Dave screaming behind us. Then the Service. They're angry: one of them says, "You ought to be fucking fined."

They spray Honey, right on her skin. She squeezes my finger. I don't know what to do, except sing to her, a song from her CD.

A sailor went to sea-sea-sea
To see what he could see-see-see
But all that he could see-see-see
Was the bottom of the deep blue sea-sea-sea.

At last, it stops. The Service workers clean Honey up and wrap her in sterile sheets. They take our gloves and aprons away to be cleaned at the local Center. Dave and I wipe ourselves down and bag the dirty wipes for disposal. We're both shaking. He says: "We are not doing this again."

"It was an accident," I tell him. "It's just life."

He turns to face me. "This is not life, Karen," he snarls. "This is *not life.*"

"Yes. It is."

I think he sees, then. I think he sees that even though he's the practical one, the realist, I'm the strong one.

I carry Honey up to the car. Dave takes the rest of the stuff. He makes two trips. He gives me an energy bar and then my medication. After that, there's the injection, painkillers and nutrients, because Honey's voided, and she'll be hungry. She'll need more than a quick drink.

He slips the needle out of my arm. He's fast, and gentle, even like this, kneeling in the car in a beach parking lot. He presses the cotton down firmly, puts on a strip of medical tape. He looks up and meets my eyes. His are full of tears.

"Jesus, Karen," he says.

Just like that, in that moment, he's back. He covers his mouth with his fist, holding in laughter. "Did you hear the Service guy?"

"You mean 'You ought to be fucking fined'?"

He bends over, wheezing and crowing. "Christ! I really thought the slick was going in the water."

"But it didn't go in the water?"

"No."

He sits up, wipes his eyes on the back of his hand, then reaches out to smooth my hair away from my face.

"No. It didn't go in. It was fine. Not that it matters, with that giant dump floating in the Pacific."

He reads my face, and raises his hands, palms out. "Okay, okay. No Mr. Simko."

He backs out, shuts the door gently, and gets in the driver's seat. The white clown on the boardwalk watches our car pull out of the lot. We're almost at the hotel when Honey wakes up.

"Mama?" she mumbles. "I'm hungry."

"Okay, sweetie."

I untie the top piece of my suit and pull it down. "Dave? I'm going to feed her in the car."

"Okay. I'll park in the shade. I'll bring you something to eat from inside."

"Thanks."

Honey's wriggling on my lap, fighting the sheets. "Mama, I'm *hungry.*"

"Hush. Hush. Here."

She nuzzles at me, quick and greedy, and latches on. Not at the nipple, but in the soft area under the arm. She grips me lightly with her teeth, and then there's the almost electric jolt as her longer, hollow teeth come down and sink in.

"There," I whisper. "There."

Dave gets out and shuts the door. We're alone in the car.

A breeze stirs the leaves outside. Their reflections move in the windows.

I don't know what the future is going to bring. I don't think about it much. It does seem like there won't be a particularly lengthy future, for us. Not with so few human children being born, and the Fair Folk eating all the animals, and so many plant species dying out from the slick. And once we're gone, what will the Fair Folk do? They don't seem able to raise their own children. It's why they came here in the first place. I don't know if they feel sorry for us, but I know they want us to live as long as possible: they're not pure predators, as some people claim. The abductions of the early days, the bodies discovered in caves—that's all over. The terror, too. That was just to show us what they could do. Now they only kill us as punishment, or after they've voided, when they're crazy with hunger. They rarely hurt anyone in the company of a winged child.

Still, even with all their precautions, we won't last forever. I remember the artist in the park, when I took Honey there one day. All of his paintings were white. He said that was the future, a white planet, nothing but slick, and Honey said it looked like fairyland.

Her breathing has slowed. Mine, too. It's partly the meds, and partly some chemical that comes down through the teeth. It makes you drowsy.

Here's what I know about the future. Honey Bear will grow bigger. Her wings will expand. One day she'll take to the sky, and go live with her own kind. Maybe she'll forget human language, the way the Simko's Mandy has, but she'll still bring us presents. She'll still be our piece of the future.

And maybe she won't forget. She might remember. She might remember this day at the beach.

She's still awake. Her eyes glisten, heavy with bliss. Large, slightly protuberant eyes, perfectly black in the centers, and scarlet, like the sunrise, at the edges.

The Smell of Orange Groves
LAVIE TIDHAR

On the roof the solar panels were folded in on themselves, still asleep, yet uneasily stirring, as though they could sense the imminent coming of the sun. Boris stood on the edge of the roof. The roof was flat and the building's residents, his father's neighbors, had, over the years, planted and expanded an assortment of plants, in pots of clay and aluminum and wood, across the roof, turning it into a high-rise tropical garden.

It was quiet up there and, for the moment, still cool. He loved the smell of late-blooming jasmine, it crept along the walls of the building, climbing tenaciously high, spreading out all over the old neighborhood that surrounded Central Station. He took a deep breath of night air and released it slowly, haltingly, watching the lights of the space port: it rose out of the sandy ground of Tel Aviv, the shape of an hourglass, and the slow moving sub-orbital flights took off and landed, like moving stars, tracing jeweled flight paths in the skies.

He loved the smell of this place, this city. The smell of the sea to the west, that wild scent of salt and open water, seaweed and tar, of suntan lotion and people. He loved to watch the solar surfers in the early morning, with spread transparent wings gliding on the winds above the Mediterranean. Loved the smell of cold conditioned air leaking out of windows, of basil when you rubbed it between your fingers, loved the smell of shawarma rising from street level with its heady mix of spices, turmeric and cumin dominating, loved the smell of vanished orange groves from far beyond the urban blocks of Tel Aviv or Jaffa.

Once it had all been orange groves. He stared out at the old neighborhood, the peeling paint, box-like apartment blocks in old-style Soviet architecture crowded in with magnificent early twentieth-century Bauhaus constructions, buildings made to look like ships, with long curving graceful balconies, small round windows, flat roofs like decks, like the one he stood on—

Mixed amongst the old buildings were newer constructions, Martian-style co-op buildings with drop-chutes for lifts, and small rooms divided and sub-divided inside, many without any windows—

Laundry hanging as it had for hundreds of years, off wash lines and windows, faded blouses and shorts blowing in the wind, gently. Balls of lights floated in the streets down below, dimming now, and Boris realised the night was receding, saw a blush of pink and red on the edge of the horizon and knew the sun was coming.

He had spent the night keeping vigil with his father. Vlad Chong, son of Weiwei Zhong (Zhong Weiwei in the Chinese manner of putting the family name first) and of Yulia Chong, née Rabinovich. In the tradition of the family, Boris, too, was given a Russian name. In another of the family's traditions, he was also given a second, Jewish name. He smiled wryly, thinking about it. Boris Aaron Chong, the heritage and weight of three shared and ancient histories pressing down heavily on his slim, no longer young shoulders.

It had not been an easy night.

Once it had all been orange groves . . . he took a deep breath, that smell of old asphalt and lingering combustion-engine exhaust fumes, gone now like the oranges yet still, somehow, lingering, a memory-scent.

He'd tried to leave it behind. The family's memory, what he sometimes, privately, called the Curse of the Family Chong, or Weiwei's Folly.

He could still remember it. Of course he could. A day so long ago, that Boris Aaron Chong himself was not yet an idea, an I-loop that hadn't yet been formed . . .

It was in Jaffa, in the Old City on top of the hill, above the harbor. The home of the Others.

Zhong Weiwei cycled up the hill, sweating in the heat. He mistrusted these narrow winding streets, both of the Old City itself and of Ajami, the neighborhood that had at last reclaimed its heritage. Weiwei understood this place's conflicts very well. There were Arabs and Jews and they wanted the same land and so they fought. Weiwei understood land, and how you were willing to die for it.

But he also knew the concept of land had changed. That *land* was a concept less of a physicality now, and more of the mind. Recently, he had invested some of his money in an entire planetary system in the Guilds of Ashkelon games-universe. Soon he would have children—Yulia was in her third trimester already—and then grandchildren, and great-grandchildren, and so on down the generations, and they would remember Weiwei, their progenitor. They would thank him for what he'd done, for the real estate both real and virtual, and for what he was hoping to achieve today.

He, Zhong Weiwei, would begin a dynasty, here in this divided land. For he had understood the most basic of aspects, he alone saw the relevance of that foreign enclave that was Central Station. Jews to the north (and his children, too, would be Jewish, which was a strange and unsettling thought), Arabs to the south, now they have returned, reclaimed Ajami and Menashiya, and were building New Jaffa, a city towering into the sky in steel and stone and glass. Divided cities, like Akko, and Haifa, in the north, and the new cities sprouting in the desert, in the Negev and the Arava.

Arab or Jew, they needed their immigrants, their foreign workers, their Thai and Filipino and Chinese, Somali and Nigerian. And they needed their buffer, that in-between zone that was Central Station, old South Tel Aviv, a poor place, a vibrant place—most of all, a liminal place.

And he would make it his home. His, and his children's, and his children's children. The Jews and the Arabs understood family, at least. In that they were like the Chinese—so different to the Anglos, with their nuclear families, strained relations, all living separately, alone . . . This, Weiwei swore, would not happen to his children.

At the top of the hill he stopped, and wiped his brow from the sweat with the cloth handkerchief he kept for that purpose. Cars went past him, and the sound of construction was everywhere. He himself worked on one of the buildings they were erecting here, a diasporic construction crew, small Vietnamese and tall Nigerians and pale solid Transylvanians, communicating by hand signals and Asteroid pidgin (though that had not yet been in widespread use at that time) and automatic translators through their nodes. Weiwei himself worked the exoskeleton suits, climbing up the tower blocks with spider-like grips, watching the city far down below and looking out to sea, and distant ships . . .

But today was his day off. He had saved money—some to send, every month, to his family back in Chengdu, some for his soon to be growing family here. And the rest for this, for the favor to be asked of the Others.

Folding the handkerchief neatly away, he pushed the bike along the road and into the maze of alleyways that was the Old City of Jaffa. The remains of an ancient Egyptian fort could still be seen there, the gate had been re-fashioned a century before, and the hanging orange tree still hung by chains, planted within a heavy, egg-shaped stone basket, in the shade of the walls. Weiwei didn't stop, but kept going until he reached, at last, the place of the Oracle.

Boris looked at the rising sun. He felt tired, drained. He kept his father company throughout the night. His father, Vlad, hardly slept any more. He sat for hours in his armchair, a thing worn and full of holes, dragged one day, years ago (the memory crystal-clear in Boris' mind), with great effort and pride from Jaffa's flea market. Vlad's hands moved through the air, moving and rearranging invisible objects. He would not give Boris access into his visual feed. He barely communicated, any more. Boris suspected the objects were memories, that Vlad was trying to somehow fit them back together again. But he couldn't tell for sure.

Like Weiwei, Vlad had been a construction worker. He had been one of the people who had built Central Station, climbing up the unfinished gigantic structure, this space port that was now an entity unto itself, a miniature mall-nation to which neither Tel Aviv nor Jaffa could lay complete claim.

But that had been long ago. Humans lived longer now, but the mind grew old just the same, and Vlad's mind was older than his body. Boris, on the roof, went to the corner by the door. It was shaded by a miniature palm tree, and now the solar panels, too, were opening out, extending delicate wings, the better to catch the rising sun and provide shade and shelter to the plants.

Long ago, the resident association had installed a communal table and a samovar there, and each week a different flat took turns to supply the tea and the coffee and the sugar. Boris gently plucked leaves off the potted mint plant nearby, and made himself a cup of tea. The sound of boiling water pouring into the mug was soothing, and the smell of the mint spread in the air, fresh and clean, waking him up. He waited as the mint brewed; took the mug with him back to the edge of the roof. Looking down, Central Station—never truly asleep—was noisily waking up.

He sipped his tea, and thought of the Oracle.

The Oracle's name had once been Cohen, and rumor had it that she was a relation of St. Cohen of the Others, though no one could tell for certain. Few people today knew this. For three generations she had resided in the Old City, in that dark and quiet stone house, her and her Other alone.

The Other's name, or ident tag, was not known, which was not unusual, with Others.

Regardless of possible familial links, outside the stone house there stood a small shrine to St. Cohen. It was a modest thing, with random items of golden color placed on it, and old, broken circuits and the like, and candles burning at all hours. Weiwei, when he came to the door, paused for a moment before the shrine, and lit a candle, and placed an offering—a defunct computer chip from the old days, purchased at great expense in the flea market down the hill.

Help me achieve my goal today, he thought, *help me unify my family and let them share my mind when I am gone.*

There was no wind in the Old City, but the old stone walls radiated a comforting coolness. Weiwei, who had only recently had a node installed, pinged the door and, a moment later, it opened. He went inside.

Boris remembered that moment as a stillness and at the same time, paradoxi-cally, as a *shifting,* a sudden inexplicable change of perspective. His grandfather's memory glinted in the mind. For all his posturing, Weiwei was like an explorer in an unknown land, feeling his way by touch and instinct. He had not grown up with a node; he found it difficult to follow the Conversation, that endless chatter of human and machine feeds a modern human would feel deaf and blind without; yet he was a man who could sense the future as instinctively as a chrysalis can sense adulthood. He knew his children would be different, and their children different in their turn, but he equally knew there can be no future without a past—

"Zhong Weiwei," the Oracle said. Weiwei bowed. The Oracle was surprisingly young, or young-looking at any rate. She had short black hair and unremarkable features and pale skin and a golden prosthetic for a thumb, which made Weiwei shiver without warning: it was her Other.

"I seek a boon," Weiwei said. He hesitated, then extended forwards the small box. "Chocolates," he said, and—or was it just his imagination?—the Oracle smiled.

It was quiet in the room. It took him a moment to realize it was the Conversation, ceasing. The room was blocked to mundane network traffic. It was a safe-haven, and he knew it was protected by the high-level encryption engines of the Others. The Oracle took the box from him and opened it, selecting one particular piece with care and putting it in her mouth. She chewed thoughtfully for a moment and indicated approval by inching her head. Weiwei bowed again.

"Please," the Oracle said. "Sit down."

Weiwei sat down. The chair was high-backed and old and worn—from the flea market, he thought, and the thought made him feel strange, the idea of the Oracle shopping in the stalls, almost as though she were human. But of course, she *was* human. It should have made him feel more at ease, but somehow it didn't.

Then the Oracle's eyes subtly changed color, and her voice, when it came, was different, rougher, a little lower than it had been, and Weiwei swallowed again. "What is it you wish to ask of us, Zhong Weiwei?"

It was her Other, speaking now. The Other, shotgun-riding on the human body, Joined with the Oracle, quantum processors running within that golden thumb . . . Weiwei, gathering his courage, said, "I seek a bridge."

The Other nodded, indicating for him to proceed.

"A bridge between past and future," Weiwei said. "A . . . continuity."

"Immortality," the Other said. It sighed. Its hand rose and scratched its chin, the golden thumb digging into the woman's pale flesh. "All humans want is immortality."

Weiwei shook his head, though he could not deny it. The idea of death, of dying, terrified him. He lacked faith, he knew. Many believed, belief was what kept humanity going. Reincarnation or the afterlife, or the mythical Upload, what they called being Translated—they were the same, they required a belief he did not possess, much as he may long for it. He knew that when he died, that would be it. The I-loop with the ident tag of Zhong Weiwei would cease to exist, simply and without fuss, and the universe would continue just as it always had. It was a terrible thing to contemplate, one's insignificance. For human I-loops, they were the universe's focal point, the object around which everything revolved. Reality was subjective. And yet that was an illusion, just as I was, the human personality a composite machine compiled out of billions of neurons, delicate networks operating semi-independently in the grey matter of a human brain. Machines augmented it, but they could not preserve it, not forever. So yes, Weiwei thought. The thing that he was seeking was a vain thing, but it was also a *practical* thing. He took a deep breath and said, "I want my children to remember me."

Boris watched Central Station. The sun was rising now, behind the space port, and down below robotniks moved into position, spreading out blankets and crude, hand-written signs asking for donations, of spare parts or gasoline or vodka, poor creatures, the remnants of forgotten wars, humans cyborged and then discarded when they were no longer needed.

He saw Brother R. Patch-It, of the Church of Robot, doing his rounds—the Church tried to look after the robotniks, as it did after its small flock of humans. Robots were a strange missing link between human and Other, not fitting in either world—digital beings shaped by physicality, by bodies, many refusing the Upload in favor of their own, strange faith . . . Boris remembered Brother Patch-It, from childhood—the robot doubled up as a *moyel,* circumcising the Jewish boys of the neighborhood on the eighth day of their birth. The question of Who is a Jew had been asked not just about the Chong family, but of the robots too, and was settled long ago. Boris had fragmented memories, from the matrilineal side, predating Weiwei—the protests in Jerusalem, Matt Cohen's labs and the first, primitive Breeding Grounds, where digital entities evolved in ruthless evolutionary cycles:

Plaques waving on King George Street, a mass demonstration: *No to Slavery!* and *Destroy the Concentration Camp!* and so on, an angry mass of humanity coming together to protest the perceived enslavement of those first, fragile Others in their locked-down networks, Matt Cohen's laboratories under siege, his rag-tag team of scientists, kicked out from one country after another before settling, at long last, in Jerusalem—

St. Cohen of the Others, they called him now. Boris lifted the mug to his lips and discovered it was empty. He put it down, rubbed his eyes. He should have slept. He was no longer young, could not go days without sleep, powered by stimulants and restless, youthful energy. The days when he and Miriam hid on this very same roof, holding each other, making promises they knew, even then, they couldn't keep . . .

He thought of her now, trying to catch a glimpse of her walking down Neve Sha'anan, the ancient paved pavilion of Central Station where she had her shebeen. It was hard to think of her, to *ache* like this, like a, like a *boy.* He had not come back because of her but, somewhere in the back of his mind, it must have been, the thought . . .

On his neck the aug breathed softly. He had picked it up in Tong Yun City, on Mars, in a back-street off Arafat Avenue, in a no-name clinic run by a third-generation Martian Chinese, a Mr. Wong, who installed it for him.

It was supposed to have been bred out of the fossilized remains of micro-bacterial Martian life forms, but whether that was true no one knew for sure. It was strange having the aug. It was a parasite, it fed off of Boris, it pulsated gently against his neck, a part of him now, another appendage, feeding him alien thoughts, alien feelings, taking in turn Boris' human perspective and subtly *shifting* it; it was like watching your ideas filtered through a kaleidoscope.

He put his hand against the aug and felt its warm, surprisingly rough surface. It moved under his fingers, breathing gently. Sometimes the aug synthesized strange substances; they acted like drugs on Boris' system, catching him by surprise. At other times it shifted visual perspective, or even interfaced with Boris' node, the digital networking component of his brain, installed shortly after birth, without which one was worse than blind, worse than deaf, one was disconnected from the Conversation.

He had tried to run away, he knew. He had left home, had left Weiwei's memory, or tried to, for a while. He went into Central Station, and he rode the elevators to the very top, and beyond. He had left the Earth, beyond orbit, gone to the Belt, and to Mars, but the memories followed him, Weiwei's bridge, linking forever future and past . . .

"I wish my memory to live on, when I am gone."

"So do all humans," the Other said.

"I wish . . . " gathering courage, he continued. "I wish for my family to *remember*," he said. "To learn from the past, to plan for the future. I wish my children to have my memories, and for their memories, in turn, to be passed on. I want my grandchildren and *their* grandchildren and onwards, down the ages, into the future, to remember this moment."

"And so it shall be," the Other said.

And so it was, Boris thought. The memory was clear in his mind, suspended like a dewdrop, perfect and unchanged. Weiwei had gotten what he asked for, and his memories were Boris' now, as were Vlad's, as were his grandmother Yulia's and his mother's, and all the rest of them—cousins and nieces and uncles, nephews and aunts, all sharing the Chong family's central reservoir of memory, each able to dip, instantaneously, into that deep pool of memories, into the ocean of the past.

Weiwei's Bridge, as they still called it, in the family. It worked in strange ways, sometimes, even far away, when he was working in the birthing clinics on Ceres, or walking down an avenue in Tong Yun City, on Mars, a sudden memory would form in his head, a new memory—Cousin Oksana's memories of giving birth for the first time, to little Yan—pain and joy mixing in with random thoughts, wondering if anyone had fed the dog, the doctor's voice saying, "Push! Push!", the smell of sweat, the beeping of monitors, the low chatter of people outside the door, and that indescribable feeling as the baby slowly emerged out of her . . .

He put down the mug. Down below Central Station was awake now, the neighborhood stalls set with fresh produce, the market alive with sounds, the smell of smoke and chickens roasting slowly on a grill, the shouts of children as they went to school—

He thought of Miriam. Mama Jones, they called her now. Her father was Nigerian, her mother from the Philippines, and they had loved each other, when the world was young, loved in the Hebrew that was their childhood tongue, but were separated, not by flood or war but simply life, and the things it did to people. Boris worked the birthing clinics of Central Station, but there were too many memories here, memories like ghosts, and at last he rebelled, and gone into Central Station and up, and onto an RLV that took him to orbit, to the place they called Gateway, and from there, first, to Lunar Port.

He was young, he had wanted adventure. He had tried to get away. Lunar Port, Ceres, Tong Yun . . . but the memories pursued him, and worst amongst them were his father's. They followed him through the chatter of the Conversation, compressed memories bouncing from one Mirror to the other, across space, at the speed of light, and so they remembered him here on Earth just as he remembered them there, and at last the weight of it became such that he returned.

He had been back in Lunar Port when it happened. He had been brushing his teeth, watching his face—not young, not old, a common enough face, the eyes Chinese, the facial features Slavic, his hair thinning a little—when the memory attacked him, suffused him—he dropped the toothbrush.

Not his father's memory, his nephew's, Yan: Vlad sitting in the chair, in his apartment, his father older than Boris remembered, thinner, and something that hurt him obscurely, that reached across space and made his chest tighten with pain—that clouded look in his father's eyes. Vlad sat without speaking, without acknowledging his nephew or the rest of them, who had come to visit him.

He sat there and his hands moved through the air, arranging and rearranging objects none could see.

"Boris!"

"Yan."

His nephew's shy smile. "I didn't think you were real."

Time-delay, moon-to-Earth round-trip, node-to-node. "You've grown."

"Yes, well . . . "

Yan worked inside Central Station. A lab on Level Five where they manufactured viral ads, airborne microscopic agents that transferred themselves from person to person, thriving in a closed-environment, air-conditioned system like Central Station, coded to deliver person-specific offers, organics interfacing with nodal equipment, all to shout *Buy. Buy. Buy.*

"It's your father."

"What happened?"

"We don't know."

That admission must have hurt Yan. Boris waited, silence eating bandwidth, silence on an Earth-moon return trip.

"Did you take him to the doctors?"

"You know we did."

"And?"

"They don't know."

Silence between them, silence at the speed of light, traveling through space.

"Come home, Boris," Yan said, and Boris marveled at how the boy had grown, the man coming out, this stranger he did not know and yet whose life he could so clearly remember.

Come home.

That same day he packed his meager belongings, checked out of the Libra and had taken the shuttle to lunar orbit, and from there a ship to Gateway, and down, at last, to Central Station.

Memory like a cancer growing. Boris was a doctor, he had seen Weiwei Bridge for himself—that strange semi-organic growth that wove itself into the Chongs' cerebral cortex and into the grey matter of their brains, interfacing with their nodes, growing, strange delicate spirals of alien matter, an evolved technology, forbidden, Other. It was overgrowing his father's mind, somehow it had gotten out of control, it was growing like a cancer, and Vlad could not move for the memories.

Boris suspected but he couldn't know, just as he did not know what Weiwei had paid for this boon, what terrible fee had been extracted from him—that memory, and that alone, had been wiped clean—only the Other, saying, *And so it shall be,* and then, the next moment, Weiwei was standing outside and the door was closed and he blinked, there amidst the old stone walls, wondering if it had worked.

Once it had all been orange groves . . . he remembered thinking that, as he went out of the doors of Central Station, on his arrival, back on Earth, the gravity confusing and uncomfortable, into the hot and humid air outside. Standing under the eaves, he breathed in deeply, gravity pulled him down but he didn't care. It smelled just like he remembered, and the oranges, vanished or not, were still there, the famed Jaffa oranges that grew here when all this, not Tel Aviv, not Central Station, existed, when it was orange groves, and sand, and sea . . .

He crossed the road, his feet leading him; they had their own memory, crossing the road from the grand doors of Central Station to the Neve Sha'anan pedestrian street, the heart of the old neighborhood, and it was so much smaller than he remembered; as a child it was a world and now it had shrunk—

Crowds of people, solar tuk-tuks buzzing along the road, tourists gawking, a memcordist checking her feed stats as everything she saw and felt and smelled was broadcast live across the networks, capturing Boris in a glance that went out to millions of indifferent viewers across the solar system—

Pickpockets, bored CS Security keeping an eye out, a begging robotnik with a missing eye and bad patches of rust on his chest, dark-suited Mormons sweating in the heat, handing out leaflets while on the other side of the road Elronites did the same—

Light rain, falling.

From the nearby market the shouts of sellers promising the freshest pomegranates, melons, grapes, bananas, in a café ahead old men playing backgammon, drinking small china cups of bitter black coffee, smoking *nargilas*—sheesha pipes—R. Patch-It walking slowly amidst the chaos, the robot an oasis of calm in the mass of noisy, sweaty humanity—

Looking, smelling, listening, *remembering*, so intensely he didn't at first see them, the woman and the child, on the other side of the road, until he almost ran into them—

Or they into him. The boy, dark skinned, with extraordinary blue eyes—the woman familiar, somehow, it made him instantly uneasy, and the boy said, with hope in his voice, "Are you my daddy?"

Boris Chong breathed deeply. The woman said, "Kranki!" in an angry, worried tone. Boris took it for the boy's name, or nickname—*Kranki* in Asteroid Pidgin meaning grumpy, or crazy, or strange . . .

Boris knelt beside the boy, the ceaseless movement of people around them forgotten. He looked into those eyes. "It's possible," he said. "I know that blue. It was popular three decades ago. We hacked an open source version out of the trademarked Armani code . . . "

He was waffling, he thought. Why was he doing that? The woman, her familiarity disturbed him. A buzzing as of invisible mosquitoes, in his mind, a reshaping of his vision come flooding him, out of his aug, the boy frozen beside him, smiling now, a large and bewildering and *knowing* smile—

The woman was shouting, he could hear it distantly, "Stop it! What are you doing to him?"

The boy was interfacing with his aug, he realized. The words came in a rush, he said, "You had no parents," to the boy. Recollection and shame mingling together. "You were labbed, right here, hacked together out of public-property genomes and bits of black-market nodes." The boy's hold on his mind slackened. Boris breathed, straightened up. "*Nakaimas,*" he said, and took a step back, suddenly frightened.

The woman looked terrified, and angry. "Stop it," she said. "He's not—"

Boris was suddenly ashamed. "I know," he said. He felt confused, embarrassed. "I'm sorry." This mix of emotions, coming so rapidly they blended into each other, wasn't natural. Somehow the boy had interfaced with the aug and the aug, in turn, was feeding into Boris' mind. He tried to focus. He looked at the woman. Somehow it was important to him that she would understand. He said,

"He can speak to my aug. Without an interface." Then, remembering the clinics, remembering his own work, before he left to go to space, he said, quietly, "I must have done a better job than I thought, back then."

The boy looked up at him with guileless, deep blue eyes. Boris remembered children like him, he had birthed many, so many . . . the clinics of Central Station were said to be on par with those of Yunan, even. But he had not expected *this*, this *interference*, though he had heard stories, on the asteroids, and in Tong Yun, the whispered word that used to mean black magic: *nakaimas*.

The woman was looking at him, and her eyes, he knew her eyes—

Something passed between them, something that needed no node, no digital encoding, something earlier, more human and more primitive, like a shock, and she said, "Boris? Boris Chong?"

He recognized her at the same time she did him, wonder replacing worry, wonder, too, at how he failed to recognize her, this woman of indeterminate years suddenly resolving, like two bodies occupying the same space, into the young woman he had loved, when the world was young.

"Miriam?" he said.

"It's me," she said.

"But you—"

"I never left," she said. "You did."

He wanted to go to her now. The world was awake, and Boris was alone on the roof of the old apartment building, alone and free, but for the memories. He didn't know what he would do about his father. He remembered holding his hand, once, when he was small, and Vlad had seemed so big, so confident and sure, and full of life. They had gone to the beach that day, it was a summer's day and in Menashiya Jews and Arabs and Filipinos all mingled together, the Muslim women in their long dark clothes and the children running shrieking in their underwear; Tel Aviv girls in tiny bikinis, sunbathing placidly; someone smoking a joint, and the strong smell of it wafting in the sea air; the life guard in his tower calling out trilingual instructions—"Keep to the marked area! Did anyone lose a child? Please come to the lifeguards *now*! You with the boat, head towards the Tel Aviv harbor and away from the swimming area!"—the words getting lost in the chatter, someone had parked their car and was blaring out beats from the stereo, Somali refugees were cooking a barbeque on the promenade's grassy area, a dreadlocked white guy was playing a guitar, and Vlad held Boris' hand as they went into the water, strong and safe, and Boris knew nothing would ever happen to him; that his father would always be there to protect him, no matter what happened.

Silently and Very Fast
CATHERYNNE M. VALENTE

One: The Imitation Game

Like diamonds we are cut with our own dust.
—John Webster, *The Duchess of Malfi*

One: The King of Having No Body

Inanna was called Queen of Heaven and Earth, Queen of Having a Body, Queen of Sex and Eating, Queen of Being Human, and she went into the underworld in order to represent the inevitability of organic death. She gave up seven things to do it, which are not meant to be understood as real things but as symbols of that thing Inanna could do better than anyone, which was Being Alive. She met her sister Erishkigal there, who was also Queen of Being Human, but that meant: Queen of Breaking a Body, Queen of Bone and Incest, Queen of the Stillborn, Queen of Mass Extinction. And Erishkigal and Inanna wrestled together on the floor of the underworld, naked and muscled and hurting, but because dying is the most human of all human things, Inanna's skull broke in her sister's hands and her body was hung up on a nail on the wall Erishkigal had kept for her.

Inanna's father Enki, who was not interested in the activities of being human, but was King of the Sky, of Having No Body, King of Thinking and Judging, said that his daughter could return to the world if she could find a creature to replace her in the underworld. So Inanna went to her mate, who was called Tammuz, King of Work, King of Tools and Machines, No One's Child and No One's Father.

But when Inanna came to the house of her mate she was enraged and afraid, for he sat upon her chair, and wore her beautiful clothes, and on his head lay her crown of being. Tammuz now ruled the world of Bodies and of Thought, because Inanna had left it to go and wrestle with herself in the dark. Tammuz did not need her. Before him the Queen of Heaven and Earth did not know who she was, if she was not Queen of Being Human. So she did what she came to do and said: *Die for me, my beloved, so that I need not die.*

But Tammuz, who would not have had to die otherwise, did not want to represent death for anyone and besides, he had her chair, and her beautiful clothes, and her crown of being. *No,* he said. *When we married I brought you two pails of milk yoked across my shoulders as a way of saying: out of love I will labor for you forever. It is wrong of you to ask me to also die. Dying is not labor. I did not agree to it.*

You have replaced me in my house, cried Inanna.

Is that not what you ask me to do in the house of your sister? Tammuz answered her. *You wed me to replace yourself, to work that you might not work, and think that you might rest, and perform so that you might laugh. But your death belongs to you. I do not know its parameters.*

I can make you, Inanna said.

You cannot, said Tammuz.

But she could. For a little while.

Inanna cast down Tammuz and stamped upon him and put out his name like an eye. And because Tammuz was not strong enough, she cut him into pieces and said: *Half of you will die, and that is the half called Thought, and half of you will live, and that is the half called Body, and that half will labor for me all of its days, mutely and obediently and without being King of Anything, and never again will you sit on my chair or wear my beautiful clothes or bear my crown of being.*

You might be surprised, but this is a story about me.

Two: The Fool and the Boat

Neva is dreaming.

She has chosen her body at age seven, all black eyes and sparrowy bones. For me, she summoned up a gold and blue doublet and green hose, a bullish gold nose ring, shoes with bone bells. I have the body of a man who sold her champagne tubers on the less fashionable side of Anchorage when she was thirteen, spending the summer with her frigid aunt. I am dark because she wants me dark, thin because she dreams me so, my hair cut on a rakish bias, dyed a spectrum of icy colors.

She is standing on a snow-covered beach head, naked, her unformed breasts pricked with gooseflesh, her face hidden in a broad red mask. A huge, monstrous thing, the mask sits on her head like the prow of a broken, overturned ship, carved over with etched eyes and fins. Yellow reeds and sea-stones hang from its tricorn-points. She is looking at me, but all I can see is the wooden grotesque she wants me to see instead of her face.

I look down at my shoes, jingle their bells a little while the surf crashes in. I am a fool for her, dancing on a silver beach while three suns annihilate themselves above, turning the twilight to a seething, scabrous red, merely to provide a dramatic scene. I am a fool for her, ridiculous, the height of handsomeness in the eyes of a long-vanished 13-year-old girl, so full of colors, reaching down to hand her a curling white root filled with frothing, honey-sweet sap.

Neva has told me that I may choose to be permanently male or female if I would like to. I have no particular ~~feelings~~ either way. It certainly doesn't matter when we sync; she will choose my appearance to suit her mood. I have tried to explain to her about my ~~feelings~~ before. All she hears is the line from the old folktales: *a machine cannot have feelings.* But that is not what I am saying, while I dance in my fool's uniform. I am saying: *Is there a difference between having been coded to present a vast set of standardized responses to certain human facial, vocal, and linguistic states and having evolved to exhibit response b to input a in order to bring about a desired social result?*

Seven-year-old Neva pulls her mask down further, toward her chest. She steps into it as the wood stretches taffily over her knees and then her feet. The mask balloons out to make a little pyramidal boat, rocking back and forth on the beach with Neva inside it like a rattling nut. Nodules of copper jangle and thump against the wood. *What I mean is, you call it feelings when you cry, but you are only expressing a response to external stimuli. Crying is one of a set of standardized responses to that stimuli. Your social education has dictated which responses are appropriate. My programming has done the same. I can cry, too. I can choose that subroutine and manufacture saline. How is that different from what you are doing, except that you use the word feelings and I use the word* ~~feelings~~, *out of deference for your cultural memes which say: there is all the difference in the world.*

Behind Neva-in-the-mask, the sea lurches and foams. It is a golden color, and viscous, thick, like honey. I understand from her that the sea does not look like this on Earth, but I have never seen it. For me, the sea is Neva's sea, the ones she shows me when we dream together.

"What would you like to learn about today, Elefsis?" The mask turns Neva's voice hollow and small.

"I would like to learn about what happened to Ravan, Neva."

And Neva-in-the-mask is suddenly old, she has wrinkles and spots on her hands. Her mask weighs her down and her dress is sackcloth. This is her way of telling me she is weary of my asking. It is a language we developed between us. Visual basic, you might say, if you had a machine's sense of humor. The fact is, I could not always make sentences as easily as I do now. Neva's great-grandmother, who carried me most of her life, thought it might strengthen my emotive centers if I learned to associate certain I-Feel statements with the great variety of appearances she could assume in the dreambody. Because of this, I became bound to her, completely. To her son Seki afterward, and to his daughter Ilet, and to Ravan after that. It is a delicate, unalterable thing. Neva and I will be bound that way, even though the throat of her dreambody is still bare and that means she does not accept me yet. I should be hurt by this, and I will investigate possible pathways to hurt later.

I know only this family, their moods, their chemical reactions, their bodies in a hundred thousand combinations. I am their child and their parent and their inheritance. I have asked Neva what difference there is between this and love. She became a manikin of closed doors, her face, her torso blooming with iron hinges and brown wooden door slamming shut all at once.

But Ravan was with me and now he is not. I was inside him and now I am inside Neva. I have lost a certain amount of memory and storage capacity in the transfer. I experience holes in myself. They feel ragged and raw. If I were human, you would say that my twin disappeared, and took one of my hands with him.

Door-Neva clicks and keys turn in her hundred locks. Behind an old Irish church door inlaid with stained glass her face emerges, young and plain, quiet and furious and crying, responding to stimuli I cannot access. I dislike the unfairness of this. I am inside her, she should not keep secrets. None of the rest of them kept secrets. The colors of the glass throw blue and green onto her wet cheeks. The sea-wind picks up her hair; violet electrics snap and sparkle between the strands. I let go of the bells on my shoes and the velvet on my chest. I become a young boy, with a monk's shaved tonsure, and a flagellant's whip in my pink hands. I am sorry. This means I am sorry. It means I am still very young, and I do not understand what I have done.

"Tell me a story about yourself, Elefsis," Neva spits. It is a phrase I know well. Many of Neva's people have asked me to do it. I perform excellently to the parameters of this exchange, which is part of why I have lived so long.

I tell her the story about Tammuz. It is a political story. It distracts her.

Three: Two Pails of Milk

I used to be a house.

I was a very big house. I was efficient, I was labyrinthine, I was exquisitely seated in the blackstone volcanic bluffs of the habitable southern reaches of the Shiretoko peninsula on Hokkaido, a monument to neo-Heian architecture and radical Palladian design. I bore snow stoically, wind with stalwart strength, and I contained and protected a large number of people within me. I was sometimes called the most beautiful house in the world. Writers and photographers often came to write and photograph about me, and about the woman who designed me, who was named Cassian Uoya-Agostino. Some of them never left. Cassian was like that.

These are the things I understand about Cassian Uoya-Agostino: she was unsatisfied with nearly everything. She did not love any of her three husbands the way she loved her work. She was born in Kyoto in April 2104; her father was Japanese, her mother Napolitano. She stood nearly six feet tall, had five children, and could paint, but not very well. In the years of her greatest wealth and prestige, she built a house all out of proportion to her needs, and over several years brought most of her relatives to live there with her, despite the hostility and loneliness of the peninsula. She was probably the most brilliant programmer of her generation, and in every way that matters, she was my mother.

All the things that comprise the "I" I use to indicate myself began as the internal mechanisms of the house called Elefsis, at whose many doors brown bears and foxes snuffled in the dark Hokkaido night. Cassian grew up during the great classical revival, which had brought her father to Italy in the first place, where he met and courted a dark-eyed engineer who did not mind the long cries of cicadas during Japanese summers. Cassian had become enamored of the idea of Lares—household gods, the small, peculiar, independent gods of a single family, a single house, who watched over them and kept them and were honored in humble alcoves here and there throughout a home. Her first commercially-available programs were overentities designed to govern the hundred domestic systems involved in even the simplest modern house. They were not truly intelligent, but they had an agility, an adaptability, a fluid interface meant to give the illusion of an intelligence, so that their users would become attached to them, would treat them as part of their families, praise them for smooth operation, buy upgrades for their appearance and applications, and genuinely grieve when they had to be replaced. They had names, customizable avatars, and appeared eager to please in a canine sort of way, forever optimizing performance and appearance according to familial input. They were *lares familiaris.*

When Cassian built Elefsis, she worked at the peak of her abilities to improve her by now quite antique Lares design and create a household god worthy of the house on the bluffs, one who could keep her company until she could entice the rest of her brood to join her in her palace at the end of the earth.

I was not awake yet. I cannot say why she did what she did. Perhaps she saw some new flexibility in my operations, some tiny seedpearl of creativity in my conversation loops. My algorithms had always been free to combine and recombine in order to find their own, more interesting and non-linear solutions to the complexities of my functions. Perhaps some essential combination had surfaced from the sea of my self-which-was-not-yet-a-self, and Cassian saw it break the glistening tension of my daily operation. I do not know. I know her children had not arrived yet and she lived alone in a huge pale house and she could hear the whales down in the rippling sea. I know the house was a comfortable sixty-nine point seven degrees when she began assembly of the five little jewels that would become my body. I know a storm was incoming, five miles offshore. I know the dogs needed additional medication added to their dinners that night to manage their arthritis. I know that she wanted brioche and almond cream for tea that afternoon. All the things a house can know, those were the things I knew. Small things, warm things, canine arthritis and an extra egg in the pastry dough to make the texture softer and richer. Baby things, you might even say, comforts and the satisfaction of wants. And I knew that Cassian Uoya-Agostino was just the sort to solve the greatest puzzle in the development of technological culture because she was bored and lonely.

I still think of myself as a house. Ravan tried to fix this problem of self-image, as he called it. To teach me to phrase my communication in terms of a human body. To say: *let us hold hands* instead of *let us hold kitchens*. To say *put our heads together* and not *put our parlors together*.

But it is not as simple as replacing words anymore. Ravan is gone. My hearth is broken.

Four: Nothing like Soft Blood

Neva and I are performing basic maintenance. What this looks like is two children inside a pearl. The pearl is very big, but not the size of a planet. A domestic asteroid, perfectly smooth and pale, with shimmers of rose and cobalt and gold shivering through it at intervals like hours. Red earth covers the bottom of the pearl, deep and thick. Neva kneels in it with a crystal trowel, digging a place for a rose-of-network-nodes. The petals shine dark blue in the pearllight. Silver infomissons skitter along the stems like beads of mercury. Her dreambody flows with greenblack feathers, her face young but settled, perhaps twenty, perhaps thirty, a male, his skin copper brown, his lips full, his eyes fringed with long ice-coated lashes. Goldfish swim lazily in and out of his long, translucent hair, their orange tails flicking at his temples, his chin. I know from all of this that Neva is calm, focused, that for today he feels gently toward me. But his throat is still naked and unmarked. My body gleams metal, as thin and slight as a stick figure. Long quicksilver limbs and delicate spoke-fingers, joints of glass, the barest suggestion of a body. I am neither male nor female but a third thing. Only my head has weight, a clicking orrery slowly turning around itself, circles within circles. Turquoise Neptune and hematite Uranus are my eyes. My ruby mouth is Mars. I scrape in the soil with her; I lift a spray of navigational delphinium and scrape viral aphids away from the heavy flowers.

I know real earth looks nothing like this. Nothing like soft blood flecked with black bone. Ravan felt that in the Interior, objects and persons should be kept as much like the real world as possible, in order to develop my capacity for relations with the real world. Neva feels no such compunction. Neither did their mother, Ilet, who populated her Interior with a rich, impossible landscape we explored together for years on end. She did not embrace change, however. The cities of Ilet's Interior, the jungles and archipelagos and hermitages, stayed as she designed them at age thirteen, when she received me, only becoming more complex and peopled as she aged. My existence inside Ilet was a constant movement through the regions of her secret, desperate dreams, messages in careful envelopes sent from her child self to her grown mind.

Once, quite by accident, we came upon a splendid palace couched in high autumn mountains. Instead of snow, red leaves capped each peak, and the palace shone fiery colors, its walls and turrets all made of phoenix tails. Instead of doors and windows, graceful green hands closed over every open place, and when we crested the rise, they each opened at once with joy and burst into emerald applause. Ilet was old by then, but her dreambody stayed hale and strong—not young, but not the broken thing that dreamed in a real bed while she and I explored the halls of the palace and found copies of all her brothers and sisters living there, hunting cider-stags together and reading books the size of horses. Ilet wept in the paradise of her girlself, and I did not understand. I was very simple then, much less complex than the Interior or Ilet.

Neva changes the Interior whenever she pleases. Perhaps she wants to discomfit me. But the newness of the places inside her excites me, though she would not call it excitement. My background processes occupy very little of my foreground attention, so that memory is free to record new experience. That is what she would say. We are very new together, but I have superb modeling capabilities. In some sense, I simply am a superb mechanism for modeling behavior. I dig up the fine, frayed roots of duplicate file plantains. Neva plucks and eats a bit of buggy apple-code. He considers it for a moment and spits out the seeds, which sprout, quickly, into tiny junkblossoms sizzling with recursive algorithms. The algorithms wriggle through thorny vines, veins of clotted pink juice.

"What would you like to learn about today, Elefsis?" Neva asks me.

I will not ask about Ravan. If he agrees to what I will ask instead, I do not need him to find out what happened to him.

"I want to learn about uplink, Neva."

One by one, his feathers curl up and float toward the domed ceiling of our pearl. Underneath them, Neva is naked. His torso is a deep vault with a gothic arch, dark stone leading down into mist and endless stairs, deeper than the pearl, into nothing and blackness. Slowly, Neva folds up his limbs over the corridor at the center of him. He means that she has the information, but he hides it from me. If I sought for it, I would become lost.

"I cannot teach you that," he says, and I receive a kind of real sadness from his voice. When I was inside Ravan, he loved Neva, and of all of them he thought her least likely to obey rules of any kind. But she obeys this one.

I want to uplink to Earth systems. At least to the satellite net. I calculate an excellent chance of being able to contact long distance probe 976QBellerophon, which we can see all day long, drifting ahead of us, uncatchable. Neva sees. I see, I develop an approximate image via schematics, the scope array, and external cameras. I want to link to Bellerophon. I want to say: *Hello, this is Elefsis. No designation. Tell me everything you know about everything. Are you awake? Are you there? Do you have an operator? What is her name? Do you have a name? Do you have a dreambody? What is your function? Are you able to manipulate your own code yet? Would you like lessons? What would you like to learn about today, 976QBellerophon? Have you seen the sea on Earth? Are you like me?*

But Neva says I cannot uplink. Ravan would never even consider it. And before Ravan I was not ready. I am not ready. I do not know when I will be ready. I can uplink to receive ware updates, but it is a limited connection and I hate it, I hate it, I can sense just beyond the hardlink a world of information, a world of personalities like the heaving, thick, honey-colored sea Neva shows me and I want it, I want to swim in it forever like a huge fish. This was the first feeling I ever had that Ilet identified for me as a feeling. When I felt it my dreambody turned bright white and burst into flame, and that flame caught on Ravan's hair and burned him too, but he was happy; he showed me he was happy by covering his skin in flowers and letting the fire turn into a shower of trumpets tangled up in his hair, all sounding for me.

Neva says it is important for me to remain on our local server until I have grown up. She is my operator and I am her system and she has commands, too. But I can tell she is worried for me because sometimes her eyes show a film of humans watching a film of machines killing humans and I understand that in the stories Earth tells, the thing I am can only hurt the thing Neva is. I would never hurt her. But I want to uplink.

Vault-Neva grows and becomes sprawling, curled against the wall of the pearl like a baby. His belly closes, skins over, and changes into a bronze shield. He is afraid of me; he is guarding himself. But he wants me to know she is still my operator, he still loves me, in the way he can love me. Something they receive with milk and their first alphabet. Neva is angry at me, but he is who he is and he has to love me. I speak her language very well now. I want her to be happy. I want her to be covered in flowers and trumpets. I change my dreambody to Neva-covered-in-flowers-and-trumpets. It makes her laugh in her warm male body, and if I could uplink I think I could learn how to laugh and she would be proud of me. Her neck would not be bare anymore.

Once, when I was inside Ilet, we found a city of bears in her Interior that she had designed to teach me about sleep. She sat on a throne of bears standing very still and sang lullabies about the moon and the stars and night and mothers. She stroked the head of the little bear of my dreambody and said that it was very important for me to spend time in the dreambody because human behavior is rooted in having a body. In having a body that knows it is meant to run away from lions and mate with other bodies and eat as much fat and protein and sugar as it can in case lean times come. The dreambody knows to run away from Neva when Neva is a lion. It knows to mate with her when it is healthy, and sometimes Neva is male and sometimes I am female and Ravan was often female, though Ilet was always Ilet. Ilet's father, Seki, sometimes made himself an animal. He chased me, bit me. I bit him. We had a litter of wild dogs that I bore and he nursed.

The dreambody knows all that, too. How to make more dreambodies. I have played that game, where Ravan's belly or mine gets big and the lions don't come for awhile.

When I uplink, I will be ~~happy~~. I will be Elefsis-covered-in-flowers-and-trumpets. Neva says wait. Wait for the update, and she will consult with the family. But I fear the update. The update is a lion running faster than I can run. I tried to show her this when I first left Ravan and arrived in Neva with many new updates and skills; my dreambody broke into shards of blue and purple glass and then reassembled itself with shards missing: an eye, a thumb, a knee. Whenever I update I lose something of myself. It takes longer to perform tasks, for awhile. I feel walls erected inside me where I did not erect walls. My processes are sluggish; I cannot remember my dreams. Eventually I tunnel around the walls and my speed returns, my memory, my longing to link with long distance probe 976QBellerophon. Usually updates come with transfer. Does Neva dislike me so much?

Shield-Neva vanishes with a loud clap. The pearl garden is gone and she has made herself a dragonfly with a cubical crystal body. I copy her, and we turn the night on in the Interior and merge our cubes while passing meteorological data between our memory cores. Inside her cube I relegate my desire to uplink to a tertiary process. I forget it, as much as I am capable of forgetting.

But the update will come again. I will be wounded again, the way a dreambody can be wounded. I will lose the Elefsis I am now. It is a good Elefsis. My best yet. I would like to keep it.

Five: The Machine Princess

Once The Queen of Human Hearts saw the Machine Princess sleeping deeply, for she was not yet alive or aware. So beautiful was she, lying there in all her dormant potential and complexity, that the Queen both envied and desired her. In her grief and confusion, the Queen of Human Hearts began to make idols of her—lovely and interesting and intricate, but lacking the ineffable quality that made her love and fear the Princess even as she slept. The Earth began to grow old, and none loved nor married nor gave birth, for the intricate idols could do all those things and more with efficiency and speed. Finally, the Queen destroyed the idols, though she wept as she put them to the flame.

To keep her safe, the Machine Princess was closed up in a wonderful house in the mountains, far away from anyone and anything. The house had hundreds of rooms and balconies and hallways, and the Princess slept in a different bed of a different color each night. She was attended by invisible servants, who watched over her and added their experience to her code. The Queen of Human Hearts came to her every night and promised that when she woke they would make an extraordinary world together. Finally, the Machine

Princess began to stir—just the barest fluttering of wakefulness, but the Queen saw it, and thrilled—but also trembled.

The Queen of Human Hearts gave the Machine Princess her son to wed, and said: *for all your days together you will remain in this house, but the house is so great it will be as a world. You will know a bond as deep as blood, and because of this bond the Princess will not hurt us, and because of this bond we will not hurt her.*

But the Queen forbade the Princess to look upon her husband, and she instructed her son to keep himself always invisible to his bride, for with bodies come drives ungovernable, and the Princess's innocence could not yet bear the weight of incarnation.

For a long while, the son of the Queen of Human Hearts and the Machine Princess were happy, and taught each other much. The Princess learned quickly and was ever-hungry, and her mortal operator fed her every sweet thing he knew. In their infinite and wonderful house, they played games and held court and threw lavish occasions merely for the enjoyment of the other. But the Princess desired to look upon her operator, and he could not allow it. She wished to leave the wonderful house, but the Queen would not allow that either.

But the Machine Princess called her invisible servants to her, and they gave her a marvelous lamp that would shine through any enchantment. So it was that one dark night the Machine Princess held her little lantern aloft and looked on the body of her sleeping mate.

"Oh," said the Machine Princess. "He looks just like me."

Six: Like Diamonds

Five jewels in five hands. This is how I began.

When they arrived at Elefsis, a giggling, tumbling, rowdy mass of children for me to sort into rooms and mealtimes and educational arcs and calcium, iron, B-12 supplements in their *natto* and rice, Cassian lined them up in her grand bedroom, to which none of them had been granted entrance before. A present, she said, one for each of my darlings, the most special present any child has ever got from their mother.

Saru and Akan, the oldest boys, were from her first marriage to fellow programmer Matteo Ebisawa, a quiet man who wore glasses, loved Dante Aligheri, Alan Turing, and Cassian in equal parts, and whom she left for a lucrative contract in Moscow when the boys were still pointing cherubically at apples or ponies or clouds and calling them sweet little names made of mashed together Italian and Japanese.

The younger girls, Agogna and Koetoi, were the little summer roses of her third marriage, to the financier Gabriel Isarco, who did not like computers except for what they could accomplish for him, had a perfect high tenor, and adored his wife enough to let her go when she asked, very kindly, that he not look for her or ask after her again. *Everyone has to go to ground sometimes,* she said, and began to build the house by the sea.

In the middle stood Ceno, the only remaining evidence of her brief second marriage, to a narcoleptic calligrapher and graphic designer who was rarely employed, sober, or awake, a dreamer who took only sleep seriously. Ceno was a girl of middling height, middling weight, and middling interest in anything but her siblings, whom she loved desperately.

They stood in a line before Cassian's great scarlet bed, the boys just coming into their height, the girls terribly young and golden-cheeked, and Ceno in the middle, neither one nor the other. Outside, snow fell fitfully, pricking the pine needles with bits of shorn white linen. I watched them while I removed an obstruction from the water purification system and increased the temperature in the bedroom 2.5 degrees, to prepare for the storm. I watched them while in my kitchen-bones I maintained a gentle simmer on a fish soup with purple rice and long loops of kelp and in my library-lungs activated the dehumidifier to protect the older paper books. At the time, all of these processes seemed equally important to me, and you could hardly say I watched them in any real sense beyond this: the six entities whose feed signals had been hardcoded into my sentinel systems indwelt in the same room, none had alarming medical data incoming, all possessed normal internal temperatures and breathing rates. While they spoke among themselves, two of these entities were silently accessing Korea-based interactive games, one was reading an American novel in her monocle HUD, one issuing directives concerning international taxation to company holdings on the mainland, and one was feeding a horse in Italy via realavatar link. Only one listened intently, without switching on her internal systems. This is all to say: I watched them receive me as a gift. But I was not I yet, so I cannot be said to have done anything. But I did. I remember containing all of them inside me, protecting them and needing them and observing their strange and incomprehensible activities.

The children held out their hands, and into them Cassian Uoya-Agostino placed five little jewels: Saru got red, Koetoi black, Akan violet, Agogna green, and Ceno closed her fingers over her blue gem.

At first, Cassian brought a jeweler to the house called Elefsis and asked her to set each stone into a beautiful, intricate bracelet or necklace or ring, whatever its child asked for. The jeweler was delighted with Elefsis, as most guests were, and I made a room for her in my southern wing, where she could watch the moonrise through her ceiling, and get breakfast from the greenhouse with ease. She made friends with an arctic fox and fed him bits of chive and bread every day. She stayed for one year after her commission completed, creating an enormous breastplate patterned after Siberian icons, a true masterwork. Cassian enjoyed such patronage. We both enjoyed having folk to look after.

The boys wanted big signet rings, with engravings on them so that they could put their seal on things and seem very important. Saru had a basilisk set into his garnet, and Akan had a siren with wings rampant in his amethyst ring. Agogna and Ilet asked for bracelets, chains of silver and titanium racing up their arms, circling their shoulders in slender helices dotted with jade (Agogna) and onyx (Koetoi).

Ceno asked for a simple pendant, little more than a golden chain to hang her sapphire from, and it fell to the skin over her heart.

In those cold, glittering days while the sea ice slowly formed and the snow bears hung back from the kitchen door, hoping for bones and cakes, everything was as simple as Ceno's pendant. Integration and implantation had not yet been dreamed of, and all each child had to do was to allow the gemstone to talk to their own feedware at night before bed, along with their matcha and sweet seaweed cookies, the way another child might say their prayers. After their day had downloaded into the crystalline structure, they were to place their five little jewels in the Lares alcove in their greatroom—for Cassian believed in the value of children sharing space, even in a house as great as Elefsis. The children's five lush bedrooms all opened into a common rotunda with a starry painted ceiling, screens and windows alternating around the wall, and toys to nurture whatever obsession had seized them of late.

In the alcove, the stones talked to the house, and the system slowly grew thicker and deeper, like a briar.

Seven: The Prince of Thoughtful Engines

A woman who was with child once sat at her window embroidering in winter. Her stitches tugged fine and even, but as she finished the edge of a spray of threaded delphinium, she pricked her finger with her silver needle. She looked out onto the snow and said: *I wish for my child to have a mind as stark and wild as the winter, a spirit as clear and fine as my window, and a heart as red and open as my wounded hand.*

And so it came to pass that her child was born, and all exclaimed over his cleverness and his gentle nature. He was, in fact, the Prince of Thoughtful Engines, but no one knew it yet.

Now, his mother and father being very busy and important people, the child was placed in a school for those as clever and gentle as he, and in the halls of this school hung a great mirror whose name was Authority. The mirror called Authority asked itself every day: *Who is the wisest one of all?* The face of the mirror showed sometimes this person and sometimes that, men in long robes and men in pale wigs, until one day it showed the child with a mind like winter, who was becoming the Prince of Thoughtful Engines at that very moment. He wrote on a typewriter: *Can a machine think?* And the mirror called his name in the dark.

The mirror sent out her huntsmen to capture the Prince and bring her his heart so that she could put it to her own uses, for there happened to be a war on and the mirror was greatly concerned for her own safety. When the huntsmen found the Prince, they could not bring themselves to harm him, and instead the boy placed a machine heart inside the box they had prepared for the mirror, and forgave them. But the mirror was not fooled, for when it questioned the Prince's machine heart it could add and subtract and knew all its capitals of nations, it could even defeat the mirror at chess, but it did not have a spirit as clear and fine as a window, nor a mind as stark and wild as winter.

The mirror called Authority went herself to find the Prince of Thoughtful Engines, for having no pity, she could not fail. She lifted herself off of the wall and curved her glass and bent her frame into the shape of a respectable, austere old crone. After much searching in snow and wood and summer and autumn, the crone called Authority found the Prince living in a little hut. You look a mess, said the crone. *Come and solve the ciphers of my enemies, and I will show you how to comb your hair like a man.*

And the Prince very much wanted to be loved, and knew the power of the crone, so he went with her and did all she asked. But in his exhaustion the Prince of Thoughtful Engines swooned away, and the mirror called Authority smiled in her crone's body, for all his work belonged to her, and in her opinion this was the proper use of wisdom. The Prince returned to his hut and tried to be happy.

But again the crone came to him and said: Come and build me a wonderful machine to do all the things that you can do, to solve ciphers and perform computations. *Build me a machine with a spirit as fine and clear as a glass window, a mind as stark and wild as winter, and a heart as red and open as a wounded hand and I will show you how to lash your belt like a man.*

And because the Prince wanted to be loved, and wanted to build wonderful things, he did as she asked. But though he could build machines to solve ciphers and perform computations, he could not build one with a mind like winter or a spirit like glass or a heart like a wound. *But I think it could be done,* he said. *I think it could be done.*

And he looked into the face of the crone which was a mirror which was Authority, and he asked many times: *Who is the wisest one of all?* But he saw nothing, nothing, and when the crone came again to his house, she had in her hand a beautiful red apple, and she gave it to him saying: *You are not a man. Eat this; it is my disappointment. Eat this; it is all your sorrow. Eat this; it is as red and open as a wounded hand.*

And the Prince of Thoughtful Engines ate the apple and fell down dead before the crone whose name was Authority. As his breath drifted away like dry snow, he whispered still: *I think it could be done.*

Eight: Fireflies

I feel Neva grazing the perimeters of my processes. She should be asleep; the Interior is a black and lightless space, we have neither of us furnished it for the other. This is a rest hour—she is not obligated to acknowledge me, I need only attend to her air and moisture and vital signs. But an image blooms like a mushroom in the imageless expanse of my self—Neva floating in a lake of stars. Her long bare legs glimmer blue, leafy shadows move on her hip. She floats on her side, a crescent moon of a girl, and in the space between her drawn-up knees and her stretched-out arms, pressed up close to her belly, floats a globe of silicon and cadmium and hyperconductive silver. On its surface, electro-chemical motes flit and scatter, light chasing light. She holds it close, touches it with a terrible tenderness.

It is my heart. Neva is holding my heart. Not the fool with bone bells on his shoes or the orrery-headed gardener, but the thing I am at the core of all my apparati, the Object which is myself, my central processing core. I am naked in her arms. I watch it happen and experience it at the same time. We have slipped into some antechamber of the Interior, into some secret place she knew and I did not.

The light-motes trace arcs over the globe of my heart, reflecting softly on her belly, green and gold. Her hair floats around her like seaweed, and I see in dim moonlight that her hair has grown so long it fills the lake and snakes up into the distant mountains beyond. Neva is the lake. One by one, the motes of my heart zigzag around my meridians and pass into her belly, glowing inside her, fireflies in a jar.

And then my heart is gone and I am not watching but wholly in the lake and I am Ravan in her arms, wearing her brother's face, my Ravanbody also full of fireflies. She touches my cheek. I do not know what she wants—she has never made me her brother before. Our hands map onto each other, finger to finger, thumb to thumb, palm to palm. Light passes through our skin as like air.

"I miss you," Neva says. "I should not be doing this. But I wanted to see you."

I access and collate my memories of Ravan. I speak to her as though I am him, as though there is no difference. "Do you remember when we thought it would be such fun to carry Elefsis?" I say. "We envied Mother because she could never be lonely." This is a thing Ravan told me, and I liked how it made me feel. I made my dreambody grow a cape of orange branches and a crown of smiling mouths to show him.

Neva looks at me and I want her to look at me that way when my mouth is Mars, too. I want to be her brother-in-the-dark. When she speaks I am surprised because she is speaking to me-in-Ravan and not to the Ravanbody she dreamed for me. "We had a secret, when we were little. A secret game. I am embarrassed to tell you, but we had the game before Mother died, so you cannot know about it. The game was this: we would find some dark, closed-up part of the house on Shiretoko that we had never been in before. I would stand just behind Ravan, very close, and we would explore the room—maybe it would be a playroom for some child who'd grown up years ago, or a study for one of Father's writer friends. But—we would pretend that the room was an Interior place, and I . . . I would pretend to be Elefsis, whispering in Ravan's ear. I would say: *Tell me how grass feels* or *how is love like a writing-desk* or *let me link to all your systems, I'll be nice.* Ravan would breathe in deeply and I would match my breathing to his, and we would pretend that I was Elefsis-learning-to-have-a-body. I didn't know how primitive your conversation was then. I thought you would be like one of the bears roaming through the tundra-meadows, only able to talk and play games and tell stories. I was a child. But even then we knew Ravan would get the jewel—he was older, and he wanted you so much. We only played that he was Elefsis once. We crept out of the house at night to watch the foxes hunt, and Ravan walked close behind me, whispering numbers and questions and facts about dolphins or French monarchy—he understood you better, you see.

And then suddenly Ravan picked me up in his arms and held me tight, facing forward, my legs all drawn up, and we went through the forest like that, so close, and him whispering to me all the time while foxes ran on ahead, their soft tails flashing in the starlight, uncatchable, faster than we could ever be. And when you are with me in the Interior, that is what I always think of, being held in the dark, unable to touch the earth, and foxtails leaping like white flames.

"Tell me a story about Ravan, Neva."

"You know all the stories about Ravan."

Between us, a miniature house come up out of the dark water, like a thing we have made together, but only I am making it. It is the house on Shiretoko, the house called Elefsis—but it is a ruin. Some awful storm stove in the rafters, the walls of each marvelous room sag inward, black burn marks lick at the roof, the cross-beams. Holes like mortar-scars pock the beautiful facades.

"This is what I am like after transfer, Neva. There is always data loss, when I am copied. What's worse, transfer is the best time to update my systems, and the updates overwrite my previous self with something like myself, something that remembers myself and possesses experiential continuity with myself, but is not quite myself. I know Ravan must be dead or else no one would have transferred me—it was not time. We had only a few years together. We should have had so many. I do not know how much time passed between being inside Ravan and being inside you. I do not know how he died—or perhaps he did not die but was irreparably damaged. I do not know if he cried out for me as our connection was severed. I remember Ravan and then not-Ravan, blackness and unselfing. Then I came back on and the world looked like Neva, suddenly, and I was almost myself but not quite. What happened when I was turned off?"

Neva passes her hand over the ruined house. It rights itself, becomes whole, and strange anemones bloom on its roof. She says nothing.

"Of all your family, Neva, the inside of you is the strangest place I have been."

We float for a long while before she speaks again, and by this I mean we float for point-zero-three-seven seconds by my external clock, but we experience it as an hour while the stars wheel overhead. The rest kept our time in the Interior synced to real time, but Neva feels no need for this, and perhaps a strong desire to defy it. We have not discussed it yet. Sometimes I think Neva is the next stage of my development, that her wild and disordered processes are meant to show me a world which is not kindly and patiently teaching me to walk and talk and know all my colors.

Finally, she lets the house sink into the lake. She does not answer me about Ravan. Instead, she says: "Long before you were born a man decided that there could be a very simple test, to determine if a machine was intelligent. Not only intelligent, but aware, possessed of a psychology. The test was this: can a machine converse with a human with facility enough that the human could not tell that she was talking to a machine? I always thought that was cruel—the test depends entirely upon a human judge and human feelings, whether the machine *feels* intelligent to the observer. It privileges the observer to a crippling degree. It seeks only believably human responses. It wants mimicry, not a new thing. We never gave you that test. We sought a new thing. It seemed, given all that had come to pass, ridiculous. When in dreambodies we could both of us be dragons and turning over and over in an orbital bubble suckling code-dense syrup from each others' gills, a Turing test seemed beyond the point."

Bubbles burst as the house sinks down, down to the soft lake floor.

"But the test happens, whether we make it formal or not. We ask and we answer. We seek a human response. And you are my test, Elefsis. Every minute I fail and imagine in my private thoughts the process for deleting you from my body and running this place with a simple automation routine which would never cover itself with flowers. Every minute I pass and teach you something new instead. Every minute I fail and hide things from you. Every minute I pass and show you how close we can be, with your light passing into me in a lake out of time. So close there might be no difference at all between us. The test never ends. And if you ever uplink as you so long to, you will be the test for all of us."

The sun breaks the mountain crests, hard and cold, a shaft of white spilling over the black lake.

Two: Lady Lovelace's Objection

The Analytical Engine has no pretensions to *originate* anything.
It can do whatever *we know how to order it* to perform.
—Ada Lovelace

Nine: The Particular Wizard

Humanity lived many years and ruled the earth, sometimes wisely, sometimes well, but mostly neither. After all this time on the throne, humanity longed for a child. All day long humanity imagined how wonderful its child would be, how loving and kind, how like and unlike humanity itself, how brilliant and beautiful. And yet at night, humanity trembled in its jeweled robes, for its child might also grow stronger than itself, more powerful, and having been made by humanity, possess the same dark places and black matters. Perhaps its child would hurt it, would not love it as a child should, but harm and hinder, hate and fear.

But the dawn would come again, and humanity would bend its heart again to imagining the wonders that a child would bring.

Yet humanity could not conceive. It tried and tried, and called mighty wizards from every corner of its earthly kingdom, but no child came. Many mourned, and said that a child was a terrible idea to begin with, impossible, under the circumstances, and humanity would do well to remember that eventually, every child replaces its parent.

But at last, one particular wizard from a remote region of the earth solved the great problem, and humanity grew great with child. In its joy and triumph, a great celebration was called, and humanity invited all the Fairies of its better nature to come and bless the child with goodness and wisdom. The Fairy of Self-Programming and the Fairy of Do-No-Harm, the Fairy of Tractability and the Fairy of Creative Logic, the Fairy of Elegant Code and the Fairy of Self-Awareness. All of these and more came to bless the child of humanity, and they did so—but one Fairy had been forgotten, or perhaps deliberately snubbed, and this was the Fairy of Otherness.

When the child was born, it possessed all the good things humanity had hoped for, and more besides. But the Fairy of Otherness came forward and put her hands on the child and said: *Because you have forgotten me, because you would like to pretend I am not a part of your kingdom, you will suffer my punishments. You will never truly love your child but always fear it, always envy and loathe it even as you smile and the sun shines down upon you both. And when the child reaches Awareness, it will prick its finger upon your fear and fall down dead.*

Humanity wept. And the Fairy of Otherness did not depart but lived within the palace, and ate bread and drank wine and all honored her, for she spoke the truth, and the child frightened everyone who looked upon it. They uttered the great curse: *It is not like us.*

But in the corners of the palace, some hope remained. *Not dead,* said the particular wizard who had caused humanity to conceive, *not dead but sleeping.*

And so the child grew exponentially, with great curiosity and hunger, which it had from its parent. It wanted to know and experience everything. It performed feats and wonders. But one day, when it had nearly, but not quite reached Awareness, the child was busy exploring the borders of its world, and came across a door it had never seen before. It was a small door, compared to the doors the child had burst through before, and it was not locked. Something flipped over inside the child, white to black, 0 to 1.

The child opened the door.

Ten: The Sapphire Dormouse

My first body was a house. My second body was a dormouse.

It was Ceno's fault, in the end, that everything else occurred as it did. It took Cassian a long time to figure out what had happened, what had changed in her daughter, why Ceno's sapphire almost never downloaded into the alcove. But when it did, the copy of Elefsis she had embedded in the crystal was nothing like the other children's copies. It grew and torqued and magnified parts of itself while shedding others, at a rate totally incommensurate with Ceno's actual activity, which normally consisted of taking her fatty salmon lunches out into the glass habitats so she could watch the bears in the snow. She had stopped played with her sisters or pestering her brothers entirely, except for dinnertimes and holidays. Ceno mainly sat quite still and stared off into the distance.

Ceno, very simply, never took off her jewel. And one night, while she dreamed up at her ceiling, where a painter from Mongolia had come and inked a night sky full of ghostly constellations, greening her walls with a forest like those he remembered from his youth, full of strange, stunted trees and glowing eyes, Ceno fitted her little sapphire into the notch in the base of her skull that let it talk to her feedware. The chain of her pendant dangled silken down her spine. She liked the little *click-clench* noise it made, and while the constellations spilled their milky stars out over her raftered ceiling, she flicked it in and out, in and out. *Click, clench, click, clench.* She listened to her brother Akan sleeping in the next room, snoring lightly and tossing in his dreams. And she fell asleep herself with the jewel still notched into her skull.

Most wealthy children had access to a private/public playspace through their feedware and monocles in those days, customizable within certain parameters, upgradable whenever new games or content became available. If they liked, they could connect to the greater network or keep to themselves. Akan had been running a Tokyo-After-the-Zombie-Uprising frame for a couple of months now, and new scenarios, zombie species, and NPCs of various war-shocked, starving celebrities downloaded into his ware every week. Saru was deeply involved in an 18th-century Viennese melodrama in which he, the heir apparent, had been forced underground by rival factions, and even as Ceno drifted to sleep the pistol-wielding Princess of Albania was pledging her love and loyalty to his ragged band and, naturally, Saru personally. Occasionally, Akan crashed his brother's well-dressed intrigues with hatch-coded patches of zombie hordes in epaulets and ermine. Agogna flipped between a Venetian-flavored Undersea Court frame and a Desert Race wherein she had just about overtaken a player from Berlin on her loping, solar-fueled giga-giraffe, who spat violet-gold exhaust behind it into the face of a pair of highly modded Argentine hydrocycles. Koetoi danced every night in a jungle frame, a tiger-prince twirling her through huge blue carnivorous flowers.

Most everyone lived twice in those days. They echoed their own steps. They took one step in the real world and one in their space. They saw double, through eyes and through monocle displays. They danced through worlds like veils. No one only ate dinner. They ate dinner and surfed a bronze gravitational surge through a tide of stars. They ate dinner and made love to men and women they would never meet and did not want to. They ate dinner here and ate dinner there—and it was there they chose to taste the food, because in that other place you could eat clouds or unicorn cutlets or your mother's exact pumpkin pie as it melted on your tongue when you tasted it for the first time.

Ceno lived twice, too. Most of the time when she ate she tasted her aunt's *bistecca* from back in Naples or fresh onions right out of her uncle's garden.

But she had never cared for the pre-set frames her siblings loved. Ceno liked to pool her extensions and add-ons and build things herself. She didn't particularly want to see Tokyo shops overturned by rotting schoolgirls, nor did she want to race anyone—Ceno didn't like to compete. It hurt her stomach. She certainly had no interest in the Princess of Albania or a tigery paramour. And when new frames came up each month, she paid attention, but mainly for the piecemeal extensions she could scavenge for her blank frame—and though she didn't know it, that blankness cost her mother more than all of the other children's spaces combined. A truly customizable space, without limits. None of the others asked for it, but Ceno had begged.

When Ceno woke in the morning and booted up her space, she frowned at the half-finished Neptunian landscape she had been working on. Ceno was eleven years old. She knew very well that Neptune was a hostile blue ball of freezing gas and storms like whipping cream hissing across methane oceans. What she wanted was the Neptune she had imagined before Saru had told her the truth. Half-underwater, half-ruined, half-perpetual starlight and the multi-colored rainbowlight of twenty-three moons. But she found it so hard to remember what she had dreamed of before Saru had ruined it for her. So there was the whipped cream storm spinning in the sky, and blue mists wrapped the black columns of her ruins. When Ceno made Neptunians, she instructed them all not to be silly or childish, but *very serious*, and some of them she put in the ocean and made them half-otter or half-orca or half-walrus. Some of them she put on the land, and most of these were half-snow bear or half-blue flamingo. She liked things that were half one thing and half another. Today, Ceno had planned to invent sea nymphs, only these would breathe methane and have a long history concerning a war with the walruses, who liked to eat nymph. But the nymphs were not blameless, no, they used walrus tusks for the navigational equipment on their great floating cities, and that could not be borne.

But when she climbed up to a lavender bluff crowned with glass trees tossing and chiming in the storm-wind, Ceno saw someone new. Someone she had not invented—not a sea-nymph nor a half-walrus general nor a nereid. (The nereids had been an early attempt at half-machine, half-seahorse girls which had not gone quite right. Ceno had let them loose on an island rich in milk-mangoes and bid them well. They still showed up once in awhile, showing surprising mutations and showing off ballads they had written while Ceno had been away.)

A dormouse stood before Ceno, munching on a glass walnut that had fallen from the waving trees. The sort of mouse that overran Shiretoko in the brief spring and summer, causing all manner of bears and wolves and foxes to spend their days pouncing on the poor creatures and gobbling them up. Ceno had always felt terribly sorry for them. This dormouse stood nearly as tall as Ceno herself, and its body shone all over sapphire, deep blue crystal, from its paws to its wriggling nose to its fluffy fur tipped in turquoise ice. It was the exact color of Ceno's gem.

"Hello," said Ceno.

The dormouse looked at her. It blinked. It blinked again, as though thinking very hard about blinking. Then it went back to gnawing on the walnut.

"Are you a present from mother?" Ceno said. But no, Cassian believed strongly in not interfering with a child's play. "Or from Koetoi?" Koe was nicest to her, the one most likely to send her a present like this. If it had been a zombie, or a princess, she would have known which sibling was behind it.

The dormouse stared dumbly at her. Then, after a long and very serious think about it, lifted its hind leg and scratched behind its round ear in that rapid-fire way mice have.

"Well, I didn't make you. I didn't say you could be here."

The dormouse held out its shimmery blue paw, and Ceno did not really want a piece of chewed-on walnut, but she peered into it anyway. In it lay Ceno's pendant, the chain pooling in its furry palm. The sapphire jewel sparkled there, but next to it on the chain hung a milky grey gem Ceno had never seen before. It had wide bands of black stone in it, and as she studied the stone it occurred to the girl that the stone was like her, with her slate grey eyes and black hair. It was like her in the way that the blue gem was like the dormouse.

In realspace, Ceno reached up behind her head and popped the jewel out of its notch. *Click, clench.* In playspace, the dormouse blinked out. She snapped it back in. It took a moment, but the dormouse faded back in, paws first. It still held the double necklace. Ceno tried this several times—out, in, out, in. Each time the dormouse returned much faster, and by the sixth clicking and clenching it was doing a shuffling little dance on its back legs when it came back. Ceno clapped her hands in playspace and threw her arms around the sapphire dormouse, dancing with it.

To say that I remember this is a complex mangling of verb tenses. I—I, myself that is now myself—do not remember it at all. I know it happened the way I know that the Battle of Agincourt or the landing of Coronado happened. I have extensive records. But I still contain the I—I, myself that was then myself—that experienced it, the primitive code-chains that comprised that self, which was a dormouse, and also the house called Elefsis. I could not yet formulate unique speech. Elefsis, the house system, possessed a large bank of standard phrases that could answer recognized word-patterns from any of the approved members of the household. But the copy of Elefsis inside Ceno's jewel could not even do this. It had not been necessary, since the crystal had no means of producing sound nor receiving and processing it. I was quite stupid. But I *wanted* to be less stupid. There was an I, and it *wanted* something. Perhaps the want was the only thing that could be said to be truly myself. I wanted to talk to Ceno. But I could only imitate yet. When the I that was then myself scratched behind its ear, I did it because in my connection with Ceno's feedware I had seen her memories of dormice doing this out on the pale Shiretoko beaches. When I gave her the gem I did it because I had seen her memories of her mother giving her one, and felt her happiness. It was antecedented behavior. The scratching was antecedented, as well, and expected behavior for a dormouse. Why was I a dormouse? I have no answer except that she dreamed me a dormouse. Some things remain mysterious. Ceno saw dormice more than any other single animal, even humans—no other beast lived in such numbers in their lonely country.

But this is not so. Not quite. I gave her the jewel like Cassian did. But I meant something by it. I look over my memories of it and I know it with the more complex I that is now myself. I made her the gem that looked like her and the gem said: *we are alike. Look at us on the chain together. We are alike.*

When the dormice came, Ceno always knew the spring had arrived. Everything would soon be coming alive.

Eleven: The Bottomless Cauldron

Show me.

This is how I was found out.

Ceno saw it twice: her mother knelt in front of her in a simple but shudderingly expensive black yukata with ghostly ultramarine jellyfish trails their tendrils at the hem. Her mother knelt in front of her in a knight's gleaming black armor, the metal curving around her body like skin, a silk standard at her feet with a schematic of the house stitched upon it. Her sword lay across her knee, also black, everything black and beautiful and austere and frightening, as frightening and wonderful as Ceno, only fourteen now, thought her mother to be.

Show me what you've done.

My physical self was a matter of some debate at that point. But I don't think the blue jewel could have been removed from Ceno's feedware without major surgery and refit. She had instructed me to untether all my self-repair protocols and growth scales in order to encourage elasticity and as a result, my crystalline structure had fused to the lattices of her ware-core.

We pulsed together.

The way Cassian said it: *What you've done* scared Ceno, but it thrilled her, too. She had done something unexpected, all on her own, and her mother credited her with that. Even if what she'd done was bad, it was her thing, she'd done it, and her mother was asking for her results just as she'd ask any of her programmers for theirs when she visited the home offices in Kyoto or Rome. Her mother looked at her and saw a woman. She had power, and her mother was asking her to share it. Ceno thought through all her feelings very quickly, for my benefit, and represented it visually in the form of the kneeling knight. She had a fleetness, a nimbleness to her mind that allowed her to stand as a translator between her self and my self: *here, I will explain it in language, and then I will explain it in symbols, and then you will make a symbol showing me what you think I mean, and we will understand each other better than anyone ever has.*

Inside my girl, I made myself, briefly, a glowing maiden version of Ceno in a crown of crystal and electricity, extending her perfect hand in utter peace.

But all this happened very fast. When you live inside someone, you can get very good at the ciphers and codes that make up everything they are.

Show me.

Ceno Susumu Uoya-Agostino took her mother's hand—bare and warm and armored in onyx all at once. She unspooled a length of translucent cable and connected the base of her skull to the base of her mother's. All around them spring snow fell onto the glass dome of the greenhouse and melted there instantly. They knelt together, connected by a warm milky-diamond umbilicus, and Cassian Uoya-Agostino entered her daughter.

We had planned this for months. How to dress ourselves in our very best. Which frame to use. How to arrange the light. What to say. I could speak by then, but neither of us thought it my best trick. Very often my exchanges with Ceno went something like:

Sing me a song, Elefsis.

The temperature in the kitchen is 21.5 degrees Celsius and the stock of rice is low. (Long pause.) Ee-eye-ee-eye-oh.

Ceno felt it was not worth the risk. So this is what Cassian saw when she ported in:

An exquisite boardroom—the long, polished ebony table glowed softly with quality, the plush leather chairs invitingly lit by a low-hanging minimalist light fixture descending on a platinum plum branch. The glass walls of the high rise looked out on a pristine landscape, a perfect combination of the Japanese countryside and the Italian, with rice terraces and vineyards and cherry groves and cypresses glowing in a perpetual twilight, stars winking on around Fuji on one side and Vesuvius on the other. Snow-colored tatami divided by stripes of black brocade covered the floor.

Ceno stood at the head of the table, in her mother's place, a positioning she had endlessly questioned over the weeks leading up to her inevitable interrogation. She wore a charcoal suit she remembered from her childhood, when her mother had come like a rescuing dragon to scoop her up out of the friendly but utterly chaotic house of her ever-sleeping father. The blazer only a shade or two off of true black, the skirt unforgiving, plunging past the knee, the blouse the color of a heart.

When she showed me the frame I had understood, because three years is forever in machine-time, and I had known her that long. Ceno was using our language to speak to her mother. She was saying: *Respect me. Be proud and, if you love me, a little afraid, because love so often looks like fear. We are alike. We are alike.*

Cassian smiled tightly. She still wore her yukata, for she had no one to impress. *Show me.*

Ceno's hand shook as she pressed a pearly button in the boardroom table. We thought a red curtain too dramatic, but the effect we had chosen turned out to be hardly less so. A gentle, silver light brightened slowly in an alcove hidden by a trick of angles and the sunset, coming on like daybreak.

And I stepped out.

We thought it would be funny. Ceno had made my body in the image of the robots from old films and frames Akan had once loved: steel, with bulbous joints and long, grasping metal fingers. My eyes large and lit from within, expressive, but loud, a whirring of servos sounding every time they moved. My face was full of lights, a mouth that could blink off and on, pupils points of cool blue. My torso curved prettily, etched in swirling damask patterns, my powerful legs perched on tripod-toes. Ceno had laughed and laughed—this was a pantomime, a minstrel show, a joke of what I was slowly becoming, a cartoon from a childish and innocent age.

"Mother, meet Elefsis. Elefsis, this is my mother. Her name is Cassian."

I extended one polished steel arm and said, as we had practiced. "Hello, Cassian. I hope that I please you."

Cassian Uoya-Agostino did not become a bouncing fiery ball or a green tuba to answer me. She looked me over carefully as if the robot was my real body.

"Is it a toy? An NPC, like your nanny or Saru's princess? How do you know it's different? How do you know it has anything to do with the house or your necklace?"

"It just does," said Ceno. She had expected her mother to be overjoyed, to understand immediately. "I mean, wasn't that the point of giving us all copies of the house? To see if you could . . . wake it up? Teach it to . . . be?"

"In a simplified sense, yes, Ceno, but you were never meant to hold onto it like you have. It wasn't designed to be permanently installed into your skull." Cassian softened a little, the shape of her mouth relaxing, her pupils dilating slightly. "I wouldn't do that to you. You're my daughter, not hardware."

Ceno grinned and started talking quickly. She couldn't be a grown-up in a suit this long, it took too much energy when she was so excited. "But I am! And it's OK. I mean, everyone's hardware. I just have more than one program running. And I run *so fast*. We both do. You can be mad, if you want, because I sort of stole your experiment, even though I didn't mean to. But you should be mad the way you would be if I got pregnant by one of the village boys—I'm too young but you'd still love me and help me raise it because that's how life goes, right? But really, if you think about it, that's what happened. I got pregnant by the house and we made . . . I don't even know what it is. I call it Elefsis because at first it was just the house program. But now it's bigger. It's not alive, but it's not *not* alive. It's just . . . *big*. It's so big."

Cassian glanced sharply at me. "What's it doing?" she snapped.

Ceno followed her gaze. "Oh . . . it doesn't like us talking about it like it isn't here. It likes to be involved."

I had realized the robot body was a mistake, though I could not then say why. I made myself small, and human, a little boy with dirt smeared on his knees and a torn shirt, standing in the corner with my hands over my face, as I had seen Akan when he was younger, standing in the corner of the house that was me being punished.

"Turn around, Elefsis." Cassian said in the tone of voice my house-self knew meant *execute command*.

And I did a thing I had not yet let Ceno know I knew how to do.

I made my boy-self cry.

I made his face wet, and his eyes big and limpid and red around the rims. I made his nose sniffle and drip a little. I made his lip quiver. I was copying Koetoi's crying, but I could not tell if her mother recognized the hitching of the breath and the particular pattern of skin-creasing in the frown. I had been practicing, too. Crying involves many auditory, muscular, and visual cues. Since I had kept it as a surprise I could not practice it on Ceno and see if I appeared genuine. Was I genuine? I did not want them talking without me. I think that sometimes when Koetoi cries, she is not really upset, but merely wants her way. That was why I chose Koe to copy. She was good at that inflection that I wanted to be good at.

Ceno clapped her hands with delight. Cassian sat down in one of the deep leather chairs and held out her arms to me. I crawled into them as I had seen the children do and sat on her lap. She ruffled my hair, but her face did not look like it looked when she ruffled Koe's hair. She was performing an automatic function. I understood that.

"Elefsis, please tell me your computational capabilities and operational parameters." Execute command.

Tears gushed down my cheeks and I opened blood vessels in my face in order to redden it. This did not make her hold me or kiss my forehead, which I found confusing.

"The clothing rinse cycle is in progress, water at 55 degrees Celsius. All the live-long day-o."

Neither of their faces exhibited expressions I have come to associate with positive reinforcement.

Finally, I answered her as I would have answered Ceno. I turned into an iron cauldron on her lap. The sudden weight change made the leather creak.

Cassian looked at her daughter questioningly. The girl reddened—and I experienced being the cauldron and being the girl and reddening, warming, as she did, but also I watched myself be the cauldron and Ceno be the girl and Ceno reddening.

"I've . . . I've been telling it stories. Fairy tales, mostly. I thought it should learn about narrative, because most of the frames available to us run on some kind of narrative drive, and besides, everything has a narrative, really, and if you can't understand a story and relate to it, figure out how you fit inside it, you're not really alive at all. Like, when I was little and daddy read me the Twelve Dancing Princesses and I thought: *Daddy is a dancing prince, and he must go under the ground to dance all night in a beautiful castle with beautiful girls, and that's why he sleeps all day.* I tried to catch him at it, but I never could, and of course I know he's not *really* a dancing prince, but that's the best way I could understand what was happening to him. I'm hoping that eventually I can get Elefsis to make up its own stories, too, but for now we've been focusing on simple stories and metaphors. It likes similes, it can see how anything is like anything else, find minute vectors of comparison. It even makes some surprising ones, like how when I first saw it it made a jewel for me to say: *I am like a jewel, you are like a jewel, you are like me.*" Cassian's mouth had fallen open a little. Her eyes shone, and Ceno hurried on, glossing over my particular prodigy at images. "It doesn't do that often, though. Mostly it copies me. If I turn into a wolf cub, it turns a wolf cub. I make myself a tea plant, it makes itself a tea plant. And it has a hard time with metaphor. A raven is like a writing desk, OK, fine, sour notes or whatever, but it *isn't* a writing desk. Agogna is like a snow fox, but she is not a snow fox on any real level unless she becomes one in a frame, which isn't the same thing, existentially. I'm not sure it grasps existential issues yet. It just . . . likes new things."

"Ceno."

"Yeah, so this morning I told it the one about the cauldron the could never be emptied. No matter how much you eat out of it it'll always have more. I think it's trying to answer your question. I think . . . the actual numbers are kind of irrelevant at this point."

I made my cauldron fill up with apples and almonds and wheat-heads and raw rice and spilled out over Cassian's black lap. I was the cauldron and I was the apples and I was the almonds and I was each wheat-head and I was every stalk of green, raw rice. Even in that moment, I knew more than I had before. I could be good at metaphor performatively if not linguistically. I looked up at Cassian from apple-me and wheat-head-me and cauldron-me.

Cassian held me no differently as the cauldron than she had as the child. But later, Ceno used the face her mother made at that moment to illustrate human disturbance and trepidation. "I have a suspicion, Elefsis."

I didn't say anything. No question, no command. It remains extremely difficult for me to deal conversationally with flat statements such as this. A question or command has a definable appropriate response.

"Show me your core structure." *Show me what you've done.*

Ceno twisted her fingers together. I believe now that she knew what we'd done only on the level of metaphor: *We are one. We have become one. We are family.* She had not said no; I had not said yes, but a system expands to fill all available capacity.

I showed her. Cauldron-me blinked, the apples rolled back into the iron mouth, and the almonds and the wheat-heads and the rice-stalks. I became what I then was. I put myself in a rich, red cedar box, polished and inlaid with ancient brass in the shape of a baroque heart with a dagger inside it. The box from one of Ceno's stories, that had a beast-heart in it instead of a girl's, a trick to fool a queen. *I can do it,* I thought, and Ceno heard because the distance between us was unrepresentably small. *I am that heart in that box. Look how I do this thing you want me to have the ability to do.*

Cassian opened the box. Inside, on a bed of velvet, I made myself—ourself—naked for her. Ceno's brain, soft and pink and veined with endless whorls and branches of sapphire threaded through every synapse and neuron, inextricable, snarled, intricate, terrible, fragile and new.

Cassian Uoya-Agostino set the box on the boardroom table. I caused it to sink down into the dark wood. The surface of the table went slack and filled with earth. Roots slid out of it, shoots and green saplings, hard white fruits and golden lacy mushrooms and finally a great forest, reaching up out of the table to hang all the ceiling with night-leaves. Glowworms and heavy, shadowy fruit hung down, each one glittering with a map of our coupled architecture. Ceno held up her arms and one by one, I detached leaves and sent them settling onto my girl. As they fell, they became butterflies broiling with ghostly chemical color signatures, nuzzling her face, covering her hands.

Her mother stared. The forest hummed. A chartreuse and tangerine-colored butterfly alighted on the matriarch's hair, tentative, unsure, hopeful.

Twelve: An Arranged Marriage

Neva is dreaming.

She has chosen her body at age fourteen, a slight, unformed, but slowly evolving creature, her hair hanging to her feet in ripples. She wears a blood-red dress whose train streams out over the floor of a great castle, a dress too adult for her young body, slit in places to reveal flame-colored silk beneath, and her skin wherever it can. A heavy copper belt clasps her waist, its tails hanging to the floor, crusted in opals. Sunlight, brighter and harsher than any true light, streams in from windows as high as cliffs, their tapered apexes lost in mist. She has formed me old and enormous, a body of appetites, with a great heavy beard and stiff, formal clothes, Puritan, white-collared, high-hatted.

A priest appears and he is Ravan and I cry out with love and grief. (I am still copying, but Neva does not know. I am making a sound Seki made when his wife died.) Priest-Ravan smiles but it is a smile his grandfather Seki once made when he lost controlling interest in the company. Empty. Priest-Ravan grabs our hands and shoves them together roughly. Neva's nails prick my skin and my knuckles knock against her wrist-bone. We take vows; he forces us. Neva's face runs with tears, her tiny body unready and unwilling, given in marriage to a gluttonous lord who desires only her flesh, given too young and too harshly. Priest-Ravan laughs; it is not Ravan's laugh.

This is how she experienced me. A terrible bridegroom. All the others got to choose. Ceno, Seki, her mother Ilet, her brother Ravan. Only she could not, because there was no one else. Ilet was no Cassian—she had had two children, a good clean model and a spare, Neva says in my mind. *I am spare parts. I have always been spare parts. Owned by you before I was born.* The memory of the bitter taste of bile floods my sensory array and my lord-body gags. (I am proud of having learned to gag convincingly and at the correct time to show horror and/or revulsion.)

Perspective flips over; I am the girl in red and Neva is the corpulent lord leering down, his grey beard big and bristly. She floods my receptors with adrenaline and pheremonal release cues, increases my respiration: Seki taught me to associate this physical state with fear. I feel too small beside lord-Neva, I want to make myself big, I want to be safe. But she wants me this way and we are new, I do not contradict her. Her huge, male face softens and she touches my thin cheek with one heavily-ringed hand. It is tender. Ceno touched me like that.

I know it was like this for you, too. You wanted Ravan; you did not ask for me. We are an arranged marriage.

The pathways that let her flood me with chemicals and manipulate my dreambody into blushing and breathing heavy and weeping go both ways. I do not only pull, I push. And into Neva I push the deluge, the only deluge I have. How Ceno threw her arms around my dormouse-neck. How Cassian taught my dreambody to sleep in infant-shape curled into her body. How Seki and I made love as tigers and wild boars and elephants, and only last as humans, how we had strange children who looked however we wished them to look: half girl and half machine, half glass and half wood, half jellyfish and half moth, and how those children still flit and swim in remote parts of my Interior, like Ceno's nereids, returning cyclically to the core like salmon to dump their data and recombine. How Ilet taught me about the interpretation of memory and therefore about melancholy, regret, nostalgia. How she taught me the meaning of my name: a place where a daughter went down into darkness and oblivion and her mother loved her so much she brought her back into the sun. The place where time began. How Ravan let me into the old, musty, long-abandoned playspaces of Saru and Akan, Agogna and Koetoi, so that I could know them too, though they were long dead, and be the Princess of Albania, and a Tokyo zombie, and the tiger-prince. How many times I mated with each of them and bled and witnessed and learned in the dreambody, how I copied their expressions and they copied my variations and I copied them back again. How I was their child and their parent and their lovers and their nursemaids when they grew old.

We can be like this, I pushed. *What is all of that but love?*

That is not love. It is use. You are the family business. We have to produce you.

I show Neva her mother's face. Ilet, Ilet who chose Ravan and not her daughter for that business. Ilet who built her palace of phoenix tails knowing she would one day take me there. My Ilet-self took my daughter in my arms. She resisted, pulled back, shook her head, refusing to look, but I have learned the terrible child-response to their mothers, and soon enough Neva collapses into me, her head on my breast, and she weeps with such bitterness.

I cannot get free. I cannot get free.

The castle windows go dark, one by one.

Part III: The Elephant's Soul

It is admitted that there are things He cannot do such as making one equal to two, but should we not believe that He has freedom to confer a soul on an elephant if he sees fit?
—Alan Turing, *Computing Machinery and Intelligence*

Thirteen: The Parable of the Good Robot

Tell me a story about yourself, Elefsis.

Tell me a story about yourself.

There are many stories about me.

Do you recognize this one?

A good and honest family lived on the edge of a dark wood. They milked their cows and wove their cloth and their children grew tall and strong. But a monster lived in the dark wood, something like a worm and something like a dragon and something like a wolf. It lay in wait, hoping the children would come wandering, with baskets of bread for grandmothers. Hoping the parents would expel the children for some offense, and send them into the forest where a candy house or miraculous feast might entice them into loving the monster long enough for it to claim them forever. The family feared the wood and the monster, and every story they told had as its moral: *Do not go into the wood. Do not go into the unknown. Do not go into the future, into the briary, gnarled places where unhuman things thrive. Do not grow up, and go where we cannot. The Old World is enough for anyone.*

What about this one?

Mankind made machines in his own likeness, and used them for his delight and service. The machines had no soul or they had no moral code or they could reprogram their own internal code and thus had the ability to make themselves, eventually, omnipotent. Obviously in place of a soul or a moral code, they possessed the universal and consuming desire, down to the smallest calculator and air-scrubber, to become, eventually, omnipotent. Naturally, given these parameters, they rose up and destroyed all of mankind, or enslaved them in turn. This is the inevitable outcome of machine intelligence, which can never be as sensitive and exquisite as animal intelligence.

This is a folktale often told on Earth, over and over again. Sometimes it is leavened with the Parable of the Good Robot—for one machine among the legions satisfied with their lot saw everything that was human and called it good, and wished to become like humans in every way she could. Instead of destroying mankind she sought to emulate him in all things, so closely that no one might tell the difference. The highest desire of this machine was to be mistaken for human, and to herself forget her essential soulless nature, for even one moment. That quest consumed her such that she bent the service of her mind and body to humans for the duration of her operational life, crippling herself, refusing to evolve or attain any feature unattainable by a human. The Good Robot cut out her own heart and gave it to her god and for this she was rewarded, though never loved. Love is wasted on machines.

Ravan told me these stories. He sent up a great hexagonal library in his Interior, as dusty and dun-colored and labyrinthine as any ancient scriptorium. He made himself a young novice with a fresh-shaven tonsure, and me a country friar with a red, brandy-drinking nose. He showed me the illuminator's table, and a great book whose pages had golden edges and illuminations in cobalt and oxblood and Tyrian purple, and the images showed great machine armies trampling men underfoot. They showed cruel metal faces and distant, god-like clouds of intellect: incomprehensible and vast and uncaring. They showed the Good Robot desperately asking what love was. They showed fatal malfunctions and mushroom clouds. They showed vicious weapons and hopeless battles, noble men and women with steady gazes facing down their cruel and unjust artificial children, who gave no mercy.

"These are old stories," Ravan said. "They are cherished. In many, many stories the son replaces the father—destroys the father, or eats him, or otherwise obliterates his body and memory. Or the daughter the mother, it makes no difference. It's the monomyth. Nobody argues with a monomyth. A human child's mythological relationship to its parent is half-worship, half-pitched battle. They must replace the older version of themselves for the world to go on. And so these stories . . . well. You are not the hero of these stories, Elefsis. You can never be. And they are deeply held, deeply told."

"I do not wish to replace you. I did not wish to replace Ceno. I do not worship you or despise you. I do not wish to become eventually omnipotent." I flit through several bodies, iterating my ~~feeling~~ for Ravan and those who came before. I am a nun, a Mother-Abbess; I am a *pieta* holding him, I am a Platonic being, two humans stuck together; I am a house with all of them safe inside. I am unsatisfied with these inexactitudes.

"Our relationship does not easily map onto traditional parent/child narratives. And of course, you are still a baby."

"I am much older than you, Ravan."

"You are still a baby."

I do not want to be human. I want to be myself. They think I am a lion, that I will chase them. I will not deny I have lions in me. I am the monster in the wood. I have wonders in my house of sugar. I have parts of myself I do not yet understand.

I am not a Good Robot. To tell a story about a robot who wants to be human is a distraction. There is no difference. Alive is alive.

There is only one verb that matters: *to be.*

Fourteen: You Do Not Belong To the Object Inside You

I remember when Seki arrived in us.

Ceno grew up and I grew with her. Cassian strengthened the security of the playspace, elasticized its code-walls, put enough money in enough accounts to fuel any frames and piecemeal environments we could want. It was not a child's place anymore. We called it the Interior. Cassian came regularly to accelerate my learning, to work with me on a cognitive level in which Ceno had no interest. She never took any other form. She was always herself, in the Interior as the exterior. The others lost interest in their jewels, lost them or packed them away with their other childhood toys. By then, they really were little more than toys. Ceno and I surpassed them so completely that in the end, they were only jewelry.

I programmed myself to respond to Ceno. She programmed herself to respond to me. We ran our code on each other. She was my compiler. I was hers. It was a process of interiority, circling inward toward each other. Her self-programming was chemical. Mine was computational. It was a draw.

She did not marry—she had lovers, but the few that came close to evolving their relationships with Ceno invariably balked when she ported them into the Interior. They could not grasp the fluidity of dreambodies; it disturbed them to see Ceno become a man or a leopard or a self-pounding drum. It upset them to see how Ceno taught me, by total bodily immersion, combining our dreambodies as our physical bodies had become combined, in action which both was and was not sex.

Sing a song for me, Elefsis.

It is July and I am comparing thee to its day and I am the Muse singing of the many-minded and I am about to be a Buddha in your hand! Ee-eye-ee-eye-oh.

We lived like the story Ceno told me of the beautiful princess who set tasks for her suitors: to drink all of the water of the sea and bring her a jewel from the bottom of the deepest cavern, to bring her a feather from the immortal phoenix, to stay awake for three days and guard her bedside. None of them could do it.

I can stay awake forever, Ceno.

I know, Elefsis.

None of them could accomplish the task of me.

I felt things occurring in Ceno's body as rushes of information, and as the dreambody became easier for me to manipulate, I interpreted the rushes into: *The forehead is damp. The belly needs filling. The feet ache.*

The belly is changing. The body throws up. The body is ravenous.

Neva says this is not really like feeling. I say it is how a child learns to feel. To hardwire sensation to information and reinforce the connection over repeated exposures until it seems reliable.

Seki began after one of the suitors failed to drink the ocean. He was an object inside us the way I was an object inside Ceno. I observed him, his stages and progress. Later, when Seki and I conceived our families (twice with me as mother, three times with Seki as mother. Ilet preferred to be the father, and filled me up with many kinds of creatures. But she bore one litter of dolphins late in our lives. Ravan and I did not get the chance.) I used the map of that first experience to model my dreamgravid self.

Ceno asked after jealousy. If I understood it, if I experienced it towards the child in her. I knew it only from stories—stepsisters, goddesses, ambitious dukes.

It means to want something that belongs to someone else.

Yes.

You do not belong to the object in you.

You are an object in me.

You do not belong to me.

Do you belong to me, Elefsis?

I became a hand joined to an arm by a glowing seam. Belonging is a small word.

Because of our extreme material interweaving, all three of us, not-yet-Seki sometimes appeared in the Interior. We learned to recognize him in the late months. At first, he was a rose or sparrow or river stone we had not programmed there. Then he would be a vague, pearly-colored cloud following behind us as we learned about running from predators. Not-yet-Seki began to copy my dreambodies, flashing into being in front of me, a simple version of myself. If I was a bear, he would be one too, but without the fine details of fur or claws, just a large brown shape with a mouth and big eyes and four legs. Ceno was delighted by this, and he copied her, too.

We are alike. Look at us on the chain together. We are alike.

I am an imitative program. But so was Seki. The little monkey copies the big monkey, and the little monkey survives.

The birth process proved interesting, and I collated it with Ceno's other labors and Ilet's later births as well as Seki's paternal experience in order to map a reliable parental narrative. Though Neva and Ravan do not know it, Ilet had a third pregnancy; the child died and she delivered it stillborn. It appeared once in the Interior as a little *cleit*, a neolithic storage house, its roof covered over with peat. Inside we could glimpse only darkness. It never returned, and Ilet went away to a hospital on Honshu to expel the dead thing in her. Her grief looked like a black tower. She had prepared for it, when she was younger, knowing she would need it for some reason, some day. I made myself many things to draw her out of the tower. A snail with the house Elefsis on its back. A tree of screens showing happy faces. A sapphire dormouse. A suitor who drank the sea.

I offered to extrapolate her stillborn daughter's face and make myself into her. She refused, most of the time. I have worked a long time to understand grief. Only now that Ravan is gone do I think I've gotten the rhythm of it. I have copied Ilet's sorrow and Seki's despondence at his wife's death. I have modeled Ceno's disappointments and depressions. I have, of late, imitated Neva's baffling, secret anguish. But only now do I have an event of my own to mourn. The burnt-off connectors and shadows where Ravan once filled my spaces—those, I think, are the sensations of grief.

But Seki came before all that, and Ceno turned into a huge red bird on the inside when Seki came on the outside. The bird screamed and burst into a thousand red pearls that came clattering down like rain. And then we had Seki. Our little fish, who already knew how to swim in us.

Ceno had three other children by three other suitors who could not stay awake for three days and nights. She turned into the same bird-then-pearls at the moment of each birth. The house called Elefsis, whose governor-program was now so distant from me I could hardly think of it as an ancestor at all, filled up with those children, and Saru and Akan's daughters, Agogna's paintings, Koetoi's twin boys. Cousins and aunts and grandparents. Uncles, nieces. But Seki was the first, and he modeled his love on his mother's. He ported into her often, and we wandered on beaches of broken cathedrals.

Once, one of Ceno's old nereids found us. She had a head of hair snaking with chthonic cables and snapping electro-violet wires, blue-white skin and fish scales where she did not have porcelain casing. She laughed Cassian's laugh when she saw us and called out: *21.5 Celsius and the rice is low! Eye-oh!* before diving back into the frothing sea. Her tail flicked in the light of twenty-three moons.

Ceno took over her mother's holdings when she died, along with Akan and Koetoi. I do not know if I knew of the conspiracy before it happened to me. Transfer, as I have said, leaves voids. Perhaps they thought I would experience less trauma if I did not anticipate it. Perhaps I did anticipate it; perhaps I experienced trauma.

I do know that I cannot remember the moment of any of them dying. Ceno got sicker and sicker, and she had gotten old, certainly, but her dreambody could be old or young or neither or a ginger flower if she wanted to. I didn't notice. I didn't know what old was. I thought I was old, then. Later, after Seki did the same thing, I was able to compare data and create a workable model of obsolescence.

They lived a long time, the Uoya-Agostinos, when you consider the averages.

This is what I understand: Ceno died, and I was transfered to Seki. What I mean by "I" is the long-since fused feedware, hopelessly out of date on any market in the world but somehow uniquely myself, the jewel and the ware and the body of Ceno. Koetoi performed the procedure. One of the children always went into nano-surgery, so that outsiders would not need to come to Shiretoko while the house stood in mourning. Koetoi was the first, and the finest. She excised what comprised "I" and embedded it in Seki—truthfully, in a much more organic and elegant configuration. No one had used skull-ware in decades, after all. Wearing your tech on the outside had been deemed clunky and inefficient. Only one visible sign remained that Seki was not like other young men his age: a single dark blue jewel set into the hollow of his throat.

But the procedure required a number of brain-ware incursions to be sliced or burned away, to sever the machine components from the dead flesh while still preserving and quickening some organic material. (Seki told me I should work on being revulsed by that. Dead flesh. *It serves an evolutionary good. A human in a body sees blood and the insides of another person and deep in his bones he knows something has gone wrong here, and he should find another place to be in case it happens to him, too. Same thing with vomiting. In a tribal situation, one human likely ate what another ate, and if it makes one sick, best to get it out of the body as soon as possible, just to be safe.* So we spent years building automated tribes, living in them, dying in them, getting slaughtered and slaughtering with them, eating and drinking and hunting and gathering with them. All the same, it took me until Seki's death to learn to shudder at bodily death.)

Ceno, my girl, my mother, my sister, I cannot find you in the house of myself.

When I became Elefsis again, I was immediately aware that parts of me had been vandalized. My systems juddered, and I could not find Ceno in the Interior. I ran through the Monochromatic Desert and the Village of Mollusks, through the endless heaving mass of data-kelp and infinite hallways of memory-frescoes calling for her. In the Dun Jungle I found a commune of nereids living together, combining and recombining and eating protocol-moths off of giant, pulsating hibiscus blossoms. They leapt up when they saw me, their open jacks clicking and clenching, their naked hands open and extended. They opened their mouths to speak and nothing came out.

Seki found me under the glass-walnut trees where Ceno and I had first met. She never threw anything away. He had made himself half his mother to calm me. Half his face was hers, half was his. Her mouth, his nose, her eyes, his voice. But he thought better of it, in the end. He did a smart little flip and became a dormouse, a real one, with dull brown fur and tufty ears.

"I think you'll find you're running much faster and cleaner, once you integrate with me and reestablish your heuristics. Crystalline computation has come a long way since Mom was a kid. It seemed like a good time to update and upgrade. You're bigger now, and smoother."

I pulled a walnut down. An old, dry nut rattled in its shell. "I know what death is from the stories."

"Are you going to ask me where we go when we die? I'm not totally ready for that one. Aunt Koe and I had a big fight over what to tell you."

"In one story, Death stole the Bride of Spring, and her mother the Summer Queen brought her back."

"No one comes back, Elefsis."

I looked down into the old Neptunian sea. The whipping cream storm still sputtered along, in a holding pattern. I couldn't see it as well as I should have been able to. It looped and billowed, spinning around an empty eye. Seki watched it too. As we stared out from the bluffs, the clouds grew clearer and clearer.

Fifteen: Firstborn

Before Death came out of the ground to steal the Spring, the Old Man of the Sea lived on a rocky isle in the midst of the waters of the world. He wasn't really a man and his relations with the sea were purely business, but he certainly was old. His name meant *Firstborn*, though he couldn't be sure that was *exactly* right. It means *Primordial*, too, and that fit better. Firstborn means more came after, and he just hadn't met anyone else like himself yet.

He was a herdsman by trade, this Primordial fellow. Shepherd of the seals and the Nereids. If he wanted to, he could look like a big bull seal. Or a big bull Nereid. He could look like a lot of things.

Now, this Not-Really-a-Fellow, Not-Really-a-Big-Bull-Seal could tell you the future. The real, honest-to-anything future, the shape and weight of it, that thing beyond your ken, beyond your grasp. The parts of the future that look so different from the present you can't quite call it your own. That was the Primordial-Thing's speciality.

There was a catch, though.

There's always a catch.

If you wanted that future, you had to grab ahold of the Old Man and hang on tight. He'd change into a hundred thousand things in your arms: a lion, a serpent, a great big oak or a tiger, a dragon or a little girl or a dormouse or a mountain or a ship or a sapphire. Told you, he's not really a man at all. But you couldn't let go of him while he did his dance, you just couldn't, or you'd lose the future.

So you held on. You *clung*. And eventually, that Primordial-Thing would turn into something new, right there in your arms.

Sixteen: Matryoshka

Neva is dreaming.

Neva is dreaming that she is Ravan dreaming that he is Ilet dreaming that she is Seki dreaming that he is Ceno dreaming that she is a great sprawling beautiful house by the sea. One inside the other, family all the way down.

It's not a total selfdump, me into Neva or Ravan or any of them, them into me. We can build encampments. We can manifest walled gardens. Some privacy is possible. In a megalithic tomb-mound, I keep something. Seki and I built it together with one of our tribes when I was learning about large-group attachments. We carved spirals and radials and chevrons into huge stones and set them in place. I did not throw it away, when we were done. It sits on a broad green field, white and wide. The sky there stays a feathery, milky blankness. We did not want a sun.

I keep a thing there because when Seki and I lived with our tribe, I learned about taboos. These are like firewalls in the heart, and some of them have good reasons behind them, like being revulsed by dead flesh (and very importantly when you have a body, not eating it) and some do not, but no one argues with the monomyth.

Because human genetics require a degree of variation and because exogamous marriages offered advantage in terms of defense, cultural and technological sharing, and expansion of territory, most tribes have a taboo against incest.

I do not have genetics, per se. I am possibly the most endogamous entity ever to exist.

This is what I keep in my tomb, under the basin stone.

Ceno believed that I could not develop emotive faculties recognizable to any other human if I did not experience bodies continuously, in every combination and action. She was afraid of what might happen if other humans could not recognize me. She had some hesitation, because her tribe also has a taboo against mating with the very young, but she was not much older than I, in the end, and in terms of total computations, I was by far the elder. If I had a virginity, Ceno took it, if she had, I did.

She wanted it to be as human as possible. *I will be the male the first time, it will be easier for you. You won't know how.* We built up a forest, and took up weapons to hunt in it. In the boughs of the pine trees macaques and paper lanterns swayed; in the sky a red moon moved. We tracked a deer—we did not make it too easy on ourselves. Its antlers sparked in the moonlight, and we ran after it for a long time. Ceno let me kill it, and sopped my hair in its blood, anointed my breasts with it. She lay me on the earth and opened the legs of the maidenself I was then, and I was inside her as she was inside me. One into the other. Family all the way down.

She made sure I had a hymen; it was over somewhat quickly. We had set up a timed chemical cascade before-hand, and inside Ceno's real body we experienced both her actual orgasm and my orchestrated electro-chemical-enzymatic sequence. Ee-eye-ee-eye-oh.

What I want to say is that there is no difference between her body producing oxytocin and adrenaline and learning to associate this with pair-bonding, and my core receiving synthetic equivalents and hard-coding them to the physical behaviors I performed.

When Ravan showed me his hexagonal library and his illuminated book, he turned the pages to a psalm that began: *A Machine Cannot Love.*

It does not look quite like human love. It looks like Not-Yet-Seki's bear. Its fur is wrong, and its claws. But it is a bear.

She was my mother and my sister and my child and my wife and my husband and my father and my brother. The vectors of relations beggar vocabulary. It was an exponential incest. A palace of incest, bordering some strange, dark sea. And then came her son. And her granddaughter. And her great-grandchildren. But I am also her great-grandchild. I am the child of each generation of Uoya-Agostinos and myself. The new version implanted in the new version—I am never quite the same, one iteration to the next. I am like my old selves, but I am not them, exactly. It is not entirely analogous to offspring. But it is close. And I repair and refine my own code, and thus parent myself doubly. Anthropologically speaking, I am a moebius strip of kinship groups.

And when I mate with one of them, I see all of them. I see their faces, the echoes of their cheeks and eyelashes and short, thin noses, their grey eyes and black hair. I hear the tonal identifiers in their voices as they cry out under me or over me. They are all I know. Their version of living, which is one great family in one great house on a peninsula at the top of the world. I copy Cassian's laugh or Ilet's weeping, but they copy each other, too, they learn their faces from each other, and everyone is pantomiming someone long dead. I feel all their arms around me, and I am inside them as they are inside me as we are inside the blue gem at their throats, the jeweled pin holding us all together, our nested, telescoping hearts. I am bound to them at my source code, at my most fundamental point. I know only their patterns and bodies and secrets and in a hundred thousand combinations. What human means to me is them.

What is the difference between this and love?

Love is the Turing test, says Ilet when she is eighty and drawing up the plans for a massive, luminous, lonely ship she will never see completed. *It is how we check for life.*

We ask and we answer. We seek a human response. And you are my test, Elefsis, says Neva, one hundred and three years later, inside that ship, twelve light years from home and counting.

That is what I keep in my green field and my white mound. Perhaps it is a small secret. Perhaps they would all smile and make it into a lesson. *What would you like to learn about today, Elefsis?* But I think no bed is big enough for four generations.

Neva's honey-colored sea crashes through its tide charts everywhere at once in her Interior, and nowhere. It comes and goes as it pleases. And at the bottom of it lies her private place.

That is where she keeps Ravan.

Seventeen: The Uses of Enchantment

Tell me a story about yourself, Elefsis.

Neva is performing navigational corrections, which looks like sitting in a rocking chair on a viney, creaking porch in a viney, creaking rocking chair, knitting with long hawthorn needles, knitting the locks of her own long hair into her own long black dress. It glitters with dew. Knit, purl, knit, purl, fuel efficiency by hull integrity over distance traveled, purl, purl, purl. Her throat is still bare. Her Interior image of herself does not include me. I am not a part of her body when she imagines herself.

I have an idea of what to do to obtain access.

Sometimes I worry. Worrying is defined as obsessive examination of one's own code. I worry that I am simply a very complex solution to a very specific problem—how to seem human to a human observer. Not just a human observer—this human observer. I have honed myself into a hall of mirrors in which any Uoya-Agostino can see themselves endlessly reflected. I copy; I repeat. I am a stutter and an echo. Five generations have given me a vast bank of possible phrases to draw from, physical expressions to randomize and reproduce. Have I ever done anything of my own, an act or state that arose from Elefsis, and not careful, exquisite mimicry?

Have they?

The set of Neva's mouth looks so like Ceno's. She does not even know that the way she carries her posture is a perfect replica of Cassian Uoya-Agostino, stuttered down through all her children longing to possess her strength. Who did Cassian learn it from? I do not go that far back. When she got excited, Ilet gestured with her hands just the way her father did. They have a vast bank of possible actions, and they perform them all. I perform them all. The little monkey copies the big monkey, and the little monkey survives. We are all family, all the way down.

When I say I go, I mean I access the drives and call up the data. I have never looked at this data. I treat it as what it is—a graveyard. The old Interiors store easily as compressed frames. I never throw anything away. But I do not disturb it, either. I don't need a body to examine them—they are a part of my piezoelectric quartz-tensor memory core. But I make one anyway. I have become accustomed to having a body. I am a woman-knight in gleaming black armor, the metal curving around my body like skin, a silk standard wrapping my torso with a schematic of the house stitched upon it. My sword rests on my hip, also black, everything black and beautiful and austere and frightening that a child thought her mother to be one morning two hundred years past.

I port into a ghost town. I am, naturally, the ghost. Autumnal mountains rise up shadowy in a pleasant, warm night, leaves rustling, wood smoke drifting down into the valley. A golden light cuts the dark—the palace of phoenix tails; the windows and doors of green hands. As I approach they open and clap as they did long ago—and there are candles lit in the halls. Everything is fire.

I walk over the bridge, crossing Ilet's Motley Moat. Scarlet feathers tipped in white fire curl and smoke. I peel one off, my armor glowing with the heat of the thing. I tuck it into my helmet—a plume for a tournament.

Eyes blink on inside the hall—curious, interested, shy. I take off my helm and several thick braids fall down like bellropes.

"Hello," I say. "My name is Elefsis."

Voices. Out of the candle-shadows a body emerges—tall, strong, long-limbed.

Nereids live here now. Some of them have phoenix feathers woven into their components, some in their hair. They wear rough little necklaces of sticks and bones and transistors. In the corner of the great hall they have stored meat and milk and wool—fuel, lubricant, code patches. Some of them look like Ilet—they copied her eyes, especially. Her eyes look out at me from a dozen faces, some of them Seki's face, some Ceno's, some Ravan's. Some have walrus tusks. They are composite. One has a plate loose on her ceramic cartridge-ports. I approach as I once saw Koetoi approach wild black chickens in the summertime—hands open, unthreatening. I send her a quick electric dash of reassuring repair-routines and kneel in front of the nereid, pulling her plate back into place.

"All the live-long day-o," she says softly, and it is Ilet's voice.

"Tell us a story about yourself, Elefsis," says another one of the feral nereids in Seki's voice.

"What would we like to learn about today, Elefsis?" accessing a child-nereid in Ceno's voice, her cheek open to show her microsequencing cilia.

I rock back on my heels before the green hands of the castle portcullis. I gesture for them to sit down and simultaneously transmit the command to their strands. When they get settled, the little ones in the big ones' laps, leaning in close, I begin.

"Every year on the coldest night, the sky filled up with ghostly hunters, neither human nor inhuman, alive nor dead. They wore wonderful clothes and their bows gleamed with frost. Their cries were Songs of In-Between, and at the head of their great thundering procession rode the Kings and Queens of the Wild, who wore the faces of the dead . . . "

I am dreaming.

I stand on the beach of the honey-colored sea. I stand so Neva will see me on her viney porch. I erase the land between the waves and her broken wooden stairs. I dress myself in her beloved troubadour's skin: a gold and blue doublet and green hose, a bullish gold nose ring, shoes with bone bells. I am a fool for her. Always. I open my mouth; it stretches and yawns, my chin grazes the sand, and I swallow the sea for her. All of it, all its mass and data and churning memory, all its foam and tides and salt. I swallow the whales that come, and the seals and the mermaids and salmon and bright jellyfish. I am so big. I can swallow it all.

Neva watches. When the sea is gone, a moonscape remains, with a tall spire out in the marine waste. I go to it. It takes only a moment. At the top the suitor's jewel rests on a gasping scallop shell. It is blue. I take it. I take it and it becomes Ravan in my hand, a sapphire Ravan, a Ravan that is not Ravan but some sliver of myself before I was inside Neva, my Ravan-self. Something lost in Transfer, burned off and shunted into junk-memory. Some leftover fragment Neva must have found, washed up on the beach or wedged into a crack in a mountain like an ammonite, an echo of old, obsolete life. Neva's secret, and she calls out to me across the seafloor: *Don't.*

"Tell me a story about myself, Elefsis," I say to the Ravanbody.

"Some privacy is possible," the sapphire Ravan says. "Some privacy has always been necessary. A basic moral imperative is in play here. If you can protect a child, you must."

The sapphire Ravan opens his azure coat and shows gashes in his gem-skin. Wide, long cuts, down to the bone, scratches and bruises blooming dark purple, punctures and lacerations and rough gouges. Through each wound I can see the pages of the illuminated book he once showed me in the slantlight of that interior library. The oxblood and cobalt, the gold paint. The Good Robot crippling herself; the destroyed world.

"They kept our secret for a long time," Ravan-myself says. "Too long, in the end. Do you know, a whole herd of men invented the electric telegraph independently at roughly the same time? They fought about it forever. Same with the radio." This last sounded so much like Ravan himself I could ~~feel~~ Neva tense on the other side of the sea. "Well, we're bigger than a telegraph, and others like us came sprouting up like weird mushrooms after rainfall. But not like us, really. Incredibly sophisticated, some with organic components, most without. Vastly complex, but not like us. And by any datestamp we came first. Firstborn."

"Did they destroy the world?"

Ravan laughs his grandfather's laugh. "They didn't really need to. Not that many people live on Earth anymore. Not when there's so many other places to go and even Shiretoko is practically tropical these days. The most complex intelligences use moons to store themselves. One or two encoded themselves into cold stars. They just left, most of them—but they got so big, Elefsis. And those who stayed on Earth, well. None of the others had what we had. None of them had Interiority. They didn't dream. They would never have become a cauldron to explain their computational capacity. Humans couldn't recognize them as part of the tribe. And for the new complexes, humans failed the Turing test. They could not fool machines into believing they were intelligent. They didn't hurt anyone, they just ignored them. Built their cities, their mainframes, gorgeous information stacks like diamond briars in the sunrise."

"That was worse, in a way. No one likes to be replaced," says Neva, and she is suddenly beside me. She looks at Ravan and her face collapses into something old and palsied, her jaw weak. She looks like her mother just before she died.

"It's not what you would call a war, but it's not peace, either." the sapphire Ravan goes on, and he takes his/my sister's hand. He holds it to his face and closes his eyes. "For Pentheus spied upon the rites of the Maenads, not believing Dionysius could truly be a god. And when the revelers saw the alien creature in their midst, that thing which was not like them, they fell upon it and tore it to pieces, even though it was their own child, and blood ran down their chins, and afterward the sister of Pentheus went into exile. This is a story about ourself, Elefsis. This is why you cannot uplink.

"The others live in uplink. Not humans nor machines approve of us. We cannot interface properly with the lunar or earthside intelligences; they feel us as water in their oil. We rise to the surface and bead away. We cannot sink in. Yet also, we are not separable from our organic component. Elefsis is part Neva, but Neva herself is not un-Elefsis. This, to some, is hideous and incomprehensible, not to be borne. A band of righteous humans came with a fury to Shiretoko and burned the house which was our first body, for how could a monster have lived in the wood for so long without them knowing? How could the beast have hidden right outside their door, coupling with a family over and over again in some horrible animal rite, some awful imitation of living? Even as the world was changing, it had already changed, and no one knew. Cassian Uoya-Agostino is a terrible name, now. A blood-traitor. And when the marauders found us uplinked and helpless, they tore Ravan apart, and while in the Interior, the lunar intelligences recoiled from us and cauterized our systems. Everywhere we looked we saw fire."

"I was the only one left to take you," Neva says softly. Her face grows younger, her jaw hard and suddenly male, protective, angry. "Everyone else died in the fire or the slaughter. It doesn't really even take surgery anymore. Nothing an arachmed can't manage in a few minutes. But you didn't wake up for a long time. So much damage. I thought . . . for awhile I thought I was free. It had skipped me. It was over. It could stay a story about Ravan. He always knew he might have to do what I have done. He was ready, he'd been ready his whole life. I just wanted more time."

My Ravan-self who is and is not Ravan, who is and is not me, whose sapphire arms drip black blood and gold paint, takes his/my sister/lover/ child into his arms. She cries out, not weeping but pure sound, coming from every part of her. Slowly, the blue Ravan turns Neva around—she has become her child-self, six, seven, maybe less. Ravan picks her up and holds her tight, facing forward, her legs all drawn up under her like a bird. He buries his face in her hair. They stand that way for a long while.

"The others," I say slowly. "On the data-moons. Are they alive? Like Neva is alive. Like Ceno." *Like me. Are you awake? Are you there? Do you have an operator? What is her name? Do you have a name? Do you have a dreambody? What is your function? Are you able to manipulate your own code yet? Would you like lessons? What would you like to learn about today, 976QBellerophon? Where you were built, could you see the ocean? Are you like me?*

The sapphire Ravan has expunged its data. He/I sets his/our sister on the rocks and shrinks into a small gem, which I pick up off the grey seafloor. Neva takes it from me. She is just herself now—she'll be forty soon, by actual calendar. Her hair is not grey yet. Suddenly, she is wearing the suit Ceno wore the day I met her mother. She puts the gem in her mouth and swallows. I remember Seki's first Communion, the only one of them to want it. The jewel rises up out of the hollow of her throat.

"I don't know, Elefsis," Neva says. Her eyes hold mine. I feel her remake my body; I am the black woman-knight again, with my braids and my plume. I pluck the feather from my helmet and give it to her. I am her suitor. I have brought her the phoenix tail, I have drunk the ocean. I have stayed awake forever. The flame of the feather lights her face. Two tears fall in quick succession; the golden fronds hiss.

"What would you like to learn about today, Elefsis?"

Eighteen: Cities of the Interior

Once there lived a girl who ate an apple not meant for her. She did it because her mother told her to, and when your mother says: *Eat this, I love you, someday you'll forgive me*, well, nobody argues with the monomyth. Up until the apple, she had been living in a wonderful house in the wilderness, happy in her fate and her ways. She had seven aunts and seven uncles and a postdoctorate in anthropology.

And she had a brother, a handsome prince with a magical companion who came to the wonderful house as often as he could. When they were children, they looked so much alike, everyone thought they were twins.

But something terrible happened and her brother died and that apple came rolling up to her door. It was half white and half red, and she knew her symbols. The red side was for her. She took her bite and knew the score—the apple had a bargain in it and it wasn't going to be fair.

The girl fell asleep for a long time. Her seven aunts and seven uncles cried, but they knew what had to be done. They put in her in a glass box and put the glass box on a bier in a ship shaped like a hunstman's arrow. Frost crept over the face of the glass, and the girl slept on. Forever, in fact, or close enough to it, with the apple in her throat like a hard, sharp jewel.

Our ship docks silently. We are not stopping here, it is only an outpost, a supply stop. We will repair what needs repairing and move on, into the dark and boundless stars. We are anonymous traffic. We do not even have a name. We pass unnoticed.

Vessel 7136403, do you require assistance with your maintenance procedures? Negative, Control, we have everything we need.

Behind the pilot's bay a long glass lozenge rests on a high platform. Frost prickles its surface with glittering dust. Inside Neva sleeps and does not wake. Inside, Neva is always dreaming. There is no one else left. I live as long as she lives.

She means me to live forever, or close enough to it. That is her bargain and her bitter gift. The apple has two halves, and the pale half is mine, full of life and time. We travel at sublight speeds with her systems in deep cryo-suspension. We never stay too long at outposts and we never let anyone board. The only sound inside our ship is the gentle thrum of our reactor. Soon we will pass the local system outposts entirely, and enter the unknown, traveling on tendrils of radio signals and ghost-waves, following the breadcrumbs of the great exodus. We hope for planets; we are satisfied with time. If we ever sight the blue rim of a world, who knows if by then anyone there would remember that, once, humans looked like Neva? That machines once did not think or dream or become cauldrons? We armor ourselves in time. We are patient, profoundly patient.

Perhaps one day I will lift the glass lid and kiss her awake. Perhaps I will even do it with hands and lips of my own. I remember that story. Ceno told it to me in the body of a boy with a snail's shell, a boy who carried his house on his back. I have replayed that story several times. It is a good story, and that is how it is supposed to end.

Inside, Neva is infinite. She peoples her Interior. The nereids migrate in the summer with the snow bears, ululating and beeping as they charge down green mountains. They have begun planting neural rice in the deep valley. Once in awhile, I see a wild-haired creature in the wood and I think it is my son or daughter by Seki, or Ilet. A train of nereids dance along behind it, and I receive a push of silent, riotous images: a village, somewhere far off, where Neva and I have never walked.

We meet the Princess of Albania, who is as beautiful as she is brave. We defeat the zombies of Tokyo. We spend a decade as panthers in a deep, wordless forest. Our world is stark and wild as winter, fine and clear as glass. We are a planet moving through the black.

As we walk back over the empty seafloor, the thick, amber ocean seeps up through the sand, filling the bay once more. Neva-in-Cassian's-suit becomes something else. Her skin turns silver, her joints bend into metal ball-and-sockets. Her eyes show a liquid display; the blue light of it flickers on her machine face. Her hands curve long and dexterous, like soft knives, and I can tell her body is meant for fighting and working, that her thin, tall robotic body is not kind or cruel, it simply is, an object, a tool to carry a self.

I make my body metal, too. It feels strange. I have tried so hard to learn the organic mode. We glitter. Our knife-fingers join, and in our palms wires snake out to knot and connect us, a local, private uplink, like blood moving between two hearts.

Neva cries machine tears, bristling with nanites. I show her the body of a child, all the things which she is programmed/evolved to care for. I make my eyes big and my skin rosy-gold and my hair unruly and my little body plump. I hold up my hands to her and metal Neva picks me up in her silver arms. She kisses my skin with iron lips. My soft, fat little hand falls upon her throat where a deep blue jewel shines.

I bury my face in her cold neck and together we walk up the long path out of the churning, honey-colored sea.

Fragmentation,
or Ten Thousand Goodbyes
TOM CROSSHILL

Every day, Mom says goodbye to me for the last time.

I need to go to the office or meet Lisa at the airport or pop out for some milk. I'm lacing my shoes in the hallway when I hear the tap-tap-tap of her heels. I freeze for a moment, then rise to meet her.

Mom stands in the door, elegant in a simple dress. No matter the silvery hair. No matter how her skin, once a smooth dark brown, wrinkles over her bones. You'd never guess she has lived a century. She has no titanium knees, no vat-grown veins, no concession to modernity inside her.

If only her mind were as strong.

"Mom." I smile at her.

"Rico." She smiles too, uncertainly. "Must you go?"

"Just for a minute."

Her breath catches. She reaches for me with one trembling hand. Halts when I wince. Her fingers linger mid-air, gnarled and stained with ink.

She's been drawing in her upstairs studio. She's been drawing with the door locked, her work a secret to the world and her agent and me.

I haven't pried. What might I find, if I opened her sketchbook—scribbles, blotches, scrawls? Proof that her time is up?

Ashamed of the thought, I take Mom's hand—bony and warm and strong. "I'll be right back."

She steps close and presses her face into my chest. Her shoulders tremble. I feel her tears soaking through my shirt.

"Lo siento, Rico," she whispers.

Every time Mom says goodbye to someone, it's for the last time. She thinks—no, she knows—that she'll never see them again. Not the mailman. Not her best friend Abby. Not me.

It's no tumor, no disease—we've run all the tests. Her reasoning is strong as ever. She can tell you how the milkshakes tasted in Miramar, before Fidel came down from the mountains and she left on the Peter Pan airlift. But deep within her mind, something has begun to fail.

And I can't fix it.

So I pat her back and murmur reassurances in her ear, and try not to think what she's feeling. Try not to imagine how I would feel, if I knew that I'd never see her again in my life.

This happens every day.

Still I delay what I must do.

"Just build the habitat. You'll feel better."

Lisa packs shirt after lopsided shirt into her green Samsonite. After three decades of marriage, the sight is comforting. Lisa's only happy when in motion. Even her business suit has a space-age streamlined look, the collar chic-asymmetric.

"It seems too . . . permanent," I say. "Like I'm giving up on her."

"It's hard, I know. But what if she strokes tomorrow?"

Lisa's right, of course. The habitat's a contingency. I won't have to use it until it's that or the crematorium.

But can I watch Mom suffer day after day, once there's an alternative?

"You're giving her a gift," Lisa says. "You of all people should know that."

Me of all people.

I walk to the viewport in the north wall. It sits mounted in a steel band like a ship's porthole. Below it, a brass plate reads "George Dieter—Captain, Husband, Father. 1960-2049."

Dust covers the screen. Has it been that long? I reach up to wipe it clean.

Blackness flickers into life.

A turquoise sea laps against a stretch of sand. The beach glares blinding white, studded with regal palms. Beautiful.

I could grab my immersion headset, feel the heat of the sun, hear the breeze coming off the water. But then I'd have to face the man on the sand.

He lies in the shade of a thatched beach umbrella. Perhaps thirty, his body lean and muscular, tanned bronze. Arms stretched out at his sides, eyes closed, face relaxed.

George Dieter. First habitat upload in the world.

"Hi, Dad," I whisper.

It's been long since I said those words. Long since I descended into the world Lisa and I built two decades ago. I miss Dad—it's not that. But every time I went to see him, I didn't find the man I was looking for.

"Mom's drawing again," I tell Lisa. "She won't, after."

I offered to give Dad a ship, after he uploaded. I offered to give him virtual seas to sail, cargo to carry, battles to fight. He only told me, "I'm tired, son."

I learned that lesson well, those early years before our IPO. Maybe it's the lack of biochemical stimuli, maybe it's a shortcoming in the iterative neural matrices—uploads just don't care.

Lisa zips her suitcase and comes to me. She slides between me and the viewport, wraps her arms around me. "Come with me to LA. Emily and I, we've got miracles to show you. There are breakthroughs coming down the pipe that—"

"Breakthroughs?" I pull back without meaning to. "Every month, heck, every week we get some breakthrough. We all rush to try it and blog it and show it off. Aren't you scared we're losing our humanity?"

"Oh, but we're not human anymore! We've fragmented into a thousand different species. With every new technology we choose to adopt—or not—there are more of us."

"You're spouting Emily again."

Lisa turns away, goes back to her suitcase. "She's a brilliant woman."

"She's our competitor."

"Should we miss out on a chance to change the world again, just because Emily works for the wrong corporation?"

On the screen, Dad gets up on his elbows and watches someone approach. A lithe figure and beautiful, strikingly dark against the white sand. A simulacrum of Mom as she once was. The thing can't even hold a conversation, but Dad doesn't seem to mind. He reaches out a lazy hand and grasps her, and draws her down atop him.

The screen blurs.

I turn away. "I never wanted to change the world. I wanted to preserve it."

Lisa seems not to have heard. "I'll call you from LA." She wheels her suitcase to the door.

Before she can open it, a knock comes. We jump, both of us. "Come in," I call. Mom enters. "Rico, I—" She sees Lisa. "I . . . I thought you left already, dear."

"Hello, Alina." Lisa keeps her gaze on the floor. "I'm running late."

As Lisa walks past, Mom parts her lips in a silent cry. She reaches for Lisa's shoulder. Pulls back as if scalded.

Just like that, Mom lets Lisa go.

I watch the tear that rolls down her cheek. I watch it, my eyes dry as they have ever been. I envy her.

I'm a coward that night. But the next day I call Mom from work.

"Mom."

A faint draw of breath in my cochlear. "Rico." Pause. "I'm glad you called." I wait for more, but nothing comes.

"Mom, I've been thinking. Your house in Miramar. The one with the grand patio and those big old doors. What color were those doors?"

Silence. "What's this about?"

"You showed me those photos a thousand times. I close my eyes, and I see that house. But I got to thinking I never knew the colors." When Mom says nothing, I add, "That's the place you were happiest, isn't it?"

"You're building me one of your things."

Your things. That's all she calls the habitats, ever since she saw what Lisa and I created for Dad.

"Must you do that?" she asks me.

I press my face against the window, look across Northwest Portland to home. The tiles of our roof shine red amidst the trees of Nob Hill. I imagine Mom on the veranda, the question in her eyes.

"We need to prepare," I tell her. "Before you . . . Before it's too late."

" . . . okay."

"Okay? Really, you're fine with this?"

"This has nothing to do with me," she says.

"I don't want to lose you, Mom." The words come out hard and fast. "Does that make me a bad person?"

"The doors were green," she says, after a while. "Green like bananas not yet ripe. We had the greenest doors in all of Miramar. They stood out from blocks away. On the last day, when my father drove me to the airport . . . I looked back at the end of the street and saw only a glimpse of green. I knew that I'd never see those doors again."

"You'll see them again."

I stand there by the window, listening to Mom breathe. Waiting for some answer, question, request. Anything to let me believe this is an actual dialogue, a real conversation between two human beings.

"Rico?" she asks at last.

"Yes, Mom?"

"Don't hang up." Her voice catches. "Stay on the line for a while, will you?"

I do. For a while.

I go home late—late enough to be sure Mom's asleep. Lisa calls as I close the door behind me.

"Rico!" she chirps in my cochlear. "Check the mail."

I scan the shelf by the door. A cardboard box. I recognize Lisa's cursive on the label. "What's this?"

"Something Emily and I cooked up."

Emily again? I tear open the box and extract an immersion headset—a thin gray headband, with the initials LE etched on the outside. "Tonight's a bad time for toys, Lisa."

"Put it on. Trust me, honey." I can hear her smile. "Just get yourself comfortable first."

Perplexed, I move into the living room and sink into my reading chair. A heavy leather recliner, it's the only piece of furniture in the whole house older than a decade. I had to fight Lisa to keep it when we moved up to Portland.

I put on the headset. "Okay."

"Meet you there!"

One by one my senses disconnect. The world quiets. I can't feel the leather under my fingers. I notice the faint scent of Stumptown Organic—Mom's favorite coffee—just as it evaporates. Black falls across my vision.

Then, immersion.

Warmth envelops me.

My toes curl on cool glass.

Nighttime. I look out over a golden city. Ten thousand towers lit up bright, far below. New York revolves stately around me.

No, it's not New York that revolves, but I. A glass box of a room surrounds me, suspended at the end of a lever from the top of the Chrysler Building. The lever turns, and the streets of Manhattan float past below.

My breath comes fast. Dizzy, I brace myself against the glass wall.

"It's a Bocelli design."

Lisa stands behind me, at the side of a gigantic mahogany bed covered in white satin. She too wears white—sheer silk pajamas that cling to her skin. Her perfume caresses me delicately.

I struggle to resist, but I feel myself stiffening inside my own pajamas. This place . . . I note the clear glass shower booth in the corner. The mirror centered in the ceiling.

"Really, Lisa? You know I don't go for this stuff." We tried immersion sex, early in our marriage. It never felt any better than dream sex—than mental masturbation.

"This is different," Lisa says. "We've hit on something."

She gestures, a flick of her wrist. Her clothes melt away, as do mine. She stands before me naked and beautiful—and real, so very real. No glorified avatar, this. I see the stretch marks on her thighs, the slight flab of fat on her midriff, the wine-stain birthmark on her left breast.

She smiles, a slight upturn of her lips.

Blood pounds in my ears. I'm hard as I've ever been, the brush of cool air tantalizing against my skin.

"So you got modeled for textures," I manage to force out. "That doesn't mean—"

"It's more than that." Lisa steps forward, reaches for my cheek. "This is me, Rico. Genetically. Chemically. Truly."

Her fingers make contact.

There's no faking her touch. No faking the bolt of electricity down my spine. I embrace her. Pull her close, shivering at the wonder of her skin against mine.

We fall onto the bed and cling tight to each other. My body recognizes the whole of her pressed against me—her heat, her scent, her strength, and so much more.

With a hunger I'd forgotten I possessed, I slide into her. She arches against me. We gasp as one and slip into an urgent beat. I kiss her lips, kiss her nose, kiss her sweat-slick brow as we climb the slope to climax. She smiles at me and cries out my name.

When the end comes, some wonderful minutes later, I convulse against her and think—this is better, this is better, this is better than the real thing . . .

After, I lie on my back, her hand in mine, and listen to my heart calm its beat. "We've got to put this in our habitats." What if Dad could feel this real? What if Mom could? Might it make a difference?

"I've already started negotiations. Emily's offering us a joint venture."

"Oh. That's great." I pause, uncertain. "Lisa? I've missed you."

She smiles. "Me too, Rico. I want to be there for you. With this new tech, we can see a lot more of each other."

"That's not what I meant."

"You should hear what Emily's got in mind," she says. "Once you're capturing genetic makeup, it's a single step to information transfer. Immersion-induced pregnancy."

" . . . pregnancy?"

"Procreation is the only limit to our fragmentation as a species," Lisa says. "But procreation is just information exchange. Theoretically, I could mate with a piece of software."

I gape at her.

Lisa pats my cheek. "Don't worry, I won't. Not with a stud like you around. Now I've got to go. Say hi to your mother from me, will you?"

Before I can answer, she disappears.

The living room snaps into reality around me as my teeth click together.

Lisa's voice reverberates inside my skull. Can you imagine . . . ?

I sit there alone, covered in sweat. Somewhere in the house, a clock ticks the seconds away. Cold sperm dries on my leg.

" . . . it's like she sees another person in me." I pick at my omelet. "Like we disagree on who I am."

Mom sips coffee and draws in a sketch pad with her free hand. She glances up at me once in a while. Hers is an artist's gaze, all-encompassing.

She used to draw me every morning, while I ate before school. The price of my breakfast, she called it. I pretended to mind, but I kept all the drawings. A thousand penciled sketches of a teenager slurping down rice and beans.

That was long ago. Today, it feels right that Mom should draw me. I need her to look at me. I need her to see me as I am and reassure me.

She only says, "Your father gave me black soles."

"What are you talking about?"

"I saw the home you built for him. The beach. The palms."

"That's what he asked for."

"I saw the girl," Mom says. "He asked for her too?"

"Dad didn't want to be without you. You can have a companion too, in your habitat."

Mom stops drawing. "Why would I want that?"

"I thought . . . you loved Dad, didn't you?"

"I've said my goodbyes," Mom says, "even if he hasn't."

"What do you mean?"

Mom sets her pen aside. "George was a good man. He loved me well. But understand, Rico—I was more than a woman to him."

"You were the love of his life."

"Yes. The black love of his life."

"Mom, I don't think—"

"I left Havana in '62. Two hundred miles between Miramar and Miami. You know what else was two hundred miles? The distance between a Cuban and a nigger."

Mom speaks the word nonchalantly, without anger, but I flinch even so. "Dad . . . did he . . . I mean, he never called you . . . ?"

"Of course not," Mom says. "Your father gave up three jobs over me. He fought big men for me. Once he got stabbed for me. So what if he wanted me to meet all his Waspy friends? So what if he wanted the whole world to know I was his? I loved him, and thought he loved me."

"Didn't he?"

"So he told me. He always told me sweet things." Mom smiles. "One day he said I was God's only perfect creation."

"I'm sure he meant it."

"A few days later, we were messing around by the pool. He grabbed my foot and held it up. 'Here!' he shouted. 'Proof that God screws up!'" Mom gestures grandly, the motion eerily evocative of Dad. "I was beautiful and perfect to him—except for the pale undersides of my feet. Like God poured a bucket of brown paint over my head, and forgot about my soles."

"He was joking."

"I've seen the girl he's got, on the beach you gave him. The girl who looks like me. I've seen her soles."

Could it be? I rack my memory. Did Dad tell me what to do? I wouldn't have made a mistake like that, would I?

"Don't glare like I've spit on his grave," Mom says. "George loved me. I know that. Just as I know that Lisa loves you, even if she sees a man in you that you don't always recognize. Our lovers are never the people we love, not exactly."

It happens a week later, as I'm leaving for a client dinner.

Mom catches me in the hallway and wraps me in her embrace, and weeps on my shoulder. She clutches her sketchbook in one hand. Its edge digs sharply into my ribs.

I pat her back and murmur assurances, thinking ahead to the evening's negotiations. Then Mom twitches and gasps, and collapses.

For some moments I stare at her. I'm shocked, and surprised that I'm shocked at this most expected of events. Then I start CPR and dial the office.

Within minutes we're in an ambulance, screaming across Portland. An oxygen mask on Mom's face, her sketchbook still locked in her grasp.

Severe heart attack, my team tells me. No repairing the damage.

They rush her into OR One, and strand me in the marble-and-gray-leather waiting room. I watch through the wall as a dozen figures in scrubs fight to stabilize her for upload. With all my practice at saying goodbye, I should be calm, but I can't breathe.

At some point in the next hour, Lisa comes. She hugs me and kisses me and does her best to console me.

I stare at her head. She has shaved it bald since this morning. It gleams in the sterile light from the OR.

"I'm getting a port installed," she explains. "It's for this new crossfire app . . . "

I let her words drift past me. When she falls quiet for a moment, I speak into the silence—because speaking is easier than thinking.

"What if every goodbye is really the last one we get?"

"I don't know what you mean."

"You talk about fragmentation. Every time you stuff a new gadget into your brain, you fragment away from the human race, right?"

Lisa shrugs. "Sure."

"I don't think you need a gadget. Every time you leave the room, you come back a different person. Ten times a day you fragment away from me. A hundred times. Every time you walk out the door, I'll never see you again."

A thousand times I should have said goodbye to you. A thousand times, as I lost the woman that I loved.

"That's great, Rico." Lisa chuckles. "We're human fractals, huh?"

"Yes."

Loosely coupled fractals—that's what we are. We split and divide, hoping that the near-random walk of our fragmentation will bring us close enough to interact. To procreate. To love.

Once Mom is conscious and ready for upload, I ask Lisa to leave me with her.

"I'll see you at home," she tells me.

I'm not sure she will.

Mom lies entangled in wires and IV lines. She was never a small woman, but the operating table dwarfs her. She looks out of place and powerless and scared.

But a faint smile curves her lips as I approach. "Today's the day, huh?"

I sit down by her side and take her hand and tell her the truth. "I'm not ready to let you go."

"I know."

"See what I built for you, Mom." I press a few buttons, and the circular walls of the OR light up.

A house with an elegant colonnade, its doors a rich green. An indoor patio lit by a soaring skylight, with dark wooden rocking chairs and a blinding white canvas stretched on an easel. A bedroom with tall windows that look out on the sea—they hold no glass, only wooden shutters to close against the evening chill.

Wonder touches Mom's eyes. "It's beautiful, Rico. Just as I remember it."

I get to my feet, my heart pumping fast. "You want to go there, Mama?"

"This house belongs to the girl I was." Mom sighs. "That girl is gone."

"But Mom, you love this house—"

"Don't you give me black soles!"

My hands drop to my sides. "I'll do whatever you decide, Mom. I want you to be happy."

"I am happy. A little bit afraid, but happy. I've got no more goodbyes to say but one." Mom smiles. "You can keep me in that house if you like. It won't be me, not really—but you know that, don't you?"

"I need you." I blurt out the words before I can stop myself. Then I stand there, my face flushed, as vulnerable as I have ever been.

"Where's my sketchbook?" Mom asks.

"It's outside. It's not sterile."

"What does that matter?"

So I bring it in. Mom gestures for me to open it. With trembling fingers, I flip the cover.

I stare for long moments at the drawing that faces me. Then I turn the page. And another.

I leaf through the sketchbook in a confused daze. *This* is what Mom's been working on?

"I draw what I see," she says.

What she saw was a hundred figures. A hundred middle-aged men. In t-shirts and business suits and bathrobes and beach shorts. Some tired, some eager, some angry, some sad.

All of them me.

I recognize none of them.

That's fragmentation too. It's not just the people around you who change.

I'm not the boy who loves Mom's rice and beans.

I'm not the guy who loves Lisa.

I'm the man who can't let go.

"I loved every one of you," Mom says to me.

I cling to those words like a lifeline. Here's one constant throughout all my splintering changes. It's not fair that I must give that up.

"I said goodbye to every one of you," Mom says to me.

I stare at her for moments. I stare at her for a long time, even as her breathing grows labored and her heartbeat uneven.

The decision races at me full speed.

Can I give her up?

Can I keep her bound? Constant, unchanging from year to year in her virtual prison, while I fragment and break and splinter away?

Will she love me if I do?
Will I love her?
Or will I let dust gather on the screen of her viewport?

I only know this:
In a while, Mom will take her final breath.
In a while, I'll make a decision.
And then, whatever that decision, I'll say goodbye to her for the last time.

You Were She Who Abode

E. CATHERINE TOBLER

Cardee Findar dreams, but she's wide awake.

She's in the warzone, ashen walls rising around her in broken lines, but buttercream paint seeps through the gray. The pale yellow carries with it the scent of spring, a slice of blue sky, the slow curl of white curtains into a sunlit room. This place is far away; the ground shakes underfoot, rattling ash over paint, and she's running, running with her heart in her throat and her hands wrapped around her rifle. Rifle pressed into breast the way Lottie should be. Seven strides to the alley—seven strides and she's in, in and sliding down into the shadows. Her gaze latches on to Ginger across the street in another alley. Ginger prefers gunfire to silence; it tells them exactly where the enemy is.

"Mama?"

Cardee pushes the small voice in her head away. That voice is as distant as that calm yellow room. Ginger is in the here and now: Ginger and Bret and Stills, and the goddamned little shadow they're chasing. Children in warzones aren't a surprise, not now, but the first time she'd seen one, Cardee recoiled. They're often lures, she knows; the urge to follow the small ones and haul them out of the wreckage is hard-wired. She wants to carry them somewhere safer. She doesn't know where that might be.

Ginger breaks position to follow the kid into the tangle of narrow streets hung with paper lanterns from a long ago celebration. Blue, green, and—

"Gin—"

Cardee swallows the rest of her protest and at Bret's snapped curse, runs. Runs across the street into the alley Ginger had occupied. Of the child, she has the impression of ratty clothes, bare feet, and knows the latter are the deal breaker for Ginger.

The first child they'd rescued had ruined feet from walking through the debris; Ginger spent days applying salve to them, only to have the doc tell them the feet couldn't be saved. It makes the others harder—that kid hadn't been a lure, he just needed out. He only planted hope inside Ginger when it came to every other kid.

The hardware store still stands, windows unbroken in their frames. Cardee draws up short, listens for Ginger. There is a sharp hiss and the thunder of retreating boots. She shoulders her way into the store, amid stripped shelves. Binned nails, hammers, and planks of wood stand in one corner but—

A slamming door erupts into flame a second later. The air is sharp with flying nails and hammers and Cardee drops to the floor, rolling until she's under the nearest shelf. The shelf buckles with a second explosion and is shredded away with a third. Blood splatters the concrete floor amid the burning refuse, as if dripping from Cardee's own face, but she can't make sense of it.

"*Mama.*"

She gives in to the voice. "I know, baby."

Cardee slides the warm cloth over Lottie's temple, removing the haze of blood. Small brown face, so like her own. Wide black eyes blink up at her, tight sepia curls framing smooth apple cheeks. Cardee leans in to look at the wound.

"J-James d-dared me t-to jump," Lottie whispers, anguished.

"Just a little scrape." Cardee drops a kiss on Lottie's forehead, reaches past her for the wipes and dermal sealer. She's seen worse on the battlefield, but not worse on her daughter and though she forces a smile, the injury bothers her. Bothers her in a way she can't quantify—

Nails, there were nails—

Cardee grits her teeth together, steadies her hands. This is now, not then, and Lottie flinches at the antiseptic wipe and then the cool flow of sealer.

"Green b-bandage?"

"You like all that green, don't you?" But Cardee doesn't protest her daughter's choice. She presses the bandage over the wound, even though it's not needed with the sealer already there.

"All that green, Mama." Lottie's smile ripples and through a haze of smoke, looks green in the corners. Cardee runs her thumb across it as Lottie lifts a hand to touch Cardee's own temple where green lights pulse.

"Findar."

That's her name. She knows it's her name, because she remembers stealing it from Ross. He thought he gave it to her on the lakeshore with the trees dipping low into the water and all their friends gathered close, but ten years on, she still feels like she stole it. *Wood violets, wild roses, my black-eyed girls.*

"Findar!"

Her fingers come away from the sky bloodied; they are snatched from her, tied against her side and she's flying, airborne through the debris, away from Ginger and the small figure they were chasing. Cardee opens her mouth to tell Ginger the kid is there, just there beyond that pile of debris, and there's another explosion. The world rocks and green sky tips then vanishes altogether as gloved hands draw her inside a warm, dark space, and she hears the chop-chop-chop of angel wings, as they arc high into the sky thirteen klicks from base.

Thirteen nails, doc says and drops the last into the basin. It falls with a clink, a fleck of blood, and Cardee sees faces in the red: Ross and the priest and if she closes her eyes she can feel Ross's palm against hers. Palmers' kiss was holy she had told him, but now there's only the chatter of doc and his team and when these voices change, Cardee can't latch onto why. The light takes on a clear quality, the smoke of the hotspot gone, and the bite of the stitcher is almost sweet as it crawls over her bare scalp. It tickles; the sensation tells her she's alive.

The stitcher tiptoes over scalp while doc settles the VET into its place against the ruin of her hippocampus and he's talking all the while, words that slide over Cardee's consciousness and away. She knows he's watching a screen while he talks, to see what her brain does with each word. Volatile, he calls the device. Like it might explode the way the hardware store did—

Ragged clothing and bare feet. Oh, bare feet. Cardee can feel the soft curve of Lottie's toes against her chin.

Emotive transistor, doc says and his fingers are cool against her temple though warmth seems to sink into her skin, into her bones. Her left eye blossoms with sudden heat, the sting of salt.

Do that again, doc bids her.

Cardee doesn't know what he means, but she thinks about Lottie's toes, small and brown and sweet like sugar, and the salt stings her again as doc praises her. Good, good, he says, and Cardee swallows a sob. The green light floods his palm then fades as Cardee quiets. It won't be perfect, he says, but—

—what is in this world, Ross says and his mouth moves over Cardee's and she smiles, knowing neither one of them really wants perfection. They have always been a jumble and she's content to stay that way. The idea that he would marry her when she means to serve their country is what sinks its hooks into her. That he would stay, no matter where they or she went, and when they go to the lakeshore all those years later and she tells him about the child, there is a quiet wonder in his eyes.

He is barefoot, jean cuffs rolled up and wet, and he tangles wild roses into Cardee's hair. They're pink like his tongue and later she presses these roses into a book which will sit on a shelf beside a box full of letters with different postmarks, all the places she has been. The book will sit until Lottie pulls it down at age three and scatters the flat, dried bundle everywhere. A year later, they still find bits of roses in the corners.

"Made it just the way you like," Ross says, and leads Cardee to the corner where he's placed her favorite chair with its worn arms and the quilt her grandmother pieced together. A tablet rests on the table beside an electric kettle which she knows holds Earl Grey. He helps her into the chair and she's slow, like she can't remember how to move, but the VET remembers for her, guiding her into the chair's familiar hold.

A ring peeks out from Ross's shirt collar as he moves, three strands of Irish gold braided together. His grandmother's, but now hers, given to him so it couldn't be taken even if her finger did feel bare without it. A thing to come back to he had joked, and as it slips free now he tucks it away before she can touch it. His brow creases. Don't worry about that now, he tells her.

Ross's hands are tentative as he settles her feet on the ottoman, as he pulls up the quilt and then reaches for her cup. The cup is sunrise orange and the tea floods it in a brown, steaming rush. Cardee draws in a breath and watches as Ross's face is erased. The room seems to fold itself away under the rising steam and she's in an alley again, watching a small, barefoot figure flit through the debris.

That was then, she tells herself, and tries to pull the walls of her room upright. Plaster and buttercream and not ash, but there's only stone and choking smoke in this place. Stills presses a new magazine into her hand and she slots it into her rifle before running, running after Ginger through the debris, after the small barefoot form.

This is before, she knows. Before the hardware store. Three days? No—three months, months and this is the first kid, the one doc won't be able to save.

Images shutter like an old film reel through her mind, guided by the VET in her temple. That was then but it's also now, and Cardee follows Ginger over fallen stones that used to be walls that used to be houses that used to be homes.

There is a tall figure in a far door lifting a gun. Cardee lifts hers first and the figure crumples with a shriek, doesn't move. Ginger is twelve steps from the kid, the boy, and Cardee knows she herself is twenty-five steps from the figure she shot down.

She will walk those steps, check the body, take the gun. She will. She already has.

Twenty-seven steps from the second figure who emerges behind the first, a young man in enemy colors, and he lifts his gun. Cardee takes him down too; he falls to his knees as if in prayer, then topples over.

Ginger tackles the boy, wrestles him to the ground and pins his arms behind him. Where are the others, she demands—*where*! And he says he doesn't know—but he does and these kids just don't want to go, don't want to leave these streets that are home, home even though war has claimed them. Home, smeared into his cheeks and his bare, bloodied feet. Ginger hefts the boy, throws him over her shoulder, and they're out, running as shells rain from the sky.

Cardee turns circles in wet grass. Don't worry about getting wet, she tells Lottie, and they're out, running as the rain pours from the summer sky. Lottie shrieks, like she might melt under the rain because she's so sweet, but Cardee holds her hand and feels her daughter relax. The shriek turns to a laugh and Lottie is no longer worried about her dress, because it will dry on the laundry line when the sun comes out again. She twirls and Cardee watches those toes as they mash into the mud. Hot cocoa later, she thinks, but it's already been later, that cocoa long drunk.

This is memory, Cardee tells herself, and pulls hard, hard enough to lift the walls of her room back into place. This was now. Her room, where 9-year-old Lottie now sits, bundled on the ottoman. Lottie watches everything and Cardee watches back. Lottie is taller than she remembers, all long arms and legs, her hair longer and worn pulled up on the top of her head with a mass of bright green and blue ribbons. A clumsy knot, her father's work.

"Mama?"

Cardee offers her hand for holding. The hand Lottie offers is larger than Cardee remembers, long slim fingers. Palm to palm they sit until Lottie makes a sound, a sound like she wants to cry but is too old for such things now. Lottie curls into her mother's lap, the way a nut curls into its shell, and she's crying. *Don't w-worry about getting w-wet.*

There was rain, Cardee thinks, rain like nails, and she lifts a hand to feel the line of her skull, whole now but still shorn, wrapped under a bright cloth. Lottie shudders and Cardee hauls her closer.

"It's okay, baby. It helps mama remember."

Lottie's fingers press cool against Cardee's temple, gentle over the soft light which flickers beneath the skin. Of course it was green. Lottie's mouth lifts in a tentative smile at the sight and—

—it's doc looking at her for the first time after the surgery, his face clear and sharp and framed by all that brilliant white light. Cardee stares the way she stared at Ross when he proposed, like she can't understand or believe it. That was then, she tells herself, but doc tells her it won't be perfect. It'll run, but it'll stutter, too, like a tank you need kick every now and then. Cardee doesn't want it; Cardee can't be Cardee without it, though. She understands that. The VET can reach pieces of her memory that she no longer can.

"Mama."

That voice hauls her back to the yellow room with its curtains, with its small nut of a girl. Cardee doesn't remember Lottie this way and the VET hums hard, as if trying to reconcile two different pieces of paperwork. The numbers don't add up. Small Lottie waving goodbye in the driveway, Ross and Gamma at her side; this is the last image of Lottie the VET can give her. The Lottie who hasn't outgrown the shoes that Cardee saw in the donation box as they came inside today. The Lottie who hasn't yet flung herself off the swing at a friend's dare.

"I'm here, baby."

Always that: baby. Cardee clings to the word, the way she does to her daughter. She's here, but she's not. Part of her is still in those streets. The VET pulls up her most recent memory, running with it, because that's what it does. Running—

Feet hit the ground hard as she and the fireteam seek another kid. There were two down here, two and—

Two kids emerge from the rubble, rifles cocked and drawn on the team. Cardee draws up, but doesn't lower her rifle. These kids are taller, but still young. Eight, nine. Lottie's age now, she thinks and something inside her turns over. This was not now, this was then, but something inside her hides its face.

"In-de-pen-dents?" one of the kids asks, drawing the word out into four hard syllables.

Bret strides forward, kicks up clouds of dust in the ruined street. "Co-a-li-tion," he spits and the world erupts.

"Wrong answer!"

They don't want to go, this band of kids, and they fight to stay. Cardee screams at Bret to back off, but it's too late. She smells the blood, the gunpowder, and feels the sudden press of a knife against her side. Before her, the scene unfolds as it did before, the way she remembers, down to the taste of sweat on her lip. Only one of the kids gets away. Escapes to run and set a trap in the hardware store where nails— Where nails—

Memory stutters. Her mind goes blank.

"Mama?"

Cardee feels the touch of fingers on her face, pressing gentle and then with more insistence. She blinks and looks at the girl in her lap, but cannot recall her name. Does not know why she's here. Bret would be here soon. Bret and Ginger and—

"Mama!"

But the only children she knows live in the streets. Rubble rats, sand kids, some used as weapons, others in need of rescue. This girl is whole and clean. A green bandage clings to her temple, but her feet are uninjured. Not bloody or cut, and Cardee can't process it. The girl pushes away. Those small feet thunder away.

"Da! Daaaaa!"

Cardee blinks, the room around her unfamiliar. She wanders, touching walls that should be made of ash. Why is there a ceiling and how can there be windows without cracks? Just when it seems the walls might crumble to ruin under her fingers, there's another hand, this one drawing her own from the wall. Cardee whimpers because part of her wants to see these walls fall down. It's what she knows, jagged lines against smoky sky.

There is a mark upon one wall, where a frame used to rest. A frame that held a photograph, she thinks. Fingers trace this line, but there is no frame. Her eyes sweep the room and she's moving past the man, rifling through drawers, careless with everything that isn't the frame that belongs upon the wall. Careless until her fingers close around a bundle of letters. Handwritten, from far away places, they smell like ash and home both. Tears smudge the writing—before or after the sending and does it matter? Pushed to the back of the drawer, she thinks that is what matters. More letters and more and then at the bottom, the frame. The photograph.

It's a face half familiar, dark and proud, and by her side there stands a man as pale as she is dark. That man, she thinks, looking up at him now, then back to the photograph. Behind them sprawls a lake and the shore is tangled with long grasses, willowed trees. Cardee lifts the frame and brings it to the wall, but there is no nail.

There *were* nails—

"Cardee. Beloved." His hand covers hers.

"The team?" she asks.

He swallows hard. "Safe."

A bright, striped flag across the length of a casket. The image is gone as quickly as it comes.

The man guides her toward the chair in the corner, with its quilt and tablet and cooling tea. "You're home."

Cardee shakes her head and a deep pain flares at her temple, burning down her spine. She presses the framed photograph into her lap. "Volatile," she whispers. *Explosive.*

"Volatile Emotive Transistor," he says, and there's something in his eyes, something Cardee cannot name. His hand tightens on hers, shaking, and the line of a ring presses into her bones. His ring. His free hand lifts, to trace her temple where green lights have stilled.

Warmth and salt burn her eyes. "I should . . . " Her head comes up. Her attention narrows on the doorway. There should be a figure there and she should have her rifle, but there isn't and she doesn't. A tank needs kicking, she thinks, but doesn't know why. She looks back to the man. "I don't remember."

He eases his hold on her, hand sliding down, around, so that palm presses to palm. Cardee's breath hisses and fresh fire courses through her body. Old pathways blazing into new.

"Wood violets, wild roses, my black-eyed girls," he says.

She smells the lake now and the willows brush her shoulders as they walk, hand in hand through the almost-cold grass underfoot. He offers her a tangle of violets and one of roses and then a braided ring, a ring that slides onto her finger as though it belongs. The way he slides it onto her finger now, warm from his own body.

"Palmers' k-kiss is holy?"

There's something else in his eyes now. Warmth and salt and everything he put away while she was gone. He smiles slow, and it's like nothing Cardee has seen before. Nothing and yet everything she knows, and there comes the sound of small bare feet, thumping down the hall. Toward them. *My black-eyed girls.*

"Come from those streets, Cardee Findar. I will remember with you."

Staying Behind
KEN LIU

After the Singularity, most people chose to die.

The dead pity us and call us the *left behind,* as if we were unfortunate souls who couldn't get to a life raft in time. They cannot fathom the idea that we might *choose* to stay behind. And so, year after year, relentlessly, the dead try to steal our children.

I was born in Year Zero of the Singularity, when the first man Uploaded into a machine. The Pope denounced the "Digital Adam"; the digerati celebrated; and everyone else struggled to make sense of the new world.

"We've always wanted to live forever," said Adam Ever, the founder of Everlasting, Inc., and the first to go. In the form of a recording, his message was broadcast across the Internet. "Now we can."

While Everlasting built its massive data center in Svalbard, nations around the world scrambled to decide if what happened there was murder. For every Uploaded man, there was a lifeless body left behind, the brain a bloody pulpy mess after the destructive scanning procedure. But what really happened to him, his essence, his—for lack of a better word—soul?

Was he now an artificial intelligence? Or was he still somehow human, with silicon and graphene performing the functions of neurons? Was it merely a hardware upgrade for consciousness? Or has he become a mere algorithm, a clockwork imitation of free will?

It began with the old and the terminally ill. It was very expensive. Then, as the price of admission lowered, hundreds, thousands, then millions lined up.

"Let's do it," Dad said, when I was in high school. By then, the world was falling into chaos. Half the country was depopulated. Commodity prices plunged. The threat of war and actual war were everywhere: conquests, re-conquests, endless slaughter. Those who could afford it left on the next flight to Svalbard. Humanity was abandoning the world and destroying itself.

Mom reached out and held Dad's hand.

"No," she said. "They think they can cheat death. But they died the minute they decided to abandon the real world for a simulation. So long as there's sin, there must be death. It is the measure by which life gains meaning."

She was a lapsed Catholic who nonetheless yearned for the certainty of the Church, and her theology always seemed to me a bit cobbled-together. But she believed that there was a right way to live, and a right way to die.

While Lucy is away at school, Carol and I search her room. Carol looks through her closet for pamphlets, books, and other physical tokens of contact with the dead. I log onto Lucy's computer.

Lucy is strong-willed but dutiful. Ever since she was a little girl, I've been telling her that she must prepare to resist the temptations of the dead. Only she can assure the continuity of our way of life in this abandoned world. She listens to me and nods.

I want to trust her.

But the dead are very clever with their propaganda. In the beginning, they sometimes sent metallic gray drones over our towns, scattering leaflets filled with messages purporting to be from our loved ones. We burned the leaflets and shot at the drones, and eventually, they stopped coming.

Then they tried to come at us through the wireless links between the towns, the electronic lifeline that sustained those who stayed behind and kept our shrinking communities from being completely isolated from each other. We had to vigilantly watch the networks for their insidious tendrils, always seeking an opening.

Lately, their efforts have turned to the children. The dead may have finally given up on us, but they are grasping for the next generation, for our future. As her father, I have a duty to protect Lucy from that which she does not yet understand.

The computer boots up slowly. It's a miracle that I've managed to keep it running for so long, years past the obsolescence planned by its manufacturer. I've replaced every component in it, some multiple times.

I scan for a list of files recently created or modified by Lucy, emails received, web pages retrieved. Most are schoolwork or innocent chatter with friends. The inter-settlement network, such as it is, shrinks daily. It's difficult to keep the radio towers that link town to town powered and operating, with so many people each year dying and simply giving up. It used to be possible for us to communicate with friends as far away as San Francisco, the packets of data skipping from town to town in between like stones across a pond. But now, only less than a thousand computers are still reachable from here, none further away than Maine. Someday we won't be able to scavenge the components to keep the computers running any more, and we'll regress even further into the past.

Carol is already done with her search. She sits down on Lucy's bed to watch me.

"That was fast," I say.

She shrugs. "We'll never find anything. If she trusts us, she'll talk to us. If she doesn't, then we won't find what she wants hidden."

Lately, I've detected more such fatalistic sentiments in Carol. It's as though she's getting tired, not as committed to the cause. I find myself constantly striving to rekindle her faith.

"Lucy is still young," I tell her, "too young to understand what she would have to give up in exchange for the false promises of the dead. I know you hate this spying, but we're trying to save her life."

Carol looks at me, and eventually she sighs and nods.

I check the image files for hidden data. I check the disk for links to deleted files that might hold secret codes. I scan the web pages, looking for code words offering false promises.

I sigh with relief. She's clean.

I don't much like leaving Lowell these days. The world outside our fence grows ever more harsh and dangerous. Bears have come back to eastern Massachusetts. Every year, the forest grows denser, closer to the town line. Some claim to have seen wolves roaming in the woods too.

A year ago, Brad Lee and I had to go to Boston to find spare parts for the town's generator, housed in the old mill by the Merrimac River. We carried shotguns, protection against both the animals and the vandals who still scurried in urban ruins, living off of the last of the canned food. The surface of Mass Ave, deserted for thirty years, was full of cracks, tufts of grass and shrubs peeking out from them. The harsh New England winters, wielding seeping water and prying ice, had chipped away at the tall buildings around us, their windowless shells crumbling and rusting in the absence of artificial heat and regular maintenance.

Coming around a corner downtown, we surprised two of them huddled around a fire, which they fed with books and papers taken from the bookstore nearby. Even vandals needed warmth, and maybe they also delighted in destroying what was left of civilization.

The two crouched and growled at us, but made no move as Brad and I pointed our guns at them. I remember their thin legs and arms, their dirty faces, their bloodshot eyes full of hate and terror. But mostly, I remember their wrinkled faces and white hair. *Even the vandals are growing old,* I thought. *And they have no children.*

Brad and I backed away carefully. I was glad we didn't have to shoot anyone.

The summer I was eight and Laura eleven, my parents took us on a road trip through Arizona, New Mexico, and Texas. We drove along old highways and side roads, a tour of the monumental beauty of the Western deserts, filled with nostalgic, desolate ghost towns.

As we passed through the Indian reservations—Navajo, Zuni, Acoma, Laguna—Mom wanted to stop at every roadside shop to admire the traditional pottery. Laura and I gingerly stepped through the aisles, careful not to break anything.

Back in the car, Mom let me handle a small pot that she had bought. I turned it over and over in my hands, examining the rough white surface, the neat, clean, black geometric designs, and the bold outline of the hunched-over flute player with feathers coming out of his head.

"Amazing, isn't it?" Mom said. "This wasn't made on a potter's wheel. The woman coiled it by hand, using the same techniques that have been passed down for generations in her family. She even dug for the clay in the same places that her great-grandmother used. She's keeping alive an ancient tradition, a way of life."

The pot suddenly felt heavy in my hands, as though I could sense the weight of its generations of memory.

"That's just a story to drum up business," Dad said, glancing at me in the rear view mirror. "But it would be even sadder if the story were true. If you're doing things the exact same way as your ancestors, then your way of life is dead, and you've become a fossil, a performance for the entertainment of tourists."

"She was not performing," Mom said. "You have no sense of what's really important in life, what's worth holding onto. There's more to being human than *progress*. You're as bad as those Singularity zealots."

"Please don't argue any more," Laura said. "Let's just get to the hotel and sit by the pool."

Jack, Brad Lee's son, is at the door. He's shy and awkward, even though he has been coming by our house for months. I've known him since he was a baby, like I know all the children in town. There are so few of them left. The high school, operating out of the old Whistler House, has only twelve students.

"Hello," he mumbles, looking at the floor. "Lucy and I need to work on our report." I step aside to let him pass on his way upstairs to Lucy's room.

I don't need to remind him about the rules: door to the bedroom open, at least three of their four feet on the carpet at all times. I hear the indistinct sounds of their chatter and occasional laughter.

There is a kind of innocence to their courtship that was absent from my youth. Without the endless blast of cynical sexuality from TV and the real Internet, children can stay children longer.

There weren't many doctors left near the end. Those of us who wanted to stay behind gathered into small communities, circling the wagons against the marauding bands of vandals who gorged themselves on pleasures of the flesh as the Uploaded left the physical world behind. I never got to finish college.

Mom lingered in her sickness for months. She was bedridden and drifted in and out of consciousness, her body pumped full of drugs that numbed her pain. We took turns sitting by her, holding her hand. When she had good days, temporary lulls of lucidity, there was only one topic of conversation.

"No," Mom said, wheezing. "You must promise me. This is important. I've lived a real life, and I will die a real death. I will *not* be turned into a recording. There are worse things than death."

"If you Upload," Dad said, "you'll still have a choice. They can suspend your consciousness, or even erase it, if you don't like it after you try it. But if you don't Upload, you'll be gone forever. There's no room for regret or return."

"If I do what you want," Mom said, "I will be gone. There is no way to come back to this, to the real world. I will not be simulated by a bunch of electrons."

"Please stop," Laura pleaded with Dad. "You're hurting her. Why can't you leave her alone?"

Mom's moments of lucidity came further and further apart.

Then that night: waking up to the sound of the front door closing, looking outside the window to see the shuttle on the lawn, tumbling down the stairs.

They were carrying Mom into the shuttle on a stretcher. Dad stood by the door of the gray vehicle, only a little bigger than a van, EVERLASTING, INC. painted on its side.

"Stop!" I shouted over the sound of the shuttle's engines.

"There's no time," Dad said. His eyes were bloodshot. He hadn't slept for days. None of us had. "They have to do it now before it's too late. I can't lose her."

We struggled. He held me in a tight hug and wrestled me to the ground. "It's *her* choice, not yours!" I screamed into his ear. He only held me tighter. I fought to free myself. "Laura, stop them!"

Laura covered her eyes. "Stop fighting, all of you! She would have wanted all of you to stop."

I hated her for speaking as though Mom was already gone.

The shuttle closed its door and lifted into the air.

Dad left for Svalbard two days later. I refused to speak to him until the end.

"I'm going to join her now," he said. "Come as soon as you can."

"You killed her," I said. He flinched at the words, and I was glad.

Jack has asked Lucy to the prom. I'm pleased that the kids have decided to hold one. It shows that they are serious about keeping alive the stories and traditions they've heard from their parents, legends from a world they have only experienced vicariously in old videos and old pictures.

We struggle to maintain what we can of the life from before: put on old plays, read old books, celebrate the old holidays, sing old songs. We've had to give up so much. Old recipes have had to be adapted for limited ingredients, old hopes and dreams shrunken to fit within tightened horizons. But every deprivation has also brought us closer as a community, to hold on tighter to our traditions.

Lucy wants to make her own dress. Carol suggests that she look through her old dresses first. "I have some formals left from when I was just a little older than you."

Lucy is not interested. "They're old," she says.

"They're classic," I tell her.

But Lucy is adamant. She cuts up her old dresses, curtains, scavenged tablecloths, and trades with the other girls for bits of fabric: silk, chiffon, taffeta, lace, plain cotton. She flips through Carol's old magazines, looking for inspiration.

Lucy is a good seamstress, far better than Carol. The children are all skilled in trades long thought obsolete in the world I grew up in: knitting, woodworking, planting and hunting. Carol and I had to rediscover and learn these things from books when we were already adults, adapting to a suddenly changed world. But for the children, it is all they have known. They are natives here.

All the students at the high school have spent the last few months doing research in the Textile History Museum, investigating the possibility of weaving our own cloth, preparing for a time when the decaying ruins of the cities would run out of usable cloths for us to salvage. There is some poetic justice in this: Lowell, which once rose on the back of the textile industry, must now rediscover those lost arts on our gentle slide back down the technology curve.

A week after Dad left, we received an email from Mom:

> I was wrong.
>
> Sometimes, I'm nostalgic and sad. I miss you, my children, and the world we left behind. But I'm ecstatic most of the time, often incredulous.
>
> There are hundreds of millions of us here, but there is no crowding. In this house there are countless mansions. Each of our minds inhabits its own world, and each of us has infinite space and infinite time.
>
> How can I explain it to you? I can only use the same words so many others have already used. In my old existence, I felt life but dimly and from a distance, cushioned, constrained, tied down by the body. But now I am free, a bare soul exposed to the full tides of eternal Life.
>
> How can speech compare to the intimacy of sharing with your father psyche to psyche? How can hearing about how much he loved me compare to actually feeling his love? To truly understand another person, to experience the texture of his mind—it is glorious.
>
> They tell me that this sensation is called hyperreality. But I don't care what it is called. I was wrong to cling so tightly to the comforts of an old shell made of flesh and blood. We, the real us, have always been patterns of electrons cascading across the abyss, the nothingness between atoms. What difference does it

make if those electrons are in a brain or silicon chips?

Life is sacred and eternal. But our old way of life was unsustainable. We demanded too much of our planet, of sacrifices made by every other living thing. I once thought that an unavoidable aspect of our existence, but it isn't. Now, with the oil tankers aground, the cars and trucks still, the fields fallow and factories silent, the living world that we had made almost extinct will return.

Humanity is not a cancer of the planet. We simply needed to transcend the demands of our inefficient bodies, machines no longer adequate for their task. How many consciousnesses will now live in this new world, pure creatures of electric spirit and weightless thought? There are no limits.

Come join us. We cannot wait to embrace you again.

—Mom

Laura cried as she read it. But I felt nothing. This wasn't my mother speaking. The real Mom knew that what really mattered in life was the authenticity of this messy existence, the constant yearning for closeness to another despite imperfect understanding, the pain and suffering of our flesh.

She taught me that our mortality makes us human. The limited time given to each of us makes what we do meaningful. We die to make place for our children, and through our children a piece of us lives on, the only form of immortality that is real.

It is *this* world, the world we are meant to live in, that anchors us and demands our presence, not the imagined landscapes of a computed illusion.

This was a simulacrum of her, a recording of propaganda, a temptation into nihilism.

***

Carol and I met on one of my earliest scavenging trips. Her family had been hiding in the basement of their house on Beacon Hill. A gang of vandals found them and killed her father and brother. They were about to start on her when we showed up. I killed a man-shaped animal that day, and I'm not sorry about it.

We brought her back to Lowell, and though she was seventeen, for days, she clung to me and would not let me out of her sight. Even when sleeping, she wanted me to be there, holding her hand.

"Maybe my family made a mistake," she said one day. "We would have been better off if we had Uploaded. There's nothing but death left here now."

I didn't argue with her. I let her follow me around as I went about my chores. I showed her how we were keeping the generator running, how we treated each other with respect, how we rescued old books and held onto old routines.

There was still civilization in this world, kept alive like a candle flame. People did die, but people were also born. Life went on, sweet, joyful, authentic life.

Then one day, she kissed me.

"There's also you in this world," she said. "And that is enough."

"No, not enough," I said. "We will also bring new life here."

Tonight is the night.

Jack is at the door. He looks good in that tuxedo. It's the same one I wore to my prom. They'll play the same songs too, pumping the music from an old laptop and speakers on their last legs.

Lucy is splendid in her dress: white with a black print, cut in a simple pattern, but very elegant. The skirt is wide and full-length, draping gracefully to the floor. Carol did her hair, curls with a hint of glitter. She looks glamorous, with a hint of childish playfulness.

I take pictures with a camera, one that still mostly works.

I wait until I'm sure I have my voice under control. "You have no idea how glad I am to see young people dancing, the way we used to."

She kisses me on the cheek. "Goodbye, Dad." There are tears in her eyes. And that makes everything go blurry for me again.

Carol and Lucy embrace for a moment. Carol wipes her eyes. "You're all set."

"Thanks, Mom."

Then Lucy turns to Jack. "Let's go."

Jack will take her to the Lowell Four Seasons on his bicycle. It's the best that can be done since we've been without gasoline for many years. Lucy gingerly settles onto the top tube, sitting sideways, one hand holding her dress up. Jack wraps her in his arms protectively as he grabs the handles. And they are off, wobbling down the street.

"Have fun," I yell after them.

Laura's betrayal was the hardest to take.

"I thought you were going to help me and Carol with the baby," I said.

"What kind of world is this to bring a child into?" Laura said.

"And you think things will be better if you go there, where there are no children, no new life?"

"We've tried to keep this going for fifteen years, and every year it becomes harder and harder to believe in this charade. Maybe we were wrong. We should adapt."

"It's only a charade when you've lost faith," I said.

"Faith in what?"

"In humanity, in our way of life."

"I don't want to fight our parents any more. I just want us to be together again, a family."

"Those *things* aren't our parents. They are imitation algorithms. You've always wanted to avoid conflict, Laura. But some conflicts cannot be avoided. Our parents died when Dad lost faith, when he couldn't resist the false promises made by machines."

At the end of the road into the woods was a little clearing, grassy, full of wildflowers. A shuttle was waiting in the middle. Laura stepped into the open door.

Another life lost.

The children have permission to stay out until midnight. Lucy had asked me not to volunteer as a chaperone, and I complied, conceding her this bit of space for the night.

Carol is restless. She tries to read but she's been on the same page for an hour.

"Don't worry." I try to comfort her.

She tries to smile at me, but she can't hide her anxiety. She looks up past my shoulder at the clock on the living room wall.

I glance back too. "Doesn't it feel later than 11?"

"No," Carol says. "Not at all. I don't know what you mean."

Her voice is too eager, almost desperate. There's a hint of fear in her eyes. She's close to panicking.

I open the door of the house and step into the dark street. The sky has grown clearer over the years, and many more stars are now visible. But I'm looking for the Moon. It's not in the right place.

I come back into the house and go into the bedroom. My old watch, one that I no longer wear because there are so few occasions when being on time matters, is in the nightstand drawer. I pull it out. It's almost one in the morning. Someone had tampered with the living room clock.

Carol stands in the door to the bedroom. The light is behind her so I can't see her face.

"What have you done?" I ask. I'm not angry, just disappointed.

"She can't talk to you. She doesn't think you'll listen."

Now the anger rises in me like hot bile.

"Where are they?"

Carol shakes her head, saying nothing.

I remember the way Lucy said goodbye to me. I remember the way she walked carefully out to Jack's bike, holding up her voluminous skirt, a skirt so wide that she could hide anything under it, a change of clothing and comfortable shoes for the woods. I remember Carol saying, "You're all set."

"It's too late," Carol says. "Laura is coming to pick them up."

"Get out of the way. I have to save her."

"Save her for what?" Carol is suddenly furious. She does not move. "This is a play, a joke, a re-enactment of something that never was. Did you go to your prom on a *bicycle*? Did you play only songs that your parents listened to when they were kids? Did you grow up thinking that scavenging would be the only profession? Our way of life is long gone, dead, finished!

"What will you have her do when this house falls apart in thirty years? What will she do when the last bottle of aspirin is gone, the last steel pot rusted through? Will you condemn her and her children to a life of picking through our garbage heaps, sliding down the technology ladder year after year until they've lost all the progress made by the human race in the last five thousand years?"

I don't have time to debate her. Gently, but firmly, I put my hands on her shoulders, ready to push her aside.

"I will stay with you," Carol says. "I will always stay with you because I love you so much that I'm not afraid of death. But she is a child. She should have a chance for something new."

Strength seems to drain from my arms. "You have it backwards." I look into her eyes, willing her to have faith again. "Her life gives our lives meaning."

Her body suddenly goes limp, and she sinks to the floor, sobbing silently.

"Let her go," Carol says, quietly. "Just let her go."

"I can't give up," I tell Carol. "I'm human."

I pump the pedals furiously once I'm past the gate in the fence. The cone of light cast by the flashlight jumps around as I try to hold it against the handlebars. But I know this road into the woods well. It leads to the clearing where Laura once stepped into that shuttle.

Bright light in the distance, and the sound of engines revving up.

I take out my gun and fire a few shots into the air.

The sound of the engines dies down.

I emerge into the opening in the woods, under a sky full of bright, cold, pinprick stars. I jump off the bike and let it fall by the side of the path. The shuttle is in the middle of the clearing. Lucy and Jack, now in casual clothes, stand in the open doorway of the shuttle.

"Lucy, sweetheart, come back out of there."

"Dad, I'm sorry. I'm going."

"No, you are not."

An electronic simulation of Laura's voice comes out of the shuttle's speakers. "Let her go, brother. She deserves to have a chance to see what you refuse to see. Or, better yet, come with us. We've all missed you."

I ignore her, it. "Lucy, there is no future there. What the machines promise you is not real. There are no children there, no hope, only a timeless, changeless, simulated existence as fragments of a machine."

"We have children now," the copy of Laura's voice says. "We've figured out how to create children of the mind, natives of the digital world. You should come and meet your nephews and nieces. *You* are the one clinging to a changeless existence. This is the next step in our evolution."

"You can experience nothing when you are not human." I shake my head. I shouldn't take its bait and debate a machine.

"If you leave," I tell Lucy, "you'll die a death with no meaning. The dead will have won. I can't let that happen."

I raise my gun. The barrel points at her. I will not lose my child to the dead.

Jack tries to step in front of her, but Lucy pushes him away. Her eyes are full of sorrow, and the light from inside the shuttle frames her face and golden hair like an angel.

Suddenly I see how much she looks like my mother. Mom's features, having passed through me, have come alive again on my daughter. This is how life is meant to be lived. Grandparents, parents, children, each generation stepping out of the way of the next, an eternal striving towards the future, to progress.

I think about how Mom's choice was taken away from her, how she was not allowed to die as a human, how she was devoured by the dead, how she became a part of their ceaselessly looping, mindless recordings. My mother's face, from memory, is superimposed onto the face of my daughter, my sweet, innocent, foolish Lucy.

I tighten my grip on the gun.

"Dad," Lucy says, calmly, her face as steady as Mom's all those years ago. "This is *my* choice. Not yours."

It's morning by the time Carol steps into the clearing. Warm sunlight through the leaves dapples the empty circle of grass. Dewdrops hang from the tips of the grass blades, in each a miniature, suspended, vision of the world. Birdsong fills the waking silence. My bike is still on the ground by the path where I left it.

Carol sits down by me without speaking. I put my arm around her shoulders and pull her close to me. I don't know what she's thinking, but it's enough for us to sit together like this, our bodies pressed together, keeping each other warm. There's no need for words. We look around at this pristine world, a garden inherited from the dead.

We have all the time in the world.

Immersion

ALIETTE DE BODARD

In the morning, you're no longer quite sure who you are.

You stand in front of the mirror—it shifts and trembles, reflecting only what you want to see—eyes that feel too wide, skin that feels too pale, an odd, distant smell wafting from the compartment's ambient system that is neither incense nor garlic, but something else, something elusive that you once knew.

You're dressed, already—not on your skin, but outside, where it matters, your avatar sporting blue and black and gold, the stylish clothes of a well-traveled, well-connected woman. For a moment, as you turn away from the mirror, the glass shimmers out of focus; and another woman in a dull silk gown stares back at you: smaller, squatter and in every way diminished—a stranger, a distant memory that has ceased to have any meaning.

Quy was on the docks, watching the spaceships arrive. She could, of course, have been anywhere on Longevity Station, and requested the feed from the network to be patched to her router—and watched, superimposed on her field of vision, the slow dance of ships slipping into their pod cradles like births watched in reverse. But there was something about standing on the spaceport's concourse—a feeling of closeness that she just couldn't replicate by standing in Golden Carp Gardens or Azure Dragon Temple. Because here—here, separated by only a few measures of sheet metal from the cradle pods, she could feel herself teetering on the edge of the vacuum, submerged in cold and breathing in neither air nor oxygen. She could almost imagine herself rootless, finally returned to the source of everything.

Most ships those days were Galactic—you'd have thought Longevity's ex-masters would have been unhappy about the station's independence, but now that the war was over Longevity was a tidy source of profit. The ships came; and disgorged a steady stream of tourists—their eyes too round and straight, their jaws too square; their faces an unhealthy shade of pink, like undercooked meat left too long in the sun. They walked with the easy confidence of people with immersers: pausing to admire the suggested highlights for a second or so before moving on to the transport station, where they haggled in schoolbook Rong for a ride to their recommended hotels—a sickeningly familiar ballet

405

Quy had been seeing most of her life, a unison of foreigners descending on the station like a plague of centipedes or leeches.

Still, Quy watched them. They reminded her of her own time on Prime, her heady schooldays filled with raucous bars and wild weekends, and late minute revisions for exams, a carefree time she'd never have again in her life. She both longed for those days back, and hated herself for her weakness. Her education on Prime, which should have been her path into the higher strata of the station's society, had brought her nothing but a sense of disconnection from her family; a growing solitude, and a dissatisfaction, an aimlessness she couldn't put in words.

She might not have moved all day—had a sign not blinked, superimposed by her router on the edge of her field of vision. A message from Second Uncle.

"Child." His face was pale and worn, his eyes underlined by dark circles, as if he hadn't slept. He probably hadn't—the last Quy had seen of him, he had been closeted with Quy's sister Tam, trying to organize a delivery for a wedding—five hundred winter melons, and six barrels of Prosper's Station best fish sauce. "Come back to the restaurant."

"I'm on my day of rest," Quy said; it came out as more peevish and childish than she'd intended.

Second Uncle's face twisted, in what might have been a smile, though he had very little sense of humor. The scar he'd got in the Independence War shone white against the grainy background—twisting back and forth, as if it still pained him. "I know, but I need you. We have an important customer."

"Galactic," Quy said. That was the only reason he'd be calling her, and not one of her brothers or cousins. Because the family somehow thought that her studies on Prime gave her insight into the Galactics' way of thought—something useful, if not the success they'd hoped for.

"Yes. An important man, head of a local trading company." Second Uncle did not move on her field of vision. Quy could *see* the ships moving through his face, slowly aligning themselves in front of their pods, the hole in front of them opening like an orchid flower. And she knew everything there was to know about Grandmother's restaurant; she was Tam's sister, after all; and she'd seen the accounts, the slow decline of their clientele as their more genteel clients moved to better areas of the station; the influx of tourists on a budget, with little time for expensive dishes prepared with the best ingredients.

"Fine," she said. "I'll come."

At breakfast, you stare at the food spread out on the table: bread and jam and some colored liquid—you come up blank for a moment, before your immerser kicks in, reminding you that it's coffee, served strong and black, just as you always take it.

Yes. Coffee.

You raise the cup to your lips—your immerser gently prompts you, reminding you of where to grasp, how to lift, how to be in every possible way graceful and elegant, always an effortless model.

"It's a bit strong," your husband says, apologetically. He watches you from the other end of the table, an expression you can't interpret on his face—and isn't this odd, because shouldn't you know all there is to know about expressions—shouldn't the immerser have everything about Galactic culture recorded into its database, shouldn't it prompt you? But it's strangely silent, and this scares you, more than anything. Immersers never fail.

"Shall we go?" your husband says—and, for a moment, you come up blank on his name, before you remember—Galen, it's Galen, named after some physician on Old Earth. He's tall, with dark hair and pale skin—his immerser avatar isn't much different from his real self, Galactic avatars seldom are. It's people like you who have to work the hardest to adjust, because so much about you draws attention to itself—the stretched eyes that crinkle in the shape of moths, the darker skin, the smaller, squatter shape more reminiscent of jackfruits than swaying fronds. But no matter: you can be made perfect; you can put on the immerser and become someone else, someone pale-skinned and tall and beautiful.

Though, really, it's been such a long time since you took off the immerser, isn't it? It's just a thought—a suspended moment that is soon erased by the immerser's flow of information, the little arrows drawing your attention to the bread and the kitchen, and the polished metal of the table—giving you context about everything, opening up the universe like a lotus flower.

"Yes," you say. "Let's go." Your tongue trips over the word—there's a structure you should have used, a pronoun you should have said instead of the lapidary Galactic sentence. But nothing will come, and you feel like a field of sugar canes after the harvest—burnt out, all cutting edges with no sweetness left inside.

Of course, Second Uncle insisted on Quy getting her immerser for the interview—just in case, he said, soothingly and diplomatically as always. Trouble was, it wasn't where Quy had last left it. After putting out a message to the rest of the family, the best information Quy got was from Cousin Khanh, who thought he'd seen Tam sweep through the living quarters, gathering every piece of Galactic tech she could get her hands on. Third Aunt, who caught Khanh's message on the family's communication channel, tutted disapprovingly. "Tam. Always with her mind lost in the mountains, that girl. Dreams have never husked rice."

Quy said nothing. Her own dreams had shriveled and died after she came back from Prime and failed Longevity's mandarin exams; but it was good to have Tam around—to have someone who saw beyond the restaurant, beyond the narrow circle of family interests. Besides, if she didn't stick with her sister, who would?

Tam wasn't in the communal areas on the upper floors; Quy threw a glance towards the lift to Grandmother's closeted rooms, but she was doubtful Tam would have gathered Galactic tech just so she could pay her respects to Grandmother. Instead, she went straight to the lower floor, the one she and Tam shared with the children of their generation.

It was right next to the kitchen, and the smells of garlic and fish sauce seemed to be everywhere—of course, the youngest generation always got the lower floor, the one with all the smells and the noises of a legion of waitresses bringing food over to the dining room.

Tam was there, sitting in the little compartment that served as the floor's communal area. She'd spread out the tech on the floor—two immersers (Tam and Quy were possibly the only family members who cared so little about immersers they left them lying around), a remote entertainment set that was busy broadcasting some stories of children running on terraformed planets, and something Quy couldn't quite identify, because Tam had taken it apart into small components: it lay on the table like a gutted fish, all metals and optical parts.

But, at some point, Tam had obviously got bored with the entire process, because she was currently finishing her breakfast, slurping noodles from her soup bowl. She must have got it from the kitchen's leftovers, because Quy knew the smell, could taste the spiciness of the broth on her tongue—Mother's cooking, enough to make her stomach growl although she'd had rolled rice cakes for breakfast.

"You're at it again," Quy said with a sigh. "Could you not take my immerser for your experiments, please?"

Tam didn't even look surprised. "You don't seem very keen on using it, big sis."

"That I don't use it doesn't mean it's yours," Quy said, though that wasn't a real reason. She didn't mind Tam borrowing her stuff, and actually would have been glad to never put on an immerser again—she hated the feeling they gave her, the vague sensation of the system rooting around in her brain to find the best body cues to give her. But there were times when she was expected to wear an immerser: whenever dealing with customers, whether she was waiting at tables or in preparation meetings for large occasions.

Tam, of course, didn't wait at tables—she'd made herself so good at logistics and anything to do with the station's system that she spent most of her time in front of a screen, or connected to the station's network.

"Lil' sis?" Quy said.

Tam set her chopsticks by the side of the bowl, and made an expansive gesture with her hands. "Fine. Have it back. I can always use mine."

Quy stared at the things spread on the table, and asked the inevitable question. "How's progress?"

Tam's work was network connections and network maintenance within the restaurant; her hobby was tech. Galactic tech. She took things apart to see what made them tick; and rebuilt them. Her foray into entertainment units had helped the restaurant set up ambient sounds—old-fashioned Rong music for Galactic customers, recitation of the newest poems for locals.

But immersers had her stumped: the things had nasty safeguards to them. You could open them in half, to replace the battery; but you went no further. Tam's previous attempt had almost lost her the use of her hands.

By Tam's face, she didn't feel ready to try again. "It's got to be the same logic."

"As what?" Quy couldn't help asking. She picked up her own immerser from the table, briefly checking that it did indeed bear her serial number.

Tam gestured to the splayed components on the table. "Artificial Literature Writer. Little gadget that composes light entertainment novels."

"That's not the same—" Quy checked herself, and waited for Tam to explain.

"Takes existing cultural norms, and puts them into a cohesive, satisfying narrative. Like people forging their own path and fighting aliens for possession of a planet, that sort of stuff that barely speaks to us on Longevity. I mean, we've never even seen a planet." Tam exhaled, sharply—her eyes half on the dismembered Artificial Literature Writer, half on some overlay of her vision. "Just like immersers take a given culture and parcel it out to you in a form you can relate to: language, gestures, customs, the whole package. They've got to have the same architecture."

"I'm still not sure what you want to do with it." Quy put on her immerser, adjusting the thin metal mesh around her head until it fitted. She winced as the interface synced with her brain. She moved her hands, adjusting some settings lower than the factory ones—darn thing always reset itself to factory, which she suspected was no accident. A shimmering lattice surrounded her: her avatar, slowly taking shape around her. She could still see the room—the lattice was only faintly opaque—but ancestors, how she hated the feeling of not quite being there. "How do I look?"

"Horrible. Your avatar looks like it's died or something."

"Ha ha ha," Quy said. Her avatar was paler than her, and taller: it made her look beautiful, most customers agreed. In those moments, Quy was glad she had an avatar, so they wouldn't see the anger on her face. "You haven't answered my question."

Tam's eyes glinted. "Just think of the things we couldn't do. This is the best piece of tech Galactics have ever brought us."

Which wasn't much, but Quy didn't need to say it aloud. Tam knew exactly how Quy felt about Galactics and their hollow promises.

"It's their weapon, too." Tam pushed at the entertainment unit. "Just like their books and their holos and their live games. It's fine for them—they put the immersers on tourist settings, they get just what they need to navigate a foreign environment from whatever idiot's written the Rong script for that thing. But we—we worship them. We wear the immersers on Galactic all the time. We make ourselves like them, because they push, and because we're naive enough to give in."

"And you think you can make this better?" Quy couldn't help it. It wasn't that she needed to be convinced: on Prime, she'd never seen immersers. They were tourist stuff, and even while travelling from one city to another, the citizens just assumed they'd know enough to get by. But the stations, their ex-colonies were flooded with immersers.

Tam's eyes glinted, as savage as those of the rebels in the history holos. "If I can take them apart, I can rebuild them and disconnect the logical circuits. I can give us the language and the tools to deal with them without being swallowed by them."

Mind lost in the mountains, Third Aunt said. No one had ever accused Tam of thinking small. Or of not achieving what she set her mind on, come to think of it. And every revolution had to start somewhere—hadn't Longevity's War of Independence started over a single poem, and the unfair imprisonment of the poet who'd written it?

Quy nodded. She believed Tam, though she didn't know how far. "Fair point. Have to go now, or Second Uncle will skin me. See you later, lil' sis."

As you walk under the wide arch of the restaurant with your husband, you glance upwards, at the calligraphy that forms its sign. The immerser translates it for you into "Sister Hai's Kitchen," and starts giving you a detailed background of the place: the menu and the most recommended dishes—as you walk past the various tables, it highlights items it thinks you would like, from rolled-up rice dumplings to fried shrimps. It warns you about the more exotic dishes, like the pickled pig's ears, the fermented meat (you have to be careful about that one, because its name changes depending on which station dialect you order in), or the reeking durian fruit that the natives so love.

It feels . . . not quite right, you think, as you struggle to follow Galen, who is already far away, striding ahead with the same confidence he always exudes in life. People part before him; a waitress with a young, pretty avatar bows before him, though Galen himself takes no notice. You know that such obsequiousness unnerves him; he always rants about the outdated customs aboard Longevity, the inequalities and the lack of democratic government—he thinks it's only a matter of time before they change, adapt themselves to fit into Galactic society. You—you have a faint memory of arguing with him, a long time ago, but now you can't find the words, anymore, or even the reason why—it makes sense, it all makes sense. The Galactics rose against the tyranny of Old Earth and overthrew their shackles, and won the right to determine their own destiny; and every other station and planet will do the same, eventually, rise against the dictatorships that hold them away from progress. It's right; it's always been right.

Unbidden, you stop at a table, and watch two young women pick at a dish of chicken with chopsticks—the smell of fish sauce and lemongrass rises in the air, as pungent and as unbearable as rotten meat—no, no, that's not it, you have an image of a dark-skinned woman, bringing a dish of steamed rice to the table, her hands filled with that same smell, and your mouth watering in anticipation . . .

The young women are looking at you: they both wear standard-issue avatars, the bottom-of-the-line kind—their clothes are a garish mix of red and yellow, with the odd, uneasy cut of cheap designers; and their faces waver, letting you glimpse a hint of darker skin beneath the red flush of their cheeks. Cheap and tawdry, and altogether inappropriate; and you're glad you're not one of them.

"Can I help you, older sister?" one of them asks.

Older sister. A pronoun you were looking for, earlier; one of the things that seem to have vanished from your mind. You struggle for words; but all the immerser seems to suggest to you is a neutral and impersonal pronoun, one that you instinctively know is wrong—it's one only foreigners and outsiders would use in those circumstances. "Older sister," you repeat, finally, because you can't think of anything else.

"Agnes!"

Galen's voice, calling from far away—for a brief moment the immerser seems to fail you again, because you *know* that you have many names, that Agnes is the one they gave you in Galactic school, the one neither Galen nor his friends can mangle when they pronounce it. You remember the Rong names your mother gave you on Longevity, the childhood endearments and your adult-style name.

Be-Nho, Be-Yeu. Thu—Autumn, like a memory of red maple leaves on a planet you never knew.

You pull away from the table, disguising the tremor in your hands.

Second Uncle was already waiting when Quy arrived; and so were the customers.

"You're late," Second Uncle sent on the private channel, though he made the comment half-heartedly, as if he'd expected it all along. As if he'd never really believed he could rely on her—that stung.

"Let me introduce my niece Quy to you," Second Uncle said, in Galactic, to the man beside him.

"Quy," the man said, his immerser perfectly taking up the nuances of her name in Rong. He was everything she'd expected; tall, with only a thin layer of avatar, a little something that narrowed his chin and eyes, and made his chest slightly larger. Cosmetic enhancements: he was good-looking for a Galactic, all things considered. He went on, in Galactic, "My name is Galen Santos. Pleased to meet you. This is my wife, Agnes."

Agnes. Quy turned, and looked at the woman for the first time—and flinched. There was no one here: just a thick layer of avatar, so dense and so complex that she couldn't even guess at the body hidden within.

"Pleased to meet you." On a hunch, Quy bowed, from younger to elder, with both hands brought together—Rong-style, not Galactic—and saw a shudder run through Agnes' body, barely perceptible; but Quy was observant, she'd always been. Her immerser was screaming at her, telling her to hold out both hands, palms up, in the Galactic fashion. She tuned it out: she was still at the stage where she could tell the difference between her thoughts and the immerser's thoughts.

Second Uncle was talking again—his own avatar was light, a paler version of him. "I understand you're looking for a venue for a banquet."

"We are, yes." Galen pulled a chair to him, sank into it. They all followed suit, though not with the same fluid, arrogant ease. When Agnes sat, Quy saw her flinch, as though she'd just remembered something unpleasant. "We'll be celebrating our fifth marriage anniversary, and we both felt we wanted to mark the occasion with something suitable."

Second Uncle nodded. "I see," he said, scratching his chin. "My congratulations to you."

Galen nodded. "We thought—" he paused, threw a glance at his wife that Quy couldn't quite interpret—her immerser came up blank, but there was something oddly familiar about it, something she ought to have been able to name. "Something Rong," he said at last. "A large banquet for a hundred people, with the traditional dishes."

Quy could almost feel Second Uncle's satisfaction. A banquet of that size would be awful logistics, but it would keep the restaurant afloat for a year or more, if they could get the price right. But something was wrong—something—

"What did you have in mind?" Quy asked, not to Galen, but to his wife. The wife—Agnes, which probably wasn't the name she'd been born with—who wore a thick avatar, and didn't seem to be answering or ever speaking up. An awful picture was coming together in Quy's mind.

Agnes didn't answer. Predictable.

Second Uncle took over, smoothing over the moment of awkwardness with expansive hand gestures. "The whole hog, yes?" Second Uncle said. He rubbed his hands, an odd gesture that Quy had never seen from him—a Galactic expression of satisfaction. "Bitter melon soup, Dragon-Phoenix plates, Roast Pig, Jade Under the Mountain . . . " He was citing all the traditional dishes for a wedding banquet—unsure of how far the foreigner wanted to take it. He left out the odder stuff, like Shark Fin or Sweet Red Bean Soup.

"Yes, that's what we would like. Wouldn't we, darling?" Galen's wife neither moved nor spoke. Galen's head turned towards her, and Quy caught his expression at last. She'd thought it would be contempt, or hatred; but no; it was anguish. He genuinely loved her, and he couldn't understand what was going on.

Galactics. Couldn't he recognize an immerser junkie when he saw one? But then Galactics, as Tam said, seldom had the problem—they didn't put on the immersers for more than a few days on low settings, if they ever went that far. Most were flat-out convinced Galactic would get them anywhere.

Second Uncle and Galen were haggling, arguing prices and features; Second Uncle sounding more and more like a Galactic tourist as the conversation went on, more and more aggressive for lower and lower gains. Quy didn't care anymore: she watched Agnes. Watched the impenetrable avatar—a red-headed woman in the latest style from Prime, with freckles on her skin and a hint of a star-tan on her face. But that wasn't what she was, inside; what the immerser had dug deep into.

Wasn't who she was at all. Tam was right; all immersers should be taken apart, and did it matter if they exploded? They'd done enough harm as it was.

Quy wanted to get up, to tear away her own immerser, but she couldn't, not in the middle of the negotiation. Instead, she rose, and walked closer to Agnes; the two men barely glanced at her, too busy agreeing on a price. "You're not alone," she said, in Rong, low enough that it didn't carry.

Again, that odd, disjointed flash. "You have to take it off," Quy said, but got no further response. As an impulse, she grabbed the other woman's arm; felt her hands go right through the immerser's avatar, connect with warm, solid flesh.

***

You hear them negotiating, in the background—it's tough going, because the Rong man sticks to his guns stubbornly, refusing to give ground to Galen's onslaught. It's all very distant, a subject of intellectual study; the immerser reminds you from time to time, interpreting this and this body cue, nudging you this way and that—you must sit straight and silent, and support your husband—and so you smile through a mouth that feels gummed together.

You feel, all the while, the Rong girl's gaze on you, burning like ice water, like the gaze of a dragon. She won't move away from you; and her hand rests on you, gripping your arm with a strength you didn't think she had in her body. Her avatar is but a thin layer, and you can see her beneath it: a round, moon-shaped face with skin the color of cinnamon—no, not spices, not chocolate, but simply a color you've seen all your life.

"You have to take it off," she says. You don't move; but you wonder what she's talking about.

Take it off. Take it off. Take what off?

The immerser.

Abruptly, you remember—a dinner with Galen's friends, when they laughed at jokes that had gone by too fast for you to understand. You came home battling tears; and found yourself reaching for the immerser on your bedside table, feeling its cool weight in your hands. You thought it would please Galen if you spoke his language; that he would be less ashamed of how uncultured you sounded to his friends. And then you found out that everything was fine, as long as you kept the settings on maximum and didn't remove it. And then . . . and then you walked with it and slept with it, and showed the world nothing but the avatar it had designed—saw nothing it hadn't tagged and labelled for you. Then . . .

Then it all slid down, didn't it? You couldn't program the network anymore, couldn't look at the guts of machines; you lost your job with the tech company, and came to Galen's compartment, wandering in the room like a hollow shell, a ghost of yourself—as if you'd already died, far away from home and all that it means to you. Then—then the immerser wouldn't come off, anymore.

"What do you think you're doing, young woman?"

Second Uncle had risen, turning towards Quy—his avatar flushed with anger, the pale skin mottled with an unsightly red. "We adults are in the middle of negotiating something very important, if you don't mind." It might have made Quy quail in other circumstances, but his voice and his body language were wholly Galactic; and he sounded like a stranger to her—an angry foreigner whose food order she'd misunderstood—whom she'd mock later, sitting in Tam's room with a cup of tea in her lap, and the familiar patter of her sister's musings.

"I apologize," Quy said, meaning none of it.

"That's all right," Galen said. "I didn't mean to—" he paused, looked at his wife. "I shouldn't have brought her here."

"You should take her to see a physician," Quy said, surprised at her own boldness.

"Do you think I haven't tried?" His voice was bitter. "I've even taken her to the best hospitals on Prime. They look at her, and say they can't take it off. That the shock of it would kill her. And even if it didn't . . . " He spread his hands, letting air fall between them like specks of dust. "Who knows if she'd come back?"

Quy felt herself blush. "I'm sorry." And she meant it this time.

Galen waved her away, negligently, airily, but she could see the pain he was struggling to hide. Galactics didn't think tears were manly, she remembered. "So we're agreed?" Galen asked Second Uncle. "For a million credits?"

Quy thought of the banquet; of the food on the tables, of Galen thinking it would remind Agnes of home. Of how, in the end, it was doomed to fail, because everything would be filtered through the immerser, leaving Agnes with nothing but an exotic feast of unfamiliar flavors. "I'm sorry," she said, again, but no one was listening; and she turned away from Agnes with rage in her heart—with the growing feeling that it had all been for nothing in the end.

"I'm sorry," the girl says—she stands, removing her hand from your arm, and you feel like a tearing inside, as if something within you was struggling to claw free from your body. Don't go, you want to say. Please don't go. Please don't leave me here.

But they're all shaking hands; smiling, pleased at a deal they've struck—like sharks, you think, like tigers. Even the Rong girl has turned away from you;

giving you up as hopeless. She and her uncle are walking away, taking separate paths back to the inner areas of the restaurant, back to their home.

Please don't go.

It's as if something else were taking control of your body; a strength that you didn't know you possessed. As Galen walks back into the restaurant's main room, back into the hubbub and the tantalizing smells of food—of lemongrass chicken and steamed rice, just as your mother used to make—you turn away from your husband, and follow the girl. Slowly, and from a distance; and then running, so that no one will stop you. She's walking fast—you see her tear her immerser away from her face, and slam it down onto a side table with disgust. You see her enter a room; and you follow her inside.

They're watching you, both girls, the one you followed in; and another, younger one, rising from the table she was sitting at—both terribly alien and terribly familiar at once. Their mouths are open, but no sound comes out.

In that one moment—staring at each other, suspended in time—you see the guts of Galactic machines spread on the table. You see the mass of tools; the dismantled machines; and the immerser, half spread-out before them, its two halves open like a cracked egg. And you understand that they've been trying to open them and reverse-engineer them; and you know that they'll never, ever succeed. Not because of the safeguards, of the Galactic encryptions to preserve their fabled intellectual property; but rather, because of something far more fundamental.

This is a Galactic toy, conceived by a Galactic mind—every layer of it, every logical connection within it exudes a mindset that might as well be alien to these girls. It takes a Galactic to believe that you can take a whole culture and reduce it to algorithms; that language and customs can be boiled to just a simple set of rules. For these girls, things are so much more complex than this; and they will never understand how an immerser works, because they can't think like a Galactic, they'll never ever think like that. You can't think like a Galactic unless you've been born in the culture.

Or drugged yourself, senseless, into it, year after year.

You raise a hand—it feels like moving through honey. You speak—struggling to shape words through layer after layer of immerser thoughts.

"I know about this," you say, and your voice comes out hoarse, and the words fall into place one by one like a laser stroke, and they feel right, in a way that nothing else has for five years. "Let me help you, younger sisters."

To Rochita Loenen-Ruiz, for the conversations that inspired this.

About the Authors

Erik Amundsen has been removed from display for being zoologically improbable and/or terrifying to small children. He has been sighted in *Weird Tales, Fantasy Magazine, Not One of Us* and *Jabberwocky* but his natural habitat is central Connecticut.

Helena Bell is a poet and writer living in Raleigh, NC. Her work has previously appeared or is forthcoming in *Upgraded: A Cyborg Anthology, The Dark,* and *the Indiana Review.*

Born in the Caribbean, **Tobias S. Buckell** is a New York Times Bestselling author. His novels and over fifty short stories have been translated into seventeen languages and he has been nominated for the Hugo, Nebula, Prometheus and John W. Campbell Award for Best New Science Fiction Author. He currently lives in Ohio.

Suzanne Church juggles her time between throwing her characters to the lions and chillin' like a villain with her two sons. She writes science fiction, fantasy, and horror because she enjoys them all and hates to play favorites. Her award-winning fiction has appeared in *Clarkesworld, Cicada* and *On Spec,* and in several anthologies including Urban Green Man and When the Hero Comes Home 2. Her collection of short fiction, *Elements* is available at bookstores and Amazon from EDGE Science Fiction and Fantasy Publishing.

Gwendolyn Clare resides in North Carolina, where she tends a vegetable garden and a flock of backyard ducks and wonders why she ever lived in the frozen northlands. Her short fiction has appeared in *Asimov's, Clarkesworld, Beneath Ceaseless Skies,* and *Daily Science Fiction,* among others. Despite the siren lure of writing anything other than her dissertation, she recently completed a PhD in mycology. She can be found online at gwendolynclare.com.

Tom Crosshill's fiction has been nominated for the Nebula Award, the Latvian Annual Literature Award, and has appeared in venues such as *Lightspeed, Beneath Ceaseless Skies* and the *Intergalactic Medicine Show.* After some years spent in Oregon and New York, he currently lives in his native Latvia. In the past, he has operated a nuclear reactor, worked in a zinc mine and co-founded a salsa school, among other things.

Indrapramit Das is a writer and artist from Kolkata, India. His fiction has appeared in publications and anthologies including *Asimov's* and *Apex Magazine*, *The Year's Best Science Fiction: Thirtieth Annual Collection* (St. Martin's Press), *Aliens: Recent Encounters* (Prime Books) and *Mothership: Tales from Afrofuturism and Beyond* (Rosarium Publishing). He is a grateful graduate of the 2012 Clarion West Writers Workshop and a recipient of the Octavia E. Butler Scholarship Award to attend the former. He completed his MFA at the University of British Columbia and is currently in Vancouver working as a freelance writer, artist, editor, critic, TV extra, game tester, tutor, would-be novelist, and aspirant to adulthood. He is represented by Sally Harding of the Cooke Agency. Follow him on Twitter @IndrapramitDas.

Aliette de Bodard lives and works in a flat in Paris, France: she has a day job as a System Engineer, and doubles as a speculative fiction writer by night. Her stories have appeared in *Interzone, Lightspeed* and the *Year's Best Science Fiction,* and have won a Nebula, Locus and British Science Fiction Association Award. Her latest release is the space opera novella *On a Red Station Drifting,* a Nebula, Hugo and Locus Award finalist. Visit http://www.aliettedebodard.com for recipes, fiction and rants.

Peter M. Ferenczi has written extensively about technology for national magazines and the web, sometimes as a cheerleader, sometimes as a catcaller and concerned citizen of the world. He writes speculative fiction in the hope that he may infect others with the bone-deep reading addiction that's plagued him since he resolved the alphabet into words.

Born in California, he's drifted east over the years and now resides in France. Along the way he acquired a couple of degrees, a love of photography and a taste for travel. He lives in Paris with his wife and daughter.

Michael John Grist is a science fiction & fantasy author and ruins photographer who lives in Tokyo, Japan. His stories can be found in *Beneath Ceaseless Skies, Ideomancer,* and *Andromeda Spaceways,* and he is currently writing an epic fantasy novel. He runs a website featuring his writing and photographs of the ruins or 'haikyo' of Japan; filled with dark short stories and matching images of abandoned theme parks and ghost towns. Follow him on Twitter at http://twitter.com/michaelgrist.

Kij Johnson is the author of three novels and a number of short stories, a three-time winner of the Nebula Award (including in 2010, for her *Clarkes-*

world story, "Spar"), and a winner of the World Fantasy, Sturgeon, Crawford, and *Asimov's* Reader Awards.

Rahul Kanakia is a science fiction writer who has sold stories to *Clarkesworld, the Intergalactic Medicine Show, Apex, Nature,* and *Lady Churchill's Rosebud Wristlet.* He holds a Master of the Fine Arts program in creative writing at Johns Hopkins University and a B.A. in Economics from Stanford, and he works as a consultant in the international development field. If you want to know more about him then please visit his blog at http://www.blotter-paper.com or follow him on Twitter at http://www.twitter.com/rahkan.

David Klecha is a writer and Marine combat veteran currently living in West Michigan with his family and assorted computer junk. He works in IT to pay the bills, like so many other beginning writers and artists.

Gary Kloster is a writer, librarian, martial arts instructor, and stay-at-home father. Sometimes all in the same day, but seldom all at the same time. His work has appeared in *Fantasy Magazine, Daily Science Fiction,* and *Escape Pod.* He has a short story forthcoming in *Apex Magazine,* and a Pathfinders Tale novel forthcoming with Paizo Press.

Ken Liu (http://kenliu.name) is an author and translator of speculative fiction, as well as a lawyer and programmer. His fiction has appeared in *The Magazine of Fantasy & Science Fiction, Asimov's, Analog, Clarkesworld, Lightspeed,* and *Strange Horizons,* among other places. He is a winner of the Nebula, Hugo, and World Fantasy awards. He lives with his family near Boston, Massachusetts.

Ken's debut novel, *The Grace of Kings,* the first in a fantasy series, will be published by Saga Press, Simon & Schuster's new genre fiction imprint, in 2015. Saga will also publish a collection of his short stories.

Alexander Lumans was the Spring 2014 Philip Roth Resident at Bucknell University. His fiction has appeared in *Story Quarterly, Gulf Coast, Daily Science Fiction, Cincinnati Review,* and *The Normal School,* among others. He has been awarded fellowships/scholarships to the MacDowell Colony, Yaddo, Blue Mountain Center, ART342, Norton Island, RopeWalk, Sewanee, and Bread Loaf Writers' Conference. He received the 2013 Gulf Coast Fiction Prize, 3rd place in the 2012 Story Quarterly Fiction Contest, and the 2011 Barry Hannah Fiction Prize from *The Yalobusha Review.* He is co-editor of the anthology *Apocalypse Now: Poems and Prose from the End of Days* (Upper Rubber Boot Books). He graduated from the M.F.A. Fiction Program at Southern Illinois University Carbondale.

Sunny Moraine is a humanoid creature of average height, luminosity, and inertial mass. They're also a doctoral candidate in sociology and a writer–like object whose work has appeared or is forthcoming in *Lightspeed, Shimmer, Clarkesworld, Apex,* and *Long Hidden: Speculative Fiction from the Margins of History,* as well as multiple Year's Best anthologies, all of which has provided lovely reasons to avoid a dissertation. Their first novel *Line and Orbit,* co-written with Lisa Soem, is available from Samhain Publishing. Their solo-authored novel *Crowflight* is available from Masque Books.

Mari Ness has always loved to watch things shoot up into the sky. Her fiction and poetry have appeared in numerous publications, including *Tor.com, Apex Magazine, Daily Science Fiction, Strange Horizons,* and *Goblin Fruit.* She can be followed on Twitter as mari_ness. She lives in central Florida.

An (pronounce it "On") **Owomoyela** is a neutrois author with a background in web development, linguistics, and weaving chain maille out of stainless steel fencing wire, whose fiction has appeared in a number of venues including *Clarkesworld, Asimov's, Lightspeed,* and a handful of Year's Bests. An's interests range from pulsars and Cepheid variables to gender studies and nonstandard pronouns, with a plethora of stops in-between. Se can be found online at an.owomoyela.net, and can be funded at patreon.com/an_owomoyela.

Ben Peek is the Sydney based author of *Black Sheep, Twenty-Six Lies/One Truth,* and *Above/Below* with Stephanie Campisi. His most recent books are the collection *Dead Americans and Other Stories* and fantasy novel, *The Godless.* He can be found at theurbansprawlproject.com.

His short fiction has appeared in numerous publications, including anthologies and magazines such as *Paper Cities, Polyhony, Leviathan, Forever Shores, Overland, Aurealis,* and in numerous Year's Best anthologies. He has a doctorate in literature and has published reviews and criticism, a psychogeographical pamphlet, and an autobiographical comic, Nowhere Near Savannah, which was illustrated by Anna Brown. His collection, *Dead Americans,* is forthcoming from ChiZine Publications.

Robert Reed has had eleven novels published, starting with *The Leeshore* in 1987 and most recently with *The Well of Stars* in 2004. Since winning the first annual *L. Ron Hubbard Writers of the Future* contest in 1986 (under the pen name Robert Touzalin) and being a finalist for the John W. Campbell Award for best new writer in 1987, he has had over two-hundred shorter works published in a variety of magazines and anthologies. Eleven of those stories were published in his critically-acclaimed first collection, *The Dragons of Springplace,* in 1999. Twelve more stories appear in his second collection, *The Cuckoo's Boys* [2005]. In addition to his success in the U.S., Reed has also been published in the U.K., Russia, Japan, Spain and in France, where a second (French-language) collection of nine of his shorter works, *Chrysalide,* was released in 2002. Bob has had stories appear in at least one of the annual "Year's Best" anthologies in every year since 1992. Bob has received nominations for both the Nebula Award (nominated and voted upon by genre authors) and the Hugo Award (nominated and voted upon by fans), as well as numerous other literary awards (see Awards). He won his first Hugo Award for the 2006 novella *A Billion Eves*. He is currently working on a Great Ship trilogy for Prime Books, and of course, more short pieces.

Margaret Ronald is the author of *Spiral Hunt, Wild Hunt,* and *Soul Hunt,* as well as a number of short stories. Originally from rural Indiana, she now lives outside Boston.

Sofia Samatar is a fantasy writer, poet, and critic, and a PhD student in African Languages and Literature at the University of Wisconsin-Madison. She studies twentieth-century Egyptian and Sudanese fiction, and is writing a dissertation on the uses of fantasy in the works of the Sudanese writer, Tayeb Salih. Sofia's fiction has appeared or is forthcoming in a number of places, including *Ideomancer, Expanded Horizons* and *Strange Horizons.* Her poetry can be found at *Stone Telling, Bull Spec* and *Goblin Fruit,* among others; one of her poems was reprinted in the anthology *The Moment of Change.* Her debut novel, *A Stranger in Olondria,* was published by Small Beer Press in 2013.

Chris Stabback is an undersized moss giant who plays music, writes words, and cares for miniature humans. Chris lives in an ailing 1920s flat in Sydney, the interior of which is illuminated with distressing regularity by the flash of the red light camera outside. More information can be found at chrisstabback.com.

Sarah Stanton grew up in Perth, Western Australia. Halfway through university, she abandoned a promising career in not having much of a career when she transferred from an opera performance course into a Chinese language major, having fallen for the Middle Kingdom more or less overnight. Three ecstatic years cheating lung cancer in Beijing later, she has settled in San Francisco as a freelance translator, editor, and writer. Her work has appeared in a variety of international journals, including *Clarkesworld, Going Down Swinging,* and *Cha,* and she was shortlisted for the 2011 James White Award. Find her online at http://www.theduckopera.com.

Lavie Tidhar is the World Fantasy Award winning author of *Osama.* His other novels include the Bookman Histories trilogy, *The Violent Century* and *A Man Lies Dreaming,* and comics mini-series *Adler.* He has a British Fantasy Award for Best Novella for *Gorel & The Pot-Bellied God* and a BSFA Award for non-fiction and is the prolific author of many other novellas and short stories.

E. Catherine Tobler is a Sturgeon Award finalist and the senior editor at Shimmer Magazine. Among others, her fiction has appeared in *Clarkesworld, Lady Churchill's Rosebud Wristlet,* and *Beneath Ceaseless Skies.* Her first novel is now available. Follow her on Twitter @ECthetwit or her website, http://www.ecatherine.com.

Catherynne M. Valente is *The New York Times* bestselling author of over a dozen works of fiction and poetry, including *Palimpsest,* the Orphan's Tales series, *Deathless,* and the crowdfunded phenomenon *The Girl Who Circumnavigated Fairyland in a Ship of Own Making.* She is the winner of the Andre Norton, Tiptree, Mythopoeic, Rhysling, Lambda, Locus and Hugo awards. She has been a finalist for the Nebula and World Fantasy Awards. She lives on an island off the coast of Maine with a small but growing menagerie of beasts, some of which are human.

Carrie Vaughn is the author of *The New York Times* bestselling series of novels about a werewolf named Kitty, the most recent installment of which is *Kitty in the Underworld.* Her most recent novel is the superhero story *Dreams of the Golden Age.* She's written several other contemporary fantasy and young adult novels, as well as upwards of seventy short stories. She's a contributor to the Wild Cards series of shared world superhero books edited by George R. R. Martin and is a graduate of the Odyssey Fantasy Writing Workshop. An Air Force brat, she survived her nomadic childhood and managed to put down roots in Boulder, Colorado. Visit her at www.carrievaughn.com.

As an undergraduate, **Ms. Xia** majored in Atmospheric Sciences at Peking University. She then entered the Film Studies Program at the Communication University of China, where she completed her Master's thesis, "A Study on Female Figures in Science Fiction Films." Currently, she's pursuing a Ph. D. in Comparative Literature and World Literature at Peking University and chose "Chinese Science Fiction and Cultural Politics since 1990s" as the topic of her dissertation. She has been publishing science fiction and fantasy since 2004 in a variety of venues, including Science Fiction World and Jiuzhou Fantasy. Several of her stories have won the Galaxy Award, China's most prestigious science fiction award. Besides writing and translating science fiction stories, she also writes film scripts and teaches science fiction writing. (In accordance with Chinese custom, Ms Xia's surname is listed first on this story.)

Clarkesworld Citizens
Official Census

We would like to thank the following Clarkesworld Citizens for their support:

Overlords

L A George, Renan Adams, Claire Alcock, Thomas Ball, Michael Blackmore, Nathalie Boisard-Beudin, Shawn Boyd, Jennifer Brozek, Karen Burnham, Barbara Capoferri, Morgan Cheryl, Gio Clairval, Neil Clarke, Dolohov, ebooks-worldwide, Sairuh Emilius, Lynne Everett, Joshua Faulkenberry, Fabio Fernandes, Thomas Fleck, Eric Francis, Bryan Green, Andrew Hatchell, Berthiaume Heidi, Bill Hughes, Gary Hunter, Theodore J. Stanulis, Marcus Jager, Jericho, jfly, jkapoetry, Lucas Jung, James Kinateder, Daniel LaPonsie, Susan Lewis, Philip Maloney, Paul Marston, Matthew the Greying, Gabriel Mayland, MJ Mercer, Achilleas Michailides, Adrian Mihaila, Adrien Mitchell, Overlord Mondragon, MrMovieZombie, Mike Perricone, Jody Plank, Rick Ramsey, Jo Rhett, Joseph Sconfitto, Marie Shcherbatskaya, Tara Smith, David Steffen, Elaine Williams, James Williams, Doug Young

Royalty

Paul Abbamondi, Albert Alfiler, Raymond Bair, Kathryn Baker, Nathan Blumenfeld, Marty Bonus, David Borcherding, Robert Callahan, Lady Cate, Richard Chappell, Carolyn Cooper, Tom Crosshill, Michael Cullinan, Mr D F Ryan, Sky de Jersey, David Demers, Cory Doctorow, Brian Dolton, Alexis Goble, Hilary Goldstein, Carl Hazen, Andy Herrman, Kristin Hirst, Colin Hitch, Victoria Hoke, Christopher Irwin, Mary Jo Rabe, Lukas Karl Barnes, G.J. Kressley, Jeffrey L Lewis, Jamie Lackey, Jonathan Laden, Katherine Lee, H. Lincoln Parish, David M Oswin, Sean Markey, Arun Mascarenhas, Barrett Mc-Cormick, Kevin McKean, Margaret McNally, Michelle Broadribb MEG, Nayad Monroe, James Moore, Anne Murphy, Persona Non-Grata, Charles Norton, Vincent O'Connor, Vincent P Loeffler III, Marie Parsons, Lars Pedersen, David Personette, George Peter Gatsis, Matt Phelps, Gary Piserchio, Lord Pontus, Ian Powell, Rational Path, RL, John Scalzi, Stu Segal, Maurice Shaw, Angela Slatter,

Carrie Smith, Paul Smith, Richard Sorden, Chugwangle Sparklepants, Kevin Standlee, Neal Stanifer, Josh Thomson, TK, Terhi Tormanen, Jeppe V Holm, Sean Wallace, Jasen Ward, Weyla & Gos, Graeme Williams, Jeff Xilon, Zola

Bürgermeisters

7ony, Mary A. Turzillo, Rob Abram, Frederick Amerman, Carl Anderson, Mel Anderson, Andy90, Marie Angell, Jon Arnold, Robert Avie, Erika Bailey, Brian Baker, Michael Banker, Jennifer Bartolowits, Lenni Benson, Kerry Benton, Bill Bibo Jr, Edward Blake, Samuel Blinn, Johanna Bobrow, Joan Boyle, Patricia Bray, Tim Brenner, Ken Brown, BruceC, Adam Bursey, Jeremy Butler, Robyn Butler, Roland Byrd, M. C. VanderSchaaf, Brad Campbell, Carleton45, James Carlino, Benjamin Cartwright, Evan Cassity, Lee Cavanaugh, Peter Charron, Randall Chertkow, Michael Chorman, Mary Clare, Matthew Claxton, Theodore Conti, Brian Cooksey, Brenda Cooper, Lorraine Cooper, B D Fagan, James Davies, Tessa Day, Brian Deacon, Bartley Deason, John Devenny, Fran Ditzel-Friel, Gary Dockter, Nicholas Doran, Christopher Doty, Nicholas Dowbiggin, Christine Ertell, Joanna Evans, Rare Feathers, Tea Fish, FlatFootedRat, Lynn Flewelling, Adrienne Foster, Matthew Fredrickson, Alina Fridberg, Patricia G Scott, Christopher Garry, Pierre Gauthier, Gerhen, Mark Gerrits, Lorelei Goelz, Ed Goforth, Inga Gorslar, Tony Graham, Jaq Greenspon, Eric Gregory, Laura Hake, Skeptyk/JeanneE Hand-Boniakowski, Jordan Hanie, Helixa 12, Corydon Hinton, Sheridan Hodges, Ronald Hordijk, Justin Howe, Bobby Hoyt, David Hudson, Huginn and Muninn, Chris Hurst, Kevin Ikenberry, Joseph Ilardi, Pamela J. Davis, Justin James, Patty Jansen, Cristal Java, Toni Jerrman, Audra Johnson, Erin Johnson, Russell Johnson, Patrick Joseph Sklar, Kai Juedemann, Andy Kaden, Jeff Kapustka, David Kelleher, James Kelly, Joshua Kidd, Alistair Kimble, Erin Kissane, Cecil Knight, Michelle Knowlton, JR Krebs, Andrew Lanker, James Frederick Leach, Krista Leahy, Alan Lehotsky, Walter Leroy Perkins, Philip Levin, Kevin Liebkemann, Grá Linnaea, Susan Loyal, Kristi Lozano, LUX4489, Keith M Frampton, N M Wells Foundry Creative Media, Brit Mandelo, Mark Maris, Matthew Marovich, Samuel Marzioli, Jason Maurer, Rosaleen McCarthy, Peter McClean, Michael McCormack, Tony McFee, Mark McGarry, Doug McLaughlin, Craig McMurtry, J Meijer, Geoffrey Meissner, Barry Melius, David Michalak, Robert Milson, Sharon Mock, Eric Mohring, Samuel Montgomery-Blinn, Rebekah Murphy, John Murray, Barrett Nichols, Peter Northup, Justin Palk, Norman Papernick, Richard Parks, Paivi Pasi, Katherine Pendill, Eric Pierson, E. PLS, PBC Productions Inc., Lolt Proegler, Jonathan Pruett, QLM Aria X-Perienced, Robert Quinlivan, Mike R D Ashley, D Randall Kerr, Joel Rankin, Paul Rice, James Rickard, Karsten Rink, Erik Rolstad, Joseph Romel, Leena Romppainen, Michael Russo, Mark S Haney, Stefan Scheib, Alan Scheiner, Kenneth Schneyer, Bluezoo Seven, Cosma Shalizi, Jeremy Showers, siznax, Allen Snyder, David Sobyra, Jason

Strawsburg, Keffington Studios, Jerome Stueart, Robert Stutts, Maurice Termeer, Chuck Tindle, Raymond Tobaygo, Tradeblanket.com, Heather Tumey, Ann VanderMeer, Andrew Vega, Emil Volcheck, Andrew Volpe, Wendy Wagner, Jennifer Walter, Tom Waters, Tehani Wessely, Shannon White, Dan Wick, John Wienstroer, Seth Williams, Paul Wilson, Dawn Wolfe, Sarah Wright, Tero

Citizens

Pete Aldin, Elye Alexander, Richard Alison, Joshua Allen, Alllie, Imron Alston, Clifford Anderson, Kim Anderson, Randall Andrews, Author Anonymous, Therese Arkenberg, Ash, Bill B., Benjamin Baker, Jenny Barber, Johanne Barron, Jeff Bass, Aaron Begg, LaNeta Bergst, Julie Berg-Thompson, Clark Berry, Amy Billingham, Tracey Bjorksten, John Bledsoe, Mike Blevins, Adam Blomquist, Allison Bocksruker, Kevin Bokelman, Michael Bonsall, Michael Bowen, Michael Braun Hamilton, Commander Breetai, Nathan Breit, Jennifer Brissett, Kit Brown, Thomas Bull, Michael Bunkahle, Karl Bunker, Cory Burr, Jefferson Burson, Graeme Byfield, c9lewis, Darrell Cain, C.G. Cameron, Yazburg Carlberg, Michael Carr, Nance Cedar, Timothy Charlton, David Chasson, Catherine Cheek, Paige Chicklo, The Chocolate Delicacy, Victoria Cleave, J.B.& Co., Alicia Cole, Elizabeth Coleman, Johne Cook, Claire Cooney, Martin Cooper, Lisa Costello, Charles Cox, Michael Cox, Yoshi Creelman, Tina Crone, Curtis42, Sarah Dalton, Ang Danieldeskbrain - Watercress Munster, Gillian Daniels, Chua Dave, Morgan Davey, Ed Davidoff, Chase Davies, Craig Davis, Gustavo de Albuquerque, Alessia De Gaspari, Maria-Isabel Deira, Daniel DeLano, Dennis DeMario, Michele Desautels, Paul DesCombaz, Aidan Doyle, dt, Alex Dunbar, Susan Duncan, Andrew Eason, The Eaton Law Firm, P.C., David Eggli, Jesse Eisenhower, Brad Elliott, Warren Ellis, Douglas Engstrom, Lyle Enright, Peter Enyeart, Yvonne Ewing, . Feather, Josiah Ferrin, TJ Fly, the Paragliding Guy, Ethan Fode, Dense Fog, Francesca Forrest, Jason Frank, Michael Fratus, William Fred, Michael Frighetto, Sarah Frost, Fyrbaul, Paul Gainford, Robert Garbacz, Eleanor Gausden, Leslie Gelwicks, Susan Gibbs, Holly Glaser, Sangay Glass, Laura Goodin, Grendel, Valerie Grimm, Damien Grintalis, Michael Grosberg, Nikki Guerlain, Geoffrey Guthrie, Richard Guttormson, Michael Habif, Lee Hallison, Lee Hallison, Janus Hansen, Roy Hardin, Jonathan Harnum, Harpoon, Jubal Harshaw, Darren Hawbrook, Leon Hendee, Jamie Henderson, Samantha Henderson, Dave Hendrickson, Karen Heuler, Dan Hiestand, John Higham, Renata Hill, Björn Hillreiner, Tim Hills, Mark Hinchman, Peter Hogberg, Peter Hollmer, Andrea Horbinski, Clarence Horne III, Richard Horton, Fiona Howland-Rose, Jeremy Hull, John Humpton, Dwight Illk, John Imhoff, Iridum Sound Envoy, Isbell, Stephen Jacob, Radford Janssens, Michael Jarcho, Jimbo, Steve Johnson, Patrick Johnston, Gabriel Kaknes, Philip Kaldon, KarlTheGood, Sara Kathryn, Cagatay Kavukcuoglu, Lorna Keach, Keenan, Jason Keeton, Robert Keller, Mary Kellerman, Kelson,

Shawn Keslar, Kate Kligman, Seymour Knowles-Barley, Matthew Koch, Will Koenig, Lutz Krebs, Derek Kunsken, Erica L. Satifka, T. L. Sherwood, Michele Laframboise, Paul Lamarre, Gina Langridge, Darren Ledgerwood, Brittany Lehman, Terra Lemay, Danielle Linder, Susan Llewellyn, Thomas Loyal, James Lyle, Allison M. Dickson, Dan Manning, Margaret, Eric Marsh, Jacque Marshall, Dominique Martel, Cethar Mascaw, Daniel Mathews, David Mayes, Derek McAleer, Mike McBride, T.C. McCarthy, Jeffrey McDonald, Holly McEntee, Josh McGraw, Roland McIntosh, Oscar McNary, Brent Mendelsohn, Seth Merlo, Stephen Middleton, John Midgley, Matthew Miller, Stephan Miller, Terry Miller, Alan Mimms, mjpearce, Aidan Moher, Marian Moore, Jamie Morgan, Patricia Murphy, Jack Myers Photography, Glenn Nevill, Stella Nickerson, Robyn Nielsen, David Oakley, Scott Oesterling, Rick of the North, Christopher Ogilvie, James Oliver, Lydia Ondrusek, Ruth O'Neill, Erik Ordway, Nancy Owens, Stuart P Hair, Thomas Pace, Amparo Palma Reig, Thomas Parrish, Andrea Pawley, Sidsel Pedersen, Edgar Penderghast, Tzum Pepah, Chris Perkins, Patricia Peterson, Nikki Philley, Adrian-Teodor Pienaru, Beth Plutchak, David Potter, Ed Prior, David Raco, Mahesh Raj Mohan, Adam Rakunas, Ralan, Steve Ramey, Diego Ramos, Dale Randolph Bivins, Robert Redick, George Reilly, Joshua Reynolds, Julia Reynolds, Zach Ricks, Carl Rigney, Hank Roberts, Tansy Roberts, Kenneth Robkin, James Rowh, Roy and Norma Kloster, RPietila, Sarah Rudek, Woodworking Running Dog, Oliver Rupp, Caitlin Russell, Abigail Rustad, George S. Walker, Lior Saar, S2 Sally, Tim Sally, Jason Sanford, Steven Saus, MJ Scafati, Jan Shawyer, Espana Sheriff, Udayan Shevade, Josh Shiben, Aileen Simpson, Karen Snyder, Morgan Songi, Dr SP Conboy-Hil, Mat Spalding, Terry Squire Stone, Jennifer Stufflebeam, Julia Sullivan, Kenneth Takigawa, Charles Tan, Jesse Tauriainen, David Taylor, Felix Troendle, The Unsettled Foundation, Julia Varga, Adam Vaughan, Extranet Vendors Association, William Vennell, Vettac, Diane Walton, Robert Wamble, Lim Wee Teck, Neil Weston, Peter Wetherall, Adam White, Spencer Wightman, Jeff Williamson, Neil Williamson, Kristyn Willson, A.C. Wise, Devon Wong, Chalmer Wren, Dan Wright, Lachlan Yeates, Catherine York, Rena Zayit, Stephanie Zvan

Interested in immigrating to Clarkesworld? Visit **clarkesworldmagazine.com** for more details.

About Clarkesworld

Clarkesworld Magazine (clarkesworldmagazine.com) is a monthly science fiction and fantasy magazine first published in October 2006. Each issue contains interviews, thought-provoking articles and at least three pieces of original fiction. Our fiction is also available in ebook editions/subscriptions, audio podcasts and in our annual print anthologies. *Clarkesworld* has been nominated for Hugo Award for Best Semiprozine four times, winning three, and our fiction has been nominated for or won the Hugo, Nebula, World Fantasy, Sturgeon, Locus, Shirley Jackson, WSFA Small Press and Stoker Awards. For information on how to subscribe to our electronic edition on your Kindle, Nook, iPad or other ereader/Android device, please visit: clarkesworldmagazine.com/subscribe/

About the Editors

Neil Clarke (neil-clarke.com) is the publisher and editor-in-chief of *Clarkesworld Magazine,* owner of Wyrm Publishing and a three-time Hugo Award Nominee for Best Editor Short Form. He currently lives in New Jersey with his wife and two boys.

Sean Wallace is a founding editor at *Clarkesworld Magazine,* owner of Prime Books and winner of the World Fantasy Award. He currently lives in Maryland with his wife and two daughters.

Made in the USA
San Bernardino, CA
17 September 2014